I0761039

ZAKHAR PRILEPIN

THE MONASTERY

A NOVEL

AD VERBUM

Published with the support
of the Institute for Literary Translation, Russia

THE MONASTERY

A NOVEL

by Zakhar Prilepin

Translated from the Russian by Nicholas Kotar

Proofreading by Emma Lockley

Published with the support
of the Institute for Literary Translation, Russia

www.glagoslav.com

ISBN: 978-1-912894-78-9
ISBN: 978-1-912894-79-6

First published in English
by Glagoslav Publications in June 30, 2020

A catalogue record for this book is available from the British Library.

ZAKHAR PRILEPIN

THE MONASTERY

A NOVEL

Translated from the Russian by Nicholas Kotar

GLAGOSLAV PUBLICATIONS

CONTENTS

BEYOND *THE MONASTERY*:
PRILEPIN, PUTIN, AND THE GULAG

How can we read a brilliant work written by an author whose ideology is deeply disturbing? Discussing Zakhar Prilepin raises a host of questions that are perplexing even by the standards of Russian literature. Given the contentious climate in Russia, it is tempting to simply dismiss Prilepin and ignore his disturbing yet original novel *The Monastery* (Obitel', 2014). Yet if those in the West are to understand Putin's Russia — a country where the leader's policies are unpopular but unopposed — we must try to untangle Prilepin's web of paradoxes. Julie Fedor, for instance, labels him a "freelancer" who only supports the Kremlin when his beliefs ally with its doctrine. Determining how this onetime opposition figure came to be a symbol for Russian state oppression explains much about how both literature and culture work in the world's largest country.[1]

The Monastery is no less bewildering as a novel — the Russian original weighs in at more than 700 pages as it chronicles the travails of Artiom Goriainov, a university student imprisoned in the Solovki prison camp in the late 1920s for murdering his father. Solovki — the informal name of the Solovetsky Special Purpose Camp — was the first and in many ways most recognizable prison camp set up by the Bolsheviks as part of the system of prisons, camps, exile, and places of execution known as the Gulag. There is a long and impressive roster of authors depicting these locations, which began under the Tsars but reached their horrific crescendo under Stalin, when the Gulag may have housed up to eighteen million people.[2] Why would Prilepin

1 Julie Fedor, "Spinning Russia's 21st Century Wars: Zakhar Prilepin and his 'Literary *Spetsnaz*,'" *RUSI Journal* no. 6 (2018), 18, 22.

2 "Gulag" comes from the Russian name for the Chief Directorate of Camps and Places of Imprisonment (Glavnoe upravlenie lagerei i mest zakliucheniia). There is a large historical debate over the number of Gulag prisoners. For an accessible overview of this mammoth system, see David Hosford, Pamela Kachurin, and Thomas Lamont, "Gulag: Soviet Prison Camps and

write a damning depiction of this system? How does this act of artistic bravery fit with his arming and fighting pro-Kremlin separatists in eastern Ukraine? This second event smacks of the Moscow-backed oppression that created the Gulag and kept the USSR's ethnic minorities (including Ukraine) firmly under the Kremlin's heel — indeed, Putin has tried to whitewash the crimes of the Soviet past as he endeavors to renew Russia's glory. Prilepin thrives on contradictions and thwarting expectations; his actions have real and deadly consequences as well as disturbing implications for the place of the author in today's Russia.[3]

Solovki is a sacred and cursed place for Russian culture. The name refers to the Solovetsky Islands, located on the White Sea in frigid northwest Russia. Constructed in the 1420s-1430s as a Russian Orthodox monastery, Solovki was one of the locations that opposed Church reforms in the mid-1660s until forced into submission. In 1920, three years after the Bolshevik revolution, it became a prison camp for political enemies and criminals. In the Gorbachev era Solovki was a symbol of the lingering trauma of the Stalinist terror; the camp's name appeared in an early documentary film about the Gulag and in 1990 a stone from the camp was placed across from the Lubyanka, the headquarters of the Soviet (and now Russian) secret police. In 2012 the stone was a gathering place for mass protests against the Putin regime, protests that failed to change state policies.[4]

The Monastery draws on the holiness and horror of Solovki. Zakhar Prilepin is the literary alter ego of Evgenii Nikolaevich Prilepin, born in 1975 to a nurse and history teacher in the village of Il'inka near the city of Ryazan in the Russian heartland of the USSR. He studied at Nizhny Novgorod State University in the chaotic and impoverished 1990s, an era that shaped the crisis, violence, and extreme emotions running throughout his prose. Many Russians saw these years as a period of national humiliation at the hands of the West, an experience that explains Putin's rise to power in 2000. Prilepin served with Russian forces in the disastrous First

their Legacy," A Project of the National Park Service and the National Resource Center for Russian, East European and Central Asian Studies, Harvard University, http://gulaghistory.org/nps/downloads/gulag-curriculum.pdf.

3 Fedor notes that in 2017 Prilepin created a group to further the patriotic image of Russia in the arts: see "Spinning Russia's 21st Century Wars," 21.

4 For an overview of Solovki before and after the 1917 revolution, see Roy Robson, *Solovki: The Story of Russia Told Through Its Most Remarkable Islands* (New Haven: Yale University Press, 2004) and the official site of Solovetsky Monastery site: http://solovki-monastyr.ru/abbey/geography/.

Chechen War, where both sides tortured and executed prisoners as Moscow subdued the Muslim region on the southern edge of its crumbling empire. His time in Chechnya was the basis for *Pathology* (Patologiia, 2005), a collection of stories about the conflict that places him alongside Arkady Babchenko and others who depict Russians fighting in this brutal war.[5]

Mark Lipovetsky notes Prilepin's series of careers and political ties: the author worked as a grave-digger and a guard, was involved with the radical left National Bolsheviks, and contributed to the rightist extremist newspaper *Tomorrow* (Zavtra). Prilepin lauded Eduard Limonov, himself a former émigré who founded the National Bolsheviks; Prilepin also contributed a respected study of Soviet writer Leonid Leonov to Russia's most popular biography series. The author envisions himself as an ordinary man who decided to take up writing, glossing over his college training in literature in an effort to distinguish Prilepin from the intelligentsia that has long dominated Russian prose. He has repeatedly linked this group to a Western, liberal culture that is alien to his nation's "traditional" values of masculinity and patriotism.[6]

Prilepin began his writing career as a poet, a choice that reflects the sacrosanct status of this genre in Russian letters. *Sankya* (San'kia, 2016) established him as one of Russia's most important beginning writers — the novel focuses on Sasha Tishin, a young man from a provincial city involved with a radical group strongly resembling the National Bolsheviks. Sasha is a violent but multifaceted character embodying the crushed dreams of those coming of age after the USSR's collapse. The novel resonated with a generation deeply shaken by the ideological vacuum of the cynical post-Soviet era. Liudmila Ulitskaia, one of the country's most prominent liberal authors (and an opponent of Putin and the war in Ukraine), praised *Sankya* as a deeply moving work because of its depictions of poverty and hopelessness. The English translation has a foreword by Alexey Navalny,

---

5 Prilepin's personal web site mixes fact with mythology as it manages his public persona: http://zaharprilepin.ru/ru/bio.html. For a short but disturbing excerpt dealing with his time in Chechnya, see "Pathologies: Zakhar Prilepin," trans. Arch Tait, *Index on Censorship* no. 4 (2005).

6 On Prilepin's contradictory activities, see Mark Lipovetsky, "Politicheskaia motorika Zakhara Prilepina," *Znamia* no. 10 (2012), http://magazines.russ.ru/znamia/2012/10/li12.html. Concerning Prilepin crafting his persona, see Igor' Frolov, "Zakon sakhraneniia strakha," *Kontinent* no. 139 (2009), http://magazines.russ.ru/continent/2009/139/fr29.html. For one example of Prilepin disparaging the liberal intelligentsia, see his Live Journal post: Zakhar Prilepin, 24 July 2017, https://prilepin.livejournal.com/tag/интеллигенция.

the political figure who in recent years has solidified opposition against Putin.[7]

His writing before *The Monastery* focuses on alienated young men scarred by the 1990s and then Putin's restrictions, implying that being Russian means being victimized by others — whether they be the new class of mobster-businessmen or immigrants from the Caucasus. This array of enemies constitutes what sociologist Lev Gudkov terms "negative identity": one's sense of self is defined by alienation from others, a trait common to Prilepin's protagonists (including Artiom). His prose promotes the superiority of his ethnicity and connects physical and political dominance to aggressive sexuality — all these, Lipovetsky notes, are hallmarks of fascist culture. This is a particularly disturbing facet of Prilepin's prose given that he, like all born after 1945, has been raised in the shadow of his nation's horrifying losses in the war against Hitler.[8]

Prilepin's *Monastery* is itself steeped in the tragedy of Russia's bloodiest century. The novel takes place in the first decade of the USSR, when Vladimir Lenin had already begun the political repressions that Stalin would expand and intensify. The novel appeared in 2014, the same year as Russia's seizure of Crimea and support for rebels in eastern Ukraine. Shortly before *The Monastery* appeared, Prilepin criticized including Aleksandr Solzhenitsyn's *Gulag Archipelago* in the high school curriculum. This groundbreaking historical study of the labor camps and prisons, Prilepin alleged, was not founded on sufficient evidence. The accusation, while having little merit, was intended to stoke reader interest in *The Monastery*. No author writing "camp prose" (prose about the Gulag) can escape comparison with Solzhenitsyn. By condemning the magnum opus by the Nobel laureate, Prilepin stakes out his own claim to camp prose, including works by Solzhenitsyn, Varlam Shalamov, Evgeniia Ginzburg, and others. Prilepin's comments exemplify the charged discourse surrounding public discussion and documentation

---

7 For brief mention of Prilepin as poet, see Frolov. On the success of *Sankya*, see Tomi Huttunen and Jussi Lasila, "Zakhar Prilepin: The National Bolshevik Movement and Catachrestic Politics," *Transcultural Studies* no. 12 (2016), 137. Liudmila Ulitskaia discusses *Sankya* with the famous liberal journalist Vladimir Pozner: "Zagadochnaia russkaia dusha. Ulitskaia-Pozner," 18 February 2015, https://www.youtube.com/watch?v=KmIBSsuWwXA. See the foreword by Alexey Navalny in Prilepin, *Sankya*, trans. Mariya Gusev and Jeff Parker (Ann Arbor, MI, Disquiet, 2014).

8 Lipovetsky notes the connection with Lev Gudkov's concept of negative identity, outlined in Gudkov's *Negativnaia identichnost': Stat'i 1997–2002 godov* (Moscow: Novoe literaturnoe obozrenie, 2004). In discerning traits of fascism, Lipovetsky draws on Umberto Eco, "Ur-fascism," in *Five Moral Pieces*, trans. Alastair McEwen (New York: Harcourt, 2002).

of the Gulag — already in the early 2000s Putin began attacking Memorial, the most prominent human rights group commemorating the nine million who perished in the camps.[9]

The Monastery, like many works of camp prose, emphasizes how the Gulag became its own civilization within Soviet society. Solovki has a hierarchy of prisoners and the work they perform, as Artiom discovers when speaking to the intellectual Vasilii Petrovich.

> "I need to find another place to live [. . .] What other brigades do they have here? Let's count them together, maybe we can figure something out."
>
> Vasilii Petrovich didn't need any convincing.
>
> "You were already in the thirteenth," he said. "You're sick of the twelfth, and I agree, you need to leave it. The eleventh is the brigade of the negative element. It's also the icebox and I don't recommend anyone go there. The tenth is the clerical workers. With your obvious literacy, that's the best place for you. You won't get into the ninth — that's the so-called informer's brigade. It's filled with former Chekists from the lower ranks, meaning they're useless for positions of authority, and so they work as guards or overseers." [. . .]
>
> "The seventh is the artistic brigade, also not the worst place in Solovki. By the by, did you happen to take part in school plays? If so, you'd be perfect for a few of the classical roles." It wasn't clear whether Vasilii Petrovich was laughing or not. "The sixth is the custodial brigade. It's good there too, but by [warden] Eichmanis's order, they only take former clergymen there." [. . .]
>
> "The fifth is the fire brigade," continued Vasilii Petrovich. "It's wonderful there, but if you can get into the artists' for your talent or into the clerical because of your ability, for example, to correctly count and beautifully write, to get into the fire brigade, you need to bribe someone. Or, as they call it here, 'the luck of the draw'. We don't burn here that often,

[9] The head of Memorial in the northwest region of Karelia, for instance, was arrested several times on fictious charges: see "Zaderzhan glava karel'skogo 'Memoriala' Iurii Dmitriev," Radio Liberty, 27 June 2018, https://www.svoboda.org/a/29324182.html. "Truth in Dmitriev's case – this is what we speak up for," message sent to the Commissioner for Human Rights, Council of Europe, https://www.memo.ru/en-us/memorial/departments/intermemorial/news/413. See also the organization's website: https://www.memo.ru/en-us/. Documenting the number of dead in the Gulag is contentious and complex — see, among others, Steven Blyth, "The Dead of the Gulag: An Experiment in Statistical Investigation," *Journal of the Royal Statistical Society* no. 3 (1995).

so they're not overwhelmed with work. They play checkers more than anything. But we don't have any money to bribe, so let's go on. The fourth brigade is the musicians of Solovki's orchestras. You haven't hidden any musical talent from me, have you? Maybe, Artiom, you can play on the trumpet? No? Too bad. The third brigade is the Chekists of the highest rank and Information and Investigation Department. So we won't even consider the third. The second is specialists in positions of authority, for example, professional scientists." Here Vasilii Petrovich looked at Artiom carefully again, but he didn't meet his gaze. So he continued, "The first is inmates from among the camp's administration — the commandants, the leaders of various industries and their helpers. You still have to grow a bit before you can get to the first… or, maybe not."

"Is that it?" Artiom asked.

"Why?" said Vasilii Petrovich. "There's still the fourteenth […] maximum security. Those are the inmates that work only within the walls of the kremlin, so they won't run away. The cooks, the lackeys, the ostlers working for the Cheka. In essence, they're supposed to be especially punished, because they don't have the freedom to walk about on Solovki, but they only made it better for them. You decide — it's one thing to carry logs, it's a completely different thing to brush the tail of the commissar's horse. The fifteenth brigade is the artisans — the carpenters, joiners and coopers. There's one more brigade that doesn't work at all. You can get there easily without any bribes, and it's called…?"

"The cemetery, I know," answered Artiom without smiling. "The cemetery of Solovki."[10]

The camp has its privileged and despised classes, with all of them subservient to the Chekists, the secret police whom the Soviets inherited from the Tsarist state. Many of them would be arrested and shot under Stalin's orders in the 1930s, including Eichmanis, the fictional stand-in for the historical figure Fiodor Eichmans.

The Monastery depicts the horrifying effects of state violence yet Prilepin actively encouraged it in another context. The author's literary works are impossible to divorce from his role in the ongoing conflict in eastern Ukraine, dominated by Russian-speakers who often felt slighted by the Ukrainian-speaking majority of the country. In 2014 two areas, backed by

---

10 Zahar Prilepin, *The Monastery*, trans. Nicholas Kotar (London: Glagoslav Publishing, 2020), 115-116.

Russian troops, tried to separate from Ukraine, beginning a war that has claimed 10,000 lives in the region that separatists (including Prilepin) have proclaimed the Donetsk People's Republic. The author's website prominently displays links to songs supporting the breakaway region as well as soliciting donations to his charity. Prilepin proudly discusses how he funded his own battalion and created his own charitable organization to aid victims of the same war he helped promulgate. In a widely-viewed clip he announces that writers are on the side of peace and then gives a command to fire, presumably at enemy forces. In December 2018, however, he announced that the war had become a struggle for big business. Given that the separatists have been connected to corrupt businessmen since the war's beginning, Prileipin's change of heart did not come from his long hatred for capitalism.[11]

In 2018 Prilepin starred in *Phone Duty* (Dezhurstvo), a film praised by the Tribeca Film Festival despite its pro-separatist stance. This role encapsulates his mutable identity — he is a former soldier who became a writer then served as a soldier while portraying a soldier. Tomi Huttunen and Jussi Lasila point out that his actions before and during the war in Ukraine share a macho "patriotic vitality" that Prilepin juxtaposes against a "'bourgeois' liberal mainstream" he derides as immoral, weak, and a holdover from the 1990s. Both Prilepin and Putin exploit Russia's desire for strong, decisive public figures who force respect from other nations.[12]

Despite upholding brawn over intellect, Prilepin sees his literary persona as an outgrowth of the books he read as a child. He devoured the collected works of Leo Tolstoy and Jules Verne, as well as Hemingway, who was popular in the last decades of the USSR. The list then becomes more surprising, combining the long-banned Vladimir Nabokov, Isaak Babel' (a Jewish modernist killed by Stalin), and canonical Soviet author Valentin Kataev. This combination rep-

---

11 Cynthia Buckley, Ralph Clem, Jarod Fox, Erik Herron, "The War in Ukraine is More Devastating than You Know," *Washington Post*, 4 April 2018, https://www.washingtonpost.com/news/monkey-cage/wp/2018/04/09/the-war-in-ukraine-is-more-devastating-than-you-know/. On Prilepin's earlier support for the war, see Sergei Aleksandrov, "'Nash fil'm o Donbasse popal v long-list 'Oskara,'" 27 June 2018, *Svoi*, republished in *Gazeta Kul'tura*, http://portal-kultura.ru/svoy/articles/zvanyy-gost/210970-zakhar-prilepin-nash-film-o-donbasse-popal-v-long-list-oskara/. On his clip, see ibid. Concerning Prilepin's criticism of the separatists, see "Prilepin ob'iasnil pochemu on brosil voevat' v Donbasse," *Gazeta,ru*, 6 December 2018, https://news.rambler.ru/ukraine/41382899-prilepin-obyasnil-pochemu-brosil-voevat-v-donbasse/.

12 On *Phone Duty*, see Aleksandrov, 45. Huttunen and Lasila, 139, 151. For a wide-ranging discussion of how Putin uses masculinity, see *Putin as Celebrity and Cultural Icon*, ed. Helena Goscilo (London: Routledge, 2014).

resents the precocious and eclectic reading tastes of the late-Soviet intelligentsia, a group Prilepin mocks in *Sankya* as estranged from the common people.[13]

Prilepin is far from the original iconoclast he tries to resemble. His blurring of political action, posturing, and talented prose is the evolution of what Andrew Wachtel calls Russian literature's "obsession with history." Wachtel focuses on authors such as Solzhenitsyn, who blend historical analysis with fiction and the philosophizing that has been a mainstay of Russian prose before and after the USSR. Prilepin updates this by cannily exploiting social media and the internet to become a household name beyond the angry young men his writing emphasizes. In this sense he fits into the celebrity culture Vlad Strukov and Helena Goscilo see as emblematic of the Putin era, where real news is subsumed by fame, wealth, and carefully managed scandal. Prilepin is the "anti-celebrity celebrity", who masquerades as an ordinary man from outside Nizhny Novgorod, a patriot, a soldier, and a writer more authentic than the liberal intelligentsia he scorns.[14]

It is thus all the more surprising that Prilepin created an original, moving, and thought-provoking novel about Solovki. *The Monastery* is at one level a thriller — Artiom escapes death multiple times and his fortunes shift by the day if not by the minute as he tries to survive the anger of professional criminals, sadistic camp officials, and the brutal Arctic climate. The prisoner's constantly shifting fate comes from the arbitrary and cruel life in the Gulag. What results is an omnipresent uncertainty and fear — depicting this is one of the affinities camp prose shares with literature of the Holocaust. *The Monastery* is a success precisely because it stretches these individual moments of possible triumph or disaster out over the course of Artiom's sentence, immersing readers in a world that it is at first alien then quickly becomes familiar.

Prilepin's novel is a strange mixture of genres that all work together. In constructing such a hybrid work, he emulates the classics of Russian literature. Solzhenitsyn's novel *The First Circle* (V kruge pervom, 1968) used the fate of imprisoned scientists in a secret lab to mediate on human nature, discuss Dostoevskii, and even develop a steamy (if unconsummated) romance plot. Mikhail Bakhtin, explaining the rise of the novel, praises this genre for its ability to incorporate aspects of many types of

---

13 Zakhar Prilepin, "Ot avtora," in *Doroga v dekabre. Vsia proza v odnom tome* (Moscow: AST, 2012), 5.

14 Andrew Wachtel, *An Obsession with History: Russian Writers Confront the Past* (Palo Alto: Stanford University Press, 1994). On celebrity culture, see *Celebrity and Glamour in Contemporary Russia: Shocking Chic*, eds. Helena Goscilo and Vlad Strukov (London: Routledge, 2011).

literature while still remaining grounded in everyday life — *The Monastery* exploits this flexibility just as its author skillfully navigates his contradictory status as critic of the state, patriot, author, and ordinary veteran. The novel's structure reinforces this mix. In the author's preface, the "real" Prilepin discusses how the plot comes from the comments of his great-grandfather: for many years the author had assumed these stories were about the Second World War, not the Gulag. The main body of the novel focuses on Artiom, imprisoned for murdering his father and thus deemed a "normal" prisoner as opposed to the priests, anarchists, and sundry actual and imagined opponents of Bolshevism populating the camp. My discussion will not reveal more of the plot than is necessary — *The Monastery* is built around the thrill of unexpected actions and their consequences, a trait it inherits from Prilepin's earlier prose. Indeed, Artiom is not much older than Sankya, suggesting that *The Monastery* is the apotheosis of Prilepin's fixation on violent men. In an afterword, Prilepin explains how he spoke to the daughter of Eichmanis. This is followed by the diary of Galina Kucherenko, Artiom's lover in Solovki — Prilepin consulted it when writing *The Monastery*, but received the diary only after he had made significant progress on the manuscript. Following the diary are a series of notes by Prilepin, explaining the fates of the principal characters after the main plot ends in the late 1920s.[15]

The Monastery also harbors traits of documentary prose: life writing that claims to be based on actual events — the novel purports to be built around the experiences of Prilepin's great-grandfather Zakhar Petrov (whose first name the author appropriated as his literary synonym). Documentary prose gained popularity in the last decades of the USSR, presenting itself as a supposedly more reliable alternative to the idealized (and sanitized) state versions of history. Yet *The Monastery* is in reality a clever manipulation of facts with many fictional additions, a scenario recalling Prilepin's critique of Solzhenitsyn for relying too much on hearsay in writing *The Gulag Archipelago*. In *The Monastery* the archival sources and family stories that Prilepin consulted are secondary to the authorial skill that makes them into a coherent fictional narrative.[16]

---

15 Mikhail Bakhtin, "Epic and Novel," in *The Dialogic Imagination: Four Essays by M. M. Bakhtin*, ed. Michael Holquist, trans. Caryl Emerson and Michael Holquist (Austin: University of Texas Press, 1981).

16 For a discussion of the relationship between fact, fiction, and genres in *The Monastery*, see Benjamin Sutcliffe, "'Pravdy ne khvataet: *Obitel'* Z. Prilepina: dokumental'nost' i roman vospitaniia," *Slovo. Journal of Slavic Languages, Literatures and Culture* no. 55 (2014).

The Monastery is also a strange and twisted version of the novel of development (*Bildungsroman*), familiar to readers of Dickens' *Great Expectations* or Fitzgerald's *The Great Gatsby*. In Russian prose Ivan Turgenev and, in a different manner, Tolstoi and Dostoevskii were the most famous authors of this genre, which the USSR chained to the cliché ideological awakening of war heroes and exemplary workers. Artiom matures in many ways, in great part due to his relationship with Galina but also because of his friendship with intellectual Vasilii Petrovich and kind priest Father John (despite both resembling the intelligentsia Prilepin scorns). Prilepin's entire corpus is a single *Bildungsroman*, but one where his male protagonists age without internalizing the 'life lessons' that shape most novels of development. This is due to the cult of violence and lack of self-reflection in Prilepin's works; likewise, Solovki as setting raises an obvious question: can characters learn anything positive from the Gulag? The camps were allegedly created to reform prisoners, yet early on any real effort at transformation devolved into slave labor for projects in the inhospitable corners of the USSR.[17]

Camp prose is, of course, another genre of *The Monastery*. Prilepin follows in the tradition of Solzhenitsyn and more terrifying vision of Shalamov, the two figures who most shaped writing about the Gulag. Leona Toker identifies the features of this writing, which also appear in Prilepin's novel: initiation into the camp (the panicked fear of prisoners arriving at Solovki), "Room 101" (a phrase drawn from Orwell's *1984*, denoting a prisoner's worst experience), and so forth. When Artiom talks to the imprisoned poet Afanasiev after the two have been hauling logs, the man tersely summarizes: "Man is a log to other men." This odd aphorism is a pun on the prisoner saying "Man is wolf to man," conveying that one can expect no mercy in the Gulag. Camp prose is suspicious of those who modify its rules: the late-Soviet author Sergei Dovlatov, for instance, was lambasted in the West for his novella *The Zone* (Zona), an absurdly comic account of the author serving as a camp guard for non-political prisoners in the 1960s. Prilepin, as is obvious from his attack of Solzhenitsyn, thrives on this sort of controversy, using it to attract more readers.[18]

http://uu.diva-portal.org/smash/get/diva2:1263773/FULLTEXT01.pdf.

17 For an examination of the novel of development, see Lina Steiner, *For Humanity's Sake: The* Bildungsroman *in Russian Culture* (Toronto: University of Toronto Press, 2011).

18 Prilepin, *The Monastery*, 96. Leona Toker, *Return from the Archipelago: Narratives of Gulag Survivors* (Bloomington: Indiana University Press, 2000), 82-94.

The Monastery also has a substantial romantic plot involving Artiom and Galina: one is a prisoner while the other is the lover of Eichmanis, the Solovki warden. This scenario is inextricably linked to a key pattern in camp prose: the irony that prisoners and guards could have easily had different fates (and sometimes changed places during Stalin's purges). Artiom and Galina's affair begins when Galina is interrogating the prisoner and he shoves his hand up her skirt, prompting her to embrace him. This unlikely scene echoes the connection that Lipovetsky makes between sex and violence in Prilepin's works: male ferocity conquers women. The power dynamics are now reversed: it is Galina who can destroy Artiom, yet she becomes his lover in response to his brutally masculine behavior.[19]

The Monastery also contains elements of the philosophical novel, that aspect of great Russian prose that uses literature to debate the purpose of life (be it holiness or building communism) or even the course of human history. Tolstoi famously discusses this last point in the second epilogue to *War and Peace*; in the twentieth century Boris Pasternak's *Doctor Zhivago* argues for humane mercy in place of the Bolsheviks' bloody utopia. Artiom has numerous conversations with more erudite prisoners, a scenario reinforcing how the intelligentsia was a group often persecuted under communism. Some of the prisoners gather for philosophical evenings, reenacting the pre-1917 literary salon (until the camp authorities send its members to the punishment cells). At one point a prisoner compares Solovki to all of Russia, which is like a fine fur coat: "'Everyone thinks it's the Bolsheviks, the Bolsheviks who ruined everything. [. . .] But it's merely the empire turned inside out, the entire fur coat! There, you find lice, all kinds of vermin, bed bugs — it was all there! It's just that now, we're wearing the fur coat with the lining out! And that's Solovki!'" This comment is important for several reasons. First, it presents the camp as a microcosm of Soviet society, a pattern found in many works about the Gulag. More importantly, the comment reveals that oppression and poverty have always been a part of Russian history — it is only now that the intelligentsia and former aristocrats are aware of it.[20]

The Monastery places special emphasis on discussions of Orthodoxy, which Prilepin sees as inseparable from Russian culture: this assumption is correct yet elides the long presence of Judaism and Islam (both predate Christianity in the country). Given the context of Prilepin's earlier works, ignoring the religious traditions of Russia's minorities is a subtler sign of his

19 Lipovetsky, 8.

20 Prilepin, *The Monastery*, 212.

muscular ethnocentrism and xenophobia. This approach is another similarity between Prilepin's fiction and Putin's policies — both fuse church, state, and ethnicity to create an exclusionary image of Russia.[21]

The Monastery is a remarkable book produced by a deeply flawed author whose politics and prose promote extremism. This does not mean that Prilepin's novel is not worth reading, but it places a special burden on the reader (and even more so on the critic). Literature — especially in Russia — does not exist without context; it echoes society's hopes, worries, and shapes how generations will view their country and its place in the world. *The Monastery* suggests the artistry and introspection that Prilepin is capable of while underscoring the sad consequences of the intolerance and bloodshed he has often encouraged.

Benjamin Sutcliffe
Professor of Russian
Miami University

21 For a discussion of the philosophical novel that emphasize Dostoevskii, see Mikhail Bakhtin, *Problems of Dostoevsky's Poetics*, ed. and trans. Caryl Emerson (Minneapolis: University of Minnesota Press, 1984), 25.

THE MONASTERY

FROM THE AUTHOR

People said that in his youth my grandfather was noisy and angry. Where I come from, there's a good word to describe such a character: *vzgal'nyj* (crack-brained).

Even in his old age, he had this strange habit. If a single cow separated from the herd walked past our house with a cowbell, he would forget whatever he was doing and run outside, grabbing whatever he had at hand—a crooked rowan walking stick, a boot or an old kettle. From the threshold, swearing horribly, he would throw whatever thing his crooked fingers grabbed at the cow. Sometimes, he would even run after the frightened beast, shouting all manner of retribution on it and its owners.

"Rabid devil!" Grandmother used to call him. She had an odd way of pronouncing this phrase, with the vowels mismatched, and hearing it like that ran shivers down your spine.

The "a" in "rabid" looked like great-grandfather's possessed, almost triangular, up-hoisted eye that twitched when he was irritated. It didn't help that his other eye squinted. Why she called him a devil, well, whenever he would cough or sneeze, it sounded like he was saying "devil" in Russian. Not "aaaa… chooo!" but "aaaa… *chiort! Chiort! Chiort!*" You could just imagine that great-grandfather saw the devil in front of him and was yelling at him, casting him out. Either that, or every time he coughed, he expelled another devil that had gotten inside him.

As I repeated grandmother's phrase by syllables — "ra-bid-de-vil!" — I listened in on my own whisper. In the familiar words, streams of wind blew in from the past, from a time when he had been completely different — young, black-hearted and insane.

Grandmother recollects that after she married grandfather and lived in his house with his family, great-grandfather used to beat "Mamania" — her mother-in-law, my great-grandmother — severely. Her mother-in-law was tall, strong and severe, a head taller than great-grandfather and broader in the shoulders. But she feared him and listened to him without question.

To properly strike her, great-grandfather had to stand up on a bench. From there, he would demand that she approach. After which he grabbed her by the hair and walloped her ears with his balled fist.

His name was Zahar Petrovich.

"Whose son is that?" — "Zahar Petrovich's."

Great-grandfather was bearded. His beard was like a Chechen's beard, barely curly and still not completely white, although the sparse hairs on his head were whiter than white, insubstantial and fluffy. If a down feather from an old pillow had gotten stuck on his head, you could hardly distinguish it from his hair.

Only we fearless children dared to take off those feathers. Not grandfather, not grandmother, not father — none of them dared touch his head. Also, if they ever made jokes about him, it was only done so in his absence.

He wasn't tall. By the age of fourteen I had already outgrown him, although, of course, by this time Zahar Petrov slouched, limped badly and seemed to be slightly growing into the earth. He was either eighty-eight or eight-nine at that point. His passport had one year of birth, but he was actually born in another year. But whether it was a year before the passport or after, he himself had forgotten over time.

Grandmother used to say that great-grandfather got kinder after he turned sixty, but only to the kids. He adored his grandkids, fed them, pampered them and washed them. By the standards of village life, this was all a little strange. All of the children took turns napping with him on the stove under his massive, curly, smelly overcoat.

He sometimes visited their house; I think I was six years old when I had a few turns under the overcoat — that rugged, woolen, sleepy overcoat. To this day, I still remember its aura.

The overcoat was like ancient tradition — you honestly believed that seven generations had worn it and couldn't wear it out. All our kin had warmed themselves under its wool. In winter, newborn calves and piglets were wrapped in it as they were carried into the hut, lest they freeze in the shed. It's entirely possible that a quiet family of house-mice could live in those huge sleeves for years at a time. If you poked around in the folds and corners of that coat, you could even find the cigarette that great-grandfather's great-grandfather hadn't finished smoking a century ago, or a ribbon from the wedding decorations of grandmother's grandmother, or even a piece of sugar that my father lost. He spent three days of his hungry post-war childhood looking for it, but never found it.

But I found it, and I ate it, although it was mixed up with old tobacco.

When great-grandfather died, my family threw away the overcoat. No matter how much I went on about it, they said it was old garbage and stank terribly.

We celebrated Zahar Petrov's ninetieth birthday three years in a row, just in case.

Great-grandfather sat, seeming, to a careless eye, to be filled with self-importance, but actually quite cheerful and a little mischievous. It's like he was saying, "I fooled you all! I lived to be ninety and forced you all to gather in my honor!"

He drank, as did all of us, no worse than the young people, even in his old age. When midnight struck and he felt that maybe it was time to stop (the parties began at noon), he got up slowly from the table and, waving off grandmother who had rushed to help him, walked to his perch on the stove, looking at no one.

While great-grandfather was walking out, everyone sat at the table frozen and silent.

I remember my godfather saying once, "He walks like a generalissimus." This was my uncle who was killed the next year in a stupid quarrel.

I found out that great-grandfather was imprisoned in a camp at Solovki when I was still a child. For me, it was as though he had walked to Persia to buy a kaftan during the reign of Alexei Mikhailovich or had reached Tmutarakan with a shaved Sviatoslav.

People didn't talk much about it, but, on the other hand, great-grandfather occasionally remembered Eichmanis or the group leader Krapin or the poet Afanasiev.

For a long time I thought that Mstislav Burtsev and "Curly" were great-grandfather's war buddies, only later did I realize that they were fellow inmates.

When I stumbled upon some photographs from Solovki, for some strange reason I immediately recognized Eichmanis, Burtsev and Afanasiev.

They felt like my near, though not always dear, relatives.

When I think about that now, I understand how short the path to history is. It's right next to you. I touched my great-grandfather; he had seen saints and demons with his own eyes.

He always remembered Eichmanis as "Fiodor Ivanovich"; you could hear in his tone that he had grudging respect for the man. I sometimes try to imagine how they killed that handsome and intelligent man — the founder of concentration camps in Soviet Russia.

To me, personally, great-grandfather never said anything about life on Solovki, although sometimes, speaking only to the grown men, especially my father, he would say something in passing. Every time it was like he was finishing a story that he had started just before — for example, a year ago, ten years ago or even forty years ago.

I remember how mother, bragging in front of the old men, checked how my sister was getting on in French. Suddenly, great-grandfather reminded father — who, it seemed, had heard the story before — how he had accidentally been given the assignment to pick berries and how he had unexpectedly met Fiodor Ivanovich, who had started speaking French with one of the inmates.

In two or three phrases of his raspy and loud voice, great-grandfather quickly sketched some scenes from the past, which turned out vivid and clear. Plus, his look, his wrinkles, his beard, the down on his head, his chuckle — it reminded me of a metal spoon scraping a frying pan — all of this added even more significance to the words themselves.

I had heard the stories of the logs in October's frozen water, the huge and hilarious "sauna switches of Solovki", the massacred seagulls and the dog nicknamed "Black".

I named my own dark-colored mutt "Black".

My puppy, in play, accidentally smothered a chick. Then it spread out the feathers of a second one on the porch, then a third… basically, one time, great-grandfather grabbed the puppy, who was hopping about, chasing the last chick by the tail. He swung the puppy around and smacked him against the corner of our stone house. After the first strike the puppy shrieked horribly, but after the second he was quiet.

My great-grandfather's hands remained, even at ninety, if not strong, then at least tenacious. The conditioning of the Lubianka and Solovki kept him healthy for the whole century. I don't remember his face, only his beard and crooked mouth, always chewing something. As for his hands, I only have to close my eyes to see them. Bluish-black fingers covered in dirty, curly hairs. He was sent away, after all, for savagely beating an authorized agent of the government. Another time, only a miracle prevented him from being sent away a second time when he single-handedly slaughtered all of the cattle that belonged to him and that had been scheduled to be communized.

When I look at my hands, especially when I'm drunk, I note with some distress that the crooked fingers of my great-grandfather, with their hoary, brass-like nails, are pushing their way out into mine more and more every year.

Great-grandfather used to call pants "skerries", a razor blade was a "washer" and cards were "church calendars". If he caught me lying about reading a book, he used to say, "O look, it's a dead body lying there." But he said it without malice, as a joke, as though he approved of it.

No one talked like him, nobody in the family or in the whole village.

Some of the stories my grandfather told in his own way, while my father told them in a different style and my uncle in a third way. Grandmother always talked about camp life from her pitying, womanly point of view, as though contradicting the male point of view.

However, with time, the general picture began to become clearer in my mind.

Father told me about Galia and Artiom when I was fifteen, which coincided with the beginning of the age of revelations and repentant idiocy. Father told this story for the record and in few words, but it impressed me, even then.

Grandmother also knew this story.

For a long time, I couldn't comprehend how and when great-grandfather told all of this to my father. He didn't speak much, but somehow he did tell him.

Later, when I put together all the stories into a single picture and compared it to what actually happened, at least according to archival evidence, personal notes from the camp and official reports, I noticed that, for great-grandfather, a series of unconnected events merged into a single tale, happening chronologically; while, in actual fact they were sometimes separated by one or even three years.

Then again, what is truer than that which is remembered?

Truth is what you remember.

Great-grandfather died when I was in the Caucasus — free, cheerful and camouflaged.

Soon afterwards, nearly all of our huge family went into the ground. Only the grandkids and the great-grandkids remained. Alone, without the adults.

Now we have to pretend that we're the adults, even though I still haven't found any significant differences between my fourteen-year-old self and my adult self.

Except that I now have a fourteen-year-old son.

It so happened that while all of my old people were dying, I was always somewhere far away. I didn't make it to a single funeral.

Sometimes, I still think that my relatives are alive; otherwise, where have they all gotten themselves to?

A few times I've dreamt that I've returned to my village, where I try to find great-grandfather's overcoat. I climb through some kind of shrubs, cutting my hands. Restless and without a purpose, I roam along the river, near the cold and dirty water, then suddenly I'm in the shed — old rakes, old scythes, rusted metal — all of this accidentally falls on me and it hurts. Later, for some reason, I climb into the hayloft; I dig around there, choking from the dust and I cough: "*Chiort! Chiort! Chiort!*"

But I don't find anything.

BOOK I

"Il fait froid aujourd'hui."
"Froid et humide."
"Quel sale temps, une veritable fievre."
"Une veritable peste…"[22]

"You'll recall that the monks here said, 'In labors are we saved!'" said Vasilii Petrovich, for a moment shifting his contented, often-blinking eyes from Fiodor Ivanovich Eichmanis to Artiom. Artiom nodded for some reason, although he had no idea what they were talking about.

"*C'est dans l'effort que se trouve notre salut?*"[23] asked Eichmanis again.

"C'est bien cela!"[24] answered Vasilii Petrovich with pleasure, and so vehemently nodded his head that several berries fell to the ground from the basket he held in his hands.

"Well, I guess we're right, then," said Eichmanis, smiling and looking first at Vasilii Petrovich, then at Artiom, then at his companion. For that matter, she didn't return his gaze. "I don't know anything about salvation, but the monks knew about work."

Artiom and Vasilii Petrovich stood on the wet grass in their dampened and dirty clothing, with black knees, sometimes shifting from one foot to the other, wiping from their faces the forest spider webs and mosquitos with hands that had ploughed the earth. Eichmanis and his woman were on horseback. He sat on a restive sorrel stallion, she was on an old piebald that seemed half-deaf.

---

22 "It's cold today."
"Yes, cold and damp."
"What horrible weather. It's like a fever!"
"A real plague!"

23 "We're saved by our work?"

24 "That's it, exactly!"

The rain began again, murky and prickly for July. An unexpectedly cold wind, even for these parts, blew in.

Eichmanis nodded to Artiom and Vasilii Petrovich. The woman silently pulled her reins to the left, seemingly irritated by something.

"Her seat is no worse than Eichmanis's," Artiom remarked, watching them leave.

"Yes, yes..." Vasilii Petrovich answered in a way that made it clear that he didn't hear Artiom's words. He put his basket on the ground and silently gathered the berries that he had dropped.

"You're tottering from hunger," said Artiom, looking from above at Vasilii's cap. It wasn't clear whether or not he was joking. "The sixth hour has chimed already. A lavish meal awaits us. What do you think? Potatoes or buckwheat today?"

A few more members of the berry brigade pulled themselves towards the road from the forest.

Without waiting for the infernal drizzle to end, Vasilii Petrovich and Artiom walked towards the monastery. Artiom limped a little. While he was gathering berries he had twisted his ankle.

He was no less tired than Vasilii Petrovich. To add insult to injury, Artiom obviously had come short, once again, of his quota.

"I won't do this work anymore," said Artiom quietly, oppressed by the silence. "To hell with these berries. I've eaten enough for a whole week, but I get no joy from it at all."

"Yes, yes..." repeated Vasilii Petrovich once again, but he finally managed to grab a hold of himself and answered unexpectedly, "At least it was without the guards. A whole day not seeing those black hat-bands, nor those stool pigeons, nor the 'leopards' Artiom."

"Plus my ration is gonna be halved, I won't have a second portion at lunch," parried Artiom. "Alas for my boiled cod!"

"I could always give you some of mine," offered Vasilii Petrovich.

"Then we both won't have met our quota." Artiom laughed quietly. "That will hardly make me happy."

"You know how hard it was for me to get today's job... at least it's not uprooting trees, Artiom." Vasilii Petrovich grew a little more animated. "By the way, have you noticed what else *isn't* in the forest?"

Artiom had noticed something for sure, but he couldn't for the life of him understand what it was.

"Those thrice-damned seagulls don't scream there!" Vasilii Petrovich actually stopped and, after considering, ate a single berry from his basket.

In the monastery and in the port, you could hardly walk through the clouds of seagulls, but it was the icebox for anyone who killed a seagull. The director of the camp, Eichmanis, for some reason treasured the shrieking and obnoxious breed of the Solovki gull. It didn't make any sense.

"Bilberries have iron, chromium and copper," Vasilii Petrovich shared his knowledge, having eaten another berry.

"For some reason I feel like I'm the bronze horseman," said Artiom gloomily. "And the chromium horseman."

"Besides, bilberries improve your eyesight," said Vasilii Petrovich. "You see that star on the church?"

Artiom looked.

"So?"

"How many points does it have?" asked Vasilii Petrovich, completely seriously.

Artiom stared for a moment, then understood everything; Vasilii Petrovich saw that he understood and they both giggled.

"It's good that you only nodded significantly but didn't talk to Eichmanis. Your whole mouth is black with bilberries," said Vasilii Petrovich through his laughter, then they laughed twice as hard.

While they looked at the star and laughed at what it meant, the berry brigade overtook them, and everyone considered it necessary to peek into the baskets of those already standing on the road.

Vasilii Petrovich and Artiom remained a little apart from the rest. Their laughter quickly died, with Vasilii Petrovich suddenly turning severe.

"You know, it's a shameful, abominable trait," he said heavily and with distaste. "It's not enough that he just decided to have a chat with me, he even spoke to me in French! I'm immediately ready to forgive him for everything. Even to love him! I will now come and swallow that foul brew, then I will climb to my bunk to feed the lice. But he will eat meat, then they'll bring him the berries that we gathered. And he will wash down the berries with milk! I really should, forgive me most graciously, spit in these berries. But instead I'm carrying them with gratitude for the fact that this person can speak French and condescend to my level! But my father spoke French too! And German, and English! And what cheek I gave him! How I humiliated my father! Why didn't I give *him* cheek, me and my old bones? How I hate myself, Artiom! Devil take me!"

"Enough, enough, Vasilii Petrovich, stop it." Artiom's laugh was different now. He had managed to come to love these monologues over the past month.

"No, it's not enough, Artiom," said Vasilii Petrovich strictly. "Here's what I've come to know. The aristocracy, it's not the blue blood, not at all. It's just that people ate well from generation to generation. The serf girls gathered berries for them, made their beds and washed them in the *banya*, then brushed their hair out with a comb. They washed off and brushed up so much that they became the aristocracy. Now we've been dumped in the mud, but they've taken the high places. They're well fed; they're washed; and they… well, perhaps not *they*, but their children… also, will become the aristocracy."

"No," answered Artiom and walked on, rubbing off the raindrops from his face in a frenzy.

"You don't think so?" asked Vasilii Petrovich, catching up with him. His voice rang with an evident hope that Artiom was right. "In that case, I think I'll eat another berry. You eat one too, Artiom. My treat. Here, even take two."

"Forget it." Artiom waved him off. "You don't have any pig lard, do you?"

* * *

The closer they got to the monastery, the louder the gulls became.

The monastery was angular, with extravagant angles, untidy in its horrible ruined state.

Its body had been burned out, all that was left was moving wind and mossy boulders for walls.

It rose so heavy and huge, as though it were built not by weak mortals, but all at once, its stone body falling from the heavens whole and catching those who ended up here in a trap.

Artiom didn't like to look at the monastery. He wanted to quickly pass through the gates and be inside.

"Already two years I've been scraping by here, and still, every time I enter the Kremlin, my hand itches to make the sign of the cross," shared Vasilii Petrovich, furtively.

"Then cross yourself," answered Artiom in a full voice.

"Towards the star?" asked Vasilii Petrovich.

"The church," Artiom cut him off. "What difference does it make? Star, no star… The church is still standing."

"But what if they break off my fingers? Better not anger the idiots," said Vasilii Petrovich after a pause; he even hid his hands deeper in the sleeves of his jacket. Under his jacket he wore a shabby flannel shirt.

"... meanwhile, there's a crowd in the church, five minutes from sainthood, filling up the three-story bunks..." Artiom said, finishing his thought. "Or even more, if you count under the bunks."

Vasilii Petrovich always crossed the courtyard quickly with downcast eyes, as though he were trying not to accidentally attract anyone's attention.

Old birches and lindens grew in the courtyard, even though above all of them stood poplars. Artiom especially liked the rowan tree. The inmates tore off generous bunches of berries to eat, steeped in hot water or to just chew something sour, but it turned out to be unbearably bitter. Now, only a few bunches remained on the top of the tree, and for some reason this reminded Artiom of his mother's hairstyle.

The twelfth working brigade of the Solovki camp took up the entirety of the refectory of the former cathedral church, named after the Dormition of the Most Holy Mother of God.

They walked through the wooden tambour, having greeted the orderlies — a Chechen whose name and crime he could never remember (nor did he particularly want to) and Afanasiev, whose anti-Soviet agitation, as he himself boasted, was that of a Leningrad poet. He cheerfully inquired: "How are the berries in the forest, Tioma?" The correct answer was, "The berries are located in Moscow, Mr. Deputy Head of the State Political Directorate. It's we who are in the woods."

Afanasiev quietly snickered, while the Chechen, it seemed to Artiom, understood nothing, but you could hardly tell from looking at him. Afanasiev sat, lounging as much as he could on the backless stool. The Chechen either walked here and there, or squatted in place.

The clock on the wall showed six forty-five.

Artiom patiently waited for Vasilii Petrovich, who, having gathered water from the barrel at the entrance, drank it, huffing and puffing. Artiom would have easily drunk the whole mug in two gulps... anyway, all totaled, he drank three whole mugs and dumped a fourth on his head.

"We have to carry that water!" grumbled the Chechen, drawing every Russian word from his mouth with some difficulty.

Artiom took a few crushed berries from his pocket and said, "Here."

The Chechen took them, not understanding what he was being given. When he realized what it was, he rolled them down the table in disgust. Afanasiev caught each of them in turn and threw them into his mouth.

As soon as they entered the refectory, the smell that they had forgotten about after a day in the forest struck them — unwashed human filth; dirty, stale meat; no cattle smells as foul as man and the insects that live on him;

but Artiom knew for a fact that in seven minutes he would get used to it, forget it and mingle with the smell, with this noise and foul language, with this life.

The bunks were built from rounded, constantly damp poles and un-sanded boards.

Artiom slept on the second level. Vasilii Petrovich slept directly under him. He had already taught Artiom that in the summer it's better to sleep on the bottom — it's colder there — while in the winter it's better on the top, "because warm air rises where…?"

Afanasiev lived on the third level. Not only was it extremely hot for him, he was constantly dripped on from the ceiling — evaporating sweat and breathing produced a rotten kind of precipitation.

"It seems you're not a believer, Artiom?" Vasilii Petrovich went on, trying to continue the conversation they had begun outside, all the while trying to take off his deteriorating footwear. "A child of the age, yes? You've read all sorts of garbage in childhood, probably? *Dyr bur shchyl* in your pants, and your brain is enthralled. God died a natural death, something like that, yes?"

Artiom didn't answer, trying to hear whether or not they'd brought dinner yet, though they rarely brought the grub before its proper time.

He had taken bread with him to the berry-picking — bilberries were always better with bread, but it still didn't appease the ever-present hunger.

Vasilii Petrovich put his shoes on the ground with that quiet carefulness that's usually seen in un-pampered women who are putting aside their jewelry for the night. Then he took a long time shaking out his things before finally concluding bitterly:

"Artiom, they've stolen my spoon again, can you imagine?"

Artiom immediately checked for his own — yes, it was in its place, as was his bowl. He squashed a louse while he rummaged through his things. They had already stolen his bowl once. Then he had taken a loan of twenty-two pennies of the local prison currency from Vasilii Petrovich and bought a bowl in the prison commissary, after which he had scratched out "A" on the bottom, so that, if they did steal it, he could find it. At the same time, he understood full well that there was no point in the etching — the bowl would go into a different brigade, and they'd hardly let him see where it was or find who had stolen it.

He squashed another louse.

"Can you imagine, Artiom?" repeated Vasilii Petrovich, not expecting an answer and once against digging through his bed roll.

Artiom mumbled something incoherent.

"What?" asked Vasilii Petrovich.

"I've imagined it," answered Artiom, and added, to console his friend, "Buy one in the commissary. For now, we'll share mine."

Artiom really didn't need to sniff out dinner. It was always preceded by the singing of Moisei Solomonovich. He had an amazing nose for food and always began to wail a few minutes before the prisoners on kitchen duty brought in the vat with kasha or soup.

He sang everything with equal gusto — romances, operettas, Jewish and Ukrainian songs, even trying out the little French he knew (he didn't know much, judging by Vasilii Petrovich's exaggerated grimaces).

"All hail freedom, the Soviet government, the will of the workers and farmers!" sang Moisei Solomonovich quietly, but distinctly and without, it would seem, any sarcasm. He had an elongated skull; black, curly hair; bulging, surprised eyes; a big mouth with an obvious tongue. As he sang, he helped himself with his hands, as though catching the words of the song as they floated by him on the air and building a little tower out of them.

Afanasiev and the Chechen, scurrying with their feet, brought in the zinc vat on sticks, then a second one.

The prisoners came up to dinner in groups; it always took no less than an hour. Artiom and Vasilii Petrovich's group was run by another inmate, a former policeman named Krapin. He was a quiet, severe man with attached earlobes. The skin on his face was forever flushed, as though boiled, and his prominent forehead was sharp, somehow impressive to look at, immediately reminding one of long-ago viewed pages from either a textbook on zoology or a medical guide.

In their group, in addition to Moisei Solomonovich and Afanasiev, there were various felons and career criminals, such as a Cossack from Terek named Lazhechnikov, three Chechens, an old Polack, a young Chinese man, a thug from Ukraine who had managed to fight for ten different Cossack hetmans during the Civil War and for the Reds in the interim, an officer of Kolchak's army, a general's batman nicknamed "Samovar", a dozen *muzhiks* from Chernozem and a satirist from Leningrad named Grakov, who for some reason avoided his fellow countryman Afanasiev.

Under the bunks, amid the utter darkness of the garbage there, the heaps of rags and rubbish, a homeless kid had settled himself there two days ago. Either he had run away from solitary confinement or from the eighth brigade, which is where most of his kind lived. Artiom had fed him cabbage once, but no more; still, the kid slept closer to their group.

"How can he know, Artiom, that we won't turn him in?" asked Vasilii Petrovich rhetorically, with the lightest self-deprecation. "Do we really have such a good-for-nothing look? I once heard that a grown man incapable of villainy, or at least murder, looks boring. What do you think?"

Artiom remained silent so he didn't have to answer and demean his manly worth.

He came to the camp two and a half months ago, having received the first designation of four possible workers' designations, which meant that he would get heavy work everywhere he was sent, no matter what the weather. Until June, he had remained in the thirteenth brigade — the quarantine — having worked for a month unloading at the docks. Artiom had tried out working as a stevedore in Moscow from the age fourteen and was adept at this kind of work, something that the foremen and the work-assignment clerks had immediately noted. If only they had fed him a little more and given him just a little more sleep, it would have been OK.

But Artiom was moved from quarantine to the twelfth brigade.

This group was also not one of the easier ones, though the regimen was a little less severe than in the thirteenth. The twelfth also worked general jobs, often slaving away for hours at a time until they met their quota. They had no right to personally complain to those in charge, they could only complain through the group leaders. As for Vasilii Petrovich and his French, Eichmanis had spoken to him first in the forest.

Throughout June, the twelfth was given different jobs — logs, cleaning up garbage in the monastery itself, uprooting trees, scything hay, making bricks or helping out at the railroad. Those from the cities didn't always know how to cut hay, while others were useless at unloading. Some people ended up in the infirmary, others in solitary. Work assignments were constantly being changed and mixed up.

Up until this point, Artiom had avoided the logs — the heaviest, dreariest and wettest work, but he had had his fill of the stumps. He could never have imagined how firmly, deeply and differently trees held on to the earth.

"If you don't chop off the roots one by one, but try to pull out the whole stump at once, with incredible strength, then in its endless tails it would pull out a piece of earth as big as the cupola on the Dormition!" Afanasiev said in his picturesque way, either angry or exhilarated.

The quota per person was twenty-five stumps a day.

Competent inmates, specialists and masters were moved to other brigades, where the regimen was less severe. But Artiom couldn't figure out where he, a student who hadn't finished school, could be useful, or even what he was really capable of doing well. Anyway, deciding that was half the battle, you still had to be noticed and called out.

After the stumps, the whole body hurt, like it was shattered. In the morning, it felt like you didn't have enough strength for another work day. Artiom visibly lost weight, began to dream about food, constantly sought the smell of edibles and experienced that smell intensely, but his youth still dragged him on without giving up.

Vasilii Petrovich seemed to have helped, having claimed to be an expert berry picker — well, clearly, he was that — and when he got the berry-picking brigade, he pulled Artiom along with him. But the lunch that they brought into the forest every day was cold and smaller than the allotted ration. Clearly, the convict-deliverymen ate to their heart's content along the road. The last time, the berry-pickers were forgotten and not fed at all. The deliverymen protested that they had come but couldn't find the pickers dispersed throughout the forest. Someone complained about the deliverymen and they each got three days of solitary, but Artiom didn't get any more food.

Today's dinner was buckwheat. Artiom had eaten it quickly since childhood. But here, having sat down on Vasilii Petrovich's bunk, he didn't even notice how the kasha disappeared. He wiped his spoon on the underside of his jacket, then passed it to his elder companion, who was sitting with his bowl on his knees and tactfully looking away.

"Thank you," said Vasilii Petrovich quietly and firmly, scooping up the sodden, tasteless porridge boiled in snotty water.

"Uh-huh," answered Artiom.

Having finished the boiling water, drunk from the tin can that he used as a mug, Artiom jumped up to his bed, risking breaking the bunks, took off his shirt, laid it under himself along with his foot wrapping to dry, put his arms in his overcoat, wrapped his head in a scarf and almost immediately fell asleep, only managing to hear how Vasilii Petrovich quietly spoke to the homeless boy, who had the habit of lightly pulling on the pants of those eating during mealtimes:

"I won't feed you, are we clear? It's you who stole my spoon, isn't it?"

Considering that the homeless boy was under the bunks and Vasilii Petrovich was sitting on them, it might have seemed from the side that he was speaking with spirits, threatening them with hunger and looking forward with stern eyes.

Artiom had time to smile at the thought, but the smile slid off his lips when he fell asleep. After all, there was a full hour until the evening roll call, so why waste time?

Someone was fighting in the refectory; someone cursed; someone wept — Artiom didn't care.

During that hour, he had time to dream about a boiled egg, a simple boiled egg. The yolk glowed from within, as though it were filled with the sun, streaming forth warmth and gentleness. Artiom touched it with his fingers reverently, and his fingers grew hot. He carefully broke apart the egg, it broke into two halves of egg whites, in one of which, shamelessly naked, alluring, almost pulsating, lay the yolk. Even without tasting it, you could tell that it was ineffably, head-spinningly sweet and soft. From somewhere in his dream, he got coarse salt and Artiom salted the egg, distinctly seeing how every salt crystal fell and how the egg yolk became more and more silvery — soft gold in the midst of silver. For some time, Artiom examined the broken egg, unable to decide what to start with — the whites or the yolk. Prayerfully, he bowed to the egg to carefully lick off the salt.

He woke up for a moment, realizing that he was licking his own salty hand.

* * *

In the twelfth brigade, you weren't allowed to leave at night. The latrine was left inside until the morning. Artiom trained himself to get up between three and four in the morning. He walked with his eyes still shut, by memory, scratching off the lice in a sleepy frenzy… at least he didn't share his business with anyone else.

As he walked back, he could hardly distinguish the people and the bunks.

The homeless boy slept right there on the floor. You could see his dirty foot, "… so, not dead yet…" thought Artiom in passing. Moisei Solomonovich snored in a singsong, multifarious manner. Vasilii Petrovich, Artiom noticed not for the first time, looked completely different while sleeping. He was frightening, even unpleasant, as though someone else, someone unknown, pushed out through the waking man.

As he lay down on the still-warm overcoat, Artiom looked, with half-drunk eyes, over the refectory with its one hundred and fifty sleeping inmates.

"It's wild!" he thought, screwing up his eyes, afraid and wondering. "Here lies man, doing nothing, and it's like this… for the greater part… of his life…"

On the other side of the refectory, a match flared. Someone, no longer able to bear it, wanted to squash at least one family of lice in the light. Even at night, the lice constantly crawled along the bars of the bunks, along the walls, falling from somewhere above.

Artiom opened his eyes at that small flare of the match and saw someone from the second group reaching into someone else's bag. He met the thief's gaze, screwed up his eye, turned over and forgot it forever.

Immediately, the morning five o'clock bell woke him up, then, after a few seconds, Afanasiev finished the job by yelling:

"Brigade, wake up!"

Today Artiom hated Afanasiev; yesterday a different man was on morning duty, yelling with a guttural voice; then, the hatred was for him.

In a minute, Moisei Solomonovich, barely visible in the repugnant half-murk, was already singing:

"Where are you now? Who kisses the tips of your fingers? Where has your Chinaman Lee gone?"

Artiom squinted at the Chinese man, who slept nearby, but he seemed not to hear the words of the song. He sat on his second level, stroking his neck and face, as though he were finding himself again under his hands, his body and his consciousness.

"Shut up, you fucking operetta!" yelled one of the gangsters who hadn't gotten up yet.

Moisei Solomonovich tripped in the middle of a word.

"I thought I was being quiet," he said to the air, shrugging his shoulders.

In any case, Moisei Solomonovich didn't remain quiet for long. Soon enough he was rumbling something barely audible — they were bringing in the food.

You could stand in line and wait forty minutes before it was your turn, but Artiom cultivated his patience, not to waste any time.

He moved to sit under a map and had time to read through the local magazine *The Islands of Solovki*, issued in the camp by the inmates. Vasilii Petrovich had loaned it from the library, apparently to keep his caustic hatred of the camp's administration at its proper level. Artiom most often read the poetry page. He had to admit that it was very bad poetry, except for maybe Boris Shiriaev, who brought attention to himself by his labored imitation of other poets. Had he been released yet or not…? The poems in the journal, no matter how bad, Artiom had committed to memory, and he repeated them to himself sometimes, though he didn't really understand why.

Only after he had finished this daily routine did Artiom get up to stand in line. As he had hoped, there were only a few people left.

"Artiom, you haven't changed your mind?" asked Vasilii Petrovich, returning him his washed spoon.

"No, I won't go," answered Artiom with a smile, immediately understanding that they were talking about the berry-picking. "Don't ask for me, it's not worth it."

"They'll put you on log brigade, my dear fellow and then you'll howl. And you won't be the first. Come to your senses," said Vasilii Petrovich severely. "For five days straight, I've done a quota and a half in the berry brigade. Today, they've made me brigade leader. Soon the currants and raspberries will come out on the north-eastern shore, keep that in mind. There's this wonderful berry that grows here, to boot, the crowberry, or the mossberry — very healthy, judging by the name."

"No," Artiom repeated. "Everything's fine with my… mossberries, thank you very much."

"And in the forest, you can see a real common carder bee, just like in our region of Tula," added Vasilii Petrovich, completely helpless. "Do you remember how we saw that nettle as tall as a man? And the birds! The birds sing there!"

"There's one bird there that chatters just like someone locking a bolt. It's unpleasant," said Artiom. "And there are three times as many mosquitoes in the forest. I don't want to go."

"You still have to survive the winter," said Vasilii Petrovich. "You don't know yet what a winter in Solovki is!"

"Why, are you planning to gather berries in winter?" sniggered Artiom, but immediately rebuked himself for his slight impudence. Vasilii Petrovich didn't seem to even notice.

Moisei Solomonovich may have been always singing, but he heard everything. Without being noticed, he appeared near Vasilii Petrovich's bunk and, interrupting his own song, asked:

"Are you freeing up a spot in the brigade? Artiom doesn't want it? Good for him, he's young and strong! Vasilii Petrovich, could I replace Artiom, even for a short time? Don't look at me like that, you don't even know how well I see the berries in the grass. I have a gift!"

Vasilii Petrovich only waved him off and left on his own business.

"So we're agreed?" called Moisei Solomonovich in his wake, looking at him with fawning eyes. "I'll make it worth your while. I'm getting a parcel from mommy any day now."

Moisei Solomonovich called both his wife and his mother "mommy", as well as several of his aunts of varying degrees of relation, and, it seemed, some other women as well.

"As for you, Artiom, you have the wonderful water treatment of the Solovki health resort to look forward to," said Moisei Solomonovich, winking with his huge eye, like an egg. "A three-year visit guarantees good health for a whole century. You're in for three years, yes?"

Artiom jumped down from his bunk and asked: "What about you?" in such a tone that Moisei Solomonovich immediately disappeared.

"Hey, moron," said Krapin, who suddenly appeared next to Artiom. "You're dead."

He had this habit — to say something rude and then stand there for a minute, waiting to see what the answer would be. Artiom remained silent, biting his lip and looking beyond the group leader, thinking two words: "Damn cretin." Artiom was afraid of getting hit and he was even more afraid that everyone would see him getting hit.

Moisei Solomonovich seemed to be taking care of his things and shaking out his coats, but by his stance you could tell he was listening with all his might to see how it would end.

The morning roll call sounded.

Everyone lined up in the corridor. At the exit, there was confusion. The Chechens, who always stood up for each other, started to bicker with someone, going at their throats. Krapin, who held a bludgeon, pushed the gangsters forward, whom he especially and vehemently hated, while they answered him with suppressed hatred of their own. In the confusion, Artiom was struck as though by accident, but Artiom was sure that Krapin knew whom he was hitting, that he hit him on purpose.

"Does it hurt?" asked Vasilii Petrovich kindly as they lined up, seeing how Artiom grimaced.

"My mother used to joke when my brother and I asked to eat in the evenings: 'For the stupid kids, a jab in the ribs!'" suddenly Artiom remembered, scowling unhappily. "If only she knew…"

While he languished in line, Krapin didn't leave his thoughts. Even though he looked ahead, he could still see, though it hurt his eyes, ten meters to his left, the sloping red forehead and the attached earlobe.

Artiom didn't want to become the reason for the beetle-browed attention and incoherent irritation of the group leader. There was no one here to whom he could complain; he wouldn't get any satisfaction here… but others would get their satisfaction at his expense soon enough.

From his very first day in the camp, he knew one thing: the most important thing was not to be noticed, remembered, or seen by all those who didn't need to see you. But today, the exact opposite had happened. Artiom wasn't afraid of pain; it wasn't all that embarrassing to get hit along with everyone else; but it was sickening when you've been marked out for some reason.

“Let that idiot choose my work detail for me!” thought Artiom sadly, yet angrily. “I’m not afraid of any work. Maybe I want to go into the shock-brigade and get my time halved! I’d never gather enough bilberries or those God-damned crowberries.”

While he thought about all this, he didn’t notice how the roll call had reached him, he only came to his senses after someone jabbed him with an elbow.

“What number is it?” asked a horrified Artiom to his neighbor, the Chinese man, who, twisting his tongue, repeated his number in order. Artiom immediately remembered that was the number that just sounded, and he called the next one.

He caught in his peripheral vision another violent glance from Krapin.

“What’s going on with me?” he cursed himself out, wanting to cry like he did in childhood when such an idiotic and infuriating series of misfortunes happened.

“Attention! On me!” yelled the brigade leader.

He was a Georgian named Curly — though whether that was a nickname or his actual last name wasn’t clear — short, with bulging eyes and shining bald spots. He reminded Artiom clearly of a demon. Like all the brigade leaders, he was dressed in a dark blue uniform with grey tabs and a military cap that he didn’t like to wear and often took off, at which point he would immediately wipe off the sweat from his head with a dirty napkin.

“Good morning, twelfth brigade!” barked Curly, bulging his feral eyes.

Artiom, as they had taught him, counted to three and yelled full voice, “Good!” If he was going to stick out like a sore thumb, it might as well be with his scream, but who notices your zeal in a choir?

The brigade leader reported to the officer in charge of the camp the number of inmates and the lack of any significant events during the past night.

The Chekist listened to the report and immediately left.

“Outcasts, frauds, lazy bums and rogues!” said the brigade leader with an obvious accent. He looked like he had been drinking all night and slept an hour before wake-up call. His eyes were red, which only increased his similarity with the demons. “I repeat my previous warning. For any games of cards or for the preparation of cards…”

At which point, unashamed of the monastic walls, he began to swear coarsely, all the while mixing up the cases — not “your mother” but for some reason “to your mother”. Then he remained silent for a long time, as though remembering and, it seemed, falling asleep occasionally.

"Secondly!" he remembered, rocking back, "in September, the school for inmates will begin again. The school has two divisions. The first is to eliminate illiteracy completely, the second is for those with limited literacy. This second division is further divided into three parts: for the beginners, the intermediate and the comparatively advanced. Other than general learning and math, they will also teach… those what-cha-ma-call-it… natural sciences with geography… and also sociology."

The inmates quietly laughed. Some of them asked whether they'll learn the fastest route from Solovki to London in geography class and will they, by the way, teach the illiterate how to speak English.

"Yes, they will," answered the brigade leader suddenly, having heard some of the discussions in line. "There will be special groups to learn English, French and German, and even groups for literature and art." He barely managed to pronounce the last words, but Artiom caught their general drift.

Next to Artiom stood Burtsev, one of Kolchak's officers, who was always ramrod straight, his hair orderly, very exact in his actions and movements. His not unsuccessfully-shaved cheek twitched in revulsion during Curly's entire speech. Interestingly, in addition to Burtsev, their group also had a *muzhik* from Ryazan and a former Red Army solider named Avdei Sivstev, who was, by the way, barely literate.

The brigade leader, while he mangled the words, seemed to wake up a bit.

"Half of you can't read or write."

"The other half speaks three languages," thought Artiom darkly, looking askance at Burtsev.

"It would be better to shoot all of you! But the Soviet government has decided to educate you, so that you can be useful. For the illiterates, attendance is mandatory, but for the others, voluntary. Those who are interested can sign up right now."

Curly wiped his mouth with a wobbly motion and waved his hand, which in this difficult morning (for him) meant, "At ease!"

"If we sign up for school, will they allow us to skip work?" someone cried out after the lines began to mix up and grow loud.

"School begins after the work day," answered the brigade leader quietly, but everyone heard him.

Someone sniggered derisively.

"What, should we give you jackals school instead of work!?" the brigade leader yelled suddenly, and everyone immediately wanted to laugh.

Right there where everyone stood, those assigning the rotas sat behind tables, ready to give their assignments.

While Artiom waited his turn, Krapin walked up to one of the tables — just looking at the group leader made Artiom's back hurt in the place where he had bludgeoned him.

The flash of pain wasn't an accident. On the way back, Krapin tossed this at Artiom: "Get used to your new residence. Soon you're moving there permanently."

Vasilii Petrovich, who stood ahead of them, turned around and looked inquiringly at Artiom, but he only shrugged his shoulders. Between his shoulder blades, a drop of sweat slipped down. His left knee shuddered fiercely and unpleasantly.

The rota assigner asked Artiom's last name and, winking at him in the dim light of the "bat", said, "To the cemetery with you."

Avdei Sivtsev kept looking for the line for those who wanted to sign up for school. But there was no line.

* * *

The worked ended up being not that difficult. No point in all that worry.

But he and Vasilii Petrovich embraced in parting, as Vasilii Petrovich again went on the berry brigade, deciding, this time, to take Moisei Solomonovich along.

"Artiom," began Vasilii Petrovich pompously, holding him by the shoulders.

"Enough, enough," he waved him off before he turned completely sour. "If Krapin wanted to really punish me, he would have sent me to the clay mill… Let's find out what this cemetery really is. Maybe they've added me to the monastery choir."

There was a single working church in Solovki — the church of St. Onuphrius, which stood on the burial grounds. As soon as Eichmanis had taken over the camp, he had allowed services in that church, and any inmate who had a "report" — meaning a permanent pass to leave the walls of the monastery, could attend them.

"The singers in Onuphrius… yes! No church in Soviet Russia has such a choir," said Vasilii Petrovich, smiling. "Moisei Solomonovich is trying to get in, Artiom. But there's a waiting list of opera stars. Such baritones and basses, oh!"

Of course, Artiom wasn't sent to the choir, but to raze the old cemetery on the other side of the island.

His brigade included Avdei Sivtsev, the Chechen Khasaev, the Cossack Lazhechnikov, who always introduced himself by his name and patronymic:

"Timofey Stepanich" — which, by the way, truly fit with his curly beard and furry eyebrows. "To such beards and eyebrows was our Fatherland beholden," said Vasilii Petrovich in his quiet, completely non-sarcastic way.

"But why break the crosses?" Sivtsev asked the guard when they got there.

In general, it was forbidden to speak to the guards, but this prohibition was constantly ignored.

"They're making a pig sty," said the guard grimly. You couldn't tell by looking at him whether he was joking or telling the truth.

"Since they've already made the monastery into a sty, now it's the cemetery's turn," said the *muzhik* quietly.

The guard said nothing and, sitting down on a bench near the last grave, pulled out a cigarette from his cigarette case.

"He probably stole it from some local chump," Artiom thought in passing.

The guard didn't have a rifle. It was typical for the brigades to travel without arms. Some work groups had no guards at all. The guards were usually taken from the ranks of former Chekists who had stumbled into the camp. In other words, they were complete bastards.

They said that if the circumstances were right — and of course, if there was a rifle — a guard might kill an inmate for rudeness or even for some shiny object, just like that cigarette case. Then they'd just lie and say something like, "He almost escaped, comrade commander!"

But Artiom hadn't seen any such cases himself and he didn't really believe the rumors. Moreover, he had no expensive things, neither was he planning on running away. There was nowhere to go anyway. His whole life was ahead of him; you can't outrun life.

The foreman appeared, after disappearing for a time in search of berries. In one hand he held an axe, with the other axe under his armpit. Even from a distance, he began yelling, spitting out the not-quite-chewed berries:

"Why are you standing? You have one day for this entire job! By evening, there should be no cemetery, no crosses, no headstones! Pile everything together! No rest until you finish! Even if you're digging around here until morning. You'll sleep in the graves, but you won't leave!"

"Do we pull out the skeletons too?" asked Sivtsev.

"I'll pull your skeleton out!" yelled the foreman even louder.

"Get to work, you damn horse!" barked the guard at Sivtsev unexpectedly, jumping up from the bench.

Sivtsev reeled as from a hot brand, grabbed an old, turned-over cross and fell down together with it.

That began the work.

"A cemetery's a cemetery," Artiom calmed himself. "If you chop down a tree, it's a living thing, but here everyone's dead at least."

At first, Artiom read off the names of the buried monks, but after an hour his memory couldn't manage it. Only a single date stood out — his birthday, but a hundred years ago, on the same day of May. The date of death was 1843 in December.

"Not much," thought Artiom with a snicker, either for himself or for the dead man. He also thought, "What's it going to be like in 1943?"

It was sunny; there was always fewer bloodsuckers in the sunlight.

At first Artiom, then the Chechen, then finally Lazhechnikov took off their shirts. Only Sivtsev remained in his shirt — as with most peasant farmers, his neck was dark from a tan and wrinkled, while the body under the collar was completely white.

Everyone slowly entered a state of trance-like rage. The crosses were broken with a kind of madness. If they didn't come down, they broke them with axes. Sivtsev was good with his axe. The fences were shaken back and forth, and if they didn't fall, they were toppled and pounded underfoot. At first, the headstones were carried to a single place and laid down reverently, as though they might still come in handy for the dead men who might later come and stick them back on their gravesites, after they had found their names.

"Excuse me, we're going to bother you a bit," mumbled the Cossack Lazhechnikov as he read out the names. "Elisei Savvatievich… Tikhon Mironovich… please excuse us as well, Panteleimon Ivanych…" But then he started to huff and puff, the sweat pouring over him and he shut up. After an hour, they toppled all monuments without any reverence or mercy, lifting them with cracking sounds, dragging them, swearing hoarsely and dumping them, however they would fall.

Occasionally, it was as though an ecstasy of blasphemy reflected in their faces.

"Is this a sin, or not?" Artiom thought distractedly, breathing heavily and constantly wiping off his forehead. "If I was lying here in the earth… would I be upset… that there was no cross over me any more… while the headstone with my name… was dropped unceremoniously among the others… far away from my grave?"

Sivtsev distracted him from these thoughts. He found an appropriate moment, and, walking past the guard, said quietly:

"My dear man, what you said about the horse, you really shouldn't do that. The whole world of the peasant rides on the horse. You must have lived all your life in the city, yes? Family of factory workers?"

"What?" The guard didn't understand what he said. Sivtsev walked past with his broken wooden cross to the pile, where there were already almost one hundred, or maybe more.

"The Bolshies… don't give any rest… to the living or the dead," whispered the *muzhik*, for whom silence, it seemed, was the heaviest burden.

They finished their work unexpectedly quickly — they routed the dead men like it was child's play.

The crosses looked ominous, as though there was a battle between bony invalids.

The foreman, not denying himself the pleasure, started the fire from one side, while the Chechen lit it from the other. He then twitched more and more angrily by the fire, fitfully fixing the blazing wood and throwing the pieces that fell out of the pile back into the inferno.

The fire was tall, dry and straight.

"They're all in heaven already," said Sivtsev about the crosses, comforting himself more than Artiom. "The dead don't need crosses; the living do, but these have no living relatives. We are all without relatives now."

When it finished burning, the foreman looked over the former cemetery with boredom. There was nothing you could with this badly torn up, almost shrunken and stupefied land. All you could do was carry the headstones even farther, throw them into the water or bury them, but no such command followed.

Artiom suddenly had the sickening thought that the dead people from time immemorial and forever were uncovered, naked in the earth. They used to be covered, but now, they were like children without blankets in a freezing house.

"And so?" he asked himself. "What am I supposed to do with that?"

He shook his head and… forgot himself, forgot.

They returned to the kremlin while it was still light.

The Chechen, externally, was his usual grim self, but he seemed to be bothered by something. Even as they approached, when the monastery walls, built of huge boulders, began to remind them of their existence through their special, foul smell, the Chechen firmly uttered: "If they told us to break our own cemeteries, no one would have touched it. We would have died before we would have touched them. But you broke them all."

"You're lying, bitch!" Lazhechnikov's reddening face immediately twisted rabidly.

"It's the bitch who's talking," answered the Chechen, almost by syllables.

Lozhechnikov's thick, almost bony sinew in the neck grew so taut that it seemed all it would take for his head to fall off was to rip the sinew. He took a step towards the Chechen, splaying out his hands in advance and curving his fingers in such a way as though he was planning to tickle the Chechen under his armpits, but the brigade guard yelled, "Come on, there!" And he pushed Lazhechnikov in the back.

"We'll finish talking inside," Lazhechnikov said in the Chechen's face.

But a minute later, he couldn't stop himself: "I'm from Terek. When we used to put you thieves down, you didn't take your cemeteries back with you. You left us your dead men, so that we could trample them underfoot."

"Yes, yes," agreed the Chechen, and those words sounded like the shriek of some massive bristled bird. "You're capable of that. At first you trample someone else's cemetery, then your own."

Lazhechnikov went rigid again. He looked around fiercely in the futile hope that the guard had disappeared somehow. But no, he was there, and his face was neutral.

"What? You don't hear how he's bad-mouthing Christians?" asked Lazhechnikov heatedly.

"Who are you asking about Christians?" The Chechen sharply laughed, looking askance at the brigade guard. "You people don't have God anymore. What sort of God is He, if this is how you lot believe in Him!"

"Chechens used to be Christians too, a long time ago..." said Artiom suddenly, remembering his childhood enthrallment with the stories of Bestuzhev-Marlinksii, back when he would devour everything he could find about the Caucasus.

Khasaev looked at Artiom as adults look at a child who butted into their conversation. Not answering anything, he just moved his jaw.

Artiom cursed himself mentally. "Why did you butt in, you idiot?"

"What an idiot," he kept repeating to himself as they walked through the monastery courtyard. "What an idiot, idiot, idiot, all day an idiot..."

He repeated it so many times that he even forget for what reason he was cursing himself in the first place.

When they arrived, each was given a cabbage pie for their successfully completed work.

"I don't even know what to do with it, to chew it or choke on it," said Sivtsev, glaring at the pie as though it were alive. But he still ate it and even gathered the crumbs from his knee.

There was still an hour before dinner and Artiom managed to sleep, having noticed that Lazhechnikov and Khasaev had parted ways and hadn't even tried to finish their conversation.

Lazhechnikov was rummaging through his shabby rags on the bunk as carefully and exactingly as he probably examined his horse's harness or his fishing tackle back in Terek, while the Chechen quietly whispered with his fellow countrymen. From a distance, it seemed that they spoke not so much in words as in signs, gestures and quick grins of the mouth.

* * *

Vasilii Petrovich shook Artiom awake; immediately, they heard the singing of Moisei Solomonovich about a forest and a sparrow — clearly, he was inspired by the berry brigade.

"I envy you, Artiom, your heavy sleep," said Vasilii Petroch, and his voice was cozy, as though it floated in from somewhere in childhood. "It's even unclear to me, how they could have imprisoned such a young man, sleeping the sleep of the righteous in hades. Dinner, Artiom, time to get up."

Artiom opened his eyes and saw the smiling face of Vasilii Petrovich close to his own face. Even closer was his hand, holding on to the edge of Artiom's bunk.

When he saw that his friend had fully woken up, Vasilii Petrovich winked at Artiom and sat down on his own bunk.

"As far as I can tell, the righteous sleep badly," answered Artiom, getting down from his bunk intentionally slowly and simultaneously stretching his muscles.

As he ate the foul wheat porridge with an appetite, Artiom thought of Vasilii Petrovich at the same time as he listened to him babbling on as usual.

At first, Vasilii Petrovich asked who was in the group breaking down the headstones, then shook his head. "They've gone mad completely, completely…" Then he told him how he found some good berry patches and that Moisei Solomonovich had lied — he had absolutely no talent for spotting bilberries. In fact, he was probably half-blind. "He'd be better working in the co-op…" added Vasilii Petrovich.

Artiom suddenly understood what he thought was strange about Vasilii Petrovich. Yes, he had an intelligent face that had managed to preserve something of breeding, a squint, the way he held his head, his penetrating glance, always preoccupied with something… But at the same time, he had dry, sinewy hands covered with thick white hairs, while Vasilii Petrovich was barely graying himself.

Artiom had unwittingly memorized those hands even while he was gathering berries. Vasilii Petrovich's fingers had that strange sureness of movement that is sometimes found in the blind when they know their surroundings exactly.

"His hands seem to belong to a different person," thought Artiom as he cleaned his bowl out with a penny-sized piece of bread. They received their week's ration of bread at the beginning of the week and Artiom still had about two pounds left. He had learned how to hoard it so that there would be enough left for Saturday evening at least.

"Do you know, Artiom, when I just arrived here, things were a little different," Vasilii Petrovich was saying. "Before Eichmanis, another man ruled the camp, named Nogtev. He was a rare reptile, even for a Chechen. Whenever a new group would arrive at Solovki, he would meet them personally and at the gates of the monastery, he would shoot one of the new people with his revolver. Bam! Then he'd laugh. Most often he'd choose a priest or a counter-revolutionary. So that everyone would know from their first steps that here, it wasn't the Soviet government that ruled, but the government of Solovki. He often repeated that phrase. Notice that Eichmanis doesn't talk like that, and of course he doesn't shoot the new people. But as for the rations, back then strange things used to happen. When the northern front of the White Army retreated, they left huge amounts of supplies here — cubed sugar, American bacon, some unheard-of canned goods. I'm not saying that they gave us those supplies, but sometimes one or two of those delicacies did make it to our table. In that year, there were still political prisoners here — Social Democrats, Socialist-Revolutionaries and other anarchists who had disagreed with the Bolsheviks in the details, though they agreed with them in essence. So they were fed like commissars' children. And they, to add insult to injury, didn't work at all. In winter, they skated on the ice, in summer, they lounged in chaise-lounges and argued, argued, argued… Now, probably, they tell everyone about their horrifying past of Solovki. But they didn't even see Solovki, Artiom."

In a bundle on his back, Vasilii Petrovich had brought some mushrooms that he apparently planned to dry, while in a tightly-wrapped bag on his chest, he had hidden a few berries. Having sat down, he shook the bag in such a way that it would be visible from beneath the bunks. Soon two dirty cupped hands appeared and he plopped the mashed berry-porridge into them. The nails on those hands were prominent.

"I still haven't even seen his face," Artiom suddenly said, nodding at the homeless kid's hands, which then immediately disappeared.

"Let's get some air, walk about the monastery," offered Vasilii Petrovich after keeping silent for a bit. "They're performing a play today, so there aren't as many people in the courtyard as usual. Plus, I have an unpleasant duty to perform."

Artiom agreed with pleasure.

Next to the marble chapel for blessing water, two old cannons stood on their carriages. For some reason, Artiom often dreamed about them and it was a frightening, unpleasant dream. Moreover, Artiom was, for some reason, sure that he had first seen that dream before Solovki.

They came as far as the square between the Sviatitel'skii and Blagoveshchenskii buildings. Artiom was not quite full and not quite rested, but still he had slept and had eaten hot food, and because of that, yawning like a child, he felt almost content. Vasilii Petrovich — always thinking about something significant and necessary — hurried just ahead of Artiom in his permanent — even in summer — English cap. It seemed he was ashamed of his balding head.

It was a bright evening, the air was sumptuous, the sky was replete with carefully-painted colors, but one could almost feel the presence of a dome behind those gentle colors, a kind of invisible firmament.

"One can ring bells in such a sky," Afanasiev had said once.

From the West, clumps of dark clouds gathered, but they were still far away.

"It's as if they're pulling that cloud down by the beard into hell," thought Artiom, intentionally copying Afanasiev's style. He smiled at himself, thinking that the image wasn't too bad. Maybe he would start writing poems? Yes, he loved poetry, but he never told anyone about it. Why should he?

A few Orthodox priests walked about or stood in the square. Nearly all of them were in old, shabby, patched cassocks, but without crosses. One of them was in a Red Army helmet with the star torn off. No one paid any attention any more to such things. Everyone wore what he could. Vasilii Petrovich attracted Artiom's attention with a nod towards the Catholic priests who sat on a bench in almost proud concentration.

"As I've noticed, you've managed to fit into the Solovski lifestyle remarkably quickly, Artiom," said Vasilii Petrovich. "Even the lice don't really eat you." He chuckled, but immediately continued more seriously. "You don't ask unnecessary questions. You speak rarely and to the point. You're not rude or stupid. Many people lower themselves in the first three months — either they fade away or they become informants or they become the gangsters' lackeys, and I don't even know what's worse. You, I've noticed, even without especially trying, have avoided all these dangers as though they didn't exist. For now, you're managing with the work. You're adept at it, which is rare for a person with a mind and discernment. You don't take anything personally and that's also an enviable quality. You're very resilient, as I see. You're intended for a long life. If you don't make any mistakes, everything will work out for you."

Artiom looked intently at Vasilii Petrovich. It was pleasant for him to hear all this, but in moderation; it was a moderated pleasure. Moreover, Artiom knew himself capable of idiotic, angry, difficult-to-explain habits; Vasilii Petrovich didn't know about them yet.

"There are many fights here, much infighting," he continued. "You, I've noticed, are companionable with everyone, while everyone else is indifferent to you, as it should be."

"Not everyone," said Artiom.

"Well, no, there's Krapin, that's right. But maybe that's an accident?"

Artiom shrugged his shoulders, thinking how strange, if not wild, everything was. Torn from his own life as from the womb, he had ended up on an island — if not the edge of the world, then the edge of the country, for sure. He was guarded by armed men, and if he acted somehow not quite correctly, they could kill him. But at the same time, he was walking in the square and talking as though any moment now he was about to return home to his mother.

"As far as I can remember, he hasn't really done any harm to anyone," Vasilii Petrovich continued about Krapin. "But if you have problems with the brigade leader, then there'll be trouble. Curly is a reptile. In any case, you're sure to be transferred to an easier work group, to do office work… you'll have your own cell. When that happens, make sure to invite me to visit, drink some tea."

"Vasilii Petrovich," asked Artiom with interest. "Why haven't you done anything yet to transfer yourself from the general duties? As you said, that's the most important rule for anyone who plans to survive Solovki. But what about yourself? I'm sure you're capable of doing much more than picking berries."

Vasilii Petrovich shot a quick glance at Artiom and, gathering his hands behind his back, answered, "Well, Artiom, I seem to have settled down here already. Why do I need another work brigade? My place is the forest. Here's a little wisdom for you — always try to choose the work where they assign the fewest people. It's easier. Plus, I'm a second-category inmate. They won't send me to topple trees. So why should I rush anywhere? I'll sit out my time thus. In childhood, I used to be spoiled. This is a good place to find humility."

It didn't sound quite convincing, but Artiom, after looking at Vasilii Petrovich sarcastically once, then again, said nothing. It was a good thing that Vasilii Petrovich changed the subject quickly.

"Look, for example, at those two. Do you know who they are? Wonderful people! On the streets of Moscow and Petrograd you simply won't find such people. Only on Solovki! Well, on the left we have Sergei L'vovich Brusilov, the nephew of General Brusilov, the very one who nearly won the second war for the Fatherland, then refused to fight against the Bolsheviks. Sergei L'vovich, if I haven't been led to believe a falsehood, is a captain in the Baltic fleet, I mean, he *was*. But even here he preserves a certain connection with the local flotilla of Solovki. He's speaking to Mr. Violar… Violar is an even rarer bird. He's the Mexican consul in Egypt."

"Did he get lost on the way from America to Africa and find himself on Solovki?"

"Basically, yes! Moreover, he got lost by first making a detour into Tiflis." Vasilii Petrovich smiled. "His wife is Russian, well, Georgian, actually. To be perfectly honest, she's a Georgian princess, a breathtaking beauty, only a little skinny for my taste."

"How do you know?" Artiom asked with unexpected curiosity.

"Listen, Artiom!" Vasilii Petrovich gently lifted his greying hand, as though stopping his fellow conversant in his haste. "Not so long ago, Mr. Violar decided to travel to the homeland of his wife, to visit, to try out the Georgian cuisine, and so on. Instead, he was arrested by the Tiflis State Political directorate and moved here. It would be useful to ask our foreman about the details, but I try to avoid excessive confrontations with Curly."

"What about the wife?" Artiom asked impatiently.

"The wife's here too," Vasilii Petrovich continued in a whisper, because they were approaching Brusilov, who indeed listened to his fellow conversant, the actively gesticulating Violar, with calmness and inarguable dignity. Their conversation was in English. "But of course, she's in the female barracks."

While they passed the pair, they remained silent.

"And here's the one I've been looking for," rejoiced Vasilii Petrovich. "*Vladychka*[25] promised to give us some sour cream with onions."

---

[25] Essentially an untranslatable diminutive. It means, literally, "little lord, or little bishop". It's a diminutive, probably deliberately insulting, a popular form of address for a bishop. It's unclear from the context of the novel whether this John is a priest or a bishop.

Artiom had just enough time to think what a great word "Vladychka" was, but the mention of sour cream with onion acted even more powerfully, and in a moment, he felt his whole mouth fill with saliva. He even laughed at himself, considering that it was somehow not even human-like, as though he were some kind of dog.

"Father John!" said Vasilii Petrovich.

Towards them, smiling, walked a tall man in a cassock, with a full and well-groomed reddish beard, with long, barely curling and not very clean hair. He was clearly not young, but rather handsome still, with a thin, slightly curved line of the nose, small ears, slightly sunken cheeks, barely noticeable eyebrows and a kindly squint.

Vasilii Petrovich bowed and Father John blessed the crown of his head with a quick motion and gave his skinny, freckled hand to be kissed.

Artiom, who didn't go to church because of a raging lack of faith, noticed that this gesture did not even hint at humiliating anyone's dignity. It was quite the opposite, raising up the worth of Vasilii Petrovich somehow.

Artiom caught himself thinking, with warm amazement, that he would also have liked to kiss that hand. What stopped him wasn't pride so much as the fear of doing it wrong somehow. He remained a little apart from them, but Father John greeted him as well, gently nodding at him, and in this gesture as well there was no challenge that could offend Artiom in any way. That is, the priest wasn't suggesting to him that it was fine that he didn't come to get his blessing because he understands how difficult and dangerous that is in these trying times. No, the priest greeted him as though nothing at all had happened, and he was sincerely happy to meet Artiom, who was most likely a good and kind young man.

"How are you, Father John?" asked Vasilii Petrovich.

"By the mercy of God, I am well," answered the other very seriously and continued, speaking as though not about his own body, but about something distant from it that he could look at from the outside in an interesting manner. "All my members work smoothly and without pain. Some kind of infection has inflamed my knee, but God willing, it'll heal on its own. As for the fact that sometimes there's a cold breeze on the heart, well, it's easier to endure winter in the heart than the winter on Solovki. The heart, if it seeks, will find its harbor in the love of the One crucified for us, but while your feet are bare and your lower back aches, you won't get very far." Father John laughed at this, Vasilii Petrovich laughed with him; even Artiom smiled, not so much because of his words, but because of the enchantment that emanated from every word of the *Vladychka*.

"But we must remember, dear ones," saying this, the slightly limping Father John looked at Artiom, who had approached from the right, and immediately then turned his gaze at Vasilii Petrovich at his left, "the powers of hell and the Soviet government are not always one and the same. We battle not against people, but against immaterial evil and its spirits. In this life, under the authority of the Soviets, there cannot be evil as long as no rejection of faith is required. You are duty-bound to protect holy Rus, because Rus didn't disappear. Here it lies under us and is warmed by our weak concern. At the very least, we mustn't forget the word 'Russian'. Everything else is earthly vanity. You can enter a collective farm or a commune — what's the evil in that? — the important thing is not to defile Christ's name. There is a governor of this camp, there is a leader of our country, and there is a master of our life — each has his own work and his own difficult task. The governor of the camp may not even know about the master of life, though he has one hundred Chekists and a corps of guards under his command, or the Bureau of Information, the clay mill and the 'Sekirka' in his back pocket. On the other hand, the master of life remembers everyone, even you and me. Don't complain, endure to the end. Through uncomplaining endurance of sorrows, we walk straight into the embrace of the master of life, and His gentleness will be incomparably more pure and brighter than all earthly goods, which are so quick to ripen, so foolish."

Artiom listened to every word Father John spoke; he was comforted not so much by the revelation of some suddenly obvious truth, but the intertwining of his words.

The only thing that distracted him was the Negro who walked past them — full-lipped, wonderfully black, tall — he smiled at Artiom, showing his excellent teeth with a missing front incisor.

"Work and cares are consuming us," Father John was saying, sweetly squinting as though from the sun. "It's easier for those inmates who are attached to their office desks as to a raft in the sea. Those who make faces on the stage — they also have it easier; they feed them well for their pains. But whoever has the common work — that's much more difficult. Our long-haired tribe..." Father John shook his barely curling mane and quietly laughed. "... is customarily assigned to be caretakers or custodians, since we don't have a habit of stealing. Of course, not everyone has that lucky fate! Moreover, many of those sufferers who come here don't take care of their brothers in misfortune, but, on the contrary, lay excessive burdens on those equally weak and humiliated as they are. And so the spark of

Christ dims without going out in the informant, in the weakling, in the one languishing in solitary. But no matter what our cares, remember that even before His birth, He exhorted us through the prophet Isaiah: 'Upon whom will I show respect, but to the humble and the peaceful.' Walk through life firmly, but practice constant meekness and reverence before Him Who will inevitably send all His servants His gracious help!"

Artiom turned aside while Vasilii Petrovich regaled *Vladychka* John with berries, while he, in his turn, passed Vasilii Petrovich a bundle.

They walked back as though half-drunk, leading a stumbling conversation while they stumbled themselves, filled with a joyful, even boyish, mood. Even the pestering, shrieking gulls flying over their heads didn't ruin their mood.

They met a woman — she wasn't bad at all, around forty, in a shawl, in worn-out boots, men's pants and jacket that she held close around her chest. Artiom ogled her until he realized what he was doing.

Above the main gates, they had attached a huge sign with the words: "We will show a new path for the world. The master of the world will be work!"

"Do you think it was our conversation that gave him the idea," said Vasilii Petrovich, meaning Eichmanis, "about the monks who find salvation in their toil?"

"You think?" answered Artiom. "Hardly..."

They ran into Moisei Solomonovich as they approached. He walked silently, but a few steps before reaching Artiom and Vasilii Petrovich, he suddenly started to sing without words, as though he hadn't found the words yet, though the music had already appeared.

They smiled to each other and walked away. After all, they weren't going to sing along with him.

"I swear to you," whispered Artiom to Vasilii Petrovich, "He senses food! In the presence of food, he begins to sing!"

"Why do you say that?" asked Vasilii Petrovich, but he held his bundle a little more firmly.

The paths inside the monastery were dusted over with sand. Everywhere, rose-beds stood, which were cared for by several inmates. Artiom once again imagined a conversation going like this:

"Were you on Solovki? What did you do there?"

"I planted rare varieties of roses!"

"Oh, the accursed Bolshevik yoke!"

On one of the central rose-beds someone had made an elephant from white pebbles. The anagram for SLON[26] was "The Camp of Special Designation of Solovki".

* * *

In order to avoid upsetting the gangsters in their brigade, and not to share or be subjected to the repeated choral inspiration of Moisei Solomonovich, Vasilii Petrovich offered a wonderful plan for dinner — to eat in the cell of his White Officer friend.

"Burtsev will join us, and he also will have something to share with us. We'll make a feast." Vasilii Petrovich was excited and agitated, as though he were going on a date. "Is there some sort of holiday today, Artiom? Preferably nothing Bolshevik, though." He inclined his head to Artiom, and, pulling back, winked at him in the most endearing manner.

In Artiom's understanding, Vasilii Petrovich presented a nearly ideal type of the Russian intelligentsia, a type that perhaps would not survive Soviet Russia. He was not malicious, was liberal, with a gentle sense of humor. The only swear word he seemed to know was the unknown word "shmorgontsy". He was slightly naïve and a little sentimental, but at the same time, he had an intuitive sense of his own self-worth.

Their inexplicable companionship happened because of, well, not the more usual circumstances.

While he was still in the thirteenth brigade, Artiom received his first package from his mother.

He had already seen how the gangsters stole other inmates' products or personal property. As he darkly considered what to do on his way back to the brigade, he bit off and swallowed huge chunks of the horsemeat sausage his mother had sent him.

Here, Vasilii Petrovich came out of the woodwork for the first time. The twelfth and the thirteenth brigades were neighbors, having their sleeping quarters in different parts of the same church.

"I see your doubt, young man," he said after introducing himself. He was either ashamed of his role or he put on the shame as an act. "You are from quarantine, yes? Part of your group was already undressed by the gangsters on the way, while you were still in the cargo hold of the ship 'Gleb Bokii'. The rest are being undressed and eaten out of house and home in the brigade

---

26 The Russian word for elephant.

itself. I've experienced it all too in my own time. I have a simple proposition for you. To prove that my intentions are honorable is difficult for me, maybe impossible. To kiss the cross in our days is not the most convincing action, and I can't give you my honest Bolshevik word, for I'm no Bolshevik. But I do know how to preserve that package. Will you hear me out?"

Artiom considered and nodded, hugging the bag with his mother's delicacies tighter against his chest.

"If you give the package into my hands, I, in turn, will hide it with my good friend Bishop Peter, who is in charge of the smoker in the First Division. He will keep your food whole and untouched. Whenever you ask, I can bring you whatever you need in portions every evening after dinner, but before the evening inspection."

Artiom examined his new acquaintance for some time, then unexpectedly decided to trust him.

"What do I owe you for this?" he only asked.

"We'll think of something," answered Vasilii Petrovich humbly.

Without waiting, Artiom found Vasilii Petrovich after dinner on the following day. He didn't ask for any reward, but Artiom, naturally, gave him some fish. Moreover, it seemed that no one had taken anything from the package. Artiom had finished off the sausage on the first day and he had counted the pieces of dried fish, while the bags with sugar and dried fruits he had tied with his own special knot. He would have surely noticed if it had been retied in a different knot.

During that second meeting, they talked with each thoroughly.

Artiom, of course, could have assumed that Vasilii Petrovich was continuing to keep up the acquaintance because he was waiting for the next package, but his instinct assiduously convinced him that things were quite different. Here, he thought, we have simple human fellowship. After all, why wouldn't anyone treat Artiom well? He treated himself well enough.

"After all, we all have to live here," Artiom concluded his reflections on the subject. "Is the intelligentsia supposed to be the first to die off?"

Later, Artiom was transferred from the quarantine brigade to the twelfth, and on that same day, the non-political prisoner who slept on the ledge above Vasilii Petrovich was released on early parole and Artiom took his empty bunk.

He hid the next package also through Vasilii Petrovich, and a second time he shared with him.

When they picked berries together, Vasilii Petrovich, during a breather from work, summarized for Artiom the story of why he ended up on Solovki.

In 1924, because of some old friends and connections, Vasilii Petrovich ended up several times at a dinner party in the French Embassy. The recent half-hungry past of war-time communism taught everyone to have their fill at dinner and the French were offering.

"They set a beautiful table, but there was nothing to eat," complained Vasilii Petrovich.

He went once, twice, but on the third time, on the way back, he was asked to sit in a car and was driven to the Joint State Political Directorate. He was accused of being a French spy, though the implication was idiotic and they were unable to prove anything definitively.

"What an outrage!" Vasilii Petrovich said angrily, though the conviction was grave: Article 58, Part 6—espionage.

"What about you?" Vasilii Petrovich had asked then, rubbing his hands together in such a way that it seemed Artiom was about to regale him with food, for example, with some boiled potatoes.

"I drank an old woman's buttermilk. Got the lash and Siberia," Artiom deflected.

"Artiom, I really don't care, but you should know that's not how we do things here," said Vasilii Petrovich with faux strictness, imitating a good teacher. "If, for example, the gangsters asks you why you got sent to Solovki, you'll have to answer. Furthermore, didn't you tell them your crime during the investigation process, when you sat in a cell? It's hard to stay silent in a cell, they might think you were an informant."

"Nonsense," said Artiom. "It's the informants who are taught to lie beautifully."

"Are you a non-political prisoner, then?" Vasilii Petrovich refused to back down. "You look just like a consummate counter-revolutionary! I don't believe you're capable of thievery."

Artiom, sniggering, nodded, but never answered his question. He walked without looking back, he lived without looking back, a healthy, frivolous man. Fate decided otherwise, so now I live in misfortune. The most important thing was never to remember my father, or shame would eat me and my soul would tear itself apart.

"… and you seem to associate mostly with the counter-revolutionaries," continued Vasilii Petrovich, looking at Artiom.

"I associate with normal people," he answered, if only because some answer was expected.

"And what does a normal person think about the Bolsheviks?" Vasilii Petrovich asked unexpectedly.

"I have a younger brother. He's a Pioneer and is very proud of his red tie. I want nothing to do with the Bolsheviks myself. They happened, and so they happened. Let them be," Artiom answered each word thoughtfully, that is, in a manner completely unusual for him.

* * *

While Vasilii Petrovich cut the onion, Artiom examined the cell.

He was genuinely surprised.

High ceilings painted white. Hardwood floors, recently painted into a brown color. A washed window almost as tall as a man. Only two couches. One wasn't prepared for sleeping — it was covered with boards. However, the other was covered by a blanket with a tiger on it. Peeking out from under it was a snow-white sheet, while the pillow was fluffed and, it seemed to Artiom, scented. Above the bed was a shelf with books — a few English novels, Racine, a certain Leonov, whose work titled "Thief" was marked with a bookmark, near the beginning of the book. There was also Dostoyevsky, Merezhkovsky, Blok, whom Artiom immediately grabbed and opened with a feeling as though what was inside was written especially for him.

He read a few lines, then closed his eyes to check if he remembered how it continued. Yes, he remembered. Then he carefully put the volume back in its place.

The table was covered with a tablecloth; on the table stood an electric lamp with a lampshade painted with watercolors. In the corner was an icon with an oil lamp and on a nail hung a silver cross. Artiom touched it, rocking it barely.

In the niche of the window were photographs of women and a porcelain dog — white with black spots, with a curly tail that was broken at its end.

"So you can live like this, even in a camp," thought Artiom. "You'll remember this later…"

"Yes, Artiom, yes, you can live like this, even in a camp," confirmed Vasilii Petrovich.

Artiom would have never believed that he could have uttered his last thought aloud. He was a young man, completely not inclined to memory loss, but for a moment, he was still confused.

"Well, yes," he said, getting a hold of himself. "It's not hard to guess. What about Burtsev? Where is he?"

Vasilii Petrovich, not answering, took a bowl from a makeshift cupboard, like he owned the place and poured the sour cream into it.

Having examined the décor, Artiom sat on the firm stool between the table and the window, trying not to stare as Vasilii Petrovich poured the cut-up onion into the sour cream and began to mix it all up with a large spoon, occasionally salting it… Oh, how he wanted to lick that spoon!

Artiom took the porcelain dog, turned it around in his hands and carefully ran his finger along the line of the break on the tail, swallowing down his constant saliva.

"Oh, Artiom, how I loved to feed my dog!" Vasilii Petrovich straightened out and, lyrically sniffing, wiped his eye with his fist. "I'm not really a hunter at all, it's more… the look of it. A rifle on my shoulder and into the forest. I'll see some bird, I'll hoist up the barrel, then it'll get scared and fly away. I'll curse, 'Oh, hell! Hell take it, Fet!' I called my dog Fet, either as a joke or because I love Fet, I don't even know… Didn't Merzernitskii have a Fet?" Vasilii Petrovich quickly looked at the bookshelf and immediately forgot what he was looking for.

He spoke as he usually did, jumping from one thing to another, but Artiom understood everything — what was there to be confused about?

"I'll curse the dog in such a way," Vasilii Petrovich continued, "as though I was really planning on shooting the bird. And my Fet, you could tell by his muzzle, is also upset, it seems, he's commiserating with me. Another time I, already an expert, will raise the barrel slo-o-o-wly. Fet will also crouch down and — he's all anticipation! And I look at the bird, and, you know, I have no strength to pull the trigger. I'm telling the truth! As a rule, I didn't even load the rifle. But when you raise the barrel and aim, it still feels like it's loaded. I feel so sickened in my soul, such trepidation."

Artiom put the dog back and took the portrait with the woman, not so much looking at her dubious enchantments — *maybe she's his mother?* — but rather hoping to catch the last rays of the sun with the glass and send splashes of sunlight running on the wall.

"This continues maybe for a minute, but probably less, because to hold a rifle for a full minute is difficult. And Fet, of course, won't be able to bear it and will start barking. Either at me or at the bird — not sure at whom. The bird flies away again… But I laugh, and my soul is filled with joy. As though I had given that bird its freedom."

"It's all so petty and vulgar," thought Artiom without irritation, occasionally raising his eyes and nodding at Vasilii Petrovich with a smile.

"So we come home," he continued, "hungry, walking on our path so that the villagers won't see that I've come back again without any fowl, even though they always knew it anyway… And Nadia had already prepared dinner for us — for me, she invented something new, while Fet got yesterday's leftovers." Here Vasilii Petrovich suddenly choked up and was silent for a few seconds. "I would also pour yesterday's cabbage soup into his bowl, crumb some bread into it and even, for example, wouldn't spare a bit of fried liver, and on top I'd even break open an egg. You know, he loved raw eggs for some reason… And so I'll bring out the bowl to him; he's sitting, waiting… I'll put it before him; he sits and watches… It's almost as though he was ashamed to eat in front of me. Or maybe it was some other feeling. I'll walk away a bit and say, 'Eat, my dear, eat!' And he, as though unwillingly, as though for the first time, begins to walk around the bowl and sniff it from all sides."

Artiom swallowed his saliva again. If he even thought about opening his mouth, it would splash on the tablecloth.

"Strange that I never thought of it myself," thought Artiom quickly, though it was less a thought than an image. "It's probably delicious — borsch, a bit of fried liver on top, some bread crumbs, mashed together so that the bread absorbs the soup… On top, to break two, or better yet, three eggs. Somewhere they'll mix with the soup, but the yolk itself will remain on top… And to sniff it for a minute, then suddenly attack it, swallowing the liver with cabbage in gulps, the bread with the eggs…"

"Artiom, are you listening?" called out Vasilii Petrovich.

"To hell with you," said Artiom with difficulty. "Let's eat quickly! Where are our hosts? How did you call him? Mezernitskii?"

* * *

Burtsev came first. He nodded at Artiom as though they were old acquaintances, even though, it's a strange thing, but for the last month and a half they had hardly spoken two words to each other. There just didn't seem to be any occasion to do so.

But this comfortable cell immediately brought all who came into it close together. They felt as though they were chosen and elected to share this clean food, this swept and freshly-washed cell, this shining pillow, this clean tablecloth and porcelain dog.

Burtsev, Artiom knew from the stories of Vasilii Petrovich, worked in a variety show after the Civil War, then somewhere in an administrative position. He didn't like to talk about the details of his arrest.

For the most part, he was quiet. If he had the time, he sometimes read something unpretentious from the monastery library, but Artiom managed to notice and be amazed that if anyone in Burtsev's presence began to speak about something curious, or if anyone risked an actual conversation with him, he spoke several times on the most diverse subjects, from the choreographic art of Duncan and the differences between the Arctic and Antarctica to the letters of Konstantin Leontiev to Soloviev and the obvious advantages of Briusov over Balmont. The last topic, naturally, was started by Afanasiev. The last time, Burtsev surprised Vasilii Petrovich by his unexpected expertise in berries and hunting, informing him that wherever cloudberries grew, you should hunt white quails, while wherever lingonberries grew, you should look for wood grouse, though you can also find bears close to lingonberries. Vasilii Petrovich laughed so sincerely at the completely serious comment about the bears that Burtsev had all the chances he would ever need to get a spot in the berry brigade, but he himself didn't want it.

Sivtsev, who was nearby and eavesdropped on this conversation, suddenly remembered how he saw a bear on the front who was trained by the artillerymen to pass artillery rounds to the gunners. But Vasilii Petrovich didn't make a spot for him on the berry brigade, nor did Burstev continue on the theme of bears.

Listening quietly to the unhurried speech of Burstev, Artiom learned that cloudberry ripens backwards — from red to amber-yellow, while its masculine flowers gave more berries than the feminine parts. Also, lingonberry can live longer than an oak, because it can live up to three hundred years.

Artiom would have found the conversation about Briusov and Balmont even more interesting than the one about the berries. Balmont was the only poet that his mother liked; however, he hadn't yet got up the courage to approach Burtsev. It all seemed too foolish — to eat some fish and, afterward, while taking a walk along the bunks, to ask: "Remember, you were speaking about the symbolists a while back..."

Moreover, in essence, Burtsev didn't seem a bad type, and despite his somewhat distant and grumpy exterior, he even sang a Jewish song along with Moisei Solomonovich, so that Moisei Solomonovich himself fell silent from amazement.

"Mezernitskii is coming already; he told us to set the table," said Burtsev. "Where does he have that...?"

Burtsev opened a painted wooden chest near the window; Artiom immediately smelled something edible.

"We have bacon today with white bread," said Burtsev simply.

"Don't you know each other?" said Vasilii Petrovich, either to Burtsev, meaning Artiom, or the other way around. As a result, their eyes met again with calm sympathy, and this quick glance contained both a young, warm sarcasm with reference to their fussy older companion, as well as a self-evident agreement that to explain to Vasilii Petrovich the reason for their not very close acquaintance was pointless, especially since no one really knew the reason — it had just turned out that way.

"This is Artiom," continued Vasilii Petrovich, who had not caught the shared glance, "a kind, generous and strong young man who is, in addition to everything else, a wonderful stevedore, a secret lover of poetry and in general a fine fellow. You will get along!"

Artiom, who stared at the table during this entire introduction, skeptically chewed with an empty mouth, but all that had little effect on Vasilii Petrovich.

"Our Solovki is a strange place!" he was saying. "This is the strangest prison in the world! More than that: here we think that the world is great and wonderful, filled with mysteries and enchantment, terrors and delights, but even we have certain reasons to believe that today, in these days, Solovki is the most incredible place known to man. It defies explanation! Did you know, Artiom, that in winter, during the tree-felling, they once left thirty people in the woods for not finishing their quota? They all froze. Did you hear about those three homeless kids who killed and ate one of those foul gulls of Solovki, whom they left 'for the mosquitoes' with Eichmanis's knowledge, tying them naked to the trees? Of course, they soon took them down, they survived, but they'll have black scars from the bites for their entire life. Oh, the governor of our camp does love his flora and fauna. Did you know that there's a biological research center here that investigates the depths of the White Sea? That, by Eichmanis's order, the inmates are successfully cultivating Newfoundland musk beavers, arctic foxes, chinchillas, silver foxes, red foxes and silvery Canadian foxes? Did you know that there's a meteorological station here? In the camp, Artiom! It's also manned by inmates!"

Artiom shrugged his shoulders. He wasn't that surprised, and he didn't really care. Mosquitoes, foxes, meteorological stations… But there lies the sour cream with onions!

"Very well, but did you know," said Vasilii Petrovich, "that in the former Petrograd guest house, the one behind the Governor's building, hired monks from Solovki to live on the first floor, while the Chekists lives on the second? And they're friends! They visit each other!"

"Just like the white man who sailed to the new world and at first visited the aborigines in their homes, then, if those did not express a desire to be baptized and share their gold, burned their homes and killed them with dogs… whom, it must be said, the Indians had never before seen. Imagine the horror of those savages!" said Burtsev, completely without any malice, clearly enjoying cutting the bacon fat into thin strips. With his final words, he raised his head and smiled at someone who had quietly entered the cell, standing behind Artiom's back.

That was Mezernitskii. He quickly nodded at Artiom to let him know that he didn't have to get up. Laughing, he immediately picked up the thread of the conversation:

"The only difference is that they didn't want baptism, while our monks don't want to stop crossing themselves."[27]

"Mr. Mezernitskii, is that really a cause for jokes?!" Vasilii Petrovich threw up his hands.

"Comrade Mezernitskii," he corrected him. "Pleased to meet you. I'm Mezernitskii, a musician of the brass orchestra." Without transition, he continued the conversation: "Very well, then here's another example for you. Vasilii Petrovich most likely began the theme of paradoxes on Solovki — isn't it curious that in the country of Bolshevism triumphant, and in the first concentration camp organized by said government, half of the administrative positions are occupied by the enemies of communism — White Army officers? While bishops and archbishops, all those who are suspected in anti-Soviet activity, guard the goods of the Bolsheviks and the camp! Even I, a lieutenant in the Tsar's army, play for them on a trumpet. This is because they themselves are not trained to do these things, but they are ready, merely because of my ability to play the trumpet, to release me from the common labors. Do you know what I will tell you? I tell you that fighting against the Soviet government is pointless. They themselves can't do anything! Slowly, step by step, we will replace them everywhere — from the stage to the Kremlin."

Burtsev looked at the door significantly, but Mezernitskii only waved him off.

"Nonsense! I was saying this to Eichmanis personally only yesterday."

"Whether you said it or not is your business, but the point is that it's frivolous," answered Burtsev without irritation, even with a smile. "You've been here three years already, my friend and you've lost your connection with reality. You know better what's going on in the brass section, but as for running the place, they're slowly getting the hang of it..."

---

[27] In the Russian original, this is a play on words. In Russian, the word for "to be baptized" and "to cross oneself" is the same, hence the joke. It's also an untranslatable joke, as most are. (translator's note)

"I don't know, I don't know," interrupted Mezernitskii, who clearly liked to hear the sound of his own voice, "Let me bring your attention, dear guests, to the following fact. The only officer who labors at the common work is Burtsev, and this is — forgive me, *mon cher* — due to his foolish stubbornness, while all the others..." Here, Mezernitskii began to count on his fingers, remembering. "The supply unit controller, the camp captain, the telephone engineer, the agricultural specialist, two production managers and two managers of the workshops! And that's not all of it, not all of it! All the people on the railroad are ours! At the electrical plant — they're ours! In the publishing office — ours! The radio office — ours! The topography office is staffed by us. Even the animal farm has our people!"

"With such talents, it's unclear how we lost the war to the Bolsheviks," quietly said Burtsev to no one in particular.

"In addition," once again, Mezernitskii was paying no one else any attention, "note that from the age of twenty, I'm completely apolitical. The stupidity and baseness of the leaders of the White Army has made peace between me and the Bolsheviks for all time. But why should we ignore reality? Solovki is a reflection of Russia, where everything is as though magnified by a lens — naturally, unpleasantly, curiously!"

Instead of answering, Burtsev bit his lips as though lost in thought. He finished cutting the bread and looked over the table as though it was a map of a successfully begun military maneuver.

Artiom examined both Burtsev and Mezernitskii, looking quickly back and forth between them.

Burtsev was not tall, with bowed legs and barely curling brown hair, dark eyes and thin lips... He had thin fingers and wrists, which seemed strange for a person who was assigned to the common labors, though not so very long ago. As far as Artiom remembered, Burtsev appeared in Solovki a month before him, with the first spring group.

Mezernitskii was tall, stooping, with straight and slightly greasy hair. He sniffed frequently like a person with a cocaine habit, something that on Solovki was impossible. His gestures were manifold; Artiom noticed he had not trimmed his fingernails in a long time.

When Mezernitskii held the white piece of bacon that had gone soft in the warmth with a black-edged fingernail, that was especially obvious.

* * *

The argument concluded quickly — the sour cream with onions, the white bread and the bacon pacified everyone.

The most difficult thing was to eat slowly — Artiom noticed that he wasn't the only one with this problem.

Then Vasilii Petrovich and Burtsev began to play checkers. The former was clearly agitated by the game, the latter was almost indifferent to the position of the pieces on the board. Mezernitskii played rather well on the mandolin and Artiom silently enjoyed the scene, half-lying on the uncovered couch, sometimes thinking: *what good people these are… I'd like to be useful to them*, sometimes almost dozing off, only waking up because a single infuriating fly kept landing on his face.

A louse fell from his jacket to the board; Artiom hurried to kill it.

Having parted with Mezernitksii, they ran into the agitated and red-faced crowd coming from the theater. Someone was still discussing the play, as was typical, while others were already thinking of tomorrow's work and hurrying to get enough sleep. But the general sense was, as always, a bit wild — the inmates walked together with the authorities of the camp and the hired workers, as well as women in makeup, some of whom were dressed quite fashionably. Even some of the men were far from wearing rags.

As soon as he saw the crowd from the theater, Vasilii Petrovich immediately returned to their sleeping quarters, hardly saying goodbye. Burtsev, having quickly smoked, also nodded at Artiom, as though they hadn't had that moment of silent mutual understanding in the cell.

On the other hand, Afanasiev appeared, having had a full rest after his day's turn of duty and looking very content.

He was a red-head, shaggy-haired, with large lips — he looked good when he was in a good mood.

"Are you coming from the theater?" asked Artiom; he thought that he probably managed to catch fifteen minutes of sleep to the playing of the mandolin — once again, he felt, not energetic of course, but slightly more animated.

Afanasiev nodded.

"What were they showing?" asked Artiom.

"Nothing special," Afanasiev shrugged off the question cheerfully. "Lunacharskii. Still, Artiom, all this inspires one, even with Lunacharskii. As though there's a bit of counter-revolutionary thought behind it all, you know? It makes you want to cry."

Afanasiev continued saying something murky about the show, as though he were trying to explain the director's vision, but in his mind, he still imagined nothing but counter-revolutionary subversion.

They walked back and forth along the quickly-emptying courtyard. Artiom nodded, nodded and didn't even notice how Afanasiev had changed the subject to the one that he liked the most.

"Tioma, only think what poems I'll write when I get back! I'll stick words into my poems that had never been there! Candlewick![28] Skerries! Sludge![29] Can you imagine an epic poem titled 'Mastyrka'? After all, we haven't yet had a poet who's done proper time!"

"What about the Decembrists?" Artiom remembered.

"They didn't have any poets," Afanasiev waved him off.

"Wasn't Mayakovskii imprisoned?" Artiom remembered again.

"That doesn't count," Afanasiev didn't agree again. "All that's not enough, not it at all! Solovki — now that's the real thing, Tioma, a special case! It's like Odysseus, when visiting Polyphemus..."

"Well yes, Polyphemus, skerries, sludge... that'll be quite a salad," sniggered Artiom, then immediately remembered the sour cream and onions.

"You don't understand anything!" Afanasiev seemed to be really angry now. "The future of poetry is in rough words, accidental ones. Lomonosov wrote about three styles — the exalted, the middling and the low. Well, we need to find even lower sources for our poetry. We need to dip into the dung, the latrine hole and mix it up with the exalted style — believe me, it'll work, you'll see!"

"As for me, I think you can only write fables in such a way: 'Polyphemus and the candlewick.'" Artiom goaded Afanasiev on purpose.

"What a curious conversation about mythology," said someone quietly.

They both turned around and saw Eichmanis. They froze in place, as though they were both nailed through.

"Good evening," said Eichmanis calmly.

"Good!" yelled Afanasiev as they always did during the roll call, as for Artiom, he feverishly tried to remember, rummaging through his thoughts as though they were clothes that had caught fire — had they uttered any counter-revolutionary stupidity in the last minute or not?

"Good, citizen governor!" Artiom yelled out as well. That was how you were supposed to answer any greeting from the governor of the camp.

28 Prison jargon, meaning "person wasting away to nothing".

29 Prison jargon, meaning "whore".

No one risked answering Eichmanis's comment about mythology.

Eichmanis nodded, meaning "at ease". Apparently, he was on his way to the gates, as always without a guard, although he was still with that woman, who was again, like the last time in the forest, looking askance.

Close up, Eichmanis ended up being taller than average, taller than both Artiom and Afanasiev. He was well-built, lean and smelled of cologne. He was in a good set of civilian clothing — a brown jacket, pants, sharp-toed shoes with a high heel.

Artiom noticed that a Red Army solider waited at the gates, holding two horses by the bridle.

Eichmanis lived four kilometers away from the monastery, not far from the St. Savvatii Skete in the St. Makarii Hermitage. They said that he had built a huge subarctic mansion there; typically, it was at a distance from the Chekist agents under his authority. Eichmanis appeared rarely at the inspections and he spent most of his time, they said, hunting, or tending to his biological garden — a nursery of both deciduous and evergreen trees that they had begun to plant all over the island…

Artiom examined his face carefully, from under his eyebrows. Eichmanis had symmetrical, large, but in some ways rare, even refined features. His hair was brushed back; he had white, rather large teeth and smiled, though the eyes seemed not to move at all during the smile. He was handsome, reminding one of some famous poet of the 1910's. He could easily have won people over. Except, in the line of his cheekbones — they were too slippery, making the face seem thinner than it was — there was something unpleasant and sallow.

Artiom didn't risk taking a closer look at Eichmanis's companion, though he wanted to.

"You're still laboring in the twelfth brigade, Afanasiev?" asked Eichmanis, smiling.

"Yes!" Afanasiev shook his red head and added for accuracy, "Exactly so!"

Eichmanis nodded again, this time in parting and the pair walked towards the gates.

"Hell!" Afanasiev laughed quietly when they heard the sound of hooves. "And here I was going on about Polyphemus… We didn't manage to say anything… did we?"

Artiom was also smiling with an incomprehensible emotion.

Not waiting for an answer, Afanasiev said, "They say that he knows all the inmates by name!"

"That's impossible," answered Artiom, having thought about it. "How many thousands are there here? Fifteen brigades…! No, impossible."

"Very well, very well," Afanasiev agreed quickly. "But at least half of them! The production managers, the brigade commanders, the foremen, the guards, the actors, the musicians, the priests — he knows them all. Everyone says so! And for some reason he's remembered me too."

"In summary: he knows the people he needs to know," offered Artiom with a certain affected seriousness.

"You think?" Afanasiev brightened, not noticing the sarcasm, though up to that moment, he had identified all of Artiom's inflections. "Maybe they'll finally take me out of the twelfth brigade. Anywhere else! Too bad I don't know how to do anything with my hands. Devil take me, I wrote poetry! If only I had been a topographer. Or a woodworker. Or knew how to play the drums. Or, finally, how to cook something delicious. Did you know that the former cook of Leo Tolstoy works here, in the infirmary? There's even a local painter named Braz. He's a former professor of the Imperial Academy of Art!"

"So ask Eichmanis to become poet laureate," Artiom offered. "You'll write odes to him every morning. 'Ode to Eichmanis's visit to the chinchilla nursery'!"

"You can only mock," Afanasiev waved him off.

"Then why did he ask what brigade you worked in? There are two possible reasons. Either he's planning to make you poet laureate, or he's planning to move you to the Sekirka. Which would you prefer?"

The Sekirka was a special isolation complex on Sekirova Hill, built inside a former church, about eight kilometers from the kremlin. The stories about that isolation complex weren't pleasant — people were killed there.

Afanasiev looked extremely hopeful but remained silent, probably because he was afraid to scare off his unexpected good fortune.

"Who's that with him?" asked Artiom quietly, not nodding or explaining that he meant those who had ridden away; it was obvious, anyway.

"That's Galia, Eichmanis's whore. She's a hired worker for the Information and Investigation Department," answered Afanasiev in a quiet recitative, with no emotion. "She hasn't called you in yet?"

Afanasiev's words made Artiom fearful and sad; he even choked a little. He hadn't had a woman for four months already.

* * *

If they had only woken them not at five, but at least at six, life would have been so much easier. But the inspections were always long and the assignments were always confused, so they still arrived at their work late, sometimes as late as nine. If you had to go far, a few kilometers away, they started even later.

The first thing Artiom remembered was how Vasilii Petrovich had praised him; well, yes, he had acclimatized to the inmate life. The most important thing was not to count the days and he had stopped counting them on the third day, accepting everything as it was. The rest was easy — to endure and to survive; basically, he hadn't yet seen any reason to die. People lived, even here. Even the weak, the foolish, the stupid, those completely incapable of living — they survived too.

Then Artiom remembered Krapin, and his positive attitude was a little shaken.

All morning he tried not to appear in front of Krapin. It worked.

Vasilii Petrovich had bought himself a spoon and he immediately bragged about it.

Afanasiev walked around thoughtfully; he was taken on the duty roster, even though it seemed that they had just assigned him. It was a good job, a warm one, especially in winter. People held on to their duty roster positions tooth and nail.

Instead of Afanasiev, they put the Chechen Khasaev on duty. Their third fellow countryman, the youngest, was also always hanging around the brigade. The Cossack Lazhechnikov now tried to walk past the duty officers quickly, staring at the ground, and he stopped drinking the water by his post altogether.

During the roll call, Curly cursed so stupidly, tediously and abominably, that Artiom even felt slightly sick to his stomach.

He was assigned to the logs. Artiom wasn't surprised — it had all been going in that direction.

"If it's the logs, then it's the logs, let's see what the fuss is about," Artiom encouraged himself, content even with the fact that Krapin hadn't measured him out with the bludgeon a second time. Instead, the foreman was beating the life out of some gangster who hadn't hurried to line up in his drawers — he had no other pants.

"Upending the forest?" asked Afanasiev gloomily. "Me too."

The same assignment fell to Moisei Solomonovich, Lazhechnikov, Sivtsev, the Chinese man, the criminal whom Krapin had beaten, two more of that ilk and some barely-noticeable short *muzhik*. All Artiom remembered about him was that he constantly mumbled under his breath, as though convincing himself of something.

They stood in the courtyard, waiting for their guard. From the early morning, you could never decide where it was best to be. In the sleeping quarters, everyone always screamed and swore, but outside there were those irrepressible gulls that had become hungry overnight. One day, when Artiom had only just arrived on Solovki, in the early morning a gull had grabbed a loaf he had saved for after. The gangsters that had noticed started to laugh. It upset him. Artiom almost seriously promised himself that before he returned to the mainland, he would tear off the wing of one gull, so that it wouldn't die immediately and so it would understand, the bastard, what it's like when it hurts.

In general, you had to be careful of the gulls — they could really attack you and peck out your eye. The bread Artiom had hidden back in the sleeping quarters, not even in his pants, but in his sheets, where he had a comfortable pocket. He hadn't planned on sharing that bread with anyone, but he didn't splurge on himself either.

"Why aren't you on the duty roster anymore?" he asked Afanasiev. "Didn't they just assign you? It's not the hardest job. You would have time to write poetry."

Artiom looked at Afanasiev and understood that he didn't really want to joke about it.

"That's decided in the Information and Investigation Department," answered Afanasiev unwillingly. "Galia and I don't get along."

Vasilii Petrovich, who stood near them, looked at Afanasiev strangely and turned away.

"As for the Chechen, Curly asked to have him assigned," Afanasiev added after a minute's silence. "After all, they're neighbors in those mountains."

Artiom nodded and, since Afanasiev wasn't in the mood, walked over to Vasilii Petrovich, who had again been assigned to the unguarded berry brigade and was awaiting his fellow pickers.

"Only don't condole with me, Vasilii Petrovich," said Artiom after a few steps, smiling from ear to ear.

"Go ahead and smile," said Vasilii Petrovich sadly, and, taking Artiom with a light touch by the elbow, turned him a little to the side. Artiom, smirking immaturely, submitted.

"I see you're friends with Afanasiev," Vasilii Petrovich uttered clearly and quietly. "I want to tell you that only informants are assigned to the duty roster, so…"

"He's just been taken off," answered Artiom a bit louder than was necessary, and Vasilii Petrovich immediately turned Artiom by the elbow even further with his firm and unnaturally strong fingers, towards the column of priests who were on their way to their guard duty.

Some of the priests walked quickly, some, on the contrary, tried to walk decorously, but the formation confused everyone. The gulls circled around them, occasionally flying towards them… Those beards, those cassocks, those gulls that sometimes sprinkled the robes of the priests with their droppings — all of it suddenly seemed to freeze in Artiom's vision and he understood that he would remember this scene for the rest of his life, even though nothing about it amazed, upset or moved him at all. He just had a feeling that he would remember.

"The sixth brigade isn't just something," said someone loudly and mockingly, "The sixth brigade is angelic! One, two, three and you're in heaven! And for what do they suffer? Not in word, not in deed, not in thought did they sin. Innocent, all in your name, O Lord."

"Look," said Vasilii Petrovich very calmly. "There's Evgenii Zernov, the bishop of Priamursk and Blagoveshchensk. That's Prokopii, archbishop of Kherson… Juvenalii, archbishop of Kursk… Pahomii, archbishop of Chernigov… Grigorii, bishop of Pechersk… Amvrosii, bishop of Podolsk and Bratsslavsk… Kyprian, bishop of Semipalatinsk… Sophronii, bishop of Yakutsk, who changed one freezing climate for a different kind of bad weather… And there's our own *Vladychka*, Father John…"

Vasilii Petrovich inclined his head in greeting, while the slightly limping *Vladychka* John, who was therefore hurrying more than the others, waved at him cheerfully. There was something either very childish or Old Testament-like in that gesture. As though a child were saying, "I'm not despairing," while an old man confirmed it: "Neither should you despair," all in a single wave.

"How do you know him so well?" asked Artiom.

"How?" answered Vasilii Petrovich. "We were just brought here in the same cargo hold. Everyone was angry and oppressed; he alone smiled and laughed. Even the gangsters didn't touch him. Next to him, you can't help feeling that we're all children. And that, Artiom, is such a warm, such a necessary feeling sometimes. You probably don't understand that yet…"

Artiom looked around and asked: "What he said in the square about the Soviet government — do you think he's right?"

Vasilii Petrovich shrugged and put his hand behind his back with a quick gesture.

"It's all true. True, for example, that you might be an informant. He had seen you for the first time in his life."

Artiom laughed sadly, noting for himself that he had not yet seen Vasilii Petrovich so severe, and he changed the subject.

"Someone told me that Eichmanis remembers almost everyone in the camp by name…"

"It's entirely possible," answered Vasilii Petrovich thoughtfully.

"And you… all these priests... when you memorized them… why?"

"Eichmanis guards them, but I have to live with them," said Vasilii Petrovich simply, looking ahead. "I will remember these faces and, if I return, I will put them up in my home like icons."

Artiom didn't say anything, but thought childishly: "How are they any more holy than I? I also devour that soup with dried fish or with the eye-less heads of salted cod and instead of meat, I eat old horseflesh. At least they get to be guards, while I'm about to go lug timber around."

Vasilii Petrovich jerked his head and, to lessen the pathos a bit, began to speak in a completely different tone of voice, much more trustworthy, immediately becoming that person whom Artiom liked so much.

"Here I was thinking… from here, from Solovki, the holiness left as long ago as the time of Alexei Mikhailovich… You probably know, Artiom, that story, how in 1666 the monastery rebelled against Nikon's reforms? After ten years of siege, they finally took it and all the rebellious monks and their workers — they were all stoned to death, lest their swords be dirtied or their powder wasted. After that, there was no more monastic asceticism, no more saints on Solovki. For two hundred years, even more, the monastery just bobbed on the waves — not a small amount of time. As though it were getting ready for something. You won't believe it, I think, Artiom, but now's the time for a new asceticism. The Russian church will be reborn from here… You were probably still a child, you don't remember how heavy the air was before the Bolsheviks came."

"How's it like in your barracks?" Artiom wanted to ask, but of course didn't.

"The intelligentsia came to hate priests," Vasilii Petrovich began to count off. "The Russian *muzhik* began to hate priests. The Russian poet — even he hated priests! I'm ashamed to admit that even I began to hate priests. And you won't immediately guess why! Because the Russian priest drank from dawn to dusk? What else did he have to do? People hate most often not because of someone else's failings, but from their own emptiness much more often. You didn't take part in the second war for the Fatherland. But

I did, and I witnessed that when soldiers were offered confession before a battle, nine out of ten refused. I saw that myself and even then — I wonder at myself! — understood that we would lose the war, that we could not escape revolution. The people had lost their faith. These were the only possible consequences…! It ended and immediately began again. Here."

"In the thirteenth brigade," suddenly Artiom remembered and was unable to stop himself, "the latrine stood in the altar, remember? In my group, there was a priest. He didn't go there a single time. At night, he would get up and go outside to the common crapper. While he went there, his place would always be taken on the bunks. When we got up in the morning, he would be sitting somewhere in a corner, nearly frozen."

"Well, what do you think?" asked Vasilii Petrovich.

Artiom vividly wanted to wound his companion — it was a firm feeling, difficult to explain.

"I think he's an idiot," answered Artiom.

Vasilii Petrovich's jaw quivered, as though Artiom had just pushed a sick person in front of him. He turned away.

His berry brigade was already waiting with the baskets. Artiom's foreman also appeared and immediately started yelling, as though someone had poured hot water on his stomach.

"I'm coming," Artiom said, more to himself than the foreman, otherwise he would have gotten it in the teeth.

The foreman was also an inmate who had been incarcerated for either three or five murders. He was a Muscovite; his last name was Sorokin. It was as though he was emitting hidden human filth — it seemed that it came out of him together with his sweat. No matter what the stink in the barracks, Artiom always smelled him whenever he got near. Under his armpits, Sorokin always had dark circles, hard with salt. His clammy hands shook slightly, the bristle on his face was always clammy and it looked as though it wasn't hair, but dirt, the kind that's left on the floor of a hay-loft — a prickly, dusty-grassy sprinkling.

Sorokin, they said, liked to come up with inventive ways of playing jokes on the inmates. Though, it must be said that he didn't hit the counter-revolutionaries. By an unspoken rule of the camp, it was generally not acceptable practice to bother the counter-revolutionaries, so those who wanted to vent their animal cruelty usually played around with the petty criminals.

They went to their work through the forest and they caught up with Vasilii Petrovich's group. He locked gazes with Artiom and immediately turned away, as though in pain from a sudden spasm in the stomach, his face screwed up.

Artiom wanted to feel sorry for himself that he had refused to go pick berries, but he banished the thought. About the reason he had, for some reason, been rude to Vasilii Petrovich, he didn't think. He didn't have an evil character, but that quality — to suddenly poke an open wound — he knew himself to be capable of that. And he didn't feel bad about it at all.

"Maybe I just don't like it when people reveal what's hurting them..." thought Artiom, smiling slightly.

"... He's telling me about faith," he thought as well, "but he himself took Moisei Solomonovich out of the berry brigade. Why didn't he feel sorry for him?"

Sorokin yelled the whole way and swore at no one in particular for no particular reason, as though he had caught Curly's bug that morning. Even the guards were looking at him sideways.

Artiom suddenly imagined that he grabbed a large bough, bigger than Sorokin's bludgeon and sharply, with gusto, began to beat the foreman in the back of the head. That would be happiness.

And such silence would ensue...

They would go berry-picking, sing a song, light a fire...

Even Moisei Solomonovich's songs were nowhere to be heard.

Artiom looked at Afanasiev, and he, it seemed, was dreaming of the same thing.

Through the forest, they came out to the canal, which, as Lazhechnikov said, joined Danilovo Lake with Pert Lake. Timber hewn down in the logging camp was floated down this canal. Artiom looked at the logs in the same way as he, probably, would have looked at some huge predatory water-monster that he had to pull out to shore by its gills.

"There are two golden days — yesterday and tomorrow," said the short *muzhik*, about a meter and a half tall, who stood next to Artiom. "Yesterday already passed; the Lord took care of that. Tomorrow I leave to Him; He'll take care of it. One day remains — today. When I prayerfully will accomplish my task."

"That one?" asked Artiom, nodding at the floating logs.

The man looked at Artiom, then at the logs and didn't answer.

"You have to carry the logs to the sawmill," explained the foreman. "The quota for the day — one hundred logs... What are we looking at?"

"Hey! Will there be barge poles or ropes?" asked one of the gangsters who had already gotten his share from Krapin that morning.

"You'll get a rope when they hang you!" screamed the foreman.

"OK, barge poles then," the criminal kept on, and, of course, got what was coming. Sorokin attacked him, blandishing his bludgeon even at a distance. The man defended himself and even tried to wave the blows off with his thinned-out, dirty hands. He got struck on the hands, on the sides and on his head. He only shrieked, "Foreman! Foreman! What are you doing?"

His flesh hung in tatters on his cheek and his hand was all bloody.

"Undress, and into the water like a bullet! Or I'll bludgeon you in the neck, so your head won't fall off!" yelled the foreman. The criminal took off his ragged pants — he was naked underneath. The foreman pulled him by his shirt into the water, and the shirt ripped in half.

So that the same wouldn't happen to them, the rest began to take off their clothes.

"What are you doing, fuckers?" screamed the foreman, leaving the criminal finally, who had fled into the water and now stood submerged to his chest, rubbing off the blood. "Getting undressed like in the ballet, fuck! The youngest go into the water and the rest pick up the logs as they come ashore. Stupid idiots, or I'll come after your mothers!"

"How about that, he knows about ballet," thought Artiom as he was taking off his pants.

"Hell, it's cold!" said one of the gangsters as he got into the water.

"Not bad, just right," thought Artiom. "At night it rained, got a little colder… At least there are fewer mosquitoes in the water…"

"Go ahead, bloodsuckers, you don't even have to bite. Just lick it off!" The beaten criminal raised his hand to the mosquitoes and laughed huskily. To look at him, it didn't seem that he really cared about the foreman's knuckle sandwich.

No one wanted to stay on the shore next to the foreman. One after the other Sivtsev, Afanasiev, Moisei Solomonovich crawled into the water. The short man also walked up and down the shore, repeating to himself, "If I only had a back, I'd find me some wine!" Then took a step into the water.

Moisei Solomonovich was taller than everyone else by a head. He walked in the water; it was all shallow to him. But the short *muzhik*, as soon as he walked into the water, somehow sank all the way to his chin and now only sighed: "Oh, my God! Save me, Lord!" He took another step and almost disappeared completely.

"Where are you crawling, you louse!" yelled the foreman. "Back to shore! What are you gonna do, louse, ride the logs along the water? And you, tall guy, get back here." He pointed at Moisei Solomonovich. "Your hands are perfect to receive the logs. You'll be our boat-hook."

Sivtsev still had a strong body. Only on his back, an eloquent scar stood out, probably from a saber. Lazhechnikov had a similar scar from his shoulder nearly to his nipple.

The gangsters were covered in tattoos.

"Look at you all, the lot of you," thought Artiom ambiguously, looking askance at his clean body, lacking even chest hair.

Afanasiev, for all that, was also without any distinguishing features, except that he was covered in slight freckles.

Artiom lurched onward, carefully walking along the lake floor, until he reached the first log — it was exactly at chest level — and pulled the tree towards himself, waving off the mosquitoes.

Quietly swearing, the beaten criminal came by to help him.

"Passport," he introduced himself.

Passport had a few pimples on his face and two more on his neck. His lower lip drooped. Artiom wanted to take it with two fingers and pull it up to his nose.

The criminal offered his hand and as Artiom shook it, said mockingly, "Take five, the GPU will take ten."

Artiom breathed in deeply and said nothing.

"Fine, don't piss in your pants, piss in the water." The criminal wouldn't back down and kept looking at Artiom.

"Are you going to continue with your proverbs or, maybe, let's get to work?" said Artiom, because he had to say something already.

"The bitch will give it to you, but you'll rinse your dick in her," said the criminal and laughed again, looking at Artiom mockingly. "So enough with the 'let's'. Got enough of it from the foreman."

"Listen," Artiom bent down to him, trying to be moderately amicable. "You've got your buddies here." Artiom nodded at the other gangsters who were listening in on their conversation with caustic interest. "You be with them, and I'll be with my friend. Fair enough?"

Afanasiev stood there, somewhat deliberately scattered and seeming as though not listening in on someone else's conversation.

Passport pushed the log so that it struck Artiom in the chest and only then took a step back. To add insult to injury, he hit his open palm on the surface of the water and splashed Artiom.

Artiom didn't answer. Splashing in retaliation seemed stupid, while to smack him immediately in the forehead also seemed an action with no brain behind it. He just wiped off his face, and that was it.

* * *

"It's better in the water," thought Artiom, distracting himself from the unpleasant thoughts of the criminal, that one, what was his name, Passport "The work here's better than on shore. Because there's only one thing to do — to push the logs to the shore. It's a totally different thing to pull them towards yourself on land."

But Artiom, of course, guessed wrong.

They had to push the logs to the shore, then grab them — wet, slippery and incredibly heavy — by one end, while Moisei Solomonovich grabbed the other end with the short *muzhik*, then to climb out to shore.

If four men could manage a log, that meant it was the smallest possible size.

At first, they lugged young trees that weren't thick in the trunk or longer than five meters, more often shorter than that. But in the water you could see such giants that if it took the whole group to carry one, there would be no shame in it.

Plus, the shore was rocky — to walk on it, barely holding on to the log, was sheer torture.

Sivtsev worked together with the Chinese man. For some reason, Sivtsev called him "little rabbit".

"Come on, little rabbit, go deeper..." he kept repeating, not without pleasure. "How awkward he is..."

The small *muzhik* couldn't get into a work flow with Moisei Solomonovich. They more or less managed to pull the first log that Artiom and Afanasiev brought them away from the water, swearing and tripping over their own feet. The small *muzhik* dropped the next log and Passport yelled at him. Immediately, the little man started to cry like a child.

"I worked in an office," he sobbed. "With papers! How many months now are they forcing me to strain my innards! I don't have any strength left!"

"Fool for Christ," thought Artiom irritably.

"Foreman! This guy's fucking useless!" Passport yelled and immediately, quickly rowing with his hands, went deeper into the water as the foreman went for him. Passport had pimples on his back too, two by two like white-legged insects along his shoulder blade, spine and down to his rear end.

By tiring out their hands, by breaking their feet, they somehow managed, with insult added to injury, to drag out about ten logs to the shore.

"… The foreman said that our quota is one hundred!" It boggled the mind, but Artiom still had enough wits to find it amusing.

From the shore, they still needed to carry them to the sawmill.

While they lifted the first log, crouching and straining their backs, Artiom had time to despise it as a living thing — frantically, piercingly.

"Bastard, you're so heavy, slippery. I wish I could chop your face off, you reptile."

Hurriedly, Artiom made the first run without his shirt. Halfway there, he rubbed his shoulder raw on the wood.

The journey ended up being long, along hills and through shrubs. Artiom constantly waved off the mosquitoes. Afanasiev not only was a poet, but ended up being sturdy as a camel. "You're a good dance partner, Tioma!" he said, breathing heavily through his nose.

Sivtsev and the Chinaman carried the front end. Artiom constantly stared at the Chinese man's black head.

The saw shrieked in the sawmill. Seeing no road, Artiom understood by the sound that they were close, closer, closer… here… looks like they made it. On Afanasiev's command of "three, four," they threw down the log. Such gratitude flared up for a moment in his entire body. If only there weren't any mosquitoes…

A grumpy, hunched-over man came out of the mill, looked at them and, without saying hello, disappeared in the doorway.

Artiom almost raced back to his shirt.

"Where are you rushing? Missing your work?" Afanasiev yelled in his wake.

His wet clothes hung off him unpleasantly. Artiom could feel his numb, shriveled and wrinkled-up scrotum. He suddenly remembered that he forgot some bread in his pocket. He stuck his hand in — yes, his hands were covered in wet and vile pulp. He slipped on the hillock, fell, unwillingly throwing forward his hand — the one that was holding the bread.

There wasn't much left on his fingers. Artiom lay on the grass, feeling the cold, oozing water with his stomach… He licked his hands, covered in bread pulp.

"Ooh, look at him hiding there," he heard Afanasiev's voice behind him. "Waiting for a deer to come by? Or are you hunting frogs?"

Artiom got up and felt on the verge of tears. He turned his head, so that Afanasiev wouldn't see.

That was his last bread. There were still two whole days on millet porridge and fish only.

He got control of himself, clenched his jaw, wiped his eyes, forced himself to turn and smile at Afanasiev. It worked; he bared his teeth.

Sivtsev wasn't hurrying back and for some reason was walking in a crouch. Artiom decided he was eating berries.

Artiom didn't want any berries. They'd managed to bring two logs, but there were ninety-eight left.

During the next run, it got hotter, though the day was cold.

He saw that Sivtsev seemed to be covered in ichor; at first, Artiom thought that the man had broken open his head. Turns out it was the berries. He had wiped them over his face against the mosquitoes, the cunning villager.

As they were coming back, Artiom also tried to find something, even a crowberry. It didn't happen at first — Sorokin the foreman had gotten bored on the shore and came to greet the late workers. Once again, he screamed his head off like a robbed man.

The next time Artiom found a patch — the devil only knows what berry — but he wiped his face with them. He rubbed them in with such ferocity, as though he knew that death was coming up to his very heart, and here he found a living berry to save for later.

At least they stopped landing on his eyes and forehead.

The little *muzhik*, whose name no one knew, cursed out everyone except for Moisei Solomonovich. Every minute or so he stopped to breathe, barely getting up, then immediately managed to trip and drop the log as he oohed and yelped.

When the sun reached midday, the little man refused to work.

He came up to the foreman, hobbling on all his legs, and said, "Kill me. I can't…"

"I'll kill you," answered the guard and began to kill him. He threw him to the ground and began to trample his face, drove his boot into his side several times, screaming all the while: "Are you gonna work, lazy bum?"

The workers stopped — it was break time. Someone even lit a cigarette. Only the Chinese man turned aside, crouched down and closed his eyes, as though he could disappear.

"I can't! Don't kill me!" The little man yelled with a weak voice. "I can't! Don't kill me!"

Artiom stupidly stared at him too. "First, 'kill me', then 'don't kill me!'" he thought to himself in passing.

If they had killed the little man then and there, Artiom would probably not have felt anything.

"What a strange expression, 'don't kill me!'" Artiom wondered again. "Never heard it before…"

When someone yelled, "Cut it out already, you hear?" Artiom, for a split-second, didn't even realize that he had yelled it. A crack opened up along his cheek — the berry juice had dried up and as his mouth opened his cheek seemed to split in half.

The foreman, without batting an eye, turned and threw his bludgeon at Artiom, like into an open field.

Artiom barely managed to duck, or it would have hit him in the head.

"Bring it back, jackal!" the foreman ordered.

Artiom didn't look the foreman in the eye, nor did he look at the other inmates. He looked askance at the two guards — they watched everything that was going on with a single and very simple emotion — they wanted someone to give them a reason to get mad. One of them even got up and started stamping — he so wanted to hit someone.

Artiom went to pick up the bludgeon — it was lying not far away on the rocks. Without raising his eyes, he gave it to the foreman.

During this entire sickening minute, he had no other thought than the repeating phrase: "The stupid boys get a stick in the ribs."

Grabbing the bludgeon, the foreman swung at Artiom, but he ran to the water, crouched over, with a speed not typical for him and an unfamiliar, even unpleasant fidgetiness — the work, the work is waiting!

He didn't even take off his shirt — just jumped in all the way to his neck.

The rest went in after Artiom.

"I don't have strength left, comrade foreman," begged the little man on the shore. "No-more-strength-left. My heart's in my throat. I'm gonna die!"

When Artiom and Afanasiev brought another log to the shore, it turned out that the foreman had come up with a different job for the little man.

He was standing on a stump and yelling: "I'm a lazy bum! I'm a lazy bum! I'm a parasite to the Soviet government!"

Passport laughed and the rest of the gangsters also snickered.

"I'm a lazy bum! I'm a lazy bum! I'm a parasite to the Soviet government!" the little man repeated like a wind-up toy.

"Two thousand times. I'm counting," said Sorokin the foreman, full of himself.

The guards, two big fellows, were rolling over, laughing, as well.

Having gathered ten logs on the shore, they once again started carrying them to the sawmill. Artiom's left arm was ragged from the bushes and when they danced along the hillocks, everything scratched at them. This time he switched places with Afanasiev, and Artiom's right arm started to get ripped up.

Behind them, the little man kept repeating:

"I'm a lazy bum! I'm a lazy bum! I'm a parasite to the Soviet government!"

On the way back, Artiom wrung out his shirt properly, but, it's a strange thing, the damp fabric seemed even colder than when it was wet through.

The berry juice had washed off his face, and he didn't find any new berries. He swung at the mosquitoes with full force — a scattering of red dots were left on his palm — that meant there was a dozen on him at once.

A new myriad replaced them.

The little man didn't have much left. After a half an hour, he barely croaked. Once in a while the foreman encouraged him with the bludgeon.

They brought lunch; the little man, staring at the food, screamed about the lazy bum and parasite with his remaining strength and was about to go get his share, but the foreman didn't understand what he was on about.

"Where you goin', singing flea? Where you goin'?" He yelled. "You think you deserve to eat? What sort of a meal for the lazy bum? A thousand extra times!"

Artiom didn't even look to see what was going on, he just heard the blows on living, unguarded flesh with that horrible crunch that he still hadn't gotten used to in all of his twenty-seven years.

* * *

"What is all this?" Artiom thought helplessly and in snatches. "Why did everything turn out like this? Up to this point, I've been managing somehow… What am I going to do with that Passport? He's got a whole posse of gangsters… It won't be Vasilii Petrovich at my back, I insulted him for some reason! And the foreman! Disgusting! I ran away from him, shame! Why didn't I just kill him…?"

No one had ever hit Artiom, except for his father. But his father… how long ago that was! He didn't even remember his name anymore.

Then there were the seventy or so logs left. As though they hadn't even started.

Afanasiev, who somehow found the strength to talk, was talking about Chechens. Artiom listened sluggishly, sometimes losing the thread. It didn't help that the little man was still going on:

"I'm a lazy bum! I'm a lazy… bum! I'm a parasite… to the Soviet… government! I'm a … bun… parasite…"

"Not bun, *bum!*" Sorokin lorded it over him. "And first it's two lazy bums, and only then the parasite. Otherwise it sounds off. And louder, louder! Well?"

Artiom found a branch on the ground that was straight and good on the teeth. He broke off the ends and stuck it in his teeth. Sitting there, he brushed his knees with his nails — moving the blood along.

"I can't become weak! I can't die before my time!" He kept repeating to himself, chewing on the branch.

Then he spit it out, bit himself on the hand several times, trying out his sensitivity.

"You can't figure out those boys' characters," Afanasiev kept saying, trying to speak in such a way that he would be heard above the cries of the little man. "The youngest Chechen went to get his ration in the smoker, but he came back with three. How he managed to convince them I have no idea… Seemingly responsive, but immediately helpless… Naïve like children, but cunning… Fascinating people!"

Artiom rested a bit during the half hour they were given to eat, though he felt a chill on the outside — goosebumps ran up and down his skin like icy lice.

How wonderful it would be for a huge, hot and golden sun to blossom and appear all around them right now, like a samovar; Artiom imagined it, squinting. At first you would be able to reach your hands up to it, nearly touching it with your hands. Then you would turn around and lean against it for a moment, so that the steam rises off your shirt with a hiss. The important thing is to remember to turn away in time before the shirt sticks to the samovar, or there'll be a hole… But if you walk away from the samovar slowly, not all at once, then the fabric will come off with a soft crunch, and how wonderful it will be for the back, how sweet. Then to turn the feet, to extend the heels — his heels were so frozen that you could just stick them right in the fire…

"Comrade foreman, can we make a fire?" asked Passport.

"It's summer! What fire? Time to work, jackals!" the foreman answered and immediately yelled, "To work, jackals! You just started and already you're dead?"

Artiom rushed to the logs already lying on shore with a certain hope of being warmed up.

The guards were throwing pinecones at the lazy bum and parasite. The little man didn't even try to avoid them, but only sometimes made soft ladling gestures with his hands, as though trying to catch the cones every time but never managing it. Sometimes they hit him in the forehead. It seems they were trying to get into his mouth but couldn't for the life of them succeed.

"Comrade foreman!" Passport kept going on. "Operetta here has lost his buddy and he's so long, he's only bothering us. Not to put too fine a point on it, but he's no worker. Let him sing, then. He likes to sing. Put Moisei on the neighboring stump."

The foreman would have preferred to send Passport to the farthest fields, but the other gangsters supported Passport's request — it wasn't so dangerous to wrangle from the water. Finally, one of the guards winked at the foreman, though it didn't matter to the guard — he, as opposed to the foreman, didn't answer for the quota.

"Come 'ere Solomon," said the foreman and immediately got distracted. "And why have you stopped? Keep going, keep going, lazy bum and parasite! Yell as loudly as you can, you iodine-filled mouth!"

They did in fact put Moisei Solomonovich on a stump. He helplessly looked around, as though he couldn't find any food around him and couldn't start singing without it, especially since the little man was clearly bothering him… but, having sighed a few times, Moisei Solomonovich suddenly launched into song.

At first it was eternally about how his own mother was accompanying him somewhere; then, having noted the enthusiasm of the gangsters, he sang "Apple", all the time slapping himself on his mosquito-infested cheeks.

"That's right! Hit that drum!" Passport taunted him.

Then he sang something Gypsy and having finished about the Gypsy girl, he started one that Artiom didn't know, about a falcon: "How sad he was, the young, bright falcon, sitting in captivity. In his golden cage, on his silver perch…"

"It's a song about Sekirka," Afanasiev quietly laughed.

They said that Sekirka had perch-poles like they do for chickens, only thicker, and that they forced penalized inmates to sit there for days on end. After a few hours, the whole body ached and moaned, begging for the torture to end, but you couldn't — any movement was given a double punishment, and then they still put you back on the pole.

The funny little man kept wheezing his chant all this time; everyone had gotten used to his sickly clucking; and, if he stopped — while the foreman made for him, swinging his bludgeon — it felt somehow strange and uncomfortable. But whenever the foreman was only a few steps from the stump, a hissing, "I'm a lazy bum!" would sound, and everything went back to normal — the water, the logs, the bum, Moisei Solomonovich singing, the ringing in the ears, the black circles in front of the eyes. The water was also swirling and the swirling black in the eyes either competed with the ripples or mingled with them…

Artiom was nauseous, his head throbbed, warm blood flowed down his shoulder.

The little man wasn't bothering Moisei Solomonovich.

"The young, bright falcon complains," sang Moisei Solomonovich, "about his wings, his fine, proper feathers: Oh, my wings, my wings, my fine, proper feathers!"

"He's fomenting counter-revolution, but those idiots don't hear a thing." Afanasiev kept laughing, though it was now edged with pain as he pushed the logs towards the shore.

Artiom noticed that Afanasiev's nipples had become almost black.

"You used to carry me away, my wings, from the wind and from the storm," Moisei Solomonovich sang, "from the strong rain of autumn, from the autumn, from the last… You didn't carry me away, my fathers, from the young man on his horse, from the Tsar's fowler!"

"What's he on about?" thought Artiom… but the thought was barely there, as though he had to force every thought to budge.

It came time to once again carry the logs to the sawmill. There they had to pile them in stacks — also back-breaking work.

As he squished the mosquitoes, Artiom noticed that there was a crust of blood on his cheek. The thought: if only there was enough bloody crust there for them to not bite through.

Towards evening, the foreman and the guards themselves became cold and finally made a fire. Sometimes they let the workers warm themselves for a minute or two.

The guards, Artiom heard, began to get on the foreman's case about it being time to go home. He kept swearing that the quota wasn't reached because of the lazy and slow cattle — the inmates.

For a little time, Artiom hoped with a fire in his cold chest that everything would end right then and there… but the foreman had somehow made a deal with the guards.

The last of the logs were already pulled to shore in the mucky brilliance of the white nights of Solovki.

No one talked any more, as though all the words they knew had been forgotten.

Moisei Solomonovich asked the foreman to help finish the work, and they let him. They had had enough. Still, the little man, standing on his stump, kept screaming about the lazy bum.

"What a mushroom," Afanasiev suddenly whispered. "You don't think he's doing it on purpose?"

Artiom wasn't thinking.

The refectory, ploughed through with filth and human swarming, where they returned in the eleventh hour of night, seemed a long-awaited and pleasant home.

The overcoat was there.

Artiom, not looking into his bowl, ate some cold porridge, drank half a mug of warm water, put his wet clothing under himself, climbed into the overcoat and disappeared. It's even possible that he died.

* * *

While the Chechens yelled, "Brigade, get up!" Artiom managed to see a long and substantial dream: that he got up, washed up, pulled out from under himself his foot wraps, pants and shirt — they had managed to dry, good — and the whole time Vasilii Petrovich was chattering on about something, jumping from one thing to another, then suddenly he pulled out a pair of felt boots from his bag and gave them to Artiom: wear them, after all, the logs are no joke, Artiom immediately put them on and in a weird way found himself to be completely inside the felt boot — it smelled musky and warm there, a little sour, but it was even better that way, after luxuriating there for a while, he got out of the felt boot and walked to the morning inspection, and all this time, while they ate and during the inspection, "Thumbel-man-a" kept yelling about the bum and the parasite, and that didn't get in the way of the call, "Two hundred and fifty, a full formation up to ten!" Artiom called out and realized that he had forgotten to eat — how's that possible, what a horror, but when did everyone have time, where was he, not on the crapper, surely, but the line to it is no less than an hour, what was he doing for a whole hour on the crapper? — he got the berry brigade, thank God, thank God, thank God. Artiom hurried back into the refectory, knowing for sure from someone that Vasilii Petrovich had taken and saved his millet with a big piece of butter that had gotten lost four months ago, he put it under his overcoat so that it wouldn't get cold, the butter poured and melted down there, that's how Artiom's mother had made his porridge when he was a child, wrapping the porridge in an old rug; trying to avoid any meeting with Passport, Krapin, the foreman Sorokin, Artiom almost made it back to his bunk, the Chechens yelled something in his wake, also offensive, everything was going to the dogs, these last days, only the porridge could save him.

"And there's a pie there too!" Vasilii Petrovich called.

Artiom climbed to the bunk, got back inside his overcoat, tucked up his feet so that they wouldn't stick out, screwed up his eyes so that even his eyes would conserve heat… but the porridge? Where's the porridge?

"Brigade, up!" the Chechen yelled aggressively; hardly a moment had passed since he had yelled it the first time.

"Brigade, get up!" he called a third time.

"What are you, a fucking rooster? What's with the three times?" Artiom had woken up already and recognized Passport's voice, though with one hand he still blindly patted the bunk under him and next to him to make sure he hadn't lain down on the porridge or dropped it.

"Who said rooster?" the Chechen asked loudly. He pronounced "rooster" with a long "oo."

Oh, how I want to sleep. Artiom would have allowed them, without thinking about it, to chop off his pinky for some extra sleep. Especially a pinky on his foot. He doesn't need it anyway. One hour for each pinky on his feet.

Afanasiev's hand appeared with a pie in it. Artiom for some reason checked nervously to see if Afanasiev still had his pinky — yep, still there — and then the smirking mug of the Petrograd poet appeared.

"You were asleep yesterday when they brought it… For the difficult work. You can't imagine what it took me not to eat it. I smelled it all night. Leave it for another day, eh? I'll smell it some more…"

Accompanied by Afanasiev's idiotic laughter, Artiom grabbed the pie and shoved the whole thing in his mouth — what if it was a dream, after all? It was a real pie with cabbage. Artiom chewed it and felt his face crumbling — that was yesterday's mosquitoes mixed with bloody berries… or was it the other way around?

"If your mother could see you now," said Afanasiev; he had somehow contrived to wash yesterday.

He had to jump down quickly. Krapin could show up at any moment, or even Curly. They walked the bunks every morning, mercilessly hustling the sleeping inmates; sometimes, they even broke a rib or two.

For the first time, Artiom didn't get up to go to the latrine at night. He had to go with everyone else; it was OK, he endured it. A tall vat with a board laid on it sideways. Opposite, face to face, the line stood and sometimes encouraged each other. Passport, so that no one would look at him, began, as though in jest, to milk himself by the dick, scaring everyone: "Here it comes! Oh, here it comes! Make way!"

Two candlewicks, Artiom noticed, brought out the latrine. They were hired by the Chechens for a bit of tobacco. They pulled a rod through the ears of the vat and carried it to the central washroom.

The Chechens brought in the vat with porridge on the same rod.

Though they didn't mix the vat with that rod, it was still unpleasant. But not enough to kill his appetite.

With the food, Artiom acted against character — he got to the front of the line, forgetting even that somewhere here was Passport's spot. Artiom realized that Passport hadn't answered the Chechen's question. "What a cowardly scumbag," he thought. It was pleasant, cramped, cheerful in line, especially since his pants and shirt had dried. Too bad there weren't any felt boots.

Having eaten, he felt a little surer of himself.

To get some hot water you also had to hurry — it had the habit of running out.

If Passport shows up, I'll hit him. Artiom decided. Vasilii Petrovich came up, looked at Artiom's face and shook his head.

"Did you hear?" he asked "Burtsev today has been assigned to guard duty."

Artiom silently rejoiced that Vasilii Petrovich had forgiven him. The morning wasn't turning out badly; maybe the rest of it would follow likewise.

"Good... Though he and I... aren't such friends... that I can... have any hopes..." answered Artiom, sipping his hot water.

Sleep kept tugging at him and a bruise on his leg smarted, his palms, torn on the shrubs, were hurting terribly. Artiom pressed them against the can with hot water and even felt a bit of pleasure from the doubled pain.

"Still, he's a decent man," said Vasilii Petrovich with regret, for some reason. Incidentally, he stank of garlic.

Artiom also wanted some garlic, but he didn't want anyone to pity him, and he keenly felt that he still wouldn't beg Vasilii Petrovich to get on the berry brigade. That was his character.

Afanasiev came and they knocked together their cans with hot water. Artiom said, smiling and feeling his mosquito-eaten cheeks, "You're not bad. I noticed it when we were uprooting the trees."

“Artiom, buddy, there were times when I didn’t eat for three days straight out there in the world,” Afanasiev answered. “I’d find a piece of bread somewhere and then there’d be another three days. But here we have soup with porridge for lunch and more porridge for dinner. If you want, you can even work a bit and make yourself a salad from pickled herring and onion. And if you’ve completely lost your mind, you can even go and buy yourself some candy in the store. Isn’t that what happiness is all about?”

“Candies?” Artiom was surprised, deciding not to continue the conversation about happiness. “Where did you get the money? Did you hoard it?”

“Why? I won it at cards. Want a candied fruit?”

Afanasiev actually did have a candied fruit, and he gave it to Artiom.

The sweetness smacked him in the brain; it was such a fragrant, tempting taste.

“From childhood I’ve worked on myself. I spun around on the pull-up bar, even did some boxing. I worked as a stevedore — but he’s a poet! How full of life!” Artiom was amazed, looking at Afanasiev. “What a simple character…! Even I have some rough edges; I keep prodding either Passport or Krapin with them… But Afanasiev has no rough edges, he flows through life along its stream… But no, didn’t they take him off the duty roster?”

“Are you listening to me?” asked Afanasiev, laughing as he was explaining something to Artiom.

Artiom shook his head, smiling again, then suddenly sang, “‘I don’t walk on plush or velvet, I walk, I walk on the edge of a knife… How do I know that song? I’ve never heard it before.”

“What do you mean, you’ve never heard it?” Afanasiev gently wondered. “Moisei performed it yesterday.”

* * *

“Man is a tenacious kind of cattle,” thought Artiom on the way to the logs.

His heart had pumped blood through his body, his eyes had woken up, his sleepiness had fallen off, his soul had come alive.

“That’s what you’re saying now, but what if you keep getting this assignment until November,” Artiom asked himself. “Imagine how it’ll be in November, in the canal, up to your neck in water…”

He waved it off without imagining it. He turned around to look at the monastery.

“I just have to grow some moss and stand stonily in any wind…”

Yesterday's group was all there; they even grabbed the funny little man again, maybe out of a sense of cruelty. His name was Philip — Afanasiev found out. Little Philip killed his mother and for that reason ended up in the monastery at Solovki.

"If you won't work, I'll pluck out your eye in the evening and make you eat it," Passport promised him quietly.

"I'll slave and slave, till they dig my grave," answered Philip, meekly and barely audibly.

After what Afanasiev had told him about the little man, Artiom unconsciously avoided him. His words were revolting, as though they were dipped in lamp oil.

As soon as they reached the place, Moisei Solomonovich walked three times around his stump — will they call him to sing today? But no one made a sign.

"Oh, how sad," said Moisei Solomonovich's entire demeanor. "How sad, oh!"

After yesterday's concert, Artiom looked at Moisei Solomonovich with interest. Judging by everything, this was an interesting person.

Without waiting for the foreman's prodding, Artiom jumped in the water. He tied his shirt around his head and rubbed the lake muck onto his shoulders.

"Comrade foreman, what? A hundred again today?" Passport asked. "It's not too big a quota?" And just as eagerly as a horse on two legs, he ran into the water.

The foreman Sorokin didn't neglect to throw the bludgeon at Passport.

"Give me back my stick, jackal!" ordered the foreman.

"It drowned, comrade foreman," answered Passport, assiduously depicting a search.

"I'll show you drowning. It's wooden, like you! Find it!"

Artiom caught himself on a strange thought — he'd like to see the foreman break Passport, force him to bring back the bludgeon and then hit him a few times with the same bludgeon.

But cunning Passport didn't give it back, no matter how much Sorokin yelled.

Having yelled his fill, the foreman went to have a smoke with the guards. Then all three of them went somewhere, probably to pick some berries. As a parting shot, Sorokin yelled that today's quota was one hundred and fifty logs. The extra fifty was for the bludgeon.

"Even if it's two hundred, there's enough work here for a week," Lazhechnikov added, looking over the canal.

"Passport, you fucker, I ought to drown you," Afanasiev swore, but without any particular anger.

Artiom was surprised again — Afanasiev could allow himself to talk with a criminal in such a tone. Not only that, but Passport answered him amicably: "Get outta here, Afanas. Go bring him his stick between your teeth. Like your little friend there yesterday."

Artiom, though he stood in the water, felt that his insides were splashed with something hot, sickly and shameful. But there was nowhere to go.

"Hey, tough guy!" Artiom called out, and the hardness of his own voice aroused and encouraged him. "Sew that mouth shut!"

Pushing himself off the logs, Artiom made his way as quickly as possible at Passport.

"What, are you nuts?" Afanasiev laughed sincerely.

"Hey, *friar*,[30] come at me," Passport called Artiom, who was only two steps away. Artiom contrived to suddenly smack Passport with a fantastically long right jab in the forehead, so that his head snapped back so fiercely that it risked breaking the neck bones, then Passport fell forward with his whole body. Good thing it was onto a log, or he would have gone under.

Two other gangsters rushed to help, but here Afanasiev butted in: "Their fight! Their conversation! When two are talking, the rest stand!"

They lifted Passport from the log. His eyes were spinning and he couldn't even talk for a time, only mooing something unintelligible.

The inmates silently went to work. Lazhechnikov scowled. Sivtsev snorted often with his nose. The Chinese man was, as usual, somewhere deep inside himself. Moisei Solomonovich as always was in a place calculated to be equally far from every possible danger. Philip, groaning and muttering, ran alongside the water as though a big fish was just about to jump out of there right into his arms.

Everything inside Artiom rejoiced and shook at the same time.

Having spit on the ground, he returned to roll the logs with Afanasiev, who was still cheerfully surprised, but still a bit thoughtful all the same.

Artiom chewed his lip and tried not to look sideways at Passport, but still attempted to listen in with a sinking feeling — maybe he would start insulting him again.

---

30 In Russian criminal slang, "friar" is someone who does not belong to the criminal underworld, but who is in submission to it. Someone who is easily robbed or taken advantage of. Can be used as an insult.

Artiom had gotten into the occasional fight. He wasn't inclined to fight, but he wasn't bad in a fight — all you needed to do was to break your inborn lack of desire to hit someone on his unprotected and vulnerable face. After that, everything worked out on its own.

The gangsters, after carrying Passport to shore, circled around him, offering help… It seems he hissed at them, and they went back into the water.

"Not bad, not bad," said Afanasiev, still smiling.

A pleasant vanity forced Artiom to show his equanimity, and the best way to do this was to remain silent.

"Why don't you read some poems?" he offered Afanasiev after a few minutes.

Afanasiev grew thoughtful, as though deciding whether or not to answer seriously, then answered completely earnestly:

"I haven't written any here yet, but the ones from before don't count. And I don't want to read someone else's. I'm going to live here without poetry, as without a woman. Later, it will be all the sweeter to taste."

And immediately, he changed the subject:

"Tioma, why you keep grabbing the heaviest logs, I can't understand. You're fucking strong, I get it. So save your strength. Pick out the switches — the thin, skinny logs. When picking girls, you go for the biggest, but here… why…"

The foreman had inconspicuously returned, probably noticing the slumming Passport from a distance, and from the wooded area he made his way almost at a jog. He had a new bludgeon in his hand.

For certain, Passport was having a difficult day. Before he managed to get to the water, he got ten whacks across the back.

After this, he worked as though half in a swoon; when it got closer to lunch he threw up in the water. A slobbery thread hung from his sagging lip, until he wiped it, looking around with evil eyes.

The bready slime and undigested porridge rocked back and forth for some time on the surface of the water.

At one moment, Artiom realized that not a modicum of pride was left in his short and obvious victory. Not because Passport could barely move, all sleepy and conked out, but because this day's work was even harder than yesterday.

It seemed that the logs had gotten heavier overnight and the wind had become more piercing, and the mosquitoes didn't even disappear because of the wind.

"Since you're flying around in such a swarm hither-thither, why don't you carry us to the sawmill, eh?" Afanasiev cursed at the mosquitoes.

In general, Artiom liked Afanasiev more and more — he would have given that a little more thought if not for the multi-colored stars dancing before his eyes.

Somewhere in the distance he heard the scream of the foreman Sorokin. He was again punishing the amusing little Philip for his lack of strength and will to work.

Philip himself offered to yell about the lazy bum, though, he admitted, his voice was completely gone.

"Did you hear?" the foreman turned to the guard. "He wants to scream about bums again, not work!"

The guards laughed; Philip was knocked down to the ground again and taught a lesson by the bludgeon. He yelped and uselessly tried to crawl away.

Today, Artiom wouldn't have even thought about standing up for him. He still couldn't understand yesterday's action and, no matter how much he wanted, he couldn't explain it.

A quiet fuzziness stole over him.

Artiom quietly repeated to himself, blinking often: there are the stars swimming in front of my eyes, there they are, they're swimming, and if I catch them, if only I could catch them, I'd boil them.

He imagined star soup — golden, aromatic, emitting a subtle fragrance.

It started to sprinkle directly into the soup, then it really came down — a deafening, loud, bubbling, pushing downpour.

It pounded his brains so badly that it rang and resounded in his head.

Artiom felt a chill that made his arms unbending, his movements blunt and his fingers wooden.

It turned out to be better in the water than on land and everyone except Philip got into the canal, standing there in the froth, the frenzy and the noise of the rain.

The foreman and guards immediately ran closer to the trees and waited there, smoking.

Philip, muttering something to himself, walked back and forth on the shore, as if looking for a place in the rain where it wouldn't drip.

The rain fell for ten minutes and banished the mosquitoes.

But the post-rain drizzle hadn't even managed to dissipate before — one by one, whining feverishly — the mosquitoes began to come back.

"Why won't a fiery, hot downpour fall?" Artiom dreamed.

The road to the sawmill and back no longer warmed them. But at least their heels hardly felt the pain. Artiom stepped on rocks, branches, cones, with something like anger.

Philip now worked together with the short but thrice-wider Lazhechnikov.

It was already evening when the constantly mumbling little Philip suddenly fell silent. For a few minutes, he acted suspiciously and strangely.

Artiom and Afanasiev, groaning and screeching, were passing on an especially heavy log from the water, when Philip, right in front of Artiom, suddenly contrived to drop his hands — clearly it was intentional. Lazhechnikov tried to hold on to the log, but there was no way! The log landed firmly with its end on Philip's foot.

"Hey! What are you up to?" Artiom couldn't stop himself.

"Ai!" Philip yelled. "Ai!" He wanted to add the prepared phrase "I dropped it!" but the pain ended up being so real that all he had strength for was "I dro! Dro! Dro-AH!"

Afanasiev and Artiom dropped their end too and stood not moving.

Only Lazhechnikov, who didn't understand anything, kept repeating, trying unsuccessfully to look at the contusion:

"Did you break it?"

The foreman, without any thought, grabbed Philip by the hair and dragged him — not anywhere in particular or for any purpose, just from fury — in circles until a curly tuft remained in his clenched fist.

"Jackal's bitch!" Sorokin screamed. "Who did you think you'd fool? I have the right to put down bitches like you personally! All self-harmers and self-wounders get death! You're gonna die right now!"

Artiom, lacking willpower or hearing, walked up to the barely alive fire that the guards had just lit.

He was completely sure that Philip would be dead in a minute.

Moisei Solomonovich loudly sighed. Artiom for some reason thought that he was praying.

Having had his fill and leaving Philip on the ground, the foreman, Sorokin, also walked to the fire. He threw the clump of hair that he was still holding into the fire and commanded: "All you fuckers in the water!"

"Don't kill me!" Philip squeaked again with a failing voice that seemed unable to find its way in his ragged throat.

Sorokin, thinking of something, called the guard, and soon they rolled a heavy twenty-five kilogram, at least, heavy stump from somewhere.

Having dried the stump by the fire, Sorokin wrote on the stump with a pencil, reading aloud as he wrote: "The bearer of this, Bum Parasitovich Self-breaker, is directed to have his foot dressed. After his foot is dressed, he is instructed to return to the logs for the conclusion of his lesson."

The guards laughed, while Artiom had a firm sense that all this had occurred sometime before and now it was repeating itself, only more loudly and obnoxiously.

"Get up, jackal!" Sorokin cried, having finished his labors. "You don't think you'll be able to work on one leg? You will! You can do it without feet at all, you iodine-filled mouth!"

"I didn't do it on purpose!" wheezed Philip with a half-whistle.

"Either I'll kill you with a bludgeon to the head and throw you into the canal, or you'll get up and go with that letter to the monastery!" Sorokin offered this with extreme seriousness, furiously brandishing his long stick.

Artiom again vividly saw a man ready to murder and even wanting to do it.

But Philip got up.

The first three steps, he carried the stump in front of him, then dropped it… He raised it on his back and for a minute he walked, taking long steps with his good foot and tiny ones with his hurt one, crying without artifice all the while… Soon he himself fell… The rest of the way he rolled the stump ahead of himself.

Artiom didn't watch him go, hearing only the groans and complaints. Sometimes Philip screeched as though they pierced him through with a white-hot knitting needle — probably when he took a bad step on his hurt foot.

They finished their quota even later than yesterday; the foreman made another deal with the guards. He was winning himself an early parole, the bastard.

"I've decided to buy a whip," Afanasiev told Artiom when they, having dragged the last log, were returning from the sawmill to the winking fire without any energy left. "I know how."

The midnight rain pursued them all the way to the monastery. They walked ankle-deep in mud. Seeing the murky monastery lights, Artiom felt that the rain wasn't hitting him in the back of the head and shoulders, but rather he was dragging the rain behind him like a huge fisherman's net, full of icy and shivering fish.

* * *

That night, an inmate from their work group hanged himself.

They raised everyone in the beginning of the fifth hour, as soon as the duty officer found the dead man.

Artiom woke up as though they broke his dream like a bone, with a crunch, and the compound fracture extended along his skull, which cracked with pain.

The brigade leaders were nervous — maybe it was murder? But the inmates knew for a fact that it wasn't. This was just a candlewick, a weakling, interesting to no one. He was already in year four of his imprisonment out of five, and he had just finished off ten days in isolation. That's what finished him.

The early-awoken Curly hit the duty officer a few times with the bludgeon for not catching it in time. The Chechen bulged his furious eyes at him, but Curly's eyes were even more furious.

The dead man hung in the far corner, contriving to hang himself from the edge of the bunks, having attached his noose to the poles of the third story. He had made the noose from his shirt, having ripped it into long shreds.

No one had heard anything. The inmate on the ground floor still had his sleeping head facing the dead man's feet until he got Curly's bludgeon.

They all cursed the dead man horribly for cutting their sleep short.

The duty officers were commanded to take down the body. The beaten Chechen obediently climbed up and cut down the noose, but the same candlewicks who brought out the latrine in the morning caught the body. The two other Chechens called out the orders.

They carried out the corpse and put it on the street at the entrance.

One of the inmates' dogs, named Black, ran up, smelled the corpse and sat next to it. A deer nicknamed Bear also lived in the yard, but today he stayed away, though usually in the morning, as soon as the inmates appeared, he rushed to them. Sometimes someone gave him bread or even a bit of sugar — not all of the inmates were poor. Later, Bear found those who had given him sugar easily in any crowd.

Artiom got up in a state of near drunkenness, not remembering even a tenth of what happened yesterday and very slowly coming to terms with what was happening today.

Without purpose, he wandered through the refectory, ready to fall asleep on his feet, or, probably, already asleep.

He came outside and noticed along the way that Passport was throwing up again, but he thought nothing about that.

The gulls were screaming, somehow especially bitchily, as though they could see the soul rising up, and they didn't like it — they wanted to peck at it as a foreign object, a leper, something unnecessary in this sky.

When one of the gulls began to lower, as though to land on the actual corpse, suddenly Black started barking with unusual ferocity. The gull flew upwards but kept the insult to itself. After a minute, several gulls circled over Black, aiming to fly over his head. He sat calmly as though he knew how to fly up at any moment and rip apart anyone he wanted to in the air; sometimes, he moved his nose a little.

Having spit his sour spittle under his feet, Artiom returned to the refectory and climbed back on his bunk. He felt sick, feverish, nauseous.

His clothes hadn't dried. It seemed his body couldn't give the needed heat during the night. On the contrary, it was his overcoat that had gotten wet and for some strange reason the inner lining had gotten somehow slimy.

Burtsev came up.

"The command to lie down wasn't given," he said.

Artiom opened his eyes, looked at him, wanted to smile pleadingly, but he had no strength. Instead, he thought sleepily: "White Army trash…" and closed his eyes. Maybe he'd go away.

And he fell asleep.

Wakeup call was in a quarter of an hour anyway, but that quarter of an hour at peace meant a great deal. Another seven-ten hours and everything would be really good.

* * *

His first thought was: did Burtsev really leave? Interesting: was he upset or not?

His second thought was: was there a corpse or did I dream it? Did I dream up Burtsev?

The corpse was still there. Black continued his guard duty. The gulls walked around, not far away, looking sideways at the unmoving human eye and taunting tongue.

"Do you remember what I said yesterday?" Afanasiev asked Artiom after breakfast.

"To buy a whip" or "to braid a whip" meant to escape.

Artiom didn't answer and didn't even nod.

They sat on his bunk with their hot water in their hands. It was only seven in the morning. Artiom shamelessly picked off yesterday's dirt from his ankles. Afanasiev didn't care.

A minute ago, before he had climbed up, he had put a candied fruit into the extended hand of the homeless boy living under the bunks. Now the two friends watched from the second story as the hand appeared again. For some time, the open, dirty hand seemed to be looking for something with a movement by which people usually check if it's raining outside or not. No more candied fruit fell from the skies; the hand disappeared.

For some time, they remained silent, quietly souring from lack of sleep.

"People don't escape from here," said Artiom, rousing himself.

"They do," answered Afanasiev roughly, accenting the "d" like a young boy.

They sat some more.

Artiom didn't even want to think about running away.

"You seem to be differently inclined towards life here," he said, his tongue barely managing the heavy words.

"Are you an idiot, Tioma?" Afanasiev hissed. "The fact that I can survive even here doesn't mean that I'm going to live here… After all, if you stay in the twelfth, they might end up killing you. In winter they will for sure."

"I want more hot water," said Artiom, climbing down from the bunk as though he had been chewed all night and was now spit out, without being fully chewed.

When he put his tin can on the bunk, he noticed that his hand was shaking from the strain. How would he lift the logs now if he could barely hold a bit of metal?

He still needed to go to the laundry room to let his clothes dry. He had extra shoes and a jacket. He got dressed in his dry extras and, in spite of the summer, climbed into his overcoat.

"I'm coming with you," said Afanasiev.

The laundry room was in the eastern part of the kremlin; for the most part, the administration used it, but some workers from among the inmates could be prevailed upon to take a few things from other inmates.

They walked past the hanged man without looking at him, engrossed in conversation. The dead tongue, noticed in his peripheral vision, barely touched something human in Artiom, something almost imperceptible.

If Artiom had thought about it, he would have decided thus: that's not a person lying there; then, he would have thought that a person was one who walks on the earth, seeing, hearing and talking. The thing that's lying there is something else, something for which you could have no sympathy.

Afanasiev kept scaring Artiom with the coming winter:

"… for unfinished quotas, they undressed him and left him in the cold. He froze to death. That's not the same as screaming "I'm a lazy bum!" And the frozen corpse lay behind the outhouse until spring, until it started to melt…"

Artiom suddenly remembered Vasilii's words that the duty roster is made up only of informants. He was talking about Afanasiev!

"Why are you telling me this?" Artiom interrupted Afanasiev.

A gloomy Chekist walked towards them from the laundry, and Afanasiev didn't answer.

There were already seven soaked-through sad sacks in the laundry and a few of them were bare-chested — they didn't have any extra clothes.

"Where are you dragging your rags? Go dry it under your ass!" The desk clerk, an obnoxious mug, was yelling.

Everything became immediately obvious.

"Man is a log to other men," said Afanasiev in the street.

* * *

Back in the sleeping quarters, Burtsev was beating the Chinese man.

He lay on his bunk and either couldn't or wouldn't get up to work.

Burtsev pulled him off by the scruff of the neck.

The Chinese man couldn't stand on his own legs, so Burtsev threw him, but then immediately leaned down and began to shake him roughly by the lapels, shrieking with a painfully fierce voice that Artiom hadn't heard before.

"Up! Up! Up!"

That "up!" sounded like someone was angrily slamming the lid of a piano.

"So that's how it is…" Artiom lazily thought. "To think, all they did was make him a guard. And look at that. Could he have done the same to me?"

Vasilii Petrovich appeared from somewhere all ruffled up like a chicken, either from horror or from surprise.

"Mstislav!" he kept repeating. "Mstislav!"

"Who's Mstislav?" Artiom couldn't for the life of him understand. For some reason he had never heard anyone call Burtsev by his first name.

Burtsev straightened, and, not looking at Vasilii Petrovich, walked to the exit. They had called out the line-up for the morning inspection.

As he walked, Burtsev wiped his palms as though he had just washed his hands.

Vasilii Petrovich helped the Chinese man get up.

"Tiom, does it seem strange to you?" chattered Afanasiev in his familiarly agitated way as the brigade tried to line up, "China is devil knows where. Over there, the Chinese walk about, living their anthill life and there the relatives of that… what's his name…? His relatives speak Chinese, eat rice, watch the Chinese sun, but their son, grandson, husband is lying about on some island on Solovki, and the guard Burtsev is beating him."

Artiom understood what Afanasiev was talking about, but all these abstractions couldn't bother him. But Burtsev had surprised him, yes. He walked back and forth, watching how the group was lining up. Burtsev had a focused expression.

Vasilii Petrovich brought the Chinese man, and Burtsev didn't give any indication that anything out of the ordinary had happened.

Walking by Artiom, Burtsev stopped, squinted and said, "Oh, I didn't recognize you. You grew up."

Artiom tried to smile, then suddenly and vividly understood that his bloated, feverish, sick face had been basically devoured by mosquitoes over the past few days and that Burtsev was mocking him.

"Fucking dandy," Artiom thought. "Do I have to smack him in the head now too? Will all this ever end or not…?"

"That's his revenge for my not getting up from the bed this morning," Artiom realized a second later.

He couldn't hope for any special treatment after that, but fate played its usual game — Artiom and Afanasiev were both taken off the logs. True, it wasn't clear where they were assigned.

"Who do I thank?" thought Artiom. "Good luck? Where is it, my good luck…? Or is it Vasilii Petrovich?"

But it seemed that Vasilii Petrovich had nothing to do with it.

Artiom tried not to look at the sloping, mottled forehead of Krapin, lest he ruin everything.

Maybe Afanasiev did something?

But Afanasiev gave nothing away, only laughed, looking at Artiom cunningly.

"The important thing is not to get assigned to clean the garbage dump. Anything else will be fine."

On the way back to their sleeping quarters, as the crowd's movement stopped, someone pushed Artiom painfully in the back; he turned around quickly. Behind him were the gangsters.

Passport stood a distance off, looking at him dimly, as though they had turned something off in his head. Naturally black circles were under his eyes.

"Time's up, scarecrow," they said to Artiom.

"What's up, boy?" Afanasiev, who was walking next to him, immediately turned around, nodding his greasy red cowlick.

"Don't butt in, Afanas," they answered him.

Artiom turned around and took a step forward. Once more, it seemed, they jabbed him with the tips of their fingers right under the shoulder blades. He didn't turn around again, on the contrary, he tried to push through quickly, but just ahead of him, as if on purpose, stomped the slow inmates, walking as though underwater.

Behind him they laughed, saying something insulting and vile.

Artiom tried with all his strength not to hear, and he didn't hear.

He was shaking, holding his balled fists in his pockets.

Outside, the gulls were screaming as usual — it was unclear why nature had made it possible for such a small bird to be able to utter such a revolting noise.

"Don't jerk about," said Afanasiev very calmly. "We'll figure it out."

Artiom felt a painful prick of a warm needle under his heart — every good word heals, and the blood warms from it. But he didn't show it of course, and there was no reason to believe him. Yes, Afanasiev, it seemed, played cards with the gangsters at personal risk to himself, but why should he go to bat for him?

"When I was a kid, I used to steal things, Tioma," said Afanasiev, as though he could hear his companion's thoughts. "I know all the Petrograd thugs. We'll try to find the right words. To make deals with them — it's like writing poetry. You find the right rhyme and you've won the game. In the meantime, move along faster, we're on sauna switch duty."

"What sauna switches? How do you know?" Artiom started.

"I made a deal, Tioma," said Afanasiev. "Krapin needs money too. We're going to make sauna switches. There's an order from the public baths in Arkhangelsk. Before the leaves have all fallen."

"So why were you going on about escapes?" asked Artiom.

"I was trying to scare you." Afanasiev laughed, and his red cowlick shook in tempo with his laughter. "But here there's a whole crowd of people trying to scare you, a whole line-up, so…"

"I'm not scared," said Artiom, though that was probably not true.

"No, buddy," Afanasiev changed his tone, "be afraid of them. When there's more than one, there's no one as scary… But you can sometimes come to an agreement. The important thing, Tioma, is that we have the switches today! And without a guard!"

Afanasiev jumped up and tried to smack a gull that was circling above. It jerked upward, screaming something mind-bogglingly insane.

"Whore!" Afanasiev insulted it back and, turning to Artiom, asked a rhetorical question: "Did you hear what she called me?"

A cart with the corpse overtook them. A fat fly sat on his tongue, unafraid of the jostling.

Artiom suddenly remembered that he hadn't seen the amusing little Philip since morning.

It turned out to be a too-long morning; it was time for it to flow into day.

* * *

"Who was that talking to me?" asked Artiom, now completely calm. "I'll weasel my way out of it," he said to himself.

"That's Shaferbekov, a gangster. He cut his wife into pieces, put them into a basket and sent it to a made-up address in Shamakhi.

"And who's Passport?"

"Petty thief. But I think he may have also scared some old lady to death."

"Where did he get that nickname?"

"Have you seen his lower lip? It's like a passport, the first thing he shows everyone..."

Artiom shook his head.

"And you hang out with that filth?"

Afanasiev smiled sarcastically. "Are there any other kinds here?"

Artiom shrugged. Obviously, there were.

"You think that any former Chekist from the ninth brigade has less blood on his hands?" Afanasiev asked. "Every single one of them has a dozen of those baskets in his personal file."

"I'm not talking about them."

"Who then? Look at Burtsev, what happened to him after a single day! All they did was make him a guard! And our Mstislav is probably a nobleman. He'll get himself a whip soon, I swear to God. You think the Chekists are all bastards, and the counter-revs are all innocent, as they all tell you themselves? Ha ha!"

"The counter-revs have different blood on their hands," said Artiom quietly.

"What other blood? It's the same blood. At first, it's wet, then it clots."

"You know what I'm talking about," Artiom repeated stubbornly.

"Can't stand your Vasilii Petrovich either," Afanasiev continued gaily, though not without a nasty note. "He's a shifty type. Do you know how we got to know each other? I was walking with a package from my mom and he caught me by the sleeve in the corridor. I was still in quarantine then. Would you like, he said, for me to watch over your package?"

Artiom was quiet, then asked, "And so?"

"Why should I share my package with him?"

"Then you'll have to share with the thugs."

"Exactly. And your first question was, 'why do you hang out with that filth?'"

Artiom sighed and said amicably, "Come off it already."

Afanasiev laughed, very pleased with himself.

"You're a cynic, Afanasiev," Artiom said in a friendly manner, though not, it must be admitted, without a certain respect. "You could have become a great Soviet poet. Not some hanger-on, but the real thing."

"I could have," Afanasiev agreed very seriously. "But I won't. My cards are enough of a swindle. I won't cheat at poetry."

"And you don't believe the Bolsheviks at all?" Artiom asked after a minute had passed.

"Me?" Afanasiev started, and even grabbed his cowlick in his fist, lightly jerking. "Some things I believe, why? It's the Bolsheviks who don't believe me at all."

He laughed again.

He chopped and broke off oak and birch branches and began tying them together with their allotted towrope. They used the same branches to wave away the mosquitoes.

Today was a sunny day, drying out yesterday's damp, they picked a place that got especially hot. So, it was very pleasant, even miraculous. Artiom didn't want to think at all about who was freezing and breaking themselves with the logs.

"Where do you play?" asked Artiom, meaning the cards. "You know you can get sent to Sekirka for that."

"Sekirka..." Afanasiev mocked him. "So what? We play where we can — it's stronger than fear. The game replaces this fucking Solovki life, it dims it... There are still plenty of spots to play. We play in the window niches... there are a few workable attics that haven't burned down yet. Behind the wood piles, there's room... They sometimes even play in the sleeping quarters, haven't you seen? But they catch us, the bastards and they squeeze us."

Afanasiev was lost in his thoughts, as though mentally he was dealing the cards.

"Do you play well?" asked Artiom.

"Play?" Afanasiev laughed. "No, it's not the game, it's something else. Tioma, it's the cheating. To play there is pointless, the only important thing is the lie. Even in childhood I wanted to be a magician in a circus, I just went crazy for that stuff. But I never properly learned the tricks, but as for the cards… the game itself is not important. The important thing, if you want to win, is to have your own pack. Or, if push comes to shove, a third person's. The whole deal is in the deck. The way you shuffle is the way you play, Tioma."

Artiom was quiet for a bit.

"Where do you get the cards?"

"To make the 'icons', that's its own sport," Afanasiev said with visible enjoyment.

"And he's a poet," thought Artiom cheerfully.

"The gangsters go to the library as part of the official plan for their re-education. They pick one of the thicker novels… They cut out pages from the books, then they glue them together with bread glue — that's when you boil bread in scalding water and then squeeze it. The remaining liquid is sticky. Then, they stencil in the pictures with soap diluted with ink. Those are the cards, aka 'icons', aka 'drumsticks,'" Afanasiev finished in a teacher's tone of voice. Raising his switch, he asked, "Too bad you can't fly away on a switch like Baba Yaga, eh, Tioma? I'd sit on one with you right now, and *adieu*, comrades!"

"Baba Yaga was on a broom," answered Artiom.

"And what's a broom? It's a sauna switch!" Afanasiev didn't agree.

They had already made one hundred and fifty switches, and they needed to make fifty more.

"Let's make a broom, maybe we'll fly away?" Afanasiev amused himself.

He walked to the pile of broken branches, picked the longest and tied a monstrous switch half the size of a man.

"Eh?" Afanasiev laughed, trying to sit on it and pick up speed.

"We're out of rope," said Artiom, chuckling. "There's nothing to tie the switches with. We won't make our quota; they'll only give us three hundred grams of bread and I'm out already."

"I know what we can use," Afanasiev immediately realized. "I saw some abandoned barbed wire here somewhere."

"You think we should?" asked Artiom, pleased with his new red-headed comrade.

"Why not?" answered Afanasiev. "They said: we need switches. Well, we'll make them some strong, revolutionary switches."

He went to pick up the barbed wire and came back with a long tail of it, straining to drag it behind him. Having broken off a few bits and falling over from laughter, he prepared a "switch from Solovki", tying together some full birch branches with the wire.

Artiom made his own too.

"A bloody switch of dawn!" declared Afanasiev, waving about his new creation. "You know the poem? 'And they thrashed their fat asses with the bloody switch of dawn!' Serioga must have had second sight!"[31]

"No, I don't know it," admitted Artiom, not really believing Afanasiev. He had probably made it up himself.

Having tied the branches with wire, leaving a single long, thorny sinew of wire hidden among the aromatic branches, Afanasiev prepared a "little switch from Sekirka".

"Oh, how it will tear them up!" yelled Afanasiev. "All the way to the kidney!" He tried it on himself and fell into an even greater ecstasy.

Artiom wasn't slacking off.

Having buried the Solovetsian and Sekirkian switches deeper among the rest, the normal ones, Afanasiev and Artiom continued their work.

"The little switch for the Chekist" already had two sinews of wire.

A switch with three horned sinews of barbed wire they called: "In honor of the untimely dead comrade Dzerzhinskii."

"Imagine!" Afanasiev was rolling over in laughter, shaking his red head and catching his cowlick with his fist; his laughter itself was reddish, freckled, crumbly. "Tioma, imagine! A Chekist mug comes into the sauna! Well there, bathhouse attendant, give me a good one! And the attendant smacks him so hard that the steam rises everywhere and you can't see a thing! Well then, the Chekist is screaming from the midst of the clouds of steam, give me a double portion! And how the attendant starts hammering him! The Chekist screams! The attendant tries harder! The Chekist screams! Is he trying to turn over? The attendant hits him even harder! Even more furiously! Even more quickly! And again! And some more steam rises up…! The Chekist is long silent! The attendant tries and tries, then calms down a bit… Now the steam dissipates, the attendant stands there and sees — blood everywhere! Bits of human meat…! Instead of the Chekist, a bloody salad…! Where's the eye, where's the cheek? Where's the back, where's the ass? Just like at a butcher's…! Instead of a switch, the attendant is holding two spits with bits of meat on them! And here another Chekist comes in. Imagine the scene,

31 Meaning Sergei Yesenin.

Tiom! Another! Chekist! Comes in! And he's looking at all this with childish eyes! Fucking painting: 'The bath attendant and the Chekist!' That's unexpected! The Itinerants would have wept!"

Artiom laughed so hard that his head was spinning. He shoved his fist in his mouth and bit himself so that he wouldn't go mad with the laughter.

They prepared the next switch — "cruel Chekist ass" — for a long time together. It was huge and fat. You could only pick it up with two hands, and even then, it wasn't easy. There were more than ten strands of wire. You could really hurt someone with one of these; the important thing was to take a good swing.

Two thin birch switches tied together with a single wire they called "crown of thorns for the counter-rev".

It was so much fun that they almost missed the foreman.

While his drunken, bluish face trudged towards them, they managed to somewhat hide their creations.

"Everything's ready, commandant!" Afanasiev delivered, holding back the laughter with such unbearable strength that it seemed it would rip him apart completely.

"There seem to be more here," said the foreman after a minute of silence.

"Much more! At an accelerated pace in the middle of our military assignment!" Afanasiev accounted for his work with an unusually bright voice.

Artiom looked aside, but the happiest tears of the last few months poured down his face.

"Take some for yourself, for your own sauna!" offered Afanasiev so loudly that the foreman might have been on the other side of the river.

"Why are you yelling?" asked the foreman.

Afanasiev cast down his eyes and bit his lower lip hard. The freckles on his face became so bright, it was as though someone had fried them.

The foreman puttered about and picked three switches, sniffing each one with an expression as though he were picking up his own foot wraps: the care and attention he took for himself were intermingled with a barely visible disgust.

* * *

A new group arrived on Solovki. Not without pleasure, the inmates watched how the new guys walked from the quay. Someone else's fear warmed them, gave them joy.

They filled the thirteenth brigade — quarantine — to overflowing. The inmates who had sat there for the last month or so got passed around the other brigades. About forty people were added to the twelfth.

When Afanasiev and Artiom appeared in their sleeping quarters, the gangsters, like curious crows, circled the two most notable newbies — the Indians Kurez-shah and Kabir-shah.

Basically, other than their names, they could pronounce little. The first Indian didn't know any Russian, the other seemed to understand, but preferred to smile.

"Not a single Russian word?" Passport asked, as usual, dressed in a jacket on top of his naked body.

"He's got his wits back..." thought Artiom with disgust.

After much annoying harassment, peppered with stupid jokes, Kabir-shah, who hadn't stopped smiling, admitted that he was a criminal and that they were imprisoned for espionage.

"Not bad, eh?" Afanasiev laughed, climbing up to his bunk. "A spy who doesn't know any Russian. How did he spy, then? Counted how many dogs and how many horses there were in Moscow? To understand whether the Muscovite would last long in case of another revolution?"

Artiom shook his head at the Afanasievan jokes.

Krapin took the Indians from the gangsters, assigning them bunks not far from Artiom. Right next to them he assigned another newbie — a very young man in a student's cap.

"You'll live here," said Krapin.

His legs hanging over the edge, Artiom watched the young man with a smile.

"That was the brigade leader?" asked the young man in a whisper as soon as Krapin turned around.

Artiom nodded.

The young man offered his hand and introduced himself: Mitya Schelkachov.

Krapin was already leaving, but suddenly turned around and stared at Artiom.

"What now?" thought Artiom, clenching his jaw.

Krapin took three firm steps, almost coming face to face with Artiom. He smelled slightly of herring. Artiom swore, not knowing how best to act — to stay on his bunk or jump down.

"Sit," said Krapin quietly and, barely waiting for an answer, said slowly and wheezily: "You don't seem a bad type, so what are you playing at?

You're not a con man, not a thief, not a Mason. Do you want to become a candlewick? You'll have all winter for that."

Artiom nodded, still not really understanding.

Krapin left, Artiom remained seated, sometimes sniffling with his nose. He was thinking.

He couldn't believe that Krapin, apparently, didn't wish him any evil. Otherwise, why had he said all that?

"My dear friend," Vasilii Petrovich called him with a whisper as he got up from his bunk. "By the way, I have some real tea. If you won't start screaming about it to the entire room, we can have a perfectly nice cup, the two of us."

Afanasiev moved in such a way above them that it became obvious that he heard. But he still wouldn't have deigned to drink tea with Vasilii Petrovich, thought Artiom.

"I see how your eyes are alight," said Vasilii Petrovich when they sat down on his bunk with the tea, drinking in the scent with such eagerness as if they wanted to absorb it all. "I see your eyes and I heard Krapin. I had a hunch before that everything would turn out like this. You're in luck, Artiom. A good star shone over your baptismal font."

"How many points did it have?" asked Artiom, and they again laughed a little, sipping their tea.

"I found out a little about Krapin's fate," Vasilii Petrovich began quietly. "When he worked for the police, one time he interrogated a thug so eagerly that he died. I think that now they call that 'exceeded his authority'. In my time, the police could beat someone up, but I can't remember a single case when the police actually killed someone during an interrogation. Of course, the gangsters we have now — we didn't have those either back then."

Vasilii Petrovich breathed in the aroma of the tea and continued, beginning certain words in a whisper and ending them with his lips alone, without sound:

"So, about your brigade leader there. The thug that he killed, he was avenged terribly — they killed Krapin's ten-year-old son. Then Krapin exceeded his authority again and, as he raided a certain gambling den, without any need, he shot several people there, including a woman and a Soviet public servant who had come to have a good time."

Artiom listened carefully, unsure what to make of it all.

"It's strange," suddenly, in his typical manner, Vasilii Petrovich distracted himself. "During the Civil War, they killed people by the thousands! Many have the blood of one, three, ten men on their hands! Here one guard was screaming that he had shot one hundred White Army officers in 1920 alone! Then, the war suddenly ended! Now, you're not allowed to kill anyone! But people got used to it! I think Krapin sincerely can't understand how he, a former Red Army soldier, was imprisoned for the death of several gangsters, an accidental woman and a government worker — after all, he had gone on an evil path!"

"Vasilii Petrovich," said Artiom with a slightly mocking tone, so that his words wouldn't sound like a request for advice, "there's one thing I don't understand. How am I supposed to apply all this history to myself?"

"Well, Artiom," answered Vasilii Petrovich with assumed strictness. "All you'd like to do is memorize poetry — yes, yes, I noted that little sin of yours, don't be upset, you move your lips too obviously, and it's one and the same phrase... You memorize poems, but you can also read some things in human souls. Here's my reading: our leader Krapin hates the gangsters. You've noticed: on Solovki, they rarely beat the counter-revs, as for Krapin — he doesn't touch them at all. As for the gangsters, on the contrary, he always finds himself at odds with them... I'm not sure that he will always come out the winner. For this government, as strange as it may seem, the scum of the earth and thieves — they're close in a social sense. Krapin can't figure it out — how can this filth of society be close to the government? Unlike the Bolshevik idealists, Krapin is sure that you can't reeducate them. Nor should you save them, either. But as for you, Artiom, maybe you're worth saving. That, at least, is what Krapin thinks. When he hit you with the stick, know that he was directing you to the right road, like a young bull. Well, he wasn't going to explain it to you in words, that's beneath his dignity! But since he couldn't knock sense into you with his stick, Krapin did something incredibly powerful — he talked to you. Value that, Artiom."

Artiom listened with such rapt attention that his fingers almost boiled on the warmed-up mug.

"Do you know what else I have?" Vasilii Petrovich got agitated. "Round crackers, believe it or not! Or rather, one cracker. A little dry, but if you do this..." Vasilii Petrovich broke it in two relatively equals halves with some effort, then, measuring them with his eyes, gave Artiom the larger half.

"Afanasiev is wrong about him, after all," thought a mellowing and grateful Artiom. "Our poet doesn't understand anything. Vasilii Petrovich is a dear, wonderful man..."

"Here, I look at the cracker and with bitterness in my heart I remember all the food that I didn't eat from satiety or stupidity in the past," Vasilii Petrovich shared. "I remember it was Lent and I, appearing at lunch having just come from outside, poked at my fried buckwheat with onions and didn't eat it! The onion seemed unappealing to me! Plus, the buckwheat was a little too fried! Also, there was frozen cranberry with sugar on the table — dessert. But I, just before, had stuffed myself with these same round crackers. My father sent me away from the table — Lent is Lent, after all…! Oh, Artiom, what a tragedy. What a terrible stupidity I committed. I'm so sorry for it, so sorry…"

Vasilii Petrovich dipped the cracker in his tea and sat there, frozen in place. Artiom kept glancing to see whether or not it would fall apart in the hot water — it wouldn't taste good then.

"I also remember how I used to walk around the market as a boy. An old woman with cabbage gave me a cabbage heart. She pulled it out of an aromatic tub like it was a magic fish! Chew it, she said. It's rough, you'll break off your milk teeth and new ones will grow. But I was so afraid of parting with my teeth that I didn't eat it. I thanked her and walked a little farther away and threw the heart into the snow. Now, I would jump into that snow with my face, like a dog, digging around and I would find it by its smell. It was — what happiness! — that crunch on the teeth! Oh. Oh, Artiom.

"And how many eggs I didn't eat on Pascha!" Vasilii Petrovich lamented. "You'd fill your pockets with dyed eggs — to battle the other boys. You'll take ten, then all your pockets are covered in red egg dye. Then you give the eggs to the birds… The birds were so full on Pascha! Not like us now. And what about the cheese pascha! My mother used to make a chocolate one! And a pistachio-flavored one! You eat one piece, another and you're full already. Mother then used to treat everyone in the yard, and I wasn't sorry at all — so full was I. Then in the morning you'll come out and there's a plate with dried-out pascha on the table, and you think: oh, I don't want any more. How much can you have…? If I could catch that rascal now — the one who didn't want to eat — I'd grab him by the ear and twist it!"

Vasilii Petrovich, laughing mirthlessly, even made the gesture of catching someone by the ear.

"Or, I remember, that bream with mushrooms… it was from a fairy tale…! It was like the white knight, Artiom!"

"Enough, enough, enough!" Artiom protested, biting his dry cracker in a kind of frenzy. "Stop it immediately!"

The dirty hand came out from under the bunks; the palm opened up.

Vasilii Petrovich bit off a piece of his cracker with visible reluctance, leaving himself only a little piece, wanting to put it in the extended hand, but then thought better of it.

"Listen," he called. "Come on, outa there. Let's at least get acquainted. What am I feeding you here without seeing you?"

Artiom quickly finished off his cracker — who knows what was going to crawl out of there, maybe something covered in scabs.

But no, the homeless boy still had a human look, only impossibly filthy, extremely skinny, and, most importantly, almost completely naked. What passed for his shirt was a bag with holes for the head and the arms, and he had nothing on his legs — only a big tin can tied with string in the area of his groin. Evidently, it replaced his undergarments.

"Yes," said Vasilii Petrovich. "What… armor… you have there. Well, sit on that bench in the corner. No one can see you here."

The boy looked no more than twelve. His hair was so dirty that you couldn't tell what color it was. Something impossible was also happening to his ears. Artiom tried not to look there — it seemed they were filled to the brim with dirt.

"Will you have some tea?" offered Vasilii Petrovich. "Only not into that can of yours, young man. I have an extra. Artiom, would you mind bringing some more hot water?"

Artiom went to the stove with Vasilii Petrovich's extra can; the Chechen duty officer was fussing about there — the same one with whom they had gone to destroy the cemetery a few days prior.

"Chechens were never Christians," he said scornfully, looking at Artiom.

"As you wish," answered Artiom. "Can I heat some water?"

Vasilii Petrovich had found another cracker and a bit of dried fruit. The homeless boy took all of it and threw it into the hot water and immediately began to drink, seemingly not afraid of being scalded.

"At least tell us something," offered Vasilii Petrovich.

"What?" the boy asked dispassionately.

"Do you have a mother?" asked Vasilii Petrovich.

The boy nodded.

"What about a father?"

The boy thought about that, then nodded again.

"Your name?"

"Serii."

"Where are you from?"

"Arkhangelsk."

"What does your mother do?"

"How should I know? I'm here."

"OK, what did she do?

"Mother? Scrubwoman in a bathhouse."

"Your father?"

"I have a father."

"What did he do?"

"Got drunk every day. Used to throw mother out into the cold — we used to get warm in the horse stables."

Serii was quiet for a long time, then, apparently tired from such a long conversation, decided to shorten the journey

"One time, Father was drinking with a *muzhik*. They got in an argument and Father killed him. He found money in his pocket. Said to mother: 'Well, what can you do? Let's get used to this line of business.'"

Vasilii Petrovich even put his mug down on the bunk, he was so upset. He quietly asked, for some reason using the informal "you".

"Did you get used to it?"

"One time they took a long time killing a *muzhik*, couldn't finish him off. He was screaming a lot and everything was covered in blood. And so, I left. Give me another cracker. I saw that you had some."

Vasilii Petrovich sighed and got the cracker.

"What did you do? Steal?"

"You can steal from the rich," said Serii confidently.

"What about the poor?"

Serii thought about that but didn't answer. It seemed he had excellent manners; he just didn't answer unpleasant questions.

"For how many years have you been stealing?" Vasilii Petrovich wouldn't back down.

"As long as I can remember; I've always stolen. You can write it down: from age three."

"We're not writing this down," Vasilii Petrovich said quietly.

"Why then? Why the curiosity?"

Mitya Schelkachov also listened in on the conversation, having moved closer on his bunk to see the overgrown head of Serii from the side.

All this time, Artiom dug around in his emotions: "Do I feel sorry for him? What about now? I think I almost don't feel sorry. What? Am I completely deaf to emotion?"

Serii was clearly no dunce — his conversation made that obvious, and Artiom wondered: how can that be?

No sooner did he start thinking about speech than he suddenly understood a strange and very important thing about himself — he truly almost had no pity. It was replaced by something that people sometimes call a sense of the fantastic, while Artiom himself would have called it a sense of tact with reference to life.

He used to steal puppies from the boys in the yard who had made fun of him or he would stand up for weak schoolboys, not out of pity, but because it ruined his perception of how things should be. Artiom remembered Afanasiev and with his words finished his thought: "… that didn't rhyme!"

On Solovki, Artiom unexpectedly began to understand that only the inborn emotions survive, those that grow naturally, together with the bones, sinews, flesh — the first things to go were the preconceived notions.

The conversation with the boy was interrupted by an angry noise from the corner where the gangsters all lived together. Serii immediately disappeared as though he had never been there and took with him the unfinished can with tea.

Artiom listened and in a minute understood what was going on.

The gangsters, more often than not, used to hide their things or rip up their own pants, shirts, and even shoes — anything not to go to work, because it was forbidden to force a naked man to work.

A ferocious Krapin began to undress one of those who had come back from the day's work down to his skin in order to dress those who were going out to night work.

"All my stuff is wet! And tomorrow morning it'll be even wetter! Am I gonna go out in wet stuff?" someone was yelling.

"But you're still gonna rip them all anyway! Rotten liars!" Krapin yelled, convincing first one, then another with his bludgeon. Burtsev seemed to be helping him, but it seemed to Artiom that he was more restrained with the thugs than with the Chinese man.

When Krapin tore the pants off Shaferbekov, lying on the bunk, with his own hands, everyone got the message that there was no way out of this one. Passport parted with his jacket — the foreman Sorokin had ripped his only shirt. Shoes, shirts and boots fell at Krapin's feet.

"We'll get even," said Shaferbekov, covering his legs with a coat that was clearly stolen from some unfortunate.

In no way warning of his intention and as though knowing in advance that Shaferbekov wouldn't be quiet, Krapin wound up and struck his face with the bludgeon, then a few more times on his hands when Shaferbekov, barking from the pain, tried to protect his head.

"You'll get even," said Krapin, breathing heavily. "In the meantime, count your teeth."

He nudged the pile of clothes with his foot and ordered the night workers: "Get dressed; it's warm."

There was clearly not enough for everyone, and Krapin, walking among the bunks, ordered Lazhechnikov, Sivtsev and the much-suffering Chinese man to get undressed. He didn't even look at Afanasiev and Vasilii Petrovich. Moisei Solomonovich was very convincingly sleeping, as though that could save him — but there you go, it saved him.

That would have been enough to finish the day. Unfortunately, there was enough time for another event.

* * *

After a tedious evening roll call, the night workers left and everything seemed to quieten down.

They brought Shaferbekov a pitcher of water and a rag — he washed his face for a long time, rubbing off the dried blood from his eyebrows and applying his palms, filled with pink dampness, to his lips. The gangsters watched Shaferbekov with rapt attention, as though that were a way he could pan out gold.

Artiom admitted that he was feeling a natural, huge, very fair and very gleeful joy at the misfortune of others.

It's possible that's what got him.

Shaferbekov, who was touching his wobbling teeth for a long time, caught Artiom's glace. Artiom immediately turned away, lay down on his bunk, was silent, ready to fall asleep. He even slept a little — the day was long, long, long and its tail was getting lost, to get to the beginning was almost impossible — the homeless Serii with his black ears filled with soot was drinking hot water, the two Indians were smiling and softly bowing, the switches were aromatic and rustling, Afanasiev was laughing, shaking his red head as though there was straw in his hair, straw and the sun, then even earlier the hanged man was taunting everyone with his tongue, while the fly…

By that time, the gangsters called Afanasiev. Artiom didn't want to think about that; he was already sleeping honestly and deeply… but they pushed him awake anyway.

He opened his eyes. He chewed with his dry mouth. A single bulb shone and the light poured through the open door from the duty officer's lean-to.

Many of the inmates were already asleep, but someone walked among the bunks, someone lazily swore, while Mitya Schelkachov was playing chess with one of the Indians.

"What?" said Artiom, trying still to find his saliva in his mouth.

"Tioma, basically, this is the deal," Afanasiev said quickly, as though he wanted to finish a boring job quickly. "You're going to share half the package with Passport. He's the victim."

"What package?" Artiom sat on his bunk. "My package? Tell him to go to hell."

"Quiet," said Afanasiev, lowering his voice. "The package hasn't come yet. Wait. Who knows what will happen before it comes. Don't be hasty."

Artiom bared his teeth — he wanted to swear terribly. Afanasiev was also clearly not himself.

"You shouldn't have hit him, Tioma," Afanasiev tried to explain, assuming that strange and false tone that adults sometimes use with children when they know in advance that they're on shaky and shameful ground. "Do you get it? In their world, you can't just fight like that. You need a good reason! You'll notice, Tioma, that the gangsters can scream at each other with awful words; it seems that any minute now they'll start fighting. But it's like a game to test their self-control. You can only hit someone for a real, deadly offense. And you let him have it for a trifle. He was kidding! Now he's puking every time he eats! I couldn't explain your action to them in a way that they would understand you being in the right."

"Fuck their understanding anyway," Artiom seethed. He was filled not so much with greed for his horsemeat sausage — though there was that too. It was more the unexpected, sickly, unpleasant offense to his mother. There she was, walking around the markets, buying him, her little son, a present with her last rubles. Now he's going to feed dratted Passport with it?

"Artiom, there are a lot of them. They can kill you, you know all that," Afanasiev whispered, holding Artiom by the knee, but now, attracted by the conversation, Passport himself showed up, stripped to his waist and very pleased with himself.

Afanasiev turned around and stood in his way, so that Passport couldn't walk up to Artiom's bunk.

"Friend or no, don't stand in my way," Passport said to Afanasiev.

"I'm standing in my own place, Passport," Afanasiev answered firmly. "This isn't your way."

"Did you tell him?" Passport asked Afanasiev, rocking from side to side and looking at Artiom mockingly. "For a year, he's got to give me half of his packages. So I can see."

"One package, Passport," Afanasiev repeated stubbornly, but not as firmly as before.

"What fucking one, Afanas?!" Passport shrieked, sensing how his power was waxing as the other's was waning. "Enough! Enough, Afanas! My advice to you? Don't stick your nose in someone else's business. You're no thief. You're a *friar*, even with all your icons."

Afanasiev didn't budge. Passport rocked once more from side to side; his hanging lower lip also rocked. Without waiting for an answer, he left.

Artiom was silent, looking somewhere to the side, head cocked. He didn't know where he was looking and didn't understand what had attracted his attention.

Finally, he realized that it was Moisei Solomonovich's foot.

Moisei Solomonovich was lying there dead, his head covered by his blanket, but his foot was jerking in a way that it doesn't when one is asleep.

* * *

Afanasiev was wandering around somewhere from early morning. They only saw each other during the inspection. He nodded at Artiom, who answered in kind, immediately remembering, not without slight revulsion, yesterday's "Afanas".

"Afanas, Afanas…" he repeated to himself several times, as though he were searching for a rhyme.

Shaferbekov's face was a mess. During the inspection, he sneezed and out popped a tooth. Afterwards, he stood, quietly growling and holding his palm to his lips.

One of the candlewicks subserviently found the tooth and returned it to Shaferbekov, for which he received a slap in the face.

Artiom tried not to look in Shaferbekov's direction, keeping close to the brigade leader Krapin and to the rest of the authorities.

"Life, like a pendulum… swings back and forth…" Artiom thought joylessly, walking from the inspection and staring at the back of Krapin's head, simultaneously forcing himself not to turn around. Most likely, Passport was sticking around somewhere not far with his vile, sickly, toothless leer. "It swings me… and I hold on to the pendulum with both my hands… soon I'll fly off and flip over…"

When they all returned to their sleeping quarters after the inspection, they were pulling the homeless kid out from under the bunks by his feet.

He and Vasilii Petrovich stood up like stakes driven into the ground as soon as they saw that.

It seemed strange to Artiom that the boy wasn't fighting back or crying out. He was preparing to make a joke about it, even turned a bit to Vasilii Petrovich, then immediately realized from his elder companion's face that laughter was inappropriate here.

The boy had been smothered. His childish mouth was crookedly open, his thin neck was broken, his eyes bulging… he stank too… the can had fallen from his loins, exposing his tiny and extremely dirty male organs.

That's the second one today, Artiom quickly thought. *What if they string me up tomorrow? Hell, no, it can't be. Why me?*

He sat next to Vasilii Petrovich, who was distracted and tired.

The Chechen duty officers carried the boy away by his hands and legs. It was obvious that he was light, as though he were empty inside.

His heart was beating, but now, it's not, Artiom thought with amazement. *That's it.*

For some time, Vasilii Petrovich rummaged about in his bag for something that he seemingly didn't need… then he suddenly stopped what he was doing and asked:

"Artiom, what do you think, what is Jesus Christ doing right now? He probably has some kind of business to attend to, no?"

Artiom swallowed, then looked attentively at Vasilii Petrovich and thought, *He's right. What is He doing right now?*

"He even returned my spoon to its place last night," Vasilii Petrovich added, and Artiom at first thought that he was still talking about Christ. "He's also a human being. He returned a stolen spoon… Or maybe he just wanted some more berries."

Artiom sat silently and rocked gently back and forth.

"Well, at least now I have two spoons, Artiom," Vasilii Petrovich concluded, though by his intonation it was clear that he wasn't thinking about spoons, but about something else.

Curly's scream rose up; he was letting Krapin have it.

"You had a homeless kid living under your bunks! Maybe the counter-revs can organize a headquarters down there? Your discipline's off! Your work is off! What is it you do again, Krapin? I'm writing you up today! In the meantime, get yourself under those bunks, examine the situation down there! Then you can let me know who else is down there!

Curly was mocking him; his voice was dripping with sarcasm.

Krapin was quiet.

Vasilii Petrovich nudged Artiom, as though to say that it's time to go outside before they were next.

The sky of Solovki had become heavier and closer. It seemed as thought the gulls flew up through resistance.

The deer nicknamed "Bear" frequently shuddered, as though he were freezing.

Black sniffed them.

Everything was heavy with sorrow and danger.

"I should get out if this brigade," thought Artiom. "But where?"

"Everything's somehow off, painfully heavy... One thing after another, one thing after another," Vasilii Petrovich said, looking about.

While they waited for their work groups, they walked a little away from the crowd, where people usually cursed a lot and fought with each other.

Vasilii Petrovich sighed, Artiom nodded to himself, trying not to look at the inmates from his group. Somewhere in the crowd were his enemies.

"I heard yesterday how Passport came up..." Vasilii Petrovich began carefully.

"I need to find another place to live," Artiom immediately continued, not even stopping to wonder how Vasilii Petrovich guessed his thoughts. "What other brigades do they have here? Let's count them together, maybe we can figure something out."

Vasilii Petrovich didn't need any convincing.

"You were already in the thirteenth," he said. "You're sick of the twelfth, and I agree, you need to leave it. The eleventh is the brigade of the negative element. It's also the icebox and I don't recommend anyone go there. The tenth is the clerical workers. With your obvious literacy, that's the best place for you. You won't get into the ninth — that's the so-called informer's brigade. It's filled with former Chekists from the lower ranks, meaning they're useless for positions of authority, and so they work as guards or overseers."

Artiom nodded. In essence, he knew all this, and Vasilii Petrovich knew that he knew, but listing them helped calm him down, put everything in its place. It also gave him some hope, maybe a false one, but hope nonetheless. What if suddenly, as they listed them, they'd find a loophole that they had accidentally forgotten about?

"The eighth is the place for the worst element; that's where the leopards live, you know. The seventh is the artistic brigade, also not the worst place in Solovki. By the by, did you happen to take part in school plays? If so, you'd be perfect for a few of the classical roles." It wasn't clear whether Vasilii Petrovich was laughing or not. "The sixth is the custodial brigade. It's good there too, but by Eichmanis's order, they only take former clergymen there. You're not a Popovich,[32] are you, Artiom?"

"Not even a Nikitich," he waved him off.

"The fifth is the fire brigade," continued Vasilii Petrovich. "It's wonderful there, but if you can get into the artists' for your talent or into the clerical because of your ability, for example, to correctly count and beautifully write, to get into the fire brigade, you need to bribe someone. Or, as they call it here, 'the luck of the draw'. We don't burn here that often, so they're not overwhelmed with work. They play checkers more than anything. But we don't have any money to bribe, so let's go on. The fourth brigade is the musicians of Solovki's orchestras. You haven't hidden any musical talent from me, have you? Maybe, Artiom, you can play on the trumpet? No? Too bad. The third brigade is the Chekists of the highest rank and Information and Investigation Department. So we won't even consider the third. The second is specialists in positions of authority, for example, professional scientists." Here Vasilii Petrovich looked at Artiom carefully again, but he didn't meet his gaze. So he continued, "The first is inmates from among the camp's administration — the commandants, the leaders of various industries and their helpers. You still have to grow a bit before you can get to the first… or, maybe not."

"Is that it?" Artiom asked.

"Why?" said Vasilii Petrovich. "There's still the fourteenth that has maximum security. Those are the inmates that work only within the walls of the kremlin, so they won't run away. The cooks, the lackeys, the ostlers working for the Cheka. In essence, they're supposed to be especially punished, because they don't have the freedom to walk about on Solovki, but they only made it better for them. You decide — it's one thing to carry logs, it's a completely different thing to brush the tail of the commissar's horse. The fifteenth brigade is the artisans — the carpenters, joiners and coopers. There's one more brigade that doesn't work at all. You can get there easily without any bribes, and it's called…?"

"The cemetery, I know," answered Artiom without smiling. "The cemetery of Solovki."

There was no loophole. The only one that really fit was the tenth — the clerical brigade, but Artiom didn't know anyone there, and why would they suddenly call him to such a privileged place? He wasn't the only one in the

---

32 Literally "son of a priest". "Pop" is a somewhat derogatory term for "priest".

camp who could read books and count decimals. At every step, you'd find someone smarter than him.

"Too bad I'm not a White Army officer. They always put them in the right places here." Artiom said thoughtfully.

"Who are you, then?" Vasilii Petrovich asked for the umpteenth time.

"No one," Artiom answered. "A Muscovite, a rake, a reader of books. You can't pigeonhole me."

Vasilii Petrovich sighed in the sense that yes, Artiom, I can't categorize you either. We're friendly, but you've never said anything about your life.

Judging by Vasilii Petrovich's eyes, something bad was about to happen, so Artiom turned around and immediately saw Passport, who was shambling in their direction. He was agitated, dressed in his returned jacket on top of his naked chest. The black bags under his eyes hadn't faded yet. On his head sat an engineer's cap that he had gotten from somewhere. He jerked his hand up; Artiom barely twitched, but Passport, leering even more, fixed his cap's bill and asked:

"You got it? I have one of my people at the post office, so if you start…"

"He's understood everything," Vasilii Petrovich suddenly said.

Passport stopped short, measured Vasilii Petrovich with his gaze, then, turning back to Artiom, finished the phrase:

"If you start anything, they'll make you into a horsemeat sausage. Horse!"

Three more thugs came up and stood five meters behind Passport. They were talking about something else, completely sure of themselves.

Is he going to come up to me every hour now? Artiom thought, looking Passport in the eyes and saying nothing.

Artiom suddenly remembered how once in childhood he saw a person who was running across a frozen river at the beginning of the ice drift. It was a frightening and brazen action — it seemed that he would fall into the frozen water any second. Where that person was hurrying, Artiom didn't know or had forgotten with the years. But he remembered his childish thoughts — that he, no matter how much the other boys were impressed by the courage and thoughtlessness of the runner, would never want to try it himself.

But here, he felt himself in the same situation as the runner, except it was as though they had pushed him in and said, "Run!" leaving him with no choice. Except, where did he have to run? He couldn't see the other bank.

Right now, he stood on a piece of ice and he could have jumped off. But he didn't.

Passport left.

"Yes. That's unpleasant," said Vasilii Petrovich calmly after a moment had passed.

"He's given me the evil eye," thought Artiom about Vasilii Petrovich with unexpected hatred, even though he had never been superstitious. "He had only just said how well everything was going for me… He cursed me, the old dog!"

"Where are you assigned today?" asked Vasilii Petrovich.

Artiom was quiet, thinking how to avoid an answer, but it would have been completely wrong not to answer at all.

"I think I'm in the kremlin…" he answered quietly. "Don't know what sort of work."

"As for me, it's the berry brigade again," said Vasilii Petrovich. "There's my group over there. I'd better go."

As he was already leaving, he turned around and added, "Artiom, don't despair. There is a God. He'll look after us, believe it."

* * *

Until lunch, Artiom had no work at all.

Mitya Schelkachov and Avdei Sivtsev were with him.

They waited for their foreman in the yard for a long time. The rowan trees rustled, their leaves flowed into each other and sparkled in the sun, especially if you looked at them through half-closed eyes. Bear the deer walked about, raising his head at the rustling.

Artiom sat on the bench, sullen, closed his eyes and tried not to fall asleep, but just warm up a bit under the sun. Passport was stuck in his head. It didn't help that Sivtsev couldn't sit still next to him. He was agitated, eager to go and find the foreman, except he didn't know where to look for him.

Seeing that his companion was sitting there with closed eyes, Sivtsev started talking as though not addressing Artiom directly, though clearly, he knew that Artiom could hear him.

"So, I guess we'll sit here, waiting, but we'll still end up in trouble…" he said quietly, but he didn't go anywhere himself, content with bothering an already bothered Artiom.

Moron, Artiom thought bitterly. *Peasant moron.*

He couldn't contain himself and asked, without opening his eyes, "What? You want to work?"

Sivtsev continued from exactly the place where he had left off, "So we'll sit here, waiting, but we'll still end up in trouble!"

"So go and do something," Artiom said, for some reason wheezing. "Go sweep the roads."

"Is that what they want us to do?" Sivtsev quickly asked with hope in his voice.

Idiot, Artiom thought once more, but now, for some reason, without any anger.

He wasn't in any mood to make fun of Sivtsev. Artiom generally didn't have any such inclination and his mood wasn't right for mocking, but the most important thing was this — as it was, he already felt superiority over that *muzhik*… And he would have felt the same superiority over Passport, if only Passport was by himself…

"How nice it would have been," Artiom imagined childishly, "if every person was on his own and only had to answer for himself. Then there would never be any war, because a big fight is only possible when huge, angry crowds gather… But here, on Solovki, who would have touched me? I wouldn't have bothered anyone either. There would be peace in all things and for all time…"

Artiom kept thinking about that, trying to force his thoughts to go along a simple, straight line, because he himself understood perfectly well that if he started thinking about all this a little more deeply and seriously, it would become immediately obvious that his head was filled with naïve and pointless nonsense.

Mitya Schelkachov was walking back and forth, examining the monastic buildings, walls dirty like the backs of homeless boys, domes cracked like eggs. He didn't walk too far, far enough so that he could still see his fellows, then coming back to confirm his presence, but Artiom was still irritated with him as well.

"Sit down, Mitya," he said quietly when Schelkachov came back again, for some reason all smiley and inspired, it was unpleasant to look at. "Sit down and don't spin about. The administration will see and put you in solitary for wasting time, and you'll know…" Artiom caught himself thinking that he was starting to emulate Vasilii Petrovich, speaking in the formal "you" to a person much younger than himself.

"But it's not our fault," said Schelkachov, continuing to smile.

"Yes, it is," continued Artiom, closing his eyes.

Sivtsev, who was standing up at this point, sat down too. Artiom suddenly realized that these two were actually listening to him.

Schelkachov — fine, he's younger, though not too much, maybe five years? Is that all that much? All the more so because Schelkachov, judging by everything, was actually educated, not like Artiom. You could tell immediately by his manners and his way of speaking.

As for Sivtsev, he was older than Artiom by at least fifteen years — Artiom could almost be his son — plus he had probably been imprisoned longer, he had more skills, was more worldly-wise… but he was listening to Artiom too!

"Well, I always make a lot of mistakes," Schelkachov suddenly admitted, somehow helplessly, like a boy. "They have already beaten me up in quarantine. I'm awfully scared when I get beaten up. OK, so they moved me from there to here. If only someone would explain to me how I need to act. What I shouldn't do."

"Don't walk around like that," said Artiom, again not opening his eyes.

Based on Sivtsev and Schelkachov's silence, Artiom understood that they listened and were waiting for him to say something else. Sivtsev stood with a slight peasant fear, trying to be duly deferential, while Schelkachov had opened himself up almost completely.

With a quiet and a kind of shameful realization that in his current state he had no right to instruct anyone, Artiom at the same moment, as it were, rose above himself.

At first, he wanted to spook Schelkachov maliciously, but he didn't. It's silly and stupid when others scare him, and they almost managed it.

"Don't make it obvious that you're resting," said Artiom. "Even if you're walking around without a job, make it look like you're working. Don't work too slowly, but not too fast, either. Work as you breathe, don't rush your breath — you'll never be late to anything here. Don't show your soul. Don't show your character. Don't try to be strong. It's better to be inconspicuous. Don't be rude. Hide. Endure. Don't complain," said Artiom with closed eyes, as though he were dictating, or, more specifically, as though he were listening to someone and repeating his words.

"Don't eat all your bread on the first morning. I saw that you ate it all at breakfast. Leave some for the day, and you'll have more energy later. If you get hungry, you'll want to steal. But if you start stealing, you'll stop respecting yourself, even if that's not such a bad thing. It's worse if they catch you. If they catch you, they can kill you. You can't catch and eat the gulls, did you know about that? Even though you'll want to. Today, when we were walking to the morning inspection, Krapin was rushing the brigade along with his bludgeon. I saw that you almost got it. It's good if he gets you on the back. The back will heal. It's worse when he gets your head. As soon as it gets cold, wear a hat and put something soft under the hat. Then, if they hit you in the head, there won't be a wound. In summer, don't wear a hat. You'll definitely take it off and hang it somewhere on a branch, and it'll get stolen. Or you'll forget it. But in general, they'll steal it faster than you'll forget it. You carry your cigarettes in a cigarette case. Lose the case, or they'll steal it. It's strange that they didn't take it away in quarantine."

"I didn't show it," Mitya said quickly.

"It's better to smoke it rolled up here anyway," Artiom continued, not getting distracted. "And don't carry it in a pouch; they'll take the pouch too. Carry it in your pocket."

It turned out that teaching was unexpectedly pleasant. Artiom couldn't figure out when and how he had understood all of it, but he realized and felt that he was saying necessary things.

While playing at being an old-timer, Artiom didn't just fill up with importance, it was as though he was growing in power and began, little by little, to be believe that he was dexterous, strong and able to deal with everything.

Having fallen silent for a moment, Artiom heard that the silence was different — it became somehow thicker and more intense.

He opened one eye. By opening just the right he made a face.

Krapin had come up quietly behind them and was listening to Artiom.

Artiom opened his second eye and slowly got up.

"Let's have a word," said Krapin in an unusual voice — tired, calm — this wasn't the brigade leader, but just a human being.

"Don't instruct Sivtsev. If you teach him, you'll only bring him harm. He's living fine as it is. As for the student, you're doing a good job," said Krapin when they had barely walked a few steps away, then immediately, without any transition, he started talking about something else. "Curly is going to get rid of me. Who's going to come instead of me? I don't know. I fixed it up so that you'll have a month of work inside the kremlin. Schelkachov too. Did everything I could. I'm out of favors. After that, you'll figure it out for yourself." Krapin spoke quickly, in bursts, as though it was strange for him to act like this. "As for the gangsters, I've sent them to the logs. Shaferbekov and Passport and the rest of that filth. Maybe they'll drown there. But if they don't, do what you can to steer clear of them. Even in prison, there are things you could learn. You've got to file down your rough edges. A ball rolls and in life, you have to roll. That's it."

Krapin left. Artiom stomped in place, wanting to calm down, but he couldn't and returned to Sivtsev and Schelkachov with a smile on his face, content and as though warmed up from within.

It's not like anything really happened. It was already obvious that recently Krapin had treated him pretty well. But here he had spoken about it openly.

But still, he brought bad news. They're moving him. Artiom tried to convince himself not to be so happy, but he still couldn't.

"What? Did he give you a ruble?" Sivtsev asked the smiling Artiom.

Still smiling, Artiom thought that it wasn't such a good thing that he had subjected Sivtsev to himself. The Sivtsevian, peasant, cunning self-importance was stronger than anything else.

"He said that there's a new law reported in the newspaper. All belonging to the peasant class will have an extra year added to their sentence because they know how to work and they love it. City dwellers are going to be released, because they're useless. What social class do you belong to, Avdei?" Artiom asked, laughing to himself.

For a moment, Sivtsev looked at him attentively and intensely, then he waved him away with irritation.

"Stupid joke. Pointless."

"Oh, I believed you!" Schelkachov laughed. "I believed you and got so happy! What a shame!"

* * *

The foreman Sorokin appeared before lunch and did begin to yell at them, "What are you sitting there for? Maybe you'd like to lie down right there too?"

Sivtsev got up, Schelkachov jumped up, but Artiom sat there, looking the foreman up and down and lightly squinting.

"What? Did your legs stop working?" Sorokin asked, flying up from his vile rattle to almost a falsetto.

"How about you stop yelling, or I'll tell Curly that you left us without work," answered Artiom, getting up.

Sorokin stopped dead in his tracks.

"Don't we have lunch now?" Artiom asked rhetorically, sensing how horribly Sorokin smelled and immediately ambled in the direction of the sleeping quarters.

After half a minute, Sivtsev and Schelkachov joined Artiom.

"You better be here after lunch, you iodine-filled mouths!" Sorokin yelled in their wake.

"It will be done!" answered Artiom without turning around and waved his hand at him… with the corner of his eyes, he noticed that Schelkachov looked at him with sincere admiration.

"Well, I beat the foreman once, but for sure he'll avenge himself ten-fold," Artiom reported to himself with a smile, and then summarized in the now usual way: "Oh, idiot. I-i-idiot!"

"I heard yesterday how that gangster came up to you. You weren't scared," said Schelkachov.

Artiom didn't answer.

Since Passport was working the logs, then at the very least he wouldn't be there at lunch.

"Or else Mitya would have every chance to immediately be disillusioned with me," thought Artiom with sad irony.

"I would have immediately given them the whole package," said Schelkachov, laughing, even a little bit more cheerfully than he should have. "Everything at once!"

When they left after lunch, Sorokin was gone again. Now even Artiom started to get worried, though he didn't show it. However, he didn't sit on the bench any more. He stood in the middle of the monastic courtyard, feigning relaxation.

A priest in a red army helmet walked by somewhere. A fop in patent shoes and with a cane — clearly from the actors' brigade. *Or from the magazine*, Artiom imagined. Three leopards were being led somewhere under guard. They were skinny, dirty, their faces covered in scabs. It was foul to look at them; they ruined his good mood completely.

Sivtsev noticed someone he knew and went to him to ask whether or not he had seen the foreman Sorokin… Schelkachov again started examining the architecture… Artiom saw a fawn, and he wanted to warm up with its gentle and aromatic warmth.

It so happened that he walked towards the fawn at the same time as a woman did, without seeing her. It was Galina from the Information and Investigation Department; she was carrying some sugar in her hand. When Artiom saw her coming up from the other side, the right, it was already too awkward to pretend that he was going in a different direction. They came up to the fawn almost at the same time, and this circumstance forced Artiom to say, "Hello!"

In general, he had absolutely no right to greet her; he, like all inmates of the twelfth brigade, couldn't directly address the authorities. But maybe she didn't know where he was from. Maybe he was a fireman from the fifth brigade.

Galina was in a blouse and skirt. Very well cleaned boots with a heel.

Under the blouse, her large breasts were very obvious.

"Are you saying hello to me or the fawn?" Galina asked Artiom strictly and quickly looked at him.

"We've met before," said Artiom, scratching the deer in one place, as though he had an itch there.

"Really?" Galina said simply. "I didn't notice you."

"What a bitch," thought Artiom with unexplained gentleness.

She fed the deer the sugar and left, without even nodding at Artiom.

He couldn't tear his eyes from her. It seemed that Galina knew it — her walk was teasing him.

The deer took a step forward, apparently unhappy that Artiom was continuing to scratch him in the same place.

"I would gladly eat some sugar too," Artiom said quietly to somehow derail his heavy and hot arousal.

He imagined that he was eating sugar from her warm hand, seeing the lines on her palm and her wrist, smelling the pure and barely obvious smell of female sweat. If he would then lick her palm in the same place where the sugar lay, it would be sweet.

Sorokin distracted him from the sugar. This time, he wasn't screaming, but he still stared at Artiom.

"You sat around all day like corpses," he whined. "Your bones aren't hurting, are they?"

"What do you mean? We had work," Artiom couldn't contain himself; some kind of madness grabbed him. "Citizen Eichmanis walked by today and told us to count all the monastery's gulls."

Sorokin stopped short for a moment, then realized that he was being mocked.

"You're still joking? I'm going to remember you now," he said.

Still, something was preventing him from crushing Artiom immediately.

The work they got wasn't the most difficult, but it was dirty. They had to clean up the pile of garbage at the infirmary.

The infirmary was a three-story building not far from the gates of the kremlin.

Near the infirmary stood several yellow monastery couches — it seemed that the most infirm, by order of the doctors, had been carried outside to warm up under the sun, lifting up their diseased feet. For some reason, the gulls were especially disgusted by this.

"After this work, she would definitely not start feeding you sugar," Artiom thought frivolously, trying not to look too closely at the puss-filled bandages and the rags that stank like half-dead human flesh.

They carried all this garbage into a cart that Mitya, then Sivtsev, then Artiom took turns pulling beyond the gates. It was most cheerful with the cart — it was a nice walk, after all, with a pleasant breeze.

Turning over yet another cart filled with garbage, Artiom suddenly noticed women's faces in the windows of the third story, and he stopped to look.

The gulls startled him. They flew after every cart, a bit aroused by the smell of disturbed filth. Truly, it seemed to them that they might find something edible there.

He had to leave. He saluted the young women with two fingers. They laughed.

"So how would you inform on me to Curly?" Sorokin suddenly asked Artiom when he, not in a great hurry, was returning with an empty cart. The foreman was probably thinking about Artiom's threat this entire time. "You devils are forbidden to address the authorities directly."

He was probably involved in some kind of perversity before lunch, Artiom guessed. *And now he's shaking.*

"I'd do it in writing," said Artiom, trying, for all that, to speak in a way that was obviously not serious.

"I'll make sure you rot," said Sorokin to his back, but not very convincingly.

Well, well, thought Artiom. *Here I'm carrying around the discharge of the sick, but Sorokin's stench is still worse. Can someone really love him? A mother? Wife? Children? God, finally?*

* * *

The evening was getting close. Thoughts of Passport returned. Artiom realized that he was vividly imagining that Passport had slipped and fell to the depths… he started to come back up, and his head hit a log with a sharp end — right on the top of his skull…

… Or he was typically rude to the foreman, and he didn't moderate his blow and hit Passport so hard on the head that his memory and reason were knocked out. Now Passport walks around with his saliva hanging down to his bellybutton, recognizing nobody…

… Or the other gangsters convinced Passport to try to escape; that sometimes happened too. But the guards quickly figured out their intentions and during the attempted escape… Artiom vividly saw Passport with a gunshot wound, for example, in the spine, and he's lying there, flopping his eyelids, not able to move.

"Oh, what happiness!" Artiom thought.

Then he brushed himself aside — what nonsense it all was! What nonsense!

He tried to think rationally: "Well, they're not killing me. While the package hasn't come yet, I'll think of something. Or maybe I should give them a portion? And why are you so mad at Vasilii Petrovich and Afanasiev? What? Should they die for you? They're getting through as well as they can. You learn from them. Krapin himself said: learn. So learn."

He ran into Afanasiev in the sleeping quarters. He smiled at Artiom; Artiom was so sincerely happy that he almost hugged the poet. He even extended an arm but limited himself with a slap on Afanasiev's shoulder.

"What actually happened was that the gangsters paid Curly to get rid of Krapin." After a minute, Afanasiev told Artiom the latest news. "As for Curly? He has a bitch in the administration, a really ugly one, like me when I have a hangover in the morning. He needs money for her — has to somehow adorn her. He'll do anything for money. And Krapin had pestered them to death, you've seen it. At first, they wanted to stick him with a knife, but then decided that it would be easier to make a deal with Curly."

Afanasiev grabbed his forelock, smiling.

"So who's in charge now?" asked Artiom.

"What do you mean who?" Afanasiev was surprised. "Burtsev is taking over his responsibilities while Krapin is temporarily suspended. But he won't be back, of course. They'll transfer him somewhere."

"Because of the homeless kid?" Artiom was surprised.

"Of course not," Afanasiev laughed. "I think you could have found ten dead leopards under the bunks and nothing would have happened… Although now, of course not. A murder in the sleeping quarters — it's no joke. Basically, I think that Curly described everything correctly in his report to the authorities. The important thing — you understand this — is how to describe it properly."

"What about Eichmanis?" Artiom asked.

"Do you see Eichmanis often?" Afanasiev continued to laugh. "He's busy with his nurseries, hunts, theaters… He's not going to try to figure out this mess. What does he care for a single brigade leader?"

"But why Burtsev?"

"Curly is cunning," Afanasiev explained. "Even though he removed Krapin because of the gangsters, he doesn't want to be left one on one against them. If they take the upper hand in the brigade, he's going to have a hard time himself. So he arranged some support for himself in the form of Burtsev."

Artiom kept asking question after question, thinking to himself all the while: "What a dog's life! I used to be interested in much more important things — what was Gorky's latest book, or why a beautiful girl is rushing by on Nikitskaia Street, should I run after her? Or I had to find the latest collection from Balmont, or mother was making some kind of cheese dessert, I'll go check it out. They said that a certain Pilniak appeared, but I still haven't had a chance to read him… But here, it's Krapin! Here's there's, to hell with him, some kind of Burtsev! What does all this matter?"

Now it was clear why Sorokin was so subdued today, Artiom interrupted himself. They removed a brigade leader, and he needed to act a little more submissively until all the noise died down… but here he was off somewhere for a half-day…"

Afanasiev wandered away somewhere, but then Vasilii Petrovich appeared, carrying berries, with the same news as Afanasiev.

"Did you notice how our general's batman is hanging about Burtsev from the morning?" He laughed barely audibly.

The former general's batman had a general's manner, though without any genuine aristocratic mien, though pompous and full of himself. That's why he got the nickname "Samovar."

"You mean Samovar?" Artiom laughed in harmony with Vasilii Petrovich. "You're right!"

"And our Mstislav doesn't mind," Vasilii Petrovich said laughingly, though with a certain amount of bitterness as he regaled Artiom with lingonberries. "He didn't have a chance to be a general while he was free, so on Solovki he'll act the part to his heart's content. Eat the lingonberries. They say that it grows here until November." He looked at Artiom significantly, as though saying, "Too bad you ran off from such a blessèd work group."

Seeing that their neighbor was coming back, Vasilii Petrovich quietly asked, "You're still with Afanasiev? Bad fortune is still walking in your footsteps. Don't flatter yourself yet."

Artiom slapped Vasilii Petrovich on the knee even somewhat chummily — as if to say it's OK! Everything's a-OK!

Vasilii Petrovich nodded his head sadly-well-well, well-well-well.

The lingonberries were sour.

"A little bit of sugar," Artiom thought again, squinting.

His member rang and demanded to live.

* * *

Artiom didn't see when Passport returned. During the evening inspection, the log brigade hadn't come back yet.

However, the next morning, no matter how vivid Artiom's imagination, Passport appeared alive, though visibly oppressed by the work and a little sick to boot. His voice was nasal and he snuffled his snot as energetically as though it weighed half a kilogram.

"I've been waiting all day — still no package, but my health is worse and worse," Passport sneered, having caught Artiom by the shirt as he was walking with a clean bowl back to his bunk. "Give me your overcoat."

"Fuck you," Artiom answered. Since he was holding his bowl in his right hand, he smacked Passport on the forehead with the same bowl. It made a loud and pleasant sound.

Passport wasn't by himself. Artiom was attacked by several other thugs, and he, as though in play, jumped to one side, then another, then for some reason hopped up onto his bunk, as though under his overcoat he had a loaded revolver.

But there was no revolver, and there was no point in running away.

Though he understood that, Artiom continued smiling and, throwing a stool under the legs of one of the thugs, at the same time managed to notice Mitya Schelkachov, who had gotten up on his bunk, Afanasiev, who was ready to jump down from his place, though he still hadn't jumped, Vasilii Petrovich, who still hadn't gotten up yet, Moisei Solomonovich, who opened his mouth wide, as though he wanted to start singing, and even Samovar, who, with an extraordinarily severe expression, ran to protect Burtsev's bunk from destruction, just in case.

Artiom didn't see Burtsev himself, but it was Burtsev himself who caught Artiom by the scruff of the neck. It's a good thing that Artiom immediately recognized him, or Burtsev too would have gotten a face full of bowl on his pale cheek.

"What's going on?" Burtsev cried out. "What sort of dance is this? Quickly to your places!"

"Stand up straight next to your bunks!" yelled Khasaev, the duty officer. "Stand up straight next to your bunks!"

Curly, a few members of the Information and Investigation Department, and Red Army soldiers from the watchman brigade were quickly entering the sleeping quarters. It was shakedown time.

They were crawling under the bunks, tearing bags apart, turning cloth ing inside out.

"Commander, why do you need to rip up the lining?" Someone was yelling in the neighboring group.

Someone got it in the teeth.

Someone tried using the noise to rummage about in his things and to hide forbidden objects. They were catching him by the leg, pulling him down from the bunk, teaching him with a boot to the sides.

Breathing heavily, his mind feverish, Artiom quickly looked back and forth from the gangsters to, for some reason, Burtsev, who was walking after Curly with a very serious face and occasionally digging into the rags of those same people next to whom he had been sleeping for the last few months.

Sorokin was here too and was as agitated as the rest, though this wasn't his responsibility at all.

"Will they knife me today or not?" Artiom asked himself and noted, not without self-satisfaction, that for some reason he wasn't afraid.

"Of course you're not afraid," he answered himself. "You're not being knifed right now. You're protected by the Red Army soldiers… I'll look at you when they start knifing you for real… Even if this shakedown continues until evening and there's a new shakedown tomorrow morning."

Little by little, Artiom's turn came. He didn't even glance down to see what they were looking for. He had few enough things as it was. Hadn't had a chance to get himself any loot.

"Whose bag is this?" asked a soldier from somewhere above. Artiom during this time was looking at Burtsev's shoes. The commanding personnel had the right to use a barrel of fish oil standing near the Information and Investigation Department for shoe polish. Burtsev, as a replacement, had no right to the barrel, but he had clearly already made use of it.

"Whose bag is this?" Curly repeated loudly.

Burtsev pushed Artiom in the chest. "Did you fall asleep?"

Looking around, Artiom saw that the soldier was holding a deck of cards.

Vasilii Petrovich took a step to the side.

For some reason, Artiom decided that they were giving him the cards, and, not thinking why he was doing it, he took them, though Curly was already preparing to take them into his hairy fingers.

For a few seconds, Artiom held the "icons" in his hands, automatically realizing that the hammer and sickle on the top card was intended to represent the ace, while the carefully-drawn Red Army soldier who was under the ace was intended to be a Jack.

Burtsev grabbed the deck from Artiom's hands and gave it to Curly; a few cards fell on the ground.

"Pick them up," said Burtsev.

"You're going into the icebox," Curly threatened.

"They're not mine." Artiom stood there, smiling.

"Uh-huh. They're mine," agreed Curly. "I've just been keeping them in your bag."

The foreman Sorokin, the Chechen duty officer, and the soldiers laughed.

"Pick them up," repeated Burtsev.

"Why don't you go fuck a mare, lieutenant?" Artiom said choppily, furious and lost all at once.

Sorokin was the first to hit Artiom — he had long been ready to settle accounts. The blow itself was so-so — he wound up but it was a stupid hit.

Khasaev, the Chechen, got involved, grabbing Artiom and pinning his arms back, trying to hold him in place — go ahead, who's next? Artiom hit the duty officer hard with the back of his head and got him somewhere in the cheek…

Then everything spun around twice as fast. Burtsev hit Artiom painfully, exactly and upsettingly in the face. At that very moment, the Chechen released his hold a bit and Artiom answered Burtsev with the same exact and offensive upper cut with a twist, so that for sure…

… After that, they all took turns hitting him, even Curly, probably took his shot…

Artiom, suddenly understanding that they could actually injure him, tried to fall, turn around and twist into the dirty floor, to stick, at least, his head under the bunks, but they kept pulling him out by the legs… A few times, he opened his eyes, saw boots, shoes, someone's hands, then he squinted again, endured it, didn't scream, tried to protect himself… then someone got him in the gut and his breath stopped. Finely sprinkled stars flew into the entire void and black firmament, then a heavy boot got him exactly in the temple.

"That's it. That's it. That's it..." Artiom repeated quickly, going to the depths like a rock.

* * *

Artiom, as all the rest of the sick and broken, lay on a monastery couch with a high back. It's wasn't very comfortable to lie there, but it was soft. Every couch had a mattress filled with straw.

He woke up while they were still carrying him.

"Are they carrying me to the cemetery," he thought, shuddering. "Have they killed me and now are dragging me to bury me?"

His entire fire was a bloody porridge, it felt like someone had driven a stake into his chest, his mouth fell somewhere to the side, his lips stuck together. Every second, something ticked in his temple and poked painfully into his eye. His eyes also wouldn't open. His temple pulsed so hard that it seemed that his head had been cracked open and his brains were falling out little by little like hot porridge out of a dropped bowl.

Artiom turned his tongue in his mouth, found his teeth and even found time to be amazed — he still had teeth, look at that! He could have had none left... Still, it was like his lips were sewn shut. Little by little, he managed to get them wet with his saliva and they came apart. He felt even more powerfully how huge his beard was on his face — a bloody, shaggy beard.

By the screams of the gulls, he guessed he was outside. By the voices, he realized the Chechens were carrying him.

He was nauseous and wanted to drink.

"Who's this? Another beaten one?" a voice called out. It belonged to someone from Asia or the Caucasus.

"No, Doctor Ali, he fell," answered the duty offer with such a tone of regret, as though he were speaking about a child.

"From a tree?" asked Ali. Based on the tiredness with which the joke was uttered, Artiom understood that the doctor was repeating it for the hundredth time.

"No," answered the duty officer very seriously. "From the ground." Then he clicked his tongue.

Artiom was laid in a private area in the foyer. They looked him over and touched him all over for a long time. It even started to calm him down — at least someone was looking after him.

They found a laceration on the temple, multiple contusions. Doctor Ali suspected that a rib was fractured and that he had a concussion.

They gave him a glass of hard alcohol. Artiom, grimacing, drank it and they immediately sewed up his temple, having washed only one side of his head, and even that was only near the wound. Ali worked fast — Artiom endured, and endured, then, when he was about to scream, he was commanded to get up and get out of there.

He got up and vomited. Good thing that he saw the bowl into which he spewed out the millet with cabbage — all of it smelled awfully of alcohol.

Vasilii Petrovich brought Artiom's things. When Artiom wandered along the corridor to the general ward, Vasilii Petrovich called to him and raised his bag, showing with a gesture that he was giving his things to the doctor.

"Did they return the 'icons'?" Artiom, having unstuck his lips, found the strength to make a joke, but Vasilii Petrovich didn't hear him.

Artiom didn't repeat the question. From the sound of his own voice, he once again almost lost consciousness.

On the first day, they didn't treat anything else, only forced him to wash in a big tub on the first floor, filled with barely lukewarm water. Artiom almost drowned in it; without fully washing off the soap, he quickly climbed back out. He forgot to wash his face; after that he remembered nothing…

… A middle-aged nurse, who was doing the rounds in her white gown and scarf, gave him a thermometer and some ice to apply to his temple.

She returned for the thermometer half an hour later; Artiom had managed to fall asleep during that time. The ice on his temple melted, while his dream had been viscous, thick, muggy, nauseating.

"What do I have there?" asked Artiom, looking at the thermometer.

"A temperature," answered the nurse.

"A high one?" asked Artiom. The whole time his eyes, then his mouth kept getting stuck together. In his temple, the blood felt thick as it moved through, like a leech.

"Yes."

He fell asleep again.

After he awoke, he lay there and touched the tall wooden headboard of the couch with his hand. Its shape reminded him of a wave. Artiom immediately remembered that he had a similar couch when he was a child; it stood in the guest room. It was his favorite place to play. He used to lead a toy caravan — a small horse and three motley soldiers — right along the top of the headboard. This entire company walked as though up a mountain and sometimes lost one of their number — either a goggle-eyed grenadier or a fusilier with a broken spear, or a Roman legionnaire. For some reason, the horse always survived.

The thoughts that came to Artiom's mind that evening were unexpected.

"Was it for this that we had a revolution?" he thought, scraping the dried-up soap from his chest with his nails, even though he had never taken part in any revolution. "Was it so that the counter-rev Burtsev could smack me in the face? That not-quite-defeated White Army bastard? Those Chechens? Why are they incarcerated? Probably quarreled with the Soviet government, the dogs! What about Sorokin, that natural cannibal! Why didn't the revolution kill them all? How dare they beat me?"

Artiom thought about this for a very long time with the same words, maybe an hour or more. He got to the point where he dimly imagined how he would write and complain to the administration about them all. What exactly would he complain about, Artiom didn't know, but he wanted revenge so badly he could cry like a child. It was so sweet to imagine that they would lead Curly, Sorokin, Burtsev away, the duty officers — all of them — and Passport and Shaferbekov too.

They called the firing squad by different names on Solovki. Some called it, "they're taking them to the left." Others, "under the sweep." Others, "to send them to the moon." Others, "into the sixteenth brigade." In general, "to send to the sixteenth brigade" was used for any death — disease, suicide or something else.

Artiom wanted their deaths very much, mixing hot anger and intolerable self-pity, and in his thoughts, he gave the commands. Curly? Under the sweep! Curly began to weep, smearing his tears along his unshaved mug. Sorokin? To the left! Sorokin begins to smell even stronger, even fouler, and he's grabbing the bunks, and they're dragging him outside. Burtsev? To the moon! He saw how Burtsev turned pale and suddenly yelled, "For what? What's the problem? What moon, damn it?" But no one listens to him.

Unexpectedly, Artiom remembered Jules Verne's novel *From the Earth to the Moon.*

"Wait, what's the full title?" Artiom asked himself and, hesitating for a moment, remembered: *From the Earth to the Moon by a Straight Path Taking 97 Hours and 20 Minutes.*

"Is there at least one other person here on Solovki who has read that book?" Artiom thought, accepting, naturally, his knowledge of Jules Verne as his obvious and incontrovertible superiority. Basically, that knowledge itself was more than enough to immediately get Artiom released from here — how much more proof did they need that he shouldn't be allowed to be beaten in front of the whole brigade! For someone else's planted cards!

"Of course! It was Afanasiev who planted them!" Artiom understood so sharply that something jabbed again in his temple, and from there into his eye.

Judging by his clothes, a former priest quietly approached him and asked, "Do you have a little bread?"

"What?" Artiom didn't understand.

"A bit of bread," the priest asked again pitifully. Above his robe, despite the heat, he wore a woman's sweater.

"I don't have anything," snarled Artiom and hid his head under the blanket.

"Afanasiev!" Artiom repeated to himself in the darkness. "Who else, after all? What a scumbag that poet is. Scum. What scum! I'm going to kill that scum!"

Someone touched Artiom right in the head, through the blanket. He, spitting out an oath, climbed out and once again saw the priest. He wasn't going away.

"What about some sugar?" he asked. "Do you have some sugar?"

"Go away!" screamed Artiom. "Go away, priest!" And once again he climbed under the blanket, managing to notice how the priest raised his hand — a bit falsely, for all that — and started to make small signs of the cross.

"Get out already!" Someone else also shooed away the beggar, but Artiom wasn't looking any more.

Until it was dinner time, he decided not to climb out from under his blanket. He was hysterical. In the darkness, surrounded by the smell of his own body and the dried-up blood, Artiom was taken by a very convincing fear — now it seemed to him that they were definitely coming for him.

"How else?" he thought. "You hit the brigade commander! They found forbidden cards on you! You started a fight with the authorities. They could easily have you shot! Good Lord!" Artiom whispered, almost crying and ready to scream out loud. "Oh my God! They're going to kill me! They'll take me outside the gates and shoot me. Then they'll cover me with dirt. And worms will start eating me. Right here, where my nipples are. Right here, where my stomach is. Right here, where my face is." Artiom touched himself all over — his ears, lips, groin, feet. "All because of that scum! Because of Afanasiev! Because of that poet! That card-shark! I should have choked him! Killed him at night! But what if I inform on him for making messed-up sauna switches? But I made them together with him. They'll punish me even worse… But how? How even worse? What can be worse than being shot, idiot? Cursed idiot! Oh my God!" He kept repeating this and grinding his jaw with all his strength to remain quiet, not to attract anyone's attention. "Oh my God! Someone save me!" And once again he touched himself all over.

"Hey! You masturbating over there?" Someone asked and pulled down the blanket. Artiom tried to catch the fabric with his teeth and couldn't, and so fell back against the headboard of the couch.

"Oh," said the person who had pulled down the blanket, evidently from the gangsters, "That's quite a mug. Why didn't you wash it, at least? You're all bloody… Got a cigarette?"

"No." Artiom didn't so much say it as gasp it out.

The sick people started to get active, rising up from their couches. The clang of vats of food was audible.

Artiom suddenly got up, licking his lips. The nurse that had taken his temperature brought Artiom's bag. He rummaged around and found a bowl.

He figured that Vasilii Petrovich had put the bowl in. Artiom for sure hadn't put it in himself; he had thrown it on his bunk when they had announced the shakedown. For some reason, he looked for the cards…

For dinner, they brought vinaigrette made of beets, potatoes, carrots, cabbage, fish and millet. Everything was unbearably delicious.

Angry at his pulsating temple, Artiom ate, swooning from pleasure that in a strange way ended up being even stronger than the fear of death that had just overcome him. He felt the tight flesh of the beet on his teeth, the crunchy cabbage, the overcooked potatoes — all of this mixed with the flavor of the millet, which he ate with bread. His head was spinning as though from love and intimacy, and his bloody beard crumbled gently.

The sick man on the bed to Artiom's right kept looking at him askance. Artiom naturally suspected that they wanted to steal his lunch, so he squinted to more intensely taste the fishy body of the cod and the fusty carrot.

"I remember that you stood up for me," said the sick man, not waiting for Artiom's answering gaze.

Artiom looked in the direction of the voice. Bah! It was little Philip. Artiom even looked for a log nearby with Sorokin's inscription. What if it's standing there under his bed, waiting for the moment when Philip's foot gets better?

"What?" Artiom wondered at Philip's words. He had forgotten standing up for him completely. "That never happened," he said.

And turned away.

* * *

He slept through the night, as though he were covered in earth that couldn't be lifted. Even his rib didn't bother him, since he lay down flat, putting his pillow on his head and didn't move all night.

There were no lice or bedbugs in the infirmary.

"How strange," thought Artiom in the morning, carefully touching the stiches on his temple. "All these months, I've been eating little and constantly working heavy labor. When I was a stevedore in the port, I worked for days on end in wet, windy weather. When I worked the logs, I was in water from morning to evening, but I haven't a caught cold. I haven't been sick at all! Not even any snot."

Artiom, its true, didn't react to his elevated temperature; on the contrary, after lunch, he felt much better and started to calm down, especially since nobody came for him.

Well, they sewed up his temple, his eye got bloated, his face swelled up, his rib hurt, it was completely impossible to lie on his left side and he was still nauseous — but it was all bearable. There was a lot of blood, but all of it had flowed from his temple to his nose. His nose was in place; they hadn't broken it.

Artiom decided not to tell anyone about that for now, but instead to take it easy for as long as he could.

Having hid under his blanket, he quietly stretched and sorted through all of his tangled, half-sleeping thoughts to find all the beautiful, fragrant and delicious things that he managed to eat recently.

Dried fruit, a bar of chocolate and horsemeat sausage were all in his mother's package… The chocolate smelled of horsemeat, but that didn't ruin it at all. The dried fruits from the second package, according to Vasilii Petrovich's advice, he soaked in hot water, and they drank it together, sweet sweat pouring down their faces.

Then the pig lard, the sour cream with onion — oh, what bliss that ended up being.

If not for Burtsev… Burtsev was there. To the *leshy* with Burtsev.

There was also the boiled egg.

But where was it? No, it wasn't anywhere; he had dreamt it up once, three days ago. Oh, what an egg it was in his dream! From such an egg, a golden cockerel would have probably hatched.

Yesterday's vinaigrette…

For the third time, they measured his temperature and again they wrote down in the notebook: 39.2.

For breakfast, they brought two roach, fried in seal fat and a baked potato — true, only one. But once again — joy, enchantment and ecstatic head-spinning.

"You would have never eaten this at home. You would have thrown the roach out the window," he tried to remonstrate with himself, at the same time trying not to believe himself.

Having gotten settled, Artiom started to study his closest neighbors and the general situation.

Along the length of an entire wall of the general ward was a fresco that hadn't been painted over; unlike most other rooms in the monastery.

The fresco depicted the sick — but among them was, it seems, Christ. He was holding up one of the sick — a white-bearded old man.

Artiom wasn't well-versed in Biblical stories and didn't know this one.

For a minute, he admired the fresco, then was distracted by the people.

Other than the fool for Christ Philip and the beggar-priest, who kept on walking amongst the monastic couches, almost all of the other sick inmates seemed to look alike, like dried fish.

He remembered that yesterday, yes, some thug had come up to him asking for tobacco, but, as he looked around the ward now, Artiom couldn't recognize him. Or rather, looking at every person, he was ready to think that any one of them could have been he.

Carefully lifting himself up by his hands — his ribs did hurt, after all — Artiom sat up, trying not to stoop and looked to see what was on the other side of his tall headboard.

There was a similar couch standing there, and the priest John sat there — the same *Vladychka*, who had given Vasilii Petrovich the sour cream and onion.

The priest was sewing up a robe.

Their eyes met.

"Good morning, *Vladychka*," said Artiom a bit unexpectedly for himself.

"How's your health, my dear?" asked *Vladychka* simply and gently. "I see they've sewn you up as well!"

Artiom didn't find the words that he thought might be appropriate, so he only smiled, shrugging his shoulders: yes, everything was basically OK, yes, they've sewn me up.

"You really don't need to find special words to talk to a priest," said John, biting off a thread. "Whatever's in your heart — the ones on the very top — those will do. Special words are often from the evil one." *Vladychka* smiled.

"So that's how it is…" thought Artiom with amazement and touched the stitches on his temple.

For some reason, this was almost pleasant.

"Well, what about poems?" he asked. "Poems are always special words."

"Do you think so, my dear?" asked the priest. "Well, I think that the best poems happen when the words are taken exactly from the top of the heart. But when special words are chosen — then the poems are futile."

Artiom scratched his barely itching cheek with nails that hadn't been trimmed for a long time. He glanced at his fingers and saw a bloody scab under his nails: he had scratched off some of yesterday's blood.

"What words are lying on the very top for you right now?" Artiom asked. For some reason, he wanted to speak to *Vladychka*.

"That our pathetic look isn't worth our sorrow," said *Vladychka*, smiling. "That since we've gathered here, then that's truly the will of God. After all, it's not just the innocent who have gathered here, isn't that true? Everyone thinks to himself that he is truly innocent and not everyone can admit to himself with what faults he has come here. One is guilty of blasphemous words, another of thieving nonsense, a third of some great and significant error. So why should we complain, we inhabitants of Solovki? They brought us here against our will, but grandfather Savvatii — the founder of this monastery — floated here himself. And he was no young man! What do you think, my dear, was it easy for Savvatii? An old grandfather appeared on this empty island. He lived here for six years and he could grow nothing except for turnips. No one fed him, he had no roof over his head, no one warmed his old hut for him, there was no infrastructure at all. But he lived, labored! And what about us? There's only offence and disturbance of the heart, instead of repentance — if not for those sins that our foolish judges ascribed to us, then for others."

Artiom touched his head and found, under his hair, a slightly wet bump. He touched it, squinting sometimes, but still continued to listen to *Vladychka*.

"For man, it's as though there is no sin if no one saw that sin!" said Father John. "But is that so, my dear? If he's not caught — he's no thief. But God is One, who knows every thief, and He had His own Solovki for all unrepentant sinners, and they are one hundred thousand times worse."

"Then why is there an earthly Solovki if they're being prepared up there as well?" asked Artiom. Naturally, he didn't believe a word that *Vladychka* said; however, he received spiritual pleasure from his quiet, gentle speech.

"I was saying, dear one, God's Solovki are for the unrepentant. That means it's better to repent in time, and the earthly Solovki are not the worst place for that. Here, for almost five hundred years, people lived lives just as difficult as we. Do you know how the *Paterikon* of Solovki describes this life? 'We labored in fasting and prayer and handiwork... sometimes we worked the earth... sometimes we prepared lumber for the monastery's buildings or carried water from the sea... among the other labors, we caught fish... and so from our sweat and our food we fed ourselves.' What has changed? Are there many differences from our days? The hardships are the same. The path is also to the same place."

Here *Vladychka* — Artiom even started from surprise — winked. But at the same moment, he returned to his quiet, though smiling, decorum.

"And here's another thing I remember," said *Vladychka*, "I read yesterday about Archimandrite Varfolomei of Solovki: 'A sweet fragrance rises from his body.' But at that time, he had been dead eleven weeks! What can we say, my dear? We smell worse than some dead men! Yes, they do wash us rarely, they feed us meagerly, the louse lives on us and there is illness in us. But the worst smell, my dear, comes from our unrepented sin! It's hardest of all to wash it off!"

The other priest who constantly made circles in the ward, asking for bread, tried not to approach *Vladychka's* couch. But, having noticed that the path of the beggar wended its way not far from him, almost within reach, if not of a hand, then of a shoe-toss, *Vladychka* John took off his shoe from his foot and manifested a sharp and obvious intention of throwing it. The beggar-priest, covering himself with his hand, ran away a few steps and stood at a distance, only extending his neck, which made him look like a frightened bird, until the moment when *Vladychka* dropped his shoe down to the floor by his foot.

"I'm gonna get you!" *Vladychka* threatened the beggar.

Artiom held back his laughter with difficulty, but by then he noticed that the freckled hand of *Vladychka*, while he threatened, didn't ball into a fist, but more familiarly, into a three-finger pinch,[33] and he shook it as though he were quickly salting himself.

* * *

The after-lunch temperature check again showed 39.2.

"What, you're not going to wash at all?" the middle-aged nurse asked, gently poking at Artiom's cheek. "Go wash yourself or the doctor will curse at you."

---

33 Familiar, because that is how one crosses oneself.

Just that light touch and something inside his soul rocked fiercely, the rocking continued to increase. Artiom had a toy in his earliest childhood, something like a small set of scales. If you rocked them, they tried to find their balance for a long time. You could watch that for a long time until your head started to spin.

Artiom even put a hand to his cheek so that the touch wouldn't disappear so fast.

"But she's probably also an inmate, no?" thought Artiom. "She was also convicted. Must she also repent for something, as *Vladychka* says? That's just silly!"

"Only don't take a shower," said the middle-aged nurse. "You can't pour water on your head. Especially with such a high temperature."

"There's a shower here?" Artiom started.

But he didn't go wash himself. He kept lazing about and stretching — it was such a pleasure not to go anywhere, just to lie there.

Lying about wasn't boring at all. Lying about was fun.

"It's strange that in my childhood I preferred to play, not lie around," Artiom thought stupidly. "I should have just lied about. I had a whole life ahead of me in which to get my fill of play..."

The doctor came. His appearance alone seemed to elicit a slight shake and a movement of air.

He was an Eastern type — very handsome, with a full beard and intelligent, dark, cherry-like eyes that reminded Artiom of a dog's. His mother was probably Russian, but his father — of southern bloodlines. Or the other way around.

The doctor moved among the monastery's couches quickly, dressed in white, like a sailboat.

"Like a sailboat with cherry eyes..." Artiom habitually imitated Afanasiev.

Behind the doctor his assistants and the nurses followed respectfully.

There were about one hundred people in the infirmary. With some, the doctor spoke for a long time, but others he didn't even approach. However, everyone expected him, even the dying tried to raise themselves onto their elbows, to cry out something — a request, a complaint...

"Doctor Ali," they called sometimes from one side, then from the other. The doctor didn't answer.

Judging by the fragmentary answers of the doctor and his entourage, Artiom figured out that the larger half of those lying here had tuberculosis, syphilis and scurvy. The other half were the beaten ones and those damaged by the guards, the foremen and the commandants. It turned out

Artiom was not alone. There were also a few self-inflicted wounded like Philip and a few who were knifed, but not finished off, by the gangsters.

"You don't happen to have some bread, do you, doctor?" asked the beggar-priest.

The priest had an awful, puss-filled rash over his whole chest that he showed not without pride — his Solovetsian rewards.

"I have no bread," answered the doctor seriously. "I do have an enema. Would you like an enema?"

It grated a little on Artiom.

"Communism-áh, just an enem-áh," answered the priest unhappily and mockingly, inserting the unnecessary ending for the sake of the rhyme, which only increased the mockery.

"If its bread you need, then God will intercede," Ali answered him in kind, which, he had to admit, immediately made Artiom like him again. Every phrase, of course, was given especial enchantment by his soft Eastern accent.

"Oh-oh-oh," *Vladychka* John said to himself, listening to this intelligent conversation.

Artiom's turn came.

"Does it hurt here? Here?" Doctor Ali asked quickly. "It seems there's nothing. Nausea? Show me your pupil?"

"How can I show it to you?" Artiom laughed, though the doctor had already taken him by the chin. "Look."

"What temperature does he have?" Ali asked the middle-aged nurse who walked behind him with an open notebook.

His fingers were strong and hot. "If I've got 39.2, what does he have? Forty-two?"

"Why isn't he washed?" asked the doctor not really of Artiom, but of all who stood behind him. "And he probably had lice. With such pediculosis, typhoid fever can begin, even in the infirmary! What a shame that would be!"

It was understood that Doctor Ali spoke not so much for his entourage, but for the sake of some general importance of his position.

No sooner had the doctor walked away then the middle-aged nurse waved the notebook at Artiom: go get washed up, right now!

"Where's the shower, then?" Artiom asked one of the monks who was working in the infirmary. The former monks wore their headgear askew — that was the easiest way of distinguishing them from the priests who had been exiled here, whom, for the record, the monks did not like.

The monk gestured "over there".

"Don't pour the water!" he called after him with a strong, but raspy voice.

There was no one in the shower. Medical rounds.

The shower was a metal vat filled with water, from which hung a metal chain. Evidently, it gave freedom to the water.

Artiom quickly undressed, pulled firmly on the chain and some sort of turbid, but warm and pleasant, water poured down in crooked streams.

Turning his head sideways, lest he get the decorative sewing on his temple wet, he stood quickly under those streams, quietly chuckling and caressing himself on his chest.

Dark water ran all over his body.

"I'm so dirty!" Artiom thought, for some reason with pleasure. "Or is it the water?"

He looked about for the soap, didn't find any, and began to furiously rub himself with his hands — everywhere except his painful ribs.

As he was thrashing around under the water, he at first decided that he imagined female laughter… he stopped moving and immediately realized that no, he hadn't imagined it. On the next story up, women were laughing — young and naked. They were washing up there too.

"Naked and white," thought Artiom, listening in to their laughter and voices with all his strength. He even opened his mouth. The shower's spray got into his mouth.

White and naked.

"You with the iodine in your mouth," Artiom uttered aloud the strange and incomprehensible oath. "Iodine. In the mouth."

He touched himself once, twice, three times. All he had stored up for a long time exploded into his hand to the laughter of the women.

* * *

Artiom walked back light, wet and filled with energy.

On the way back, he once again met the monk and thought that he would curse him for pouring out the water, but the monk only nodded — go that way. And he pointed with a crooked finger at a cubicle.

Inside the cubicle, on a bench, sat Vasilii Petrovich.

Next to the bench were thrown some bloody and ragged stretchers, a few buckets — one filled with old bandages, the other with some other medical garbage.

"In vain, Artiom, do you look so little like a sick man," said Vasilii Petrovich with kind strictness. "In your place, I would try to look the part more.

But as I see, it's all water off the duck's back for you." He even extended his hand to touch the hair of his young companion, but of course he didn't touch it.

Artiom smiled.

"They almost killed you in there, by the way," said Vasilii Petrovich. "Do you remember?"

He didn't really want to remember it and Artiom made an ambiguous face. While he had such a high temperature and stitches in his head, they wouldn't drive him back into the brigade. As for later, let the chips fall where they will.

Judging by everything, they would eventually do him in, Artiom understood that. But he couldn't fear that for very long; he could just about handle a few hours' worth of fear.

"What's the news over there?"

Now Vasilii Petrovich remained quiet, pausing and not answering. Judging by everything, he was preparing for a different conversation.

"How's Burtsev?" asked Artiom, faking iron indifference, not so much for Vasilii Petrovich as for himself.

"Burtsev?" asked Vasilii Petrovich in turn, in clear aggravation. "Mstislav. Yes, he's befuddled me. At first, when it happened with the Chinese man, I thought that… That he did it to the Chinese man because there were too many Chinese in the Red Army. Burtsev is from Kolchak's army — they had especial trouble with them. But now you as well…"

Artiom snorted.

"But, you know, you shouldn't have called him 'lieutenant.'" Vasilii Petrovich continued with a bit more animation, as though up to this point he was having difficulty understanding Burtsev. "He was upset at the 'lieutenant.'"

"In other words, if I had called him a colonel, he wouldn't have been upset?" asked Artiom, smiling.

Vasilii Petrovich didn't answer, pursing his lips: Artiom was right.

"They just beat up Lazhechnikov," said Vasilii Petrovich. "I was walking to you, and they carried him into the brigade. He was lying behind the wood pile… all black and blue. Not sure who beat him up. Not the authorities, I don't think."

"I think I know who it was," said Artiom, remembering the conversation at the cemetery between Khasaev and the Cossack.

Vasilii Petrovich for some reason didn't ask who Artiom had in mind.

"Everyone is slowly going wild here," said Vasilii Petrovich after a short silence. "It's frightening. They have souls, after all."

Artiom thought and answered very firmly, "I don't give a damn. It's just a state of mind."

With that, they started to say goodbye.

Vasilii Petrovich brought some berries to share with Artiom.

"Thank you," said Artiom sincerely, weighing the baggy in his hand with pleasure. "You probably had to give some to the monk at the entrance?"

"I gave him some," said Vasilii Petrovich calmly and a bit dryly. "In general, you're not supposed to bring them here. I had to bribe him… I hope you've now understood everything about Afanasiev?" he asked, already standing.

Artiom winked in the sense that he understood well enough. He had known for a while now.

"Artiom, do you know how one gets the evil eye?" Vasilii Petrovich suddenly introduced, it would seem, a different topic. "When there is the seed of some kind of disease in a person — then the same disease or foulness becomes immune to him. Everything, as much as possible, was good for you here, because everything inside you was properly aligned. I was impressed with you. Even learned a few things. 'Well now,' I thought, 'he shows no signs of human self-indulgence, weakness, or meanness.' But then something happened and everything collapsed. Do you know how they all beat you? If they did that to me, I would have been killed. But here you're running around. Maybe your bravado has set you up, Artiom? You should think about that… You can't win here, that's what you have to understand. You can't be a victor in prison. I understood that even at war, you can't win, but I still haven't found the right words for that…"

Artiom got up and shook Vasilii Petrovich's hand. He decided not think about his words this very moment, but to leave them for later. Let's say, he'd try to make sense of it all as he was falling asleep. The most important things are understood at the threshold of sleep — that's how it seemed to Artiom sometimes. There was one hitch, though — the next morning you don't remember what it is you understood. Probably you understood something, but what? You forgot.

But maybe you don't have to remember?

"Artiom, you're going to get solitary, don't you understand that?" said Vasilii Petrovich already in the corridor.

He ruined Artiom's good mood.

* * *

"Well, what did you think?" Artiom mocked himself as we walked back. "That they would give you a double ration? A pie with cabbage?"

"Whatever he brought you over there, share," said the criminal, catching Artiom as he walked into the ward.

If he had said it forcefully, Artiom would have answered him badly. What did he have to lose now, after all that happened? But the gangster asked it with a smile; it was even a bit ingratiating. He could have easily refused, saying cheerfully, "None of your business!" And everything would have been fine, Artiom was sure of it. If only because the gangster wasn't with his posse here. He tried playing cards with anyone he could. He even offered *Vladychka* John to play once. In general, he was bored.

"You want a berry?"

"Exactly right," he answered and immediately cupped his hands.

Artiom had a hidden, and not quite acknowledged, desire to appease, if he could be allowed the expression, the god of the gangsters. Maybe, if he fed this one, then Passport would fall off him like a leaf in the sauna?

"It's good that you don't have four hands," said Artiom, pouring different berries into the dirty palms.

"Huh?" The gangster didn't understand.

His hands were covered by incomprehensible tattoos; Artiom noticed some kind of bluish drawing on his chest underneath his shirt, which was three sizes too large.

He had sunken cheeks, there was a bit of puss in his eyes, and his face looked similar to a fish — his lips protruded forward, then came the eyes, and his chin seemed almost completely chopped off. If you punch someone like that in his beard, you'll break his Adam's apple.

His nickname was "Gills".

"You want a girl?" asked the gangster, immediately tossing almost all of the berries in his mouth. He opened his mouth also in a fishy way. Artiom tried not to look into the criminal's mouth, lest he see a fish's small, gnawed-off teeth.

"Well now," Artiom said with clear and deliberate sarcasm, looking at the criminal's forehead, which was also sloping and barely visible. "'Where did you get a girl?"

"I don't have a girl," the gangster started to say in a somewhat nasty tone — Artiom knew that manner — to win every male conversation with every single word, so that at the first change, he could squash his companion like a bedbug.

"So who has one?" asked Artiom cheerfully. Be that as it may, he hated that manner of speaking and it was obvious that he hated it. Even someone with a sloping forehead could figure that out.

The gangster figured it out and said a bit more moderately, "The female ward is over there." He pointed with his finger upward. "There's the one-ruble girls, there's the fifty kopeck girls, then there's the fifteen kopeck girls. The local monk can arrange a meeting. Half a ruble for him, half for me. I'll guard and have my turn after you. As for the girl, your choice."

"I don't have any money," Artiom immediately said.

"What do you have?" asked the gangster and even grabbed Artiom a bit by the sleeve, with two fingers smeared with berry juice.

"Get your hand off quickly," said Artiom gently.

The criminal removed it, but a little more slowly than he should have. He immediately offered, "What about cards?"

Artiom didn't even answer. They were carrying a new sick man through the corridor. The bearers were familiar faces. The twelfth brigade had once again done its job to fill the ward.

The monk walked forward, showing the way. Lazhechnikov — by all appearances no longer alive — was carried by Khasaev with his fellow Chechen and a third person who was blocked all the time by the monk.

It was someone Artiom definitely didn't expect to see — but he appeared. Afanasiev. Not only that, but as he was trudging by, holding the edge of the horse cloth on which Lazhechnikov lay comatose, he winked. His face was sleepy — he was probably playing cards with the thugs again.

Behind them, the middle-aged nurse prodded the whole procession forward.

"I wanted to see you! I foisted myself on the Chechens to help them out!" Afanasiev whispered as he left the ward. "You can't get in here just like that. But the local medical assistants don't want to carry the sick, so... What do you have? They beat you like that, but you only have a swollen nose and those stitches on your temple! Did they set you up?"

"They sewed me up," repeated Artiom, trying to stoke hatred inside himself for that red-headed wretch, but it wasn't working, no matter what.

Afanasiev grabbed his forelock familiarly, as though trying out the firmness of his head. Will if fall off? Will I tear it off?

"I don't walk on plush or velvet, but I walk on the edge of a knife," Afanasiev sang, looking at Artiom with gentleness.

Against his will, the thought appeared: "No, it's not him, not him…" It was as if Artiom wanted to convince himself, even though there was no way of getting out of it — Afanasiev had planted the cards. Who else?

"Let's go, Afanas," called Khasaev.

"Yep, be right there," answered Afanasiev, not looking back.

"It was they who did the Cossack in?" asked Artiom, indicating the Chechens with his eyes.

"Who else?" answered Afanasiev with false strictness and immediately decided to ask: "You probably think that I planted those icons? Artiom, I swear to God…"

Artiom suddenly understood how to finish it all.

"Afanas, can you give me a ruble on loan? Better yet, two."

Artiom would normally never ask for money — he didn't have the habit — but at this moment it seemed easy and even salvific.

Afanasiev gave it with relish and winked one more time to boot.

"I'll come back again," he said, grabbing his forelock.

"Uh-huh," Artiom answered. "Only don't bring anyone else from the brigade. There aren't any more free beds here."

Very content with the joke and also, it seemed, with the fact that he gave two rubles, Afanasiev laughed.

"Hey," Afanasiev came back after leaving half-way. "Here's another ruble. Go ahead. Buy yourself something to eat…"

* * *

Lazhechnikov awoke, but he couldn't speak, he could only blink and breathe. They tore out a few bunches from his beard and the ripped-off skin on his jaws seeped blood. The bushy eyebrows of the Cossack stood almost on end, as though they were horrified. It was hard to look at him.

"Maybe he should drink something?" Artiom asked Timofey Stepanovich.

The middle-aged nurse shooed Artiom away: "Go to your place. They know what to do without you telling them. We'll give him everything."

He left, climbed under the blanket and soon hot and wearisome thoughts overtook him. That's what a single adventure in the shower means for such a youth!

He couldn't bear it; he climbed out. He took the rumpled ruble out of his pocket and admired it with the same intensity as though it were a picture of a naked girl.

The ruble promised an earth-shattering and long-awaited pleasure — so huge that he could hardly contain it in his consciousness.

"Dark-haired? Brunette? Red-head?" Artiom thought feverishly. "Who'll she be? For a ruble, she might be very beautiful… Curly hair or straight? And what? Can I undress her completely? Take off all her clothes?"

On the ruble was written: Camp of Special Designation of the OGPU. Below that: "currency voucher." Even lower: "Acceptable as payment from inmates only within the institutions and enterprises of the Camps of Special Designation of the OGPU."

"Why is there nothing written about payment to one-ruble beauties?" Artiom joked.

Truth be told, he was a little ashamed, but this long-awaited, bestial joy — it was far stronger, and it deafened him so much that his rational mind seemed to go underwater.

"After all, doesn't she need the ruble?" Artiom reported to himself, touching the stitches on his temple. "No one is forcing her, right?"

The beggar-priest, taking advantage of the fact that *Vladychka* John fell asleep, once again came to Artiom's couch. He quickly hid his ruble in his pocket.

Seeing Artiom's unfriendly mood, the priest began to poke the sleeping little Philip.

"Do you perhaps have a herring's tale left over from lunch? Some bits of leftover potato, maybe?"

"Go away, father, I don't have anything. We're all hungry," little Philip, in contrast to many others, said this with pity. But it was with him that the priest got angry.

"'We're all hungry…'" he mocked him. "No matter, no matter. If you had a pig, you'd have some bristle too."

"What are you talking about, father? Why are you reproaching me?" little Philip complained with tears, but no one was listening to him anymore.

The beggar-priest only looked insane at first glance; no, after careful examination it became clear that he was quite healthy — no worse than any inmate. His speeches guaranteed it.

Often, they did give the priest food, especially whenever there were new sick men from those brigades where life was a little better and they got paid double or even triple salaries. These were the artisans from the fifteenth, the clerks from the tenth and the specialists from the second. Then, he would become exact in his speech and very observant.

He was called Zinovii.

Father especially liked a bit of sugar.

The sick inmates — first of all from among the believers — were drawn to him until they met *Vladychka* John and then transferred, so to speak, into a different parish.

Father Zinovii was clearly jealous.

He had a nondescript face, as though it were sprinkled with sand, and it was small, as though gathered into a pinch. His hair was thin, brown, long and willful.

His tiresome begging was quickly replaced with brazenness and disgust, especially with reference to those sick who never gave him anything and never planned on giving him anything in the future — evidently, little Philip was one of these.

In general, the beggar-priest was afraid of violence and, whenever there was a threat of severe reprisal, he immediately retreated and kept a low profile.

His conversations were always accusatory and agitated — he hated the Soviet government in many imaginative ways and he didn't conceal it.

However, he approached the subject tangentially every time.

"How well everything is organized in the human primer," explained Zinovii to one of those sick with scurvy, with horrible sores on his gums that in no way distressed the priest. "Move a single letter in the entire primer, just one small letter, to a different place and everything becomes nonsense. The same is true of human consciousness. It's fragile! Man thinks that he thinks, but he is not even in a state to understand his own consciousness. Thus he, who is unable to understand his own consciousness, risks to think and explain God. But you can only attend to God. Change a single letter in man's consciousness, and though he may be noble in appearance, soon it will become clear that all his ideas are a jumble and a hell. The same is true of the Bolsheviks," he continued in a whisper. "They jumbled all the words and we all became insane. It seems like it's all the same labors, all the same difficulties, but if you really examine them, you'll immediately see that our eyes are looking out the back of our heads and our ears are turned inward."

The sinewy former monk of Solovki, unnoticeably having come up behind him to pick up the linens of a cured and discharged inmate, stuck like a burr to a single word of the loquacious priest and got so angry that it seemed he had been storing up an answer to this word long ago:

"Why are you complaining?" He even stomped his dirty booted foot. "Even before you came, we lived here on Solovki and it was even harder. We got up at three in the morning and you get up at six! And we worked until dark. The monks drove the workers here no less than the Chekists drive you!"

Father Zinovii immediately fell silent and did not offer a rebuttal.

Artiom raised himself on his couch to look at *Vladychka* John. He wanted to hear an explanation of the preceding argument.

He was eager to answer Artiom's glance, as though he was waiting for it.

"They used to call Solovki the island of white gulls and black monks," said Father John after a minute. "They had it difficult here, it's true."

"So you're on his side?" Artiom said loudly, meaning the monk.

"There are no sides, my dear," answered Father John. "The sun goes in a circle; it's everywhere. And God is everywhere too. On all sides."

"Even on the Bolsheviks'?" asked Artiom. He didn't really like the priest's answers.

Father John smiled and, it seemed, decided to start over from scratch.

"Even in previous times, monks experienced a lack of love for the priesthood. After all, they live as celibates, in constant labors and in considerable poverty. They probably thought that they had the right to rebuke some of us for indulging the flesh. Well, I won't say that it's a completely false accusation. But here on Solovki, as soon as the Bolsheviks closed the monastery, many monks went to work for the Chekists. Now they, my dear, are considered members of the OGPU — helpers with the housekeeping, if you will — and they treat the inmate-bishops extremely badly, as though they were carrying out a secret vengeance. But what did we do to deserve this vengeance? Every one of us is in his proper place. We are in prison, they are free."

"That monk was complaining that their freedom was always like your imprisonment," said Artiom.

Vladychka John nodded his head, smiling warmly and without malice.

"It will be a great miracle if the Soviet government will overcome all offenses, tear asunder all false bonds and be able to establish a right community!" He answered as though he were singing a short musical phrase.

"Where their freedom will be like our pris…" Artiom started mockingly, but Father John put his finger to his lips: Shhh!

"Listen to that Renovationist!" the beggar-priest suddenly cried out from his place. It turned out he had the hearing of a predator. "The Red Army soldiers raped his wife and he's still talking about building community! Listen to him! He'll talk your ear off!"

Artiom was afraid to look at *Vladychka*, but, when he eventually turned his head, he saw how Father John sat quietly, intertwining his fingers and muttering something. He waited for the abuse to finish, lifted his gaze and again smiled at Artiom. Well, that's how it goes.

* * *

"Did you find a ruble?" asked Gills in the evening. As though he could smell it.

"Yes," said Artiom with a voice not his own, immediately overcome by a hot and excruciating agitation.

When they brought dinner, the gangster once again turned toward Artiom, but it turned out he wasn't coming to him.

Gills sat at little Philip's couch and said, grabbing his bowl with his fingers: "Wait, don't eat. Gimme."

Philip, not understanding anything, gave him his bowl. Gills lifted it and carried it to his place. On the way, he ate everything that lay in the bowl, and, turning around next to his own couch, he brought back the empty bowl, having put it into little Philip's hands.

All of it was so insolent and obvious that Artiom smiled against his own will. His smile was crooked and surprised.

Having noticed the smile, Gills nodded to Artiom as though they were accomplices.

The whole situation was ugly and foolish.

At this point, it was the farthest thing from Artiom's mind to stand up for anyone… But he had absolutely no desire to appear as Gills's partner in crime.

"It looks like I kept quiet only because of the ruble." Artiom was irritated.

Little Phillip examined his bowl for a minute, then quietly began to cry.

Vladychka John, who hadn't seen anything, but only noticed his crying neighbor, got up and, limping a bit, went from his place.

"What happened, my dear?" he asked Philip.

"Nothing," answered Artiom, feeling that he would still feel guilty before *Vladychka* for all this. "Go ahead, eat." He gave little Philip his untouched bowl.

He accepted the gift.

"What is it?" Vladychka asked Artiom this time.

"He's hungry," he answered.

Quickly, occasionally sniffling, Philip scraped it all clean.

"Millet porridge," Artiom told himself, trying not to watch the others eat.

"If the robber gets his loot, he'll be hanging by his crook," Philip suddenly said loudly.

At first Artiom didn't understand to whom he was speaking or what he was saying. When he thought about it, he figured that the words were addressed to Gills. But what was even stupider was that Philip once again accepted Artiom as almost an intercessor. That's why he raised his voice.

Luckily, Gills didn't figure that out.

Philip extended the bowl to Artiom.

"Why are you giving it to me?" he asked irritably. "Go and wash it. Return it clean."

Only when Philip started to get up did Artiom slowly remember that, up to this point, he hadn't really gotten up at all. He certainly didn't wander about the ward but kept on sleeping or stupidly staring at the ceiling.

A hand-made crutch lay under his couch. Leaning on it, he got up and having awkwardly picked up the bowl, he took a step. One leg was amputated under his knee.

"Fuck!" Artiom swore, sitting down with a jerk and feeling a sharp pain in his ribs. "Fuck!" he repeated, this time from the pain.

The scared Philip got up and turned around to check if someone was yelling at him. *Vladychka* John frowned so sorrowfully and pitifully that it seemed someone had painfully poked him in the chest. Only Gills, quickly returning from somewhere along the corridor, walking around Philip quickly, as though nothing had happened, found the opportunity to make a joke, leaning down toward Artiom's couch.

"Are you calling her already? You can't bring her here. You'll have to go to her."

Trying to overcome his pain, Artiom sat for a while, then asked, "What, now?"

"What? Do you think they need a long time to get ready?" asked Gills with his fishy mouth. "Just lifts her ass and carries it with her."

"You could easily catch him on a hook, with a worm," thought Artiom, looking at that mouth.

The monk waited at the end of the corridor, as though he were fixing a windowpane that he promptly forgot about as soon as Artiom and Gills came up.

"Give me fifty kopecks," said the monk.

He had a voice as though born from the chest, from where it resounded.

"Where's the girl?" asked Artiom, not showing his money. It seemed that he really didn't want her anymore. It wasn't joy anymore, but something like a duty, except he wasn't clear to whom he owed it.

"Did you think you've come to a brothel?" asked the monk from his womb. "What? Do you want me to show them to you, too?"

"Hey, *friar*, give him his fifty," said Gills, for some reason once again sensing his position of power.

Artiom sniffed and couldn't come up with a plan of action. If he was going to leave, then he'd better leave, but suddenly he really wanted to see if she was a red-head, brunette or dark-haired. Only to look, that was enough.

"Here you go. Split it." Artiom lifted the Solovetsian ruble. The monk took the paper into his fist, hid it somewhere with a single gesture and walked away.

Gills pushed Artiom painfully in the side. *Go after him.*

"I'm going to have to tear out his gills," thought Artiom, but he followed the monk.

"This is my room," said the monk, standing at the doorway. "The bitch is in there. Don't turn on the light. While I go throw out the garbage, you have to get it done. Don't lie down on the bed. Do it standing."

Artiom remained silent.

The monk pushed the door — it turned out to be open. Inside was a pungent half-murk in which you could hardly see anything.

"I repeat. Don't even think of lighting a candle," said the monk as he left. "You can get thirty days solitary for a girl."

"And eternal fires in hell," said Artiom, as though to himself.

"For a repeat offense, half a year in solitary," droned the monk from his womb. "And serves you right."

"Holier than thou," thought Artiom, still not deciding to walk in.

"Fuck it, get in there already." Gills pushed him, and it hurt again.

"Listen, dog," Artiom turned on him. "If you touch me one more time… You got it, dog?"

Gulls gaped at him, but his eyes were stupid and brazen. Artiom stared at his whites point-blank.

He walked into the room and closed the door behind him. He felt for the hook and found it, latched it.

He turned around and, trying to see something at least, got used to the half-darkness.

"I'm here," sounded a female voice.

She was sitting at the window on a chair.

Artiom took two steps and she stood up to meet him.

"Here, I'll lean against the windowsill, and you go ahead," she said. Her breath smelled of millet porridge. Artiom couldn't make out her face for the life of him.

"You gotta hurry," she said, lifting her clothes, which in the darkness looked like a repurposed bag. It's possible that's exactly what it was.

"What color hair do you have?" asked Artiom, taking a lock of her hair in his palm. From the shut-up window the lantern light barely made it through, but he couldn't discern the color of her hair.

"What, did you come to give me a haircut?" she laughed in a smoked-up voice.

"Shut up," said Artiom, touching the woman's face with his right hand — her eyebrows, her nose, her lips…

"Fuck, why are you creeping around me like a blind man?" She slapped his hand.

Her nose was thin, her forehead clean, her skin dry and weathered, her lips feminine and soft.

Artiom put the ruble in her hand and left.

He forgot where the hook was on the wall and fumbled around for it. The woman laughed behind his back quickly and unpleasantly.

"Anyone else?" she asked, having hiccupped, when Artiom finally opened the door.

"No," he answered.

In the corridor, he immediately saw Gills, who stood at the ready.

"My turn," said Gills, hurrying to squeeze his way past Artiom.

Catching him by the scruff, Artiom whispered in his ear very firmly: "Here's your ruble. Don't touch her, there's a good fellow. Let's go."

Gills swore but grabbed the ruble and hid it in his pocket.

"Let's go, let's go," Artiom repeated, pulling Gills by the jacket.

He didn't know himself why he did it all.

* * *

His mood from the morning was foul. Everything fell on him again and crushed him — the expectation of solitary, Passport, Burtsev, Sorokin, Curly… or maybe they would execute him? They could execute him, couldn't they? A package will come from his mother, but he'd be in the ground. There's a sausage in the package. Who's going to eat it? Or will they send it back? "We consider it necessary to inform you that for reasons of your son's execution, we return your package to you as useless."

Artiom clutched his blanket and sat like that.

They were changing the dressings on a new self-inflictor without two fingers. He was roaring.

"In the summer, a self-inflictor is a rarity. It's in winter that they come in here in packs." Someone was saying not far away. "On one of the jobs, there was a foreman who cut off an ear for every self-inflicted wound. And he'd hang it above his door. He had a whole necklace hanging there. The administration of the camp came for an inspection, and he reported: forty self-inflictors punished with the cutting off of their ear! And they rewarded him!"

"They're lying, all of them," thought Artiom.

Lazhechnikov was barely regaining consciousness. He didn't eat anything and couldn't speak. His chest became black and his beard withered as though cut off at the root.

Artiom remembered how he caught a ladybug when they were breaking the monuments in the cemetery. Lazhechnikov had noticed it and said, "We used to call that bug an 'Alionka.'" Then he had boomed at the ladybug: "Alionka, Alionka, fly up to the sky, there your children are sitting by the bee skep."

He had pronounced "fly up" oddly. It was a comical scene — a strong Cossack with his full beard and bushy eyebrows whispering over a little bug.

"What's a skep?" Artiom had asked, laughing.

"A woman's genitals," said Lazhechnikov, squinting. "But if we're talking properly, then it's a wicker basket. It's a little joke."

"I should have done it with that whore yesterday," Artiom berated himself, hurrying from one thing to the next in his thoughts. "I should have torn to her to shreds, undressed her completely, looked her over, smelled her, fingered her everywhere… because when will I ever now? Never!"

But at the same time, Artiom felt no arousal at all, his member was withered and sleepy.

Philip had hidden his leg under the blanket before, but now he stuck his stump out and was airing it out. Flies were flying around it.

He didn't wash his bowl. Maybe he was hoping that Gills wouldn't take his food away for that reason.

The one sick with scurvy, not long after each meal, would pick at his teeth. Artiom, once he had noticed the horrible sores on his gums, couldn't forget the image again.

They measured Artiom's temperature. This time it was 39.3.

"Maybe I've got the ague?" he thought. "Why don't I feel it? To fall unconscious — maybe they wouldn't touch me then. Damn consciousness, go away!"

Gills appeared. It didn't seem at all obvious that he was in any way sick. He now looked at Artiom as though he were a louse and all that was left was to squish the louse with his fingernail.

"They told me that they'll put you in solitary," Gills began immediately. "Do you know where they're putting you? The clay mill."

Artiom said nothing.

"Do you know what the clay mill is? It's a basement under the southern wall. Its floor is clay, which you have to work with your feet. From morning to night in clay up to your knees. Your ration is 300 grams of bread. If they did it right, they'd only fit about thirty people there, no more, but they push in about one hundred there at a time. Everyone lies on the cement floor — no blankets, nothing. You're only left with your clothes. If you have no clothes, you go naked. They feed everyone from the same vat, but they don't give you any bowls. So they eat with their hands. You need about a week to die. You'll get a month for sure, but probably more."

"Why are you saying all this?" asked Artiom.

"Give me your jacket. You don't need it anyway," said Gills.

"Bug off," said Artiom.

Gills smiled, opening his fishy mouth. And truly, his teeth were like a fish's — small and dirty.

"And find me five rubles," said Gills. "Or I'll inform on you that you were with a girl. They'll add another month. Make sure I have them before lunch."

At these words, Philip hid his stump under his blanket.

Vladychka John, who didn't quite hear the conversation, but figured some of it out, stood up from his place and asked Gills in his gentle way, "My dear, go and sit in your place, lie down and rest. You're so restless, you can't stay in one place."

Gills listened to him and walked off, but then remembered something and returned for two more words: "They've passed a message from your brigade. You've got a package; it's waiting for you at the post office. You should have it brought here, I'll take care of it... yeah? Hello from Passport, got it? Write a letter, so that they can get the package. We'll find the right person for it. Write down, 'I am in the infirmary and request that the package be handed over.' You can do that. I'll give your letter to the monk. He'll take care of it."

Vladychka John, having waited for the end of the conversation, lay down again, but he was uneasy and kept tossing and turning.

Soon, not waiting for breakfast, he got up and, limping heavily, left the ward. He was gone for a rather long time, but he returned in a better mood.

He ate his cold breakfast — which no one had touched, of course — and afterward, rosy-cheeked, he sang something to himself, barely audibly.

In another hour and a half, they called *Vladychka* out. He made his way with difficulty, from one couch to another, until he reached the corridor. But only a minute later, he returned with a bag that he put on Artiom's couch.

Artiom reached for the bag — his ribs flared — then, twisting himself around, he grabbed the bag with his left hand and put it on his knees. Yep, it was a package from his mother.

What a fragrance! It was just impossible. Artiom looked around; everyone must sense this gorgeous, multifaceted, stupefying fragrance.

Without even opening the bag, but only closing his eyes for a moment, Artiom could list nearly everything that was in the bag. Mustard tickled his nose; the white fragrance of lard diffused heavily about the room; the yellow smell of lemon undulated subtly and sharply; the multicolored smell of dried fruits enveloped him; the rice had a dusty, sprinkly smell; the tea diffused foggily and heavily; the sugar was light and barely shining; the dried fish basked and sparkled in sugar and mustard, and the sausage — that horsemeat sausage — it didn't smell at all of horse. It smelled of meaty debauchery, of flesh, of life…

"*Vladychka* John!" Artiom turned to the priest, moved and surprised. "How did you know? How did you retrieve it?"

Vladychka gestured with his finger to not speak so that all would hear.

Artiom covered the bag with his blanket and walked over to *Vladychka's* couch.

"Our long-maned brother is working alone at the post office," said *Vladychka* in a whisper, laughing. "I convinced him! Otherwise, as I see, too many hands are reaching for your package. The important thing is that it came to you. Now, my dear, it's for you to decide with whom to share, with whom not to. And don't be angry at them! Don't insult Philip. He was walking from work, wounded, with a broken foot, carrying a huge log. He fell, lost consciousness from the pain and exhaustion. He lay there for a whole day. The administration thought that he had run away and they searched for him with dogs. As soon as they found him, the dogs ripped up the leg again for good measure. Then they interrogated him for two days. Then threw him in the clay mill. While they figured out that they were punishing him unjustly, his leg was so damaged that they had to cut it off. Now, he has to hop around without a leg until his death! You're kind; don't rebuke him for his empty words. Through his empty words, he's also coming closer to God… And don't be angry at Gills, either! Is it easy for a person with such a nickname to live? He's also created in the image and likeness, but everyone calls him Gills, worse than a dog. No one would even call a dog by that name, my dear… And don't be angry at all this lack of order around you. If the Lord shows you this disorder that means that He wants to inspire you to restore the order in your own heart. Everything that you and I see is an illumination of our consciousness. For this we must only thank God, not blame Him…! Well, go on, go on and enjoy your gifts."

Artiom decided that disemboweling the package in front of everyone was completely unnecessary, but he couldn't restrain himself from eating the horsemeat sausage.

He bit it once, he bit it twice and he locked gazes with Gills. He looked deflated.

Artiom didn't turn away his gaze and angrily ripped off another chunk of the sausage. Without looking, he dug in the bag with his hands, found a pack of dried apples by their scent alone, then got it and ate it with the sausage.

Gills motioned towards the door in the corridor.

Artiom nodded with a happy smile: I'm coming, I'm coming right now, dear comrade.

"Don't go anywhere, my dear," said *Vladychka*, but it was too late. Artiom came out into the corridor with the sausage and apples in hand.

"You didn't get it, *friar*," Gills started.

"What do you mean I didn't get?" Artiom was surprised. "I understood everything."

Artiom put the pack of apples in his mouth, so they wouldn't bother him.

Gills skillfully avoided the first blow, but the second — the left — got him. The problem was that Artiom still had the sausage in his left and the blow was weak. Artiom got the answering blow in his ribs — it seemed Gills knew where to hit him. It was so painful that it seemed a rib had broken off and pierced the softest pulp.

Artiom went berserk. He spit out the apples. His eyes were swelling. Gills now tried to get his temple, holding his hands like a bird does its talons.

"He's trying to untie my stitches," Artiom realized with playful fear. "He'll untie the stitches, and my head… like a show… will open wide, and everything will fall out…"

The apples crunched under his feet.

Someone jumped from the ward, shouting, "Hey! Idiots! Hey!"

Artiom noticed how the monk was walking through the corridor with a block of wood in his hand — he was out to get them.

Artiom feinted with his left, then ducked under Gills's strike so well that he ended up behind him, then he gave him a right hook in the back of the head.

The door into the ward was open, and Gills flew into the room and crashed somewhere there.

Artiom lifted the sausage from the floor — the apples were already not worth picking up — and hurried after Gills.

The monk, realizing that he wasn't going to make it in time, wound up and threw the block, as though he had lived with it his whole life and hated it and now decided to throw it out.

It hit the wall so hard that it cracked.

* * *

His temperature was elevated again.

However, he slept like a fish in ice — deeply, without hearing anything, without remembering anyone.

In the morning, he took the food and brought it to *Vladychka* John.

"I don't need anything, my dear," he sorrowfully refused. "Why don't you give some to the beggar? I don't need anything. How will I pay you back, my dear? I only take when I can give something to others, but here you can feed anyone you like. I won't hand out your mother's gifts to others in the ward right in front of your face, will I? It'll look bad. It would be better if you went and fed him whom you'd least like to give joy to. Now you can. Now that you've beaten him, be good to him. That would be becoming of you, my dear."

"He'll get by," said Artiom.

That morning, they took out Artiom's stitches. As for Gills, they stitched him up yesterday. When he fell, he split open his head and half his fish-face, including his lips. He looked incomparable and in a strange way now resembled two fish at once.

"Is your tongue also forked, you snake?" asked Artiom, sitting down next to Gills on his way to the outhouse. Gills moved, making room for his guest, but was silent, moaning from pain and shuddering with his jaws.

On the way back, Artiom looked in on Gills again, wiped his wet hands on his blanket and blew his nose in the same place.

For some time, he examined the gangster.

He found the stitches across his entire face to be amusing.

"How about we change your nickname? You'll be not Gills, but Corset," offered Artiom, mocking him.

Gills silently swallowed; it was painful to swallow.

For lunch, Artiom took Gills's bowl with the lunchtime vinaigrette.

"You can't chew anyway," he said. "You can only chomp and move the food around. I'll dig up some worms in the dung for you, Gills. You can swallow them without chewing.

Gills was so stupid that he couldn't understand what Artiom was saying, and he didn't even try to defend his ration.

Artiom didn't need him to understand; he was just amusing himself.

He gave the vinaigrette to little Philip. He didn't want to take it. Artiom just dumped Gills's portion into little Philip's bowl and brought the empty bowl back to the gangster.

He extended it: take it. Gills decided to belatedly show his character; he didn't take the bowl.

Artiom couldn't restrain himself and sharply struck Gills on the head with the empty bowl.

Gills grimaced from the unexpectedness; the stitches on his lips came apart and blood flowed out.

Having gotten his fill, Artiom went to his couch, lay down, watching after the gangster. He was shaking and in pain.

Finally losing his patience, Gills ran to Artiom's couch, though he was afraid to touch him and only cried out, "They'll sew you up! They'll sew you up!" On every "s", he spit blood, and — Artiom was childishly amazed — the tears from his eyes didn't flow, they sprayed. Well, well.

"Your mouth got ripped," Artiom quipped, not getting up. "Go to Doctor Ali, ask him to sew your lips back in place. Or you'll get your gills cold."

"Ah!" Gills yelled without words. "Myah!!"

"O Lord, my merciful God," whispered *Vladychka*, whom Artiom didn't see behind the headboard of the couch. "O my God, my Lord!"

Soon they took Gills away to sew him up again.

After a minute, the middle-aged nurse came in and walked straight towards Artiom. He thought that she would start yelling at him about Gills, but it turned out to be something different. She touched his forehead and immediately yelled no worse than Gills: "You have a normal temperature!

You're healthy! Why do you constantly show 39? Where are you warming up the thermometer? You know how to do that? You're a faker! You! A faker!" The words tumbled out of place and confused.

Until this moment, she had seemed to Artiom to be completely intelligent — he even thought she might be some kind of unfortunate Counter-rev. She even had a nice-sounding last name, something like Veromlinskaia, but here — it's like they switched her with someone else.

"How should I know why I'm showing 39?" Artiom wondered. "I'm not warming up the thermometer anywhere! You're warming it up yourself somewhere!" He would never have used the informal "you" with an older nurse, but she was screaming so loudly, so loudly.

"What are you doing?" *Vladychka* was almost crying, having gotten up and coming to calm down the fuss. While the middle-aged nurse berated Artiom, Doctor Ali announced himself with a slamming door. He was all disheveled and enraged. Even his beard took part in his agitation.

"People like you won't be in my infirmary!" He hissed, stopping ten steps away from Artiom's bed. "Take your things! You're going to fly out of here like a bullet!" He waved with his white sail and shoved off.

Artiom sat without moving, holding his bag in his hands.

His dumbfounded heart was loudly beating.

He tried to lead at least a single thought to its logical conclusion — within the scope of a single phrase — but could only bounce back and forth from the thermometer to Doctor Ali to the lips of the gangster and back again. He didn't understand anything at all.

Vladychka John sat down next to him.

"You're like a child, my dear," he said quickly and compassionately. "Except that here they don't put children in the corner for bad behavior, but immediately put them in the coffin! Pray yourself, and I'll pray for you day and..."

From the other side a sick man, who always lay quietly in his own place, sat down next to *Vladychka* John. He was a large man who had not shaved for a long time, with a big nose, big lips and rumpled cheeks.

"I'm an actor. My name is Shlabukovskii," he said, wiping the sweat from his face and breathing with difficulty. "But that's not the point... I heard how they just took you to task... I noticed something that you didn't pay attention to. She always gives you the thermometer after me... and she doesn't shake it first... I have a fever... many days now, a fever... And they measure your temperature, but they're actually recording mine... I only just understood this... These people — whom can they treat? This staff is only capable of burying everyone. Keep it in mind — I'm ready to confirm that your thermometer had my temperature readings…"

Artiom didn't have time to rejoice before a Red Army soldier came for him from the guard brigade. A rifle hung on his shoulder.

He loudly called Artiom's last name, incorrectly and with a wrongly stressed syllable.

Artiom's mouth dried up and his legs grew weak.

He knew for sure that they were calling him and that there was no mistake.

The soldier once again repeated the last name, making a different mistake and once more moving the accent — again to the wrong syllable.

All these mistakes sounded as though Artiom was already being turned in the meat grinder.

The soldier swore and called the last name for the third time, adding, "Whose name is, may he be bludgeoned in the throat, Artiom!"

"There he is!" said little Philip, sitting up and pointing at Artiom. "Over here!"

Artiom took his bag and, not looking at anyone, walked towards the exit.

The last thing he saw was *Vladychka* blessing his back with a freckled hand.

* * *

"Where are you taking that bag? Might as well take a blanket with a pillow," said the soldier, baring his teeth. "Take the couch too. You'll be like Ivan the Idiot on the stove."

His face was a baked potato that had popped into a smile.

"Gift of gab, that one…" was the only phrase that Artiom's consciousness was capable of retaining, but it was enough to give birth to his thought process.

He had to return to his couch.

Vladychka took the bag into his hands and said with conviction, "I'll keep it until you return."

It was raining outside. Artiom was brought into the Information and Investigation Department; he managed to get a little wet, get cold and take a breath of fresh air.

Until this moment, he had not been inside the building and he hadn't had any such aspirations.

Having walked past the duty officers, who were drinking hot water, they went up to the third floor. The soldier barked, opening a door without any inscription on it.

"I've brought the inmate from the infirmary!" And he read out the last name, pronouncing it wrong a fourth time.

Artiom even laughed — not loudly, but sincerely. They definitely didn't bring him here to be shot — that in itself was joyful.

Galina sat in the office behind a ponderous and ugly table.

Or maybe it was that she was so well put together and no-nonsense in a feminine way that the table seemed excessive and crude.

A typewriter stood on the table, large and heavy, like a tractor.

The entire room, except for the windows and the walls behind Galina, was covered with stacks. Evidently, that's where the inmates' files were kept.

She pronounced Artiom's last name without a single mistake: "Goriain-ov?"

"Yes. That's me."

"Artiom?"

"Artiom Goriainov. Yes."

Galina was fiddling through the papers on the table, but it was obvious that she remembered everything very well.

"Sit down," she said after a minute, as though she didn't remember that he was standing.

"You remember everything..." he thought and sat on a stool at the table.

The stool was shaky.

He tried, standing up a bit, to settle it a bit more firmly, but Galia said, "Sit still."

Artiom sat down, but he was forced to tense his legs — the entire time it seemed he would fall on the floor together with the stool. His temple began to ache and pain jabbed his ribs.

"It would be better to stand..." thought Artiom.

"Here's the report..." Galina read one of the papers and squinted: evidently because of the corrections and the absurdity of the writing style. "... during an inspection, we found playing cards in Goriainov's bag..."

"The cards aren't mine. I don't even know how to play. Someone planted them," Artiom said quickly.

Galina raised her eyes — they were green — and very calmly, almost without emotion, uttered, "I. Have. Not. Yet. Asked. You. Any. Thing."

Artiom was silent.

Galina scratched her forehead with her pencil so hurriedly that it seemed a fly had just been sitting there and all that was left was the tickling from the fly's feet.

Behind Galina's back, on the wall hung a pair of sparkling, clean — evidently, wiped — portraits of Trotskii and Dzerzhinskii. For some reason, Lenin wasn't there.

Trying not to attract attention, Artiom first tilted his head one way, then another — maybe the number one Bolshevik is hanging there somewhere, as yet unnoticed — anyway, he didn't have to tilt his head. Galina moved the papers slightly and Artiom saw on the table, under the glass, a portrait of Lenin from "The Fire" and next to him, a portrait of Eichmanis, cut out of a newspaper and glued onto thick paper or cardboard, so that he wouldn't be bent or become worn down.

"Where did the cards come from?" asked Galina.

"I'll explain," Artiom repeated patiently. "They weren't mine. They were planted."

"Afanasiev?" Galina quickly asked.

"Why?" asked Artiom, tottering on his stool and barely preventing himself from falling.

"Afanasiev plays cards."

"Maybe he does, but he doesn't draw them." Artiom shrugged.

"But he could have had cards?" asked Galina.

Artiom again shrugged his shoulders, but this time said nothing.

Galina assessed the gesture with a sarcastic glance. Artiom felt stupid: "I shrug my shoulders like a schoolboy…"

"Does the Indian Kurez-shah really not know how to speak Russian?" came the unexpected question.

"I don't know. He just arrived when I… found myself in the infirmary." Artiom smiled.

"Vasilii Petrovich didn't say anything about his past?"

"There was something…"

"What?"

"He used to hunt. He had a dog named Fet. He is from an educated family; his father spoke several languages…" Artiom unexpectedly realized that he really didn't know anything about Vasilii Petrovich.

"What did he do during the Civil War?" Galina asked without emotion, once again looking through the various papers on the table and touching her temple with her pencil from time to time. Seeing that, Artiom really wanted to scratch the place where yesterday there were still stitches.

"He fought," Artiom said uncertainly.

"With whom?"

Artiom remained silent in thought. Somehow, he had to answer properly and without causing offence: With you? With the Bolsheviks?

"Listen, why don't you ask him? I really don't know very much. I was just always sure that he was imprisoned as a counter-revolutionary," Artiom answered.

He was much more worried that the room unmistakably smelled of perfume. He even got a little drunk from the smell — he hadn't smelled any perfume in such a long time.

"You didn't fight?" asked Galina.

"With whom?" Artiom asked this time.

Galina, unlike him, didn't take long to answer.

"With us," she answered simply. "Or against us."

Artiom noted in his mind that "with us" and "against" could really mean one and the same thing, and there was no real choice here.

"You know that I was too young to be drafted."

"Did Afanasiev never say whether he met with the poet Sergei Yesenin on the eve of his suicide?" asked Galina.

"She's jumping from place to place," Artiom quickly thought and immediately answered, "No."

Galina carefully caught the very end of the pencil in her teeth. In one of the neighboring rooms, someone cried out abruptly in pain, as though a person had been struck and immediately lost consciousness.

Galina didn't react to the cries, not even raising her eyes, only removing the pencil, and quickly licked her lips with the tip of her tongue.

"Look here, Goriainov," she said a little louder than she had been speaking up to this point. "They found cards on you — a forbidden object. Where they came from, you don't know. That's point number one. You've deserved a week of solitary just for that… You started a fight with the brigade commander and the foreman — that's another week, up to half a year. As for attacking a member of the administration — that's the highest degree of social protection, that is, execution. That's point number two."

"I didn't attack," said Artiom, but in answer Galina raised her pencil vertically — silence, you got it?

"I could finish here, but that's not it," she continued. "Forcing a woman to cohabit — that's another month of solitary."

"Was it the monk who informed or Gills?" thought Artiom, as unpleasant sweat covered him. He thought for a moment — should he say that there was no "cohabitation", or was it not worth it? But he didn't have the chance.

"Falsifying a signature when receiving a package as a result of a deal with an inmate from among the clergy with an anti-Soviet inclination. That's another three days up to two weeks of solitary." Artiom blinked as though something unnecessary, like hay dust, were dropping on his head. "Finally, faking sickness while in the infirmary. '…The sick man Goriainov… faked a fever…'" Galia read from one of the pages.

"Why should I fake it if I'm 'the sick man Goriainov'?" You can see for yourself what nonsense they write!" Artiom answered quickly, with a certain mocking rudeness that even surprised him. "There's that nurse. She's not trained; the devil knows what she…"

"Shut up," Galina suddenly said simply. Artiom's heart dropped at her voice. Her lips, which just a moment ago seemed beautiful and arousing, immediately appeared thin, angry and old-womanly. "You could be executed immediately. Or you could be put in solitary until the end of your term."

"So that I can die there? Before the end of my term? I can explain every single one of these accusations." Artiom wouldn't back down. His head was spinning; he understood that he had to hurry with all his strength, to hurry terribly.

"Shut up," Galina repeated, but only more loudly and angrily.

Artiom shut his mouth with the word halfway out, as though he had caught a fly in his mouth. He sat with that fly in his mouth; he wanted unbearably to open his mouth and utter another hundred words, even a thousand of the most necessary words. They were all itching and bouncing around in his mouth.

For three minutes, they remained silent.

"That's it," Artiom repeated to himself. "This is the end… that bravado that they were telling me about… This is definitely the end. Or maybe I should say something? No, this is the end. Why am I not falling unconscious from fear? This is the end, after all…"

"Are you scared?" Galina asked. In the corner of her ugly, old-womanly lips, a smile flickered.

Artiom swallowed his saliva and didn't say anything.

In the corner of her office, behind her back, stood a chest instead of a safe, locked with a padlock. That was probably where the most important documents were kept.

"Or maybe that's where she keeps her panties?" thought Artiom in a frenzy.

"There is another way out," said Galina. "Because you are a young man, and there's a chain of accidental occurrences that could have brought you here."

"I'm not much younger than you, bitch," thought Artiom and immediately, without a break, thought, "You lovely, dear, most lovely, dearest woman, don't kill me. I will kiss your feet, please!"

"I believe you can start down the path of reeducation." Galina clearly spoke with words that were unfamiliar to her, but there were no other words for this situation. "You can be released at the end of your term — or even earlier — as a normal, good, proper Soviet man. But you have to prepare yourself, so that no other such situations repeat themselves, yes?"

"Of course," said Artiom.

He was breathing through his mouth. His tongue was dry. He felt his dry tongue and his dry, cold palate.

"To prevent any cards from being planted on you, we have to know who could have planted them in the first place, is that not so?"

"Exactly so," answered Artiom, understanding where this was going.

"We must prevent people faking sickness. To prevent inmates coupling like dogs. To prevent people, who came here because of crimes against the Soviet government, from compounding those crimes. Better to prevent all that in advance, instead of going the way of solitary or the highest degree of social protection. Yes?"

"Yes," Artiom repeated, feverishly thinking what he should do after this listing was finished.

"You and I will sign a paper attesting that you will help me — me, personally! — in all difficult situations. And there are many! Because the foremen, brigade commanders and duty officers, especially those taken from among the inmates, often understand their responsibilities improperly and, as they take care of the work and discipline, they often angrily destroy that same discipline. Because the counter-revolutionaries, to whom the Soviet government has given the chance to correct their mistakes, only make them worse by anti-Soviet speeches, which, as in the Civil War, can then become actions. Because thieves and murderers — all those gangsters! — heartlessly take advantage of their social closeness to the working class, turning them into rampant asocial elements, jointly responsible for drunkenness and gambling. You don't want to live in the midst of all this, do you…? How much time do you have left here on Solovki?"

"More than two and a half years," answered Artiom.

"So think of how you could survive them," said Galina. "In solitary? Or… to leave with a well-deserved amnesty, having only been here for half your time? Who do you have at home? A mother? A bride?"

"Mother."

"Your Mommy is waiting for you… Why doesn't she write letters to you?"

Artiom hesitated.

"It just turned out that way. She sends me packages. Just sent me one, actually," answered Artiom, immediately remembering that Galina knew about the package and even how Artiom received it.

"Oh," Galina said somehow very domestically, seeing yet another paper on the table. "There's still that fight in the infirmary. You beat up Aleksei Yahnov."

"Who?" Artiom wondered aloud. "Is that Gills?"

"What gills?" asked Galina, without, it must be said, any interest. She was already extending to Artiom some kind of important paper with typed-out letters. "Here's that form. All you have to do is sign it."

"Listen." Artiom even unconsciously tried to move the stool back, but again almost fell. "I still have nothing…" he stood up a bit and tried to settle the stool firmly. "Absolutely nothing to tell you about any delinquencies. But I agree with everything, with every one of your words. This is important work!"

"So sign then," said Galina, still holding the paper in the balance. She even stood up so that it would be easier for Artiom to take it. With her left hand, she fixed her skirt in the back.

Artiom, against his will, glanced over her figure. She was fine… that skirt… and that, damn it! That perfume… Her stomach — what does it smell like? If it's exposed?

"Why don't we do it this way?" asked Artiom, smiling, putting in all his energy, all his essence, his gentleness, everything human, noble, heart-felt into that request. "I'll go, I'll think about everything and then I'll definitely be useful to you. I'll help you. And you can summon me then, even tomorrow, if you want… or the day after, and I'll come then…" *How do I say it? With a report? How vile! With my tale? Why not with a novel? With poems?* "And I'll come and tell you… something important. So that you can see that I'm capable of this kind of work. That I'm necessary. And then, I'll sign it immediately. But now… I've done nothing yet, but already I'm signing? What if I'm not capable of doing anything?"

"You will, I can see that, Artiom," she called him by his first name for the first time. It sounded so naked, so sharp, so pleasant, as though she had exposed a little bit of her bare midriff to him… Or she had seen a bit of his naked body and called that body by name…

"No, I implore you," Artiom didn't know how to address her properly. "Please. And I promise. What if I sign right now, and then I'm not useful at all. During our next meeting…"

"Meeting…" Galina quietly mocked him, sitting down in her place.

She remained silent for another minute, clearly annoyed.

"Well, I hope so," said Galina with slight hostility. "Then take your things and go back to the brigade. You're healthy, aren't you?"

"Healthy," Artiom confirmed, though he thought with conviction: "I'm horribly sick. I'm going to die soon."

Galina once again touched her temple with her pencil.

Her temple was pale and slightly concave. A dark lock fell on her pencil.

"So they weren't your cards?" asked Galina.

"Of course not. I told you, I don't even know how to play cards."

"What do you know how to do?" Galina was speaking absently, thinking of something else.

"I don't know…" Artiom looked at the lock, and, surprising himself, he made the stupidest joke that could possibly have come into his head at such a moment. "I know how to kiss."

Galina removed the pencil from her temple. As though it was preventing her from lifting her surprised eyes.

She looked Artiom over sarcastically. The swelling on half his face, where he had been stitched up had not yet come down… His nose was puffy, his forehead sweaty, his lips dry… Eyes staring forward with an expression of simultaneously mixed rudeness and slight fear…

She made a quick gesture with her pencil: get out of here, you idiot.

* * *

On the upholstered, trampled threshold of the Information and Investigation Department, made from two wooden blocks, Artiom stood for a bit, looking for his soldier.

Having thought about it, he decided to come back. He couldn't afford another infraction.

"What would they call it?" thought Artiom tiredly. "Fleeing from his guards?"

He was stopped at the post downstairs: “Who are you looking for?”

The Red Army soldier who had brought him was sitting there, chatting with the commander of the post.

“Him,” Artiom pointed.

“What do you want?” asked the soldier.

“They’re letting me go back to the infirmary,” said Artiom.

“So what’s that got to do with me? Should I carry you?” asked the soldier, ribbing his comrade: look at that weirdo!

They both guffawed, showing dark mouths with black teeth.

“Need a compass?” the guard cried out in his wake, and they guffawed again.

“He’s a sailor,” thought Artiom indifferently, as though slightly frozen.

Outside shone an evening sun, piercing through the clouds with its rays. The rays gently slipped about the kremlin walls and everything in the air seemed sweetened.

On the way to the infirmary, Artiom thought about everything at once, avoiding thinking about the most important thing, but that attempt was pointless.

“… The sun shines so…” he remembered and ridiculed Afanasiev, “Only on sleds can you ride such a sunset…”

“… He’s afraid that I’ll turn him in…” he laughed at Afanasiev without a smile. “Gave me three rubles! Cunning red-headed bastard…”

But he still couldn’t be mad at the Leningrad poet.

He remembered about *Vladychka* John with his bag, in which his package lay, and he thought, “… I’m going to eat everything right now… Even though I may choke on it, I’ll eat it. In any case, I have to go back to the brigade… Maybe they’ll let me stay the night in the infirmary? Should I beg Doctor Ali? No, that won’t work…”

Then he thought, “How can people come to love God if He alone knows all about your villainy, your thievery, your sins? Don’t we hate everyone who knows bad things about us? I hate that bitch Galina. She knows that she can put pressure on me. She did put pressure on me! What am I going to do now?”

Then he thought, a little confusedly, about Burtsev, Passport, even about Gills. Then, remembering how pitiful Gills had become, how stupid with his stitched-up fish-face, he laughed aloud.

But his own laughter made him sick — that unnecessary and now-impossible smile on his face forced him to return to that which needed to be understood: “They’re going to make me an informant. Or they’ll kill me in the brigade. How am I going to get out of this? How? Maybe everything will work out again?"

But to himself, he answered, "Tonight, the gangsters will cut you into little pieces. Yep, it'll all work out…"

His weak human judgment offered him a solution: go back to Galina, sign everything and ask to be immediately moved into a different brigade.

With one half of his mind, Artiom tried to convince himself that it was shameful, that he would not do that, because he's not a snitch and because he doesn't want to be beholden to anyone, especially that creature… But at the same time, he understood that he wasn't going back to the IID for a completely different reason.

And he spoke the reason out loud for his own benefit: "She's not going to transfer you anywhere, you idiot! Who are you going to inform on in a brigade where you don't know anyone? And what reason does she have to move you? Because you're a coward? They have nothing better to do than transfer all the chickens from one place to another…?"

"What do you mean, coward?" Artiom violently argued with himself. "They're going to kill me today or tomorrow! They'll knife me! How am I supposed to take that? With an open damned heart? What? Am I a bull for the slaughter?"

Tortured by this two-faced conversation, he fell on his couch in the infirmary.

After a minute, *Vladychka* John brought his bag with the package. It was clearly hard for him — his knee was bothering him — so he sat down next to Artiom.

"Thank you, *Vladychka*," said Artiom, taking the bag.

Generally, he should have sat up on the couch — it wasn't good to be lying down next to a priest — but he had no energy left. He moved his hand a little and changed his mind.

"Stay down, don't worry," said *Vladychka* John. "You'll need your strength yet…"

They were silent a while.

No sooner did Artiom want to hear his voice than *Vladychka* started talking, as though he could, for the umpteenth time, read his thoughts.

"You keep seeking, my dear, for truth or honor. But truth and honor are here." *Vladychka* pointed at the Gospel. "Take it as a gift. You need it, I can see. As soon as you understand with your whole soul that the Kingdom of God is within you, it'll be much easier for you."

"No," said Artiom firmly. "I don't need it."

"Oh, you're wrong, my dear," said *Vladychka*, hiding the Gospel. "Well, in that case, God give you… God help you overcome it all."

Vladychka didn't even have time to leave when the middle-aged nurse and the monk entered. "Follow me," understood Artiom.

"I'm coming, I'm coming," he said loudly from his place, because the nurse had already opened her mouth to yell at him.

He had nothing to gather. His bag of things was still unopened, and all he had done was take out his spoon and bowl.

Vladychka John had tied his bag with food into a bundle.

Philip lay there with closed eyes, his sawed-off leg lying exposed on the bed. Lazhechnikov looked at Artiom, but it was as though he didn't quite recognize him. Artiom turned towards him on the way out, untying the package as he walked. He took some sugar and poured a full bowl for the Cossack.

"You?" asked Lazhechnikov barely audibly. It sounded like the word was lying on his tongue, and he had pushed it out.

Artiom didn't answer.

Gills hid under the covers. Artiom wanted to expose him, to pull off the covers as a parting shot, but he got lazy. It didn't help that the middle-aged nurse was stomping her feet, as though she were standing on a hot floor.

"Do you have anything else?" asked Father Zinovii, having noticed how he gave Lazhechnikov some sugar.

Artiom looked into his bag and pulled out the unfinished horsemeat sausage. He put it in the priest's hand.

"What about some sugar?" He asked Artiom's back. "A little bit of sugar too?"

They stopped Artiom at the infirmary's post. It seemed they were looking for his record card, then Doctor Ali as well, so he could sign it. They did everything hurriedly, just so they could throw him out as soon as possible.

Vladychka John, despite his painful limp, came out to say goodbye and whispered quickly, lest someone see them: "Here's what I think. You didn't sin today, and Rus survived."

It's as though he could guess what happened in the IID, and this made Artiom even more sick at heart and irritable.

"Everyone sins here," Artiom answered quickly. For some reason, he felt as though he were in the train station and it was time for him to depart, and now all words were excessive, but for some reason he uttered them. "They sin one hundred times worse than we do."

"You don't have to answer for them, but you do have to answer for Rus!" *Vladychka* John answered quickly. "They sin, but you must balance them out. A righteous deed weighs more than a sin!"

"No!" Artiom answered, containing his anger with difficulty. "You sin and you still get saved. But righteousness doesn't raise you even a foot above ground. It only pulls you under."

"God sees truth, but He doesn't speak it quickly." *Vladychka,* helpless, was already not speaking, but begging.

"He should go to the IID and tell them everything," answered Artiom with a smile that felt fake on his face — even his jaws recoiled from it.

"God send his angel to help you, my dear," said *Vladychka*, when the monk opened the door: get out of here.

"Wherever it's easy, there are hundreds of angels, but where it's hard, there are none at all." Artiom offered his final, insolent shot. He said it loudly, but not turning around. He didn't want to see *Vladychka* anymore.

Artiom was all business as he walked to the brigade, as though he were going to fish. He ladled out the sugar from his bag and ate it from his hand. After a minute, his hand grew sweet, sticky and rough. The flies few around his face and kept flying into his cheek or his forehead from greed and amazement. Artiom waved them away, then rubbed himself with a sugary hand.

"Answer for Rus!" he mocked the absent *Vladychka* aloud, crunching the sugar between his teeth. "Well, tomorrow, they'll summon me to Galenka,[34] and I will answer for all of Rus. I'll tell all for the sake of that Rus."

And he chortled. The sugar flew out of his mouth in all directions.

A Chekist, walking by from the direction of the sauna, dressed in a sealskin coat on top of his naked body, not noticing the cold, looked over, upset at the laughter, but Artiom couldn't care less.

"Your Gospel," Artiom continued, "couldn't even make peace between *Vladychka* John and the beggar Zinovii, or both of them with the monk. How can it make peace between me and anyone else?"

He met Bear, the deer, who also reached for the sugar.

"Will I survive the night, or not?" he thought, sitting down on the bare earth and offering the deer first his face, then his hands. The deer licked him, blinking often and hurrying.

Above them, hysterically screeching, the gulls thrashed about.

In the entrance room for the duty officers, the Chechens smiled at Artiom as though they had long waited for him.

---

34 A diminutive of "Galina."

"Hey there, brother!" said Khasaev and even slapped him on the back. "Why aren't you in solitary?"

Artiom mentally snorted, didn't answer and firmly walked into his stinky twelfth stable, dog kennel, pigsty, meat grinder.

* * *

No sooner had Artiom entered the sleeping quarters than Moisei Solomonovich started to sing.

The song was unfamiliar and sad: "He was in a leather jacket, thirty wounds in his chest..."

Artiom wasn't expecting to see Passport, but immediately locked gazes with him. He smiled, looking, with even a bit of gentleness, at the bag in Artiom's hands.

Artiom, pushing the inmates aside and not answering the greetings of those who greeted him, rushed to his bunk.

Vasilii Petrovich got up to meet him and was just about to hug him, it seems, but Artiom muttered something incomprehensible, climbed up and when he was already there, he began to do that which he planned to do.

"Mitya," he called Schelkachov. "Don't listen to me. Live by your own mind... Better yet, have some food."

He pulled out two dried fish with missing eyes from his bag.

"What about you? What about you?" asked Schelkachov.

"They're moving me to a different brigade with a higher allowance. Triple rations! Moisei Solomonovich, come here, come here. Stop singing for a second.

He didn't force them to wait long.

"You sing well, Solomonovich. You don't ruin the songs. Can you sing me this one, do you know it? 'I don't walk on plush, not on velvet, but I walk, I walk on the edge of a knife...' I used to have velveteen pants and though it wasn't velvet, I did have a silk shirt. And my father, through a special board with cutouts, used to polish the buttons of my school uniform. Can you imagine? I used to have a father. Will you sing?"

"Not on plush?" Moisei Solomonovich asked with pleasure, nodding and smiling. "Yes, yes." But he didn't start singing, instead carrying away the hermetically sealed tin can of sunflower oil, in case they all changed their minds.

"Afanasiev! You red-headed bastard!" Artiom was happy when the sleeping redhead poet dangled from the third level with his amazing forelock.

"I've got a surprise for you! What do we have in this canister? Candies! To chew! For you!"

Kurez-shah and Kabir-shah received the remainder of the sugar in a separate baggie and bowed and smiled at him for a long time. Avdei Sivtsev got the last piece of sausage.

"May your horse wait for you, Sivtsev," Artiom said.

The journalist Grakov, standing silently to wait his turn, was found worthy of a pack of dried crackers.

"Oh, you're here too, Samovar?" Artiom was surprised. "Take some of this mixed flour and don't give it to the general. They feed him well enough now."

"What general?" asked Samovar, accepting the gifts with dignity.

"Field-Marshall," Artiom apologized. "Field-Marshall Burtsev."

Samovar vividly got offended with his entire supraciliary arch, but he didn't give back the flour.

"Eat, my dears, I'm going to rat all of you out, together with the offal. If I live that long."

They did truly start to eat immediately. It would have been strange to hoard that which was gifted.

"Vasilii Petrovich," Artiom jumped down lightly. "Look, look at how much tea I've brought you! You'll have enough until winter for sure… And nuts. Where's our rabbit flesh? Where's our yellow-faced Chinese man? I've got rice for him too."

"The Chinese man? Our duty officer Mstislav Burtsev transferred him into solitary," answered Vasilii Petrovich, looking at Artiom more with sorrow than with curiosity.

"Well now," answered Artiom with the same tone as if someone had told him an interesting bit of social news. "Vasilii Petrovich, I would have given you the entire package, but our gangsters would have killed you for it," said Artiom in a whistling whisper.

Vasilii Petrovich grimaced. It seemed he felt sick from this situation in which Artiom was forced to play the buffoon. He couldn't stop him, but he couldn't bear it either.

At least, that's what Artiom thought, but he couldn't stop now.

When Passport arrived, having delayed while looking for his buddies, the bag was empty.

"I was preparing a half for you, but more's the pity! They took it all," Artiom told him. "At least take the bag. Maybe you can sew yourself a dress from it."

Passport looked at him silently, his jaw muscles rippling. His lower lip hung down thoughtfully at the same time, barely moving.

They announced the evening inspection and the loud and drunk voice of Curly was heard. Burtsev walked through the ranks. He had a stiletto in his hand. He was swinging it.

"Zagib Ivanovich will come to you at night," said Passport. "Are you going to wait up? Or maybe you'll just hang yourself right now."

"Why hang myself?" Artiom asked. "I'll wait."

Afanasiev sat on his bunk and watched all of it without saying a word.

"Zagib Ivanovich" is what they called death around here.

* * *

Death didn't come for Artiom. Passport and Shaferbekov were sent out to do night work. Krapin hadn't lied… The other gangsters from their corner looked over at Artiom several times.

He waited for them a long time — it seemed like he waited until dawn. He was afraid, clenching his jaws, imagined how he would scream if they approached… or would start jumping from bunk to bunk, stomping on everyone and ducking under other people's blankets…

… He squished the bedbugs, and every time, he thought: they're going to do you like this bedbug, just like this bedbug…

… Sometimes he fell asleep, and in his head, something fell, shrieked and the gulls screamed right above his head.

From every cough or creak of a bunk he would jump awake, all covered in sweat. But no one stood next to him, there were no gulls, only the snoring and the grinding of teeth.

"I should get myself a goose," thought Artiom. His thoughts were slow, as though he were walking through mud and every thought, like his foot, needed to be pulled out of viscous slush. "Get myself a goose… Tie him on a string… They'll come to kill me and the goose will honk, beat his wings… everyone will wake up."

Before morning, Khasaev began to rumble with the vat in the anteroom for the duty officers, and to Artiom's mind, raw from horror and tiredness, it seemed calming. Well, since they're making that racket, what can happen now? Nothing… Do the duty officers really want to deal with murder? Not at all…

Except now he fell deeply asleep and he had a dream that he was in the IID again and had signed everything.

And it was so light on his soul, so pleasant…

During the morning inspection, Artiom stood as though plague-stricken. Sounds were twisted in his head, coming to him from a distance, seemingly underwater. The people were walking around murkily. There was no air outside, only inside. Any moment now the fish of Solovki would float by between his legs.

The fish did, in fact, appear.

Before the line-up, they brought out a thief who had stolen herring from the kitchen. It was probably Curly who had thought of the punishment, though Sorokin administered it. They beat the delinquent across the face with the herring. He didn't try to break free, endured it, and only closed his eyes. After the third strike, his cheek started to bleed.

Artiom thought, distantly and without compassion, "Well, if they offered me, instead of being knifed, to be beaten with a herring for the next two and a half years, I would have agreed. What's the big deal? Beaten with a herring."

"Will they throw out the herring or put it in the soup later?" asked someone nearby.

At the line-up, an unknown, fit, young man in glasses appeared. During the punishment, he looked to the side, sometimes touching his glasses. Clearly, all of it didn't appeal to him.

After the traditional idiotic swearing session from Curly, they gave the unknown man the floor.

"My name is Boris Lukianovich," he said drily and not very loudly, though in a bass voice. "I am preparing the camp's Spartakiade, which will be dedicated to this year's anniversary of the October revolution. I'm interested in anyone who was seriously into sport — running, jumping, swimming, boxing, lifting and football."

"Is running across the border acceptable?" asked someone. Everyone laughed.

"What about swimming for logs?" They laughed even more cheerfully.

"What about counting mosquitos? Is that a sport or a private entertainment?"

Everyone thought it was very funny.

"Here it is!" Artiom understood. He stepped out of the line-up.

"Me!"

"Get back in line!" Burtsev hissed.

Artiom didn't move. They might not notice him, but it was necessary, absolutely necessary that they notice him, call him, save him.

Call me quickly, you, in the glasses! I will jump for you in all directions! With a ball on my head and with a kettlebell on my foot! Come on!"

Boris Lukianovich whispered something to Curly.

"Get over here!" Curly poked Artiom with a thick and curling finger. "But if you've lied!" Then, turning to everyone, he added, "All impostors will get three days in solitary!"

Boris Lukianovich furrowed his brow. Talking about solitary also seemed inappropriate to him.

Now Artiom looked at the line-up, thinking that he had never seen the brigade from this point of view.

"It's nice to stand like this..." he thought, surprised. He immediately liked the feeling of being in charge.

Afanasiev was smiling and winked at Artiom.

"So it's like that, Afanas? Well, tricksters and card-sharks aren't allowed here," Artiom thought with sarcastic vengefulness.

He saw Schelkachov and added, "Nor do they take chess players, Mitya!"

Grakov the journalist was stomping in place, apparently trying to remember some kind of sport that he had taken part in at some point, but for some strange reason, he forgot about it. Boxing? No, definitely not. Lifting? Clearly not. Swimming? Probably not. Football? He'd never even seen what that looks like. Maybe jumping? But what sort of jumping was it? How was it done?

Moisei Solomonovich was suffering similar doubts. He had already tried to break into the actors' brigade and they seemed to have been ready to move him there but were still considering it. Now he was thinking — to swim or not to swim. Anyway, do they even swim at Spartakiades? Plus, it's the anniversary of October. You'll hardly swim far in October.

Sivtsev stood downcast and detached, as though he didn't understand what was going on. He didn't even laugh when the clowns bellowed about running away and logs.

Only three volunteered. Evidently, Curly's threats worked.

Immediately after the line-up, they went with Boris Lukianovich to examine their sports acumen.

Artiom wasn't worried; instead, he felt a completely inappropriate apathy. For some reason, he was sure they would take him. He breathed through his nose, smeared the mosquitoes across his face and walked, staring at his feet.

Artiom did some boxing when he was just a kid — around three months' worth. In general, he was good at it, but then the war started for real... a lot of things started then.

Having absolutely no inclination towards violence or towards the putting down of the feeble and shy, Artiom was still the strongest in his school year, the best at the parallel bars and the pull-up bar and sometimes even flaunted his natural strength and ability to dexterously punch people in the teeth, knocking them off their feet.

At the same time, he was never able to really get mad.

After school, he had much fewer occasions to fight.

Once, when he was about nineteen, two slightly older men tried to rob him by taking off his coat. Artiom weighed his options and wisely chose to run. He at first ran well, but the coat kept getting tangled in his legs and slowing him down. Suddenly, he turned around and hit the first with such strength that it seemed that he popped open a cheek.

That really wasn't supposed to happen, but Artiom saw it so obviously and so clearly, that he actually scared himself and ran twice as fast as a result.

He also fought once when he worked as a stevedore. There was a man, also a stevedore, who was twice his size and he would have beaten Artiom down, if he hadn't been extremely drunk and therefore careless in his swing. Artiom bloodied his fist when hitting him, but, pushing his breathing and himself beyond his normal endurance, he did beat him… It's true, he didn't work there any more afterward. He had already decided to drop that line of work and here he'd have to deal with that hulk again. Though compared with everything that was going on around Artiom now, that fight seemed comical.

In general, his credentials didn't look too convincing, but that didn't stop Artiom from feeling confident.

The only problem was that he hadn't slept. And that scar on his temple. What if someone were to smack him there and it would come apart again? Would they take him into the infirmary anymore? Probably not. He would have to walk around with his brains on the outside until they all poured out.

"Who am I going to fight?" thought Artiom. "Not that guy in the glasses? Will he take off his glasses? It would be good if he couldn't see anything at all without them."

They had decided to build the sports center beyond the monastery. Next to the new, long, still roofless barn; you could see a field that looked decent enough for football. A little farther off, they had put up a bar — that was it.

The builders were at work — inmates, obviously — two below, handing the boards up to the two who were above. The foreman had brought hay from somewhere and was now lying inside the barn and watching. He had a billiard-cue in his hand that had been broken in the middle.

"This is where we'll be…" said Boris Lukianovich, looking around near-sightedly. He was carrying a folder, but there was nowhere to put it.

He crouched down and wrote onto a bulletin that had been grabbed with dirty fingers, all the names of those brought from the twelfth brigade. Artiom looked at the page — there were around thirty or so names written down already.

"Who's going to start?" asked Boris Lukianovich and immediately decided for himself, nodding at Artiom. "How about you? Tell me, you say you did boxing? How seriously…? Well, we'll see right now… You'll probably have to take your jacket off, yes? We don't have any boxing gloves, but I found these wonderful mittens… try them on. Good? On top of these mittens, we'll adapt these gloves! Since we don't have any sports inventory, we'll use the workers', ha-ha."

"What an intelligent man! Will he really start beating me on the face right now?" Artiom thought, gently mocking. "But since it's the workers' inventory, I wish he'd give me the haft of a shovel, I'd get a great head start…"

The only thing that Artiom seriously didn't like was the annoying attention of the builders, who had stopped working and were joking about something.

"What, are you guys having down time?" Artiom asked the foreman. When he didn't sleep enough, he often acted as though he were drunk.

"Mind your business. They've got a smoke break." The foreman answered, clearly peeved.

"Pay no attention," said Boris Lukianovich quietly. He was generally quite amicable and pleasant, but you could hear his weighty sense of self-worth behind every word. Artiom respected such people.

"Right here?" Artiom asked when Boris Lukianovich, also putting on the mittens, then the workers' gloves, carefully took off his glasses with those paws and passed them to an inmate from the twelfth who was standing nearby and who had claimed to be a runner and jumper.

"We can go outside," said Boris Lukianovich, his joints cracking as he warmed up.

The cracking was impressive.

"If he's cracking like that," Artiom thought coldly, "I can imagine what sort of a cracking you're going to hear from my bones right now."

For the sake of appearances, he hopped on one leg, then the other, but immediately realized that he was too unsteady on his feet and began to warm up his neck and head, as though trying to twist it on or off.

"I should have said I'm a runner," he thought finally. "At least they wouldn't have hit me on the head for it."

Boris Lukianovich led the fight slowly and carefully, only marking out the hits. After half a minute, Artiom calmed down and after a full minute, he thought with some irritation about his opponent: "He's so confident in himself, as though he couldn't even imagine that I could beat him down…"

Unexpectedly for himself, Artiom went on the offensive, was met with a jab to the head, but didn't retreat, and, getting closer with a persistent jerk, attacked with a combination of hits.

Boris Lukianovich didn't budge; on the contrary, he nodded with a pleased smile: keep going, keep going, not bad at all.

"You're too agitated," said Boris Lukianovich, once again taking a defensive posture and giving Artiom the chance to work himself.

The inmates who were working on the roof crawled closer so they could see the duel better.

Understanding that he had little energy left, Artiom began to attack Boris Lukianovich more openly, but his opponent moved smoothly, holding his hands high, at his face, glancing out invitingly through the opening between his two strong hands.

"How can I get at you…" repeated Artiom, "how can I get at you... how… can I…"

Then all the air in Artiom's chest disappeared and there was a huge, hot cloud that filled up all his insides at once. Artiom looked around with eyes full of tears and, opening his mouth, torturously waited for the moment when he could breathe again.

He had missed a single, very short and completely invisible blow to the solar plexus.

Two inmates who were watching the fight were now laughing, while Boris Lukianovich had disappeared somewhere completely.

"Are they laughing at me?" thought Artiom with slow and humid sorrow. "Am I really that comical?"

He found the strength in himself to twist around and look at those who were laughing. No, they weren't laughing at him, glory to… At the exact moment that Artiom missed the jab, an inmate who had been sitting on the edge of the wall had lost his balance and fallen down right on the foreman.

Boris Lukianovich immediately ran to them, afraid that the foreman had been crushed… but it all turned out alright.

In a strange way, together with his breath, Artiom's hearing returned as well — the foreman was swearing terribly — and for some reason his sense of smell also. It smelled of freshly sawed wood, which he hadn't noticed before. And his brain clicked on as well — he suddenly understood that Boris Lukianovich, having been distracted by the inmate's fall, didn't notice in what a pitiful state Artiom was, almost killed through the chest.

"What do you have on your temple?" asked Boris Lukianovich, when he returned. His breathing wasn't labored in the least. "A scar? Recent? Well, that's alright, it'll get better in a month and a half. I tried not to hit you there."

"You didn't try to hit at all," Artiom thought gratefully.

Boris Lukianovich threw off the gloves, took off his mittens, then waved at the other candidates — your turn.

"What about me?" asked Artiom, hurriedly taking off the mittens and still not finding enough air to breathe. "What about me…? Can I stay with you for a bit?"

"What do you mean 'for a bit'? We're taking you on," said Boris Lukianovich, going outside. "We'll have to train a bit, of course," he added, looking around. "You've got some natural talent, but as for professional technique — a little less."

"'A little less' meant 'not at all,'" Artiom figured out, but in spite of that knowledge, in a single instant, he became so happy that he desperately wanted to play some stupid trick on someone.

The foreman kept swearing and even wanted to fight, but the fallen inmate had run away and climbed up the wall again for safety, waiting for it to blow over.

Artiom was just about to hurry after everyone to watch the runner or jumper, but then remembered what a joy he had laid up for himself. As though he had known!

When he had given away all his gifts, he couldn't give away the baggie with the pig lard, the mustard and the lemon. No matter what his state after returning from the infirmary, no matter how much he was preparing to die, he couldn't part with those. He hid them in his jacket.

Now he sat next to the walls of the barn, spit out a single, long line of spittle, then spit again… Looking up at the sun, he began to bite the lard, angrily ripping at the rough filaments. He followed it up with the lemon. The mustard had crumbled in his pocket, and Artiom occasionally dug into it with his fingers then licked off all that bitterness, then once again pressed the lemon juice into his mouth and ripped the lard with his teeth.

All this time, he looked up at the sky, squinting…

It was like he was squeezing the sun into his mouth — sour, fatty, bitter.

* * *

"You're going to live in a monastic cell," said Boris Lukianovich. "Come to the trainings yourself, without a foreman. There are no foremen for this. Then the workouts, then…"

"What about today?"

"What?"

"The cell…"

"When else?"

Artiom didn't even go into the twelfth to get his things. He decided he could wait until Vasilii Petrovich got back from his berry brigade, then he'd ask him to bring them.

He couldn't scare off what was happening to him.

For the first half hour, Artiom didn't even walk away from Boris Lukianovich — it was like he had become the pledge of his miraculous good fortune. Especially since the other two from the twelfth were sent back to the brigade: "You'll get called as soon as you're needed," he said, and those idiots seemed to actually believe him. Still, Artiom understood it all and realized that he was feeling a quiet and self-satisfied malice: but they picked me! They picked me!

While Boris Lukianovich looked over the barn and counted, for a long time, through the names he had written down, biting his lip, Artiom hung on the pull-up bar, though he had absolutely no desire to work out.

"I'm acting as if I'm fourteen years old and trying to attract a girl's attention," Artiom thought, waiting for the moment when Boris Lukianovich would appear in the doorway, so that he could mount the bar with a proper swing at the moment he came out. He had once been able to do that trick.

But his wrists soon started to ache, and just hanging there proved impossible. He had to mount the bar without waiting for the attention of the sports administration.

"But he's just the same kind of inmate as I am, thought Artiom, jumping down from the bar. "Interesting. How did they entrust him with all this…?"

His hands smelled of metal, pig fat and mustard.

While Artiom licked himself like a cat — his cheeks pleasantly and sweetly burning from the lemon and the pig lard — he almost missed Boris Lukianovich, who walked off on his own business.

Despite all his human attractiveness, Boris Lukianovich, it seems, was not very convivial and after about three minutes, he threw Artiom, who was hurrying behind him, a quick and thoughtful glance.

"He might think that I'm a snitch and send me back to the brigade," thought Artiom with a revolting, oppressive fear that he didn't even experience from Passport or Shaferbekov's threats.

But what could he do?

They stopped at the entrance to the Cathedral of the Trinity, where Artiom's familiar thirteenth brigade was situated. Boris Lukianovich had apparently come here to find some more fortunate ones. It was almost time for lunch.

"You can eat in your brigade, then later go set yourself up in your new rooms," said Boris Lukianovich strictly.

"But will they let me in?"

"Damn, you're right," answered Boris Lukianovich and smiled so sweetly that Artiom, if he'd beckoned to him, would have jumped to embrace four-eyes' neck, as though he were a long-lost older brother.

"I should have left the lemon and given it to him! Idiot!" Artiom cursed himself.

Boris Lukianovich, having asked for Artiom's last name, wrote down the dictated details onto a paper that had already been signed by the careless administration. Then he gave it to Artiom. It said something like, "To this so-and-so give the order to direct… and to make provision to the aforementioned…"

"It will be done!" Artiom said loudly, taking the paper, though no one had commanded him to do anything.

"Why don't you go eat something?" Boris Lukianovich called in his wake. "And I think you can sleep in tomorrow." At these words, Artiom turned around. "I have a lot of work! I have to find athletes somewhere!"

The monastic cell that Artiom got was found in the former abbot's wing on the second floor. It was an austere, white building with tall windows. For some reason, it reminded Artiom of his school.

The duty officer at his post carefully explained where he needed to go.

When Artiom opened the door to his cell, he saw a person. He was lying on a wooden, crudely jury-rigged bed with no sheets, having put a bag of things under his head. His external appearance made it very clear that he could never take part in any competitions. The best one could say was that he had played ball in childhood with his cousins, but even that was doubtful.

Hesitating a bit, the man sat up and gazed at Artiom — more with irritation than with fear.

He had huge, unseasonably warm shoes on his feet, as though he had only now come from the street… But his face was well-slept, and his hair was rumpled.

"Who are you?" he asked in an unfriendly tone.

"They've determined that I'm to live here," said Artiom as he looked over the cell, which was exactly the same as Mezernitskii's. At the same moment, he noticed that his companion had a half-eaten, unpeeled carrot in his hand.

"That bed is reserved for my mother," he noted very severely, and even extended his hand, as though indicating that even sitting on the second one, which was also wooden and without any sheets, was forbidden. Only at that moment did the man notice that he was holding a carrot and he tried to put it on the wooden table next to the bed, which he managed with some difficulty, since the carrot had stuck to his palm. Evidently, having come to eat, the man had fallen asleep without managing to finish the carrot.

"So that's how it is," thought Artiom, looking at the carrot and trying to understand what mother he was talking about. However, his confusion was almost cheerful; obviously, there was some kind of nonsense going on here that should definitely be resolved happily.

"So where is your mother?" asked Artiom.

"She hasn't arrived yet," the man answered importantly, brushing his rumpled mane with five dirty and post-carrot-sticky fingers. This only made his hair stick out more in all directions.

"Maybe I stay here until she arrives?" Artiom asked with a smile.

"No," answered the rumpled man. "I know how it can be. At first you just take her place, but then there will be nowhere for Mummy to live."

"But I have a document," said Artiom. "And I will sit down for a bit after all. We won't tell your mother anything about how I sat down on her bed."

When Artiom sat down, the rumpled man immediately got up and his face was so angry as though he was planning on immediately throwing out his guest, which of course seemed comical when combined with his concave ribcage and his long arms, which were little more than thin bones.

"Well, look," said Artiom, smiling and extending the document.

He took it in his hands.

"Your name is Artiom?" He asked. "Goriainov?"

"Yes. And you?"

"We are called Osip," answered the rumpled man in extreme disapproval and, waving about the paper, firmly announced, "This is a mistake! You must immediately go and figure it out. To tell them that this announcement has no validity in reality!"

"Why don't you … give me that aforementioned document?" Artiom asked gently, because Osip was waving his arms around a little too widely. "I will definitely find out what happened, just let me rest for a bit please."

"You will take care of it? You promise?" asked Osip, with that strictness that adults assume when speaking with a child.

"When will your mother come?" asked Artiom.

"Soon," answered Osip and quickly added, "But you must leave much earlier than that, so that I can have time to," he waved his hand over the cell — three steps in length, three in width, "prepare everything…"

"It will be so," Artiom promised.

For some time, they remained in silence. Artiom had no things and he had nothing to do, but he didn't want to leave the cell.

However, he was sure that there were vegetables in the room, not only the carrot on the table.

"I believe you have a dry ration?" Artiom asked him directly. "Why don't I prepare a salad for both of us and then I'll return it all when I receive my allotment?"

Osip thought about it, but more for appearances sake, raising his eyes to the ceiling. Having paused appropriately, he answered with conviction, "Why not." And with that, he pulled out a crate with edibles from under his bed.

There were potatoes, cereal, salted fish — Osip significantly mentioned that it was a carp — some carrots, onions, turnips, macaroni, mixed flour and tinned meat.

Artiom's head began to spin from it all.

"I don't know what to do with all of this," Osip suddenly admitted, taking a carrot into one hand and a potato in another, so that he reminded Artiom of a monk holding an orb and scepter.

But Artiom knew.

Soon Osip Vitalievich Troianskii loudly and expansively shared his observations and conclusions on a large number of different subject.

"In the Northwestern part of the island, they changed the name of the White Sea into the Red!" His pockmarked, big-nosed and not very handsome face became inspired and almost attractive. "The Holy Lake at the kremlin?" Here, Osip raised a thin and long finger, like a pencil, "They call it Labor Lake! What constant confusion! It's hard for me to order all my thoughts about the island. But the most important — they!" And Osip raised his finger even higher, as though trying to poke someone who was hanging above his head. "They think that if they rename the world, the world will change. But if your name wasn't Andrei, but, say, Seraphim, would you become a different person?"

"I'm Artiom," he corrected him. He put on the table a crudely chopped salad of turnips, carrots and onions, and began to clean the fish vigorously.

"Yes, of course, terribly sorry," agreed Osip and continued, from time to time licking his lips, for which reason, evidently, they were chapped even in summer. "Instead of changing the names, they should instead give us better food. You can't even imagine what a diversity of fish you can find in these waters. Herring and cod — that's obvious, even we get some of that, though terribly prepared, I ate it in the quarantine brigade. But in these waters, we have three types of flounder, saffron cod, wolfish, smelt, goby — the coast-dwellers call them "sculpin", up to ten varieties of loach — one of the rare kinds of fish that give live birth! And the lakes? There is a great multitude of lakes, more than three hundred! In them we have ruff, carp, perch, pike, roach. You can even find trout! And all of this is edible! But we don't eat it! Why not?"

Artiom didn't have time to find an answer before Osip began to lay out his next series of reflections: "It's worth thinking about the kinds of mirages that exist. You haven't yet seen the local mirage? Oh, it's amazing. The shore of Kemi, usually invisible, especially from the low places, sometimes appears on the horizon and seems to be very close! Small islands that are at some distance from us, sometimes seem to be flattened and raised upward. As for Kutuzov Island, it sometimes takes an absolutely phantasmagorical form. Either it looks like a giant hat, or a mushroom, or it seems to hang in the air like an airship…! Its worth thinking — maybe we are also a mirage? It may seem to you and to me that we are sitting in prison, but perhaps we are the inhabitants of a mushroom? Or the passengers in an airship?"

"Or lice under a hat," said Artiom, as it seemed to be appropriate to him.

But Osip looked at him severely and immediately put everything in its place.

"The French geometrician Monge explained a long time ago what's going on here. The reasons are, in the different density of the lower and higher layers of air, and the resulting refraction of the rays of the sun!"

* * *

Notwithstanding the geometrician Monge, Artiom still felt as though he were in a mirage. He had to hold on to the airship more tightly, lest he fall out.

It seemed that he was now attached to the second brigade.

Vasilii Petrovich had said that it was filled with specialists in artisanal work, but it was actually somewhat different. Other than the business managers and economists — most of them were counter-revs, there were also scientists, including this same Osip, and even accountants and office workers from the administration and the educational section. The future sporting event, as Artiom understood it, was part of the reeducation and enlightenment of the inmates, therefore, the motley crew assembled by Boris Lukianovich was also transferred here.

Wake up time in the second brigade was nine in the morning.

There was some small difficulty in calming down Osip, because he spoke endlessly. But the first night, Artiom, without any pangs of conscience, fell asleep exactly in the middle of yet another monologue of his learned comrade, who, it seems, didn't even notice.

However, in the morning, Osip woke up in real suffering. It seemed that someone had smeared his entire face with woodworking glue.

Artiom went to get some hot water and as he did, he looked around carefully.

The monastic cells were situated on either side of a long corridor. The stove, Artiom noticed, was common. There were neatly piled logs in a niche in the wall — it seems the monks still kept them there.

Next to the wood stood footwear — boots, shoes, galoshes.

"People don't rob each other here!" Artiom understood in shock.

The day that had begun measuredly continued very well. An overworked Boris Lukianovich ran in for a minute and handed Artiom eight rubles and twenty-seven kopecks of Solovetsian currency. With the money came a special permission to freely visit the store and to walk around beyond the territory of the kremlin without a guard.

Osip already had such a paper; not only that, he also had the right to freely visit the shore of the sea, while with Artiom's pass that was explicitly forbidden.

"Well, I don't need that anyway," thought Artiom, examining the pass that he held in his right hand, while his left held the money.

"Drop by the office tomorrow and sign a receipt for all this," commanded Boris Lukianovich, hurrying onward. "Otherwise, I'm handing all this out under my own authority."

From sheer joy, Artiom invited Osip to come shop with him in the monastery store — it was right in the kremlin, inside the chapel to St. Herman.

But the store was closed.

Then they walked to the retail store beyond the kremlin.

Artiom felt himself triumphant and agitated, almost like a bridegroom.

He was sure that the guards at the gates would immediately take away his papers as fakes and send them under guard to the IID, where, probably, Galia was already missing Artiom… But no, they calmly and even somchow ordinarily let them out.

"How strange everything is," Artiom admitted to himself, feeling a constant tickling itch in his chest.

Even the gulls screamed joyfully and ecstatically.

It happened previously that Artiom had picked berries without a guard, but that was still with his work group, and no one would take it into their heads to go do their own thing instead of the job at hand. But here, he was walking around, not beholden to anyone and without any escort.

Osip, by the way, had no idea that this was so rare — he only took part in the general labor for a week and a half before they determined to transfer him to the Iodine production plant, which they produced, as he explained to Artiom, from seaweed.

Every day, Osip left for the laboratory that was situated on the shore of Prosperity Harbor. Incidentally, he already had the time to berate the lab for lacking everything necessary for his work.

"You should be sent to the logs; there you'll find everything you need for your work," Artiom thought without malice.

The retail store turned out to be a tidy wooden hut that stood in a green meadow far from all the other buildings. There was something fairy-tale-like about it.

It smelled like his mother's package inside — edibles and soap, satiety and cares.

Four inmates sold the goods. They were filled up with their significance — you couldn't get this sort of a job without having friends in high places.

"The retail store doesn't have a mind-boggling variety, just a simple and self-confident assortment," Vasilii Petrovich had said once.

That's exactly how it was.

A kilogram of herring cost a ruble thirty, sausages cost two fifty, sugar — sixty-three kopecks. Perfume was five rubles twenty-five. English safety pins cost thirty kopecks each.

There were two kinds of candies and candied fruits — one of which was the same kind that Afanasiev had shared with Artiom. Wheat bread, tea. Tin plates, spoons and mugs. Tooth powder, face powder, blush, lipstick, hair brushes. They also sold kerosene stoves, wood stoves, cast iron stoves and a huge cooking pot.

In the clothing section, they offered felt boots, felt shoes, pants, sailor jackets, hats and a huge number of different shoes, disorderly thrown about into several crates.

"Should I buy some perfume?" said Artiom. "And some candied fruit to add to it. Let's rub perfume on ourselves and eat candied fruit. How do you like this plan for our evening?"

"Yes, we can do that," Osip answered, completely serious. "But I have no money," he quickly added. "Would you buy it for me…? That…" And almost guessing, he poked his finger in the direction of the safety pins.

"What a little devil," thought Artiom, but of course he bought it. After all, he had dragged him here in the first place.

Osip, for his part, immediately put the safety pin in his pocket.

Artiom also bought half a kilogram of sausage, six candies and a plate with a spoon — he hadn't seen Vasilii Petrovich yesterday.

"I should also buy a stove," thought Artiom and then immediately started to make fun of himself: "Are you sure you're going to stay in that cell? You're going to go back, my dear, to the common work again! And then you'll drag the stove around with you through the forest in winter!"

On the way back, they met three candlewicks near the kitchens, who were waiting for the scraps of food to be dumped in the landfill. You had to arrive exactly at the moment when the cook pulled out the vat, then, according to ancient and venerable tradition, he returned for a minute into the kitchen. During that minute, the candlewicks dug around in the vat, finding a cabbage leaf or a fish head.

They themselves looked either like a special kind of fish that had grown sparse, slick hair, or mangy birds with their feathers fallen out and their scales dirty.

Artiom was a little upset that they were ruining his good mood.

"Why are they doing that?" Osip asked, horrified. "Listen, we have to give them some sausage." He grabbed Artiom by the sleeve. "These people are hungry and we have extra."

"Sure, I'll give them some right now," Artiom said, ripping his sleeve out with unexpected anger. "Better give them your safety pin."

"They don't need a safety pin," Osip persisted. "They're hungry!"

"Go to the devil," said Artiom and walked faster.

In a minute, Osip joined him.

He held his hand in the pocket where he had placed the safety pin.

"Did he really want to give it to them?" Artiom thought with slight disdain.

"What, have you never seen any candlewicks?" he asked, a bit more calmly.

"Candlewicks?" Osip asked, and then, understanding what they were talking about, answered, "No, for some reason, I hadn't encountered it before."

"The word 'it' sounded as though Osip was holding something unpleasant with his long fingers, something like a dirty diaper.

"Well, imagine that 'it' is a mirage," said Artiom, "according to Monge."

"Monge?" Osip asked and, being silent a while, answered, "No, it's not a mirage."

"How did you get here anyway?" asked Artiom quickly.

"They put me in prison," Osip explained.

"Really? I never would have guessed," said Artiom.

They were already near their own abbot's wing.

"Hey!" It sounded like they were calling for Artiom. "Stop!"

Artiom turned around and saw Passport, Shaferbekov and Gills, hurrying to cut them off.

"Six rubles, twenty-two kopecks, half a kilogram of sausage, six candies," Artiom listed to himself, as he pushed Osip through the door, everything that he could lose in a moment.

Not counting his life, about which he had forgotten.

"They seem to be calling us," said Osip, barely pushing back at the duty officer's post.

"No-no-no, not us," whispered Artiom, pushing him painfully, ready to throw Osip on his shoulder and run up to the second floor. The scientist was spindly and generally unpleasantly flexible under his clothing, as though he were made of herring bones.

Leaning down under the opening in the staircase, invisible from below, Artiom heard the thud of the doors and the immediate shout of the duty officer.

"Where do you think you're going?" asked the duty officer, getting up, judging by his voice, from his seat.

"Those two who just walked in… they're needed," quickly said the toothless Shaferbekov, lisping slightly in his abhorrent voice.

Artiom's heart was beating as though he were having a heart attack.

"For me?" asked Osip, held back by his sleeve by Artiom. "Maybe they're from the laboratory?"

"Don't move!" Artiom commanded in a whisper.

"Where are you coming from?" asked the duty officer.

"We need Artiom Goriainov," said Gills.

Artiom jumped. To learn his name was no difficult matter, but he still experienced a short burst of disgusted fear, hearing Gills pronounce his name. It was one thing if that foulness was looking for who knows what person who happened to look like Artiom, but it was a different thing to be called by name. It felt as though Gills had caught Artiom by the scruff with his untrimmed fingernails.

"I don't care who you need, go get a pass," answered the duty officer.

Artiom leaned down and saw how the duty officer was pushing the gangsters to the exit.

As though he knew that someone was eavesdropping, Gills turned around and yelled, "You're not gonna get away, got it, *friar*?"

* * *

"What was I thinking?" thought Artiom at night, his thoughts accompanied by the never-ceasing screaming of the gulls and Osip's cutting conversations. "Why am I acting like a child? I can go straight to Galina and shoot my mouth off about Gills and about Passport, and about Shaferbekov — they'll all get permanent solitary… But what can I say? I don't really know anything. Damn it, I'm going to have to ask Afanasiev. Or just lie. Make up something horrible and they'll finish off that foulness in the clay mill…"

Barely moving his lips, Artiom convinced himself, not listening to Osip's continual paradoxes about the boring, ice-bound, garbage-ridden, alluvial landscape of Solovki.

Judging by the passion with which Artiom tried to convince himself, it seemed that everything in him was ready for that step and that first thing in the morning he would go to the IID…

… But of course, Artiom didn't go anywhere, and, drinking his morning hot water while munching on the sausage from the store and a carrot from Osip's ration, he didn't even remember his nighttime inspiration or his feverish mumbling.

At ten in the morning, Boris Lukianovich led a warmup session for all of the future passion-bearers of Solovetsian sports. Then they were divided into groups — the runners ran, the jumpers jumped, the footballers chased a rag-ball — they hadn't been given a real one yet — there was only one in the entire camp. Two wrestlers appeared and a dozen *bogatyrs*, chosen from all the brigades to lift weights. There weren't many weights either, so they waited their turn, without, it must be said, much enthusiasm.

Other than the wrestlers and weight lifters, there was a group of young, student-aged men from the city. Therefore, the whole atmosphere was boisterous, comical and there was much joking about.

At one point, the ball flew away, while Father Zinovii was walking by, God only knows from where. They yelled at him, "Hey, long-skirts! Pass it back!" But he spit on the ball and that only made everyone laugh. Someone immediately offered to include a competition of censer swinging among the clergy and the students again all fell over from laughter.

Artiom suddenly noticed that only he and Boris Lukianovich did not laugh.

By age, Artiom ended up among the average of all present — the students were all younger by five–seven years, while the heavies with their kettlebells were seven–ten years older.

When he looked more attentively, he realized that Boris Lukianovich was about the same age as he, perhaps a few years older. In general, it was obvious that he had much more experience of interacting with different kinds of people, including the Bolshevik authorities.

Artiom mentally admitted Boris Lukianovich's superiority, but he didn't let it show. He held himself with dignity, as though they were equals, one step away from back-slapping familiarity. Boris Lukianovich seemed to have noticed this and he turned to Artiom once for some small help, then again — Artiom ended up exact, fast and quick on the uptake. The third time, Boris Lukianovich even shared a jest with him, talking about the rest of the sportsmen in the third person. Artiom didn't run with the joke and laughed seemingly from the heart, but in moderation — he felt that was exactly what was needed.

"Boris Lukianovich has the right to place himself a bit higher than the rest, and that's none of my business," Artiom understood.

Before lunch, Boris Lukianovich left, having asked Artiom to take care of discipline.

Why not? Artiom wisely didn't touch the wrestlers and the lifters, while the students played with enthusiasm until lunch.

Boris Lukianovich returned around four in the afternoon with some pale-faced fellow.

"I may have found you a partner." He nodded at the new guy. "In solitary! The only place they're not letting me go is Sekirka, so far."

"He's switched to the informal 'you,'" Artiom noticed, not without pleasure, as he looked over the pale-faced fellow. Until this moment, Boris Lukianovich had only once used the informal "you", when they were fighting. But that situation presupposed a degree of intimacy.

The newbie ended up being half a head taller than Artiom, with a rare, unkempt stubble, frightened and sweaty.

"Did I look like that too?" thought Artiom, twitching his shoulder in revulsion.

"Why don't you have a go?" offered Boris Lukianovich, offering Artiom the gloves. "Why should I do it? You're the boxer."

Glancing at his opponent, Artiom acknowledged his superiority. It was an unattractive, but still an insurmountable feeling. The pale-faced guy probably didn't even know that Artiom himself was only here the second day. On the contrary, he was sure that he had ended up in a group of washed-up former experts who had long been taken off common work. The obvious fear of the pale-faced fellow only strengthened Artiom's sense and he underlined it with the most independent mien he could adopt — yeah, we're having fun here, yeah, I'm going to beat in your ribby sides, you sweaty pipsqueak.

This time, the attention didn't worry him, it even excited him a bit. The lifters were the first to leave their weights, then the wrestlers came soon after. The footballers kept playing, but many were already slowing down and openly staring at Artiom and the pale-faced guy.

"Ready?" asked Boris Lukianovich.

Artiom touched his glove to his forehead.

"What about your temple?" Boris Lukianovich suddenly remembered.

"I'll lead with the other side," Artiom answered. Boris Lukianovich nodded, repressing a smile.

Everything happened very quickly. Artiom feinted to the left, then feinted to the right. He quickly understood that the pale-faced guy was swimming, although he held his hands correctly and seemed to know how to move right, he was still very afraid… so Artiom smacked him, at the first obvious chance, right in the teeth, a lot harder than he should have.

The pale-faced guy fell.

The gulls, who were already acting shamefully, actually laughed.

One of the students who had run up to look, gasped in mockery, but the others didn't support him. The pale-faced guy looked very pitiful.

He didn't bother getting up. Leaning on his right arm, he pulled off the glove from his left, holding its edge in between his jaw and his shoulder and quietly touched his lip with the mitten underneath.

Artiom at first almost stretched his mouth into a grin — look at me! — but then he quickly realized that there was no reason to rejoice.

Boris Lukianovich helped the pale-faced guy get up.

Artiom understood what he should have done.

"Next time, be a little more careful," said Boris Lukianovich, winking at Artiom, and he led the fellow into the barn.

The wink calmed Artiom down a little.

"So what?" he said to himself. "They told me to try him out. I tried him out..."

But another ten minutes passed and Artiom unexpectedly understood what a complete idiot he was.

"I should have danced around him at least five minutes, and only then dropped him!" He berated himself sorrowfully and angrily. "After all, who knows who they'll find as a replacement?"

Boris Lukianovich, having given the fellow some water, offered him some food and returned.

He clapped Artiom on the shoulder. Artiom twisted a smile, saying nothing.

"Will you hold my glasses?" Boris Lukianovich asked and energetically ran into the ranks of the footballers.

Artiom painfully wanted Boris Lukianovich to calm him down somehow instead of fooling about with the ball. At least he had given him his glasses; that was something.

He caressed the curve of the glasses and continued to quietly berate himself.

There was also a mixture of another, shameful feeling — they had probably just pulled out the pale-faced guy from solitary, where, as everyone was always saying, the devil only knows what goes on. Maybe he came from that same clay mill that Gills was scaring him with... He had a salvific chance to remain in the sports brigade, but then Artiom showed up.

"How awful! How disgusting!" Artiom repeated to himself in a whisper, simultaneously wishing the pale-faced guy to finish his food and get out of there finally.

"Where?" Artiom asked himself. "Back to solitary?"

The journalist Grakov appeared at a very opportune time, though it was unclear when he came from, or from where.

"What are you doing here?" asked Artiom, hurrying to speak, not so much because he was interested in Grakov, but because he wanted to distract himself. "Have you decided to try out for the Olympics?"

"Of course not," answered Grakov. "I'm working for the printing section now — newspapers, journals…"

"They took you into the *New Solovki*?" Artiom was almost happy for him, though he had only spoken to Grakov a few times and took absolutely no liking for this silent and not very conspicuous type. He almost added: "Make sure to drag Afanasiev out with you, since you're both from Petersburg," but then he remembered that they avoided each other.

"Where's Boris Lukianovich?" asked Grakov. "I've come to talk to him. I'm getting an article ready about the coming competition."

"Over there," Artiom pointed.

Boris Lukianovich, squinting nearsightedly, was watching out for the ball, this looked cute and funny. It seemed that he couldn't see a damn thing on the other side of the football pitch without his glasses, and he watched for the ball only by following the clustering of cheerful students.

The students — Artiom noticed from the morning — in spite of their serious, yet forcefully interrupted, education, knew how to swear like sailors. Only Boris Lukianovich, even in the heat of the game, expressed himself only in a proper fashion.

"Looking for me?" He ran up, slightly winded and amicable.

"Here, from the newspaper," Artiom said, offering him his glasses. "Comrade Grakov."

Boris Lukianovich looked at Grakov first without his glasses, then with them, as though comparing the impressions.

"I'm writing an article about…" began Grakov, but Boris Lukianovich immediately grimaced sorrowfully.

"Listen, I'm no good at this. Here, Artiom speaks well. Tell him something, Artiom."

"What? Why does he think…?" Artiom was surprised, though, it must be said, pleased. Grakov immediately opened his notebook and got out his pencil from behind his ear.

"The participation of inmates in sporting events is…" Artiom began very confidently, then looked over at Boris Lukianovich, who slowly nodded his big head with a look as though he were listening and simultaneously translating a foreign language into Russian, "is no diversion. It is a reflection of the competence of the cultural work of the Camp of Solovki. It is a reflection of the path walked by those members of society who are correcting themselves, but still guilty before the law."

"Perfect!" said a more than content Boris Lukianovich, and in confirmation of his words began to clean his glasses on his undershirt.

"Sport is the purification of the spirit, equally important to labor," Artiom etched his words as though he were doling out combinations of words that he had never in his life used or even thought about. "In sport, as in work, there is beauty. Sport is the hands of the strong holding up and leading the weak. Comrade Trotskii says, 'If man hadn't fallen, he would never have been able to raise himself up.' Sport teaches the same thing that the Camp at Solovki does — how to get up after falling."

"Oh, beautiful!" Boris Lukianovich razzed him amicably. "It's simply a garden of nightingales. Artiom, you could have been a wonderful political agitator. Boiling with thunder!"

"Does he like Tiutchev or Severyanin?" Artiom thought in passing, a bit flushed from the praise, no matter how sarcastic it was. "Probably Tiutchev. And Blok, of course."

"Wait," said Grakov, inflicting squiggles on the notebook that looked a great deal like Khokhloma painting, but definitely not words. "One moment… yes, I'm listening."

Artiom mocked for another half an hour until the pages in Grakov's notebook ran out.

"Yesterday they came for you to the twelfth brigade from the IID," said Grakov in parting. "I was collecting my things to move… did they find you?"

Artiom looked at Grakov without blinking, even forgetting to answer.

He hadn't even thought of Galia for a whole day.

"It's time to snitch, Artiom, your time has come," he sang silently and without saying goodbye to Grakov, slowly walked to the barn; near its wall he had eaten the lard with lemon the last time. It's a wonderful place to think about the future… As though anything depended on his thoughts.

"That's what you get for the pale fellow," Artiom said to himself.

"Yep," he answered himself, "Because if not for the pale fellow, Galia would have forgotten about me, right? Maybe I can ask her: 'Aren't participants in the sports section freed from the responsibilities of snitch and informer?'" Artiom tried to amuse himself, but it still wasn't funny.

On the way, Boris Lukianovich caught him.

"Listen, Artiom, you're still a bit thin," he said. "Let's issue you a dry ration as well, what do you think? Starting tomorrow? The monetary allowance is for the boxer, and the dry ration is for the agitation, right?"

Boris Lukianovich talked to no one else with such a kind and joking tone.

* * *

"Since I didn't come yesterday, that means that they'll take me right out of my monastic cell," thought Artiom, feeling a heaviness in his heart.

For some reason, the call from IID was even more frightening than the possibility of meeting the gangsters at the entrance to the abbot's wing.

"That's because dishonor is more frightening than death," Artiom uttered pathetically about himself, knowing in advance that all of it was stupid words, a fantasy.

On the way to the kremlin, Artiom resolutely turned into the retail store and bought a small iron pot. "At least I can feed myself with something warm before I fall into sin."

Now he carried his money on his person — it seemed to give him strength; it led to a delusive sense of freedom and importance.

"But as soon as you start snitching," Artiom goaded himself, "they'll give you yet another ration, a third! You'll always have money in your pocket. You'll get fat. You'll get greasy, slow, fat-cheeked…"

He imagined how he would walk through the kremlin's courtyard, hiccupping, as fat as any NEP-er. He got a little more cheerful.

In the main kitchen, the first chef gave him a dry ration according to Boris Lukianovich's paper. He even added some cabbage with a head of garlic and some lard…

The chef — he stank unforgivably of gruel, fish, millet porridge and buckwheat, with a completely shaved head and a single eye — carefully examined Artiom, trying, just in case, to understand what sort of a character stood before him and why he was receiving an increased ration.

Artiom winked at him. It was a bit wild to wink at a man with one eye.

"Let him think that I am the camp's most important snitch," Artiom continued to mock himself, carrying back his ration. "Let him guess by my brazen mug that I've done my time and remain a freebie in the monastery because of a natural inclination towards villainy, a true lickspittle! That's why they feed me!"

Neither the gangsters nor any soldiers awaited Artiom at the abbot's wing.

He hurried to the entrance as though there were forty loving sisters waiting for him in his room.

… Or better yet, only one, and not a sister at all.

"Maybe Galina has forgotten about me?" thought Artiom, crunching his cabbage leaf and energetically ascending the staircase to the second floor, while no one was calling him. "Or maybe IID won't be able to find me? They'll lose me in the papers, thinking that the inmate Goriainov was sent on a distant business trip, and they'll forget about me until the end of my time? That happens, right?"

He was ready to believe in anything, just to avoid meeting that thin-lipped creature ever again.

In his monastic cell, a sullen Osip half-lay on his sheets-less bed, reading some kind of textbook without a cover.

"Osip is home," Artiom remarked with a warm feeling, as though his learned comrade would also serve as protection. At the same time, he caught himself thinking that he's calling this cage a home, while he had never called his previous loathsome louse-house, the twelfth brigade, home.

"Osip, shall we make some cabbage soup?" Artiom offered from the threshold.

"You know how to?" Osip asked without confidence, licking his lips.

Artiom knew.

Osip only licked his lips when he was in a good mood, Artiom noticed. While he was in a bad mood, he held his mouth sealed and dry.

Someone had already lit the stove in the corridor. Artiom added some logs and added his iron kettle so no one else could occupy his place on the common stove.

After an hour and a half, everything was ready.

"The storms throw the seaweed out to the shore," Osip explained about his work, holding his bowl with both hands by the edges, as though the bowl might jump away somewhere. "Sometimes the waves are several kilometers long. The seaweed is all edible; there are no poisonous kinds. In England, Japan, Scotland, they make many delicious things from seaweed. Candies, jams, blancmange."

"Is that what you work on?" Artiom joked, sweating after bustling a long time near the stove, as he poured the cabbage soup. "Will you bring me some blancmange made from seaweed to taste?"

"No, that's not my work," answered Osip, carefully examining first his bowl, then the kettle. "Yes, they make blancmange. Also, ice cream, crème brûlée, cookies. But we are working on something else for now, for the Soviet government has no time for cookies. They need the aforementioned iodine to treat their own wounds."

Osip always joked extremely caustically and completely without smiling. The humor confirmed that this person was not as absentminded and lost as it might seem at first glance.

"More than that," he continued in the same tone, "you can make a kind of glue from it called algin, or cellulose, even potassium salts."

"But for now, you only make iodine?" Artiom clarified.

"Yes," Osip answered curtly, ladled some soup with his spoon and held the spoon for some time above the bowl, paying no attention to it. "They incinerate the seaweed, soak it in water and from this water extract the iodine from potassium iodide. It's all very simple. For more large-scale work, we don't have the facilities. Even so, Comrade Eichmanis, naturally, has huge plans."

Osip finally tasted the soup. Artiom was sure he wouldn't even notice that he ate it, but quite the opposite happened.

"This is very good," said Osip with dignity. "Will you teach me?"

Artiom nodded sweepingly. For some reason he was in a very good mood.

"The Bolsheviks in general love to plan everything, make a graph of it and delegate it," continued Osip, raising the next spoon to his mouth. "It's some special kind of psychological disease. They're insane, but they approach everything in a strictly scientific manner."

Artiom cheerfully looked at the door and changed the subject.

"Have you socialized with Eichmanis?" he asked as simply as he could and even frivolously, in order to attune Osip to this new melody.

"Naturally, I have. I immediately demanded that he bring my mother here."

"To prison?" Artiom wanted to joke but didn't.

"And what did he say?"

"He immediately agreed," Osip said proudly.

"Why do you need your mother, Osip?" Artiom asked.

"She can't do without me," he answered confidently, "while I absolutely need her to be able to work normally."

"What do you think of Eichmanis?" Artiom asked.

"He's the head of the camp. That means he's a piece of shit; otherwise, how would he have gotten to the top?"

"Yep..." said Artiom, raising his spoon vertically, as though he was planning on striking Osip on his intelligent forehead. "What other delicacies do they make from seaweed?"

* * *

During the morning warm-up, Boris Lukianovich was called into the cultural and educational section.

"Artiom, can you lead it?" he asked simply, as though it were obvious.

It wasn't a hard job. Artiom led the warm-up.

An hour later, Boris Lukianovich returned, but only for a minute, and he asked Artiom to make sure that they'd dig in the parallel bars where they needed to be, not just wherever.

They brought the bars soon afterwards.

It wasn't a difficult job. He made sure.

The rest of the time, Artiom tortured himself on the pull up bar. All of this was incomparably better than the logs.

"And no one is guarding me," Artiom basked. "If I want to, I hang here. If I want to, I sit here. If I want to, I stare at the sky."

For that matter, he stared more at the road from the monastery, even as he spun around on the bars — were there red army soldiers hurrying from the guard corps to lead him to the IID? Galina must be tired of waiting there.

Instead of soldiers, Artiom saw Passport, who schlepped under guard from the forest work group to go eat lunch, together with other inmates as exhausted as he was.

From this distance, it wasn't clear whether Passport looked at Artiom or whether he couldn't care less.

After lunch, there was a bit of a lull in the sport section — it was hard to fervently lift and run energetically from morning until evening on a single dry ration, even with added bread and carrots. But Boris Lukianovich returned and Artiom decided with pleasure that this was no longer his headache. Let the boss watch everyone and drive them forward.

Boris Lukianovich appeared without any added food, though he did have good news.

"Friends and comrades!" he announced. "From this day, in addition to your monetary allowance, we will also have daily hot food for lunch!"

The students whooped; Artiom was also not upset — as before, he wanted to eat constantly.

"Only for some reason they didn't bring it to us," Boris Lukianovich, smiling, ruined everyone's mood. "Artiom, maybe you can go and find out what's the trouble?"

Hoping that Passport was already in the sleeping quarters and that they would miss each other, Artiom hurried to the monastery, through the St. Nicholas gates, to the main kitchen.

He walked through the main entrance, past the guard, with an iron expression on his face. They didn't even call to him, though inmates were naturally not allowed to enter the working area of the main kitchen.

The head chef walked towards him in his boots, in a dirty black apron, holding an ax. He recognized Artiom and looked at him with a certain amount of tension, not winking his only eye with its burned-off eyelashes and missing eyebrow.

Artiom again didn't introduce himself, but immediately asked about the hot lunch for the sports section, who were preparing for the Olympics according to the personal command of the head of the camp in honor of the anniversary of the revolution. Perhaps, he suggested, he should write a complaint to Fiodor Ivanovich?

Artiom said "Fiodor Ivanovich" on purpose — it sounded more convincing, as though he had just sat with him at the table and came to know the names and responsibilities of saboteurs.

"What's going on?" the chef growled. "I told them to do it!"

His words were as though they had been chopped with his ax, like pieces of meat: "Whassgoinon! I tol'em t'do it!"

Artiom walked out of harm's way outside to wait, as though he, in his authoritative irritation, had decided to take a smoke break.

They carried out the vats with hot food in three minutes.

"Next time," Artiom declared to himself, hurrying after the kitchen staff, "when the gangsters, Burtsev and Sorokin are planning to beat you up, a one-eyed chef with a soup ladle will join them and take your head off with the ladle finally.

The courtyard was almost empty — only Bear the deer watched out for someone with sugar, while Black watched after the deer.

The gangsters didn't leave him waiting — Artiom heard their voices and turned around; they were right there.

"I saw that bitch from the window," Gulls said, leering with his fish-teeth. Apparently, while Artiom was going to the kitchen, he had time to find Passport and Shaferbekov in the twelfth. A fourth — some leopard filled with interest in how they were about to catch the *friar* and tear him into pieces or at least knife him — hurried along with them.

"Comrade warden! Comrade soldier!" Artiom yelled, calling the serviceman a "comrade", which was forbidden — only "citizen"! — and ran to the monastery's gates, hearing stomping feet behind his back.

"Passport's shoes are falling apart; it's not easy for him to run," Artiom managed to remember.

Behind them, Black started to bark, then run after them, soon reaching Artiom.

"Hey! Don't bite! Hey!" Artiom asked while running, because the dog was running right at his feet, baring his teeth. At least Bear didn't run anywhere, though he jumped in place, raising his tail.

The leopard, who was running barefoot, reached Artiom almost at the gates, then grabbed his jacket, ripping the sleeve.

"What's going on here?" asked the soldier. "Whoah there, all of you! I'll shoot you between the eyes!" He actually racked the slide and raised his rifle.

Only the kitchen staff stopped with their vat, while Shaferbekov, Gills and Passport ran right up to the post and now stood next to Artiom.

He quickly looked from one vile face to the next.

Black was getting tangled up in everyone's feet, barking shortly at the people.

"I need to leave," said Artiom, showing the pass to the soldier, then pushed the leopard in the forehead, because he still hadn't dropped his sleeve.

"Why were you yelling?" asked the soldier, returning his pass.

Artiom said nothing and walked through the gates, taking his paper and putting it in his pocket without looking at it.

On the other side, he stopped and, heavily breathing, turned to the gangsters, who were still standing there next to the post.

Artiom felt that his back was hot and the back of his head flared as though burned. But he immediately recognized the comedy in the situation. He stood here, they stood there and they couldn't get out. They didn't have any passes. Even Passport went to his forest work under guard.

They let the kitchen staff with their vats pass as well — they, egged on by the head chef, hurried towards the sportsmen.

"Gills, come over here," Artiom called him gently. "I'll give you a candied fruit. Want a candied fruit?" He did pull a candied fruit bought this morning from his pocket. "Catch!" And he threw it. "Just make sure that you don't rip your mouth open again."

The leopard picked up the candied fruit and immediately swallowed it without chewing.

"Passport!" Artiom yelled. "Don't piss sideways!"

He remembered Shaferbekov too. Afanasiev had told him, while they were preparing the sauna switches that he had chopped up his wife, put her in a basket and mailed it to Shemakha.

"Shaferbe-e-e-ekov!" Artiom drawled. "They say that your wife sent you a parcel from Shemakha? Or was it that they send *her* in a parcel? Not sure which one! Why don't you go to the post office and find out?"

Gills and Passport stood in place, their mouths open, beside themselves with fury. Passport's nose even turned blue. Shaferbekov was smiling and squinting, as though Artiom were blinding him.

"Get out of here," the soldier commanded the gangsters, and, turning around to look at Artiom, added, "You go take a hike too, jokester."

The gangsters walked away and sat near the monastery's walls.

"Are you feeling better, jester of Solovki?" Artiom asked himself, shuddering with pleasure, as though a beautiful, buxom girl with long, painted nails had just scratched his back and blew on his neck.

"Oh yeah!" he answered himself, with excitement. "But how will I go back? It's not like I can ask the soldier to lead me back to my cell."

He caught and smashed a big drip of sweat with his finger as it poured down from his hair down to his forehead.

Boris Lukianovich was hurrying towards him — from a lack of anything to do, Artiom examined him carefully — flared pant legs, sailor shirt, all full of energy, his shoulders bulging with muscle, the neck of a boar, his ears — like the ears of all healthy people — small.

"Listen!" Boris Lukianovich said a few steps away. "I'm impressed! I see that they're carrying the lunch at a trot! What did you say to them in the kitchen?"

Without answering, Artiom waited while Boris Lukianovich drew level with him. He only smiled.

"I was looking for you; good thing I found you." Boris Lukianovich said, coming up and not noticing a certain nervousness in Artiom's face, although he did pay attention to something else: "Oh, your sleeve is ripped… Listen, there's going to be a meeting with Eichmanis right now. Tell them that you're my assistant and we'll go together, OK? You speak well. Butt in if you have to. Especially since Grakov will be listening in again and writing it all down. So we need the right speeches. I'm not good at those."

"Me neither," answered Artiom, still not calmed down after all that had happened.

"You can do everything very well!" Boris Lukianovich said with conviction. "Can you do without lunch? I'm hungry too. After the meeting, you'll go straight to rest."

Artiom hoped that the gangsters had left, but no, they were still sitting there. They jumped up in amazement. The leopard got up and scratched himself in the nether regions.

"What, back again?" the soldier asked Artiom.

Having searched for it, Artiom found the pass in his pocket — it was covered in mustard and grease spots.

"You can use it to flavor your soup," said the soldier, returning the pass.

Sighing, Artiom walked after Boris Lukianovich.

The gangsters rose up and slowly walked towards them.

"Why aren't you back at the sleeping quarters?" Burtsev yelled at them, arriving like a storm. "Did they cancel your work group? Did they announce a rest stop here? Or did they open up a boulevard here?"

Seeing Burtsev, Passport took two steps back, Shaferbekov took one.

"Who are you?" Burtsev yelled at Gills. "Which brigade?"

Gills sniffed and quickly walked in the direction of the infirmary, his entire face screwed up, as though he were counting the remaining teeth in his mouth.

Burtsev didn't touch Passport or Shaferbekov, but he swung his stiletto at the leopard.

"Get out of here, trash!"

After half a minute, everyone walked away, leaving only Burtsev. Artiom and Boris Lukianovich walked past.

Burtsev was wearing new, excellent boots that had been polished so much they shined.

He didn't greet Artiom.

* * *

They walked through the monastery courtyard and exited from the other side — the administration of the camp was located in a building at the quayside. They didn't allow inmates to leave through those gates, but evidently Boris Lukianovich had a special document.

Eichmanis's office was large and airy. A carafe of pure water stood on his table. There were no portraits on the walls, only a handwritten map of Solovki with many small flags.

"Probably one of the inmates drew that," Artiom thought.

When they walked in, Eichmanis raised his eyes and said nothing.

In the bright light of day, it became obvious that he was tanned. His hair was brushed back evenly, his high, bare forehead had a white stripe right under the hairline — evidently, he sometimes walked outside in the heat in a hat or cap. There was a deep groove between his eyebrows. He had full, pursed lips. His immovable gaze was directed right at Boris Lukianovich.

There was something in him that was… Artiom searched for an appropriate word… It's like he was a foreigner! Any minute, it seemed that he would switch to a different language, his native tongue and not at all Latvian or German or French — something else with shrill, commanding words, crunching like broken glass.

Grakov sat apart from them in the corner, making notes in his notebook with an incredibly intelligent look.

"… Fiodor Ivanovich, I know that the actors are now due an addition to their ration, as they've been taken off common labor… but we sportsmen, I think, need a triple ration. At least until the competition. Many of them are underweight… That could have a visible effect…" Boris Lukianovich said, a little shyly, but at the same time insistently, as though forcing himself to utter everything that he considered necessary.

"Boris Lukianovich, there's only one problem with your team," answered Eichmanis loudly, as though on the parade ground. He spoke with a somewhat deliberate sharpness, despite the fact that, judging by appearances, the situation seemed amusing to him. "Twenty-three of your twenty-seven prospective participants in our games are incarcerated under the section dealing with 'terrorism.'"

Boris Lukianovich touched the curve of his glasses as though he wanted to take them off, but changed his mind, as though he had decided — what if I miss something important?

"How small Boris Lukianovich looks next to Eichmanis," Artiom noticed. "Or is it the authority? What if Boris Lukianovich was sitting in Eichmanis's place…? Would I think differently?"

"Terrorism!" repeated Eichmanis and raised his pencil in the air, turning it with a light circular motion with a look as though he was ready to hurl it to the far side of the office or at Grakov, whom he simply did not notice.

Artiom remembered inappropriately that Galia also always talked with a pencil in her hand.

"What? Do we not have any other kinds of criminals?" asked Eichmanis. He lessened the grip on the pencil, and it slipped down. Eichmanis caught it by its tip and shook it in the air, as though it were the second hand on a clock. In this unconscious game, there was an attractive boyishness. "Do we have thieves? Yes. Robbers? Yes. Conmen? Ve-e-ery many! So why have you only chosen terrorists? Is that your favorite article of the criminal code? Or are you preparing some kind of surprise for the October anniversary?"

Boris Lukianovich coughed and looked from side to side. Artiom guessed that he was looking for a glass. He wanted some water. But only Eichmanis had a glass.

"Ivan!" Eichmanis called somewhere, lightly slapping his palm on the table. Boris Lukianovich and Artiom jumped, and the water in Eichmanis's glass quivered. "Bring a mug, there's a good fellow!"

Eichmanis, despite the fact that he loved drilling, parades and military inspections, was himself dressed in civilian clothing. No matter how many times Artiom saw him, he noticed it every time. While all the rest of the camp administration wore uniforms, he appeared in public in a red sweater or in a sailor's shirt, whilst he now sat in an elegant jacket, the three top buttons of which were unbuttoned. His strong neck was visible. At the same time, there was something young, almost boyish about him.

Artiom caught himself in an obviously shameful emotion — in this moment, he liked Eichmanis as a person.

He gestured so exactly, so convincingly, and behind every one of his words there was an extraordinary level of self-confidence and power.

If Artiom had had to go to war, he would have wanted such an officer.

They brought a mug and Eichmanis abruptly, familiarly moved the carafe from his own table to the conference table that stood right next to his.

"You understand…" began Boris Lukianovich, having filled his mug and cautiously taking a drink; it was obvious that it was hard for him to express himself. "Most often those who are arrested under the article concerning terrorism are… students. If a student becomes a terrorist, he is, as a rule… in good physical shape. That is, many of them prepare themselves…"

"Well, yes, so I've heard," Eichmanis answered in harmony with Boris Lukianovich, apparently without irritation. However, Artiom felt that the sportsman was afraid to lift his eyes to the head of the camp.

Boris Lukianovich once again fell silent for a few seconds.

"No matter what you say about the working class or the peasants… or the NEP-ers. Or the majority of inmates — many of whom have had their health destroyed. There are, I think, among the counter-revs, some people who might…"

"Yes, yes, terrorists from among the new and counter-revs from among the old," Eichmanis laughed. Artiom finally decided to look at him in passing and immediately met his gaze. The commissar's eyes were grey, a bit arrogant and a bit tired, though with full and long eyelashes. How he was able to keep them this long, Artiom didn't know. What, did he never smoke on a windy day?

His laughter sounded as though it was clear that only he could laugh in his office, while everyone else wasn't required to.

Eichmanis's teeth were straight, his ears firm, seemingly carved by a carver, there was an obvious dimple in his chin… Only the cut-off, even slippery line of his cheekbones, once again noticed by Artiom, slightly ruined the general effect. With such cheekbones, Eichmanis's head didn't seem large enough for his body. It reminded him of something like a cliff in the see that the waves had eroded after a long time, then it was as though the waves spit, smoothing out that which needed to look sharper and more distinct.

"That would be quite a team," finished Eichmanis and then immediately asked Artiom, looking at him for the first time, "What are you in for, Artiom?"

Artiom almost choked when he heard his name — he remembered clearly that Boris Lukianovich had only introduced him as his assistant, not giving any name; after all, it would have been stupid to acquaint the head of the camp with a simple inmate.

This knowledge of Eichmanis's could mean anything, but Artiom painfully sensed a deafening pride — they know me! I've been noticed!

"Me?" repeated Artiom, a habit that wasn't usual with him.

Eichmanis gave a short and patient nod: yes, you.

"For murder," said Artiom.

"Domestic?" Eichmanis quickly asked.

Artiom nodded.

"Whom did you kill?" Eichmanis asked just as quickly and ordinarily.

"My father," answered Artiom, losing his voice for some reason.

"You see!" Eichmanis turned to Boris Lukianovich. "There *are* normal ones."

Boris Lukianovich looked at Artiom and said nothing, only drank his water one more time.

Grakov didn't take his eyes off his notebook and it seemed he wasn't even writing, but drawing or scribbling something.

"I have a suggestion," suddenly Artiom offered, trying to redirect their attention to something else. "Maybe it makes sense to include the Information and Investigation Department and look into the files? We might find something there, information about people who used to do sports, but for some reason or another didn't announce their desire to take part in the competition. They can be asked separately and insistently. You just need to know who."

"Ivan!" Eichmanis called, and immediately the secretary's face appeared in the doorway. "Send someone to IID to summon Galia."

"It's an obvious idea, but it didn't occur to me. Thank you, Artiom," said Eichmanis very simply, and Artiom didn't redden from pleasure, only with difficulty, but the head was already speaking to Boris Lukianovich. "So. You can get your third ration. As for the composition of the participants, we'll work some more on that. Now for the general organization. You have my full attention."

Boris Lukianovich gave a full report. Before every new item, he took a breath, as though every time he needed to swim up to the next section.

Eichmanis didn't interrupt him anymore.

Artiom thought with some doubt: will his initiative result in a new, separate meeting with Galia, whom he had absolutely no desire to see?

She still hadn't arrived.

He had to butt into the conversation one more time when they started talking about the educational content of the competition. Here, Grakov puffed his chest out anew and loudly turned over his ink blobs to a fresh page.

Artiom had already thought of several cracking slogans for the competitions and immediately offered them to choose from. He had put neither heart nor soul into them, so this sort of work came to him very easily. However, Eichmanis was more than serious about it and he wrote down every single slogan, contracting words or sometimes whole sentences, in which you could clearly see the habits of a student who had seriously attended lectures in the past. Grakov, Artiom noticed, was writing much more exactly, so wasn't keeping up, in vain trusting in his memory.

At the end of the conference, without any pathos, Eichmanis summarized the complete picture and added a few ideas for Boris Lukianovich to consider.

His conversation proved him to be a collected and attentive person.

When everyone got up, Eichmanis asked once again, "Artiom, you are responsible for general discipline, but you are also a participant in the competitions?"

"Exactly so," Artiom calmly answered, already settled in.

Eichmanis cast his eyes over Artiom with a careful gaze; Artiom immediately guessed what the head was about to ask him.

"Boxing," said Artiom, barely smiling.

Eichmanis nodded.

"Evidently, Galina is busy with something," he said. "They'll take you to her and she will prepare the necessary information in the meantime concerning possible sportsmen.

Artiom wanted to say, "Galina and I have already met," but immediately thought better of it.

Waiting in the corridor for their summons were a priest, a young man — a leopard judging by his appearance — and a counter-rev — his deportment and gaze gave him away.

All three carefully examined Boris Lukianovich, Artiom and Grakov.

Artiom, unable to stop himself, had his special election into esoteric mysteries, unknown to everyday inmates, stamped all over his face.

As for Boris Lukianovich, he didn't even notice the other visitors, but was merely thoughtful.

* * *

"Mezernitskii is having a get-together tonight, will you come?" Grakov offered Artiom when they came outside. "He speaks well of you."

They were looking at the sea. A gull flew over the water, first lowering, then rising up, as though it was swinging on an invisible swing set.

Artiom interpreted this new mode of address from Grakov as yet more proof of his new position.

"Yes?" Artiom asked amicably. "At what time?"

He had suddenly decided not to fear the gangsters any more — who would touch him after Eichmanis had called him by name? Artiom would trample all of them.

"As for Boris Lukianovich finding out for what reason the inmate Goriainov was imprisoned — people here are imprisoned for all kinds of reasons!" Artiom made excuses for himself.

At the very least, they parted normally. "Not a bad idea to find new sportsmen," said Boris Lukianovich, not very sure, for all that, judging by his appearance, in what he was saying.

Never mind, Artiom decided. The important thing was that Eichmanis had liked it.

"But what about the fact that they're going to take you back to Galina?" he asked himself one more time. "Does that mean that you are a complete cretin with all your good ideas?"

"Why would she make me a snitch if I'm working on a separate project for the head of the camp?" Artiom answered himself with a bit of challenge.

In general, he calmed down. It had all turned out not badly, even well.

He walked back to his building — confident and strong. A gull obnoxiously circled just over his head — he jumped up and almost hit its tail with his palm.

There was only one question: whether or not to invite Osip.

"Do I need that neurotic or not?" Artiom asked himself. "Is it right for every person to bring his own friends to the get-together?"

He wisely decided not to remember how Vasilii Petrovich had himself invited Artiom to Mezernitskii's the last time.

"After all, he was speaking so badly and stupidly about Eichmanis. He completely misunderstood him," thought Artiom, meaning Osip, and kept trying to come up with a good reason to go alone. But for all that, what had Eichmanis to do with it? You're not going to Eichmanis's get-together," he quietly mocked himself.

Of course, he invited Osip.

Osip had returned from work irritated as usual. Artiom knew in advance that Osip would immediately begin to complain about the lack of tools or about the stupidity of the limitations of the camp, or about the rudeness of the administration; therefore, he cut it all off immediately.

"Osip, we've been invited to a get-together!" he announced triumphantly, chomping on his carrot — he hadn't had time to have a proper lunch, after all.

Osip, squinting, looked at Artiom for some time. Then he answered, "You think that's appropriate? I, probably, don't want to go anywhere."

"Come on," Artiom said confidently. "They'll feed us very well there… But you and I will also bring a few things with us." With these words, he pulled out his own dry ration from under the bed.

Osip glanced at the dry ration, as though he might find something new and unexpected there.

In Mezernitskii's room, Grakov and Vasilii Petrovich were already sitting down. Grakov was on the bed, Vasilii Petrovich sat near the window on a chair. The host himself was addressing them.

Artiom barely stopped himself from laughing aloud like a child. He was extraordinarily glad to see his old comrade. Vasilii Petrovich's eyes also sparked, as though someone had blown on the coals.

"Oh, Artiom, my dear Artiom," Vasilii Petrovich's entire countenance seemed to say.

"There was the empire, it shone all over," Mezernitskii expounded, waving about his hands. His nails were, as before, untrimmed and with a black edge. “Now, Solovki. Everyone thinks it’s the Bolsheviks, the Bolsheviks who ruined everything.” Grakov, listening to Mezernitskii, looked at the table, his eyebrows barely twitching, as though he had a nervous tic. “But it’s merely the empire turned inside out, the entire fur coat! There, you find lice, all kinds of vermin, bed bugs — it was all there! It’s just that now, we’re wearing the fur coat with the lining out! And that’s Solovki!”

For a minute, Osip looked around in all directions until his attention settled on the table, which was laden with a variety of food.

Vasilii Petrovich got up, silently calling Artiom to his place with a look saying that he had been sitting there for more than an hour and was already tired of resting, while Artiom, who was tired after his journey, must definitely take a seat.

All of this, of course, moved Artiom even more. He put the fish he had wrapped in paper on the table and firmly embraced Vasilii Petrovich.

“What, you don’t see each other in your brigade?” asked Mezernitskii seriously, though with a barely evident sarcasm.

“They moved me,” Artiom answered. “This is my friend Osip. He’s a scientist.”

“And day and night the learned cat kept walking round and round the chain…”[35] said Mezernitskii, extending his hand to Osip. Osip grasped it with a certain disapproval.

“I brought you your things, Artiom. After all, you haven’t visited at all,” Vasilii Petrovich said quietly. “But you are right not to, of course.”

Artiom realized that Vasilii Petrovich smelled. It was an unpleasant, but strangely familiar, stench.

“That’s the smell of our sleeping quarters! My own twelfth brigade!” Artiom realized. “When did I have a chance to forget it?”

It somehow made him feel better and relieved him: “Our good old familiar smell!” He didn’t even think about it, but rather commanded it to himself. He commanded and submitted.

“… begun to see clearly what sort of a nation it is,” Mezernitskii continued his topic, setting up the various foods brought by the guests in different parts of the table — that’s to cut, that’s to clean, that’s for the salad, that’s for later. “Maybe it’s like this? Or maybe it’s like that? And here, they’ve finally brought them all to one place to see what sort of nation it is. Now they see clearly! Except their clear sight is darkness. Clear sight into darkness! They see darkness! And now they try to describe it in the correct language. The nation, you

35 Pushkin’s *Ruslan and Ludmilla.*

know, is dark and taciturn. 'Yes, dark and even frightening!' 'Truly so, dark, frightening, and smells somehow damp too!' 'And prickly too! Smelly and prickly!' But all this is the fur coat pulled inside out! They wore that fur coat and had no idea what sort of smell was in the sleeves or armpits!"

"What is that?" asked Osip, pointing.

"That," Mezernitskii interrupted himself, completely nonplussed that he had been interrupted, "is seal meat." Immediately, he asked Artiom, "Where have they moved you?"

"Into the second," said Artiom, smiling.

"What do you do now?" asked Mezernitskii, without the "w" at the end of the phrase.

"I invent slogans," answered Artiom, continuing to smile.

Mezernitskii, pursing his lips in a unique way, nodded: yes, I see, not bad.

"Is it easier than at the logs?" he asked.

"A bit easier," Artiom answered, just as seriously.

"Mezernitskii, here you're saying that they saw the light on Solovki. But I think that they had a chance to see and understand the nation during the Civil War, no? Don't you think so?" said Vasilii Petrovich, smiling.

"No, don't say that," said Mezernitskii, immediately distracted from Artiom, while Artiom thought that all this was wonderfully quaint — this conversation that everyone had with everyone at the same time. "First of all, the war has a different set of circumstances. There is much less of the quotidian there. Secondly, even at war, where there were enough kinds of vermin, there was still not such a variety of types as on Solovki, especially considering that certain types had not come into existence at all. Yes, they somewhat knew the peasant and the worker. The Cossack and the Ossetian. The priest. The orphan, etc. But at war, strange as it may seem, people always show themselves a bit better than they actually are. So many are killed and this is very effective — at least, in my memory of the events, they killed us more often than we killed them — and I still haven't learned to stop sorrowing about that. Maybe that's because those whom we killed — we didn't know them at all, maybe didn't even see their death close at hand. However, those who were killed from among our ranks — we knew them well and saw the departures of all kinds of souls."

Moisei Solomonovich, completely unexpectedly for Artiom, entered and made a charming gesture to everyone with his hands and eyes — sit-sit-sit, I will be completely inconspicuous.

Mezernitskii nodded to him as if to an acquaintance and began to energetically cut the seal meat.

Grakov even stood up to see it.

Artiom noticed his cheeks — they always seemed paralyzed, as though he were still sleeping.

Moisei Solomonovich, standing at the doors, licked his lips, ready to sing, though battling that desire.

"And here, as I was saying, is a prison," continued Mezernitskii, "and people suddenly show their true colors. We very rarely kill each other here, but we chafe against each other, chafe and chafe with all our rough angles, having no strength to stretch out, and suddenly, we understand the essence of things. It's as though we were put into a full railcar compartment, but it went insane and drove us around for a whole year or three. Like it or not, we have to get used to each other… Here we've become acquainted with yesterday's enemies at point blank range and even begun to break bread with them. Here we've been left almost naked — most of us have neither calling, nor awards, nor regalia, only the length of our incarceration. Here we have come to know the Soviet NEP-er and the Soviet homeless child — these human types were unknown to me, personally, before now. Here I have seen the camp guard and the convoys of soldiers — and this is the ideal image of the working class, who has, for a time, with sorrow in their hearts, left the plough and the lathe."

Grakov, at these words, quickly looked from the seal meat to Mezernitskii and back again.

"His eyes are too fast, considering his slow cheeks," thought Artiom distantly.

Osip, on the contrary, was now listening to Mezernitskii with interest, having forgotten about the seal meat.

"Do you not think that it's not the nation, so much as the mold growing on it?" asked Moisei Solomonovich with his beautiful and deep voice. "How can we judge the taste of cheese by the mold on it?"

"There are certain cheeses with mold on them," said Mezernitskii.

"I fear that the Soviet government is preparing a different kind of cheese, on which any kind of mold is forbidden," said Moisei Solomonovich. "Only milk! A new nation of only milk and cream. No mold at all."

Vasilii Petrovich looked attentively at Moisei Solomonovich. There was something… unpleasant in his gaze.

Moisei Solomonovich, having asked for permission, began to help Mezernitskii prepare and set the table, and he did this not without some ingenious dexterity.

Grakov asked Osip how his investigation of the seaweed was proceeding. It became clear that they had met before and had already spoken on the subject several times.

"You won't survive to the end of your time if you continue like this," said Vasilii Petrovich to Artiom quietly, but distinctly, through the general hubbub. "They want to kill you for sure. It's as though you're carried away in some game. I don't even know how to help you."

"Vasilii Petrovich!" Artiom even head-butted his comrade into his much-wise forehead, which he had never allowed himself to do before. "Don't ruin my green mood of June! Nothing's going to happen to me..."

Vasilii Petrovich looked deep into Artiom's eyes and only sighed.

Artiom rummaged through his bag — if there was anything he was afraid to lose, it was the pillow that his mother had sent from home. For some reason, it was dear to him. He didn't even put it under his head but hid it somewhere under his heart and slept on it thus, but not always. The pillow, in its striped sheet, was there. True, it also smelled of the twelfth.

In the meantime, Moisei Solomonovich, without even noticing it, quietly began to sing: "Mania's heart is longing, 'I want, I want the open air... the luxurious carriage... to drive up the yard in regal splendor.'"

Mezernitskii, looking over the table, angrily rubbed his hands.

"Oh, poor Mania was so bored! Her dress was light as fuzz, Mania was bored with all the Italian paintings," Moisei Solomonovich sang prettily into his nose.

He performed the song as though all the whores and slags of all Rus had asked Moisei Solomonovich, "Tell them about us, have pity on us, man!"

The man pitied them for a while, but then, without noticing it, he began singing something completely different and unexpected.

When Moisei Solomonovich sang Russian songs, it seemed that behind his shoulders stood silent *muzhiks* — their ranks reaching almost to the horizon. His voice became so huge and high that in its space you could see the subtle ray of the sun and the swift that cut through that ray.

If he sang a romance, Moisei Solomonovich's face took on an aristocratic mien, and if you looked closely, you could see a dandy's mustache above his lip, which at other times was absent.

Only one thing unified the performance of all these songs — or rather, a verse from each of them, or even less — somewhere, barely evident, there was a constant, distant note of sarcasm. No matter what Moisei Solomonovich sang, he always remained as though not within the song, but outside it.

"They've moved our tenor," said Vasilii Petrovich to Artiom. "Now he's in the coop."

Moisei Solomonovich, by the way, had brought a dozen cabbage hand-pies and just as many with egg.

The table wasn't exactly rich, but was quite varied, full and set to an excessive degree.

"To eat all this at the same time is no sign of a man of breeding, but if there is tea, then, that's a different story," Mezernitskii announced. "Then, the combination of fish, cabbage hand-pies, seal meat, lingonberries and carrots become completely appropriate. Therefore Grakov, go get the samovar. It's bubbling on the stove in the corridor.

"Is that an analogion[36]?" Osip asked Mezernitskii.

"Not an analogion at all," answered Mezernitskii. "That's a bedside table! We've adapted it!"

Everyone laughed.

It seemed that the samovar took the last remaining space in the room, but when, "in harmony with the analogion," as Artiom thought, *Vladychka* John appeared, limping as before, then everyone enthusiastically moved to make space for him.

"Here… I brought some candies," said *Vladychka,* looking for a place to put his sweets.

"For now, keep your candies," said Mezernitskii, "first we will ask our guests to taste this seal meat, and when its place is vacated, we'll put your candies there…"

Before eating, only *Vladychka* John and Vasilii Petrovich crossed themselves, but no one else did, Artiom noticed.

In spite of its enchanting smoked and salty smell, the seal meat turned out to be as tasteless as a rag. Although, if they ate it with the hand-pies with cabbage and followed that with hot tea, it turned out to be not bad at all.

Everyone was chewing, everyone had tears of tension and sweetness on their eyes.

"Your time is almost finished, Mezernitskii," said Vasilii Petrovich, who literally dropped a tear when he had finished the seal meat.

"Don't even mention it, Vasilii Petrovich," Mezernitskii answered, as though a bit out of place and, therefore, comical.

"Where will you go? To Crimea again?" asked Grakov.

---

36 A stand used for icons in churches.

Mezernitskii looked at Grakov with caustic humor, simultaneously not denying himself a cabbage hand-pie. So, with his mouth full, he answered, "Of course to Crimea. I've got a common law wife there, then to Turkey, from Turkey to Paris, then to Moscow, then back to Solovki… I'll make the full circuit, you see." He drank it all down with tea.

Moisei Solomonovich laughed silently at Mezernitskii's words. Artiom found them funny as well. However, Vasilii Petrovich didn't smile at all.

"But really, where are you planning to go, my dear?" asked *Vladychka* John.

"Moscow, where else?" Mezernitskii answered calmly.

"Why Moscow? Run to the countryside, or they'll get you by the scruff and stick you in an envelope," said *Vladychka* John, and even gestured with his hand to show how they would grab Mezernitskii by the scruff. At this, everyone laughed, even Osip, to whom laughter was always unusual. These words, coming from the priests' mouth, were extremely unexpected and therefore all the more touching.

"Did they cure your ailment, *Vladychka*?" asked Artiom a minute later.

Everyone was already steamed up and were gradually becoming satiated. The biggest appetite ended up belonging to Moisei Solomonovich and Osip, who was not talkative today — apparently, he preferred a single attentive conversant to several rowdy ones at the same time.

"No, my dear," answered *Vladychka*, "They did release Zinovii. They only allow me to walk around in the fresh air and to stretch out my knee. So I came to you by invitation of Vasilii Petrovich," and he nodded at Vasilii Petrovich.

The door opened and Artiom was once again surprised. It was Burtsev.

"On the other hand, he was here before, so why shouldn't he come in for a bit," said Artiom to himself, calmly looking at Burtsev. "No one here knows your problems with him."

Burtsev immediately sized all the guests up with a single glance in that special manner that gives one the opportunity not to lock gazes with anyone in particular.

"Quite the… full house," he said.

There truly was no place for Burtsev, but, it seems, this didn't upset Mezernitskii in the least.

Vladychka John started as though to get up, but Moisei Solomonovich made to get up from his place entirely — having, it must be said, taken two candies with him, but Mezernitskii stood opposite Burtsev in a way that stopped all movement behind him.

"It's been a while, brother," said Mezernitskii and Artiom immediately sensed something even brazen in his address, as though he had gotten drunk off the tea. "Is everything well?"

Burtsev looked directly at Mezernitskii and said nothing.

"They say that you have a new job. I'm guessing that you've come to visit me, so that I would also share in your joy," said Mezernitskii.

"They offered me a transfer to the IID," Burtsev answered calmly.

He carried himself with much dignity.

"How great you've become," said Mezernitskii. "Soon you'll take Eichmanis's place, you're rising so fast..."

Burtsev looked at his now former friend and answered, "I am no clown, Mezernitskii."

Only after Burtsev had gone did Artiom realize what the point of the conversation was.

Burtsev, a member of the administration, had called Mezernitskii, a musician of the brass orchestra, a clown.

* * *

"Let me," said Boris Lukianovich to Artiom.

Artiom took off his makeshift gloves with pleasure — the real ones, as Eichmanis had promised yesterday, were supposed to arrive with the first ship from Kemi.

"He's a champion of Odessa," Boris Lukianovich nodded when the new candidate for the sports brigade arrived under guard.

Artiom said nothing, lest he make his sad doubts obvious. Judging by Boris Lukianovich's thoughtful manner, it was obvious that the Odessa school was no joke.

The forehead and nose, the shoulders and hands — everything revealed this fellow to be a real boxer. When he took off his bedraggled jacket, Artiom felt sick. His muscles reminded him of those wet and ten-times-twisted shirts that Artiom had sometimes wrung out with his mother.

Moreover, the fellow was incensed that they had pulled him out of his brigade. He had no desire to fight with anyone. But it seemed he had no plans to forfeit either.

He looked at Boris Lukianovich with dislike. He didn't look at Artiom at all.

The fight began at such a blistering pace that it seemed it would be over in seconds.

Boris Lukianovich, who up to this point had looked like an ideal among sportsmen in his combination of speed and power, now looked beefy, slow and worried.

The champion of Odessa struck everywhere and from all sides, as though he had six hands and every hand was doing its best to show itself as the fastest and fiercest.

In a minute, to Artiom's surprise, Boris Lukianovich even began to be a bit flustered, but he could do nothing about it. It was enough that he had not yet fallen, though one eye had already swollen up and one ear was livid as though fried.

In general, there was nothing stopping him from saying, "Thanks, friend, we're taking you on," but Boris Lukianovich, it seemed, had lost some of his wits from the frequent knuckle sandwiches.

The champion breathed through his nose and his very breathing was angry, irritated, thirsting to humiliate his opponent.

"There are no ropes here," he barked with disdain. "Would you do me the honor of honoring at least the semblance of a square? I'm not a runner to keep up after you."

Upset to his core by these words, Boris Lukianovich threw himself at the champion, and in a moment, he was lying, beaten down, his arms and legs akimbo.

Artiom crouched down near him, slapped him on the cheek, called him — thank God, he started to come up to the surface, slowly coming to terms with the objects around him, the sounds, the colors and the reason for Artiom to be right next to him.

In a minute, he sat down, holding his temples in his fists.

The champion, taking off the gloves and mittens, with extraordinary revulsion threw them on the ground, stood with his back to Boris Lukianovich, pulled on his jacket and eloquently put his hands in his pockets.

Boris Lukianovich asked for his glasses with a gesture at Artiom — as though he couldn't speak without his glasses.

"You work extremely well," he said loudly. "I am compelled to request your transfer to the sports brigade."

"I am disgusted by this entire sham," said the champion.

"Do you refuse?" asked Boris Lukianovich.

The champion remained silent for some time.

Boris Lukianovich had enough time to get up, not refusing help from Artiom, who had offered him his hand.

"I don't care," said the champion.

"It's a deal, then," Boris Lukianovich said indifferently and went into the sports barracks, which now had a roof. He waved at Artiom — come here, I want a word.

"Artiom, you're no match for him," said Boris Lukianovich simply. "First of all, he's heavier than you… But of course, that's not it… You have to find an opponent equal to your strength and preparation. Otherwise, it will be a quick and shameful beat-down. That also means that we need an opponent for him."

Artiom was silent and waited — what could he say?

"I think there is an opponent for him," Boris Lukianovich continued calmly, sometimes barely grimacing from the pain in his head. "There's a new inmate here — a British spy. Judging by his deportment, I've already decided that he's good…"

"But what if you don't find me a partner?" Artiom finally decided to ask.

"It would be better, in that case, to leave you in the sports department as a trainer and my assistant," answered Boris Lukianovich and, looking at Artiom, added. "You're not going back to your brigade yet, don't worry. But still, you understand, all this is temporary."

"Here's temporary, there's temporary, but you know, my time here is also not forever," answered a very grateful Artiom.

He had never needed much to be joyful.

Boris Lukianovich kept trying to fix his glasses, as though his face had changed shape, now his glasses became small and, in a strange way, also protruding.

"I think that means we have to go to IID," he said, touching his nose then his ear in turn. I'll write down the spy's last name for you. I keep forgetting it…

Artiom walked into the kremlin, enjoying his superlative good mood.

There was no need to figure out why. When there was so much vileness around you, there was nothing left to do but wear a gentle smile across your face.

"So here I'm going to Galina myself," Artiom thought as though in a half-dream. The day was warm, pleasant, the sun was gentle and the mosquitoes were slow. "I'm going to Galina, and something is going to happen there… and along the way, Passport may find me with a knife… and Gills with a garrote… and Shaferbekov with a crutch… and here I'm walking about… walking about."

The same sailor with a brazen mug and black teeth was at the post in IID.

Artiom suddenly realized he knew neither Galina's last name nor her title.

There was no time to stand there thinking, so he just said, "I'm here for Galina."

"She's not here," answered the sailor and got up for his smoke break outside. He walked straight at Artiom, there was no point in standing in his way, so Artiom, whether he liked it or not, hurried outside. The sailor still pushed him, just out of spite and rudeness.

"How nice it would be to turn around and smack him right in the teeth," thought Artiom, without being all that offended.

And, to pamper himself completely, he decided unexpectedly: "I'm going to the library! No one will even notice that I'm not here."

During his entire time inside, Artiom had not yet once been in the library, and remained sure that you couldn't just go there.

But no, no one stopped him.

He walked through into the reading room — the people sitting there were either inmates or hired workers. They were leafing through magazines, paying Artiom absolutely no attention. Everything was so quotidian, and therefore surprising.

Artiom walked up to the librarian, who was, judging by appearances, a priest.

"Good day, young man," he said. "What would you like? You, as I understand it, are not yet signed up here?"

"No, this is my first time," Artiom answered quietly, even squirming with pleasure.

"Which brigade?"

He quickly signed Artiom up and even opened a separated log-book for him.

"I'd like some poems," said Artiom in the same way a child asks for candy.

"Whose?" asked the librarian.

"Anyone's," Artiom continued in the same joyful whisper.

He received several ripped-up booklets — Nekrasov, Nadson, a volume of Briusov, a pile of papers from *The Red Virgin Earth* and something else with typography of different sizes, the letters either sitting or standing on each other's heads.

He sat next to the window. A gull flew to the window, knocked on the window with its beak: give me some food. It looked at him with an impudent eye.

Artiom didn't even begin to read it all. He just leafed and leafed through all these journals and books, reading two or three lines at a time, rarely a full stanza to its end, then leafed again. As if he had lost a line somewhere and wanted to find it.

He kept repeating a single poetic phrase without meaning, not understanding it and not trying to understand it.

"Whose feet will walk over our rust?" he kept whispering and his face looked like he was working out an impossible geometric equation out loud.

He wouldn't have noticed that it was getting dark, but hunger reminded him.

He walked out with the packet of books and papers. "Whose feet… over… our rust… damn it. Some kind of feet, rust. What will I say to Boris Lukianovich? Something. I'd better go buy some candied fruit for my evening tea…"

The store in the kremlin was already closed.

Artiom didn't dare go to the other store that was beyond the kremlin, because the way there walked right past the sports department. They might notice him; it would be awkward.

Artiom noticed that there was another store here — the retail store at the quay, at the far end of the camp administration building. He had noticed it when he and Boris Lukianovich had gone to visit Eichmanis.

It's true, only hired workers, soldiers and Chekists were allowed to shop there, but Artiom felt himself to be almost free after the library... At least, he really wanted to feel so and was happy to fool himself into believing it.

His pass indicated that any passage to the sea was forbidden, but he wasn't going to the sea, just to the administration building, where had already been.

This retail store was a bit richer. Artiom momentarily lost his breath when he saw the liver — oh, how much he wanted some fried liver! — the butter, the smoked sausage, the boxes of tea.

In general, he couldn't make it that obvious, so he hurried to the counter. Ahead of him stood a single soldier from the guard brigade, and the cashier was weighing candies and not looking at Artiom.

When the soldier, having put the candies in his pocket, left, Artiom resolutely walked up to the counter, but he didn't have a chance to open his mouth before the cashier butted it.

"Where are you from, buddy?"

"Released by amnesty, remained as a hired worker!" Artiom suddenly lied loudly, which he had not expected from himself a mere second before. "Let's get acquainted! I'd like some candy."

In actual fact, he wanted liver, but to buy that seemed a much more serious step that would have immediately uncovered his deception. But candies? What are candies? Nonsense.

It seems that Artiom was right about that, because the cashier, whose face, with its frozen smile, still registered doubt, dropped the remaining candies onto the scales along with the paper on which they lay in a sticky heap.

"We're actually closed already," said the cashier, quietly unhappy with himself.

"Thank you!" said Artiom, quickly giving him the money, so that the cashier, God forbid, wouldn't ask anything else like a document or the place where he worked.

But that's exactly what happened. As he gave Artiom his change, the cashier, scowling ever deeper, asked, "Where were you hired?"

Artiom extended his palm to receive the change that the cashier did not release from his paw.

"On rabbit island," he answered, smiling with all his strength.

"And what do you do there?"

Artiom, continuing to smile, grabbed the tip of the paper ruble and pulled it towards himself. The cashier loosened his grip.

"I breed chinchillas," said Artiom, looking back at the cashier from the doorway. "A special Solovetsian breed! They only eat counter-revs!"

Outside, after he had closed the door, he couldn't contain himself and laughed.

"Ha!" he was thrilled with himself. "Look at me!"

He popped a candy in his mouth and, biting through it immediately, enjoyed the evening sun and golden waves — what sweetness there was in everything.

Somewhere nearby a rifle went off.

Artiom jumped.

He didn't need any time to figure out what had happened — he understood immediately and at once.

There was a prison under the store. They put all the worst offenders against the regime there. And there, from time to time, people got shot.

That's why they called execution being "swept under."[37]

The sun shone; the gulls screamed; the waves crashed.

Artiom looked up to see where the human soul flew. It had to fly somewhere, right?

The candy was huge, revolting and sticky. It filled his entire mouth. Artiom unmistakable felt that he had a piece of soap in his mouth.

---

[37] There's an untranslatable play on words in the original Russian "pod razmakh" (swept under) sounds like "pod Rozmag" (under the retail store).

* * *

They woke him up at night — the knocking on the door was horrifying. Artiom never thought you could get covered in sweat so quickly.

Or maybe he was sleeping already wet?

Only rising halfway on his bed, he understood that if they had come for him, to "sweep him under", no one would have knocked on the door so cautiously, though insistently. After all, there were no locks on the doors.

"Who's there?" asked Artiom with a voice dry from sleep.

Osip kept sleeping as though nothing was going on. Before going to bed, he had eaten all the candies that Artiom had given him with pleasure.

"It's me," came the voice from beyond the door, without giving a name, but Artiom guessed it was Boris Lukianovich.

He opened it quickly.

"Artiom, please forgive me, for God's sake, but I can't do anything about it. We have to go. Get ready immediately."

"What is it?" It wasn't enough that Artiom was all wet, his heart was bouncing like a ball, painfully ribbing him.

"Some Chekists arrived either from Kemi or even from Moscow to visit Eichmanis," Boris Lukianovich whispered, glancing at Osip. *At such a minute, he's afraid to wake up that sweet tooth…* Artiom thought in passing, not knowing exactly what this minute even was or what awaited him. "Evidently, the head of the camp boasted about the Spartakiade, and they demanded immediate entertainment," Boris Lukianovich explained. "You'll have to fight him."

"Whom?" asked Artiom, not finishing pulling up his pant leg. "The champion of Odessa?" Even so, he had time to realize happily: *At least it's not execution.*

Boris Lukianovich only nodded.

Artiom finished dressing in silence. In the window, the night sun of Solovki shone, blending with the light of the lamps. The sun was like cottage cheese that his mother used to hang in cheesecloth — it seeped with pale liquid into the pan underneath. The light of that liquid was the light of the night of Solovki.

Outside, it was fresh, quiet, expansive. Artiom realized he had never seen the monastery at night.

There was not a single gull.

Black the dog ran up to see who was walking by. He wagged his tail.

After him appeared Bear the deer, who was standing under the rowan tree.

“The guests probably woke up our beasties,” Artiom guessed. “I should have left the sweets for the deer. Not given them all to Osip…”

“Where are we going?” he asked Boris Lukianovich.

“To the theater,” he answered. “They’re all there…”

The theater was located in a part of the former kitchens.

Artiom was immediately led into the green room.

He heard noises on the stage.

“Who’s there?” he asked Boris Lukianovich.

“The wrestlers,” he answered curtly.

In the corner of the green room, his eyes closed, sat the champion of Odessa. His face was pale and his lips were pursed together firmly. Occasionally, his jawline rippled.

“He’s going to kill me without any retail store,” thought Artiom calmly and fatalistically.

At the mirror stood a lifter whom Artiom knew, all sweaty and smelly. Judging by everything, he had already done his bit and was now upset at how much weight he had lost recently. He had not seen such long mirrors in a while.

On the table, a bit out of place, lay a chandelier.

“A stage prop,” Artiom realized. “Interesting, if I hit the champion of Odessa right now with the candelabra on the back of the head, will that affect the result of the fight at all?”

They brought in another performer — this time a circus performer.

He had only appeared in the sports department that morning and had promised to prepare a special act — breaking a stone on the chest of an athlete.

“So why is he without his stone?” thought Artiom, trying to sit down, though he didn’t want to sit at all. “And without the athlete? Will he ask one of the Chekists from the audience to lie down for a minute? Then he’ll bonk him on the chest with a hammer!”

He wanted to drink.

But not really.

“Maybe we can warm up a bit?” asked Boris Lukianovich without any real enthusiasm.

“Why not,” said Artiom and got straight up.

In the darkness of the offstage wing, he followed the noise towards a band of unpleasant light: at least let’s see what’s going on.

The Chekists were whistling there and soon Artiom saw the wrestlers too — they were bare-chested and dirty as the devil knows what.

One lay on his stomach, his legs tucked under him, sticking out his enormous back side, while the second was trying to lift him, his hands encircling his chest.

Artiom took one step forward and saw the guests.

They had placed a table near the stage. On the table stood many bottles and there was some chopped food — salad, cucumbers, sausage, bread.

About six people sat in chairs. Eichmanis and one more, unknown to Artiom, stood next to the table with glasses in their hands.

Eichmanis was in uniform but sweating, with an unbuttoned collar. The second was without a jacket at all, and noticeably drunker.

They were all armed.

"Lord, why did I get myself into all of this?" Artiom sorrowed. "How simple it would have been to fix it all. Nothing simpler! I would have just given the package to Passport, and that's it! Did you really need that package? You wouldn't have starved to death! Why did you volunteer? What, do you really know how to box? You don't know a damn thing about it!"

"Shut up!" He answered himself aloud.

He went somewhere. He needed to go somewhere, not to just stand in place.

Only there was nowhere to go and it was really dark for all that. Artiom immediately bumped into a chair and almost fell over with it.

He straightened out, dusted himself off and realized how badly his legs were shaking.

How was he going to move about on these legs?

He lifted the chair and sat on it. It seemed a little better — in the darkness, it was almost as though you weren't even there, only your mind was left, but if you turned that off, you'd be completely empty.

He tried to remember today's, or rather yesterday's poem — that line that he repeated for a while. Something about rust and feet. Rust and feet. Rust and feet.

"Interesting. How can those go together?" thought Artiom intently. "In a single line? Feet! And rust! And most importantly, that didn't seem to bother me at all! What a nightmare! What nonsense! Lord, what was that line? It's so terribly important! Nothing will work out if I don't remember that line!"

"Damn!" Artiom answered himself aloud again. "Damn it, stop already."

Getting up from the chair, he silently and angrily berated himself.

"What about the guy who got shot in the head while you ate candies? Was it easier for him? Was it? Wasn't he worried at all? All you have to do is go on stage and get a fist in the face. But they won't kill you! They won't shoot you!"

"Artiom!" called Boris Lukianovich in the darkness. "Artiom, where are you? It's time!"

Once again dropping the chair to the ground, Artiom hurried to follow the voice.

"There are no gloves," Boris Lukianovich fussed next to Artiom as he took his shirt off. "And they're not going to bring any. They've sewn these out of the cloth of an overcoat. Try them."

Artiom did. The fact that he was going to hit with these — that he liked. But the fact that he was going to be hit with them — that he didn't.

The champion was pulling on his gloves completely indifferently.

As before, he hadn't looked at Artiom once.

"There's no way out of this. Hang in there. I'll be referee," Boris Lukianovich said as they hurried to the stage. "I'll try to help you out."

"Sure," Artiom answered. "Just get him in the liver, why don't you, while no one is looking."

It was a bit brighter on stage than he'd like. It took a little time to get used to it.

By now, there were four Chekists standing at the table, and all, except for Eichmanis, were red-face, meaty — and all of them were chewing.

Eichmanis was pointing with his empty glass at the champion from Odessa and was saying something quietly.

Artiom didn't listen on purpose.

However, he did hear how Boris Lukianovich asked his opponent, "Can you hold off, please? At least one round."

His opponent didn't answer, hitting one glove against the other.

The fight started, as was expected, terribly. Artiom found himself in a meat grinder and the fact that he didn't immediately fall was an objective miracle.

Boris Lukianovich saved him, when he stood between the fighters at the first opportunity, once again, quietly, trying to impress upon the champion: "I'm asking you, do you hear?"

The fighter just pushed Boris Lukianovich aside with both hands, powerfully squeezing him in the shoulder.

"Fuck you, dog!" Artiom said to the champion.

He didn't answer. It seemed that he understood Russian badly.

"I'll just manage half a minute; it'll be enough," Artiom decided desperately and threw himself towards his dishonor.

Seven seconds later, he ecstatically realized that he had managed to avoid a hit that would have taken his head off his shoulders like an over-ripe pear.

He didn't manage a counter-punch, but at least he vigorously sketched out an attempt at it.

He didn't manage to keep his opponent at arm's length — he could hit him hard from three steps away.

Artiom was trying with all his strength, and he was utterly powerless.

Once again Boris Lukianovich intervened.

"Hey!" Someone yelled from their seat. "Get out of there! Fiodor, tell that fucker not to butt in. He's ruining it!"

Eichmanis smiled at the one who was yelling and commanded, "Boris, please move to the side for now. This isn't the actual competition, after all!"

Artiom, his hands on his knees, was trying to catch his breath, looking at the champion from under his eyebrows. The champion stood in place and seemed not to be the least winded.

Boris nodded to Artiom finally: I did everything I could. It's up to you now.

Artiom looked at the hall one more time and suddenly saw Galina, whom he hadn't noticed yet. She sat farther off, holding an apple in her hand. He couldn't make out her expression.

The rest Artiom remembered only in fragments.

The face of the champion appeared, then someone yelled, "Come on!" Artiom, protecting his head and absorbing hit after hit, threw himself forward again with a firm intention to scratch out that scum's throat. He realized he had only managed one hit — from below, into the chin — so hard that the champion took a step back and shook his head, as though he were trying to stick his eye back in its place. Looked like he managed to put it back in.

Because all Artiom saw after that was the ceiling and round lights.

He didn't notice the hit.

At first, the light was under his eyelids, and the circles were red.

Then he opened his eyes and the circles remained, only now they were yellow.

The stage underneath him swam.

* * *

The Chekists were screaming like huge, fat-faced, drunk gulls. Their voices were very pleased.

Artiom recognized Eichmanis's voice, also pleased and excited.

"But they're in different weight categories! He's much heavier! That one's lighter! But he stood for a while, didn't he!"

"Yeah, yeah, he stood," they answered him. "Then he lay down."

Everyone laughed.

He heard the noise of clinking glasses.

Boris Lukianovich helped Artiom get up.

"Not bad," he kept repeating. "Not bad. Not bad at all."

Artiom noticed that Galina was no longer in the audience. There were fewer Chekists in general, as two or three of them had gone out. Maybe to smoke…

"Boris, Artiom, come down here, have some food. Call in the wrestlers, the circus performer…" Eichmanis called.

"Thank you, but we…" Boris Lukianovich began in an apologetic tone; Eichmanis simply rocked his head back as though he were amazed: "… What?" And Boris Lukianovich, though he was nearsighted, immediately ran into the green room.

Artiom was slightly nauseous.

"I'm just going to put on my shirt," he said to Eichmanis.

"Go on, go on," he answered, smiling.

When Artiom returned, everyone except for the champion from Odessa was already standing by the table. No one was eating yet.

"Go ahead and pour some for yourselves," offered Eichmanis to the wrestlers. "Where is he? Mr. Rapid-fire?" he asked Boris Lukianovich.

"He's washing up, he'll be here soon," he lied. Artiom had seen that the champion was sitting in the green room in his own place, his eyes closed.

The wrestlers didn't need any convincing, the circus performer poured himself an entire glass to the brim, though Artiom couldn't remember when he had managed to perform.

"To the Spartakiade!" said the fattest Chekist, extending his glass to Eichmanis. "The inspection has determined that…" he didn't finish his phrase and drank almost the whole glass in one gulp.

Eichmanis, in contrast to his guests, clinked glasses with every single sportsman and even said something to each of them.

"That was beautiful… how do you do that? Boris, thank you, not bad at all… Artiom, I understand what sort of an opponent that was! I drink to your impudence! Chekists know the value of impudence. It costs a great deal sometimes! Especially since you almost knocked him off his feet."

Artiom still hadn't come to himself fully and couldn't understand what to think of himself and of his defeat — was it a total disaster or not quite?

"Well, have some food," Eichmanis said in parting and the Chekists left. Only the fattest, having gone five steps, returned to take an unopened bottle.

"You know I've got a cellar over there," Eichmanis laughed. His eyes though were immovable.

"They'll get drunk, all right," the other answered. "The food's too greasy."

Artiom noticed Boris Lukianovich's face — he looked at the fat Chekist with hatred. He held a glass of vodka that he hadn't even touched to his lips.

"So, here's the list," continued Eichmanis, having waited for the Chekist with the bottle to leave with him. "Wrestling. Boxing. Gymnastics — there's some real masters there. Football. And the final — a pyramid made of all the participants…"

Boris Lukianovich, relieved, put the glass back on the table.

"You're not gonna drink, Lukianych?" one of the wrestlers asked him.

Other than the cucumbers and sausage, there was also a bowl of red caviar and a bowl of black. In a tin can that used to hold cocoa, there was melted butter that no one had touched.

But Artiom knew that if you put some melted butter on a piece of bread and salt it — it's very delicious.

There was salt as well.

He tore off a bit of bread and put the butter on it, thick as his finger, then black caviar on top, red on the top of the black, then sprinkled it with herbs and decorated it with a cucumber slice. The cucumber had been bitten in places by the Chekists, but that didn't seem important.

"One more?" offered the circus performer.

They drank, but Boris Lukianovich once again abstained — he didn't eat anything either, only rolling a bread ball between his fingers and holding it.

"Lukyanich, what's up?" asked one of the wrestlers, already half-drunk.

"I'm full," he answered quietly, but Artiom saw that he was revolted.

Artiom remembered that when Boris Lukianovich raised him and he sat up on the stage, after the yellow orbs, a Chekist's face appeared. He was holding the bowl with the red caviar, which he ate with his fingers, then licked them clean.

"So what…" said Artiom to himself, biting the bread, smudging himself and gathering the bits of caviar that had fallen on his shirt with his free hand.

"I'll go bring him some to the green room," said Boris Lukianovich, taking the sausage. There was no bread left.

"I'm drunk too," thought Artiom pleasurably. He couldn't remember the taste of the first glass of vodka or the second, but suddenly the wave came and it immediately became cheerful and pleasant, and in his chest a fuzzy, tickly, gentle knot formed itself. He wanted to hug someone, he wanted there to be a good song.

The vodka ended after the third round, they almost licked the bowls with caviar clean; they finished the greens to the very last leaf.

They went outside — the sun rocked back and forth and quivered.

Somewhere near the gates of the kremlin, they could hear the voices of the Chekists. They were swearing loudly, and someone was calming down someone else.

In his room, Artiom was purposefully loud, hoping to wake up Osip, but without success.

"How nice would it be to have a shot of vodka right now," said Artiom out loud. "Or a beer or two… What do you think, Osip?"

Osip didn't even move.

Just as quickly as it had appeared, his cheerful mood left him.

He suddenly felt himself to be beaten, offended, pissed off and pathetic, all at the same time.

"I hate to lose!" Artiom told himself out loud, drunk and smelly and hating himself. "I hate it! Should I pay Passport to kill him? I've lost my edge! I've only just started and already I've lost it! Let Passport knife him…"

Suddenly, Artiom needed to hurl and he quickly turned to his side to save everything that he had eaten up after the Chekists.

He had no strength to change. He wanted to cry.

Artiom rummaged with his hand in his bag next to the bed and took out the pillow his mother had sent him. He put it over his heart, bit his blanket with his teeth, breathed with his nose and felt the wet under his eyelids.

Everything around him was wet, black fog roiled and in the fog, Artiom barely noticed himself, sitting on a mount in the middle of an enormous body of water.

"If I move, I'll fall into the water and drown," he understood.

He heard the lapping sound of an oar.

A boat floated out of the mist — first its nose, then gently and soundlessly the rest of it slipped out. Artiom saw an old man who was standing in the boat. He had an oar in his hands.

You couldn't see his face, only his beard and high forehead and, it seemed, blind eyes.

His long robes were wet on the bottom.

In the boat itself, dirty water splashed. The old man was standing in it almost to his knees.

"I can't go on that boat. We'll drown…" thought Artiom. He pushed the boat onwards powerfully, so that it would float farther away.

He was left to sit alone.

* * *

Eichmanis was in a good mood, though slightly hung over — by his eyes, you could see that he had gone to sleep in the early morning, but got up energetic and active around nine, immediately drank some vodka, and when he saw his guests off, drank another shot right at the quay.

He rode to the sports department to see how the building and field were coming along. Jumping down from the horse, he spoke about something to Boris Lukianovich.

"Oh, Artiom," Eichmanis said. "You fought well. I wanted you to win."

Artiom felt the smell of alcohol — not a stale and old smell, but a fresh, strong one, like the bottom of a winter cabbage barrel.

"The thing is that Artiom came out as a replacement," began Boris Lukianovich. "We now have another heavyweight…"

"The English spy, Robert?" asked Eichmanis.

"Yes, Robert."

"And no middleweight?" Eichmanis quickly asked, looking at the footballers.

"Not yet. But I do need Artiom's help in the sports department," Boris Lukianovich added, not understanding where the head of the camp was going with his conversation.

"Oh, you'll be fine by yourself, since that's the situation," said Eichmanis.

Artiom went cold — his fate was being decided, and, he thought, not in his favor.

Boris Lukianovich looked at Eichmanis silently.

"He's coming with me," Eichmanis said abruptly. "Today. On a trip. I need smart people, but not counter-revs. 'Not a very common product!'" He laughed, but immediately grimaced. It seemed that he had drunk a great deal the night before, and sometimes his hangover asserted itself.

"So what do we do?" asked Boris Lukianovich.

"You?" Eichmanis asked in his characteristically commanding tone, which immediately chilled the blood. "Nothing. Practice. Artiom, go to your room, gather your things and wait for me outside. I still need to gather a few people. They say there were a few draftsmen in the twelfth? Kabir-shah?"

"Yes, he's there," answered Artiom, feverishly trying to decide what had happened — something good or bad?

Nodding, Eichmanis rushed back in the direction of the kremlin.

"I don't even know what to think," said Boris Lukianovich.

Artiom silently gave him his hand, said goodbye and left.

Osip wasn't in the cell.

He divided the money he had in two — one half he took with him, the other, he rolled into a tube-shape and put inside his mother's pillow, right there where the threads were coming apart…

He thought about whether or not to bring his dry ration.

He decided to take the potatoes and the carrots, the salt in a box and some tea. He rolled out a piece of fabric, put everything in it, then tied it into a bundle to put on his shoulder, having tied the ends into a knot.

He didn't take a change of clothes, only tying his jacket around his waist and putting on his cap in case of rain.

If he was lucky, they'd feed him and put him to sleep under a roof.

If not… well, that meant he wasn't lucky.

"But I'll still get my edge back," decided Artiom, still afraid to scare off his good fortune.

He quietly sang: "I don't walk on plush, on velvet, but I walk on… the edge…"

Outside, he immediately saw where to go. At the tower where they used to bless the water stood Kabir-shah and his brother Kurez-shah, Mitya Schelkachov and one more unknown young inmate.

A little farther off, Passport shifted from one foot to the other.

Artiom, paying no attention to him, nodded at Mitya, walked up to the tower and sat on the grass.

They didn't wait long for Eichmanis — it seemed he had drunk another one hundred grams. This time, he appeared on foot together with Galina and two soldiers, and he looked over the assembled men.

Everyone immediately stood straighter. Artiom also, naturally, got up, noticing that Passport had disappeared as though he was never there.

"Good! Citizen comman—" Schelkachov tried to yell, but Eichmanis cut him off with his hand: not necessary.

"The cart is at the gates, let's get in," he commanded one of the soldiers.

"I've been looking for him for several days," Galina said quietly, but he heard it.

"Anything urgent?" asked Eichmanis.

Galia moved her eyebrows eloquently: why are we discussing this in front of the prisoners?

"Well, where is he going to go?" Eichmanis brushed it aside. "You'll finish your work later. After all, I just gave amnesty to my entire projects services group. I got no one else…"

It was clear that the head was eager to get away from his girlfriend, Artiom decided.

He walked slowly towards the cart, expecting any moment to be called back.

But that didn't happen.

When he was sitting down, he saw that Galina was walking back to the IID with a disgruntled expression.

Some of the inmates who were walking along the courtyard did not address Eichmanis properly. He, only a minute ago in a positive mood, suddenly yelled in unfeigned rage: "Who! Who are they? Which brigade! What? Get the commander of the brigade here!"

The soldier who stood closest immediately ran off, not quite knowing yet where he was going.

The inmates stood pale-faced, looking at Eichmanis with bulging eyes.

The commander of the brigade wisely did not allow himself to be found, but the group leader did show up and Eichmanis took him by the scruff.

"What sort of discipline is this?" he yelled with a strong, but angrily raspy voice. "They don't know how to greet the head of the camp? What is going on in your brigade? Hear my command! The commander of the brigade is transferred to the thirteenth! All of these — into solitary! After work hours, line up the entire brigade and drill them for three hours!"

"Serves you right," thought Artiom, sitting comfortably on the cart, "Next time make sure to cultivate the habit of greeting the head, got it?"

He wasn't quite serious when he thought this; he mostly mocked himself. But he still thought it.

And he wasn't ashamed of it.

* * *

Their work ended up being unexpected and strange.

At first, after crossing a dam built by the monks, they arrived on the island Greater Muksol'ma. There, from the time of Abbot Philip, at a fitting distance from the monastery, cattle had been bred. Eichmanis didn't end that tradition, apparently. From a distance, you could hear bulls bellowing, huge cattle ranges came into view, and it stank.

"Where are we going? Do you know?" asked Mitya.

Artiom shrugged his shoulders.

"In any case," he said after a short silence, "I don't see any reason to worry. They'd hardly drive up to some secret Solovetsian mine while accompanied by Eichmanis."

Mitya smiled, but he didn't stop looking around.

Eichmanis either rode far ahead or returned back; he noticed a rowan tree near the road and rode horseback towards it to tear off a bunch of berries.

Artiom thought and thought, and, waiting for Eichmanis to ride away, he jumped off the cart and ran to the rowan tree. Though he had doubts — to tear off berries after the head of the camp… there was a bit of a challenge in that…

"But it's not his rowan tree," Artiom convinced himself, running after the cart and seeing how the soldiers who accompanied the head of the camp were looking at him darkly.

He gave each of them several berries. Mitya, grimacing, chewed one, while Kabir-shah and Kurez-shah didn't dare eat one. They kept holding them in their hands, sometimes smelling them.

They didn't enter the cattle ranges, they only left the cart there. Their final destination was on the island of Lesser Muksol'ma.

Eichmanis once again disappeared somewhere.

It was low tide and they walked from Greater to Lesser Muksol'ma by foot, along the rocky seabed. Everyone looked with interest at their feet.

Artiom, unable to contain his boyish enthusiasm, from time to time picked up small rocks and threw them.

It was obvious that Schelkachov wanted to do the same thing but couldn't bring himself to do it.

On the left, you could see Mount Tabor; Artiom found, perhaps for the first time, that twilight at Solovki was beautiful. The drying out, broken, tall grass, the rare boulders in the grass, the small evergreen wood.

There were only three huts and a chapel on the island.

Eichmanis sat on a log next to one of the huts. Next to him stood a bearded monk who looked like one of the former monks. They were talking, very slowly. Judging by their way of speaking, it was clear that this meeting was not their first.

Eichmanis's horse, untied, was munching grass nearby.

There was nothing servile in the old man's pose.

It seemed that the local warden hadn't been warned of Eichmanis's arrival and greeted the guests after a notable delay.

He ran out in his shirtsleeves, still tucking it in as we walked and only noticed the inmates and soldiers. He overlooked Eichmanis completely.

"Warden Gorshkov..." began a soldier, running up to Eichmanis.

Eichmanis, unhappily grimacing, showed him with his hand that he should shut up and immediately made a circular gesture with his finger: turn around and go back to the place where you came from.

Gorshkov, tripping as he walked, froze on the spot and frantically tried to figure out what to do. Finding no other way out of the situation, he turned and walked back a little, secretly expecting to be called.

"Go ahead and finish sleeping," said the head of the camp to the warden.

"I wasn't sleeping, Citizen Eich..." he began, turning around sharply, his small eyes spinning, but Eichmanis repeated a short chopping gesture with his hand, as though he was chopping off any speech directed towards him, except monastic speech.

The warden moved off, perplexed, but his back and the back of his head continued to reveal a torturous expectation of at least some kind of command from the authorities.

"Gorshkov!" Eichmanis relented. "Take care of these people."

The warden quickly returned and indicated the third hut to the soldiers in a whisper, while the rest he led to the old man.

Artiom, who had already sat down on the grass, decided not to fuss — or else he might not find the doors to the hut.

"Gorshkov wants to invite Eichmanis into his hut," Artiom realized.

Something suggested to him that there was no point in hurrying anywhere. Occasionally, he would tear off a single rowan berry and then roll it around his mouth for a long time, from tooth to tooth, as though he were making fun of it.

"Hey, let's go," Gorshkov called Artiom, clearly feeling leery of calling the prisoner a jackal in front of Eichmanis, as was usually the accepted practice.

Artiom started to pretend to get up.

Gorshkov turned around and Artiom sat back down.

The old man reached into the pocket of his coarse pants and pulled out a pipe and a tobacco pouch.

"Are you still smoking, old man of the seals?" Eichmanis asked looking carefully at the old man's hands.

"What else is there to do? This way I can get rid of the stench," answered the old man without smiling.

Eichmanis nodded in his way.

Artiom thought that this nod could mean anything — it could mean, for example, that the head of the camp appreciated the wit of the old man, or that he was offering him to keep talking until they led him under the retail store, where he belonged.

Eichmanis looked at Artiom, and for a moment he regretted that he didn't leave; however, now it was too late to move.

The head of the camp looked at him as though he had only now discerned him amid the surrounding nature.

"Father Feofan," said Eichmanis, not taking his eyes from Artiom. "Why don't you bring us a pair of mugs?"

Artiom didn't look away and looked right back at him calmly, barely smiling.

"How strange it is to hear 'Father Feofan' from his mouth," thought Artiom slowly, without moving. Something was going to happen right now.

"Go get it," said Eichmanis to the soldier.

He untied the bag that he had brought with him and got a bottle of vodka out.

"Anything to eat with it?" he asked quietly.

Eichmanis barely noticeably and with slight impatience shook his head, which was interpreted thus: no, get it over here quickly.

Father Feofan brought out two mugs, having hung them by the handles on his wonderfully long and seemingly burnt trigger finger, which, to top it off, was crowned with a bony and twisted nail.

He didn't take them off his finger, just stuck them under the bottle of vodka. Only when each was filled to the brim did he careful pull of the outer one and give it to Eichmanis.

"Artiom, come here," the head of the camp called. "You're not allowed, soldiers," he added, looking at the soldiers, though they hadn't even hoped to be included in such company.

Artiom accepted the invitation with external calmness, but inside everything was rejoicing.

"Feofan here doesn't drink," added Eichmanis, raising his squinting gaze at the old man. "Or have you started?"

The old man didn't smile, nor did he answer, only curtly and indeterminately rocked his head.

"I know you monks," said Eichmanis. "You always prepared your home brew out of the berries. Sinners!"

"It happened," Father Feofan answered calmly.

Eichmanis downed his mug without clinking Artiom's. Then, not looking at him, he extended his hand. Artiom quickly figured out what the gesture meant and gave him the bunch of rowan berries. Eichmanis, contentedly nodding, pulled off one berry and ate it.

Artiom also drank without closing his eyes — he couldn't miss a thing.

Eichmanis lifted his empty mug and Father Feofan also figured out what to do and offered him his long finger. The head of the camp once again put the mugs on his finger.

"Twenty-five years on Solovki." Eichmanis nodded at Feofan, though he was speaking to Artiom. "It's your twenty-fifth, right?" Father Feofan blinked his heavy eyelids in assent. "Four years he was in the monastery, then he came out here… to Letter Muksol'ma… He built himself a hut and began to… combine his labors of prayer…" here Eichmanis pulled off another berry from Artiom's bunch of berries and threw it in his mouth. "… with fishing and hunting sea beasts… and when the Bolsheviks appeared, he didn't leave this place. All he started to do was smoke baccy. For him, as a specialist," Eichmanis smiled, not so much at either Feofan or Artiom, but rather at the pleasant alcoholic warmth in his chest and head, "we've assigned eighteen silver rubles as a salary… He continues to do what he did before — he fishes, hunts, gives the kitchens of Solovki its fish and the farms their seal meat. Our pigs eat it. That's why I call him 'the old man of the seals'. And he answers. Do you still go to the chapel to this day, old man of the seals?"

"Why should it stand empty?" answered Father Feofan simply.

"Does Gorshkov pray with you at least?" Eichmanis asked.

"He hasn't been noticed," answered Father Feofan, provoking the head of the camp to laugh from the bottom of his heart.

The camp leader's laugh was not very pleasant, but Artiom also laughed — a little quieter than Eichmanis, but a little louder than the soldiers who stood nearby.

"Go, Artiom, get your assignment," said Eichmanis.

In Feofan's hut, all the vessels were handmade. In the icon corner, there was an entire iconostasis — the "Burning bush", the "Mother of God of the Firs", the "Mother of God that Comforts my Sorrows", and several "Kazan Mothers of God". Seal skins were drying on the walls. The smell was heavy, muggy, but it didn't smell of man and that was good. The icons in all this indestructible and heavy fish-smell had a strange effect. Artiom thought that if he were to carry the smallest "Kazan" icon from here to another house, then the entire house would smell of fish in a single hour. From the farthest chest to its very foundation. You would pull out your lace cuffs and you would jump in surprise, as though a fish had put them on for its fishy holidays.

… They didn't let them rest — what was the point of resting anyway, when they hadn't started working yet.

Until the evening, the inmates dug holes wherever Eichmanis indicated.

At first, they would unearth one place, then move a half a kilometer, then do the same thing.

Kurez-shah and Kabir-shah's job became clear very soon — it turned out that they were both draftsmen. They were given a meter-stick, a pair of binoculars, an old map and they were sent without guards to study the local area. Judging by everything, they were going to make a new and very detailed map.

Artiom worked deftly, quickly, even with pleasure; he didn't show any tiredness. Eichmanis noticed this, Artiom was sure of it and for that reason he started working even harder.

Mitya Schelkachov, on the other hand, was constantly getting tired. He was a Petrograd lad, booking and not used to physical labor.

The third inmate, though very young, was also remarkable for his peasant way of working and his quiet constancy in work. His name was Zahar.

What they were all doing Artiom only guessed when the sun was already setting and his back, wet from sweat, began to get cold.

They were looking for old monastic treasure.

… He guessed, but he told no one.

* * *

"This place had always been a slaughterhouse, that's why the monks didn't leave. They're used to it!" Eichmanis laughed, following Father Feofan with his gaze.

Father Feofan didn't have lunch with everyone else. He thanked them and said that he had to go check the tackle.

Eichmanis didn't argue with him.

It seemed that Eichmanis was drunk, though it was an unusual drunkenness that did not remind Artiom of his father's dark alcoholism.

At first glance, there were no signs that the head of the camp was drunk, except maybe that his skin was a little paler and his eyes heavier. His speech was still well-formed. The only thing that surprised him was that he spoke a lot more.

Now they were sitting on the shore and eating: Artiom, the two soldiers, the inmates… Artiom sat closest to Eichmanis.

The soldiers wisely held themselves at a distance and from time to time looked at Artiom with displeasure: he had settled himself in definitively. Whenever he'd notice any disorder on the tablecloth, Artiom would slice either some more sausage or some more greens. The soldiers didn't like his high-handedness, nor did they like that he was holding a knife in his hand. But it was inappropriate to put a prisoner in his place when he was invited to eat by the head of the camp.

Eichmanis, from time to time, nodded at the empty glasses, then Artiom would pour vodka for himself and Fiodor Ivanovich. The rest either immediately refused or it wasn't even offered to them.

Kurez-shah and Kabir-shah didn't even dare sit at the self-styled table in the presence of the head of the camp — as it was, they awkwardly crouched and kept getting up at Eichmanis's slightest movement.

Even when he started to talk, they got up, as though they could not even imagine that you could listen to such a big leader while seated.

Eichmanis saw this with the corner of his eyes and it seemed he was enjoying it, but he didn't let it show.

Schelkachov and the other young inmate also tried to sit in a way that wouldn't block Eichmanis's view of the water or irritate the soldier with their closeness to the authorities.

From time to time, Artiom, by what right no one knew, took from the tablecloth either a piece of sausage or a cucumber, or a piece of bread and passed some of it off to Mitya.

Mitya shared it with his comrade and they chewed very slowly and silently.

Artiom had a high tolerance for alcohol. If anything made him drunk, it was the ecstatic madness of this situation.

He terribly wanted everyone to see this. And mentally Artiom counted off the list of everyone: Afanasiev… Burtsev… Sivtsev… the Cossack Lazhechnikov… the Chechens and the gangsters… Grakov, of course. Curly and Krapin… Doctor Ali! And that bitch Galina too…

For some reason he didn't want Osip or Boris Lukianovich to witness the proceedings, but Artiom didn't start contemplating that topic and just mentally deleted them from the list of names called to witness the feast.

Vasilii Petrovich was still up in the air, and Artiom, in his blessed contemplations, either sat him across from himself or got rid of him entirely.

This was perhaps the first time during his time at Solovki that Artiom was truly happy. Then there was that sun, right in his eyes. All that smell of smoked sausage — he didn't hurry to give too much of it to Mitya, though he tried not to think about that, instead eating as much of it as possible himself, thrilled with its natural delight.

The soldiers, in addition to everything else, also, evidently, wanted some sausage, but you can't just walk back and forth in front of Eichmanis to grab stuff from the tablecloth. They took an egg each and some fish — and he, content with that, comrade soldiers!

Eichmanis himself ate little, following each shot either with some dill or parsley. Squinting at the sun, he said, "The monastery: over a kilometer in circumference, walls a height of nine meters, six meters thick. Eight towers. A fortress! A monk-stonemason had made niches in the wall and inside the towers; at first, they wanted to use them to store powder and ammunition, but then they changed their mind and did something else. They used those niches for prisoners! Each niche was two steps by three steps. A stone bench and that's it. You slept half-bent! The window was three timber frames and two bars. Eternal half-darkness. And a chain on the wall, to boot… No royal pardons were every given to Solovetsian prisoners. No amnesty…! They couldn't correspond with their families! Their terms were thus — 'for all time', 'until correction', or 'until the end of his life nowhere and interminably'. Eh? Nowhere and interminably!"

Eichmanis chewed some parsley together with the stem and sucked his teeth.

"And they had underground prisons!" He said quietly and clearly, turning to Artiom, though Artiom felt that Mitya Schelkachov, sitting behind him, was listening with all his strength. "Do you know how they looked? The roof was the floor of a threshold. In that roof, there was a crack — to pass down food. The defrocked priest Ivan Buianovskii was imprisoned in 1722 — Peter imprisoned him — and in 1751 he was still in prison! Thirty years! The rats ate off his ear! One of the guards felt sorry for him and gave Buianovskii a stick to beat off the rats — well, they beat that guard with whips…! The underground prison, a huge one, as they wrote then, 'horribly frightening, completely soundless' — was found in the north-west corner of the Korozhansk tower. Under the exit threshold of the Dormition Church was Saltykov's prison. There was one more hole in the ground in Golovlenkov's Tower at the Archangels' Gates. The Cellar Prison was under the kitchen cellar. The Transfiguration Prison was under the Cathedral of the Transfiguration… How did they feed them? Water, bread, rarely some cabbage soup and kvass. They insisted that no fish should ever be given to them to eat!"

Artiom looked at the tablecloth and took a fish tail just in case, then sucked on it, deferentially looking at Eichmanis.

"Do you know what happened later?" said Eichmanis. "The Synod forbade underground prisons — too cruel! But the monks of Solovki didn't fill them up! Why? It was convenient! You never had to carry out the latrines! I tell you, it was always a slaughterhouse here! Our Father Feofan had nowhere to go! You won't scare Solovki with a prison."

Artiom really wanted to ask: if it was a slaughterhouse before, then, does that mean that Fiodor Ivanovich considers it to still be a slaughterhouse?

But he didn't ask that. He wasn't an idiot.

Gorshkov arrived on a horse, heavily dismounting to the ground.

You could tell by his look that he had spent no less than half the night with Eichmanis at the same table.

"Sit down, Gorshkov," said Eichmanis.

He sat down, looking at Artiom with surprise, who this time poured the vodka without being asked.

Gorshkov was, as most other Chekists were, a fat-faced, large fellow. Their breed, Artiom had long noticed, had amazing cheeks — such a cheek you definitely could not pinch. The meat on those cheeks was tight, hardened in constant work, as though these mugs only did one thing — sucked the marrow out of the toughest bones.

"I know what you're thinking," said Eichmanis to Artiom, once again drinking without clinking classes and paying absolutely no attention to Gorshkov. "You're thinking, in what way does our version differ from the previous? Do you know the answer or should I tell you?"

"I know it," said Artiom.

"Is that so? Tell me," commanded Eichmanis.

Gorshkov — he also led with his cheek in Artiom's direction.

"If I say it wrong, he'll bite my neck," Artiom understood. "Then they'll fry me up and eat me."

"It's not a prison here," Artiom answered firmly. "Here, they create a factory for people. Back then, people were put in underground holes and held, like worms, in the earth until they died. Here, a choice is given — either you become a person, or…"

"Aha, or we'll grind you to powder," added Eichmanis. "Do you truly think that?"

Artiom became sober. In his ears was a slight ringing. The day around them was also ringing — all the trees, movements of air, voices of birds.

One of the soldiers broke a branch nearby. He was preparing the bonfire.

"I think you have a government within a government here," said Artiom. "Your own dominion, your own kremlin. Your own palace, your own monks. Your own army, your own money. Your own newspaper, your own magazine. Your own means of production. Your own hairdressers and courtesans. Your own executioners." Here Gorshkov twitched his cheek and looked at Eichmanis, but he didn't react. Artiom continued, "Your own theaters, your own servants, and, finally, your own inmates… As I was entering, I heard that they yelled to us, 'Here it's not the Soviet government, but the government of Solovki.' That's true. The religion here is common — a Soviet one, but the religious offerings are personal. And on all this, you create a new man. It's civilization!"

Artiom fell silent and sat looking at the tablecloth, not daring to lift his gaze at Eichmanis. But unexpectedly, Eichmanis laughed.

"And our own language too, yes? Little by little, we're developing our own tongue here." It wasn't clear whether or not Eichmanis was joking, and Artiom nodded, just in case. "A mix of the criminal and the aristocratic, Bolshevik newspeak and the lexicon of the White Army officer, the languages of actors and prostitutes. 'Everything is confused: the nobleman's coat, the peasant's kaftan, and the blouse!' Maybe Kurez-shah and Kabir-shah will add something of their own. What do you say, you innocent victims of the Bolshevik dictatorship?"

Kurez-shah and Kabir-shah nodded.

Eichmanis watched this unquestioning agreement for a few seconds with obvious pleasure, then became suddenly serious, and, turning to Artiom, continued crisply, "We have our own class system, our own class hatred, and even our own social structure — something, I think, similar to militant communism. There's a pyramid — we, the Chekists, are on top. Then the counter-revs, then the former clerics, priests and monks. On the bottom is the criminal element — the backbone of our workforce. Our proletariat. True, it's been de-classed and demoralized, but we are obligated to reeducate it and raise it up again."

"Why are the counter-revs placed so high, Comrade Eichmanis?" Gorshkov unexpectedly spoke.

"Who's in charge of the scientific research?" Eichmanis answered quickly. "The bourgeois intelligentsia and the former counter-revolutionaries. Who acts in the theater? The same. Who organizes all the activities in the club, who organizes the educational work in classes, who gives the lectures…?"

Eichmanis turned away from Gorshkov and finished his thought, looking Artiom in the eyes: "This is not a camp. It's a laboratory!"

* * *

Artiom woke up at night with that wonderful feeling when you don't know where you are sleeping, but you remember that nothing frightening, you think, is going to happen — quite the opposite, in fact.

It was half-dark in the hut, but in a minute, Artiom could discern the eyes of the Kazan Mother of God, who watched the white night without blinking.

Having stepped over Mitya and Zahar, he went into the yard.

Having heard a noise, Kabir-shah immediately awoke and sat up — you could see the frightened whites of his eyes in the half-murk.

"They're shining just like the icon, you heathen," Artiom thought sarcastically, but aloud said, "It's just me. Go to sleep. It's still night."

Gorshkov's window was alight again; it seemed half-open — the voices came through very clearly. Who or what was talking wasn't immediately obvious, but you could discern a frequent laughter that was Eichmanis, barking fiercely, as though mocking.

Forgetting where the outhouse was, Artiom sprinkled the corner of the house.

"Like a dog," he thought, yawning.

His head was especially clear — whatever he drank didn't stay in the body. He had dug hard, sweated, drunk a lot of water and in the evening, he had even bathed, though the water was autumnally cold.

On the way back, he jumped — Father Feofan was standing by the hut. It he hadn't been smoking his pipe, Artiom would have walked right by him — because the monk looked like an inanimate object, something like a tree stump, for example.

"Hell, that's awkward," thought Artiom. "He probably heard how I… on the corner… Who prevented me from turning around and pissing in the grass? Honestly, I'm an idiot."

"Good night," Artiom said hoarsely and killed a mosquito on his cheek.

"Good," answered the former monk calmly.

"Listen, Father Feofan," Artiom was happy that someone was talking to him, and he promptly forgave himself for his bestial behavior — youth does such things all the time. "Is it true that Eichmanis is looking for buried treasure?"

"Is that a secret?" answered the old man. "He's looking everywhere. He's dug up half of Solovki already. Now he's looking here. And he's asking me where best to look."

"Why haven't you found it yourself, Father Feofan? Since you're giving the advice, you should have looked."

"What use is it to me? I'm not planning on leaving anywhere. If you take out the gold into the sun, it'll ask you why you've taken it out. I've got enough to answer for already. But Eichmanis isn't afraid of that question. Let him look."

"Feofan!" someone yelled from the warden's hut and Artiom recognized Gorshkov's voice.

At the same moment, Artiom realized that the old man had only just left Gorshkov's hut as though to smoke, but in actual fact he wanted to run away back to his place, since the nighttime revelry with the Chekists was grating on him. He smelled not of the fresh night of Solovki, but of human vigilance and his clothing smelled, not of the air and the evening, but of people and wine.

"Like a dog," Artiom had time to think again. "I'm sensing everything like a dog."

"Eh?" answered Father Feofan.

"Who are you blabbing with over there?" asked Gorshkov and stuck his head out of the window.

"The inmate Artiom Goriainov," answered Artiom after thinking for a bit, and immediately heard how Eichmanis clearly said behind Gorshkov's back, "Let them both come in!"

"Both of you, over here!" commanded Gorshkov and loudly returned to the table, rocking the plates. Someone loudly moved a few chairs.

Saying nothing to Artiom, Feofan humbly ambled back to Gorshkov's hut.

Led forward only by good premonitions, Artiom returned to his bed for his shirt and getting dressed along the way, hurried after the old man. Good thing that he had left the door open, or it would have been awkward, swearing, to climb into another's, much less a Chekist's house. On the way, there would have definitely been some kind of damned bucket, and he'd be lucky if it'd be empty, not filled with the host's slop.

Gorshkov lived austerely. There was a stove in the middle of the hut, next to the stove was a bed, but, judging by the bed roll right next to the entrance, it seemed that today Eichmanis took his host's bed. Except for the table and chair, the only other furniture was a chest. A bunch of dried fish hung above the window; above the bed was a saber and a watch hung on a nail close enough to be grabbed while lying down.

Eichmanis sat at the head of the table, not in the least, despite Artiom's unclear expectations, tired or bloated from the night-time revelry, unlike Gorshkov. On the contrary, it's as though Eichmanis had become a bit sharper and quicker in his glances and movements. Gorshkov, with his scowling, slow manner and his tight cheeks, clearly did not correspond to his superior's mood.

"Have you come up with an answer?" Eichmanis asked Father Feofan.

"I never had any, Fiodor Ivanovich, any answers, that is," said the monk.

"The proletariat is better than Christ," Eichmanis said quickly, as though not listening to Father Feofan. "Christ persecuted me from the church, while the proletariat put everyone there — those who betrayed, those who shot and those who stole from their neighbors… The revolution may be one thing, it may be another, but where is the great truth that can withstand the Bolshevik truth? To preserve that Russia that was falling apart into pieces, rotting from within, but covered in tinsel gold on the outside? Preserve for whom? Why?"

Eichmanis quickly looked at all those assembled, and Artiom calmly met his gaze.

"Solovki is direct proof of the fact that everyone is at fault in the Russian slaughter. What? Were the brigade and platoon leaders from the 'old guard' kinder than the Chekists? Artiom, tell me. Feofan doesn't know."

"They're all… great," said Artiom with an intentional pause.

Gorshkov shook his tight cheeks and for the thousandth time looked with fury at Artiom, then at Eichmanis: how dare this jackal…? But Eichmanis didn't look at Gorshkov again.

He silently looked at Artiom without winking.

Artiom for a moment thought that the head of the camp's eyes were completely insane. There was nothing human in them. He shifted his gaze to his hands and saw that Eichmanis's wrists were not manly, but almost like a musician's and his fingers were thin, his nails pale, groomed and clean.

"Why didn't you pour him one?" Eichmanis asked Gorshkov. "Pour it, he's your guest."

Gorshkov, not looking at Artiom, shoved the bottle and a glass towards him, grabbing one and the other in a single hand with meaty and almost red fingers, with no nails.

Eichmanis sniggered.

Feofan looked at the table.

Artiom poured himself enough for a large gulp and immediately drank it.

Some unevenly cut herring lay on a platter — it smelled enticing and tremulous. Artiom decided not to reach out for it, but in a strange way, he felt that this herring had something in common with female enchantments… the same kind of engorged, flowing, incredible…

He even bit his lip to distract himself.

"Not long ago, in Finland, there was a soldier who deserted," Eichmanis continued from a place that only he understood. "And they immediately published a book, in Russian, think of it! Bokii just brought it for me," explained Eichmanis, looking at Gorshkov curtly. "That filth writes in his little book that in a single year we shot six thousand seven hundred people here. Over there the fine ladies are probably swooning as they read it. We are capable of executing six thousand, sure, or sixty-six. But in a single year, we only had seven thousand inmates on Solovki! And whom did I execute? Three orchestras, two theaters, the fire brigade and the breeders of foxes? Together with the foxes!"

Artiom thought about it, then he reached for a piece of pie that lay on a platter next to Gorshkov.

It turned out to be filled with cabbage — it was light and sweet, and it seems that Artiom even got goose bumps of pleasure.

After that, he grabbed a piece of the herring and threw it in his mouth… O-o-oh. He chewed with eyes full of ecstasy.

Gorshkov swallowed his saliva and sighed heavily: "Haven't you stuffed yourself enough?" his look said.

"As if you didn't have enough," thought Artiom.

"They also write that we torture inmates here," continued Eichmanis, as though not noticing what was going on at the table, even though, in actual fact, he saw everything. "For some reason, they don't write at all that it's the inmates torturing other inmates. The foremen, work group leaders, superintendents, commandants, brigade commanders, wardens, bursars, the entire medicinal and cultural-educational infrastructure, all the clerical workers — they're all inmates. Who tortures you?" Eichmanis again looked at Artiom, and he immediately stopped chewing, not from fear, but more as a quiet and unassuming joke. "You torture yourselves much better than any Chekist does!"

It seemed that Eichmanis was starting to lose it. Artiom guessed it by looking at Gorshkov, who slowly removed his hand from the table and straightened out.

"Naked!" Eichmanis loudly said in the same tone that actors use when reading poetry from the stage. "They write that our inmates go out to work completely naked! But what if they're the gangsters that gambled away their own clothes? Have I undressed them myself? What idiocy! Do you know what would happen if I handed out boots to everyone right now? Tomorrow half of those who have them will be left with nothing!"

Eichmanis grimaced, as though he were holding back a heart attack.

"They write that we house prostitutes with nuns! Well, what did you expect? That we would have one house for nuns and one for whores? What about a special wing for baronesses? And then, the prostitutes walk around naked, and you're surprised? I put them together exactly for that reason, because immediately I have fewer fights and less syphilis and debauchery and degeneration and hell!" Eichmanis took a glass and on the word "hell", slammed it on the table.

"We've only separated the political prisoners!" Eichmanis was lecturing either someone here or someone absent. "And the priests too! And we dig, with our hands, we gain the money to make it all to everyone's liking! Because that which Moscow sends is enough only for your coffins! And that's right! We have to know how to make our own profit; we're not in paradise. What do you want? The whole country is living like this! War awaits this country! They're squeezing the juices out of the peasant! Out of the working man! And we should leave you in peace?"

Artiom, to his good fortune, had already managed to chew through half the pie and sat, looking either at the bottle — it was still half full — or at the herring — it was completely untouched, arousing him in natural fashion, agitating the manliest parts of him.

The carousing of that night was stupendous. Sometimes Artiom pinched his leg: was he dreaming this? A sweet drunkenness spread once again through his head; he would have drunk more.

Artiom wasn't afraid of Eichmanis in the least. He didn't understand why Gorshkov feared him.

They said that Eichmanis once personally shot someone for Dzerzhinsky's birthday. Maybe he did, but why would he shoot Artiom?

"To read what they write about us, it seems that there are only political prisoners here and that they're all sitting on pikes on Anzer," Eichmanis was saying. "But we have housebreakers, lock picks, pickpockets, thieves from railroads and thieves from train stations, thieves of bicycles and horse rustlers, thieves who steal from churches, from stores, from exchange offices, thieves who rob the guests of their prostitute-partners, keepers gambling and drug dens, misers, counterfeit money makers that fool the peasants... But they write that the best people of Russia sit here and suffer their *via dolorosa*. By the way, Artiom, did you know that there are more Chekists imprisoned here than White Army officers? No? Well, know it!" Eichmanis suddenly laughed, looking at Gorshkov.

That laugh relaxed nobody.

Now the monk looked at the window, as though he were expecting the dawn — they say that all evil spirits disappear with the dawn. Gorshkov now looked at the table.

"And we take worse care of them than many others!" Eichmanis said with some inspiration, "Artiom knows in what sort of monastic cells the counter-revs and priests reside! Chekists don't get those rooms! They're all in the same barracks. Although, it would seem, whose merits are greater before the revolution? The Chekists or the counter-revs? What do you think, Gorshkov?"

Gorshkov bit his lip and began to look straight ahead of him intensely, as though the answer were written in small letters on the wall across from him.

"No one's!" Eichmanis answered for him mockingly. "The revolution cares for none of your merits! They've all been a-nn-hi-la-ted! And we've started counting anew! Whoever works, he eats the pies! Whoever doesn't work, the worms will eat! There Artiom sits, but what if he runs away tomorrow?" At this, Gorshkov jumped again and even looked for his revolver on his hip — it was there — should he shoot the runner? But Eichmanis wasn't giving the signal and continued, "He'll run away and tell them all the whole truth. But what truth does he know? He was in two brigades, worked the logs five times, picked berries five time and interacted with about twenty other inmates. He can describe his barracks, but it's not as if that were the limit of the world… And here, it's not so much a camp as a huge farmstead. Count on your fingers!" He commanded Artiom. "Timber preparation — the sawmill and woodworking factory. Fishing and catching seals. The Beef ranch and the dairy. The lime and alabaster factory, the ceramic factory, the mechanical factory. The coopers, the shipwrights, the rope-makers, the sand-paper makers. More workshops: tannery, leather-making, cobblers, blacksmithing, brick-making… Add to that our shoe-making factory. The electrification of the entire island. The distillery. Oh, you're out of fingers. Let's start from the beginning…"

Eichmanis poured himself a glass and Artiom thought that everything here drinks by the hands on the clock, skipping over Feofan… His turn was next.

"… The railroad, peat harvesting, salt factory, the animal farm and the agricultural farm. The monks couldn't grow anything here, they said, 'it's the wrong climate', but we've done it! Potatoes and oats! Dispatches by boats and steamboats. Building new buildings, remodeling the old ones. Upkeep of canals that the monks dug out. The nature reserve and the biological garden inside it. Tar works, radio station and publishing house. Theater. Even two theaters! An orchestra. Even two orchestras. And two magazines. And a journal. And an infirmary, a pharmacy, and three retails shops… By the way, where did you buy that cap, Gorshkov?"

"In the shop," Gorshkov quickly answered.

Eichmanis, looking at Artiom, nodded as though Gorshkov's cap was the clearest proof of everything he had said.

"They write that we feed our prisoners badly. But where am I to get the food? The nature is severe, there is a minimum of natural riches. All of our factories and industries can only be a support. For. Our. Inner. Needs. Of. The. Camp. But we're cunning and we feed more people than the monks ever managed. If they had been brought so many prisoners, they would have all died in a week… They write: their medical care is bad. But we order, every year, medicines worth over two thousand rubles! Where are they? I ask you! Where? Maybe they steal them? But if I only torture the Chekists in solitary for that, will they write about that? What about our school for the illiterate? They won't write about that! What about the church I opened, allowing former priests and monks to walk around in their cassocks. They don't write that!"

Feofan suddenly opened his tightly closed mouth with a smacking sound and uttered, "To first forbid the use of cassocks, then allow it — and you're saying that it's a good deed you've done? You could also whip someone, then put oil on the naked bones — that's another good deed."

Eichmanis suddenly got cheerful, otherwise it started to seem as though he was getting more and more bored by the minute.

"Oh!" said Eichmanis, as though Feofan, together with Gorshkov's cap, once again proved his point. "And he said that he had no answers. I knew he did!"

Feofan was silent, but Artiom, in a strange way, continued to hear what he had said. The old man uttered his fricatives as though they were something round and shaggy, something to grab into your arms and pet.

Gorshkov twice creaked with his teeth and almost choked on his low-browed fury, but Eichmanis stopped him with the meekest possible glance.

"Feofan, other than his holy stories, has never read anything probably. As for Artiom, he's read Dostoyevsky, I think. I remember that Dostoyevsky wore fetters during his penal service in Siberia. For every infraction, they whipped them. Like children. Have they whipped you here?"

Artiom remembered how Krapin beat him with a bludgeon, but what was the point of talking about that? Therefore, he just shook his head: no, they haven't whipped me. It's true. No whip had been applied to him.

"And I see no fetters on you," said Eichmanis, raising his voice. "What? Do you take them off for the night?"

Feofan again made a smacking noise with his mouth — it seemed that he had another Northern-accented word with furry fricatives ready, but this time Eichmanis stopped him.

"What you just said, I like it. And if Gorshkov thinks to get back at you later for that, I'll force him to hunt for seals himself. But now, be quiet. In general, it's time for you long-robed ones to shut up once and for all. Artiom and I will speak, for no one else will explain these things to him. Artiom, do you like poetry? I sometimes read poetry. They say that poets know how to say the most… yes. If they will write poems and sings songs about us, that means that we will be justified for all time. And they do write and sing of us already. But this is what you have to pay attention to, Artiom. The common folk in the Russian village never read poetry. The most important things were explained to them by the priest — everything about God and Russia and the Tsar. Every time Blok published a book, the print run was no more than a thousand copies! But any priest in any village has three thousand parishioners. That's much more powerful than any theater! Now there's the moving pictures, but the priest is still stronger than they are, because the moving pictures are silent, and everything rushes about there. But the priest — he doesn't rush. And the monk never rushes at all."

Eichmanis looked at Feofan, checking if he was hurrying to get a bit of sleep in before the dawn, or if he was enjoying himself.

"And if the priests say that the Soviet government is from Antichrist — and they say that constantly! — that means that we will not be able to establish any kind of socialism in that village while the church stands there," said Eichmanis, looking sideways, maliciously at Feofan, as though he were enjoying his silence. "It's not even spoken in our wheels! The priest is pulling our cart in the opposite direction and he's carrying it with much more success! In the best-case scenario, we are equally matched. The *muzhik* listened to his priest for almost a thousand years, but we have to teach him to listen to us in ten! That's quite a challenge! And we will accomplish it!"

Eichmanis sat for half a minute, looking at the table and lightly rolling the empty glass between his thumb and middle finger.

"They say that we have killed the Russian priesthood," he quietly continued. "Not a bit of it. In Russia, there are forty thousand churches, and in each one, there's a priest, and each of those priests has his superiors. While in Solovki we only have a single brigade of them — one hundred and nineteen! Even those are only the most obnoxious and pernicious. Where are all the rest? They're still in their places. They're still preaching about the kingdom of Antichrist. No, Feofan?" Eichmanis suddenly screamed and commanded even louder, "Shut up!"

"It would be fine if they were only preaching!" Eichmanis continued, twisting a smile as his voice became metallic and frenzied. "But no one is talking about what was actually found in the monastery on Solovki when we got here in 1923. Here's what we found. Eight three-inch-thick cannons. Two machine guns. Six hundred and thirty-seven rifles and Berdans with a hu-u-u-ge reserve of bullets. Feofan!" Eichmanis again roared unexpectedly and angrily. "Who were you planning to hunt? Seals? From cannons? Eh? Shut up!"

"We know what this is, right?" asked Eichmanis, now definitely not speaking to those seated here, but someone behind their backs. "An impregnable fortress that the English couldn't even take, while Tsar Alexei the Most Peaceful besieged it for ten years. And it's full of weapons, like a pirate ship. By the way, the monks here have long been specialists not only in prayers, but in firing guns. And what would you have the Soviet government do with this place? Leave it to be a monastery? That's… fantastic! What wonderful good-heartedness. But I think it's enough that we didn't execute all of them immediately, but let them live here. It's true, we took away their cannons… But if Feofan writes an official request for a cannon, I'll take a look at it…"

Eichmanis shook out his tobacco pouch and finally rolled himself a final cigarillo.

He looked for a light with his eyes, but he only found the old monk and Artiom, who immediately felt something unpleasant.

"… Go to sleep," said Eichmanis tiredly and unhappily.

But his face looked as though he didn't just really want to rest, but quite the opposite. He suddenly woke up and noticed that he was talking to people who were not his friends, even strangers.

Artiom was already walking out when Gorshkov unexpectedly, in a single moment, fell asleep.

Outside, he and the monk heard a terrible ruckus and someone's sharp cry.

Artiom stopped, but Feofan, on the contrary, hurried on even more quickly.

In the house, Eichmanis's laugh rang out.

Having thought about it, Artiom walked after Feofan. In a few steps, he understood what the noise was. Eichmanis had knocked the stool from under the sleeping Gorshkov.

* * *

That herring, with all its butter and gold, didn't leave Artiom's head… except his head had nothing to do with it.

As he left Gorshkov's hut, he at first felt completely safe, but then he suddenly felt how painfully it ached below his belt, as thought there was some kind of wire that was uncurling of its own volition — and there was less and less space. It felt simultaneously frightening and worrying and shameless.

Feofan, who had entered the hut, came back out and asked, "Are you going to bed?"

"I'm going to breathe for a bit," Artiom answered hoarsely, knowing in advance what he would do.

From the alcohol, he was brazen and reckless.

"Well, breathe, then," said Feofan. "I'm going to close the door… mosquitoes, you know."

The mosquitoes were spinning about in front of Artiom's face, but below that wire was pulling more powerfully, and, barely managing to wait before Feofan closed the door, Artiom rushed behind the hut, far away from the windows — and grabbed himself with his whole hand — his member was alive, hot, bulging, filled with humming blood.

Eichmanis laughed again, but Artiom couldn't care less.

The forest that stood nearby was full of rejoicing songbirds.

It was as though it were a huge factory. Someone was carefully sewing on a sewing machine. Someone was striking the silver keys — key to key, key to key. Someone was washing crystal cups in a vat. Someone was turning a screeching bolt. Someone was shaking a stopped clock. Someone was pushing spools of cloth against each other. Someone was dropping resonant rings onto a wooden finger. Someone was pulling water from the well, pulling it up by the chain. Someone was snapping with scissors, measuring the paper. Someone was chipping at wood, someone was rolling nuts in his hand, someone was trying out a golden coin on his teeth, someone was clip-clopping horseshoes, someone was hurrying everyone else, ripping the air with a whip, someone was tut-tutting at the lazy, someone, finally, shrieked — it was as though the entire forest was singing along to Artiom's ecstatic blood.

"How are there so many birds here?" Artiom thought dimly, as though with his last effort. "The forests on Solovki are usually so quiet, as though dead… but what's this now?"

Barely making it to the corner, Artiom already got on with pleasuring himself. The mosquitoes were flying around his bare hand that shuttled back and forth, they couldn't land on it — that was funny, but not funny enough to laugh, because inside his stomach, painlessly and quietly, the wires were popping one by one, more and more freedom and space opened up inside, and on this freedom, a huge flower bloomed — sticky, sunny, full of honey.

And all the crazy birds…

He imagined a woman — white in her white parts and dark in her dark parts, breathing with an open mouth, not knowing how much more to twist herself to open up even more.

In the last minute, Artiom couldn't bear it and smashed three mosquitoes who were sucking his blood, fiercely pressing his cheek to his shoulder, and simultaneously feeling as though the stars were falling into his moving hand.

A boiling, gentle wave passed through his entire body — from his brain to his heels, and it went somewhere underground, into its very core.

"This is how the world was born!" he suddenly understood, as though he had screamed it inside himself. "This! The world! Was born!"

It all came out. It took a very long time to all come out — like that, like that, like that… will this ever end? It was already not sweet or tantalizing, but a bit painful and nauseous and chilly. The barely-opened flower was closing, cooling, hiding — but the mosquitoes increased seven-fold, Eichmanis laughed without stopping, and in the house where Artiom was spending the night, someone had turned around. It was very close and very audible.

Artiom squatted. His head was spinning. He felt the ground with his palm, and on the ground was something thick and wet, as though someone had coughed up phlegm.

He got up quickly and wiped his hand on his pant leg.

No world was created. There were white spots on the trees, visible in the light of the night of Solovki. He stomped them with his foot.

* * *

No one had seen Eichmanis since the morning.

Artiom, no sooner had he woken up and gone to wash, couldn't stop himself — he went behind the hut to see if anything was left of yesterday's debauchery.

"Or else, Eichmanis will appear, find everything immediately and ask strictly, 'Who messed about here yesterday?'" Artiom laughed at himself.

He felt a bit grossed out. But bearable, bearable…

Feofan got six herrings for breakfast — in the morning they no longer reminded him of anything feminine, but the taste was as good as before.

Everyone ate greedily, quickly, with pleasure. They licked their fingers and smiled at each other. At the table, they almost didn't speak — they were so absorbed.

Artiom noticed that the whites of Kabir-shah's eyes were turning red from intensity.

Schelkachov had the best manners — you could tell he was well brought up. Sometimes he attentively looked at the icons in Feofan's corner, squinting slightly.

"I think that if I ate herring like this every day, that would be what real human happiness looks like," Schelkachov suddenly said, looking at Artiom.

Artiom nodded with a smile; he appreciated what was said.

"Thank you, Father Feofan!" Artiom loudly thanked him on his who-knows-by-whom-granted rights of primacy here, when the herring had been finished off.

He would have been ashamed to admit to himself that he wanted Father Feofan to talk with him. For some reason, it seemed to Artiom that Feofan understood why Artiom needed to take a breath last night, and Artiom felt nauseously uneasy from that thought.

Instead of an answer, Feofan threw some kind of rag on the table — possibly his old underwear. Everyone began to wipe their forty-times-licked hands, and no one was disgusted with it.

Feofan left the hut.

"And may the devil go with you, old demon," thought Artiom, "who knows what you've done during your whole impoverished life…"

When all the others had little by little wondered out into the light of the sun, Schelkachov smiled so sweetly at Artiom that they immediately started talking. It helped that Artiom didn't get enough sleep and still felt the fermentation of the alcohol inside — in this state for some reason he was always talkative, opened up wide and curious about others. He wanted to talk twice as much because of Feofan — that quiet and insistent shame demanded distraction.

"Have you understood what we're doing?" asked Artiom with a cheerful whisper.

Schelkachov shrugged just as cheerfully, meaning that it would be hard not to figure it out.

Artiom still widened his eyes questioningly: how did you figure it out?

Here they both laughed, because they both realized that after Artiom's first question they could exchange a few phrases without actually saying a word.

"They called me here," said Schelkachov, "because my business is in icons."

"Where?" Artiom didn't understand.

"They moved me out of the twelfth," answered Schelkachov. "To the museum that Eichmanis established."

"There's a museum here too?" Artiom was amazed, remembering yesterday's list. He hadn't mentioned the museum as he had counted off his fingers.

"Yes, yes," said Schelkachov. "In the church of the Annunciation. Two and a half thousand icons. Among them, miracle-working images of the 'Sosnovskaia' and 'Slavianskaia.'"

Here Schelkachov attentively and quickly looked at Artiom, who immediately figured out the meaning of that glance — Schelkachov tried to understand if all this was significant for Artiom or not. Judging by everything, Schelkachov himself was a believer — which you couldn't say of Artiom, though he didn't make it obvious — on the contrary, he nodded respectfully and with interest.

"They say that the 'Slavianskaia' is the work of Andrei Rublev, and that Abbot Philip of Solovki himself prayed in front of it. Later he became the metropolitan of all Rus, then later he was suffocated by Ivan the Terrible's command."

Artiom once again nodded with an expression indicating he had heard all about those stories, and he did know something about them in the past. He had just forgotten it all a long time ago.

"What do you do in the museum?"

"I sit in the altar to the Annunciation and I draw the plans for the exhibition. I determine the century, the value and the content of each icon… The head of the museum bartered me from the twelfth for the price of three church robes." Schelkachov laughed, and Artiom joined him. "I know a bit about icons and other antiquities — I studied them. So I figured it out quickly why… Fiodor Ivanovich… needed me. If we uncover some accidental thing, he needs to know immediately if it's thirty or three hundred years old, if it's valuable or just take it or leave it, whether or not it's worth it to continue digging in any given place."

"Do you know if he's found anything yet?" asked Artiom.

"Who's going to tell us?" Schelkachov shrugged. "Maybe he did. Those are the rumors… They say that he found a note in some document that the treasures are in the place where the third head leaves a trail on the day of the Trinity, and that you have to dig exactly three meters deep. Under the head, let's assume that means under a cupola. So they found the necessary head, they dug on the day of the Trinity — they set up a whole shock brigade here, but found nothing… But I have heard that he studies all the church documents and they're constantly bringing him monks from the former monastery."

The third young man in their company, Zahar, came up to them.

He was short, bow-legged, big-nosed, with more bristles than expected for his age. You could see that he hadn't shaved for three days, and already he was overgrown. If he didn't shave for a week, though he was twenty years old or whatever, he'd have a full, curly beard.

Artiom had wanted to ask him yesterday where they had met before, but he kept forgetting.

"You don't remember?" Zahar smiled. When he smiled, squinting, it was as though his eyes disappeared under his eyelashes. "They brought us on the same boat, we almost suffocated in the brig, and in our stupidity, we were the first ones out — but we should have done the opposite. Then there would have been some space at the exit and we would have been able to breathe a bit."

Artiom nodded: yes, that did happen.

"We were together in the thirteenth also, but we rarely crossed paths in that crowd, and I was without a beard then, they kept sending us to different work groups… Then they moved me to the twelfth exactly when you…" Zahar, again squinting, looked at Artiom and added, "Started fighting with the gangsters, then landed in the infirmary."

Artiom was pleased that it had looked, from the outside, like he was fighting with the gangsters, not jumping away from them like a maddened louse, from one bunk to another…

"I heard that they moved you to the sports division?" Schelkachov asked him, and Artiom realized that he had long been using the informal you with Mitya, while Schelkachov still used the formal address.

"Let it be," Artiom quickly decided.

He nodded: yes.

"Boxing?" Schelkachov said with admiration.

Artiom snickered. It was doubly funny because Zahar, judging by his expression, was hearing the word "boxing" for the first time and didn't know what it meant.

Though he had never really taken time to think about the people surrounding him, Artiom easily guessed that Zahar wanted to be friendly with him — with Artiom, that is — and the reasons for that were simple enough. If you become friends with the gangsters, you have to sell yourself and lose yourself, but with Schelkachov it was hard, because he's smart. Zahar wanted to be friends with a man he understood, in the hope that in a difficult moment, he would maybe help him out.

But Artiom had already long abandoned friendship with anyone, since he figured out that no one can help anyone. More than that: it was better not to burden yourself with anyone — what was the point of Vasilii Petrovich or even Afanasiev watching how the gangsters were beating up Artiom; that would have driven him to an early grave if Burtsev hadn't broken his head first.

"And I'm still mad at Burtsev?" he suddenly thought, or rather, he understood. "I should find some herring to bring him as a gift. If wasn't for him, I'd be torn to pieces already."

Schelkachov was also not against becoming friendly with Artiom, if only for the reason that they shared a lexicon, used participial phrases and obviously shared a love of books. But Schelkachov was not necessary to Artiom for all that, and he was friendly with him only because it was pleasant and amusing, and today, it seemed, no one was going to kill him — and isn't that a reason to be joyful?

Moreover, any morning that begins with herring from the kremlin is an extraordinary, excellent morning.

Before lunch, they worked for a short while — some of them dug, some of them drew maps, but Artiom spent most of his time waving away the thousand-winged bloodsucking monster with his shovel.

A soldier watched them, but didn't get involved or rush them — he was probably ordered not to: watch, but don't butt in.

By lunch, Gorshkov appeared with a swollen face and a fresh abrasion that went across his cheekbone all the way to his temple. In his hand, he carried a scroll.

Artiom looked at Gorshkov with a bit of worry — who knows what's on his mind after yesterday's humiliation.

"Good, citizen warden!" Artiom barked just in case, kicking Schelkachov in time for him to support Artiom. Zahar only managed to join them by "… warden."

"You're going to shave and wash right now," said Gorshkov, as though he didn't hear the greeting. "You've already brought lice to our little island. And we need it about as much as a bullet in the head."

Feofan came after him with pies.

The pies were yesterday's or the previous day's, possibly even a week old, but who cares when you spend the entire day outside with a shovel? Everyone rushed to eat, choking on it and breathing with their noses, looking around with their eyes from time to time, checking if a bottle of milk had grown up from the ground somewhere nearby or maybe even some water.

"You'll drink from the lake right now," said Gorshkov.

Not only that, but the pies were not only with cabbage, but some were with jam, and when that jam appeared on Artiom's fingers, he even squinted: where am I? Who am I? Why am I eating jam? Am I asleep?

At the lake, Artiom and Zahar quickly threw everything off themselves and climbed into the water. Schelkachov stopped thoughtfully, while the Indians froze on the spot completely.

Artiom quickly figured out why Schelkachov dallied. Around his neck, around his waist and on his ankles hung little bags with camphor and garlic — Vasilii Petrovich also adorned himself thus, to the terror of the lice — but these smelly wards, it seemed to Artiom, didn't really help. Artiom had once also thought about wearing them, but quickly decided that to eat the garlic was much more pleasant.

"Why are you standing there, stupid-eyed?" Gorshkov yelled at the Indians. "Get down to the water!"

Artiom swam farther but didn't drink the water. He did wash out his mouth with the water, gargling the water in his throat and spitting it out three times — so it was almost like he did drink.

When he swam back, everyone had already gotten their soap, while Father Feofan walked with a razor blade along the bank, as though waiting for the first one to decide to return.

Kurez-shah and Kabir-shah stood up to their waist in the water, weekly splashing themselves and looking at Father Feofan with a certain amount of fear.

Zahar was the first to get out — judging by everything, he didn't like to swim and quickly got cold.

"Maybe I can get my bristle myself, while you take the head?" he offered.

"Don't be afraid, I won't cut off more than one ear," Father Feofan unexpectedly joked, and everyone took their turns laughing. Even Gorshkov smiled, but yesterday's abrasion made its presence felt, and he immediately scowled.

"Interesting: does he call Eichmanis a bitch in his thoughts, or is he too afraid? Or has he convinced himself that he fell from the stool of his own free will?" Artiom amused himself.

Without hair Zahar became a kid, though his nose grew twice as large and became sharper.

“Are you from the Caucasus?” asked Artiom, all lathered up and not getting out of the water, continuing to rub himself thoroughly.

“From near Lyptsi.” Zahar answered, as though expecting to be mocked for it, though not wanting it. “We’re peasants. But we do live on a hill. It’s small, but it’s a hill.”

He kept caressing his own head, amazed at how he looked — it wasn’t a done thing to shave your head in the villages. In the old days, a shaved head marked one as a convict, and now, he *was* one.

Artiom felt that the kid didn’t like the joke, so he didn’t pursue it.

He saw how the skinny, though leanly muscled Schelkachov was getting out of the water, and as he came out slowly behind him, spraying the soap off himself, Artiom caught himself thinking — perhaps it was an inappropriate thought, but he had it just the same — that he was the most good-looking one here.

All it took was not working for a few days and to eat pies and herring, and all sorts of nonsense starts crawling into the brain…

Schelkachov, though shaved bald, didn’t look that different. He used to be a big-headed kid from Petersburg with attentive eyes, and he still was that. The only difference was that he now had larger ears and his bluish pate was somehow funny.

It was Artiom’s turn to get shaved — Feofan did his job effectively and carefully.

Artiom kept waiting — especially in the moment when Feofan firmly took him by the chin with two fingers, shaving under his lips — that he would whisper: “And as for you, you swindler and masturbator, I’m going to chop off your nose for messing up the grass near my window.” But nothing like that happened.

The sun already lost its heat when Artiom rinsed off the small, shaved hairs and the bits of skin from his shoulders, and suddenly, looking at his reflection in the water, he almost laughed aloud — his entire face shone with such cleanness and youth, his body felt such ecstasy — what sort of a prison was this anyway, and why is it here, in this place? — if his entire life, all the way to the sun, was ahead of him. The sun danced in the water next to him, like a piece of butter.

In the meantime, the Indians couldn’t bring themselves to trust their faces and hair to a bearded monk with a blade. They kept standing in the lake to their waist, covered in goose bumps and completely frozen.

Artiom was just acquiring the taste to savor the spectacle of the shaving of the Indians, but unexpectedly, Eichmanis appeared, sober and energetic.

"Good!" Artiom yelled very sincerely. Eichmanis familiarly chopped off his scream with his hand: be quiet.

"You're in which brigade, Artiom? I forgot." Artiom started to answer, then quickly pulled on his shirt — it's not good to talk with the authorities naked — only realizing whilst in his shirt that Eichmanis was talking to him not as an inmate, but as a fighter, soldier, army officer. "And that's just wonderful," thought Artiom, diving out from inside his shirt so quickly that he almost tore off his ears. "That's wonderfully pleasant..."

"And where do you live?" asked Eichmanis. "In a monastic cell?"

Artiom answered yes, in a monastic cell with two beds, and for some reason he added, "With Osip Troianskii, a botanist."

"Oh, I know about him," said Eichmanis.

"He said that they should move me out of there soon, because he officially requested that his mother come live him with in his room," Artiom added, for some reason thinking that Eichmanis might find that curious.

"His mother in his monastic cell?" Eichmanis asked with a smile and looked at Gorshkov. "How droll." Gorshkov nodded, just in case. "I think he may have misunderstood something," said Eichmanis and Gorshkov again nodded, this time with much more conviction.

"In general, Artiom, I've seen how you all work," Eichmanis continued. "You're going to continue working with me, I'll explain the job and you'll be in charge of the work group."

Artiom would have clicked his heels if he wasn't barefooted, but he still brought his heels together and lifted his chin a little higher.

"Gorshkov, write him a document saying he's commanded to go to the monastery and back," Eichmanis instructed, not looking at Gorshkov. "You, Artiom, will get uniforms for everyone and produce. And a few more tools. Gorshkov will write it all down in the letter."

"It's too bad that in military etiquette, it's not customary to add a jump in the air to the usual 'Sir, yes sir!'" Artiom thought completely calmly and very seriously. "To jump in the air and scream."

* * *

He got ready quickly, smelling all the while how Feofan had clearly prepared something delicious with mushrooms. A thick smell wafted in from the oven.

When they were leaving, the rest of the inmates came towards them, their faces tired from extended laughter — Kurez-shah and Kabir-shah had finally been chased out of the water and shaved.

"You're getting soup with mushrooms, convicts," declared Father Feofan, who was also a bit cheerful.

Everyone sat down immediately in reverent expectation — their faces lengthened and became more attentive.

Artiom decided to stay — he didn't want to miss lunch so badly that even the shaved — and for some reason Russified — Indians didn't make him laugh.

The soup smelled like a symphony of the forest. Those devilish mushrooms had grown to the clamor of one hundred thousand birds, and no they hadn't started singing themselves — their voices flowed all around and agitated everyone considerably…

But Gorshkov appeared.

"Why are you stuck here?" he asked Artiom with moderate strictness. "You expected me to come get you?"

Artiom hesitated, not knowing what to answer; it was good enough that he didn't sit at the table in front of him and started to each the soup.

"Here's your paper," said Gorshkov, displeased. "Your escort is waiting; hurry like a bullet."

"… And for the hundredth time, he wanted to call me a jackal, but because I'm the head of this work group, he once again didn't," Artiom guessed and immediately laughed at himself. "You're starting to guess a little too much, you guesser. Maybe all of your realizations are nonsense? Everything isn't the way you think, but you're the idiot, eh Artiom?"

He didn't introduce himself to the soldier, just sat on his horse and rode after him.

It must be said that he rode a horse for the first time in his life. At first, he was scared that the horse would end up balking and throw Artiom down to the group — and then what a "group leader" you'll be! — but no, it calmly walked after the soldier's mare.

He shook, of course, but once he got used to it, it wasn't so bad. The soldier wasn't hurrying anywhere, for which Artiom gave silent thanks. After a few minutes, Artiom calmed down.

"How soon will you turn into Burtsev, friend?" he asked himself contentiously. "Will you start beating Schelkachov on the back with your shovel?"

He laughed at himself, but he didn't quite know the answer to the question.

No, of course not, he couldn't even imagine himself in such a situation. But… what if?

"What if Eichmanis would ask him? To do what? Hit Schelkachov with a shovel?"

Not able to come up with an answer, Artiom stopped thinking altogether, he merely looked around and petted himself on his own head — it was a pleasant feeling.

If any inmates crossed their path — from the number of those who worked outside the kremlin walls — Artiom straightened his back and the expression of his face became independent he so wanted to show them that he wasn't just a jackal, like everyone else; he was a jackal seated on a horse. Even the soldier ahead of him wasn't so much guarding him as accompanying him.

Judging by the fact that Artiom was generally looked at with hostility, it seemed that the inmates had understood at least part of what was going on. For example, they understood that this guy with a shaved head had caught a lucky break.

They got to the monastery when it was almost night.

Artiom of course wanted to ride into the monastery, maybe Vasilii Petrovich or Afanasiev would see him, and how good that would look! But the soldier forced him to go on foot at the gates, taking his reins and going in his own direction.

"Hey! Where do I go?" Artiom called him quietly.

"What do I know?" said the soldier, without turning around. "Wherever you've been ordered to go, that's where you should go.

Then he had a change of heart and turned around.

"Tomorrow, you'll gather everything that's been ordered and we'll go back. As soon as you've gathered everything, stand in the square and wait for me. We have to leave before noon."

At the gates, Artiom showed them his document and they let him pass. He hurried to his monastic room.

"I hope Osip's mother hasn't arrived yet," Artiom said aloud. "Or Osip is going to have to sleep on the floor…"

An unbidden thought intruded itself on him, that maybe Osip's mother could end up being quite young… Why not? If, for example, he was a bit over twenty and she had given birth to him while young… but Artiom cut himself off immediately: what vileness, vileness, stop it.

The monastery's courtyard was empty. Artiom thought about it and decided that it had probably never happened before, that he was here completely alone.

"What if everyone's left?" he either laughed or hunkered down in hope. "Two gate guards left, but no one else?"

"Yeah right," he answered himself.

Only two gulls were screaming and circling above the yard, tortured by insomnia and migraines.

Towards this lonely passerby, Bear the deer and Black the dog approached from different sides — each in their own manner. Black approached with dignity but dancing a bit with his muscular body and wagging his tail with restraint. Bear was less noble and hurried as though he were afraid that if he arrived late, the dog would get all the goodies.

"These are the inmates," Artiom joked to himself. "If I walk right now into any sleeping quarters, the bunks will be filled with all kinds of animals. Moles, rats, foxes — everyone is gnawing at each other, everyone is fighting each other, smelling each other… Who was it that checked my document at the gate, I forgot?" And Artiom seriously turned around to look at the post. "Maybe two goats were sitting there with their goatish eyes, and I didn't even notice."

Bear and Black approached.

"But I don't have anything," Artiom thought with the usual chagrin, looking at the beasties, but then he stopped short when he felt a piece of pie in his pocket. He didn't even remember when he had grabbed it. Maybe after being shaved at the lake… probably yes… someone's leftovers were lying there after they had overeaten. Or it wasn't leftovers, but someone had left it while shaving and Artiom stole it without a second thought.

He broke the pie, extending the left piece to the dog and the right piece to the deer. They both took the offering without even smelling it. The touch of the animals' wet lips remained on both hands.

Artiom still felt it when he entered his wing — a slightly wet warmth.

The animals ate it all at once, then the deer followed him for a few steps, but understood that there would be no more and stopped. But Black immediately knew that if someone gave something, then left, that meant there was no more. He gratefully waited while Artiom disappeared behind the doors of the building, then he went back to sleep.

It smelled sour in the room. Osip, as usual, slept deeply. Artiom, without standing on ceremony, took off his shoes, pulled the jacket from his shoulders — then, his neighbor unexpectedly jumped up, scared by the noise. Artiom froze, still with his jacket half-off on his arm.

"Who? What?" Osip cried. Horror ran in his eyes; he didn't recognize his comrade and moved his feet, crawling back into a corner. "Go away!" He was either commanding or begging. "Out of here! I don't need this!"

"Osip! Osip!" Artiom wanted to wave his hand, but the jacket was in the way. "It's me, Artiom!"

For a few seconds, Osip tried to understand the meaning of what he said.

"You scared me…" he said, whispering. "I thought you were a Chekist."

Then he rubbed his temples for a long time.

* * *

"We've made a machine to precipitate and filter out the iodine," Osip was telling him the next morning as they ate. "A big vat with two filters. A mixer and a tube moved by electricity. The tube also has a fan. Do you know how it was before?"

"How?" asked Artiom; he still understood nothing and only thought from time to time, should he blindside Osip with Eichmanis's words that they had no plans to move his mother there, or should he mind his own business? It should be said that to Osip, Artiom had no desire to boast about his new position. Though he still prevented himself from boasting, only with difficulty, in spite of his better judgment.

"Up to this point, we precipitated it by hand, in bottles," Osip explained. For some reason, when he said "bottles", he extended the carrot he held upwards. "First of all, that's a difficult process for the workers, but, more importantly, it's a dangerous one. Bromides, Nitrogen oxides, acid, iodides — and people breathed all that stuff."

"Awful," agreed Artiom and repeated. "Nitrogen oxides. Iodides."

"Yes," Osip said, nodding, happy that someone was listening to him. "But I fixed it up so that there would almost be no smell. No need to push yourself, everything happens by itself." Suddenly, without transition, he quietly laughed, even jumping up a bit on his bed. "How scared I was yesterday! Why did you shave your head? Someone without hair walked in, like a demon, no hands to be seen, and, it's as though there's a monastic robe hanging off him. I thought they'd come for me… not for me, but for my soul!"

Osip just as suddenly stopped laughing.

"Eat the carrot," said Artiom, nodding at the vegetable that he held in his hand.

"I've gotta go," suddenly Osip answered and started to gather his things.

"What about you mother?" Artiom couldn't stop himself. "Is she coming soon?"

"Oh," Osip started. "Thank you for reminding me. Mama has already begun her journey. You must go to IID and tell them of the necessity to find you a new place to live."

Artiom choked down his laughter, but said nothing, only thinking, "What a little devil! It's *his* mother that's coming, and I have to go to IID? I'll see him in hell first!"

While Artiom was thinking this, Osip left without remembering to say goodbye.

Artiom washed one more time and even decided to look at himself — their wing had a common mirror. From the mirror, a wild and bright-eyed overgrown boy who had seem much of the world looked back at Artiom. He was so tanned he almost had white spots on him like a salted bit of dark bread. His head was gorgeous — it would look great, even on the Arbat, oh!

"You've eaten your fill lately, you wolf," Artiom thought with pleasure, barely stopping himself from clicking his teeth.

He really liked himself.

He was full of summer strength.

After showing his letter, he received clothing for his group at the camp warehouse — he guessed the sizes by glance; no one gainsaid him, letting him choose for himself.

For himself, naturally, he picked things that fit perfectly — tall water boots, breeches with leather pads and a service shirt with sloping pockets.

He got dressed immediately in his new clothes. Washed and impudent, he walked outside with the feeling that the soldiers were about to salute him.

Filled with joy, he forgot to get a necessary tool. He had to go back to the warehouse, received three shovels, a pickaxe, an axe, a dustpan, canvas, bucket, brush, and broom — the last Schelkachov ordered.

"To sweet the earth off the golden decorations and then to put them into the buckets like fish," Artiom laughed. Everything was funny.

Also, some pencils and paper for the Indians with their scribbling.

With all this garbage — the parcel of clothing, the bucket — bristling with the handles of the shovels, swearing and occasionally losing something, he barely managed to get out into the monastery courtyard — there, he dropped everything again.

Afanasiev ran up and hurried to help — he was just as cheerful as always, with the same cowlick, a candy in his mouth. Evidently, he had won at cards yesterday.

"Tioma!" Afanasiev sang, playing with the candy in his mouth. "What? They haven't killed you yet?"

"No, I'm with Eichmanis now?" Artiom immediately blurted out — how much longer could he be expected to hold it in?

"As what?" Afanasiev asked cheerfully and grabbed his forelock, evidently so that his head would not fall off.

"That, brother, is a secret!" Artiom answered him in harmony, fooling about a bit.

"But you're not joking?"

"My honest Solovetsian word!" Artiom sneered. A month ago, it wouldn't have even occurred to him to joke like this. "What about you?"

"I'm also getting ready for a transfer," Afanasiev boasted. "Theater business. But you're way cooler. You're quite the cool cat, aren't you? And how they've dressed you! Devil tear me to shreds!"

In answer, Artiom only winked with dignity — yes, super cool. Yes, the devil tear you to shreds!

"Well, I'm off," Afanasiev continued in the same style. "We've got a rehearsal. Premier soon. Citizen Eichmanis himself will be there. You'll be sitting at his right hand? Or at his left?"

Artiom laughed, Afanasiev too — they nudged each other like boys and parted, only Afanasiev looked back three more times.

Only after he'd gone some distance, looking back quickly and carefully, he yelled, "Where are you taking the shovels? The bucket? Are you going to wash him or bury him?"

These were already dangerous jokes, especially since you didn't know who was about, but Artiom didn't care as before. He dramatically spit in Afanasiev's general direction and turned around.

As he turned around, he saw Passport in his line of sight. He was carrying his hanging lower lip somewhere.

Artiom, who had all the garbage underfoot, picked out something that he would need the most, choosing the pickaxe.

"I'll knock his block off," he decided, not really deciding whether or not he was serious.

It seemed Passport figured out what it was all tending towards and assessing the situation at once, he rather quickly went his way and even picked up his lower lip.

Artiom stood there a bit, playing with the pickaxe: well, who else is here? Come out, you devils — seven against one, if you like!

Coming back to his parcel of clothing, he sat on it, "Or someone will carry it away, and then what are you going to say?"

For a moment he thought that he might look a little funny in his swamp boots in the middle of the yard, but he didn't want to think about it, so he didn't.

Black came up and rubbed against him with his side. Artiom scratched him in that place where a dog would have had a beard, had it grown at all. Black gratefully rolled his black eyes back. He smelled sweetly of dog — Artiom loved that smell from childhood.

Bear the deer awaited nearby — are they only scratching over there, or is there sugar?

Even Solovki's sad, shabby, blackened walls, the empty monastery windows, as though they smelled of the after-smoke of a Chekist, the silly stars on the cupolas — even all of this rejoiced in today's sun, even dancing a bit. If he half-closed his eyes, they all doubled and tripled in his vision.

But when one misfortune passes you over, but your fate demands it, another misfortune will still take its place.

In actual fact, somewhere, like a brook, a weak foreboding bubbled — he should have hidden and disappeared in such a morning, but he wasn't able to hear that feeling well enough.

From nowhere, the foreman Sorokin appeared with his sweaty armpits that smelled like a fish that had been caught that morning and was already rotting in the sun, with his sticky, dirty hair, like bits of hay, with his dimwitted glance of a rabid dog and his lips filled with saliva, as though they were an envelope that had been licked but not sealed.

He was very drunk.

In his life, very obviously, an important event had taken place. This sense of significance wreathed around him like a cloud of flies over garbage.

The gulls accompanied Sorokin with their frenzied cries; they also, probably thought that he was carrying a fish under each armpit.

Sorokin saw Artiom immediately and kept looking at him, winking from time to time, trying to remember where he had seen that fellow. His swamp boots, breeches with leather pads and his service shirt with angled pockets were throwing Sorokin off, but he tried very hard and finally remembered.

Before him stood that same jackal who had once humiliated him in front of the other inmates.

Sorokin had promised to remember him; would you look at that! He did remember him.

"I still need to buy food," thought Artiom randomly and with slight sadness, looking around. It was uncomfortable to walk into the store with these shovels… Or maybe he should go to the kitchens? What was written in Eichmanis's letter?

"You, jackal! Did you think my pardon would save you?" Sorokin started from a distance. He wobbled, but not too much and in general, Artiom thought almost with detachment, that foreman was a strong fellow. “I’m going to beat a long string of snot out of you right now,” hissed Sorokin, walking ever closer. “Then I’m going to choke you with it.”

When Sorokin only had a step and a half left, Artiom, without any effort and not even thinking about it, quickly stood up from his parcel and gave the former foreman a wicked upper cut on the chin.

Sorokin fell.

Artiom once again sat on his parcel.

He sat and stared at the sky. Next to him lay the shovels, pickaxes, Sorokin, the bucket and three steps away, his ears perked up, stood a surprised Black. Bear the deer, on the contrary, ran away, but ended up still in the way of the soldiers who had seen everything and were rushing towards Artiom.

They raised him up by the scruff as though he were a naughty puppy, lifting him up from his parcel and boxing his ears.

Artiom wanted to punch the soldier too, but he was cooling down like an iron pot taken from the fire and dumped into water — he was still hissing and steaming, but with every second, he was getting colder and colder.

“Where should we take him?” asked one soldier of the other.

The other, down on one knee, was shaking Sorokin.

“Is he dead?”

Not hearing the answer, he got up with a crack and looked around with mild annoyance, evidently hoping to see Doctor Ali appear at his side immediately, but for some reason the doctor wasn’t there.

Saliva was pouring out of Sorokin’s mouth. A fat fly sat on the saliva and almost got stuck in it.

“I have a commanding order from Eichmanis,” Artiom said angrily, but he was still looking at Sorokin. Did he really…?

“Shut your trap,” answered the soldier and he started that phrase as soon as Artiom started talking and managed to utter it while Artiom was saying “commanding order”, but when he heard “Eichmanis”, the soldier understood something, and no second box on the ears followed.

“Get him to IID,” he said.

“You will answer before the head of the camp for the loss of his property,” announced Artiom, feeling the metallic taste of every word. Sorokin stared at the sky with half-open eyes that seemed to have no life in them.

“What about him?” asked the second soldier, nodding at Sorokin.

“First take the shovels, we’ll take them to IID,” the other answered. “Then we’ll get the doctor for the foreman.”

In a strange way, Artiom walked into the IID empty-handed — the two soldiers walked after him, carrying his parcel of clothing, tools, and bucket. They themselves realized that they looked ridiculous, but it was too late — they weren't going to just drop it all now.

At the entrance, Artiom turned around and almost yelled from joy, as though he were pricked — Sorokin suddenly sat up and started to rub his face with his hands with unexpected passion. Seeing this, Black started to bark, as though he were angry that the dead man had resurrected.

Sorokin's manner and all his movements made it obvious that he didn't understand anything and remembered nothing. Only for some reason he was drooling over his face…

"He's alive!" said Artiom to the soldier joyfully.

"Get in there," answered the soldier and pushed him into the doorway.

The tools and clothes they left with the duty officer, and when they led Artiom upstairs, he realized by the second flight of stairs whom he was going to see right now.

It was already the third floor… where else?

The helper of the duty officer tried to announce him, but a familiar female voice answered, "No need. I saw in the window."

Galina sat at her table. On the wall, behind her back, hung the portraits of Trotskii and Dzerzhinskii, as before.

"Sit down," said Galina, momentarily raising her eyes at Artiom. Naturally, she was writing something. But, raising her eyes and immediately lowering them, she couldn't stop herself from looking at him again.

Artiom approached her table. The stool was the same, he remembered it. While he was sitting, he had time to notice that the portrait of Lenin was still in place, under the glass of the table, while the portrait of Eichmanis, which used to be there as well, was no longer in place…

"Or not," Artiom suddenly realized. "It's on the same place, but it's been turned around. As though Galina didn't want to look at it!"

"Finally, Goriainov has returned," said Galina and quickly, even somehow in a business-as-usual manner, licked her lips. "Our papers have been waiting for you for days. Concerning the voluntary aid to the Information and Investigation Department that you are obliged to undertake."

She was out of uniform, in a blouse with her sleeves rolled back. Two of her top buttons were undone, showing a short neck, but a beautiful face, slightly sweaty, dark skin, eyes widely set apart, an attentive and slightly malicious glance, pierced ears without any earrings, firm cheekbones, white teeth, chapped lips, like a teenager's, which were flaking.

"Have I gotten myself in a jam?" Artiom thought almost calmly, "Or not?"

"Citizen Eichmanis sent me here with an order," answered Artiom and reached into his pocket to pull out the document…

"I'm not asking you, Goriainov, who sent you or where," Galina interrupted him. A barely evident drop of saliva flew from her lips and landed on the papers spread out before her. "We are speaking of the fact that you have violated discipline and proper order many times while you are serving your time in the Solovki Camp of Special Designation, for which you must be immediately punished. Your new room is now solitary, you got it?" Her voice rang and soared.

"Yep, in the soup, in the soup, in the soup," it beat at Artiom's head.

"I am trying to explain," he began hoarsely, "that the former foreman Sorokin tried to get in the way of a direct order given by Comrade Eichmanis…"

"Citizen!" the crazy woman interrupted him. "Citizen Eichmanis! He's not your comrade, didn't they explain it to you yet? Have you not been here long enough yet? Maybe we should double your time here? Still, you won't even live out this term in solitary!"

Galina even stood up from behind the desk, looking at Artiom uninterruptedly, trying to burn a hole through him, kill him without waiting, immediately, as though Artiom himself was the foul conglomeration of everything that she hated and that she angrily wanted to destroy.

Artiom felt this and got more and more scared.

"… Lord, save me," he thought feverishly. "Send me to the gangsters, to Passport, to Gils, anywhere…"

"Citizen Eichmanis assigned me," Artiom almost yelled and immediately forgot, or didn't have chance to hastily come up with a word, that would determine his exact assignation, "assigned me as his orderly! And I must fulfill his order!"

"What am I blabbing, my God…" everything inside him screamed. "They're going to kill me for this!"

And they both, it seemed, were screaming — he with the voice of a child hiding his face with his hand from horror, she with the voice of an abandoned and insulted woman, demanding that her lover immediately prove that she was beloved, necessary and without her the world would be empty, while with her…

"Who? Who, did you say? Repeat it!" she demanded, ready to laugh and, circling the table, walked right up to Artiom, as though ready to clutch his face with her talons. She was wearing a tight skirt.

She stood before Artiom and leaned her buttocks against her own table.

"His orderly," Artiom repeated stubbornly and loudly, looking at that skirt. "How dare you detain me?"

In his head, a completely incomprehensive phrase appeared, as though from somewhere outside, "She's doing it on purpose."

"She's doing it on purpose," someone thought instead of the frightened and numb Artiom. "She's doing it on purpose. She's doing it on purpose. You have to figure it out. You have to figure it out. Otherwise she'll turn back, sit at her desk, and you're done..."

Without being aware of what he was doing, still seated on the stool, he suddenly leaned forward slightly, took her by the leg and reached, reached, reached with his insane arm into her tight skirt, as much as he could, and that was only up to the knee. But that was already... that was already a nightmare, execution, a pit full of worms.

"Have you figured it out?" some demon screamed inside Artiom's head. "What? Have you figured it out?!"

"You bastard!" said Galina clearly and, as it seemed, completely without emotion.

But Artiom was already on his feet, the room rocked, frozen sideways... somehow. And he saw this in passing, as though he were falling out of an uncoiling sky and flying together with this entire room down at an incredible speed. Her thin, chapped lips and sweaty cheek appeared and he latched on to those lips, trying to save himself and not to shatter on impact.

He immediately felt how with one hand she took his service shirt, gathering the fabric into a fist, while her other grabbed his neck painfully, not with her nails, but with her talons — bastard, bastard, you're a bastard! That's what her hand was screaming.

Her frenzied, thin, snake-like tongue was in his mouth, and it was resisting and battling as though scalded.

"She has just drunk tea with sugar," someone thought instead of Artiom, who had lost his mind.

Tearing out her talons from his neck, she just as fiercely groped for something in his groin, unable to find it.

"Hurry up and unbutton everything down there ..." she commanded him in a maddened whisper.

* * *

Those swamp boots — they were so out of place. He was coming down from the third floor on the staircase, his legs unbending. They were shaking.

"Swamp boots, because you're in the swamp," the first thought swam up to him, and he carried it, while it rattled about in his brain like a leaf falling on water.

He went outside, not realizing it, remembering only that while he was going down, he could hear the tapping of several typewriters that reminded him of some kind of birds. The birds were pecking the letters. The letters were flying around in all directions.

He was very surprised that it was sunny outside — it blinded him. He thought it should be evening already. So much seemed to have happened already. An entire life had shot upwards, exploded like a firework, and dissipated.

His hands were also shaking.

He licked his lips. They smelled of something foreign.

A gull almost flew into his very face, squawking something.

He breathed in, looked around and remembered something.

At first, he remembered that Sorokin had been there, but now he wasn't.

Then, he remembered that he had had shovels. Pickaxes. A bucket. An axe. A parcel with clothing and swamp boots. Paper for map making and pencils.

Artiom turned around and walked back into the IID.

Saying nothing, he approached the tools that had been piled right there at the exit.

"Hey!" called the duty officer. "Put that down!"

Another soldier entered IID and Artiom recognized yesterday's escort.

"You birchen bloodsucker! Where you been, you idiot with iodine in his mouth?" He yelled.

Artiom looked at him as though he were concussed.

"Grab the tools, why have you dumped them here?" the soldier demanded.

"Petro, you can't," the duty officer said. "Confiscated."

"What do you mean I can't, are you nuts?" The soldier raised his arms. "Comrade Eichmanis is waiting for them."

The duty officer was slightly upset by this bit of news, but he didn't retreat.

"What did they tell you in the office?" he asked Artiom.

"She told me to get out," Artiom remembered, but he didn't say it. Her voice had been hoarse and a lock of hair had stuck to her temple.

"Nothing," Artiom answered quietly. Even his voice was shaking.

"We'll figure this out in a minute," said the duty officer and, calling his assistant out of the store room, told him, "Run up to the third, ask Galina what to do with the confiscated tools."

Yesterday's escort-soldier spit. Artiom now knew that his name was Petro.

Petro, calling Artiom a bloodsucker one more time, went out to smoke, rolling his cigarette as he walked.

Artiom waited two minutes, sometimes touching the cold wall with his fingers.

Petro returned, asked, "Well?"

No one answered.

Finally, the assistant returned and reported, "The tools are to be returned to Eichmanis, while Artiom Goriainov is ordered to remain in the kremlin until a special order is given and to return to his brigade."

Artiom breathed heavily with his mouth, trying not to look from side to side, lest he meet Petro's glance.

"You're a bastard yourself," he thought very distinctly and confidently.

"She's not afraid that I'll tell them all that I just…" he asked himself, exasperated.

"And this very evening they'll shoot you, you moron," he answered himself.

"Why are you getting up, you ugly mug?" Petro yelled at Artiom. "At least carry this garbage to the horse." For emphasis, he pushed Artiom in the side.

Artiom gathered what he could, Petro held the door open and let him out.

"How am I going to carry all of this by myself? Did you think of that, shithead?" asked Petro, looking at the stuff Artiom dumped next to his horse.

"There's still the foodstuffs," Artiom answered with a dead voice.

"Give me the paper," said Petro.

He went to get the food and Artiom waited half an hour for him, feeling like scum, dust, the dirt under his own feet… And he was still wearing those swamp boots.

The gulls were screaming in his ears.

"May you burn!" Artiom thought of himself, not so much with exasperation as with some unaccountable sadness that he couldn't just catch fire immediately. "May you die, rot immediately! How were you born such a driftwood! A crooked driftwood! A crooked, worm-infested driftwood! With your empty head! With your damned empty head! What? I hate you! I hate you so much!"

He looked around on both sides, seeking some kind of salvation, but then he saw her windows — there they are! — she stood at her window, that filthy, debauched bitch…! But she immediately walked away, disappeared, as soon as she caught his glance.

Oh, how happy he would have been to throw a rock over there — what joy! What a hysterical fit he would have! How he would scream that that bitch had just taken off her panties in front of an inmate, like a whore. I'm telling the truth! Cut open her stomach — there's my seed! What are you doing, you bitch! You're destroying a living person! Look at that window! Where are you, you bastard, where have you gone? She asked, "Where is it down there?" Do you want to see? Here it is! Should I show it to you again! Right here!

It was insane, but Artiom once again felt aroused, a hot male arousal, sharp and very strong.

Naturally, he didn't scream anything, but only suddenly understood that a huge, unsummoned tear had just fallen out. He caught it as it fell, like a cold insect and he clasped it in his fist.

"Your body has gone crazy!" he said to himself, not understanding how what went on in his groin could possibly correspond with what went on in his head.

Petro returned with a bag of foodstuffs.

A crowd of gulls circled around his head, as though he were carrying offal on his head.

"Get out of here, bloodsucker."

Artiom turned and went.

In three steps he remembered, and, not turning around, he answered, "You're the bloodsucker."

He walked another seven steps, expecting that someone would run him down, but no one did.

* * *

It seems he even fell asleep. It was as though he were walking, walking on thin ice and fell into icy water, but under the ice, it wasn't water, but earth — and hot earth, as though warmed up, and very muggy.

He slept in that muggy ground.

Then he lay there, his eyes closed and tried not to hear anything, not to understand anything, not to remember anything.

"Right now, I'm going to open my eyes and I will see my mother," he prayed. "And it will turn out that I'm actually at home and I'm twelve years old, and there's jam waiting for me, and in the corner a spider has caught a fly, and it's buzzing there, and I will move my chair to it, and standing on my tip-toes, I will look at how he will wind his web around the fly, then he will carry the fly into a crack between the boards of the wall. And mother will say, 'Tiomka, why don't you feel sorry for the fly? Me, I feel sorry for it! Lord, why is it buzzing like that over there! Go and drink some tea quickly!'"

"Why is it buzzing like that, Mama?" Artiom asked aloud.

He opened his eyes. There was no mama there.

Someone knocked on the door.

Artiom sat up. His swamp boots lay on the floor. He wished he could just cut them into pieces.

"Why the devil won't they open it themselves!" thought Artiom, not exactly sure whom he meant by the word "they". The door isn't locked.

"Who's there?" he asked loudly.

The door slowly opened, though it creaked, and on the threshold appeared Vasilii Petrovich.

Artiom breathed out as if at least part of the weight on his soul, if not all of it, fell off suddenly.

"I saw you, how you walked across the courtyard. So handsome, so muscular and young… When they send you over to Moscow, the communist young ladies will melt before you… and such boots!" Vasilii Petrovich bubbled on from the threshold, squinting like a fisherman.

"I spit on them!" said Artiom, looking at his boots and once again felt how near the tears were.

"Why do you say that?" Vasilii Petrovich wondered, also noticing the boots lying in front of him. "These would come in handy very much. Autumn is coming, autumn, and mine are completely falling apart."

Artiom suddenly remembered and squinted from the pain in his chest — he had put his own personal clothing in the bundle where he had put the uniforms of all the rest, and now the soldier had carried it all to Eichmanis. When was this all going to end already!?

He ran to the window — maybe that Petro was still standing in the yard? But of course not. Bear the deer was shifting from one leg to another in the place where Petro was.

The day had long passed; the white evening of Solovki had crawled in.

"What's the matter, my friend?" asked Vasilii Petrovich, worried. "Why are you darting about like Chatskii?"

Artiom turned and looked at Vasilii Petrovich for a short time, saying nothing.

"To hell with him anyway!" he decided aloud, waving his hand.

"They might execute you tomorrow," Artiom told himself. "And you're worried about an old pair of pants!"

But if he listened to his conscience, he would admit that he didn't really believe that they would kill him. For what? They detained him in IID; it wasn't his fault. He struck a foreman? Well, he wasn't even a foreman anymore, but a former inmate pardoned by amnesty. Plus, he was drunk.

Of course, all that did look rather flimsy, but it was still the truth.

"How do you come to be here, Vasilii Petrovich?" asked Artiom, not smiling yet, but coming back to life little by little.

"I share my berries first with one group, then with another," his old companion answered eagerly. "I've got people everywhere, you can't do without favors around here, after all. And of course, they won't all come to the twelfth to get their lingonberries, so I bring it to them from time to time... Here, I've brought you some too." In every word of the dear Vasilii Petrovich there was a mix of sarcasm, self-deprecation, kindness and cunning, and the newly-acquired wisdoms of life in Solovki.

He put a bag of currants mixed with raspberries on the table. Artiom didn't even remember the last time he ate those berries.

"May I?" he asked.

"No-no-no," Vasilii Petrovich answered with faux severity. "You can only look. Feast your eyes on them and then I'll continue on my rounds in the brigades, to tease everyone to my heart's content." Then he laughed. "Eat! Eat, Tioma!"

Vasilii Petrovich sat across from Artiom on Osip's bed.

Artiom grabbed the bag, immediately took a handful and downed it.

As a well-bred person, he offered Vasilii Petrovich some, who, still squinting as though looking at the sun, answered by raising his open palm and rocking it to the right and left.

"How are things in our brigade?" asked Artiom, licking his lips.

"Everything's somehow... difficult and messy," answered Vasilii Petrovich. "Lazhechnikov died. Didn't you know? I think he died while you were still in the hospital, no? Afanasiev's been moved to the actors. The gangsters do their criminal deeds sometimes."

"I feed them with berries too, Artiom, can you imagine? What humiliation for this old man. Burtsev... well, you've understood everything about Burtsev already. He's not getting better, only worse. I think he's finally finished off the Chinese man completely — our Chink went to solitary, and so it goes... Krapin is on Fox Island breeding someone. I don't think they're quite foxes..."

"And you, that means, are still gathering berries?" asked Artiom, as though continuing the conversation, though the berries were incredibly delicious and he had no desire to talk.

"And I'm still gathering berries," agreed Vasilii Petrovich. "What about you?"

Artiom let it be known that he would finish chewing and answer then, but thought to himself, "Now I will tell my dear Vasilii Petrovich that the head of the camp Eichmanis assigned me as head of the group searching for buried treasure — yes, yes, buried treasure! — on the islands of the archipelago, and after we drank moonshine with him for two straight days — yes, yes, I drank moonshine with him! — I came here today and during an interrogation on the third floor of the IID I raped an employee of the camp… or she raped me. Yes, yes, we undressed almost completely. All I had on were these boots that you liked so much and my dropped breeches, while she still had her blouse on with their rolled-up sleeves, and we unexpectedly entered into a carnal — hell! — union. I'll tell him and Vasilii Petrovich will think that I've gone mad. And he'd be right… I forgot to add that Galina is Eichmanis's lover, Vasilii Petrovich."

Having finished this monologue in his head, Artiom felt his head spinning and a strong desire to vomit.

"This is all so completely off the wall," he said to himself, sensing drops of sweat appear on his forehead and temples.

Since Artiom continued not to answer, but only to make strange signs with his eyes — I'm eating! Still eating! And I'm chewing it all, and now I'm swallowing! — Vasilii Petrovich decided to answer for him, "I thought that you had become part of the… how do they call it? The Spartakiade…? But I've been passing by the sports fields the last few days and I haven't seen you."

"Yes," Artiom answered very firmly, but said nothing more.

And he didn't eat any more berries, holding the bag in his hand. His hand was wet.

"Well, that's fine," the tactful Vasilii Petrovich nodded. "You can tell me later. Why have I come? Since you're here, will you come to our Athens of Solovki? We're gathering today. Mezernitskii was asking about you again. And *Vladychka* John also."

"When?" Artiom came back to life.

"Right now," said Vasilii Petrovich, rising up. "As I can see, you're not too busy. Believe it or not, but we actually have a certain quantity of alcoholic beverages. Do you have any snacks?"

"Me?" Artiom reached under his bed, still not letting go of the bag with the berries.

"Why don't I hold it for you?" offered Vasilii Petrovich.

Not looking at him, Artiom gave him the berries. Then he gave him the tinned foodstuffs he found under his bed.

"Oh, meat with peas..." said Vasilii Petrovich with interest. "And another one! Where did you find them?"

"I can't remember," answered Artiom from below.

"You're living well," said Vasilii Petrovich.

"Well enough," Artiom answered.

* * *

"What, you don't have any other footwear?" asked Vasilii Petrovich when Artiom started pulling on the boots. "You know, it's not very wet where we're going."

"Vasilii Petrovich, stop," asked Artiom with even a measure of pain.

"Well, as you wish, as you wish," said Vasilii Petrovich placatingly.

They met again at Mezernitskii's.

"We greet you, Artemii, our dear fellow-sufferer," boomed the host, extending his arm either to indicate the set table or the guests at the table.

"What do you mean?" answered Artiom thoughtfully, looking at the table.

"Why 'fellow' or why 'sufferer?"

Artiom, as though not understanding anything, looked at him with a smile. That was the end of that exchange.

A rainbow shone over the table. The following drinks were there: purple methylated spirits, yellowing varnish liquid, shellac purified with salt — all in black rags. Next to it stood the impurified version — "not to everyone's taste," Mezernitskii explained. Greenish hair tonic. Floral perfume for women, though there were no women present.

"The bouquet of my grandmother," Mezernitskii explained the last drink.

By the way, in Solovki's stores, from time to time even vodka was sold for three rubles fifty. But to buy it, you needed special permission; it appeared very rarely, disappeared quickly, handed out for favors, so the inmates of Solovki had to make do.

"What are we celebrating today?" asked Artiom amicably, looking over Mezernitskii's shoulder to see who else was there.

"Do Russian people drink to celebrate a holiday?" asked Mezernitskii.

"They celebrate, so they can drink," said Grakov with feigned lack of emotion; he stood and took Artiom's hand.

"*Vladychka* John will bless you," said Mezernitskii, turning to the priest.

"God forbid, my dear!" said *Vladychka*, smiling at Artiom, but speaking to Mezernitskii. "I pray the Lord that this poison will not harm you all."

"It's Mezernitskii's birthday," whispered Vasilii Petrovich.

"Why didn't you tell me? I've come empty-handed," Artiom answered, concerned.

Vasilii Petrovich shook his head in the sense that nothing was needed.

"The wheel of history rolls past entire swathes of people, but it struck us while we still live," Mezernitskii answered *Vladychka*. "We are treating our wounds." And once again he pointed at the joyful table and the jiggling drinks.

"It rode over us!" Grakov added, in harmony to Mezernitskii, evidently meaning the wheel of history.

"They've wound all of us on this wheel," continued Mezernitskii, sedately nodding at Grakov in a sign of approval. "You can't understand where the head is, where are the buttocks, the hands and feet are sticking out in different directions. One eye has leaked out, while the other's been sucked into the skull and it's swimming inside there, between the brain and the nasopharyngeal cavity, frightened of looking out, but! But! My friends!"

"Are you urging on your horse, my dear?" Vasilii Petrovich asked Mezernitskii gently.

"No!" Mezernitskii answered very seriously. "But I am placing a division in my argument. But! Because our entire youth was spent speaking about the folk. We spoke of the folk as though they were aborigines. We spoke of its greatness and its fates. Of its inscrutability. Even the idea of God —" Here Mezernitskii quickly looked at *Vladychka* — "we have come to understand and destroy, but we haven't even approached the idea of the folk. And here it is! This is the place of meeting! The place where the Silver Age and the folk will meet! The Silver Age is dying, while the folk is coming awake. What must we do? That which the Tolstoians and the populists did not do — we must breathe the spirit of illumination into the aboriginal mouth and... leave in peace."

"Mezernitskii's worldview is a bit self-contradictory," said Vasilii Petrovich with a gentle smile. "No less than two visits ago, he said that the aristocracy, or rather he expressed himself even more precisely — the White Army officers and counter-revs — because of their natural superiority, are capable of gradually replacing the Bolsheviks. For the simple reason that the Bolsheviks know how to do little, while the crushed and dishonored aristocracy knows how to do everything — which is easy to prove, if you pay attention to the cadre of administrators of the camp here, where, as Mezernitskii expressed it, they are 'ours.'"

"… Yes, everything changes," Mezernitskii agreed. "Man changes, I change, there is a constant exchange of substances, entire nations exchange their blood for the blood of other races, an eye for an eye, fire for fire — what do you want from me? Everything flows forward! I do as well."

As he spoke, Mezernitskii managed, somehow, to ask Artiom with his eyes, indicating the drinks: this one? Or this one? What would you prefer?

"Any one of them," said Artiom aloud. "It's all the same to me!"

"Tell me about it," answered Mezernitskii and poured Artiom something green.

"One thing I have not understood," said Vasilii Petrovich. "Why must we breathe in the spirit of illumination in this place in particular? Is there no better place in all of Russia in which to do it?"

"No!" firmly and even shaking his head a bit, Mezernitskii said, "Here we are mouth to mouth. There the Red Army soldier, the proletarian, the homeless boy — any one of them will run away, hiding their heads in their mother's or their wife's skirts, into the moss, into the rhizomes — and then how will you force his face to turn back to you? Here, his face is everywhere, no matter where you breathe."

"You're carrying on this conversation… like an acrobat," Vasilii Petrovich said with slight, though amicable, irritation.

"Here we see the end not only of the Silver Age," Mezernitskii said, as though he hadn't heard, even though he was actually answering Vasilii Petrovich, "Here the last Harlequins end their journey. The final dandies. Look, for example, at these swamp boots." Mezernitskii pointed at Artiom's boots, clinking glasses with him at the same moment.

"Listen, stop that," Artiom asked with a smile, feeling, to his surprise, that he was blushing. "I didn't do it on purpose…"

"Very well, very well," quickly agreed Mezernitskii and searched with his eyes, looking for someone else to use as an example — *Vladychka* John didn't really fit. Grakov — not him either. Vasilii Petrovich… alas.

The example appeared, as though they had ordered him off a menu.

Artiom immediately remembered who he was and his name — Shlabukovskii, an actor. The one who had been lying in the infirmary with a fever and who had explained to Artiom that for days they had been giving Artiom a thermometer with someone else's readings. Or rather, with Shlabukovskii's readings…

But he was a different man now! First of all, he was in black gloves with white piping. Secondly, he carried a cane. Thirdly, he was wearing suede shoes and excellent pants that had been tailored. Finally, he wore a tweed jacket.

"You've once again put on the entire costume wardrobe of the theater, my soul," said Mezernitskii.

Shlabukovskii indifferently waved him off, but there was suppressed joy in that gesture. It seems he recognized Artiom as well.

"Well, has your temperature come down?" he asked.

"We have the same temperature," answered Artiom. "Judging by your appearance, it has indeed come down!"

Shlabukovskii laughed almost without sound; it seemed he was very pleased with the joke. Artiom had never before seen such laughter — inaudible, but infectious.

"Shlabukovskii, cease your choking fit. When will you finally learn how to laugh out loud?" Mezernitskii beleaguered him, though, it seemed that they were so friendly that they had every right not to pay each other the least attention.

"Your charlotte is burning," said Shlabukovskii with great dignity and put his cane in the corner, then placed his gloves on top of it.

"Damn!" said Mezernitskii about the charlotte. *Vladychka* John crossed himself; Mezernitskii downed his garbage.

Artiom understood that it was his turn as well, but he asked Shlabukovskii, "What about you?"

He looked over the table and answered, "A little later!" with a look as though in seven minutes exactly they were supposed to bring him his favorite champagne from 1849.

Artiom drank. It felt as though someone sprayed paint mixed with acid in both his mouth and his eyes. It didn't go down easily; it burned and choked.

For some reason, he remained faintly sure that he would die at any moment.

He opened his mouth, tried to breathe, but the air had disappeared.

Mezernitskii appeared miraculously, as though he knew in advance how it would all end. In his hands, he carried four mugs of barley "coffee".

"Here you go, here you go," he fussed next to Artiom. "Drink it down. It's cold already."

Artiom quickly drank and diluted the paint.

But, strange as it may seem, no sooner had the air entered his lungs again than it became warmer and somehow cleaner inside him.

Vladychka John was looking at him as though he were his own child, and as soon as Artiom breathed, the priest did as well.

He had an amazing quality, though he didn't speak with anyone, he upheld all conversations. This was how full his gaze was of understanding and involvement.

Mezernitskii again left and returned with a platter on which was placed something luxurious and very aromatic, despite the fact that it was slightly burnt. Evidently, this was the selfsame charlotte.

"My God! And I didn't believe you," Vasilii Petrovich exclaimed, flinging his arms up. "I thought it was a joke. How did you ever prepare it, my dear?"

"As we know, everything is possible on Solovki," answered Mezernitskii, putting the platter on the table, which needed to be quickly cleared — the bottles and phials hung in different colors in the extended hands of the guests, searching for a place to alight like birds. Only when everything alcoholic and edible found a modicum of calm, he explained. "We bought a dried wild pear, Vasilii Petrovich. That was half the battle. Then we found some butter and jam. Seal fat. Finally, some dark breadcrumbs. And voila! Enjoy. Artiom, would you like another. Everyone else here is tee totaling."

"With some charlotte, I would risk one," said Vasilii Petrovich.

"Let's risk it!" said Mezernitskii and poured Artiom and himself a second shot, while he poured Vasilii Petrovich his first.

"Artiom," said Vasilii Petrovich a bit pathetically, though his eyes sparkled with cunning, "you and I have eaten..."

"... So many berries," offered Artiom.

"Yes," agreed Vasilii Petrovich, as though he were drunk in advance. "But we have never yet drunk together. That must be fixed!"

"And we will drink again, and not once," said Artiom, getting as emotional as he was capable of getting.

"Do you think so?" asked Vasilii Petrovich very seriously, as though Artiom knew something that he didn't.

"He does!" answered Mezernitskii, tired of waiting with his glass full in his hand. "*Ergo bibamus!*" Then he translated for himself, "therefore, we drink!"

And he drank.

Artiom lost his breath for a second time and once again froze in expectation. Vasilii Petrovich endured the imbibement of what seemed to be an even worse drink, the one in black rags, and he quickly reached for a mug of "coffee" to give to his younger comrade. At the same time, he willingly broke of a piece of as-yet-uneaten charlotte. Not for himself, but for Artiom.

By this time, Mezernitskii forced everyone to grow thoughtful for a moment.

"Do you know, my educated friend, that the expression *ergo bibamus* can stop any argument and transform any phrase at all into a toast?"

Artiom at first drank a sip of coffee, and only then did he try to understand the meaning of what was said. Inside, his consciousness was precipitating in waves of sand and a heavy drunkenness approached.

"Grakov, will you drink?" asked Mezernitskii as though to offer an example to prove his words.

"You know that I don't drink," said Grakov, a bit scared.

"I do not drink… *ergo bibamus!*" concluded Mezernitskii and did in fact pour another shot.

"My dear, give the boy a chance to breathe. You're like a bull at the gate!" *Vladychka* John couldn't contain himself.

"Yes!" Having finished his third, Mezernitskii exclaimed, "Exactly! Bull at the gate, *ergo bibamus*!"

Everyone laughed. *Vladychka* also quietly laughed, covering his eyes with his hand.

"That is one definite way to prevent any conversation," complained Vasilii Petrovich with a tear in his cunning voice. Naturally, he took the bait and got hooked.

"Prevent any conversation, *ergo bibamus*!"

They had to drink another one.

Everyone grew still, like children at a play, looking around and suppressing their laughter. Artiom suddenly had a wonderfully sweet feeling inside: Eichmanis, and the soldier named Petro, and the parcel with clothing, and the foreman Sorokin with his sweaty armpits, and that bitch all went far far away; but then that same bitch, turning around in the soft and enchanting air, returned and he unexpectedly sensed her smell and her breathing and her chapped lips…

The rest, in the meantime, tried to find at least some kind of word that wouldn't lead to the immediate consumption of the rainbow-colored alcohol.

Mezernitskii, either severely or jokingly, looked over the guests as though he were besieged, but he cut the charlotte at the same time. This time, Artiom noticed with pleasure, his nails were clean and trimmed.

"Of course! It's his birthday," he explained to himself.

Vladychka John, it seems, was ready to read the prayer before consumption of a common mean, but, evidently, was seriously afraid of immediately hearing about *ergo bibamus*.

"I've shut you all up," Mezernitskii said strictly, but with a sarcastic note to his voice that relaxed everyone. "After all, we can speak of anything you like! Just know that we've predetermined the result of any argument!"

And everyone, at the same time, as though desiring to socialize to their heart's content, until they might be caught by the sleeve, started to talk.

* * *

"I was in Crimea. There were still the fine ladies, there were still epaulets, but now, none of that is left. That life has died...! There are dead cities, where no one lives anymore and there is nothing but ruins. But this was a dead city with living people!" said Mezernitskii, who got drunk in a strange way, as though a warm, barely foggy cloud enveloped him slowly — it dampened all sound and every word came to him with a certain difficulty. "Sad? Sad! But why shouldn't we be sad now? There won't be any of that left soon either."

"Any of what?" said Shlabukovskii, who didn't understand.

"Everything," and Mezernitskii waved his arms around. "The brigades, logs, leopards, foremen, Eichmanis... nothing! You don't think that we've only gone from one myth to another? Troy, Carthage, Sparta... Kulikovo, Borodino, Bastille... Crimea, Solovki. Do you understand?"

"I don't want to be in a myth," said Shlabukovskii. "I want to go into a carved bed with painted cupids on the headboard. And in my pajamas... Moreover, I see no difference between Crimea and Solovki. In my opinion, Crimea, at the moment when the Bolsheviks and Makhnovists broke into it, broke off from the rest of the mainland. For some time, it traveled across the seas and now it arrived here. The audience is pretty much the same, only it forgot to sail away to Turkey in time."

"You, Shlabukovskii, are an anarchist and a member of the bourgeoisie in the same person," said Mezernitskii. "Although, from a different point of view, what else should you be if you want to become an actor?"

Grakov was looking through the books on the shelf.

Vasilii Petrovich sat at the table and thoughtfully chewed something that was no bigger than a leaf of grass.

Artiom climbed into Mezernitskii's bed with his feet up, having taken off his boots, in which it was too hot. He was listening at once to Shlabukovskii and *Vladychka* John, who had just finally sipped a shot of something purple.

"The Church is the people of Christ, but you are outside the Church. You are an orphan," *Vladychka* John quietly said. "The one who believes in Christ and lives in Christ is a god-man. You are only a man. It's difficult for you."

Artiom listened to *Vladychka*, and it seemed to him that his head was clearing up like an onion — layer by layer, and at first it was so light, lighter and lighter, as though he had learned how to breathe with his entire body at once, and everything around him became more transparent… but at the same time, a terror grew within him — what was inside him, in the very heart of him, what?

Yet another word from *Vladychka*, and Artiom was like an onion on his palm — there's one layer peeled off, there's another, there's a third — and what if suddenly he were to take off the last layer and there would be a worm writhing inside? A worm!

It's as though catastrophe was averted — or so Artiom felt — when Mezernitskii, it seems, who was able, despite his little cloud, to speak and listen at the same time, suddenly stopped his monologue and interrupted *Vladychka*.

"Now here's what I sometimes think, Father John. How is Christianity possibly after such a horror?"

Vladychka John looked at Mezernitskii with a slightly tired, but easy-going look. His eyes were very sleepy — he had overextended himself, poor man.

"What about the first Christians?" he asked quietly, but with a tone which suggested that the first Christians had just sat somewhere nearby. "Lions tore them apart. What about Christ Himself? He was nailed to a cross. And He was the son of God! God gave His own son!"

"All of Russia nailed each other with nails," said Mezernitskii. "And now it doesn't want to believe in God. Let God believe in Russia. It's His turn."

Vladychka forced a smile, as though he were looking at a mischievous child that was about to calm back down.

"He does believe. He believes," agreed *Vladychka*. "It's always His turn, it never stops being His turn. It was said, whoever loves his soul will destroy it, but whoever hates his soul, he will find it. Russia has come to hate its soul, in order to find it again."

"And it is finding it," Mezernitskii answered a tone, or even two, higher. "It finds it!" Even Grakov turned around at that tone, while Vasilii Petrovich stopped chewing his blade of grass.

Mezernitskii made a gesture with both hands, as though he were tearing apart the invisible cloud and finally came outside, covered in sweat and exhausted.

"Our dear priest doesn't read books. In Russia, priests in general don't like education very much, since it tries to usurp the place that they already hold… the place from which they preach," said Mezernitskii very clearly. Vasilii Petrovich, at the word "priests" raised his angered eyes but remained silent. "But nonetheless, Russia already has lived for a hundred years in two faiths. Some are fed by prayers, others, by Pushkin and Tolstoy. Grakov, what do you have over there? Tolstoy or Pushkin? Turgenev? Turgenev is good too! Because an impartial reading of Russian literature, written, by the way, as a rule by the nobility, will impart us with a single, but very firm, bit of knowledge: 'The peasant is also a human being!' The most important word here is what? No, not 'human being'. The most important word here is 'also'! The Russian writer — noble, aristocrat, genius — entered the Russian world as one enters a zoo! And his heart wept. Look at them — in the dirt, in filth, in bestiality — they are almost as we are. That is, they are almost like human beings. Look, there's the peasant woman — she's almost like a fine lady! Look, that *muzhik* knows how to talk and he once said something that wasn't stupid, almost on the same level as my six-year-old nephew! Look, those peasant children — they're just as beautiful and joyful as my borzois! Have you read those stories that Leo Tolstoy wrote for that… how do you say it… that *folk*? If Tolstoy himself had been read such stories, he wouldn't even have reached the level of a Nadson!"

"What is your point?" asked Vasilii Petrovich, a bit perplexed.

"Wait a minute, Vasilii Petrovich," answered Mezernitskii. "*Ergo bibamus* awaits us in any case; it is unavoidable. Until then, concerning Tolstoy, and even so only as an example. You can switch Tolstoy with Chekhov — Grakov, put that book back, don't squeeze it any more — it's the same story. Chekhov — he loved no one at all. But he doesn't love all people as people, while the *muzhik*, for him, is something like an animate and angry tree that might attack you and scratch you. Our peasant walks across the pages of our national literature as the Indians do in Fenimore Cooper, except they're worse than the Indians. Because the Indians at least have pride and honor, while the Russian *muzhik* never has that at all. Only, in the best cases, a bit of resourcefulness… But he has no honor, because at any moment his pants might fall down. What sort of honor can there be?"

"And?" asked Vasilii Petrovich, who didn't like Mezernitskii's monologue from its inception.

"The Bolsheviks give faith to the people that they are great!" said Mezernitskii, clearly cutting himself off — he had many more words in reserve. "And the people believe them. The Bolsheviks told the *muzhik* that he is not 'also a human being', but only that he is a human being. And you want him not to believe them. The Bolsheviks have only one problem — the people are wild. Maybe the *muzhik* is not just a human being, but more than a human being, but he is still wild. It's our own fault, of course, but that's no longer important. What can the Bolsheviks do? It's obvious — they must not despair but say to the *muzhik*: 'We will now mold you into what you must be. We will forge you.' The *muzhik*, naturally, doesn't want to be forged. He's been whipped, you understand, for almost a thousand years, and now they've decided to exchange the whip for a hammer — is that joke? However, it's too late. He already agreed."

"So what do we have to do with it, my dear?" asked Vasilii Petrovich.

"We?" Mezernitskii was genuinely astonished. "We have nothing to do with it at all. We're already gone. We're mad at our German tutor that he screams at us — how dare he? We should kill him! We run around the meadow and catch butterflies with a net. Then they lie and dry up in boxes that we've forgotten. We seduce the maid and don't even feel very bad about it. We steal cigars from our father's cigar box… we are in epaulets, but at the same time we're sick with gonorrhea — in that same Crimea, in the heat, hungry, sick with the slowness of the brain that presages death… and we still plan on taking Moscow, we plan it and we plan it, though we really don't want to fight — oh my God, how we hate to fight! Especially since the Indians beat us — they had more anger, faith and strength. The Indians won and they drove us into our reservations — to Solovki."

Mezernitskii sat and poured a different drink into each of the glasses.

Artiom thought, why is *Vladychka* silent? He turned to him, but he was asleep.

For some time, Artiom looked at him with gentleness, even if it was inspired by drunkenness — otherwise he never would have looked at him like that. *Vladychka* suddenly opened his eyes, as though he sensed that someone was looking at him.

At the same moment as his eyes opened, *Vladychka* smiled at Artiom, as though his good humor was only waiting to show itself, enduring the priest's sleep with difficulty.

Vladychka quickly crossed himself, saying, "It's time, it's time, or I won't get up tomorrow…" He quietly got up — with a look as though everything around him was in a glass and he needed to disappear as quietly as possible. Mezernitskii, having gathered air, continued during this time to say something, picking Grakov as his listener, for some reason. Grakov agreed with him in various ways: "That makes sense…! Yes, yes… Of course…! And why not?"

"Vladychka," thought Artiom, "probably had many wondrous words in reserve, but there was no point in wasting them on drunk and broken men."

"My dear lost ones..." that's what *Vladychka*'s entire apologetic and quiet mien said.

"Just don't think that I'm going mad," said Mezernitskii, not even accompanying *Vladychka* with his gaze, but already speaking to everyone.

"No one thinks that," answered Shlabukovskii. "Pour me some as well."

"... So are they going to reforge the *muzhik* in the camp as well? They can't do it in the free world?" asked Artiom as soon as *Vladychka* left. He didn't want to take part in it while the priest was there.

"Have you seen many peasants on Solovki?" asked Mezernitskii. "The Bolsheviks are waiting to see if and how the *muzhik* understands what they're doing... If he doesn't understand, they'll bring him here to finish his instruction... If he understands it himself, it'll be better for him. But in any case, Tioma, it's easier to forge in the blacksmith's shop. *Ergo bibamus!*"

* * *

"These conversations are painful... ragged! But appreciate them, Artiom. They were in Petersburg before. Sometimes in Moscow, though more rarely... Now they are only held here and they will never be repeated anywhere else," said Vasilii Petrovich on the way back, accompanying Artiom. "What horrible heartburn from these drinks...?"

"What about *Vladychka*?" Artiom asked the question he had intended to ask the last time. "Why is he with you all? Does he really need it?" Artiom tried to find the right work, and, not finding it, added. "Is it appropriate for his status?"

"For him?" Vasilii Petrovich chuckled. "No, during our whole lives none of this was appropriate for our status... Do you know, when I was a child, and my father — he was a nobleman, though he had lost his money — when he invited a priest to our estate to perform a service, we didn't invite him to sit at table with us. Not we, not our neighbors — no one sat with the priest. That was bad form. He was fed separately from us... We carried out snacks, even a shot of vodka once. And he ate there by himself like a servant. And I'm not even speaking about the Petersburg high society. There it was easier to bring a devil on a leash — O, everyone would have been extraordinarily pleased! — than to invite a priest. We all knew how — and wanted — to talk without the priest present... But now, we want to speak in his presence, that's how it all turned out! So that he can hear us! And feel sorry for us!"

Vasilii Petrovich became thoughtful about something, but then another thought led him away in a different direction, and he, having run after it, immediately spoke it aloud.

"However, I will say one thing. Mezernitskii changes his mind faster than the weather. No one can understand the essence of his position. He often says things that contradict each other."

"But right about some things," said Artiom thoughtfully. He felt a little sick, but it was endurable. "About the forge, for example."

Vasilii Petrovich ruffled his feathers, as though he was a bird and someone had thrown a rock at him, but he didn't yet know who.

"You can say it in a different way. This is a laboratory," continued Artiom with strange words that he had heard not so long ago, though he did notice Vasilii Petrovich's gesture.

"Tioma, my gentlest heart, what are you going on about? I can't understand it," Vasilii Petrovich said, and then he stopped.

Artiom shrugged and looked directly at Vasilii Petrovich.

"Artiom, have you ever been to the circus?" asked Vasilii Petrovich. "No…? I mention it because this is not a laboratory. And it's not hell. It's a circus in hell."

He was silent for a moment, then added:

"A phantasmagoria."

"I socialized with Eichmanis," said Artiom very calmly. "He says many intelligent things. And he sees everything from a different point of view."

"Oh yes," agreed Vasilii Petrovich with an almost mocking readiness to agree. "But what about you, Tioma? Do you see from your own point of view?"

"Don't get angry, Vasilii Petrovich. You yourself know very well that I do."

"Do I?" Vasilii Petrovich was sincerely confused. "I thought that I do, yes. But now I am not so sure! What are you doing next to Eichmanis, anyway? Have you never heard the phrase, 'Near the Tsar, near to death'?"

Artiom quietly looked Vasilii Petrovich in the eyes and didn't answer.

"Very well, very well, very well," Vasilii Petrovich agreed with who knows who. "Just tell me what he said, in summary… Eh? Something about reforging? Re-smelting?"

Artiom continued to be quiet.

"I, of course, don't know exactly," said Vasilii Petrovich in a whisper, "but I can guess." Even though it was evening, inmates and soldiers still walked in the courtyard here and there. "I know for sure what he did not tell you." Here, Vasilii Petrovich took Artiom by the shoulder and said, "Let's walk this way," then literally pushed him against the nearest wall.

Above Artiom's head was a semicircular arch made from white stone, behind his back was a huge boulder of a wall that smelled of water, grass, the massive amount of time that was imprisoned within it.

"Did you discuss such subjects as imprisoning inmates in solitary in their underwear, in a place that is nothing more than a meter-deep hole in the ground, whose ground and ceiling is covered in thorny branches?" asked Vasilii Petrovich, breathing in Artiom's face. "Did Eichmanis tell you that such inmates can bear it for three days, then they die? Did he make you laugh with his jokes about dolphins? That's when inmates, hearing the following command from a soldier: 'Dolphin!' must jump, for example, from a bridge, if they are being led to a bridge, into the water. If there is no bridge, the guards sometimes place the inmates on the boulders lining the shore. And those, having heard the command, also dive. And it's a good thing if it's August outside, not November! And if they don't jump, they're beaten, very seriously and then they're still thrown into the water…! Did Fiodor Ivanovich remember that one of the punishments for the inmates is carrying water from one hole in the ice to another on our local lakes? Did he tell you how here, in the skete of St. Savatii, political prisoners lived — those same ones who made the Revolution together with the Bolsheviks, then differed in their view and immediately received Solovki as their reward. Yes, they didn't work here, yes, they only arranged disputes and quarrels. However, when the politicals once refused to leave earlier than usual from an evening stroll — our administration called in a Red Army platoon and they gave a few volleys straight into the living, defenseless people! The heroes, I tell you, of their own Revolution…! You, Artiom, by some miracle have avoided the common labor, and already for how many weeks are doing the devil knows what and you've stopped understanding some very simple things. Should I remind you of them? Do you think that if you are no longer sent to the logs that means that no one is carrying them anymore? Do you think that if things are good with you, then everyone else's lives have become better? People die here! Every day, someone dies! And this is the daily life of the camp of Solovki. Not a tragedy, not a drama, not Sophocles, not Euripides — just daily life. Quotidian!"

Vasilii Petrovich squeezed Artiom's shoulder more and more firmly, then suddenly relaxed his fingers, removed his hand, and turned away.

They remained silent for another half a minute.

"… They almost killed you here," he said with an impossibly tired voice. "They almost trampled you to death. How can this be?"

"That's not all," suddenly said Artiom. "Eichmanis was speaking of something else. He said that we ourselves... we do it to ourselves. And I see that it's true."

"We do it to ourselves — yes!" Vasilii Petrovich continued, immediately understanding the point of the conversation. "But why then is he placed as our authority? So that we can torture ourselves even more painfully?"

Somewhere nearby a gull cried painfully, as though someone had stepped on its tail, and several others shrieked in answer.

Vasilii Petrovich leaned with both hands against the wall near Artiom's head and loomed over him.

Artiom almost turned his head aside — to look at a drunk, grown, irritated, almost fifty-year-old man in the eyes was not the greatest pleasure in the world.

He didn't want to answer any more.

Vasilii Petrovich cried out in a whistling whisper, as though something had illumined him, referring to Artiom in the informal you: "Oh, you have fallen under his spell, Artiom! That's not difficult. I know it for myself! But remember one thing, I beg you. Eichmanis is a whitewashed tomb! Do you know what that is? A painted, beautiful tomb, but inside it's still full of filth and bones!"

Artiom finally lifted his arm and freed himself, almost pushing aside Vasilii Petrovich.

He stood a step away from him, looking at the ever-present cap of his friend, now cocked to the side.

"I loved you because you were the most independent of all of us," said Vasilii Petrovich very simply and sincerely. "All of us were broken more or less, if not in spirit, then in character. We were all becoming worse; you alone were becoming better here. There was courage in you, but there was no anger. There was laughter, but no sarcasm. There was a mind, but there was also breeding... What now?"

"Nothing," Artiom answered in an echo that had unexpectedly found its reason.

What else could he answer?

He searched out his sleeping quarters with his eyes and jerked in that direction. In two steps, he did finally vomit. He didn't even stop, only stepped over the foul puddle, wiped his lips with his sleeve — it smelled terribly of perfume and bile, and he rushed towards his wing.

The gulls flew down in a cloud to peck at what was left after Artiom.

* * *

In the morning, a soldier walked it, and said, “Get your stuff!”

Artiom had slept badly and little, he woke up before dawn and lay facing the wall for a long time without moving. At first, he tried not to think at all — but that didn’t work. Then he tried to think — that didn’t work either.

While Osip gathered his things for work, Artiom pretended to sleep.

“Why does it smell like perfume,” Osip asked several times, smelling the air. “Artiom! Artiom, are you asleep…? Or is it *eau de cologne*?”

“No, fuck, I’m not sleeping. I’m chopping wood,” Artiom answered mentally, desiring Osip the fate of the proverb: let him grow hoarse and fall to the devil.

… And then, the soldier.

Artiom sat on his bed, trying to gauge by the soldier’s appearance what was about to happen to him.

He couldn’t understand anything. All that was left was to gather his things.

Oh, those damn swamp boots.

The soldier examined Artiom as he put them on.

It would have been no less abhorrent for Artiom to pull on women’s tights.

“Why is he looking like that?” thought Artiom. “Maybe he’s planning to take them off me as soon as they’ve executed me?”

At other times, Artiom had managed to energize himself with similar thoughts, but here nearly the opposite happened — he suddenly felt nauseous, his hands lost their strength, his boots wouldn’t go on, and wouldn’t go on, and wouldn’t go on — it was a joke and some kind of humiliation…

Artiom got up — he didn’t manage to get one of his feet fully into the toe, so he walked like a lame horse for his first few steps.

“Pull on your boot already,” said the soldier indifferently. “Don’t you have any other footwear?”

“No,” answered Artiom, barely hearing his own voice.

… Their path lay towards the IID.

He met Burtsev on the second floor — he was quickly going downstairs, carrying a packet of papers under his armpit. He didn’t give way, so both the soldier and Artiom had to move out of his way — so that piece of shit sloughed off past them without even nodding, as though they had never known each other.

On the third floor, in the same office, Galina waited for him with her lips pursed, with her glance icy… but she smelled of perfume.

She nodded at the stool.

Artiom sat.

Eichmanis's photograph under the glass was turned face-up again, he noticed with surprise.

"Too bad she didn't draw horns on him," thought Artiom from the depths of his hot spiritual underworld.

Galina moved closer to the table, right to the edge, so that her expansive bosom froze in place right above the table.

"If you," said Galina with her lips alone, "say even a single word, you'll live exactly as long as it will take for you to be led 'under the store'. You can forget about solitary — there are enough reports about you to give you exactly three executions. And it would only take one bullet to take you down."

Artiom raised his eyes to Galina and nodded.

She also nodded: good.

"You didn't boast to anyone yet?" she asked, slightly louder. "What were you whispering about with Vasilii Petrovich in the yard yesterday?"

Artiom swallowed his saliva, not knowing what to say.

"Something else," he pushed out.

Galina examined Artiom, but not for long.

"Since you've been left without any work," she said, returning to the paper on her desk, "I've had to… assign you a new task… From this day, Artiom Goriainov is assigned to guard duty in the Iodine Plant. Your neighbor Osip Troianskii works there, so… now you'll work together. When you get there, they'll show you everything… Usually, it's the clergy that works these jobs in the sweat of their brow… So you'll be like a priest's son."

They sat in silence for some time.

Galina tapped her pencil on the table.

A flush crept up her cheek, Artiom noticed.

The icy expression of her eyes softened a little to something slightly more alive — as though she had just thought of some feminine mischief.

"Thank you," said Artiom quietly and distinctly.

"Uh-huh," said Galina with a careless voice, the same voice that the fine ladies probably use on the Arbat.

Artiom nearly ran down the staircase, just as he had done in school many years ago.

"I'm alive, alive, alive," he kept repeating. "I'm alive. I'm so alive. And I don't want to be a god-man. I want to be a living orphan. Without a cross and without a tail… Yes!"

For some time, he rushed about his room like a lover before a rendezvous with his beloved. In general, he had basically nothing to gather. He no longer received an increased ration as a member of the Spartakiade and he only had his winter things left, while the weather was still fine, swelling sunnily in the threshold of August.

"And what does that mean? Now I'm to go hungry?" Artiom complained, completely forgetting that if they had told him half an hour ago that they would no longer feed him at all, but they wouldn't shoot him, that he would have agreed and been grateful and limitlessly happy.

He really wanted to eat. He had vegetables under his bed, he remembered. And though there were many of them, Artiom really wanted something like a big piece of meat.

Without thinking, he pulled out the chest from under Osip's bed.

Osip was rich — it seems that he had only just received his package. Dried sweet and sour cherries. Poached pears in sugar. Macaroni in a cheesecloth bag. Rise, buckwheat, peas. Mustard, lard. Nuts… Bread.

"Only a few sour cherries and a handful of the sweet…" Artiom decided and immediately filled him south.

"And the lard…" he allowed himself. "One piece."

Good thing that it was already sliced and not yet finished.

"His mother probably sent it to him like that — already sliced." Artiom decided. "Otherwise Osip himself would have just gnawed at it until he dislocated his jaw."

One piece wasn't enough. Three pieces wouldn't have been enough if Artiom had not commanded himself: enough, enough, go away. But really — dried cherries and lard is a miraculous thing.

"As soon as I get home, that's all I'm going to eat," Artiom decided.

The iodine plant was two kilometers away, through a spruce forest.

Artiom knew the road, and it's wasn't difficult. From the kremlin to the north, past the most peaceful lake (like Aleksei Mikhailovich) along the granite shore, through the narrow-gauge railway. Then, a few minutes later, you'd see no more inmates or guards at all, because the rest of the way is straight, straight — forest to the right, forest to the left. Very calm, almost without sound, only if you listened attentively could you hear the river that emptied into the Holy Lake.

"I don't walk on plush or velvet… but I walk on the edge of a knife…" Artiom sang quietly along the way. It seemed to him a very cheerful song.

"If I knew how to think," thought Artiom, "I would be like Mezernitskii — I would be sure of everything at once, especially in the most unpleasant things. And that conviction wouldn't bother me…"

"… How difficult to understand are all people," thought Artiom. "No one is easy to understand. Inside the external man, there is always the internal man. And inside him there's someone else still."

"Shlabukovskii, for example. Who is he? Afanasiev — who is he? Grakov — who's inside Grakov? Moisei Solomonovich — is he really who he appears to be — the one singing his never-ending songs? Burtsev? Krapin? Curly? Boris Lukianovich? Schelkachov? Zahar? Lazhechnikov…? But no, he's dead already… Passport? Gills? Was every one of them a child once, climbing up to his mother's knee? How did they get off those knees?"

He didn't want to remember yesterday's words of Vasilii Petrovich, though, on the other hand, he did say that Artiom was getting better in this place — how strange that is, because he didn't notice anything like that in himself. He didn't notice himself at all — he was just here and did everything he could not to die.

"But other people want the same thing," thought Artiom. "Or maybe not…? How do other people do it? How am I different from them? I should ask Vasilii Petrovich. I don't understand it myself."

Artiom on purpose did not call Eichmanis and Galina to mind, because those were difficult thoughts and they frightened him. In different ways, but they both frightened him, and he didn't want to be frightened.

The more so, because if Artiom let his mind wander freely even for a moment, he immediately and vividly felt Galina's breast in his hand. He had found it in her shirt, having torn off the fourth button from the top, and pulled it out. Her nipple, terrible hard, pushed exactly against the middle of his palm… what could he do with such thoughts…?

… If they came, he had to run away from them just like he did from the mosquitoes, or they would eat him alive. Even now, Artiom ran forward a little and once again felt how light, young and handsome he was. He was convinced that if he struck a tree full force with his shoulder, the spruce, croaking, would fall over.

In one hundred meters, he slowed down, and his breathing almost didn't change, but at least that hallucination was left behind, and his palms were once again empty — grab the air with them and walk on!

At the road, a fallen birch lay. Its leaves were red, as though filled with blood.

To the left of the road, then up to a wooden gate, and there, on a hillock, stood a while building, tidy as a cake, with three windows on the back end and four on the front, with a porch in the middle with stairs. St. Philip's Hermitage — this is where the iodine plant was now. It used to be in a different place; apparently, they had just moved.

Next to the building, in the front yard, he saw something like a hen house made of logs with a small window and a small door — it's possible this was the cell of that same Philip, who knows? But how did he walk through that door? Only by bowing every time to the ground.

A little farther off from the house stood a tall cross and under the cross was a well.

Artiom, as though he owned the place, went over there to drink some water.

Now this would be his new place of residence.

He didn't think about that out loud, but his entire soul begged that he be allowed to stay here to the end of his term — in the middle of the forest, invisible to all, not needed by anyone, forgotten by all.

"She probably doesn't want me to talk to anyone and to shut up," thought Artiom. "I'm ready to seal my mouth shut and take an oath of silence…"

The water was cold and delicious.

"Well, then, grandfather Philip," said Artiom aloud. "Accept your new lodger! Without a cross and without a tail."

Osip met Artiom with surprise; he even asked as though joking — he didn't know how to joke well, so it sounded severe: "Should I watch out for you? Did they send you to bring us all in?"

Artiom scoffed.

Osip himself — finally, he got it! — understood that he was a bit tactless, and so immediately changed the subject.

"We moved here very recently. It's not bad here. Let's go, I'll show you how we live here."

Osip's colleagues paid absolutely no attention to Artiom — they were educated people, very busy. Artiom didn't strive to get to know them either.

"Don't touch anything here," Osip warned, nodding at all his myriad devices and solutions, which, of course, only inspired Artiom's quiet desire to break and confuse everything by tomorrow morning.

In the laboratory, there were six rooms — three under the laboratory, two empty: "We're going to make bedrooms out of them and eventually move here completely, so we don't waste time walking back and forth," said Osip. There was also a kitchen, six guinea pigs lived there.

"Do you eat them?" asked Artiom completely seriously.

"No, no, they breed them," answered Osip. "It's not just the iodine plant here, but the biological garden too. They breed animals… by the way, they told us that the guard would see after them. So, maybe I should introduce you to these creatures?"

"Later, later," Artiom declined. "I'll have plenty of time."

Artiom noticed that there was a constant racket coming from the attic.

"What are they doing there?" asked Artiom. "Building a conservatory?"

"No," answered Osip. "The bunnies live upstairs. Twenty of them. Should we go see?"

"Later," said Artiom. "I'd like to see my room."

He suddenly realized that he didn't get enough sleep and that he would immediately fall asleep in an incredible sleep that he had not had for many days already. After all, someone was always interrupting his sleep, even Osip, who snored next to him, and someone from the guard brigade might come in at any moment, make him get up and do something humiliating; the foremen were always yelling, and the work group leaders beat everyone with bludgeons. But here, there were only bunnies in the attic… And those, what-cha-ma-call-it… piggies.

"There's nothing here, just that blanket… maybe that sweater can serve as a pillow," Osip showed him, opening the door, but Artiom, without even waiting for him to finish, fell on the floor, pushed the sweater in to the corner, stuck his head in it, though it smelled horrible — paint and, he thought, rabbit droppings, and man-smell, and who knows what else. Artiom was already sleeping the sleep of the dead.

In his dream, he heard impossibly distant, though audible, human speech, but as though it were not in the next room, but forty rooms away.

"And what's this? What about this? And here?" repeated the same voice, so thick and unpleasant as though it were coming from a caterpillar with a cold.

Artiom understood that some uniform from the kremlin had arrived with some soldiers, because there was a constant racket of boots stomping here and there and at any moment they would walk into the room of the guard, and the guard was asleep, doing nothing, and this would be a wonderful chance to immediately kick him out by the scruff of the neck, or even send him into solitary; but Artiom still could do nothing with himself and lay there without moving, buried under his entire term with black earth in which he was looking for treasure, buried by Eichmanis's gestures and words, by Galina's heat and the moist smell that came from her, the whispered mumbling of Vasilii Petrovich, the hanging lower lip of Passport, little

Philip's stump, the logs, the cross of *Vladychka* John, the poached pears from Osip's parcel…

"Here we don't have anything yet, it's closed," Osip lied nearby, almost above Artiom's ears, and the caterpillar crawled away behind him; once again it became almost quiet, only the rabbits kept looking for something in the attic, found it, ate it and once again searched for it, moving as though not on paws, but on square wheels.

"Or was that Eichmanis?!" someone growled inside Artiom. "What if it was Eichmanis? He'll come in and ask, 'Who's that? Artio-o-o-m! And what are you doing here?'"

Artiom hid his head in the sleeve of the sweater and died there. He had no more strength left to worry.

"Hey! What's wrong with you?" Osip pestered him. "Are you going to begin your duties or not? It's time to guard. Let's go, I'll warm up some tea. And I'll teach you how to feed the piggies."

Artiom got up, as though completely drunk with a head boiled from the unexpected and powerful sleep. Tripping over himself, he went after Osip.

He didn't even ask if it was Eichmanis who came or someone else. He preferred to decide that he had imagined it.

"I will feed the guinea pigs with the rabbits," said Artiom hoarsely. "And the rabbits, with guinea pigs."

* * *

Osip was a man who remembered that decency and orderliness had the same root.[38]

In the kitchen, where the guinea pigs lived in their cages behind an ingenious wooden barrier, Osip hung a paper where he had written their names: Red, Gypsy, Blackie, Yellow, Daughter and Mommy.

"What, does he think I'm going to talk to them?" Artiom thought with dark sarcasm.

Still, Osip did show him where the teapot was, though he didn't warm it up, in spite of his promises.

It turned out he had to feed the guinea pigs with oats, rutabagas and turnips. In a separate cage, there were another thirty white mice.

---

38 In the original Russian, not in English.

Artiom looked around to see if there was another paper with the names of the mice, or — God forbid! — he would mix them up and they would die from humiliation.

"I hope they don't send you to solitary for each dead mouse," thought Artiom in the same tone. "Or I'm going to ask to be transferred to the logs."

"What are the logs, anyway?" he answered himself a little more seriously. "I could do them now."

Without admitting it to himself, he was talking with Vasilii Petrovich, arguing with him about yesterday's words.

Artiom didn't really remember anything clearly — not the mosquitoes that ate human flesh, not Curly's swearing, not the bestial labor, not the feeling of the slippery and unwieldy tree on his shoulder.

"... If only I could find something to eat with my tea. Here. There's a carrot. It's probably for the rabbits. The rabbits will go without their carrot today."

The hot sour-cherry tea with carrots in an empty house in the middle of the forest, a few kilometers away from the IID, guards, and watchmen...

"... No, really, how can I manage it for them to forget me?" Artiom imagined again, looking now at the turnip.

In answer to his thoughts, someone knocked on the window.

It seemed that this was enough to scare a grown, strong, young man.

Artiom felt that his legs got cut out from underneath him, even though he sat on a chair.

"Who is that?" the thoughts hopped around like fleas in his head. "For me? I'm the guard — how I am supposed to guard? To die in defense of the guinea pigs? Maybe I shouldn't answer at all? Who needs to come here in the evening? Or did Osip forget something? Or maybe St. Philip's come here to preach to me? 'Who drank from my well?'"

Someone knocked again.

Artiom put down his mug, got a knife from the table and went to the door.

"Who's there?" he asked loudly.

"Open up," said a woman's voice very calmly. It was Galina. "Come on, quickly," she said dully. "I can't manage the key."

Artiom quickly opened the door.

Galia was alone and whisked into the room lightly, without making a sound, as though she were some unlisted animal in this biological garden.

"I was waiting for them to leave," she said, rubbing her cheeks, which were bitten by mosquitoes. She walked in the direction of the kitchen as though she knew the place. "They're slow, like all scientists."

She spoke to Artiom as though they were old friends. He remained silent, and inside him everything trembled again.

"I'm going to turn into jelly soon from all this freaking out."

After entering the kitchen, Galina put her hand on the teapot and stood there for some time without turning around, as though she were looking at the animals but not quite seeing them.

"Did you know that I'd come?" she asked.

"Yes," said Artiom, though he knew nothing of the sort and didn't even dare to think about her.

"Bastard," she said contentedly, turned around and kissed him on the mouth.

* * *

She left around an hour later… or a little later. Artiom wasn't quite sure.

At first, getting dressed in the darkness, she commanded him with a firm voice, slightly mocking and demanding, as though she were a teenager.

"Now talk to me. I want you to talk."

Artiom blinked and got confused — he no longer knew a single word.

Ten minutes before, a step before the now almost inevitable loss of consciousness, he had whispered, with a voice heavy from piercing ecstasy: "Galia…" and lightly bit her on the shoulder.

Now he didn't even dare pronounce that name — who was he anyway? How dare he?

"No, first we have to feed you," she said, without waiting for a single word from him. "Where did you drop my purse? Did I have a purse?"

"I didn't see," Artiom said quietly.

"Didn't see… Well, go find it now," she answered.

It lay right at the entrance. In the purse, there were tins of meat and — my God! — oranges! Four of them.

"I'll eat one," she said, cleaning the orange, "And you eat the rest. Have you eaten these before?"

"Where did they come from?" asked Artiom, not touching the yellow, strange fruit.

"They rolled in," answered Galina seriously.

They were in the kitchen — Galia sat on the chair and Artiom stood.

She had let down her hair — it lay a bit lower than her shoulders, and as she talked, she sometimes blew on the falling hairs or fixed them with her hand, quickly looking up at Artiom.

"… They coo like pigeons," she said, nodding at the guinea pigs, then gave Artiom an orange. "Eat. Do you know how?"

Artiom took the orange.

He stood barefoot — he wasn't about to put on his swamp boots.

All the more so because they warmed up the iodine plant — evidently, the scientists required warmth to be able to work.

"What, you don't have any other shoes?" she asked more with concern than ridicule. "Why are you always in those swamp boots…? And you take such a long time to take them off."

Artiom shrugged. Then he quietly said, "No."

She looked at him again, a bit longer than usual this time, and said, "Well then. I'm going to go. Guard."

Artiom was about to go with her to the exit, but Galia stopped him.

"Sit here until I leave. Don't… see me off. You can close up later."

She slammed the door.

He didn't turn off the light and sat in the kitchen for a long time.

The guinea pigs fell asleep.

Artiom ate one orange — it was delicious. But in his mouth, no less powerful than the orange, was the taste of that woman — her skin and sweat.

He had neither joy nor wonder — it was remarkably easy not to think. And if he entered into himself, trying to find at least some kind of feeling, some kind of thought, then it was like he was walking in an empty house, looking into every room and finding nothing other than a quiet draft.

It wasn't a bad draft and it wasn't a frightening emptiness, as though he had just moved someone for a time, or forever. But where?

He fell asleep a bit before morning. His sleep was like this — as though he had been performing some extraordinary and rare work all night through a terrible racket and flickering fires. The work required not only strength, but endurance, and also angry joy… maybe a sailor in the tropics? Something like that. In his dream, that tropical noise and flashes of fire and trilling of birds went on constantly, circling about and rising up into the heavens.

He woke up from the voices of the scientists. He hadn't locked the door behind her… What a guard!

"Oranges!" someone was amazed. "The guard feeds himself with oranges!"

Artiom quickly came out of his little room. Osip was, it seems, coming to him — they almost knocked heads.

"My friends were asking if they could use the orange peel — we're going to add them to our tea. I think it'll turn out to be… unique."

“Of course,” said Artiom quietly, trying to remember if anything else had accidentally been left.

By the morning, the warmth in the iodine plant diminished. Artiom felt chilly and his head ached slightly.

“Where did you get them?’ asked Osip.

“They rolled in,” Artiom answered in an echo.

In five minutes, he went back to his room to finish his sleep.

On the way to the monastery, he felt a little better — a breeze blew the brouhaha of his short sleep away, inspiring a seemingly impossible, and yet completely palpable carelessness.

The trees stood thoughtful — the summer had turned to autumn, after all.

“Autumn — that’s good,” thought Artiom.

The thought of Galia was sweet, bitter, sour — like nettles. It quietly clenched his jaw.

“Galia… that’s good too,” Artiom thought carefully, attentively watching to see how his consciousness would react at these words uttered silently within.

His consciousness pulsed.

“You were supposed to be digging for treasure. And when Eichmanis returns, they’ll bury you instead,” Artiom thought, almost cheerfully. “And no one will search for you… Except for Mama?”

These thoughts didn’t sadden him at all — if only for the reason that in this forest, in this solitude, it was very difficult to believe in them.

Suddenly, he realized that he was still carrying an orange in his hand. He had taken it from the kitchen.

He began to peel it with his teeth and even tried to chew the peel, but no, it’s not good, bitter. But the orange — yes, it’s magical, thank you, Galia.

From this second utterance of her name in his thoughts this morning, his head started spinning, and a desire to scream appeared…

“… My God, there’s solitary ahead, and there, they’ll truly — Vasilii Petrovich is right — they kill people there… But here, there’s this silence and I alone am free. How is it? Maybe I should go somewhere?”

Something rustled in the forest.

Then two soldiers came out to the road. They started to smoke, standing next to a huge black boulder, looking at Artiom from time to time.

When he was passing by, the soldiers had already forgotten about him and were speaking about something, cursing angrily, heavily and bitterly, like cheap tobacco.

Not far away, Artiom heard the striking of axes and someone swearing terribly. They were probably beating someone.

Artiom hurried on.

At the entrance to the monastery gates, he met Curly, who bulged his eyes at him — not very much, though — it seemed that he didn't recognize him.

Artiom even touched his face, caressed himself on his shaved head — maybe something changed in him, making him completely different.

People were walking in the monastery courtyard, but he didn't want to meet anyone and kept looking at his cobbled path, hurrying forward.

No one was in the abbot's wing. Everyone was working except for Artiom…

He fell onto his bed, face down, as before stunned by everything that had happened, smiling into his mother's pillow, invisible to anyone in the world.

In two minutes, or maybe only one, the door opened and he quickly looked up.

"What, it doesn't lock?" she asked. "That's right, you can't. Let's move your boots over here…"

She quickly moved the swamp boots to the doors with her little feet, and, taking off her skirt with difficulty as she walked, returned to Artiom's bed.

She stood next to it, leaning against its edge with one knee. Galina was still wearing brown boots with heels. They had silver buckles.

It was all terribly seductive, so much so that he spasmed in his chest.

"Only quickly," she said strictly. "Do you know how to do it quickly?"

"I don't know," answered Artiom, looking her up and down.

* * *

Breathing heavily, with widened eyes, painfully clasping the back of his head, she suddenly called him "Tiomka", with her lips alone, somewhere into his temple. But he heard how his name pushed with her breathing against his skin…

It was as though when he had said "Galia" last night, unexpectedly for himself, he had said the first half of a password, and now she was uttering the second half.

They had named each other — and only after this did they learn how to talk a little bit. Or at least Artiom did.

She stood at the door, looking at him with drunk eyes.

"Do you have any water?" she asked.

"No… there, in the carafe."

"Give me some."

Artiom did.

"Br-r-r," she grimaced comically and gave him the carafe back.

"They sometimes do inspections," said Artiom, nodding at the door.

"So what?" she asked. "Here I make the inspection, checked..." and she laughed quietly, very appealingly.

It turned out that Artiom had not yet heard how she laughed. He quietly smiled, trying to sketch out the line of her lips with his own crude, awkward lips.

"Are you worried for me or for yourself?" she asked, becoming severe again.

"For you," he answered firmly, choosing the informal you.

"What about for yourself?"

Artiom shrugged without looking away from her and received a piercing pleasure from the fact that he could look directly into her eyes.

"Can you imagine what he is capable of doing to me?" he asked, smiling, though the smile was more one of anticipation.

"He's going to kill you," answered Galia. There was something childish in her voice, like a child saying that Papa is coming to punish everybody.

Artiom nodded.

Galia left.

"Good!" someone barked in the corridor.

Artiom almost jumped up from that cry.

For a moment he sat there, then, as soon as her severe heels quieted down, he lay down again.

He lay there with frenzied a heartbeat. His mouth was dry, his eyes were dry — and it was as though a dry draft had blown through his head.

"... What if they really do execute me because of her?" he thought.

"But for what?"

"What do you mean for what? 'Cohabitation with inmates from the female barracks' is punished by solitary, but here..."

"What about here? There's nothing there about female employees of the IID."

"... Uh-huh. You're not laughing? Idiot."

Artiom tried not to think of the head of the camp. Even the name "Eichmanis" sounded like the snap of a pair of scissors as they cut off someone's head.

Having lain there another minute, he felt that he was covered with sweat — it was slight, almost feverish.

"No-no-no," he calmed himself down. "Everything will be otherwise. She won't want me to be here anymore and she'll arrange a pardon from me. She's cut down my time by half or even more... and I'll go home."

Then he thought about her again. "Has she gone insane? Has she gone totally insane?"

The word "phantasmagoria" surfaced — as though someone had said it recently. But who?

Vasilii Petrovich, that's who.

Artiom jumped. Vasilii Petrovich had brought berries yesterday, and he hadn't finished them. Where were they? Or had he finished them? Or maybe he had left them here?

On the table near to Osip's bed, there was an empty bag — that's who finished it.

"Oh, so that's how it is," said Artiom completely forgetting that he had enjoyed Osip's reserve lard and sweet and sour cherries.

He pulled out the chest with the produce — there were only cereals and poached pears left. The rest Osip had probably taken to work with him, Artiom decided.

He didn't really want any pears. He wanted lard again or at the very least some cheese, but in any case, some animal product, something connected to flesh, blood and milk.

"But I had some money!" Artiom remembered, grabbing his mother's pillow, where he had hidden it. He felt with his fingers: yes, it was still there.

"I'll go to the store right now… buy myself everything for… how much do I have there? Some sausage, oh… do I have enough for sausage?"

He had to put on footwear to leave. Again those damn boots.

"What if Eichmanis orders me to return the uniform? He probably will. Let's say that I have a spare set of shirt and pants. But I only have felt boots to put on my feet. I'll have to buy something. Maybe I shouldn't waste it on sausage? Or else I'll be barefoot, prowling around like a leopard. I'm not going to put on the felt boots, after all… But no, I really want some sausage… I'm going to get some sausage, for sure… But what about Passport? Gills? Shaferbekov? They promised to make sausage out of me… Damn it, damn it all. I need some sausage right now… By the way, do I get a ration now or not? Whom should I ask?"

Artiom hurried down, his legs barely bending in the boots, and, no sooner had he left his building to go outside than he met Mitya Schelkachov.

He gasped from pleased surprise and immediately fixed his eyes on him: well, what news have you brought?

"Thank God!" exclaimed Mitya, very pleased. "Your foreman wasn't allowing me to come to you, but he didn't want to come get you either. I've brought you some things. They brought us the uniforms, and… here it is, your bag. What happened to you? We haven't figured it out yet."

"It's not important, not important," Artiom said. "How is… Fiodor Ivanovich... Eichmanis… did he… say anything about me?"

"Eichmanis!" Schelkachov repeated contentedly. "There's been no more Eichmanis at all. After he sent you off, he hasn't come back. They say he's gone to Kem."

"And what have you been doing?"

"Nothing," Schelkachov laughed. "We've been listening to Gorshkov's swearing. They swear so curiously here that I decided to put together a dictionary…"

Taking up his parcel and looking at Mitya — as though his face would hold the confirmation of everything that he had just said — Artiom felt as though he were a child who woke up at dawn on new year's morning, running with bare feet to the tree, and there, a wooden piebald horse — huge, half the size of a real horse and a whole army of wooden soldiers from three armies, not counting the guerillas, three bottles of lemonade, a winding clock, a saber and something else buried in the tinsel — it's scary to even go there, his heart might burst from it.

"Mitya," said Artiom with a suppressed voice. "Wait a moment for me. I'm going to take off these… boots. I'll change and let's go to the retail store. I unbearably want to buy you something.

"Enough," said Schelkachov. "Not worth it."

"Shut up," commanded Artiom and ran back.

How wonderful it was in his own shoes, in his own shirt. He felt as though protected with his own body's warmth, which had heated his clothing before and in a miraculous way had not escaped.

There was no sausage. They ran out the previous evening. So they bought some cheese and Artiom said "… for everything!" and on the way back, paying no one any heed, they began to eat it.

Two leopards immediately ran up. Artiom broke them off a piece — he didn't mind, but he commanded them: "Don't come up anymore, or I'll kick you."

"And I'll spit in your face!" answered the leopard, and his mouth was already full of cheese.

Artiom laughed, nudged Mitya — ha-ha, that guy's funny — but he only moderately smiled, evidently, not all that amused.

In the courtyard bustle, Bear and Black easily made Artiom out. They also got a piece and some caresses. Only the gulls bothered them, frantically and incessantly demanding their own.

The cheese was magnificent, soft, sour, and milky — you could cry from it.

"How are our Saracens doing?" asked Artiom. Schelkachov thought for a minute, then laughed with pleasuring, understanding that he meant Kabir-shah and Kurez-shah.

Behind Artiom, someone slapped him on the shoulder.

"The gangsters…" his heart jerked.

But it was Boris Lukianovich.

"Artiom!" They hugged with sincere pleasure. "Where are you now? How are you? Has the head of the camp released you? It's a bit difficult for me without you. There's hardly anyone I can rely on here."

"Oh, I'm well, yes," Artiom smiled from ear to ear. "Want some cheese…? They've moved me to a new job, but I'll ask if I can be returned to you," he answered, though he knew he was lying — with all his heart, but still lying — after all, what damn Spartakiade when he had such a… what? Job? Life? Song?

When he was living in such a phantasmagoria.

"Yes, yes, do ask," said Boris Lukianovich. "Considering that they've continued to issue a ration for you all these days and I haven't even received a document confirming your transfer. So you can take that which belongs to you. Not… cheese. Though that's good too, of course, thank you. You'll take your dry ration tomorrow, yes?"

Artiom closed his eyes, opened them, grabbed his ear and walked like that for a few steps.

"No. I'm not sleeping."

* * *

"What did you call me?"

"A con woman."

"I like that. It sounds like a candy in the mouth, rolling around in the teeth… Call me something else."

"Ladette."

"What's that?

"Like a lad. Except female."

"Ladette… ladette. That's good too… so why didn't you do it with the prostitute? You gave her a ruble. And didn't do anything. Idiot."

Artiom was silent for a time, drawing an invisible design on the wall. They were lying in darkness in his guard room.

I gave her one, but spent three, he remembered.

"Just didn't," he said.

"What a proud man," she quietly laughed. "And now your wait is over?"

For a moment, Artiom stopped drawing on the wall — what if she suddenly gets angry? His other hand lay on top of hers, not grasping it, not trying to intertwine fingers, just — above. These hands were the only things that were touching right now.

Artiom tried to sense through his hand — is she angry or just joking? Is she just provoking him? Or is she making herself angry on purpose?

Just in case, he didn't answer.

"In that case, go get me some tea," she commanded.

Artiom threw his nonexistent drawings off the walls and went into the kitchen.

It was a strange thing — when he left her for a moment, he immediately lost any faith in the reality of what was happening, even more so in her human and — how insane to say it! — feminine emotions.

"Osip made a thermos. Himself," he reported, quickly returning. "Now we'll always have hot water."

Even though he had only left her for two minutes, he had already managed to become afraid — what's her mood now? Did it come apart at the seams? Did it transform into something impossible and horrid? Artiom always felt that the chance of that happening was great. Blink, and the world around him would become unrecognizable.

With his voice, uttering the words into the darkness of the room, it was as though Artiom tested whether or not there was life there, and if there was — what sort of life was it? Warm, mammalian? Or cold, contentious, consuming people whole?

In the same way, people search with a trembling lantern or hissing torch underground, every minute fearing to see something that would make their hair turn white for all time.

"Troianskii?" She asked from the darkness.

Artiom at first didn't understand what she was on about.

"Oh, yes. Osip. Troianskii."

A few hours before, Artiom, having argued with that same Osip, pulled a couch from the scientists' smoking lounge to his own room.

"Where are my friends going to smoke when it gets cold?" Troianskii asked angrily and a little bit into his nose.

"Standing! You have to smoke standing!" Artiom answered quietly, moving the couch. No one helped him; the scientists in general tolerated his presence less and less.

Neither had Osip offered Artiom to use the thermos, but he hadn't asked.

Instead of a table for the tea, Artiom, once again leaving the room, brought back a bedside table on which the scientists jotted down the weights of the guinea pigs and other observations concerning their rich lives.

When he returned the second time, Galia was sitting completely dressed, only with her hair down, and she was touching the self-same couch with her hand.

"You don't have any lice, do you?"

"Are they necessary?" Artiom asked with a smile.

She didn't laugh.

"I brought some pie with a jam filling. Let's eat. I haven't eaten anything all day. Turn on the light! Only the window… cover it with something."

Artiom did everything she commanded.

He sat near the table on his knees. He poured himself and her a cup.

By that time, she had reached for her purse.

The purse wasn't quite feminine — it was leather, military, with a strap, only it wasn't very large and it was almost new. However, inside it had everything a woman needed — powder, lipstick, perfume — Artiom noticed when she opened it and began, in her womanly way, to rummage for something quickly and with slight irritation — where is it?

It seems she was looking for her brush, but she didn't find it. However, she did find something else.

"Look at what notes I have here," she said.

"To whom?" asked Artiom, blowing on his tea, even though it wasn't all that hot.

"To no one, really. The inmates write them. We confiscated them. Listen. 'I'm going to go to the nurse's station, and you come there. Without you, I'm melting like a candy. I'll remain your faithful lover until the grave.' Eh? There's love for you. Listen to this one too." She chose some from her purse, there were many in there, and Artiom didn't understand why she carried them around with her. 'That Gala that you know wants to get to know you.' Understand? Gala! Fa-mous!" It's as though she were waiting for him to laugh.

"Yes," Artiom answered very seriously.

She looked at him for a second and not finding something in his face, breathed out, "Fine…" And put away the notes. "… What shall we have with our tea? It smells of herbs."

"I added pine leaves into it," said Artiom, looking at her nervously. Something was going on and it had to be stopped.

"Really?" she asked and looked into the cup. "Interesting… I don't want that. I'm going to go."

She got up suddenly, grabbed her purse and the purse opened up, dropping a single note. Galia didn't notice it, walking around the seated Artiom and rushed towards the exit.

He got up too, walked after her, sorrowfully understanding that this is it. The end was coming and what would happen after, no one could explain to him. Nothing good, probably would follow.

She would leave right now and goodbye, incredible good fortune.

And if he would try, for example, to kiss her on the cheek in parting, then something completely awful would happen.

But if he didn't come out to accompany her, it would be even worse.

Basically, there was not much of a choice, and it was bad either way.

"The Gala that you know," he explained quietly. "I understood it like this: she who's made of spring."[39]

She stopped, holding the door frame, and once more looked back at him.

It was dark in the threshold, and Artiom couldn't see her eyes.

Then he added, guessing, "You."

* * *

It was all painful and impossible, holding on by some kind of ancient, invisible threads that, if you breathed in, would rip apart… But by some miracle, it continued.

He walked towards her, and she had nowhere to go — behind her was the door, and he was before her.

Then they drifted somewhere into the kitchen, frightening the guinea pigs. The animals all got scared, the people dropped the teapot, the thermos and everything was covered in boiling water… until they found themselves a space in some new corner, on an old armchair, biting each other all over and thus made peace.

Artiom didn't come back to himself immediately. His mind was cloudy and kept disappearing — now Artiom, almost already without a mind, thoughtless, felt himself floating for some reason, jerking, jerking, jerking — down underneath he had a fish, but it had caught him, or he had caught it, it wasn't

39 There is a play on words in the original Russian that does not translate well into English.

clear anymore, and at any moment, he would pull that fish out into the wide world and it's all wet, golden, fantastic, hungry — or, on the contrary, it would pull him down to the bottom, floating once again and he would finally choke. This feeling of indeterminacy kept going and going and that, devil take it, fish kept biting, the circles in the water kept getting more and more rough, and the water simultaneously turned thicker, like molten metal, and you can't survive in that water, in that water you die forever, yes, that's for sure, yes, yes…

Then suddenly someone turned the entire river upside down, together with the sun reflected in it, or the stars, or the fish, and everything flew from above, as from a trough — the sun, the fish, the stars.

She had tanned hands, with downy hair. Her breasts and… another part of her body were blindingly white like ice cream…

"I want your tea. With trees," she said hoarsely. She had screamed herself out. And she couldn't get up yet; he had to do that first.

He got up, left, and for the first time felt much more confident that he would return and now everything would be well. Now it couldn't end badly. At least, not immediately.

The thermos, thank goodness, didn't break.

"What about the pie?" she cried from the room, where, judging by her voice, she was dressing. "You forgot the pie. Get the pie!"

They drank the tea, and Galia said, "Ask me, 'why me?' I have to explain myself."

"I have no right to address you without permission," Artiom answered.

She laughed quietly and warmly.

She had her fill of laughter and said, "You struck Sorokin. I knew that they would put you in solitary and kill you soon after. You were walking towards IID — all young and sweaty — and I even sensed your smell; though how that's possible, from the third floor… And that was it. Everything collapsed."

Artiom looked into his cup.

"I had seen you before, but you were different. When you were boxing in front of Eichmanis and his guests—" the name 'Eichmanis' she uttered with some kind of especially vengeful, it seemed to Artiom, feeling… but perhaps he had imagined it. "… There, I didn't feel sorry for you. And it was generally vile over there. Only… well, it's not important."

Artiom raised his eyes and very quickly, carefully looked at her, lest he ruin that tone, that voice… though he thought to himself, "Yes, it's very important!"

"Oh, no, I had called you out before that, didn't I? That time, you played the fool and at the end of our interview you said that you knew how to kiss. I thought, 'Right now, I'm going to call Tkachuk and he'll knock all his teeth out. At least his front teeth, top and bottom… And after that we'll see how you can kiss.' Your brazen green eyes… speckled…" and she suddenly looked him in the eyes, as though checking.

Artiom inaudibly swallowed his saliva and didn't think anything about what he was hearing. "Well, yes, there you go." With such a phrase you could summarize what he felt both about Tkachuk and about his eyes.

"Then I needed to… hire you," she continued. "Not because there aren't enough informants — every fifth person here is an informant — just because… I needed to. And I was angry. Maybe I was angriest at the fact that I had started to like you. I never like any of the… local men. You were all to me… for example, like wolves or horses. A different species."

Galia was silent for a short spell. It seemed to Artiom that she had surprised herself with her inappropriate sincerity, but immediately waved the thought away: what now? After all this? After the armchair that they had almost crushed into seven pieces?

"If you hadn't have made a move on me, nothing would have happened," she said with an imperceptible, as though internal, smile that was hiding in her cheekbones. "You would have gone to solitary. But you guessed exactly when you needed to do it… Everyone pushes himself on me when it's not necessary. But when it's necessary, quite the opposite, no one does… With some I have to humble myself, but others I have to pester. Neither one nor the other is pleasant. But here you guessed it. For the first time. You don't believe me?" She asked, unexpectedly loud.

"Why? I do believe you," said Artiom. "Can I eat the pie now?"

She laughed again, this time leaning her head back, and he saw her neck — naked and unprotected. She usually laughed as though her laughter was a bit frozen, but now it thawed. And with such a thawed-out laughter, she had not laughed for a very long time. A day. Or a month. Or even all summer. All the time, things weren't funny for her, but now it suddenly became hilarious.

"Eat, eat," she said. "I want to as well. Did you feed the animals today?"

"Yes," he said, not remembering whether he was lying or not. "Why are they here anyway?"

"What do you mean why?" She was eating the pie and drinking it up with some tea, becoming completely at home and without a care. "There's a biological garden here, after all."

"I know. What is it?"

Galia turned her head, in the sense that she was already too tired to laugh and her pie and tea were preventing her anyway… but it was still funny.

"I know… what is it?" She mocked Artiom without rancor. "It was commanded by Fiodor. Eichmanis."

In a strange way, she injected his last name with a clear sense of respect.

"In May… when? Last year, or the year before… long time ago. He declared the entire North-western side of the island a wildlife reserve. The lakes, the fens, the forests that you can never chop down — everything around it was protected."

"Why?"

"Because they were chopping down a lot of wood and the animals started to disappear, and we don't want the island to be bald and lifeless. Fiodor planted a nursery of deciduous trees… then some other kinds of trees. Then the biological garden appeared. Fiodor needed to breed some deer, and those… what are they called? Guinea pigs… and he also wants to raise musk beaver, so that it settles here. They've added them to your lake — have you seen the lake nearby…? Both of those who were here before and some species that never existed here at all. They bring all the beasties here from somewhere else…" She turned her head again; either to brush away her hair or to push aside a thought, or because it all seemed silly and unnecessary to her. Still, it wasn't clear, maybe it was the opposite — maybe it was all very serious and necessary.

"At first, when they were first organizing the camp, they hunted from morning to night. Nogtev loved it… That's the head of the camp before Fiodor, you know? Then Fiodor forbade the hunt… He even forbade people from destroying the gulls — but I would have shot them all down, my head's splitting by evening and I can't open the window… Though Fiodor himself does hunt sometimes. But only those animals that are in abundance… Not like Nogtev. He would have continued to shoot from morning to evening.

"They told me that the politicals were shot here when Nogtev was…" Artiom said, biting the pie, which had become soft and limp.

Galia, on the contrary, had stopped chewing and asked with that other voice that Artiom had forgotten too soon it seems.

"Who said that?"

Artiom, half-lying down, continued to chew his pie and only after that answered very calmly and as amicably as he could: "Everyone knows about it here. It's not a secret for anyone."

Galia sighed.

"Well, what else do you want me to speak with you about?" Artiom thought quickly. "I know nothing other than the camp. And I think that you, Galia, also know nothing other than the camp. Maybe it would better if you asked me why I killed my father? Or maybe I should ask why you're working on Solovki, not ambling down Red Square arm in arm with someone in uniform and riding breeches?"

She thoughtfully bit her lower lip.

"Basically, listen," she said. "If everyone speaks about it here, then someone should know how it was in actual fact… They were treated specially, because they were neither gangsters nor counter-revs. Yes, they were revolutionaries, but they didn't understand the truth of the Bolsheviks, and they persisted in that… But no one needed to execute them. They themselves kept asking for it for an entire year. Fiodor wouldn't have done it, but Nogtev listened to them. Even so, he had to try hard to make it happen. They lived in Savvatievo. No work, no guard, complete self-government. They read lectures to each other there, breaking up into factions… inter-factional dispute." Galia scoffed loudly. "They fought, then made peace, anything you like! Walks around the island night and day. The electricity didn't turn off until early morning. Seven hours of partying a night! With Nogtev, they didn't socialize. They yelled at him, 'Go away, executioner!' and he would leave. Fiodor was his second in command then; he would come instead of Nogtev, but only the elders would socialize with him, the others also… expressed their disdain… The only ones whom the political would admit were the soldiers on the watch towers. But Fiodor forbade them from socializing with the political. So they came themselves to the watch towers — at first rarely, then daily and then several times a day. They yelled all sorts of nonsense; it's unpleasant even to remember… They only addressed the soldiers by one name: 'rams'.[40] Then — you don't think this is wild? Many people work here and sometimes they die from only eating fish. At the very least I know that the eleventh, twelfth and thirteenth brigades have a difficult life… but these disputes — and what disputes! All empty words, all quarrels because of some minutiae… Here, the whole world is upside down, but they…"

Galia, it seemed, had calmed down again and even took another bite of pie and drank it down with tea, and then remembered, as though in passing:

"Did you know that they had a better ration than the soldiers? They ate better than their guards! They even received packages, while the soldiers

---

40 In Russian, an insult meaning "dim-wit".

weren't allowed! Do you know how many packages came to them? Seventy-five thousand kilograms worth a year! If only someone had stolen at least a cracker from them! But no. For all that, the soldiers never had scurvy, while the politicals somehow managed to catch it. Do you want to know how? Because they lazed about for days on end, fermenting from their own idleness… Do you know what sort of demands they had? Every section of the prisoners needed to be inspected by their elders, who would then decide who was a political, and who was not. No, but think of it! What do they think? That in France or in… I don't know… Finland, they would be allowed to do that? The elders were rude to Fiodor. They screamed that we better give them everything that they need, and even twice that. They openly badmouthed the Soviet government."

Galia finished her tea and pulled out a pine needle from it.

It seemed that she had only started explaining all of this because Eichmanis had some reference to this story.

Artiom, to be honest, wasn't very happy that he had started the conversation.

On the other hand, everything that Galia had said was very interesting — he could now answer Vasilii Petrovich.

He noticed another thing: Galia herself was bothered by this story, and, as she told it, it's as though she wanted to justify Eichmanis. You could sense that.

"Then an order came from Moscow to limit their walks to six hours," she continued. "Fiodor read them the command by himself, without a guard, inside their skete — he always went like that. But they, naturally, have their own knives and axes… In the command, it was stated that they could only take walks from nine in the morning to six in the evening. After all, you can get your fill of walking around if you start at nine in the morning, yes? Especially if you don't work. But they decided that it wasn't enough. Also, now the electricity was turned off at midnight. Also, a command from Moscow… The politicals refused to accept these requirements."

Galia threw the pine needle back into the cup: it bored her.

"Nogtev made the final decision. After all, they were doing everything out of spite — they were told three times to go back to their buildings. But they were walking under the lamps on purpose. Someone gave the command and the shooting started. By the way, the soldiers were firing in the air. Only three people fired into the crowd. I know them all — Nogtev's flunkeys. One of them, Gorshkov, was moved far away to one of the islands here. Another was sent to Kemi… Only Tkachuk remains here. If all the soldiers had fired into the crowd, they would have mowed down all the politicals. That wouldn't have been hard."

Galia raised her eyes and looked at Artiom.

"Now you can't talk about any Galia from spring," thought Artiom, comically rather than in fear.

"Then they," Galia remembered, "started a hunger strike with a demand that they be returned to the mainland. And they took them off, no problem. Only I don't think that they'll have it better there. They lived here in an ivory tower. All the work they needed to do was chop the wood for their own heating. Even that they didn't want to do! To prepare their own logs — that was beneath them. But to burn those logs that other inmates had chopped for them — that's fine. Even the twigs to use for cooking — even that they wouldn't chop, but they didn't have any issues accepting other people's labor! All that was left was to demand their own batmen for horse rides all over the island… It was all so stupid on their part, Tiom."

Since she called him Tiom, then why not be completely brave? It seemed that he could manage it.

"They say that Nogtev shot one or two who were just coming off the boat several times," said Artiom, pronouncing every word firmly, but as though he were cajoling, as though he were leaving himself a chance to take back any of them in case they once again irritated her.

Galia, as though completely exhausted, just shrugged.

"How do you imagine that for yourself? Do you know how rumors are called around here? Latrines! It's a very foul and exact word. He probably shot once into the air. Killed…! Maybe he killed someone at some point. I don't know, and no one saw it. Don't believe it. And if anyone did see it, he's buried in the earth of Solovki… And where's Nogtev now? He won't end well, mark my words."

"What about you, Galia? Will you end well?" Artiom almost asked.

He even almost said Gala.

* * *

After the evening inspection in the camp, he was walking towards the iodine plant.

The cuckoos were chattering in his wake, but he didn't count how many times.

He hurried as though Galia were already waiting for him there.

He didn't even properly notice the road — it became shorter and shorter every day. Just a stone's throw away, two thousand meters, hilarious! You can cover that in a single run.

Then he was terribly angry at the scientists — they didn't want to gather their things and part with their beloved piggies.

"Take them with you to the camp, into your rooms and sleep there hugging your guinea piggies," Artiom added aloud, having locked himself in his room. He was so bothered that he couldn't do anything.

He got his dry ration, upended it on the floor and built a tower from onion bulbs and tins. The bulbs kept falling. He took them in hand, smelled them. They also smelled of flesh, soil, lusty life.

In a total rage against the scientists, he even wanted to throw the onion bulbs against the wall, but he stopped himself — he remembered how for weeks his stomach ached from hunger, and even spoiled millet porridge made him salivate…

… Yes, he was walking by the infirmary in passing and he smelled something horrible. He even started, but in a moment, he remembered that it was the vinaigrette that he had eaten and that he had found so delicious when he was there. That's how the vinaigrette smelled!

He got up suddenly and walked to the scientists.

Troianskii almost walked out on tiptoe, putting his finger to his mouth.

"Shhh! They scare easily."

Artiom sniggered.

Troianskii put a paper into his hand — the same one, with the names of the piggies — so that Artiom would probably memorize them overnight or at least repeat them a few times.

"Red, Gypsy, Blackie, Yellow, Daughter and Mommy, I remember," said Artiom.

"No, I added short descriptions of their distinguishing marks. You don't know how to distinguish them, do you?" said Osip. "We try to call them only by their names."

"Do they do the same to you?" asked Artiom.

Troianskii didn't answer. He probably thought it was a bad joke.

In the crack in the door, Artiom saw that the piggies were lying on the large windowsill, evidently sunbathing.

"You should talk to them more," Troianskii offered.

"What do you mean?" Artiom answered. "I read them poetry and sing them lullabies. I even tell them funny stories…"

Troianskii quickly looked at Artiom.

"Decent ones," Artiom added.

"I've never noticed your habit of making a fool of yourself before."

Artiom shrugged — he didn't care.

"Maybe I should smack him in the forehead..." he thought, almost indifferently.

"You already did that to Sorokin not long ago," he answered himself.

The scientists barely managed to leave, traditionally not taking leave of Artiom.

He waited for another minute. Maybe someone had stayed, carried away with enthusiasm for making marmalade from seaweed?

No, it was quiet.

But what about the piggies? Artiom jumped. "Are they still on the windowsill? Will they freeze there? I'll be accused of negligence."

He hurried to the kitchen, opened the door suddenly and the frightened pigs, though they were on the floor, rushed towards each other in a frenzy. They were scared.

They wanted to gather into a single pile, but the top ones didn't want to be on top and kept trying to dig into the center, and because of that, nothing seemed to work.

"A-a-a-ah!" a pleased Artiom called absurdly loudly. "Sca-a-a-ry!"

For some time, he enjoyed the bestial confusion and agitation, then he quietly closed the door.

He waited another minute until it was quiet in there, then he repeated it all again, getting a completely intoxicating, childish pleasure from it.

"Why are we sle-e-e-e-eping!" he yelled, opening the door towards himself. The animals got even more scared, but the scrum wasn't working out as before, and their fear was persistent, sincere and volatile.

"This is a great way to while away my term," Artiom rejoiced, laughing aloud. "Just make sure all of them don't die from a heart attack..."

He almost got one himself, because a horrible shriek and racket exploded from above.

"What? Did they drag a moose up there?" Artiom swore, running to see what the problem was.

As he ran out of the house, he managed to notice that the piggies, for the third time, tried to make a scrum with that same stupid — and already no longer hilarious — desire of each piggy to be under all the rest.

It was even worse in the attic — a crime scene revealed itself to him immediately.

A fat tawny cat sat in the rabbit enclosure and held a rather large bunny in its teeth.

It was clearly not long for this life, barely foaming with quiet rabbit blood and quivering in its death throes.

The cat had completely evil eyes.

Those eyes angrily assessed Artiom.

It seemed that two profound thoughts lived in those eyes. The first was, "And who are you then?" The second was, "Oh, now I won't have time either to eat it or hide it!"

"Motherfucker!" Artiom swore heatedly — that's how his grandfather used to swear. He was a Moscow merchant of the third guild.

The cat blinked, but didn't let the rabbit go, only holding on to it tighter.

Now it seemed to Artiom that the cat was ready to negotiate, something like this, "OK, let's each of us eat one half. Why are you yelling like that?"

The rest of the rabbits, in utter terror, huddled into the different corners of the enclosure. Some of them even closed their eyes. They were all black and grey colored.

"I'm going to kill you right now," Artiom confidently promised the cat, looking around for something with which to accomplish the deed.

He found a metal dustpan into which they gathered the rabbit droppings.

Seeing the dustpan in the human's hands, the cat immediately left his quiet prey — Artiom almost thought that the predatory bastard was going to jump him next, and he even had time to be a little scared — but the cat just needed to reach the peephole behind Artiom's back. It had been left open.

Scraping with its claws and screeching like a fighter, the cat flew past Artiom and the dustpan flew in its wake, but there was no way he could get it.

Artiom ran to the lifeless rabbit, grabbed it by the scruff and ran after the cat.

Still, there was no reason to hurry. The cat was gone.

"Where did you go?" Artiom asked loudly, all green from natural anger. "And where did you come from? I haven't seen you even once! Go, finish your rabbit. Why did you drop it? Go, you pest!"

Three times he walked all around the iodine plant, but without success. All the doors and windows were closed, devil only knows where that vermin had hidden. He moved the couch, looked under all the tables, the chairs. Once more, he bothered the guinea pigs. Nothing.

Stupidly, he measured the corridor with his feet, speaking somewhere to the ceiling in the manner of a hero of a Greek tragedy, "What will I do now? How will I explain the death of an animal in my care? Answer!"

"Maybe I can find a rabbit in the forest? Lay a snare and catch one?" Artiom thought seriously. "Who's a hunter here? Vasilii Petrovich did some hunting, I think. Maybe he can tell me how to make a snare? But no, what sort of a damn hunter is he? He was telling me that he couldn't kill anyone, not even once..."

"Or maybe I can ask Burtsev? 'Brother Burtsev, let's forget the past! Catch me a rabbit! I won't ever forget it!' There have got to be long-ears living here! No one will be able to tell the difference. Let Osip come up with a theory about how domesticated rabbits living in the wild slowly transform into wild rabbits..."

"Or maybe I can take the skin off that bunny and put it on the cat?" Artiom thought aloud. "Do you hear that, pest? I'm going to put its skin on you, and you'll walk around with long ears, you moron."

He returned to the kitchen with nothing, opened the thermos, and poured himself some tea. He decided that at the very least he could feed the piggies — they were terribly ravenous.

He offered them some carrots and cabbage; they didn't refuse.

"Why do you eat so much, you swine?" Artiom asked, amazed.

Once again, the bunny nursery came alive. They sat down on their bicycles with square wheels and rode back and forth in circles and slantwise.

"Oh," thought Artiom. "One of them was eaten, they were afraid for three minutes and then again started to look for something to gnaw on... everything just like on Solovki with the humans. No difference."

In his thoughts, Artiom named the cat "Chekist". He was a chip off the old block after all.

"Here, kitty-kitty-kitty!" called Artiom. Maybe it would respond to caresses.

At least I'll get to kill one Chekist. Except it'll never work. Chekists don't need caresses. Only Chekistettes sometimes.

Galia still hadn't come.

The rabbit — damn it. With every minute, Artiom longed more and more vividly for Galia.

He tried to distract himself, thinking of whatever, but his desire for a woman creeped up on him. At first the insistent touch of her body appeared in his hands like an itch — her shoulder blades, neck and other places — then Artiom hid his hands in his pockets, balling them into fists until the itch disappeared. Then his lips would sense her taste, her sweet sweat, the goosebumps on her neck and Artiom would bite his lips and lick them like that cat did.

"Push off, Galia!" he begged. "Or I'll start yowling here… All the animals will die from terror…"

But Galia didn't leave him.

Undeterred, the thoughts once again creeped up on him, warm and insistent.

"Why, if the prostitute that one time commanded me to 'do it quickly', then it's vile?" Artiom asked himself, "While Galia…" He kept trying to catch his breath to finish the thought… "When she asked, 'Can you do it quickly?' your heart stood still? Why? It's the same thing, no?"

He caught himself thinking that he was going on again about Galia, Galia, Galia… And he hurried far away, somewhere to freedom, to Moscow, to Zariadie Park, to any public house with platters of peas on the tables… or to the cinema…"

He suddenly imagined so vividly and distinctly how he sat in the cinema, having brought a bottle of bear and on the screen, women — naturally, looking like Galia — were ringing their hands and opening their huge black and white eyes, and were silently screaming…

… He left the cinema, having decided to take a walk — "where, where, where do I want to go?" he asked himself in a tongue-twister. Maybe to Prechistenka Street, just to wander about. He had a friend who lived there…

I'll meet him, he'll ask me, "… Where've you been? Haven't seen you in a long time, Tioma!"

"Oh, I was on Solovki… Didn't you know?" Artiom answered as though unwillingly.

Everyone knew about Solovki since '23. To say that you were on Solovki — that was impressive. There was cosmic terror in that and a dark manly dignity.

Although… His friend would start asking him why they imprisoned him… Better to not have that conversation.

"OK, so I'll do something else," Artiom imagined. "I'll get to know a girl… a young one in a skirt with a ring on her little finger. 'How did you live?' she'd ask, looking at his already grown-out hair…"

"There was a lot… it was Solovki… Better not to ask…" that's how Artiom would have answered in a tired voice, his eyes half-shut.

He caught himself thinking that he's lying there right now with his eyes half shut, all soft, as though he had drunk ice-cold beer in the heat.

He sat up and laughed audibly at himself.

He roused himself with the question: "What about Galia? What girl with a ring when there's Galia? Maybe we'll come back with her and start living together? And why not? We'll have kids. They'll grow up. 'Papa and Mama,' they'll ask at one point, 'Where did you meet?' 'In prison. Papa killed your grandfather and was imprisoned for it. And Mama wanted to put Papa in solitary and kill him too. But then she changed her mind, and, calling him into her office, she said, where's your… down there… Well, children, how do you like that story?'"

Artiom laughed again.

Someone was knocking. It was very cheerful and promised much.

"Open, orphan," he commanded himself. "You without the cross or the tail!"

* * *

Artiom noticed that she could speak about Eichmanis at any moment and during any conversation — as soon as he mentioned him, but even if he didn't…

He could peek out of any event, as though the world were full of his reflections and well-defined tracks.

"He's forgotten about you already," Galia was saying, looking at the ceiling, as though calming Artiom down. But in actual fact, there was a bit of disdain in her words; who are you, that Fiodor would remember you? "For him, it doesn't matter if you're an inmate or not. Not because he considers you all human beings — he doesn't consider anyone to be a human being. Therefore, he sometimes seems humane, because he just doesn't care. It's only prisoners working here, everywhere, so he converses with them — who else is he going to talk to? You think you're the only one — oh! Eichmanis called me to himself! You did think that, didn't you? He was just bored with the Red Army cattle — and most of them are cattle. If they imprisoned all the soldiers tomorrow and assigned him to reeducate them, nothing would shiver inside him. Why? Because Eichmanis is much more a swine than all of them put together…"

"I think you're just in love with him," Artiom thought, but didn't say. What business was it of his?

"To tell the truth, he doesn't want to talk to anyone. He couldn't care less," Galia continued her difficult and painful speech. "But he saw how Trotskii was with people, and he wants to be like him. He worked with him… That's where we first met…" She suddenly decided not to continue this subject and quickly summarized, "But if he has to execute you, he won't even blink. Fiodor has killed hundreds of people."

Today, they didn't do anything with each other. Galina appeared somewhat unusual, she didn't start kissing him. Artiom, naturally, didn't start pushing himself on her.

She lay down on the couch — it was immediately obvious that she was tired, and when she started talking about the Red Army cattle and Trotskii, it dawned on Artiom: she was drunk.

Galia felt that he realized it.

"Want some vodka?" she asked.

Artiom didn't answer, still looking at Galia. She wasn't expecting an answer.

Every time, he already knew it by heart, she brought something in her purse. Galia never came without gifts.

"Where did you get such vodka?" he was amazed, seeing the pulled-out bottle with its many-colored label. He hadn't seen anything like that since before the NEP, and after that there was prohibition, and they had long ago drunk all the good stuff.

Galia looked at Artiom mockingly and answered, "There is always good vodka available for operational and investigative activities."

Artiom nodded, though he didn't understand a thing.

"For executions…" she explained after a minute, not finding a glass, though she searched all over the room, turning her whole head, like a bird.

He got a mug.

When he came back, Galia was already sitting on the couch, slightly rocking.

"After executions, you always want to drink. It's difficult manly work," she explained as she poured.

Artiom breathed in with his nose, sensing the vile smell of the vodka.

"And what about now?" he asked indistinctly, though she still guessed the point of his question.

"They'll shoot them dry. Then they'll drink it down with water," Galina answered and put the mug in his hand with an uneven gesture. The vodka rocked and licked his hand. The feeling was like a slight burn. He wanted to blow on it.

He drank it in one gulp.

It was like drinking a stone.

It stuck somewhere in the middle of his ribcage.

"Eichmanis was laughing so hard today," she suddenly remembered, starting from some place where she herself had stumbled. "In the administrative section, only the White Army swine got together — he was the one that chose them. Now they're assigning supervisors for various jobs. And do you know what they came up with? They're handing out assignments alphabetically. Don't get it? Well, look. Bookkeeper? Well, naturally, that's for Bulannikov. One of the White Army officers. Zoological station? Zveroboev. Electrical station? Podtokov.[41] They're planning an observatory — and they assigned Medveditsyn, but he's only good for looking through binoculars." Galia laughed herself, remembering something. "Do you get it, why Medveditsyn? I didn't get it myself at first. The big dipper, that's why![42] Eich immediately got it. He thought it was funny."

"So it's 'Eich' now, is it?" Artiom thought.

"Then there's the dendrological nursery," Galina remembered. "Vladimir Dendiarev works there… same nastiness. But, not like Zveroboev and Medveditsyn, he actually knows his work. And he senses that he's valued. He's become so brazen that he's demanded a horse-drawn buggy for himself! So, Fiodor ordered that a goat be presented to him! Dendiarev didn't refuse it, and now he leads the goat up to the St. Nicholas gates, then sits on it and rides it into the monastery. Then he gets off and hands the reins to the soldier, and he ties the goat next to his post!"

Galia laughed again, though her laughter was angry and sounded as though she were unpleasantly splashing him, like the vodka, away from herself.

Artiom, for some reason, found none of this funny. It was probably some kind of un-funny vodka that had gotten into his throat.

"He's unleashed them all here," said Galia with greater and greater irritation. "That goat — fine. Seletskii, who runs the sawmill, is a former head of a Tsarist prison. He said that he needed a revolver. An inmate was issued a revolver, Fiodor ordered it! Burtsev, who was transferred to the IID from your brigade, also wanted a revolver, and he gets it no problem! Osip demanded his mother, and they'll bring her too. It's unpleasant for him to sit in prison without his mommy! He's also demanded a business trip to the mainland, and they're going to send him, without a guard…! Grakov was

41 Roughly translated as "flow of current".

42 Medved means "bear" in Russia, while the big dipper constellation is also called the "big bear" (Ursus Major).

telling me…" She started telling him some new story, Artiom briefly nodded off, but didn't show it. She stopped short and continued with another story:

"All the specialist inmates that run the factories — the brick makers, etc. — live with their own women. Fiodor allowed them to cohabitate. And you think that anyone values that or talks about it outside? 'I sat in Solovki, they gave me a temporary wife, the right to wander over the island, they even paid me a wage. I had enough to buy the best cigars in the shop, some sweets for tea and even enough to feed my dog or cat, which decorated my life in the concentration camp.' No, no one talks about that! Everyone has real wives at home! But they're still upset! I'm sure that all of them describe their *via dolorosa* — the whole country knows about Solovki! Parents use Solovki to scare their kids! At least the local Chekists inform on Fiodor every week… And if not for his relationship with Bokii — Gleb Bokii, you know…? Fiodor himself would have been incarcerated long ago."

Galia once again started to look for something, twisting her whole head like a bird, and Artiom figured out that she needed a mug for herself too.

He went to the kitchen again and came back with carrots, bread and two mugs — one with tea, the other empty. When he had walked up to his guard-room, he heard with surprise that Galia had continued talking, as though she hadn't noticed his absence.

"Because you're all just people, but he's a demigod," she concluded and raised her empty, black eyes at Artiom.

"They've canceled God," said Artiom, carefully laying out the food and quietly placing the mugs.

"There never were any gods. There were only ever demigods," said Galia, laying out every word separately and with a pause, lest they all stick together in her drunken larynx.

"From two demigods," Artiom thought distantly, "You can make a single god. Lenin and Trotskii — there you go… though I think Trotskii's been torn out of the iconostasis. Like a tooth."

He was uneasy.

"It would be better if she left," he thought, looking at Galia.

Galia poured herself some vodka and immediately downed it.

Artiom thought that she would start coughing, but no, she drank it and sat half a minute with closed eyes, not moving.

He also didn't move.

Then she breathed out and only after that, it was as though she woke up. Quietly, with difficulty, she opened her eyes — and there's Artiom! Tiomka. Galia smiled.

Her smile was also foreign and dangerous.

"Is it true that they use young boys in the sleeping quarters?" Galia asked cajolingly.

"I don't know. I haven't seen it," said Artiom, looking at her. Only not at her eyes, but at her lips, which had strangely lost their shape and were all the time unpleasantly twisting, as though the teeth in her mouth had grown hot and were burning her.

"It's true," said Galia in a convinced whisper. "Use me. I'm your… how did you say it? Lad! Come on, pretend I'm lying on a bunk here… scared."

"No," said Artiom very quietly. "I don't like it. You haven't seen what it's like there. Don't play at it. Please."

She didn't care; her lips continued to twist.

"Then I'm going to use you," she said.

Slowly she crept from the couch, moving the stool that was between her and Artiom. The bread fell, the carrot rolled off, the mugs jumped, their sides ringing…

Then Galia shrieked very sincerely, completely not drunkenly. In her voice, there was such horrible fear that Artiom himself was petrified.

She was looking somewhere beyond the couch.

"Galia! What it is?" He called, getting up.

"You…" not finding any air, she breathed out the answer without a voice, evidently still barely coming to her senses. "You eat raw meat…? Have you gone completely mad, you jackal?"

Artiom finally saw what the problem was — a bit to the side of the couch lay the rabbit that he had dropped somewhere while he was looking for the cat.

The horrible thing was that the rabbit had been half-eaten — it seemed that he lacked a leg and half of his stomach, from which tiny rabbit intestines were hanging.

Artiom grabbed the rabbit by the ears and the intestines unrolled even longer.

"Shit, I'm going to vomit!" Galia shrieked.

"It wasn't me!" Artiom yelled. "Chekist ate it!"

"What Chekist?" Galia yelled in answer. "I'm going to shoot you right now, you counter-rev!" She did actually reach for her holster, which she didn't have on her hip, and, noticing that, she kicked the mug that was lying near her foot.

"It was the cat! Shut up, already!" Artiom barked, beside himself and in that second while both of them were quiet, a noise erupted.

Someone was knocking on the door.

At full speed, Artiom ran to the door, thinking of Galina all the way — where was she? How was she? — he ran back, but she wasn't there, and they were knocking on the door again…

"Damn it!" Artiom swore and again rushed to the door and opened it.

Two guards were standing there — well, how can you say that — they weren't really standing, they were holding on to each other.

"Jackal! Where were you?" asked the first and pushed Artiom in the chest.

He smelled terrible, as though he were chasing his vodka with frog caviar seasoned with bog silt.

"I was checking on the rabbits in the attic," Artiom answered without a pause.

"Ha! I told you," said the second and pushed Artiom as well.

They walked into the room where the light was turned on — Artiom had left it on when he was running after the mugs — but they didn't find what they were looking for.

"There are only fucking water rats here," said one of the soldiers. He pulled the word "water" out of his mouth as though it were long and disgusting, like a worm.

"Hey, fucker! Where are the rabbits?" one of them called Artiom.

"He said already: in the attic," the other remembered.

"Turn on the light, jackal," the first commanded. "Can't see shit."

Artiom thought about it, then turned it on.

"There you go, fucker!" The guards rejoiced at the light, and, making a racket, climbed to the attic.

Stomping broke out in the attic, swearing and counter-swearing, more stomping — someone, it seems, had fallen down… then laughter.

"One's enough," said the soldier, coming down and hawking up phlegm.

Artiom turned aside, lest they spit on him. Then he took one more step back, lest they push him again.

"Is there anyone else here?" asked a soldier without looking at Artiom.

"No," he answered.

"Any whores?"

"No," Artiom repeated.

"Well, skin it and fry it," said the soldier, shoving a rabbit with a broken neck into his hands.

"They're going to be here all night," Artiom thought feverishly.

The second soldier appeared, missed the last few steps and he counted them with the noise of his falling body.

He sat on the floor, then got up moaning. He noticed the rabbit in Artiom's hands, silently took it, barking at his friend who was lost in the kitchen.

"Why the fuck did you give it to him? What, are we going to sit here with him? Let's go get that… Lial'ka… in the female barracks. She'll prepare it.

Artiom stood in place, praying that all this would end soon.

The guards moved something in the kitchen for another three minutes and then left without saying goodbye, leaving all the doors open.

Artiom slowly moved to follow them, afraid to curse his good luck. Outside, he saw it was a gorgeous white night — lighting up everything, as though naked. He quickly shut the door.

"Galia!" he called quietly.

She wasn't in his guard-room. Nor in the laboratory. Nor in the other rooms.

Finally, he pulled aside a curtain in the kitchen and saw her. She was sitting on the windowsill, petting the cat.

The cat purred with his eyes closed, but he still peeked at Artiom with one of his eyes.

"He wanted to eat the pigs too," she whispered, nodding at the cat.

"The soldiers were standing right next to her," Artiom realized. He almost laughed. Good thing the curtain was opaque; what if it weren't?

Galia was completely sober.

"I've scratched myself," she said with a clear voice. "There's a nail here somewhere." She showed him a finger with a crimson drop on it.

Artiom took Galia by the wrist and licked off the blood, immediately wiped his tongue on the back of his own hand and licked off her blood again.

"The water's singing. Like a grouse," she said, listening.

It was pouring from the faucet and then, with a barely audible gurgle, poured out somewhere under the floorboards.

* * *

In the morning, Artiom, when he was admitting the scientists, forgot the most important thing.

That same evening in the iodine plant, Troianskii met him with a look as though he had just found out everything about Artiom — the most horrible and most impossible truths. And now Osip didn't know what to do with that knowledge.

"I didn't tell you in the morning, I'm sorry," Artiom said with a quick apologetic whisper. He took Troianskii into his room and in vivid, yet mainly invented, details told him about the drunk soldiers.

He also added the fib that they took not one rabbit, but two.

"You have to write an official complaint about this to the administrative section," Osip immediately said. "Otherwise, they'll demand it of us."

"What are you talking about?" Artiom answered quietly. "I won't write anything. Tomorrow they'll come and twist my head off."

"Are you a coward?" asked Osip, spitting the word coward from his lips to such a degree that it was as though it still hung to his lips, stuck on the last letter.

"Only insofar as you're an idiot," thought Artiom, sincerely bored from this stupid conversation and only thinking about how best to accompany these devils out of the building.

"Osip, did you ask your friend?" asked another learned fellow, coming into the room. He had a rabbit head in his hands, complete with its ears, its backbone, and a few other furry scraps.

"Yes, by the way," Osip raised his hands. "What's this then?"

Artiom had thrown the rabbit out the window last night, together with the cat. The cat immediately started to gnaw at the dead rabbit meat. Artiom was sure that no traces would be left.

All the more so considering there were bushes under the window. What sort of demon the scientists were looking for in those bushes, he had no idea.

"... At least it could have chewed off the ears, the Chekist pest," thought Artiom, and, snickering, asked, "You're trying to say that I ate two rabbits? Raw? Together with their fur? And didn't finish the second's head?"

"And you're trying to say that the Chekists ate the rabbits raw?" asked Osip.

Hearing about the Chekists, the second scientists, coughing, left the room. He carried away the rabbit's head, holding it by the ears.

"They didn't eat them; they took them away," Artiom repeated patiently.

"Oh sure," Osip sarcastically grimaced. "Then they tore off the head of one of them and threw it under the window. Can you describe to me in detail how that looked?"

"I wasn't watching it, Osip, I don't know," said Artiom, looking Osip in the eyes and grudging the fact that he had absolutely no energy left to strike that thin and sarcastic person on the face. That would have been completely wrong — he was no Sorokin, nor a Passport with his wet lip.

"So," said Osip with a look as though he were standing on a cathedra. "Either you write a complaint to the administration or we will be forced to write it ourselves."

"Go ahead," Artiom offered amicably. "Only get the hell out of here quickly."

"What does that mean, 'get the hell out of here'?" Osip squawked. "It's you who have nothing to do here! We're not going to be returning to the city any more. Too much time lost in the journey."

"What 'city'?" Artiom didn't understand.

"The monastery, the kremlin — there, that prison," said Osip quickly.

In the crack in the door the learned fellow appeared again, this time without a rabbit, but behind his back a third figure shone from his wise, bald head.

"You have no right. Go away!" Artiom repeated again, understanding that now he was looking completely stupid.

The scientists looked at each other and each smirked in turn — it seemed that this was how they socialized with each other.

"Look at what he has, my friends!" said one of the scientists, pointing.

All three stared at something confounding.

Artiom looked aside, expecting this time to see a half-eaten guinea pig.

But no, it was a half-drunk bottle of vodka.

All the scientists laughed as one, only not Osip.

He left, disdainfully flapping the edge of his coat.

Artiom, forgetting himself, ran after them into their lounge, grabbed the first bottle that he saw and threw it against the wall.

It's not that the learned people expressed an immediate readiness to start a fight, even with their superior numbers. However, neither did their eyes show any fear.

"He's still drunk," said one of them.

"Tomorrow we will write a detailed report concerning your behavior," another one quietly promised Artiom, though he sat with his back to him and didn't even turn to look at him.

Artiom ran outside, he wanted to immediately go into the kremlin, but immediately changed his mind. He had to meet Galia and tell her everything.

"Where does she usually wait?" thought Artiom, looking around. His heart thumped in his chest, his lips quivered — everything was impossibly upsetting and stupid.

Suddenly he understood that he had to climb the roof — he could see better from there.

He returned to the building, immediately climbed to the attic; a thought flitted past him to choke the rest of the rabbits and throw them down for the enjoyment of the scientists…

He couldn't see Galia anywhere.

As strange as it may seem, the birds were still singing in the soft evening light, in the gentle warmth of the approaching white night of Solovki. The singing was also quiet and warm.

A cuckoo flew up somewhere very close and trilled. Artiom looked for it — there, it sat right on the post in the yard — what a large bird! It was the first time in his life that he saw a cuckoo.

It also saw Artiom and immediately flew from its place, quickly flapping its big wings.

Turns out you could also see the sea from here.

It lay immovable, as though dead. You could see stony islands in it. Artiom stared into the depths of the waters for a long time.

His heart slowly calmed down.

The sun didn't set downwards as it did over there, in Russia, but it seemed to roll along the horizon, gradually descending.

The sun looked as though it were melting and oozing like ice cream, and by the time it got below the horizon, nothing would be left. Tomorrow it would rise, but instead of a huge sun, it would be a clipped, barely warm ball, all frazzled with embarrassment.

They say that the sun here rises and sets almost exactly over the North Pole. That means North is over there.

"… What if we go into Philip's cell?" thought Artiom, noticing the log hut in the front yard. "Grandfather Philip, allow us our sin, we'll do it quietly…"

The mosquitoes were completely gone.

The clouds were pink and purposeful, foaming beautifully and aromatically, like French soap.

He could also see the lake. On the water, from time to time, quick circles appeared — probably those were the same musk beavers introduced by Eichmanis.

If not for the circles, the lake would have appeared to be as immovable and hard as steel. The setting sun licked that steel, just like children who used to lick metal when it was frozen during their Russian childhood — but the sun's tongue didn't stick to the lake.

They're going to take this job away from me — what am I guarding here anyway?" Artiom was suddenly afraid. "Am I guarding the scientists…? Plus, with their report, oh!"

Galia needed to appear quickly and resolve all his doubts.

Artiom searched with his eyes first here, then there, then once again he grew quiet, not breathing. While he was on the roof, nothing was happening and nothing would happen. Only the rabbits romped about underneath him.

Artiom heard someone climb to the attic. "They're checking if I'm eating another rabbit, my eyes sparkling in the half-gloom."

He was barely calming down when once again his heart began to ache unpleasantly. Why couldn't he live in peace at least for a week? Artiom imagined himself to be either an animal or a person who was climbing up a cliff — at first, one stone collapsed under his foot, then another… then some bird began to circle around his liver — he couldn't push her away with his hands or spit on it…

He felt all this so keenly that he caught himself holding the roof with all his might.

Good thing he was holding on, because he suddenly saw someone in the forest.

For a moment, he stared at him — maybe it was a mirage… He waved at the person, but the person didn't answer.

"Galia? No? If it's Galia, then why is she coming from the other side of the road? In some kind of strange, unfamiliar shirt…"

Artiom, trying not to make too much noise, descended… It turned out that all the scientists had gone to sleep already. The most uneasy of them, it seems, had just checked the rabbits and went to bed.

Beyond the well, through the gate, turning off at a little distance, Artiom went into the forest to the place where he saw the person.

"It's probably Galia, or who else? I won't even say hello, but I'll just kiss her," he decided.

In the forest, it was much darker than on the roof, but he thought he had memorized the direction well enough.

From the unexpectedness, Artiom uttered a completely new noise: "Khak!" it was torn from him, as though a small bone had just fallen out of his throat.

An old man stood before him.

Possibly an old man.

Afterwards, Artiom tried to remember what he was like, but it was as though someone added color to the white night — a thick, foggy-white color — again, and again, until the entire face was rubbed out.

He wasn't naked — he had a shirt on, and on his legs, it seems, there were some pants; but were there any shoes, or bast woven slippers, or boots? It was more like he was grown into the earth like a tree — or what?

His feet probably drowned in the grass.

He was as tall as Artiom, his beard was as white as the white night of Solovki. You couldn't see his eyes.

"Who are you?" breathed out Artiom, staying a few steps away. But he himself didn't want to know who it was — he only spoke to make sure that he hadn't lost his wits from terror.

Artiom was suddenly covered in sweat up to his waist and, without waiting for an answer, in mid-stride, turned around and ran back to the windows where there were people — living, domestic, human people.

No one called after him.

In the morning, after an accidental, absurd, short sleep, it seemed to Artiom that when he ran, the old man was extending his hand towards him, and there were berries in that hand. But how could he have seen that?

* * *

When the sun had come up, all of yesterday had become not frightening and even, to use the proper word, idiotic.

Artiom walked to that place and naturally he found no footprints; but he didn't really search for them. He needed to see Galia as soon as possible.

"Maybe she changed her mind?" he asked himself, kicking up moss and grass with his feet.

"Changed her mind about what?" he answered himself.

The scientists were still sleeping.

To not meet with them, he decided to immediately go — as it was now, apparently, acceptable to call it — into the city.

When he was already leaving, he heard the squeaking of the guinea pigs; they had grown accustomed to their morning feeding; but he didn't go back — let the scientists feed them.

Some kind of bird accompanied Artiom, flying from tree to tree.

Fireweed flowers, which not long ago had covered everything, were falling off and everywhere stood clipped broom handles.

But at least he could smell mushrooms.

People were walking toward him — probably on their way to their morning work. In a minute, Artiom recognized with surprise some people from his former brigade — the feeling wasn't the most pleasant.

It seemed that they would all begin to point at him and yell: "Look! A lazy bum! And he's avoiding his work! Make him go to the logs with us!"

He almost jumped; he wanted to turn back and go in the opposite direction. But it would have looked completely stupid.

They recognized him as well; the faces almost came back to life.

Artiom suddenly understood how much better he looked than those who were walking towards him. They looked wrung out, with black shadows under their eyes, with sunken mouths — grey old people.

Passport shook his lip in such a way that it seemed that it was swinging back and forth like a censer and he kept prodding Shaferbekov, who was walking ahead, but he wasn't answering. He had seen Artiom himself well enough.

Shaferbekov was thinking about something but couldn't come up with an answer.

Sivtsev kept looking at Artiom as though with hope: maybe he would give them some good news or a piece of pie.

"Even Samovar's here!" Artiom was surprised to see the former general's batman, who had begun to serve Burtsev in faith and truth; however, his new master didn't take him with him to the IID — he was a relic, after all. So go on, uncle, to your logs. We Soviet people know how to clean our own boots.

"Should I greet them or not?" Artiom quickly tried to decide. By that time, they had gotten close to each other. Artiom nodded at Sivtsev. The batman, not greeting him, carried his samovarian face onward. "Old idiot," Artiom laughed, without looking away, for all that, from Passport's lip or Shaferbekov's red cheek.

It was a good thing that the group was accompanied by a foreman and two soldiers, or who knows what would have happened…

With every step, like a blind, half-buried turtle, the monastery crawled towards Artiom.

But it was closer than he realized and he had a slightly different impression. He saw the red cupolas of the kremlin, covered in gold — and if he squinted, the feeling arose that the sun was pouring with warm waves along the golden metal.

"I should tell Afanasiev about this, maybe it'll be useful," Artiom made a note to himself.

He walked towards the gates by the wide arc — so that he could see the building where Galia lived — next to the monastery, in the Petrograd dormitory where all the Chekists lived, on the second floor. Artiom had walked past that house several times, but he didn't know her window. However, he did know many other things, and that knowledge made his head spin.

"Your pass?" asked the soldier.

"Our pass," answered Artiom, giving him the paper.

The soldier didn't like his tone, but what could he do? You can't eat an official paper.

There it is, the green arrow of the Cathedral of the Transfiguration. Afanasiev said that this church was joyful, light, even droll. He also said that the cupolas were filled with kissel.

"What if I told Galia about that? Would she understand?" Artiom asked him.

The former metropolitan of Solovki was chopping wood for the workers' kitchens.

A hoarse whistle sounded — that was the arrival of the "Neva". Artiom remembered the voice of that tub from the time that he used to load barrels with fish on the quay.

"… Well, it turns out I'm hungry," Artiom understood, looking at the metropolitan and hearing the "Neva".

He received his ration as Boris Lukianovich's helper — there was plenty to animate him there.

"While your previous brigade is dragging logs in cold water," Artiom said to himself and then answered, "So what's that to me? Should I burn from shame? I dragged them too."

A little late, Vasilii Petrovich was leading his group.

Artiom was already on the road and he couldn't walk around them. He wanted to begin his morning by being forgiven, then the day promised to work out well.

Vasilii Petrovich nodded, touched his cap and it was clear that he was still angry as before, but what now? Was he going to just pass by that shaved, tanned villain?

"Just for a minute, just for a minute," said Artiom, hugging Vasilii Petrovich a bit, speaking quietly and quickly. "I don't know how often your Athenian evenings gather, Vasilii Petrovich, and what you talk about there, but I did see Grakov there… Please be careful in his presence, OK? He's repeating your conversations to whoever will listen."

Vasilii Petrovich, not saying anything to Artiom, nodded severely, squeezed Artiom's elbow and hurried back to his berry brigade.

"And I could have been gathering berries this whole time!" Artiom remembered, looking at them leave. "Vasilii Petrovich tried to convince me… Would that have been better? Maybe nothing that happened would have happened? What do you choose, Artiom?"

His choice was clear; however, at the moment, it was unattainable.

He didn't end up going to eat after all — what if suddenly Galia appears and leaves on her work, travels to Kemi or to Moscow, and that's the end of the charlatanette, that ladette, that… Artiom once again felt his heart grow bold, and for a second a black, dissipating dragonfly with many quivering wings appeared in his eyes.

"What's wrong with you?" He almost laughed aloud at himself.

If he were smart, he should have long ago left the courtyard, but Artiom wandered under the windows of the IID on purpose: "Maybe they'll take me," he thought, huddling into himself. "Or maybe I should go in myself with a complaint… Comrade Red Army soldier, I ate two rabbits on duty and I demand to be taken into Galina's office. She's going to punish me."

"They'll take me all right, but not there… You'll know…" Artiom called himself to order for the hundredth time and yet still didn't listen to himself.

There were many people in the yard, but everyone was hurrying to do their work, and no one was just hanging around without purpose or care.

Three soldiers walked past without looking at Artiom. He thought that the gangsters and the soldiers all looked the same to him — like Chinese people. The gangsters were dirty as soap suds, with sharpened teeth. The soldiers: dog-faced with sunken eyes. How was he to distinguish them? It was easier to distinguish one gull from another.

Every gull that flew past him tried to scream as loudly as possible in his ear. From the early morning, they were always hungry and angry. Those creatures had completely lost their ability to hunt in the recent past and ate exclusively in garbage dumps or next to the kitchen. They even stole quietly or blatantly in the open. A real case of natural Cossacks, like they were even before Catherine.

Black and Bear circled Artiom but left him alone. He smelled of the sun, of idiocy, but not of food.

"Oh, I know that person…" Artiom thought.

He noticed Violar, the former Mexican consul, Vasilii Petrovich had talked about him. Violar had gone to visit his wife's family in Tbilisi, and from there, together with his beloved, he landed in Solovki.

Violar was also not hurrying anywhere, but waiting for something, being in a state of obvious spiritual unease. He stood at the corner of the nearest building, stepping from one foot to another and languishing.

"Maybe he's waiting for Galia," Artiom laughed, immediately feeling his joke like a slight blow to the solar plexus — no, it's wasn't funny at all.

"… They're about to lead the females out right now, you doofus," he explained to himself and in confirmation of his guess, a lineup of women appeared on their way to the common labor. "… Peat, most likely," Artiom thought.

In the row closest to Violar walked a tall, thin woman — her appearance was proud and her chin held high, but her eyes were emitting such sorrow that it pinched his heart.

It was astounding, but the women, who usually swore much worse than the men, fell silent when they saw Violar — it seemed that everyone knew that they had a meeting, and they didn't want to bother them. They even walked a little more quietly — everyone, including the guards.

Violar held the stone corner, picking at it with thin fingers, and smiled — or here it would be more appropriate to say that he smiled with all his might. If the lineup of women had walked past him only a minute longer, Violar's face would have suddenly popped with a sharp lengthwise crack…

But no sooner had the women passed than Violar suddenly gathered himself and walked on, even somewhat relieved. It seemed he worked somewhere in the retail store.

But Artiom felt even worse.

"I see you, I see you," a woman's voice spoke quietly behind his back. "You're standing like an idiot. Maybe you should have waved your hand too: I'm here, I'm here!"

Her voice was very pleased.

Artiom didn't look around, lest he scare off this miracle. Inside, it was as though a flock of small birds had just taken wing.

"Go into the Transfiguration Cathedral, to the roof where the windows are burned out. Say that you have an assigned job there… to clean garbage. Here's the key, in your pocket, since it's locked. Go through the covered gallery, not through the sleeping quarter."

* * *

"Save me or not, I don't care. My life is not dear to me. Just bring me the one that I love…" Galia sang quietly and maliciously as she dusted off her skirt and knees.

She was like a domesticated pet today.

Artiom didn't say a word, he only watched.

He couldn't even think that she was in love with him — why would she be? But he wasn't upset; think of it! She's in love with someone else, but she's still singing that song here, to me.

If she only sang, dear people…

"Don't be bothered that all this was burnt out. It was a church. You got it?" said Galia.

Artiom nodded.

"You understand everything," Galia agreed.

The light here was unclear, dusty and it smelled of burnt garbage. Galia looked at Artiom as though she were planning on taking him away from here and carrying him home with her.

The walls still had some icons — Christ looked with one eye and another from various corners. The bears poked out in tufts and a pink ankle of a child was clearly obvious.

"There are people for whom thoughts are desires and desires are thoughts," said Galia. "But you have neither desires nor thoughts. Your thoughts are your actions. But all your actions are accidental. You're borne by the wind along the road. You think that the wind will carry you away, but what if it carries you to the wrong place?"

Artiom shrugged, slightly smiling.

"Your understanding lives separately from yourself," said Galia. "You expend no energy and usually don't even know what you understand. But if I were to ask you, you'd answer, and it would suddenly seem that you again understand everything."

Artiom smiled again — everything she said was very pleasant to him; only sometimes he listened to hear if someone might be climbing up to this garret.

"How did someone so cheerful end up here?" Galina asked not him, but more herself. Therefore, Artiom didn't answer, though he thought, "Many kinds ended up here…"

"Your place is… by the sea, so that you could dive and the young ladies would be afraid of your drowning."

"I'm diving right here," Artiom wanted to answer, but once again didn't.

"Except your understanding is excessive for your joy, so you don't think of anything," Galia concluded, once more examining him. "But I just can't decide — should I explain at least something to you or should I just leave you in your enchanted half-consciousness?"

Artiom, barely biting his lower lip, looked at her. A drop of sweat rolled down Galia's neck.

She suddenly squinted and sneezed, and immediately after that she laughed.

Artiom listened yet again — was anyone coming here?

"The roof of the church," said Galia, raising her finger up, "was where the artillery was stored. When it started to burn, the cartridges exploded and were carried by the wind all the way to the holy lake! A *verst*, probably! They say it was very beautiful... When, five hundred years ago, the monks arrived here, there was a green meadow here. And when we came here five years ago, there was an inferno."

"They built a church, and you built a prison," thought Artiom distantly, even amicably, without feeling the weight of his incarceration.

"I know what you just thought," said Galia.

Artiom was sure she didn't, but was still slightly afraid. "It's going to start again," he thought indistinctly.

"Eichmanis said that there was always a prison here," Artiom said placatingly just in case. What if she did know?

"Why are you worried about Eichmanis?" Galia asked, as though she were waiting for it.

"Why?" Artiom was sincerely surprised. "I'm not worried."

"You're always talking about him."

"I'm not always talking about him, you are," it rolled off Artiom's tongue, but he shut up and didn't continue that conversation.

"During the Tsars, sure," Galina hurried, without listening to him. "Do you know who built a new prison here? After the revolution? The 'allies' — the White Army folks. They exiled the representatives of the Provisional Government from Arkhangelsk, those who seemed too 'red' for their tastes. What do you say to that?"

Artiom almost didn't care, but she clearly did.

"Here they now persecute seven thousand people," said Galia, talking about something that she clearly wanted to say for a long time. "But up to this point, they had beaten all of Russia for a thousand years! The *muzhik* — they beat him and beat him!" Artiom huddled into himself — they would definitely hear them and how would she explain it all? That she had arranged a lecture specifically for the inmate Goriainov?

"Only five years have passed, but who would now dream of taking a grown man into the stables, taking his pants off and beating him on the buttocks with a whip?" Galia was almost screaming. "Have you not thought about that? How quickly everyone forgets about that!"

"At least here they beat people with bludgeons on the head," said Artiom quietly — that was the least that he could say.

"And so?" asked Galia with a challenge, pushing her mad eyes at him.

"I thought that things would be different under the new government," said Artiom, not thinking about anything. Why should he be quiet now?

"It didn't quite work out how you thought!" Galia barked with someone else's words. Her face was angry and unpleasant. She got up with a look that suggested that she wanted to slap Artiom across the face, to scratch his cheeks and eyes until they bled, so that he would hurt, hurt, hurt, more than she already hurt.

Artiom got up too. She screamed, "You!" She wanted, probably, to add the usual "jackal" here. But she didn't. They had disturbed the dust on the floor and it was unpleasant to breathe. "Creature!" she finally said and struck him not with a fist, but as though with talons right on the chest under his left shoulder.

"Stop it!" he almost yelled as well, grabbing her hand, pulling it to himself. He was clearly stronger, but she was also no weakling. At first, she resisted him, then with anger and in all seriousness, she bit his wrist. Artiom had nowhere to go; he couldn't yell, after all, so he shut his eyes, clenched his jaw and endured. It was really painful and the blood immediately poured down his hand — she bit through, look at that!

Galia recoiled, and he grabbed his wrist with his other hand, compressing the wound.

She stood with sparkling eyes: what? Understand now? You understand everything, right? Have you understood this time?

For some reason, she had no blood on her lips.

Artiom breathed through his nose.

"You've fouled me up, and now you're even leading counter-revolutionary discussions," said Galia with feeling, as though she had just accomplished her vendetta.

Artiom looked at her for almost a full minute without speaking, then he laughed. It was funny, what she said about counter-revolutionary talk.

She also tried to laugh, but suddenly she started to cry. Artiom saw her tears for the first time, and he was afraid.

"Galia," he called her and embraced her, expecting her to push him away, but she didn't. Neither did she lean into him. She cried quietly, not pitifully, but confidently, as though it was necessary to get her crying out of her system immediately.

He tried to turn her face to his; she finally submitted and turned.

Suddenly, he said, right into her mouth that smelled of his blood, "I love you."

She heard it but acted as though nothing happened.

She moved back a bit, wiped her face with her hands; it wasn't irritated, but neither was it domesticated any more. It was just a face.

"For a woman, you have to apply yourself, my dear," she said, not looking at Artiom and gently straightening out her cried-out eyelids and rubbing her cheeks. "By the way, do you remember that they can shoot you any day? And then how would I be? When I want a shawl with swirls, slippers with elastic bands, or 'Swan Down' face powder?"

"You make the effort," said Artiom quietly with an accent on the "you". "Then, your whole life will be like swan down."

"I did. Your *Vladychka* John was supposed to be guarding the piggies, but you went instead. While the priest is guarding the infirmary and sweeps in the yard next to it."

"If you let me out, I'll apply myself like the last slave," Artiom repeated.

"I'll let you out," she suddenly answered simply. Then she followed with, "Let's go to the theater tomorrow? It's a premiere."

And, without waiting for an answer, she took her purse and walked towards the exit.

"Galia. Where should I work?" Asked Artiom, feeling small and embarrassed.

"You're a guard? Go guard. You have a responsibility," she answered without looking around and, leaving, quickly started to descend the staircase.

After a few minutes, Artiom followed. At the doors, when he was closing the door — it almost didn't close, even when he slammed it — on the floor, near the entrance sat a homeless boy, a leopard with empty eyes. He wasn't scared of anything anymore because of his hunger and wildness. Among all these burnt-out icons and soot-darkened saints he looked a real, underaged demon.

"Get out of here!" Artiom scolded him with fear, almost dropping his key.

He didn't even move but gathered the snot in his mouth and spit.

What he needed — that wasn't clear. Was he eavesdropping? That did happen here sometimes.

Artiom walked away with fear, hurrying. What if that little devil jumped on his back?

He only calmed down when he saw some grown inmates in the light — gangsters and candlewicks — human riff-raff. They were familiar, and everything went back to normal.

"Did you clean up, shit-head?" the duty officer asked when he came down.

"Go and check it out," Artiom answered across his shoulder. "It's as clean as a children's nursery."

He walked outside, raised his head.

Two windows in the burned-out cathedral.

* * *

Their eyes met when he walked into the hall. Artiom's place was exactly in front of Galia in the third row.

She did that on purpose, Artiom guessed. "So that I would think of her throughout the entire performance."

At the last second before sitting down, Artiom raised his eyes and saw Eichmanis in a low side box. Thankfully, he was talking with someone and didn't notice Artiom.

Artiom quickly sat down, feeling his head ringing from the onrush of blood. Not without difficulty, he overcame his desire to crawl under the chairs and hide there.

Galia, in the meantime, wouldn't back off. She needed to call someone, but it seemed uncomfortable to do it seated, so she got up, pushing Artiom's head with her hip.

It may have been pleasant, but not in front of Eichmanis.

Artiom lowered his head barely, to give Galia the space to twist about freely, but as soon as he straightened out and sat up, he immediately felt her hand on his shoulder, and she twice quickly tickled his neck with her little finger. Leaning over Artiom, Galia said to someone who was sitting in front of him, "Frenkel, Eichmanis is looking for you. Go to him in the box." Only after that, she took away her hand.

The person whom Eichmanis was looking for quickly got up. Turning about, he barely nodded at Galia, examined Artiom — exactly at the moment when Galina's hand was coming off his neck. He noticed the hand, but pretended that he saw nothing, turned aside, and, begging pardon, moved to the front of the row.

He was short and unremarkable, but something in his movements, in his firmly clenched, faintly wet lips revealed him to be a man of unpleasant, stubborn will.

"Naftali Aaronich," Artiom heard Eichmanis's voice. "Come here, I need to speak to you quickly."

Frenkel raised his head, smiled with restraint and nodded again — but slightly differently, in a military fashion.

Together with Frenkel, Moisei Solomonovich also slowly walked along the length of the first row. He had noticed Artiom a while ago and waved to him with unexpected affability. Truth be told, he greeted nearly everything, in the most different ways, as though his greetings were souvenirs from the gift shop, and everyone got a unique one.

"... Mara, Mara, what will I do when they drive me to the island of Solovki! You will remain here, getting your fill of pleasures, while I will perish, die of sorrow..." Having greeted pretty much everybody, Moisei Solomonovich sang beautifully. Artiom was almost sure that he was doing it for him as well — to show how the former unfortunate who had lived next to Artiom was now so well settled that he could sing a dubious song right in front of the Chekists, and nothing would happen to him.

Frenkel, seeing Artiom, glanced over at Moisei Solomonovich with a quick look, and in that look, there was spite — but it was so momentary that hardly anyone noticed it.

The hall was filling quickly; it had about five hundred seats.

Artiom accidentally noticed that Violar and his wife were sitting next to him. Their hands interlocked, they looked directly ahead of them, seemingly seeing or hearing nothing.

Everyone sat intermixed — soldiers and prisoners. The high levels of the administration, however, did sit in the two side boxes, while the first rows were mostly filled with employees of the administration and superiors.

No one from the brigades assigned to common labor was anywhere near him — however, three places away from Artiom, Burtsev was touching his cheek with his thumb — "Did I shave well enough?" — And next to him, on both sides and almost halfway up the row, sat all the dregs of the IID, as Artiom mentally determined.

"Burtsev probably wants to know how I ended up here," thought Artiom without especial pleasure. It would have been better if Galia had put him in the very farthest corner.

Galia could have sat in the first row, but from there, Artiom realized, she wouldn't have been able to look at Eichmanis.

And, maybe, Artiom too.

Or she wanted to see both of them at once.

Artiom stared at the gray curtain with a white gull. In the camp, the gulls were everywhere. He had so long become accustomed to them, that only when they raised the curtain did he remember that that gull was the symbol of the Moscow Artistic Theater.

He didn't even understand the first few minutes of the play — Galia was behind him, Burtsev not far away, Eichmanis to his left… Artiom took several sidelong glances there, into the royal box and saw that Frenkel hadn't left — he was still sitting there next to the head of the camp. He had seen that Frenkel in the lineups at some point — he was a simple inmate, what was he doing sitting in the box?

Young ladies, wringing their hands, were running back and forth along the stage. Judging by everything, they were the daughters of a merchant who sat in the center and was tugging at his beard with such irritation that it seemed it would fall off at any moment.

Especially since it was Shlabukovskii in the beard, and he didn't have one normally.

Shlabukovskii's voice, in contrast to his beard, was his own and overwhelming — it was enough for two theaters — he even whispered in a way that was clearly audible.

Another thing that surprised Artiom was that those who sat near him, and especially behind him, didn't just pay attention to the action, but appreciated every double entendre ambivalently.

"What do you expect of me, tell me please?" asked the merchants of a young man who had appeared on the stage.

Other than four daughters, the merchant ended up having two sons as well — the younger was the first to appear before the audience.

"Give me the freedom to sleep, walk about and eat whenever I want!" the son exclaimed, half-turning to the audience, and he heard laughter and encouraging noise in answer.

Artiom barely looked about and immediately saw Eichmanis, who was also laughing and indicating the audience to Frenkel with his hand. Frenkel lowered his head with respect, but there was no smile on his face.

Burtsev, by the way, also was not smiling, but, it seemed, was carefully examining the merchant's daughters. The audience was driving him mad.

"There would be no order," said Shlabukovskii, drawing out the necessary pause, and Eichmanis again smiled and someone in the front row laughed.

Then the mother appeared, as is the custom in Russian literature, all tender-hearted and quiet, trying as much as possible to protect her children from evil fate and their hard-fisted father.

"We are all quiet and meek," she whispered to one of the sons with a tear in her voice, extending her arm with a flourish that included the hall as well.

"In front of father," her son interrupted her and almost pointed at Eichmanis, "but under our coats, we all have knives!"

The audience was hooting again, for some reason very pleased with themselves, the chairs were creaking and a wonderful animation ruled over all. It was as though everyone that was sitting in the former culinary wing of the former monastery was going to sit on a tram — or even get into a personal automobile — and go wherever they'd like right after the curtain fell.

Eichmanis enjoyed the proceedings in an obvious way. He only got distracted from the stage when the audience responded especially loudly to the actors' retorts.

"He has the right!" the merchant cried.

"Your right is a two-edged sword!" the elder son answered.

"Bludgeon!" someone yelled, and that was the source of much rejoicing, which, for all that, quickly subsided, because no one was forgetting to pay attention to the plot of the piece, and their involvement was clear and heart-felt.

Artiom was unable to say that the acting was without comparison, but without a doubt, this was a real theater, not an amateur one.

Eichmanis had clearly not skimped on the props — the furniture was typically merchant-style, stolid, the curtains were so nice that you could make dresses from them, and at the end, they opened a bottle of champagne — it even foamed, it even smelled real.

Everyone was absorbed in the action.

In the last scene, the merchant's daughters and the elder son with his bride, standing with their backs to the audience, peering through nonexistent windows, looking with horror at their father who had just shot himself. Off stage, a shot actually rang out, it sounded like a revolver — and, to see what was actually happening backstage, many got up, especially the back rows… someone by that time was already clapping, someone cried, "Bravo!" the daughters of the merchant ran backstage, but immediately ran back, leading Shlabukovskii by the hand — thank God, he wasn't actually dead and everyone was indescribably happy to see him, even Eichmanis. Only Violar, who understood Russian badly, looked at the stage with surprised eyes, still not releasing his wife's hand.

Artiom couldn't stop himself and turned to look at Galia, as though he had something to do with all that had occurred. She smiled and winked at him with eyes in a familiar way, like a dear and beloved person. Artiom was taken aback and hurried to turn around, then he met eyes with Afanasiev, who was looking out from backstage, holding on to his red forelock. It seemed that in his eyes, there was understanding that Artiom had absolutely no need for.

Still, he might have imagined it.

When everyone was getting up to leave, Afanasiev again appeared and cried out, "Tioma! Tioma, don't leave yet."

Artiom, apologizing but not looking into the faces of those walking towards him, moved towards the stage, trying to keep his distance from Eichmanis's box.

He loudly embraced Afanasiev.

"Let's go, I'll introduce you to Shlabukovskii!" he called. Artiom didn't have time to answer — the flushed and red-faced Afanasiev spoke without stopping. "You saw how he played the merchant? I was watching Eichmanis — he was even rubbing his hands." And Afanasiev showed him how.

Goriainov had already been in that green room.

"This is my friend Artiom," Afanasiev introduced him, though from behind Afanasiev, Artiom couldn't see to whom he was being introduced. "He works with Fiodor Ivanovich," Afanasiev added with a distinct whisper.

Artiom finally took a step to the side. Shlabukovskii laughed soundlessly and a little tiredly; that is, he raised his chin and opened his mouth, having breathed out three times.

Artiom now understood why he laughed like that — without sound. With such a voice, if he started to laugh, he could break all the dishes.

"We've met," explained Artiom.

"Oh, damn!" Afanasiev laughed, grabbing himself by the forelock and leading him to the table, where sausage and cheese were generously piled on two platters and the bread lay nearby. Someone was already bringing the samovar, and someone else was slipping a shot with something green to Shlabukovskii.

"It was wonderful, fantastic!" said Artiom, smiling.

"Another…" and Shlabukovskii raised two fingers at the person who had brought him the shot glass.

They immediately appeared —an entire set of ringing bells — the two actors who played the sons, Afanasiev, Artiom and someone else.

There were no women — it seemed that they had a different green room. Occasionally, they heard female voices.

"They're coming, they're coming!" someone at the doors said.

Everyone quickly downed their shot glasses, cups and mugs, and threw them all into a dexterously placed knapsack.

As Eichmanis walked into the green room, the knapsack was being pushed under the table.

Behind Eichmanis walked in Frenkel and Boris Lukianovich.

Artiom had almost turned around in the hope that he might crawl over into a far corner and remain undetected — Shlabukovskii's beard showed up before his eyes, and a mischievous thought to put it on passed through his mind. He would look good in a black beard without hair… but suddenly Artiom saw that Galia appeared in the doorway, deliberately calm.

"To hell with it," thought Artiom distinctly. "To hell with it. What does she need?"

"What about the theater?" Eichmanis asked Boris Lukianovich, continuing a conversation they had just started. "You've seen our theater's repertoire?" Shlabukovskii started, but no one paid him any attention. "Here, half the plays couldn't be performed on the mainland. And have you seen the caricatures in our journal? And our symphony orchestra?" Eichmanis chuckled. "You think I don't know that they play Rachmaninov? A hater of Soviet Russia and an émigré? The same orchestra plays 'A Parting of Friends'. That's a march that I know from my youth, but then it was called 'The Two-headed Eagle'!"

"I heard," answered Boris Lukianovich dully. "I know that march too."

"Have you heard the expression, 'My yoke is easy'?" continued Eichmanis; Artiom suddenly realized that the head of the camp was tipsy — he had already seen him in this state before. "Or how was it that your merchant put it just now?" Eichmanis turned to Shlabukovskii, and he immediately stood up, trying to remember and understand which of his retorts he meant, "'… I want first of all to think of your souls,'" Eichmanis repeated by heart.

"… It seems to me that there is only avarice and enmity there," Shlabukovskii ended it.

"Exactly!" said Eichmanis, and without any transition, he asked with sincere affability, "Artiom, how did you do with the uniforms? Did you get them?"

"Yes," answered Artiom, looking at Eichmanis with eyes that seemed to his own self to be completely round from embarrassment and horror.

"Well, sit down," Eichmanis said to everyone, and immediately turned to Frenkel with a quiet question, "Have you brought them?" Frenkel, in his turn, made a gesture to someone behind Galina's back, and from there, over people's heads, bottles of wine appeared — two, three, four...

"Celebrate," said Eichmanis, widely extending his arms. "The show was..." Artiom felt that the hearts of everyone who had any part in the play stopped for a moment, especially Shlabukovskii, who, apparently, was also the director, "... worthy of our theater."

Saying not another word, Eichmanis turned and slowly walked to the exit. Frenkel walked next to him, pushing aside the actors that were in the way.

Galia, Artiom saw, let Eichmanis pass as though unwillingly, not looking at him and at the same time inexplicably directing the action at him.

Eichmanis, sensing this, walked past Galia as one does past a kerosene lamp without a glass cover.

* * *

They came back to their rooms in a proper state — Shlabukovskii was arm-in-arm with Tioma, after them Afanasiev stomped, not in rhythm with them, singing in long refrains that were either double entendres or just drunken repetitions: "Rip, soldier, it... to... shreds! Especially... the ... black... color!"

Artiom thought that the poet was staring right at the back of his head when he was singing.

"Could he really have guessed? How?"

"Look, the light's on at Mezernitskii's," Shlabukovskii announced to the company, pointing with his cane. "Now we will invade! Afanasiev, don't you think? Artemii?"

"Oh, I have to go work," Artiom only now remembered. "I should have gone ages ago."

"Come on, your work will wait for you," Shlabukovskii said. "You work for Eichmanis," Afanasiev was saying. "Well, Eichmanis commanded us to celebrate. That was a direct order!"

In a strange way, Artiom found Shlabukovskii's words convincing.

"What's going to happen anyway?" he said cockily. "Who's going to demand it of me? The scientists? I'll feed them all to the rabbits..."

But Afanasiev remained firm, "No, no, I don't go there."

"Listen!" said Shlabukovskii, looming over the poet. He was a head taller than Afanasiev and quite large in general. "You haven't gone there because you've been hanging about only with the gangsters and basically lying on the sea floor with the crabs and … leeches. But now — now you've been admitted to the church of art, and, one can say, you have the right to swim upward…"

"I always had that right," Afanasiev answered with an unexpected and rude pathos. "But I don't need to go there."

Shlabukovskii only opened his mouth to utter another monologue, but Afanasiev, having said "Adieu," went his way. More exactly, he suddenly whistled prettily, called Black to him and raced against him along the yard, swinging around a sausage he had hidden.

"We should also have hidden sausages in our pockets," said Shlabukovskii thoughtfully. "Well, never mind. They'll take us even with empty hands… I've fed them often enough."

The duty officers, it seemed, know Shlabukovskii's special status. No one asked him about anything. He walked into his wing in the same way as he walked into the best Moscow and Petrograd restaurants not so long ago.

They were already next to Mezernitskii's room when Vasilii Petrovich came out of there.

"Oh, unexpected guests," he wondered, tiredly and not very joyfully. "We're already on our way out."

"There's not even any charlotte left?" Shlabukovskii asked and boldly walked into the room.

It so happened that Vasilii Petrovich remained in Artiom's path.

"Well, what's up?" asked Vasilii Petrovich, not moving.

"I was in the theater," answered Artiom, still not sure about his old friend's mood.

"And how was it?" asked Vasilii Petrovich in the same tone.

"I liked it very much," Artiom answered sincerely, and since Vasilii Petrovich remained silent and the silence could be interpreted as one of expectation, he continued, "Ivan Komissarov, a former bandit, played the elder son of the merchant. He used to rob secret money barges with machine guns, but he makes a very convincing nobleman." Artiom laughed. "You've never been? After the play, the local orchestra also played a few pieces. Also… inspiring."

"Orchestras, hell!" Vasilii Petrovich, for the first time in Artiom's memory, swore, looking somewhere to the side. "The landowners also had their own serf orchestras! Why the hell did we have to switch one for the other?"

"I'm in a really stupid situation," Artiom thought meekly, though with cheerfulness. "Galia is biting me because I remembered the bludgeon, Vasilii Petrovich is ripping me to shreds because of the serf theater. What am I doing between them? Put me back in my old place again..."

"What did this wonderful orchestra play for you?" Vasilii Petrovich asked with mocking gallantry.

"Rachmaninoff," Artiom answered, sniffing. He understood everything now; he had to finish the conversation somehow, only he didn't know how — should he just walk through to Mezernitskii's, go to his room, or go straight to the iodine plant?

"Rachmaninoff?" Vasilii Petrovich was falsely astounded.

"Yes. And also '... branded by a curse.'"

"And how was it?"

"Sounded good," answered Artiom.

"I've heard, I've heard how the piano sounds," Vasilii Petrovich continued vengefully. "It was also exiled to Solovki for playing the wrong notes. Only deaf people are incapable of hearing that!"

Artiom shrugged, but in the darkness, it wasn't visible, and clearly no one cared here about his gestures.

"If you had listened in, you would have immediately recognized that everything around you is a cacophony! Cacophony and nonsense stories! And barbarians, explaining themselves in an incomprehensive tongue, who have decided to teach us — us! — their lowly speech! They've stolen everything — the country, freedom, God... Now they're even stealing the language — those words are piled into my head and they're sticking out in odd angles... 'branded by a curse' — what does that even mean? An opera about the lives of Indians? 'The dictatorship of the proletariat' — how's that? Maybe that's a dish? What's it made of? 'The intrigues of the Entente,' the 'spring of the revolution', 'the glorious future', the heaviness of Tsarism', 'class warfare' — what is all that? Are those the names of gunboats? What gobbledygook! Do you know the meanings of those insults? In such a language, can you even ask, 'what time is it?' Or, perhaps, make a bow and say, 'Good morning to you!' Why did they reward us with this ugly language? 'Extraordinary commission!' Eh? I know what a coffee shop is. I know what a boulangerie is. I know what a tea house is. But extraordinary? What is so extra about this ordinary? Or does it mean that we had no work until this moment, but now, suddenly such important work has begun that — Good Lord! After all, they're not just important, they're extraordinarily important! Their eyes are climbing up their forehead from importance! Everything is new all around, in red cloth, everything in red cloth! Back then we called each other 'chere' and 'ma chere', but now we've added 'ka-ere' to it.[43] I hope they shot your merchant's son in the final scene. Was it one of the new plays? About heaviness and exploitation?"

"No, it was an old one."

"There you go!" Vasilii Petrovich raised his finger. "An old one! Everything around us is an old play! In the oldest play of all, it was said, 'Fear not those who kill the body, but cannot kill the soul, but rather fear those who can kill both body and soul in Gehenna.' Do you know the author, mister comrade Artiom?"

Artiom turned to walk away, but Vasilii Petrovich grabbed him by the sleeve. His fingers really were iron-strong.

"The Chekist who first raised a red flag over Solovki was brought here as a prisoner," he began whispering in his ear, it seemed that he was drunk to the gills, but he didn't smell of alcohol at all. "Have you understood nothing, Artiom? All of them will again be imprisoned here. And they'll all be buried here too. God is near here. God doesn't allow his fallen children to go far from His side. He doesn't abandon this monastery! Never! There was a revolt in 1666; it was put down by Ivan Mescherinov. The soldiers under his authority killed the monks with rocks, they slaughtered them, and then they didn't bury the bodies. Well, Ivan Mescherinov ended up here soon afterward! And the Greek Arsenios, who fixed the ecclesiastical books — which was why, in the first place, the revolt even happened — he was also imprisoned here! And they were here together! They ate from the same bowl! And you also will sit together with your Eichmanis." Here Vasilii Petrovich began to speak only with his lips, "And all his whores, and you, idiot, together with them! This monastery has teeth! Have you seen the watch towers? They're stone fangs! It will crush anyone who thinks highly of himself!"

"Vasilii Petrovich," Artiom said very clearly, "let go of my hand. Or I'll hit you."

"Oh, of course," agreed Vasilii Petrovich and very gently let go his hand. "Without a doubt you will. In parting, I am obliged to tell you that Mezernitskii has asked that you no longer visit him."

"Why, what happened?" Artiom didn't understand.

"You're an intimate of Eichmanis, yes? And you're proud of it. And we are all happy for you. I've already been told in what company you were sitting at the theater. And they also say that you and Eichmanis drink vodka far into

43 In Russian, "ka-ere" is "counterrevolutionary".

the night and discuss immense questions. That's charming… Such success, and still so young, oh…! However, such people are… inappropriate… in our little circle."

"What the…" Artiom almost screamed, but he waved his hand and in anger almost ran downstairs.

"Inappropriate!" Vasilii Petrovich called in his wake.

"What nonsense!" Artiom said feverishly as he lumbered down the stairs. "Pharisees! Pharisees and brainless lunatics! Mezernitskii himself plays in the brass orchestra! Shlabukovskii is in the theater! And Grakov writes for the paper… And I, pull my leg, warned them about Grakov and now I'm forbidden entry? Me! Because I dug holes for Eichmanis twice and one time sat amid the swine from IID? Well, they can all go fuck themselves! I don't want to know them. And that old idiot too! Let him gather his berries until he drops dead…"

Artiom even stopped, barely overcoming the desire to run back upstairs and tug Vasilii Petrovich by his old ears with their blue veins, grab him by the scruff and smash his nose into kitty corner full of piss.

"I should have gone to work, to work. There I can calm down, but here there's nothing more for me to do, I might as well never come back here."

Artiom ran up to the post, gave the officer his pass and stomped in place with frenzied impatience, until he tried to catch the lantern's light on the paper.

"Should I read it aloud?" asked Artiom with a voice suppressed with anger.

"You can give your whole lessons aloud," said the soldier and without reading anything, asked, "Where did you sleep, you seal?"

Artiom blinked, was quiet for a bit, then stupidly asked, "W-who?"

The soldier folded the paper four times over, put it in his pocket and loudly spit to the side.

"Leaving the monastery is already forbidden. You're late by two hours. Plus. I'll take your paper tomorrow morning to the IID. You can explain everything to them. Meanwhile, go to your sleeping quarters and tell your commander everything I said here. Let him figure it out for himself. Since you're not going to your place of work, you're definitely going to get solitary.

Artiom clenched his teeth and went back into his wing.

If he had unclenched them for even a moment, he would have howled.

* * *

He saw the same half-dream several times during the night — he went to Galia, explained the highhandedness of the soldier in detail, she took a revolver, together they rushed to the gates, and — boom! Boom! — everything's in smoke, the soldier's on the ground, Artiom grabbed his rifle. The second watchman, having taken off his helmet and pressed it to his chest, fell on his knees…

Artiom didn't want to let these self-invented visions go so badly that he bit his blanket. He woke up with it in his mouth, with a bad hangover — it didn't seem to be from yesterday's wine, though, then again, it could be from it as well.

It was still morning and immediately, as soon as he opened his eyes, a siren shrieked from the electrical station. It turned out that wake up time was now at six, and no longer announced by the bell.

With a troubled heart and nausea, Artiom began to dress, but then he suddenly stopped.

"Why am I?" he asked, "Where? So that the head of the brigade can yell at me? And who is he anyway? I'm supposed to be in the iodine plant, what am I doing in the line-up? As soon as they all go their ways, I'll go to Galia. She can return me my pass… And that's all! What hell was in my head in the night! Nothing's happened!"

People were hurrying to make breakfast in the hallway; it smelled of food. Artiom pulled out his crate from under his bed, broke off some bread, started to eat, without anything. Then he thought about it, looked for the salt, salted it and it turned out very good.

The camp was revealing itself in constant new qualities, thought Artiom. Turns out, you could not only die on the logs here, but you could also fall into a kind of interstitial space, hide and disappear, and you might never again be noticed, forgotten.

"And why not?" Artiom summarized for himself, biting his bread. "There are seven thousand people here, and do they care if one of them stays in his room? Won't the other manage without me?"

"They'll manage," he answered himself and fell on his bed. He pulled out the blanket from underneath himself and crawled under it with his head. For some time, he continued eating bread in the darkness — this was a new, curious sensation. He thought that even in childhood he had never eaten under the blanket.

The company commanders, the brigade leaders, the foreman, and the duty officers — they all knew that Artiom had a special job and that in the mornings, he slept.

"So here I am, sleeping in!" said Artiom to himself, and he did fall asleep.

His wakening was unsettling — a woman was speaking animatedly in the room, and it was definitely not Galia — her voice was elderly, gentle and hurried.

This just couldn't be borne. Artiom sharply sat up in his bed.

"Oi!" The woman shrieked in fear.

She wasn't an old woman — her voice just shook from worry; she looked a little over fifty, but young for her age. A high forehead and, as Artiom determined it, long cheekbones — these immediately revealed her to be intelligent first of all, but, more importantly, the mother of Osip Troianskii, who also stood there, extremely unhappy with Artiom's presence.

"This is your neighbor?" asked the mother of Troianskii, simultaneously smiling at Artiom, but with a look as though on the bed next to her son slept some strange animal, like a musk beaver, who was possibly not capable of human speech.

"Doubtless," said Troianskii, "And he was supposed to find himself another place a long time ago."

"Yes, I'd like a two-storey apartment on the Prechistenka," answered Artiom, rubbing his cheekbones with his fists.

"What? Are you quarreling?" asked the mother, still scared.

Artiom even felt sorry for her, especially since Troianskii scornfully refused to answer.

"I'm always bothering Osip," Artiom explained, very amicably. "And here I'm extraneous, and there, where we work, I'm a burden to him."

"Where we work?" answered Troianskii, stressing the *we*. "But what you do there, I still can't figure out."

Artiom looked at the mother: see, it's like I said.

Completely unexpectedly, the mother took Artiom's side.

"Osip, you can't do that," she said, very firmly. "They're teaching us now that there are laws of communal living; and you, apparently, will have to abide by them until everything gets resolved."

Strangely enough, that actually had an effect on Osip — at the very least, it was as though his temperature dropped and he continued to do what he was doing before — move food from his mother's bags to his crate.

"Why don't I feed you both?" offered the woman. "I am called Elizaveta Averianovna, and I have borsch. I managed to cook some in Kemi and bring it here. The duty officer warmed it up, and I gave him an egg for that."

"… Well, why not, it's borsch after all," thought Artiom, cunningly explaining to himself his morning agreeability. "Plus, I do have to explain to Troianskii about the rabbits... otherwise, it's all so ridiculous."

"My name is Artiom," he introduced himself and threw off the blanket, which momentarily disconcerted the women — there would have been a reason if he introduced himself and then, unexpectedly uncovering himself, would have presented himself naked under the blanks. But Artiom slept dressed, even in socks.

"He's never even liked to travel by train — there are other people there, but here…" Elizaveta Averianovna simply explained her son's behavior and looked over the whole room.

Artiom also looked around: yes, you're right, other people, they're crowding…

In the meantime, the borsch smelled so good that Artiom had to hold back, with who knows what reserves of energy, from any desire to grab the bowl and run out with it into the corridor.

"Osip?" his mother asked expectantly.

Troianskii finally moved back the crate with the produce that had tripled in a single morning.

"Yes, Artiom, please sit," he said ceremoniously, indicating the table.

Artiom once again sat on his bed with extraordinary readiness, this time closer to the table.

"Osip, I want to unburden myself to you," Artiom said triumphantly, looking, however, at the borsch, where a piece of shaggy meat that took up half the bowl floated. "One of the rabbits was in actual fact taken by soldiers. But the other — a cat killed it.

"Then why did you remain silent!" Osip flung his arms up. "We would have taken measures!" he even laughed, which was completely unnatural to him. "That villain got the knack of climbing in through the hearing window, can you imagine? Today he killed another one. We were ready to kill him! But in our milieu, unfortunately, no one is capable of that."

"What are you talking about?" Elizaveta Averianovna asked and put some sour cream in the borsch.

Immediately, so much saliva gathered in Artiom's mouth that he couldn't speak.

The first spoon went to his head so fast that it felt that Artiom had downed a miraculous, fiery vodka straight from the Tsar's table, then the Tsar himself passionately kissed him, shall we say, in the forehead.

Artiom, in a single moment, sweated all over and became completely, to his very last fiber, happy.

This happiness wanted to go on and on.

That borsch was not just food, it was an epiphany of nature and self-knowledge, the continuation of one's race and the search for God, the finding of peace and an ecstatic joy of all the human powers, contained in the hot, blossoming body and the immortal soul.

They ate three bowls each, until the container was completely empty.

A few times, Artiom almost bit through his spoon.

By this time, Elizaveta Averianovna got some halva from her purse — it emitted a gentle, sweet fragrance that smelled like the ruins of a Buddhist temple covered in powdered sugar.

Having drunk the dregs of his soup and grabbed a leaf of cabbage with his fingers, Artiom reached with his other hand to the halva and Osip, from his side, did the same.

With four hands, they broke that temple and immediately began to eat its crumbled pieces. On his lips, Artiom tasted salt, fat, the sticky enchantment of the halva, ecstasy and drunkenness.

After the halva, they ate another three puffy, sensual rolls with homemade apple jam, and they were finally full.

"How do you live here, tell me now," Elizaveta Averianovna said insinuatingly. It was obvious that she had around one hundred or even one thousand questions saved up, and for now, she was limiting herself to one.

"You should eat something yourself," Artiom remembered. "Why don't I put on the tea kettle?"

"No need. I've brought the thermos..." said Osip, getting the thermos from his purse; opening it, he smelled it. "It's warm. Completely."

"He made that thermos himself," Artiom praised Osip.

"He was always an inventor," said Elizaveta Averianovna, wiping the mugs. "Even at school..."

"There has never been any profound life of the mind here," Osip suddenly interrupted her. "A work commune, husbandry — yes. Did Christ appear? It's possible. But Russian thought always slept here; there are only boulders here, what kind of thoughts can you have? And Eichmanis surely won't awaken that thought; everything that he does is a caricature."

Artiom eloquently pursed his lips and attentively looked at the door.

Elizaveta Averianovna looked at her son with a smile; then, not smiling any more, she looked at Artiom; finally, with a request and sorrow in her eyes, she looked at Osip again.

"But you do work," said Elizaveta Averianovna, "and quite successfully."

"Artiom, did you know that Solovki, in its shape, looks like Africa?" asked Osip. Evidently, he was continuing some incessant battel with his mother, who was quite stuck on her adoration of him. "You haven't noticed? Solovki is exactly Africa-shaped. And we here are the black slaves of the Bolsheviks."

"Fiodor Ivanovich spoke to me today," said the mother quietly, trying to be weighty and heard by her son, though she spoke for some reason to Artiom, "Fiodor Ivanovich says that Osip needs a trip to the mainland to continue his research. And he's ready to let him go, if I'm willing to promise he comes back."

"I like that," Troianskii answered extremely cuttingly, as though he had prepared an answer in advance, "I'm here in cold storage. There's no real work to speak of. And so they'll unseal me, like canned meat and they'll say, 'Bird, go fly!' I'll fly a bit, then I'll come back, and they'll seal me up again in a tin can. How wonderful, Mama."

"Why is he so nasty to his mother, what a moron… He's ruining our lunch," thought Artiom, smiling distractedly.

Elizaveta Averianovna rarely looked at him and also tried to smile, expecting, though not quite able, to wait long enough for the proceedings to become a big joke.

"A little while ago," continued Troianskii, seemingly feeling pleasure from this brazenness, even if it was to his mother, "Eichmanis quoted, you won't believe this, Pushkin's letter to Zhukovskii. Pushkin wrote… one moment…" and Troianskii moved his fingers in the air as he remembered, "… 'This situation smells of exile. Save me at least with a fortress, at least with the monastery of Solovki.' And do you know why he quoted this? Because he sincerely believes that he is saving us. As he eats us, he saves us!"

Troianskii looked over everything with a look as though they were supposed to laugh at any moment; but for some reason, they didn't.

No one touched the tea. It stood on the table, cold, without a bit of steam.

"What about the mazes, Artiom?" Troianskii suddenly remembered. "Do you know that on a few of the islands, there are mazes made from the stones? Not tall ones, like a man, but a single stone high — even for a cat, such a maze would be small. I think that these mazes are very old. Probably five centuries BC. At first, the Germanic tribes built them, then the Laplanders took them up… doesn't matter. No one knows their purpose… I think that in the center of each maze is a burial place. And the stones are a difficult path to prevent the soul of the dead man from leaving."

Troianskii looked at his mother once more, but to expect understanding from her was pointless — she was only a woman, after all. He tried to find interest in Artiom's face, but Artiom was rolling a bit of halva on the table.

"So," Troianskii concluded confidently, "today's Solovki has become just such a maze. Not a single soul must leave this place. Because we are all dead men. And here, they're releasing my dead soul from the maze. That kindest Fiodor Ivanovich, our protector, guardian and all-merciful one. Mama, have you ordered a service in his honor yet?"

Elizaveta Averianovna blinked in such a way, that it seemed that her son had caught her doing something improper, such as if he had walked into his room, and she was reading his diary.

The son snickered crookedly; everything's clear, mother, everything's clear.

"And so, raising my wings, I will soar over the mainland, breathing with a full chest…" Troianskii suddenly began to cough and his mother made a gesture as if to help him, but he stopped her with his hand — don't! "I will soar," he continued, having finished coughing and extended his arms, "like a bird, and on my leg, there will be a long, invisible, one-thousand-*verst* long chain. And if the desire arises, in the middle of a word, or a cry — CARK! — and they'll pull me back."

"I've referred, Osip, to all the possible departments, and it's possible that they'll reinvestigate your case," the mother repeated quietly, but audibly.

"The important thing is that you can't tell anyone over there what's going on here," Troianskii continued, as though he were deaf. "It's like I'm a bird, and seemingly free, but I must keep my beak shut."

"You've eaten your fill, you nobleman's son, and now you've started mocking your mother," Artiom thought in serious irritation.

"I would tell them, too. Or at least I would have listed my complaints," Troianskii whispered confidently and sharply. "The dog-awful sludge! The oubliettes! They shoot at us! They put is in frozen iceboxes!"

"Who put you there? Why are you lying?" Artiom unexpectedly interrupted him, grimacing, using the informal "you" for the first time with Troianskii. "Everyone wants to talk about the iceboxes that they've never been in themselves, but about the fact that the prison population goes to operettas, the politicals take walks all over the island and the counter-revs walk around in top hats and patent shoes eating marmalade — no one will tell about that. Have pity on your mother."

Troianskii opened his surprised eyes and looked at Artiom for a moment without even blinking.

"Plebeian," he concluded some long and convoluted thought aloud. "Cad. Slave. Get out of here. They'll feed you marmalade over there from their hands."

* * *

Artiom hurried to the street, caressing his hand barely — he had punched Troianskii in the lips, as he wanted, and he fell back so sharply that it seemed he had broken his neck. The head flew back sharply and unwillingly, and Osip hit the stone wall with the back of his head. His mother gasped, someone dropped the canister with the borsch, and at the exact same moment a very clear shot rang out outside, and a few others came in answer…

"Że to będzie, że to będzie," Artiom repeated, trying to remember where he heard that phrase… then he remembered. Mitya Schelkachov told him how in childhood he used to make fun of the Poles who lived in the neighboring village. "Że to będzie" meant "something's about to happen."

Right towards him, from below, making a horrible racket, soldiers were running. Artiom leaned against the wall to let them pass, but it turned out they were aiming for him. Very hard, they smacked him in the head, then grabbed him by the head, scraping off some skin, then threw him down the stairs.

"On the street, jackal! Line up in the square!"

Artiom flipped over his head, cracked open his cheek against the metal railing, and, he thought, twisted his arm.

"Why me? For what?" he tried to understand with all his might.

"Are they going to beat and kill me in front of all the people? Even Galina?" Artiom asked, getting up with difficulty and feeling the blood pouring down his face.

But downstairs, at the doors, he noticed that all the rest who were in the monastic cells had been also, with blows and swearing, sent outside with wounds and contusions.

Tens of inmates were already crowding in the square. Soon there were hundreds, also sent out from the sleeping quarters or from the nearest work groups, from the port, from the narrow-gauge railway, from the administrative buildings, from the laundries, from the kitchens, from the carpentries and metal working shops. Several musicians ran out frightened with their trumpets, one with a violin… They beat the actors out into the street from a rehearsal of something historical — Shlabukovskii at first stood in a crown, then took it off and held it in his hands, not knowing where to put it. Next to him, pages in hilarious pantaloons stood in a crowd.

It started to rain, and Shlabukovskii, not thinking, put the crown back on his head — as though it could save him from the downpour.

Artiom, looking around from underneath his eyebrows and keeping away from the bestializing guards and the foremen who were constantly laying about with their bludgeons at whoever they could find, took his place in the line. He stood in the second row — it was harder to get to it, because the first was constantly being straightened with fists and rods and the last rows were just as energetically beaten to get the desired formation.

Someone was yelling, someone was crying, someone was wailing, someone was hysterically asking, "Why, commander?"

Over all of them, the hysterical screaming of the gulls hung, and through that screaming, through horrifying human swearing, through the din and roar, through the maddening rain in the monastery's courtyard, Artiom finally heard the most important thing:

"Mezernitskii shot at Eichmanis!"

"What? Did he go insane?" Artiom didn't understand. "Why?"

Immediately, whispering hoarsely, turning their identical, black, dirty heads, they asked each other, "Did he kill him? Did he not?"

It was unclear what was behind that question — more a secret hope at Eichmanis's death or, on the contrary, an earnest desire for everything to work out, because the death of the head of the camp meant that everyone would die immediately.

"How did I not notice it?" Artiom suddenly wondered.

Mezernitskii lay in the middle of the square, dead. They shot him in the face, because he had no cheek, and then they shot him in the back. He lay in a pool of blood and Black barked not far away — it wasn't clear who he was chasing away — the soldiers, the inmates, or death itself...

When the square was filled with people, Eichmanis flew in on a horse through the southern Jordan Gates, which were always closed.

The soldiers took the rifles off their backs, ready for any order.

Everyone fell silent.

The land was bubbling, as though it boiled.

The rain made another turn and then left somewhere under the red roofs, rushed away to the green spire of the Transfiguration Cathedral.

Only the gulls continued to scream and constantly rain down their droppings on the inmates from above. No one wiped himself.

"On your knees!" yelled Eichmanis in pale fury and pulled out his saber from its scabbard.

The lines fell as though everyone had been hamstrung in a moment — several thousand hamstrings by a single, merciless blade.

On their knees stood priests, peasants, horse thieves, prostitutes, Mitya Schelkachov, Don Cossacks, Yaitsk Cossacks, Tersk Cossacks, Curly, mullahs, fishermen, Grakov, pickpockets, NEP-ers, artisans, Frenkel, house thieves, safe-breakers, Passport, rabbis, coast dwellers, noblemen, actors, the poet Afanasiev, the painter Braz, misers, merchants, forgers, Gills, anarchists, Baptists, smugglers, office workers, Moisei Solomonich, owners of gambling dens, offshoots of the Tsar's family, shepherds, gardeners, drovers, ostlers, bakers, lapsed Chekists, Chechens, Estonians, Shaferbekov, Violar and his Georgian princess, Doctor Ali, nurses, musicians, stevedores, craftsmen, Catholic priests, homeless boys, everyone.

Eichmanis was only in his shirt, and it seemed that he didn't freeze, though an icy steam rose from the earth and many in the lines chattered with their teeth, unable to stop, and they leaned with their hands on the ground, as though they were constantly seasick.

Artiom had time to notice that Troianskii didn't want to go down on his knees and immediately got a gun-butt to the back of the head… now he lay on his stomach behind the lineup… where his mother remained was unclear.

Burtsev also stood on his knees and stood strictly, his eyes half-closed, as though he were giving an oath.

"Well, who's the clown now?" Artiom thought, breathing raggedly, looking back and forth from Burtsev to Mezernitskii…

Artiom himself hadn't noticed how he fell on his knees.

Only a minute later did he understand suddenly that he also, together with everyone, stood there, licking the rain off his lips, desiring only one thing — to live.

However, one astounding feeling lived in him — that everyone who stood right now on their knees stood for some good reason. Only he also stood for nothing — he just didn't want to defy and was ready to share the common guilt.

Uttering nothing, Eichmanis flew — ferocious, with an unsheathed saber — along the lines.

The horse under him rejoiced and snorted.

The fear spread by his movement was palpable, almost visible; this fear could be cut into pieces, together with the people.

The gulls now didn't just scream, they teased in both human and bestial voices.

Black recognized the familiar speech and suddenly barked with a frenzy in answer, and the gulls barked back at him.

Eichmanis chopped an invisible chain with his saber, and at the same moment, unrolling from the spire and extending over their heads, a heavy rain, like berries, began to fall.

"He's gone Satanic," someone whispered next to Artiom.

It seemed to be the voice of *Vladychka*.

Artiom tried to raise his eyes to look up.

A heavy drop fell exactly in the apple of his eye.

BOOK II

The last gulls were flying away from the island, taking with themselves their feathery, spotted chicks who had gotten brazen over the course of the summer.

The summer in that year, though it had breaks for cold rains, was unexpectedly long, and the gulls were a bit late in their departure, went a bit soft, though, they say that some years they even waited until August to get their stuff together.

"Maybe the gulls will fly away for the winter, but won't find their way back?" Afanasiev thought aloud. "They'll land next spring somewhere in Yaroslavl… or maybe even in the kremlin in Moscow. They'll say: it's not so bad here; let's stay here and yell!"

Artiom laughed, smelling a torn fir branch — it barely had any scent. It was strange, but even the flowers in spring didn't smell here, nor the trees in autumn. It was as though the expansive sky of Solovki sucked in all smells, leaving only a slight vertigo.

Sometimes you'd look to the left, then to the right, but it seemed that everything around you was the same, and the sky with its multi-colored clouds spins around you, and it's as though you're in the center of a child's spinning top, going mad.

"No, but imagine," Afanasiev wouldn't shut up. "I was always sure that only Solovki had such horrid gulls. A cursed place should be cursed in all things. Only here could such a foul bird exist with its hungry, whorish, villainous character. But if they fly away, that means that there's at least one other place on the earth where they also scream from morning to night and torture some other innocents with their cries. Who could that be, and where, Tiom? In Africa?"

Artiom seriously looked his friend in the eyes, as though he were planning on answering, and Afanasiev almost seemed to open up to him, expecting that he would explain everything to him. Instead, Artiom exploded in laughter. No, he was really very happy to see Afanasiev.

"Fine," said Afanasiev, little red devils swinging on swings in his eyes. "Maybe there's a different side to the world, where everything is inside out? And these gulls have angelic characters there?"

"Oh, yeah," agreed Artiom. "That place also has a concentration camp where Curly comes into the sleeping quarters with a container of warm milk and gives everyone a drink from his own hands, from a white cup."

At this, Afanasiev laughed too.

"I actually found that one of the gulls had a ring on its foot. It said 'Rome' on it," explained Artiom, having had his fill of laughter. "They're from Rome."

"You're not serious!" Afanasiev wondered and familiarly grabbed his red forelock. "How about that!"

For some reason, that surprised him; but at least it gave a new direction to his crackbrained thought process.

"Let's take it a step further," Afanasiev offered. "So, the Roman Empire collapsed, falling apart into pieces and lumps, and these same gulls were then flying to Solovki, where there was absolutely nothing! The Russian people hadn't yet been born, Christ hadn't come to them, because neither a *leshy* nor a mole needs Christ."

"Uh-huh," Artiom agreed. "So, it's we who are the strange whatchama-callits to them! After all, it was quiet, calm, transparent here before. Winter in Rome with its parades and gladiators, and summer on their dacha in Solovki, in the quiet — what a life! But then two monks appeared. Then another hundred. They dragged about a bunch of rocks, began to knock, shop, serve their *moliebens* from morning to night, build their walls, put up their crosses. Then later, there were even more! A whole circus came to join the monks, together with rifles and balalaikas, and something completely insane began… And who, one might ask, is bothering whom?"

"Maybe," Afanasiev was inspired, as though he had gotten high off of Artiom's words, "the gulls have gotten used to it and now say to each other: 'Hey, look here white-tail, it's all like it was in ancient Rome again — the same mugs, the same foulness, the same bestiality and slavery…'"

Artiom breathed in deeply through his nose and decided to put a temporary stop on this successful conversation.

It strongly smelt of fox and the disorderly life of a fox here on Fox Island.

This island was about two *versts* away from the main island of Solovki, and a fox nursery had been established on it.

In charge of it was Artiom's former brigade commander from the twelfth — Krapin.

They got along famously and lived in peace.

Artiom had already been here five weeks. Other than taking care of the foxes, he also did an idiot bulletin newspaper, conducted political propaganda meetings, he was listed officially as a caretaker and janitor. There was enough work, but nothing to complain about.

Afanasiev only appeared an hour and a half before — they had sent him here to replace a prisoner whom the silver-black fox named Glasha had bitten in the hand. The hand had gotten infected, and they had to send his partner to the infirmary; still, Artiom had never expected to see the Petersburg poet here — why suddenly?

As for Artiom, he was sent here by Galia immediately after the Mezernitskii mess, the very next day.

"You also attended those Athenian evenings," said Galia not looking at him and even, it seems, annoyed. "Everyone is going to be pulled into IID, and they're going to try to uncover a conspiracy… go to Fox Island… Hopefully they'll forget about you."

Artiom felt such gratitude then that if it were even a little bit appropriate in her office, which was covered in shelves filled with files, he would have fallen to his knees and kissed Galia's feet.

"Well, tell me the news. What's going on in the kremlin?" Artiom asked Afanasiev. They specially went to the shore to have a chat.

Afanasiev finally released his forelock — it stayed in place like a red shrug hanging over a chasm.

"We have a new head of the camp," Afanasiev said while walking. "He came two days ago."

"From where?" Artiom breathed out, bulging his eyes and throwing away the fir branch as completely unnecessary in such a conversation.

"How should I know?" Afanasiev answered. "From hades, like the rest of them. His last name is Nogtev. They had been the boss here before Eichmanis, but you and I weren't here then."

"So where's Eichmanis?" asked Artiom, thinking about Galia — what's she up to? Did she leave together with Eichmanis? And what will happen to him now, to Artiom? Strange, but all the good fortune he had, he associated it with the former head of the camp, and without him, it was as though he were naked and unprotected.

"What a strange question!" Afanasiev crookedly smiled with one side of his mouth. "I think Eichmanis took that place in hades that's gotten cold since Nogtev's departure… Listen to this rather. After Mezernitskii's attempted assassination, they took everyone who attended those Athenian nights. You've got some special good luck, Tioma, that you came here. Don't even know what sort of star is looking after you. Mezernitskii shot from a revolver that Eichmanis had issued Shlabukovskii for one of the plays — only for theatrical needs, and not for shooting at the head of the camp. Either Shlabukovskii forgot to return it or something else, but that very evening he came to Mezernitskii with a revolver in his pocket. Remember? We were accompanying him. And I left, and you went there, into Mezernitskii's room.

"I didn't make it," Artiom said quickly.

"Really?" Afanasiev answered without believing it. "Good for you… Shlabukovskii seems to have forgotten the revolver there. Or Mezernitskii stole it. Or Shlabukovskii gave him the revolver on purpose. In any case, you're supposed to be executed for any of those.

"They executed Shlabukovskii?" Artiom asked quietly, but still he only had enough breath to get to the middle of the last word.

"Wait," Afanasiev interrupted him, his jaw twitching, as though he were pushing away Artiom's premature words. "At first, they punched out a few of Shlabukovskii's teeth, during his first interrogation. But then, Tioma, Eichmanis himself called him in. And… can you imagine! They've let Shlabukovskii go! And a week later, they sent him home with a pardon — he had already sat half his time! That's how fate turns its wheel. What do you think?"

Artiom looked at the sea and even made a gesture as though someone slightly poked him in the forehead. As though someone had tried to put his brains back in place, because Afanasiev's look still didn't explain anything.

"But why did they let him out?" Artiom asked, not of Afanasiev at all, but who knows of whom — the dirty foam on the shore.

Afanasiev shrugged and continued after a brief pause, "Maybe because he founded the theater here… Maybe Eichmanis believed Shlabukovskii, that he wasn't involved. Who knows? Except Nogtev, as soon as he arrived, immediately promised that there would be no amnesty for anyone, because a place where they shoot at the head of the camp is a diseased place, and he's going to treat it. And Doctor Nogtev, judging by his vile mug, knows exactly how… So our dandy Shlabukovskii's floated away on the last ship!"

"What about Vasilii Petrovich?" Artiom remembered. He didn't hold any grudge against him, nor did he against Afanasiev for that matter, though he still remembered that he had framed him for the cards; but all sorts of things happen in life — you can't get mad at everyone! "What about *Vladychka*?" He, of course, wanted also to ask about Galia — did she leave? But how would he ask that? Galia didn't come to the Athenian evenings.

"They took Vasilii Petrovich too. Put him in solitary, only let him out for Nogtev's arrival… I think your Vasilii Petrovich's given up. As for *Vladychka*, he's still sweeping the infirmary's floors like he was before. Though they may have interrogated him; I'm not sure."

"And Grakov?" asked Artiom, of course without any heartfelt interest, just for the company.

"Grakov's an informant," Afanasiev said lightly, as though it were an obvious fact. "Even when he was outside he was an informant, even when he hung around our Petersburg poets. Everyone knew about it."

"Why didn't you tell anyone?" Artiom truly couldn't understand Afanasiev's behavior.

"Me?" Afanasiev was sincerely surprised. "Why? Do I look like a fool for Christ that I would stick my finger at him and say, 'Look, a demon!' Anyway, they were your Athenian evenings. I'm not from Athens. I came to Petersburg from a sma-a-a-ll town, where there wasn't a single straight fence, and all the toilets were wooden. I only studied three years; I still make mistakes in my writing."

"There was nothing there," Artiom quickly answered. "Nothing Athenian."

"Yes there was," Afanasiev insisted. "You're a Muscovite, you're a schoolboy, you've grown up looking at the Moscow kremlin, you've gone to the theater since you were five, you've got a special nature, you had a right to go there. I'm a yard boy..."

"You're talking nonsense, and that's final," Artiom repeated a little annoyed. As far as he understood it, Afanasiev was really talking total nonsense.

Afanasiev sniggered.

"Since you're so smart, Tioma, explain this fact to me," he said insinuatingly. "Four... yes, four days ago I heard this bit of news — the sauna switches that you and I made — the whole thing — they sent them back to the monastery. With a demand that they figure it out and punish whoever was responsible. Remember? We made those delicious switches with the barb wire? The Chekist switch, the switch of Solovki, the bloody switch of dawn?"

Artiom felt the heat strike his head — every hour, worse and worse! What sort of idiots had they been? How could such a folly have ever entered their heads! He hadn't even managed to grow his hair properly after being shaved and already he was ready to turn white from such news.

"Well, I thought," Afanasiev continued. "It's all over. Farewell, stage! I'm off to Sekirka...! But the night passed, and I found out that for those switches, they took Avdei Sivtsev and one other one — Zahar, from near Lipetsk... Remember him?"

"Yes, I remember, I remember," answered Artiom, intending for Afanasiev to go one.

"Maybe they also had a turn with the switches, I don't know," said Afanasiev. "Though I doubt it would have dropped into their heads to do what we did, to tie them with wire… It's not like Sivtsev at all. But now they're in solitary, paying for our little joke."

"Fuck! I'm going to kill her!" It tore out of Artiom unwillingly. He understood it all, of course. The whole thing went through Galia, she quickly figured out who was at fault in the preparation of the jolly switches and once again she protected Artiom, because you couldn't punish Afanasiev alone for such a thing. So she had to send off the poet as well — and how convenient that the bitten inmate appeared, exactly from the same island as Artiom, freeing a place for Afanasiev.

Though, of course, the story was much more complicated. Galia could have sent Afanasiev to any distant island work, to carry logs or to dig up peat. But she sent him to Artiom as a hello: look, you creature, I remember you.

There was only one thing in this whole story that he could be happy about — Galia hadn't left.

"Whom are you going to kill, Tiom?" asked Afanasiev, grabbing his forelock again and holding it, lest his head roll away.

"But couldn't you have chosen a different way to protect me, Galia?" asked Artiom silently. In this wind, his tears were always near and he sighed several times, trying to cool his jumpy heart. "Galia!" He called her mentally again, looking over the sea.

There was no answer, though Afanasiev continued staring at him.

"That fox Glasha," Artiom answered dryly, getting up. "Have you seen what a bitch she is?"

… Afanasiev caught up with him in a minute, walking behind him as though nothing had happened — OK, let's check out Glasha — and continued to weave his usual word-decorations.

"Tiom, you know what I've noticed? In Moscow, the sun sets like a cold samovar they've carried away. In Petersburg," Afanasiev waved his hand somewhere to the side, "it's like they've hidden a nickel in their sleeve. In Odessa," here his hand waved in the opposite direction, "it's like they've rolled by a rabbit in a drum… In Astrakhan, the sunset looks like they're frying a red fish. In Arkhangelsk — like they were feeding you frozen fish, but then took it away. In Ryazan, it's like a deck of cards eaten by ants. In Riga, it's like you've put a pill under your tongue. Only here, it's like a blade," Afanasiev quickly slashed across his throat with his index finger…

Artiom had no interest in all that poetry.

There was no more poetry on earth.

Taking two catch-up steps, Afanasiev quietly took him by the sleeve and said, with a smile in his voice, "I'm still going to run away."

* * *

You had to get used to the smell.

Fox-stink hung over the island. Sometimes the salty sea-breeze chased it out to sea, but then drove it right back — no we don't need that smell over here, you can have your animal stink.

Afanasiev was clearly not a squeamish guy — no wonder he was a poet. He immediately thought nothing of the smell.

Artiom had also gotten used to it in his own time.

The small island was surrounded by shields to prevent the foxes from running into the sea.

No one guarded the people — there was not a single soldier here.

In the fox nursery, every fox had its own accommodation with lamp-heating and a small lawn, separated from the others. For this reason, Krapin, who had turned out to be an intelligent, competent man, jokingly called them "minor landowners".

Only Fura was allowed to take walks — she was Krapin's favorite — as a reward for her almost domestic manner. Artiom, naturally, nicknamed her "Fury". She and Artiom didn't get along, though he assiduously fed her fish. As for Krapin, she almost embraced him every time he appeared.

Krapin's attached earlobes no longer seemed to Artiom, as they did before, a telltale sign of limited intelligence. Instead, they were proof of his trustworthy character. Also, his red, broad back of the head, so red, it looked like he had just been pulled out of borsch.

Krapin and Artiom showed Afanasiev the nursery, preparing him for his new work.

To a degree, Krapin wasn't thrilled to see Afanasiev, remembering his previous friendship with the gangsters and his constant card-sharking. But here on Fox Island, there were no gangs, and Krapin was ready to give the red-headed conman a second chance.

"There are seventy-three old foxes, seventy-six young ones, twenty blue foxes and five sables…" Krapin was saying, hissing through his teeth. "And a dozen cats."

"The cats are for mittens?" asked Afanasiev.

Krapin didn't answer, as though he hadn't heard.

“When the foxes can’t feed their young with milk, we use the cats to give them extra milk,” Artiom explained quietly.

“And the kittens go to the foxes for extras too,” Krapin explained. Of course, he had heard everything, and he summarized thus: “Husbandry!”

The nursery was divided into angles.

The entrance to every fox apartment was made in the form of a tube to remind the fox of its hold, otherwise the animals got agitated and were afraid to sleep.

Foxes, like people, try to live monogamously, but there were not enough males on the island, so they had to enter into a bit of a contradiction with nature — they pushed several black-silver males to mate in various apartments.

The foxes’ pairing, it was shameful to admit, constricted Artiom’s breathing.

“Why can’t we have the same arrangement with the women’s barracks?” Artiom’s friend imagined aloud. “Why do they want to breed foxes, but not the poet Afanasiev?”

Krapin once again pretended not to hear the evil speech of the new worker.

He was one of those people who couldn’t bear frivolous wordplay and jokes — though he was fully capable of answering them, sometimes amazingly to the point. But Krapin still saw the humor of life quite well.

“… What do we feed them?” he answered Afanasiev, who clearly envied the foxes’ way of life. “With fish, and with thrown out vegetables from the main kitchen in the monastery. At first it was a problem: what to feed them. For some reason, they decided to feed them with crows. There are many crows, you only need to set a trap. But you know how smart crows are? Ha ha! Basically, they tried to make a trap with a candy wrapper and bait. The candy wrapper was dipped in glue. They didn’t have to wait long; the crow came, pecked at it, and the candy wrapper stuck. Well, they thought, we’ve caught it now! Then another crow came, grabbed the wrapper and pulled it off its friend. And both of them few away, the cheats.”

Krapin rolled himself a cigarette. His fingers, in their brown glaze of tobacco and fat, worked deftly.

There was something homely in such conversations here, which were frequent, and Artiom realized that this wasn’t the first time he left that way. He did sometimes wake up to think: where’s Passport? Where’s Shaferbekov? He would look down from his bunk, but there was nothing but floor before his eyes.

In every fox apartment stood Krapin's pride and joy, and his own invention — a foxophone. In order to avoid having to run around one hundred small yards, Krapin asked the kremlin for the tools to wiretap every single fox.

"You sit in the office," he explained to Afanasiev, "and let's say you've decided to see how Glasha is doing. You turn on the number of her apartment, and you listen on the foxophone. If her kits are barking and rustling about — that means everything's fine. If they're whining, that means Glasha doesn't have enough milk.

"But if there's silence, then they're all dead," Afanasiev answered in the same tone; during his time in the theater, he relaxed a bit; though even before, he wasn't remarkable for his excessive obedience.

"... They're all dead," Krapin continued in the same tone, "and the person responsible, that is you, goes to Sekirka. In other words, you'll go chasing after the dead fox. And you won't be far from it."

"Not bad!" thought Artiom and winked at Afanasiev: did you hear? And you thought you were the only one who knew how to joke, you red-headed poet?

Krapin even read books — this was a serious surprise for Artiom. In the monastery, Krapin would never have allowed himself such a luxury, but on the island, there were few extra eyes — why not read a bit? Though even here Krapin tried not to read alone, and Artiom only accidentally noticed Jack London in the hands of the former policeman, when he had rushed to his little house last week to tell him that Glasha had just given birth to eight kits — an extraordinary situation.

Naturally, none of the foxophones worked properly, so Artiom walked from apartment to apartment, checking. To be honest, he didn't really like the animals and was even a bit afraid of them.

"If only we were breeding goats," Artiom laughingly complained about his fate. "I should ask Galia if there's a goat nursery here... I would drink some milk, gain a little weight..."

"Here's our clinic," Krapin showed him sedately; Afanasiev didn't stop being amazed, which, it seemed to Artiom, Krapin secretly enjoyed.

The clinic was a single room. In the room was a cupboard filled with foreign medicines and all kinds of vials. There was a table for writing, above which hung a cardboard paper with a drawing of an anatomical cross-section of a fox. In the middle of the room stood a soft, wide shelf laden with belts for examining the foxes.

Galia had only once come to the island, two weeks before. On the same boat that had brought her, Krapin, having quickly shaved, departed to make a report of his accomplishments. Galia spoke with his assistant about all manner of paperwork and, while the workers of the nursery sat to eat, she walked with Artiom to examine the apartments of the foxes.

On that shelf for examining foxes, they had grappled with each other, as though they were mad. Basically, Artiom knew for a fact, of course, that the medical room was the only one that locked from the inside.

In the middle of their encounter, someone had knocked on the window…

Gasping, Galia looked with wide eyes at Artiom, and he felt her frenzied legs on his back…

It turned out that a gull had flown down to demand bread — this was their usual habit on Solovki — knock, knock, feed me!

But it was only funny later. At first, not at all.

Artiom, even now, looked at that shelf with arousal and quiet sorrow.

"There's even a microscope… a Reichert tester," Krapin continued. "Do you know how to use it?" he asked, not looking at Artiom.

"Not the Reichert, no, but…" Afanasiev answered quickly, though even now there was an air of red-headed nonsense about him.

"And you don't need to," Krapin interrupted him. "You'll use this thing." He turned around and pointed a popgun at Afanasiev's forehead.

Afanasiev looked askance at Artiom: what's going on? Artiom shrugged: we make such jokes here too.

"I surrender," said Afanasiev, though he didn't raise his hands up.

"All the foxes have worms," Krapin explained. "We have American capsules to help with that. But the fox doesn't know that it's supposed to swallow it, so we have to use this tool."

Krapin turned the popgun aside and shot at the picture of the fox. Having popped off the wall, a white capsule fell onto the table.

"The important thing is to get accustomed to this work," Krapin explained, still not looking at Afanasiev. "Our former colleague was experienced at breaking into houses, so he walked with this popgun to all the apartments. He knocked, and in answer to 'Who's there?' he popped the lady of the house right in the mouth. But Glasha got sick of the arrangement, and she bit him… By the way, I got bit three days ago too," Krapin announced, speaking only to Artiom. "They brought three young foxes from Kemi… The shaking, the gasoline — evidently, one of them was completely overwhelmed. I started to rush them out, already on the island and she grabbed me by the hand. I was afraid it'd get infected, but it looks all right."

Krapin pulled back his sleeve and showed the dryly healing traces of the fox's jaws.

"So you should figure out how best to do your work," said Krapin, finally turning to Afanasiev and giving him the popgun.

"Maybe I can toss the fox a fish, she'll open her mouth and then I'll shoot her in the mouth: bang!" Afanasiev offered, completely seriously.

"That's possible," answered Krapin no less seriously. "But for a single lost capsule, the worker receives one blow on the back with a bludgeon. I brought my bludgeon with me, didn't forget it… And for a second lost capsule, the worker departs to the aforementioned Sekirka, to sit on a pole and repent of his ways belatedly."

Afanasiev quickly folded his face into an understanding expression, having folded one eyebrow under another and sorrowfully pursing his always pink, and seemingly a bit puffy lips, the joy of faraway ladies.

"Here we have a dental room." Krapin pushed the next door. Afanasiev whistled his approval. "Except we don't treat bad teeth, but good ones — the sharpest canines…"

In a separate, covered small shed there was also a photography room — especially for the foxes. Krapin himself photographed them — the former policeman had revealed many useful talents.

"Take a picture of me, citizen commander," asked Afanasiev, for some reason pulling up his new cotton pants. "I can't remember the last time I was photographed."

"Here, after we photograph, we take off the skin," Krapin answered without smiling, rolling another cigarette.

Next to the photography room, a fox was playing with a local young dog, who had been born in prison, something she probably hadn't guessed.

The dog kept pouncing and seemed to grab the fox every time with superior strength and boldness, but every time, the fox silently extricated itself. She held her beautiful tail out like a stick the whole time, lest she get it dirty. What a coquette!

"The dog is happy that he's stronger," said Krapin. But the dog is an idiot. He only thinks about biting her. But she's a natural born killer. If he does something wrong, she'll kill him immediately.

Artiom inconspicuously kept rubbing his thumb against his index and middle fingers, as though he were trying to remember the feeling of his fingers grabbing the shelf… as he stared at Galia and breathed.

* * *

At night, a fox walked over the roof.

They warmed the house in earnest for several day. Not only did the old stove crackle with the heat, but even the walls responded — groaning, and the ceilings — surprised, and the floors — rebuking.

The dark nights returned, as though they had been smoked and frozen to their very hearts during the time while the summer kept them under lock and key.

The night smelt either of fox tail or herring tail, and, if you had to go outside to relieve yourself, a wet, foul-smelling wind pushed you in the back of the head.

The stars appeared — Artiom hadn't seen them all summer. They were freckled, like *Vladychka*'s hand, but they also seemed to smell of herring.

When outside, he always wanted to go back inside where it was warm; too bad there was no tea, nor any berries — because it would have been so nice to have some tea when the stars were in the window and the over-salted wind, moaning, tore about here and there as though it had lost its leash.

Afanasiev was installed in the same room as Artiom, and they occupied a single bedroll that had been set up on the floor.

"Right next to the iodine plant," said Afanasiev, who couldn't sleep, "they caught — you're not going to believe this, Tioma, some old grandfather. It turns out he was a monk who lived in some hole and ate roots and berries… maybe someone fed him sometimes, but he said himself that he was nourished by prayer."

Artiom, who was already preparing to fall asleep, opened his eyes and saw the cracked ceiling, long in need of whitewash, in the light of the street lamp.

"They say that the old man didn't even know that there was a camp here. He hadn't come out to see anyone for seven years." Afanasiev quietly laughed. "They held him for three days in IID, got nothing out of him and sent him to Kemi: go work, grandpa, the Antichrist has come, and you can't hide from him in the forest… But he, no one knows how, returned to the island, thinking to dig deeper into his hole and not come out anymore… But they quickly caught him and this time they assigned him to the fourteenth brigade."

Afanasiev told his tale while leaning his red head on his hand, but his hand fell asleep and he fell down to his back.

"So?" asked Artiom, after some time had passed.

"Who, the grandfather?" Afanasiev answered indifferently. "He's on his way out. It seems it was easier to live in a hole than in the fourteenth."

"I know that hermit," thought Artiom, but he didn't say anything.

Instead, he asked, "What about your friends? They haven't croaked?"

"What friends?" he asked, as though he didn't know what Artiom was talking about.

"The gangsters," answered Artiom. He secretly hoped that a crazed and high-spirited wave had once engulfed them and pulled all of his enemies at once into the sea.

Afanasiev sighed.

"No, Tioma, they're not my friends. A criminal can't have any friends. Maybe you think that being one of the criminal underground means just taking what doesn't belong to you and having a bad character and foul habits? And the language-that too. You know how they talk..." Artiom knew, but he had forgotten; Afanasiev reminded him, a bit: "'I almost landed in the soup at grandmas while shaking the elbow — a regular gentleman of ours! Then the dry snitching began and they almost got the *friar* up with their heat wave. It was two minutes from the dance on the blacktop!' I know all those phrases, Tioma, and I can memorize their habits and I can ruin my character and get into the habit of taking others' things and not feel bad about it. But, Tioma, I still can't repaint my *friar*'s colors! A gangster is a different species than you or me! Instead of a soul, he has a middle finger, and it's sniggering and showing its dirty tongue. You can't become a thief for a time, nor can you play at it. A thug is forever. They're not the way they are because they act like thieves, but because they don't know any other way to be... In the best-case scenario, for them, I'm a wartycabbage. Do you know that word, Artiom? A wartycabbage isn't a *friar* or a criminal; he's a fake. Left the *friar* life, but didn't become a gangster — that's the first roll they'll eat... It's better to stay a *friar* and not try to pretend."

Evidently, Afanasiev remembered something important and significant, for which reason he stood up on his elbow again.

"You know what they called you once? I heard it by accident. 'The beaten *friar*.' Just like that! A beaten *friar*, Tioma — that's good, that's almost respect. They'll still kill you, and with a lot more pleasure than a regular *friar*, but in your case, it'll be so they can boast about it later... You've earned it, Tioma, I'm telling you for sure. As for me, brother," Afanasiev lowered his voice, "I never expected you to survive this long... You've got a good star. Are you carrying around in your coat pocket, eh?"

Artiom, not understanding the movement, put his hand on his chest, as though under his shirt there truly was something.

A fox ran over the roof again, as though it were trying to get into the warm rooms where it smelled of food.

Afanasiev looked up and asked, "Listen, you're not afraid of death? Do you think it doesn't exist?"

In the half-dark, Artiom noticed that his friend even nodded up, as though it weren't a fox, but death itself walking up there.

"What do you mean? It exists?" asked Artiom.

He knew for a fact that it was a fox.

The red-headed poet again fell on his back, but extended both arms in front of him, spread out his fingers and started examining them.

"Kabir-shah… or was it Kurez-shah…? One of them told me that death is a journey. The most curious journey in life. So curious that all you have to do is sit and rejoice, as before a play…" Dropping his arms, Afanasiev was quiet, gathering his thoughts. He breathed out and said, "You wait for it, wait for that journey, then you peek your head beyond the curtain, and — snap! — they've cut your head off with a pair of scissors. Huge ones, rusty ones. Your head fell off, there's your journey. Except that out of your headless corpse different-colored liquids pour out in finality, from both directions."

Unexpectedly, Afanasiev started to scratch his cheek — it was a rapid, dog-like movement. It was a wonder no sparks flew from under his nails at that noise.

Artiom looked at all this as though it were the usual Afanasievan ruse. And of course it was.

As for Afanasiev's words — Artiom seemed to understand their meaning, but he could only appreciate the beauty of the language, because — his friend was right — he didn't feel any scissors and he hadn't learned how to imagine their snapping right under his own chin, though during the last few days the possibility of that happening was very real. It must be that the knowledge of one's own mortality wasn't the most important science on earth.

"… In general, such journeys are not my cup of tea," said Afanasiev, having had his fill of scratching. "I have a different proposal from the arena of geography. Are you ready to hear me out, Tioma?"

"Go ahead, Afanas," said Artiom, though from somewhere he knew in advance that what he was about to hear would be useless and extraneous.

Afanasiev, having turned over, got up, and, squeaking the floor boards, walked to the window — he looked out for a long time, even holding the frame.

Then he returned and stood at the door, listening.

"Are you sure no one is here?" he asked.

"There's the fox," said Artiom.

"What about that… foxophone… Could Krapin extend it to here?"

"Everything that you will say right now will go immediately by radiogram to the IID," answered Artiom. "In the morning, they'll summarize it over the official radio station."

Afanasiev twisted about for another minute, in the half-murk, either sitting down on a stool or on his own shoes that he had brought into the room–an old prison habit–not leaving them outside like Artiom did, on the threshold.

Then he finally sat next to Artiom and said something like the following, gasping either from ecstasy or from worry: "Burtsev has been assigned head warden for the entire camp of Solovki."

When he heard that, Artiom only shook his head. All it took was his departure and the devil knows what started in the camp. He wasn't sure whether to rejoice or be sorrowful.

"While Eichmanis gathered information and Nogtev hadn't yet taken up his responsibilities, Burtsev managed to shoot up the ranks. While working in the IID, he cunningly gathered all sorts of information on the leadership of the Cheka. As it turned out, half of them are cocaine addicts and the other half – syphilitics. Taking advantage of this information, Burtsev gathered serious power to himself and all sorts of authority."

"It got to the point that he actually started to stick some Chekists of the middle ranks into solitary and no one could complain about him, because all complaints went through his former office in the IID, where Burtsev left his own people, also former officers of Kolchak's army.

"He left the most interesting stuff for now," Artiom thought, as he also began to pace back and forth after hearing such news, looking first at the window, then the door. "He kept it until night… his fried game…"

"Burtsev is keeping the Red Army guard battalion in a constant state of fear. He's introduced beatings for drunkenness and disciplinary infractions. But at the same time, Burtsev is oppressing anyone who comes near him — the gangsters, the counter-revs, the domestic criminals, the former socialists, whom he can't stand with an especially vengeful hatred."

It turned out that the situation with Mezernitskii was even useful for Burtsev. He was the one in charge of interrogations, so his own dark deeds could remain in the shadows. For example, it was our Mstislav who beat out Shlabukovskii's teeth.

Eichmanis saved Shlabukovskii, but overall didn't get in Burtsev's way. And basically, there was no reason to — the guards stopped raping the girls in the women's barracks, the Chekists stopped their bacchanalia, their tortures to make examples of inmates, like leaving people out to be eaten by mosquitoes overnight and their drunken rifle-fire during general formations.

But Burtsev's most important undertaking was the selection of a special squad for escape. Afanasiev didn't know who comprised that group, but he guessed that it was mostly former White Army officers and a few longshoremen. Very soon, while the seas are still navigable, in a single night, that group would disarm the guard platoon, blow up the lighthouse, destroy the radio station, tear up the telephone wires, grab the ship "Gleb Bokii" and escape to Kemi, and from there-to Finland.

Artiom was silent.

"Well, who's the clown this time?" he asked himself.

It seemed to him that even his thoughts were a whisper.

Afanasiev sat, not moving, expectantly looking at Artiom.

The fox overhead found the warmest place near the chimney and also grew silent.

"I won't flee," said Artiom.

They were quiet for a while longer.

"You won't?" asked Afanasiev a second time, as though something could have changed over the space of a minute.

"No. Why did you tell me this?"

"Well, since you're not running, then..." Afanasiev began, but faltered... having thought about it, he continued, "Tioma, I know for a fact that you can call in favors. I've got to get off this island. The sooner the better. I don't want to come up with my plan of flight. Krapin won't listen to me. Except maybe if I injure myself... or break something, but then how will I run away with a broken leg or with a finger missing? Help me out, Tiom. Send me back to the island. For medicines, for whatever! Let them even put me in solitary on the main island. I can endure it. When Burtsev's plan will begin, they'll let me out... Tiom?"

"Let the foxes bite you, Afanas, and you'll land in the infirmary," Artiom wanted to joke, but didn't. What sort of joke could there be now? Everything had stopped being funny.

"Let's sleep till tomorrow," he said firmly and ducked under his blanket. He covered his head, turned to the wall and quickly fell asleep.

He slept heavily; for some reason, he found it comforting that the fox had wrapped itself around the chimney, protecting their fragile house. At least no one would dare climb down the chimney.

* * *

In the morning, Artiom, as he put on his pants, dropped a folded punch of Solovetsian money from his pocket. On Fox Island, he received the highest salary of his time at Solovki, and he had no place to spend it — all the stores had remained on the big island.

"I owe you three rubles, Afanas," he said cheerfully; Afanasiev was still asleep, but was beginning to respond to the sounds of human voices and tried to dig himself deeper into his blanket. "Do you remember? You gave me some in the infirmary," Artiom wouldn't back off.

"I remember," Afanasiev mumbled into his pillow.

"Here, take it," said Artiom; he waited until Afanasiev turned around, opened his eyes, and extended his hand for the money — there you go. "And please don't speak to me any more about what we were discussing yesterday," he asked amicably and distinctly.

Afanasiev rubbed his eyes and sat down, looking from under his eyebrows at his friend. Artiom shook his wrinkled, fox-smelling jacket and, not without a flourish, throwing it over himself, landed with his arm exactly in the sleeve.

"Will I have a chance to get back to the monastery?" Afanasiev asked dully.

"There will be opportunities. You'll go; I'll help," Artiom said lightly, as though they were talking about a cup of tea that he had promised to pour. "But I'm not going to invent something just for that, sorry, Afanas."

He nodded and rubbed his eyes again with his fists.

"What time is it?" asked Afanasiev. "I didn't hear a bell or a siren…"

"It's eight already, my dear, you overslept a long time ago. No bells or sirens here, its freedom, equality and freeloading! Let's go feed the foxes, then we can eat ourselves… Today's washing day — we have to get as dirty as possible before evening so that we don't just waste the water."

"There's a sauna here?" Afanasiev finally woke up.

"You bet!" Artiom laughed. "You know how Krapin steams you up with that bludgeon?"

"We should ask them to send our switches over from the monastery," Afanasiev joked.

Artiom laughed as well. The morning was beginning well. There was absolutely no reason to run away.

From the moment that he no longer worked under the threat of beatings, Artiom felt that he had grown up a lot, expanded in his soul and everything inside him became twice as large. He remembered how in his youth, when he was about fourteen, he caught himself thinking that when he walked into the food pantry, he had to lean down a bit — finally he had grown! Now, he walked along the earth with the feeling that he had to lower his head a little bit somewhere; otherwise, his head might come off, or walk sidewise, because his chest wouldn't fit — but where could he lower his head? Where could he walk sideways?

It turned out that heavy, exhausting work didn't help him grow, but instead knocked a person into the ground all the way to his throat. A person grows wherever he can run around, jump up, scare a bird from its highest perch, almost catching it by the tail.

A little before morning, a dilapidated and garrulous rain fell, chasing the fox off the roof, churning up all the dirt. The smell rose even thicker, but Artiom found all of it to be quaint; he had mud boots after all, and he got a pair for Afanasiev. They both squelched, stuck in the mud, then swore, all the way to the nursery, from which they could already hear the nervous bark: food! Food…! No need for any foxophone.

They fed the foxes once a day, during lunch, but nursing females and growing kits got an extra meal in the morning.

They made the food beforehand and then handed it out. The kits lived on verandas covered in chicken wire so that they could also walk around in the sun, not just sit in their holes.

To be sure, the sun today was very distant, as if it had cooled down, in the throes of a chest cold.

Carelessly arguing with Afanasiev, who was armed with the popgun and offered to try it out at least on Artiom — "maybe you have intestinal worms too, eh?" — Artiom tried not to think about Burtsev, because even the mental utterance of that name scared him, bringing up dark clouds, though there was also a mixture of respect — Look at how he turned out, that wanton officer, a proud, stubborn, wild man. But his wildness was organized, not in the least improvisational, iron, like a machine.

"I couldn't do it," that's all that Artiom understood. And he understood this, probably, for the first time in his life, because, seeing the rest of the people and knowing their actions, he guessed that he either could do it like they, or even better, or he didn't even want to resemble them in the least.

Among such was, naturally, Eichmanis himself. Artiom wouldn't dream of comparing himself with Eichmanis. It would be like comparing himself with Caesar or Robespierre.

Eichmanis was older than Artiom by five or seven years — it was worth mentioning that those years were the years of the World and Civil Wars — but the heart of the matter was somewhere even deeper… Artiom secretly guessed that Eichmanis was older — *forever.*

What was hidden in that resonant word, he didn't have to understand. Forever, for a whole life, for a single amputated soul, finally, for one hell itself… But even these words, to speak honestly, didn't mean anything for Artiom, and he couldn't weigh their significance. Well, soul, well, hell — he put one word on one palm, the second on the other — neither weighed anything. His palms were empty and freezing.

Potatoes with fish weigh more than the conscience, and lice are more vivid than hell.

However, his unextinguished (even in such a frozen place) boyish wonder scratched at his insides with a question: who would have ended up the stronger if they faced each other — Eichmanis or Burtsev? Not in a fist-fight, but in another kind of encounter, where everything would be thrown into the balance — bayonets, brazenness, intelligence and the murky past of each.

Artiom smiled and turned his head — he seemed to have come into his own, enveloped in new skin, thicker than before, while the stupid, childish thought was just about to splash its tail.

He wouldn't even have been able to decide for himself who he would prefer to win such a battle, who he'd like to see lose.

"… Maybe Troianskii is right and you have become a slave who's in love with his slaver?" asked Artiom.

"… But if Mstislav Burtsev had to execute me right now — not for any reason, just in the name of the fulfillment of his great idea — would he do it?" Artiom thought.

Having caught himself on a hook with that question, Artiom even shivered: of course he would have shot him.

"… Then why do I wish him good luck?" Artiom continued to torture himself.

"… Only because Eichmanis took you in a for a moment and your pathetic human soul put a ring into your lip on its own — and it runs after the shade of its master, who left, leaving you as a gift to his former slut…" Artiom laughed at himself, and once again banished all such thoughts, because his life didn't need them at all. His life only needed continuation of life.

"… Don't say that about Galia," he implored himself. For Galia's sake it was always much more painful than for anything else — he included himself in the "anything else".

Afanasiev, whose voice Artiom had heard for the last two minutes without listening to what he was saying, continued to fool around, asking about everything like a red-headed late-bloomer, left for the third year straight in the same grade.

That's probably why the poet's soul kept getting attracted to Artiom, because with him he could be himself — something that you couldn't afford to do with anyone in the camp.

And is that also why Artiom valued Afanasiev?

"Why is that fox three-legged?" Afanasiev asked with fake fear. "Did you and Krapin eat one of the legs? You thought no one would notice? You decided that the Chekists can only count to three?"

"That's Marta," answered Artiom, thankful to Afanasiev for delivering him from his depressing thoughts. "She ran away last month," Artiom looked at Afanasiev significantly, "and she got caught in a trap. She chewed off her own leg so she could run away farther. Can you imagine such strength of will?"

Afanasiev became serious, but not for long, and the seriousness was dubious, because as he thought about it, he was staring at his hand, as though imagining — what if I get caught in a trap? How will I get out?"

A while ago, we brought Marta a male fox, and they lived together and started to settle in well. Artiom watched yesterday, enjoying it for a minute, until he got slight spasms in his chest.

"But the male — it doesn't bother him that she has three legs?" Afanasiev asked with interest and doubt.

"No," answered Artiom.

Afanasiev thought a little more and said, for the first time without the slightest smile, "I couldn't do it."

"Well yeah," Artiom agreed. "Although these days it's rare to find a woman with three legs."

They laughed so much about the three legs — Afanasiev, with his imagination, it seems, imagined it very vividly — that at first, they scared Marta, her male, and then they didn't notice Krapin.

"Good, citizen commander!" Afanasiev yelled as they do on the big island — on Fox Island there was no such custom.

Krapin grimaced and made a gesture like he was planning to crumple him up and hide him in his pocket to then throw him out into the stove.

"Artiom, what do you think, who's there?" Krapin asked, pointing at the sea.

A motor boat floated on the sea. The people in the boat were still indistinguishable.

Afanasiev, Artiom noticed, was so happy, it was as though Burtsev had summoned him — well, are we going to Finland or not?

Krapin, however, was a little worried. He had recently reported about all the foxes, brought them the photographs, what else did they need? Maybe the new head of the camp, Nogtev, was requiring his presence now?

All three stared, and though Afanasiev and Artiom's eyes were younger, the former policeman was still the first to recognize their guest.

"Galina is visiting," said Krapin. "She's become quite the frequent visitor. She's probably decided to find herself a fur coat in advance, the bitch."

Afanasiev stared at Artiom and didn't look away, his lips faintly trembling.

Artiom at first endured that glance, but then he turned and without especial friendliness asked, "What are you staring at, Afanas? Your eyes are gonna catch cold."

"I wanted to tell you, Tioma," whispered Afanasiev amicably, not offended at all, looking now at the back of Krapin as he walked towards the small wooden quay. "You know what else happened in the camp? You can lose your mind from it all!"

"Tell me quickly." The guests were already landing, and Galia stood up, but the boat started rocking, and she sat down again in the boat.

"Your Troianskii has a colleague in the iodine plant," Afanasiev said, cheerfully squinting. "He's just as high-browed. Troianskii's mother came, but as for his colleague, on the same boat, his daughter came to meet him. I saw her — angelic beauty, as though born with the flowers of spring…"

Artiom breathed out — hurry, hurry, why do I care about Troianskii and that daughter from the flowers!

"Two weeks later," Afanasiev continued steadily, for some reason sure that Artiom needed to hear this, "Citizen Eichmanis called this young woman to himself and said, 'If you agree to marry me, I'll let your father go immediately!' And the father had only finished three months of his five-year sentence. She immediately answered, 'Yes, I agree, only let him out first!'"

Artiom jumped, and, not believing it, stared at Afanasiev. At first glance, the story had nothing to do with Artiom at all, but from another perspective, not entirely understood, it had everything to do with him. And Afanasiev, the bastard, somehow knew about that.

"Then what?" asked Artiom, looking at the disembarking Galina or Krapin who was greeting her or Afanasiev.

"He let him go," said Afanasiev.

"You're lying," Artiom hissed through his teeth.

"The whole camp knows about it," Afanasiev calmly answered. "The father of this beauty left together with Shlabukovskii, on the same boat, while she's already with Eichmanis, only a few days ago. They say that they already got married in Kemi, not wanting to wait until Moscow…"

Artiom pressed his temples in with his fingers, quickly trying to understand how to relate to this most recent head-spinning news from the island.

"Oh, Afanas," Artiom almost groaned. "You don't have any more news, I hope? Did the allies arrive in the monastery on an airship? Did Lenin come back to life? Did the Tunguska meteorite fly back into the sky?"

Afanasiev thought about it and answered, "No, that didn't happen."

* * *

"My swoon. My darling. My dear one, my heart's desire. How I need you," Artiom repeated all day. He had never said such words to anyone.

But he couldn't say them to Galia. Krapin grabbed her into his loop and didn't let her go at all. Only one time he came for a minute, ran into a different hut, returned from there in cleaned boots and smelling of cologne.

He was extremely pleased that he had guessed the reason for her visit — it seemed that Galia immediately, even at the quay, had whispered to Krapin about the fur coat. Having found a quick moment, he mockingly whispered to Artiom in triumph: "I can see right through her. She's come to pick out her winter wardrobe, the bitch…"

"Hey you, Pinkerton," Artiom thought, "You've caught so many rascals, but one lady, and you're out to sea…"

Galia was wearing a prettily-tied head scarf. It looked very good on her.

It's true, Galia was giving off such feminine electricity, so full was that woman of readiness for hot human sport, that all the other workers of the nursery — the fox-cook, who was also the procurement officer — he was a former proprietor of a gambling joint — and the old Soviet embezzler of public funds, who was officially Krapin's assistant — he was also in charge of the radio, which, by the way, didn't work at all, as well as the motorboat captain, who had brought Galia — he had a completely criminal look, with two teeth beaten out and a predatory face — how was she not afraid to go with him? — and, of course, Krapin himself, his chest puffed out — all of them visibly cheered up and become almost the worse for wear.

Only Afanasiev held himself at a distance, though he still stared at the skirt as it walked passed him, examined how she sat and on what.

"What, did you announce a dance for the evening?" Artiom thought angrily, looking at all the men with distaste.

"No one guesses," he thought without any pleasure. "That all this — is here for me! So go away!"

He remembered how Galia, crazily, almost with anger, took off her blouse over her head, revealing her white armpits, washed with pure soap but still slightly smelling of sweat, her breasts bouncing up and down like the freshest bonnyclabber in huge bowls, and with her hungry, strong, angry hand she pulls Artiom to herself, and with quick gestures she touches him with her other hand on his back, his neck, the back of his head, his hip, not even caressing, but as though searching: where? Where is it? Where was that which you had there?

… Artiom's heart started to constrict; he stopped for short spells, looking around, as though he had sunstroke. Afanasiev also stood and silently waited, sometimes continuing to go on about nothing, familiarly mixing beautiful words with ugly ones and enjoying the resulting picture, but sometimes he was quiet and stared at Artiom with sarcastic gentleness.

"How is it that no one guesses," Artiom corrected himself, "when Afanas knows everything! How does he know, the dog?"

… And he once again got distracted by Krapin. For the first time in his life, Artiom felt jealous — so that's what it's like, I didn't even expect that. At least his jaw didn't creak, but when Galia went to Krapin's house to drink tea he was doused with heat, then with cold. He got all wound up when Krapin led her into the clinic… that shelf is in there… who knows what that crazy bitch would do? It would serve her right if he ran through the bushes to the window and, like a gull pecking with its bill, knocked on the glass.

All day he walked as though not himself. He didn't eat.

"You're not going to finish?" asked Afanasiev, nodding at his bowl with millet and fried fish tail. "Good." And he finished it off himself.

"Will she really leave without anything?" repeated Artiom, going outside, pulling in his stomach and swallowing his saliva with difficulty.

By the evening, a heavy, dreary wind rose up, the shields guarding the island started to rattle and a few of them fell. They raised them up again, reinforced them, freezing in the process… the foxes all hid in their apartments…

The sea was jumping, as though it was peeking in — what's there behind the shields? Is there something living there?

The motorboat captain said that it was dangerous to go back — they could flip over.

Galia waited for Krapin to offer her to stay, which he did immediately, and, seeming to think about it at first, agreed.

"Thank you, Lord!" exclaimed Artiom silently, almost snapping his teeth in his joy — that maddened wind: he would have hugged it if he could have grabbed it.

He looked at Krapin and realized that the old wolf had the same thought, only with the Lord — who did they, Artiom wondered, thank, these former policemen…?

"That's the right decision, a wise one," he kept repeating, squinting gently. "After all, today is our sauna day. Do you like saunas?" And he looked Galia in the eyes with a question, as though he had already decided who would be with her in there, whipping up the steam. "We even prepared the switches in advance," Krapin added, though it sounded as though he said, I have long waited for you and prepared everything.

Artiom wondered — should he jump on Krapin's shoulders to pull off that red, balding head off his broad, borsch-boiled neck?

As for the sauna, Galia, as was appropriate for a young, well-bred woman, much less a Chekist, said nothing… but she went there first, contrary to village custom, according to which the women always went last.

The wind hadn't calmed down, but the men still sat in the covered veranda of the clinic, exactly opposite the sauna. Krapin walked outside, as though to smoke, but in such a wind, no matter how much he hid his cigarette in his hand, it went out in half a minute and he walked back.

The rest in their turn examined the sauna in the hope either that Galia would forget herself and come out naked onto the porch to breathe, or they might find a previously unnoticed crack in the wall, or perhaps an entire corner of the sauna might suddenly fall down in this wind? Why? Doesn't that sometimes happen?

Artiom spit and took a walk around the island — maybe the shields had fallen again.

The sky had blackened, the sea was like boiling lead, it was truly cold — the wind in the open places seemed to be trying to take off one's clothing: get naked, boy, I'm going to tear you to pieces and throw the chunks to the fishes…

"Go back to all your salty demons of Solovki!" Artiom suddenly called aloud while walking.

"How do people survive winter here?" he thought for the first time, waving the wind away with his hand.

The shields stood in place, trembling.

Next to the quay, he came to the shore — the sea was rising to an ever-increasing, angry, blackening hysteria. He realized he was a little scared that he was all alone in front of this monstrosity. He stood at a distance, enchanted and slowly freezing.

In the foaming waters, he unexpectedly saw a large log. In a half minute, the waves cast it out to shore lightly.

It was a full six meters long.

Artiom approached carefully, looking at the sea: who had thrown it? He was still out there…

He gingerly touched the log with his hand — as though it could suddenly come alive and yell at him.

He noticed a sign on it, carved out with an axe. A bit more confidently, he cleaned off the seaweed that had stuck on it and read the following: "Save us. Solovki." Every "s" was sharp, like an arrowhead.

He thought for a short while and with unexpected anger rolled the log back into the sea, as though someone could have seen him reading this dangerous sign and he had to quickly get rid of the evidence.

"I can't read," he whispered. "That means this wasn't intended for me…"

He pushed the log into the water, and, not looking around, quickly left. At first, he felt that the log, once again returned to the sea, could fly back and strike him in the back … but the feeling passed.

There is no sea, no wind, nothing. Only the small window in the sauna.

How wonderful it would be if there was no one here on Fox Island, Artiom imagined. He alone would meet Galia on the beach, and they would immediately kiss on the mouth — oh, how wonderful it is to kiss the woman you love on the lips. Can there be anything better in this world?

The kiss would be salty at first, then slightly stale from the long wait, then immediately sweet, and sweet, and sweet again from joy.

… Into the sauna Artiom fell in, ready for the heat and to be beaten without pity by the switches of Solovki.

The men were already warming up there.

Galia had not called Krapin into the sauna after all, and so he tried to tear the fox-cook's soul from his body. That one screamed and ran away to cool down. The embezzler of public funds held on for a minute or two, but, when Krapin, angered by his tenacity, sprinkled a healthy portion of water on the stones and spun the switch around in a new, fiery arc, he also, his eyes bulging, ran towards the tub with cold water, into which he plunged his head in the hope that it would prevent his brains from being boiled into hardened yolk…

Only Afanasiev managed to endure the torture — he, pulling on his forelock, got red all over his body, but didn't scream once, enduring, biting his hand and screwing his eyes shut…

Tottering on his legs and grabbing the blackened walls, he walked naked outside.

"Where are you going? There's that… woman," the fox-chef tried to stop him, but Afanasiev heard nothing.

Krapin had no strength left to torture Artiom.

Artiom got on the top ledge that was strewn with birch leaves and got lost in his blessedness, his legs extended, his head covered with his arms, breathing out as though he were floating in a boiling river… suddenly he caught himself thinking that he was still happy — even in this Solovetsian middle-of-nowhere, in bondage, surrounded by human pain, on a small island that stank of fox, not far away from a crazy woman with whom he had fallen in love — he did love her, right…? And she had lain here, just before, on this very ledge, naked… if only he could find just one drop of sweat that had fallen off her…

"Hey! Move!"

Artiom turned onto his back, then sat down, his legs hanging, from time to time rubbing off the sweat and dirt off his chest with his right hand and listening to the confident beating of his heart.

Afanasiev added water to the stones.

They hissed like Zmei Gorynich, caught on a chain and tortured by people, whom he, given his freedom, would immediately devour. The breathing of that dragon was heady, aromatic, because they had fed him with only grass and tree bark since his capture.

The back of his head was burning and Artiom leaned forward a bit, got used to it, and in a short time felt that his heart had started to beat faster, as though it were trying to beat its way out of his ribcage. The sweat poured in four new streams, and his joy became thicker and hotter.

"My soul's been cooked like a baked potato," Afanasiev said huskily. "With such a soul, it'll be easier to live now…"

The evening turned out to be quite astonishing.

The chef laid out dinner in the administrator's hut on the large table. Krapin had probably commanded it, and it was clear why — he couldn't invite Galia to his own hut, now could he? But to send her alone to drink tea in an empty hut — that was simply inhospitable.

There was no wine on the table — it seemed that Krapin didn't drink, and if he did, he wouldn't have given it to anyone else. But after the sauna, everyone was in a pleasant, clean state of mind, smiling and amicable.

Artiom walked in when his friends had already gathered, and Galia sat unexpectedly happy, while the fox-chef hurried about her with pies — apple, cabbage, fish and one even with cheese — you could go mad, and then some.

"This is my house," Artiom suddenly imagined. "And she's my wife. I can't be jealous of anyone and can't feel bad about it, because when everyone will have drunk their tea and chatted to their heart's content, she will be left with me, and all night I will breathe in her warm neck.

"… Can that really be?" he asked himself.

"… It can. And it will," he answered himself. "Only I will never again drink whortleberry tea from the berries of Solovki."

And he pushed against the empty mug.

He looked somehow anew at the frivolously-talking Krapin, whose eyes even sparkled and became clearer.

"… But the day before yesterday," Krapin hoarsely laughed, then coughed, but also somehow cheerfully, continuing the conversation he had started himself. "I went with a fishing rod to catch some fish for myself to fry. With me came Fura — that's one of the foxes," explained Krapin, especially for Galia. "I pulled out my first. Fura's spinning around next to me: give me some! 'No,' I say, 'You've eaten already.' She barked, but I keep on fishing, we've got nothing more to say on the subject. Hey! Another one! And Fura does her dance again. My answer is the same. She says, oh, so that's how it's going to be? And grabs my tobacco pouch and runs away into the bushes. I left the fishing rod and went after her. She ran about for a while, then dropped the pouch in the bushes and continued on her merry way. Good thing I saw where she dropped the pouch, found it quickly. Rolled up a cigarette, walked back. Laughing. I got back to the shore and she, can you imagine? She'd eaten all my catch! She knew in advance, while she was carrying around my pouch, that she'd come back and have her revenge! But that's typical: she came closer just to enjoy the show of me jumping around with fury. But she picked a perfect distance, so that if I wanted to throw a rock at her, she'd have a chance to run away…! Eh?" And Krapin again looked at Galia, "Most people wouldn't come up with such an elaborate plan!"

He told another dozen stories about foxy characters; the chef played second fiddle and inserted a well-aimed word here and there. Artiom suddenly saw in his buttery eyes the afterglow of his previous, NEP-er life in Moscow's hot spots. The official assistant didn't know how to talk; however, he didn't ruin the general, pleasant picture. It was truly entertaining to listen to Krapin; Galia laughed in moderation, as though aware of her status, which even the sauna and tea hadn't fully removed, but still, she laughed from the heart. On the other hand, Afanasiev was crying from laughter and it seemed that he was filled with the gentlest emotions towards the former policeman. He hadn't even expected such solicitude and kindness from Krapin. But whoever sees and knows the beasts is inevitably wise also in the affairs of man.

They finished the pies, collected the dishes — Galia, of course, didn't even touch the empty cups, neither did she allow Krapin to help her with her Chekist's leather jacket: I'll do it myself, thank you.

Krapin determined that Galia would sleep in Artiom's house — where he used to sleep together with the inmate who had been bitten and now where he shared a roof with Afanasiev. The procurement officer found some clean sheets and pillow cases for their guest.

The motorboat captain slept in the sauna. Krapin was in his own hut, where, as the head of the nursery, he lived alone.

As for Artiom and Afanasiev, Krapin sent them to the third house on the island, where the chef (who was also the procurement officer) and his assistant (according to the paperwork) resided.

That house had an attic, dusty, but good enough for a single night's sleep.

Having laughed his fill and eaten his fill of pies, Afanasiev immediately fell down and snored.

Artiom tried with all his strength not to move and kept listening to what was going on downstairs. From the attic, he could have come down into the hut itself, or he could also exit along a ladder leading to the attic window. He still wanted to wait until everyone calmed down, not having to worry about making some noise, which was inescapable. The chef, as is the custom among chefs, started snoring immediately, while the paperwork-assistant kept his lamp lit an entire hour, apparently inspired by Galia's visit, he was writing something there, filling up tables and counting fox tails.

Finally, even he fell silent, having put out the light.

With a heaviness in his chest — as though he lay under a bag of wheat — Artiom waited some more time, trying to recite poems in his head — but he stopped halfway through, not making it after the first lines either to the executioner with his wife, nor to the devil who croaked by the swings, nor to the rabbits' eyes, nor one teasing under the trees…[44]

---

44 References to various famous poems of the Silver Age.

He hoped that more than half an hour had passed, but it was more likely fifteen heavy minutes instead.

Trying not to make any noise, Artiom got up and moved to the attic window… naturally, the floor creaked so loudly that it seemed the house would fall apart any moment… Artiom froze in place and decided to take two decisive steps, he thought it would be quieter in the end — and instead he smacked his head into a beam — he almost screamed from the pain... he sat for a moment to enjoy the golden dust in his eyes… he touched his forehead, licked his hand, was sure that he had cracked open half his head and was all covered in blood… but no, his hand was dry…

He pushed open the attic window; it howled into the darkness — good thing that the rain was falling a bit, its light knocking and tapping at least covered something.

But maybe not so much…

From the window, a completely not autumnal cold began to blow.

He spit at everything: "What if I need to go relieve myself? What? Do I have to prowl?" So he confidently climbed down, almost making a racket on purpose.

While he was going down the stairs, he leaned his head back so that the drops would fall on his cracked-open forehead. The rain was almost white in color, but he felt nothing on the wound, as though the rain was evaporating as it fell.

Having stepped on the ground, he felt like an animal that had escaped its cage — freedom, and nothing else.

Without looking around, he hurried to the hut where Galia was spending the night.

She looked out the window as soon as he had barely touched it with his finger.

"She wasn't sleeping," it pinged his heart.

"You didn't see Krapin?" she asked, smiling. Her voice was well audible through the glass. "He came an hour ago, asked to give his report."

"What did you say?" asked Artiom, standing at the window, as though he were not hurrying inside.

"What do you mean what did I say? I asked if he wanted to visit Sekirka — there he could give as full a report as he'd like."

* * *

… She was doing awful things… Asked him to touch everything, to scratch her, to brag, and she herself scratched him and knew no shame in anything, as though she had never before met a person with a different anatomy and wanted to learn it by heart forever, in the most excruciating detail…

It was the first time she was completely naked with him; he went completely mad from it.

"How can it be?" Artiom thought afterwards, without any sorrow, but only in a tremulous and grateful astonishment. "In bodily union, this woman from the beginning nestles so much closer than with any emotional connection. And she is filled with the physical so much earlier than with the emotional. Shouldn't it be the other way around?"

"How could it be the other way around here?" Artiom laughed at himself. "You would have taken her arm-in-arm on walks to the sea for three months first?"

Any possibility for it to be otherwise simply didn't exist. To know each other, they had to get completely naked.

The fox once again ran across the roof, constantly changing its place — Galia had yet to hear such noise and scrabbling.

"Who's that?" Galia noticed the foxy footfalls a bit late; before that, she only heard what was going on inside her.

"It's a fox, a fox."

"Why is it on the roof?"

"It's warm there."

"Oh yes... Krapin warmed it up…" And she threw the blanket off herself.

She lay — quiet, like a saint. Only a bit giggly, and she didn't want to look him in the eyes. While the saints do look, and always in the eyes.

Artiom leaned on his elbow and caressed her stomach.

My meek one. My delight.

She smiled. Her lips stuck together slightly and she finally looked at him, squinting in the darkness, as though she were nearsighted, and Artiom felt such an awful gentleness towards those eyes and those lips, such pain, such life inside him.

She knew what he was thinking.

"When you take my clothes off, it's as though I've come out of the ocean, I'm purified," said Galia. "I'm not ashamed. Right now, I'm so clean, as clean as I've never been."

"Yes," said Artiom, not meaning that he agreed, but that he was listening to her.

Then he thought and leaned towards her face, whispering into her ear, because to say this aloud would have been embarrassing: "Un-bear-a-ble… joy… though I'm inside… you…" and the rest in a quick patter, "with only a small part of me…" then was quiet, and finished, "What if it was possible to be completely inside you? With all my blood to flow through all of you, all… its heaven there!"

"… Stupid, stupid, stupid…" Galia answered, having thought a bit, as though listening in to her temperature inside. "It's not heaven in there. It's so hot that only I can bear it…"

Artiom laughed quietly and breathed on her a little above her chest, his mouth almost on her skin — in childhood, he used to breathe on windows like that, trying to see the street, the cabby, the posters on the corner.

"Why did you ask that time about Esenin?" he suddenly remembered that day when Galia had called him in and scared him.

"I love him," she answered simply. "And also, Utkin, Marienhof, Lugovskii… Tikhonov."

"Really?" Artiom asked.

"Why not?" she asked with a certain, barely evident, annoyance. "Who else should I love?"

He looked at her in surprise and joy, as though every time he took off her clothing, it was a new set every time, then, he took another layer off her already naked body, then another, third invisible cover, and every time he found her again, only even better.

Galia found her blouse and asked him to turn around.

He listened, but thought to himself, "She was just lying here without anything on and didn't ask me to turn away, but as soon as she starts dressing, it's 'turn around!' She's funny."

Now Galia sat in her blouse and nothing else, and it looked very good on her.

But, looking around and finding nothing nearby, she covered herself up to her waist with the blanket — evidently, she was planning on saying something that you shouldn't say while undressed.

"I have some very good news for you," said Galia triumphantly and with a completely unknown voice, not in her feminine, gasping, blubbering voice, but also not in her authoritative, unbearable and chilling one. It was a third one. "Your mother's come to visit you. She asked permission to visit you, and I gave it to her." Galia looked Artiom in the eyes.

Artiom blinked and turned away.

"And she came immediately," Galia repeated; and, not waiting for an answer, asked, "What's the matter?"

"Yes, good," he said, but the lie was too obvious, all the more so because internally, with sorrow and disgust, Artiom kept repeating, "Why all this? What are you doing all this time, Galia! I didn't ask you for the favor with Avdei Sivtsev and Zahar either… no sooner had I fallen greedily on your white titties… I'm cattle, cattle!"

"What's wrong with you?" Galia kept asking him in a different intonation, a lot louder. "You don't want to see your mother?" Artiom raised his eyes but didn't say anything. "I got a boat on purpose to come and get you… to give you… joy! Your mother is waiting for you! And you don't want to go?" As though she couldn't at all understand what was going on, she kept asking, but instead of answering, Artiom caressed his cheek, it was bristly, rough, but hot and kissed. "What are you? A monster?" she asked with powerless anger, and even her hands — ready just a moment ago to slap him across the cheek — seemed to lose their strength.

Her questions made it sound as though he were rejecting her — Galia — not his mother. As though she had found out something about him, something that made any intimacy between them impossible — what right had he, after such behavior, to see her and breathe on her skin?

"Everything's going to end badly again right now…" Artiom understood. "Why does everything end so badly for me every time…? As soon as I'm happy, that everything is fine, everything goes wrong."

"I will go, I'll go," he said hurriedly, though he dimly understood that he didn't have to go anywhere, someone whispered to him that he couldn't do it, but he didn't hear the hint and repeated a second time, "I'll go, I'll go, I'll go. I was just very surprised. I'm here… and suddenly my mother." Artiom was trying to charm Galia and he even began to believe his tongue-twister; after all, how could she expect him not to be surprised? But now he understood everything, and he was very grateful to her — not everyone got a visit, and here she made a holiday for him — what a good, good, good, Galia she is. Kind and gentle, he must do everything not to offend her.

At first, she didn't believe him at all, then she believed him a little bit, the very smallest bit, then she gave up a little and believed a little more, later, she even let him kiss her, without pleasure, half turning away… but the next kiss landed on her lips and her lips opened, and though her mouth was tired, it was hot… Artiom threw off the annoying blanket and discovered that she was hot and ready all over — only her eyes were cold, but we'll kiss those eyes right now, kiss them and warm them up, only the blanket… it's completely unnecessary, even on your feet.

* * *

While he was at Galia's, an unexpected snow fell — evidently it was falling constantly while they were scratching each other in there. It wasn't a puffy snow, but it fell in an even, brittle layer.

It fell and went on its course towards the big island.

Everything around was new, never before seen.

"What? It's not bad," Artiom decided, having had his fill. "The stars above, the snow below."

"It's good!" he repeated, deciding to leave the thoughts of his mother for tomorrow, and hurried back to his room.

In about fifteen steps, he looked back in hope — maybe Galia was looking at him — and at that moment terror pinched his heart — his clear tracks led directly from the hut, and he stood at the end of his path like an exclamation point.

"Damn! Devil take me!" Artiom suddenly swore.

Sweeping the tracks aside with his feet, he returned back.

Behind him remained a black, unkempt line, leading still to the hut. As though Artiom flew by on a broom, jumped off near the house and walked the rest of the way on hands and knees — accept your slave, O princess! Warm him in your skirts!

"What do people do in such cases?" Artiom thought, still drunk from his unimaginable joy, still sure that he would think of something. "Maybe I can confuse the trail? What if I walk backwards?"

Artiom tried it. It was even worse, as though he came to Galia and decided not to go back.

"Krapin will come out in the morning — he's a policeman through and through — and immediately he'll determine, by the size of the footprint, who slept at Galia's. He'll ask, 'What are your footprints doing there?' 'How do I know?' I'll answer. 'What if Afanasiev was walking about in my shoes?'"

"Good idea!" Artiom rejoiced. "He's sleeping soundly. I'll put my shoes on his feet. Take that, Afanas, for your cards!"

"And what about Galia? She'll be under suspicion of being visited during the night by red-headed poets."

He tried once again to walk like all people walk — face-forward — the same picture turned out. It was impossible to tell how he ended up at Galia's, and how he walked back to the attic. The entire nursery in the morning would see that path.

"Maybe I should lead the trail to the sea?" Artiom thought. "Everyone will think I've drowned! But then — hello! — I'm in my room, sleeping. 'What's the matter?' I'll ask in confusion in the morning, when Krapin's huge head will announce itself in the attic. 'Why aren't you in the sea?' Krapin will ask, his policeman sense unhappy with the loose ends. 'Why should I be in the sea, what am I, the ship Gleb Bokii?'"

No, that wouldn't work either.

Artiom grabbed a rake that stood near the threshold and went a little towards his attic, dragging away the snow behind him.

That ended up as completely incomprehensible nonsense. Everywhere the snow lay like snow — lying down, not moving — but next to the house, where Galia slept, it looked like a tractor had driven by.

"Well, let them figure out who drove to her on a tractor at night…" Artiom tried to make himself laugh, but it wasn't funny anymore. The tractor still plowed its way directly from the attic to her hut.

"Maybe I can sweep up the snow on the entire island?" He approximated. "It's just enough work till morning… Or at least near Galina's house. Krapin will come out and say, there's a miracle! Snow fell on the entire island, but this house was covered as though with a dome… Maybe the policeman will come to believe in God?"

There was nothing else to do. Artiom decided to overturn as much snow as possible with the rake and to return by crooked paths through the clinic. The important thing was for no one to appear, or he would have to explain himself. Well, yes, I decided to clean up a bit, or else there's snow everywhere. It's untidy…"

Attracted by the bustle, three eternally hungry cats descended on Artiom. The dog too, in the hope that someone would play with him — with that rake, for example! Fura herself got down from the roof, licking the snow off her paws… Artiom stood in the middle of all the animals like a young, lost Santa Claus. He tried to scare them off — that didn't work. The dog, for example, only got excited and started to bark, while the cats didn't stop hoping that Artiom would pull out a fish from his pocket, and Fura wasn't afraid of anything. She only looked at the cats with a secret thought — maybe she should eat something other than constant fish, fish…

The sound of an opening window rang out; dumbfounded, Galia looked out in her blouse.

Artiom raised the rake and greeted her, trying to smile. He had to say something, but what?

"What? Have you lost your marbles?" she asked vehemently, looking at the animals and his beloved in their midst. "What are you doing with that rake?"

He had no answer.

* * *

By morning, the snow was all gone. Only yesterday they had brought forty buckets full of snow from a lost storm cloud, but today every trace of it had evaporated.

No one noticed anything. The traces of cat and dog paws remained in the freezing dirt, but nothing else.

Only a fir tree next to the clinic stood like an idiot in a not-quite-melted dirty-white cap and a shabby apron.

"We have to go, or there'll be another sudden storm," Galia said to Krapin.

They met on the open space between the clinic, sauna and administrative building.

Artiom and Afanasiev sat on the covered porch of the clinic. Afanasiev was quiet and nervous. He was intensely expecting Artiom to fulfill his request.

"Of course," Krapin answered Galina.

It seems that he was uncomfortable about last night; he himself couldn't understand how such a thing could have occurred to him; with the reports… at night… But everything was easily explained. Today, yesterday's stupefying electricity didn't emanate from this woman.

But her black, small head, surrounded by the cloudy sky, agitated Artiom.

"Goriainov's mother has arrived for a meeting; he's coming with me on the boat," said Galina.

Krapin smiled and waved at Artiom.

"Did you hear?"

Artiom got up and smiled in answer, a little forced, "Yes sir!"

"Why didn't you say anything?" Krapin yelled; they were generally talking louder than they should — you could hear everything as it was. "Bring the package here; don't eat everything on the say!"

Artiom nodded, and this time it wasn't hard to smile.

He had nothing to gather — he hoped to come back soon — and what was there to do on the big island? It was better to wait here for his Galia. He only took his pass through the St. Nicholas gates and put on his wool socks, or his feet would freeze.

His room had been cleaned by a feminine hand — he didn't even understand how that looked exactly, but his heart was warmed. As he was running out, Artiom grabbed his pillow and smelled it — it smells! It smells of her hair! — and at first threw the pillow back on the bed, then returned and hid it under the blanket: maybe that would preserve the smell.

"Well, goodbye. I'll let Nogtev know about your accountability," Galia said dryly to Krapin, who was about to accompany her to the boat. Artiom guessed that she didn't want any sendoff — damn all those sentiments…

Krapin himself was uncomfortable with all that was going on, so he took it under advisement, turned around and hurried back to the nursery. His Fura, gentle to the point of obsequiousness, ran to greet him.

"It's a good thing she can't talk," thought Artiom, "or she'd let it all slip right now…"

They walked silently to the quay. Artiom kept slightly behind her.

The captain was already sitting in the boat.

Finally, Galia, not looking around, hiding her obvious enjoyment in her strict voice, said, "Go ahead. You're staring at me."

Artiom, chuckling, walked around her and quickly turned around to look in Galina's face. At the same time, he saw Afanasiev, who was walking at a distance, without a hat, unbuttoned, not daring to speak up — like a forgotten dog.

There were about twenty steps left until the quay. Already at the boardwalk, Artiom turned with his back to the sea and nonchalantly said loudly, so that his friend, who had felt something was about to happen and hurried forward, could hear, "We have to take Afanasiev with us!" He showed Galina with his hand: over there. "Citizen Krapin sent him to get some medicines from the monastery."

"You have the papers?" Galina asked, looking the unbuttoned Afanasiev over from head to toe, but avoiding his fawning glance.

Afanasiev, smiling from ear to ear, slapped his pocket — there it is!

Saying nothing, with her usual distant face, Galia sat in the front.

Of course, Afanasiev had no papers.

When they disembarked, the motor roared and Krapin ran out to the shore, waving his hands; however, only Artiom saw him, because he was seated with his face to the island, and he looked away at once.

Yesterday's log was lying again on the shore, waiting for a person who had been taught to read.

Their trip wasn't long, but Artiom had time to freeze till he was blue.

Galia didn't look at Artiom a single time, always past him.

"Is she really that mad… about my mother?" Artiom guessed, twitching. "No… She just doesn't want Afanasiev to notice… Damn shore, when's it going to draw near?"

The kremlin appeared in the fog like a threat.

On the landing, Galina, saying goodbye to no one, walked away silently, as though she had been alone in the motor boat; if something had been lying there, it was only some packages with dirty garbage — let someone else deal with it.

Artiom understood everything, of course, but he still shivered from the cold gathered during the journey as well as his foolish resentment.

"Passion makes a person suspicious," for the first time in his life, he formed a thought that wasn't a shot in the dark, but paid for by experience, even if it was small.

Along the way to the St. Nicholas gate, Afanasiev touched him by the shoulder and stopped him on the road.

"You took me, and I owe you, Tioma," he said.

Artiom didn't feel his toes at all. If only he could climb back into yesterday's sauna.

"Nonsense," Artiom said, unclenching his lips with difficulty, glancing at the soldiers who were stomping in place at their posts — their shoes were still meant for summer. He nodded: let's go quickly, Afanas.

But the other made a face: wait, listen, this is important.

"Tioma, you need to know this," said Afanasiev, looking to the side. "When they sent me here… Burtsev told me to try you out casually about Galina. And if she were to come to Fox Island — Burtsev knew for some reason that she would — he commanded me to spy on you both."

Artiom felt slightly nauseous. And immediately — as though someone had picked him up, flipped him over feet up, then put him back down harshly — his head started spinning.

"Did you spy on us?" he asked and suddenly understood that Afanasiev didn't sleep last night, but pretended to fall asleep immediately on purpose, to allow Artiom the chance to leave.

"He knows everything about you two, Tioma," said Afanasiev, continuing to look away, "You two should be more careful. Especially you. All they'll do to her is kick her out of here, but they'll add five years to your time and put you in such an icebox that… well, they'll kill you, Tioma."

"It's none of your goddamned business, red," said Artiom and clenched his blue jaw until his gums hurt.

"You're right; it's not," he agreed without being offended.

Artiom, pushing him slightly with his shoulder, walked on towards the St. Nicholas gates on stiff legs.

Afanasiev immediately followed, talking quietly, audibly, but as though without punctuation, "If you were released, you'd never even look at her. She's totally average. She's only beautiful because she's in authority. If she were a train conductor, you would turn away and forget her. Have a care, Tiom."

Artiom turned around fiercely, but Afanasiev, figuring it out immediately, took two deft steps back, though without any fear in his eyes: "Yes, I know, I know. You can. I've seen it. No need, brother. I love you."

"Love?" Artiom asked with unexpected hoarseness in his voice, as though he had ripped off an old bandage with the scab. "Did you plant the cards on me, pig?"

Afanasiev grimaced, as though for a moment something seized up under his ribs somewhere, and he didn't answer.

"So go ahead and f…" Artiom commanded.

In the monastery courtyard — he would have been happy not to see it for another age — things seemed to have changed, but at first, they weren't clear.

Yes, there were hardly any gulls left and their screaming was much weaker. Yes, they had swept and cleaned up for the arrival of the new head of the camp. And there were a lot fewer loitering inmates, as though they had found work for everyone.

Black was the same and recognized Artiom, but Bear was a little skinnier and looked frozen.

Near the entrance to IID stood a soldier from the watch brigade and Burtsev stood next to him, holding the solider by the chin as though his arm was stuck in a cramp.

"What sort of unshaved cheek is that, pig?" Burtsev kept repeating. "What sort of bristle? Eh, pig? Maybe you're planning to be a conquistador?"

Artiom hurried to run back into his former room, realizing that he had two thoughts at the same time — Afanasiev was right, that dandy's gathered some serious power if he's taking the soldiers to task like that! And: the soldier probably thinks that "conquistador" is a German swear word.

It was so cold that Artiom forgot all his thoughts, even as he was running up the stairs. The important thing was to get warm, to get warm, or he would get sick, he was probably already sick.

In his former rooms — O, wonder! — it was almost as warm as in a sauna, clean, joyful.

Troianskii's mother looked at her son in confusion, but Artiom didn't notice the answering glance or gesture, because while he was walking, he threw off his frozen shoes and immediately fell onto the bed, facedown.

"That's my mother's bed, you know," Troianskii said angrily.

"Hit me on the back with a pillow, musketeer," thought Artiom blessedly.

He suddenly remembered how he smacked Troianskii a month and a half ago on the lips — not hard, but with a rebound so sharp that his neck had almost snapped.

However, judging by Osip's speech, his mouth had healed.

"We're leaving anyway, Osip," said his mother quietly.

Artiom felt that they were talking about him as though he were a drunk or crazy person.

"Where are they leaving?" thought Artiom. "Are they actually letting him go on an unguarded research trip?"

"Oi!" Osip unexpectedly shrieked.

Artiom tensed a bit, but still didn't turn around.

"What's that?" said the mother.

"A safety pin," answered Osip some time later. "It was in my pocket."

"You never did let me wash your pants, Osip," said his mother rebukingly. "Where did you get a safety pin? Why?"

"I bought it for him," said Artiom, constantly wiggling his melting toes and sweetly breathing in the smell of clean sheets that had been washed no longer than a day ago.

Judging by the silence, Artiom guessed, in an incredible way, that both the mother and the son were looking at his wriggling toes in their wet socks. Osip had disgust on his face, while his mother was filled with an automatic desire to take off the socks and dry them on the stove.

"I think I've learned how to see with the back of my head," Artiom chuckled.

It was good to lie with his face in the pillow — he could even stick his tongue out at people, and they wouldn't see it.

A minute later, the Troianskiis left. It seemed that Osip went to bid goodbye to his colleagues in the iodine plant, while mothers will always find womanly things to do.

Artiom turned his head, squinted and saw a huge suitcase and a canvas bag — they were actually leaving! What's going on…?

… Afterwards, he was never able to figure out how that simple and at the same time horrible thought appeared in his mind, so horrible that it literally made him jump up from the bed.

It probably started from the fact that he registered the departure of the Troianskiis, then he thought that he was alone and to hell with the Troianskiis, he'll wait it out here, then he remembered that the red-headed Petersburg swine was planning to flee and to hell with him too, but then he vividly saw Burtsev, rebuking the Red Army soldier and Afanasiev's words about Burtsev's plan to seize the artillery during their flight surfaced in his mind… but they're going to kill all the Chekists! It pierced through Artiom. And then, more importantly — they're going to shoot Galia! They're going to shoot Galia for sure! All the Chekists from IID live in the same building — the former Petrograd dormitory behind the Administrative Building. They're going to go there at night and shoot everyone!

All these thoughts fit into a single moment, less than a moment — Artiom even had time to imagine how Galia would open her door to see about the noise and shots — she was probably used to the drunk debauches of the Chekists, but this time the uniformed scum had gone overboard and hurriedly putting on an overcoat over her half-naked body, she takes a step into the common corridor, angry and sleep-deprived, turns to the sound of feet and they immediately stab her with a bayonet into the stomach, because the maddened, bloodied inmate didn't have time to reload his rifle — Galia didn't even have a chance to look at his face.

Artiom grabbed his head, lest it explode.

"Idio-o-t!" he sang aloud. "Idiot! What an idiot! Your habit of thinking nothing and floating downstream will kill you! And enough about you, it'll kill her!

He had to do something. This isn't brushing away the snow with a rake. Yesterday's fears seemed idiotic, childish… What's the importance of prints in the snow when this was taking shape! This… what? Evildoing? But Artiom didn't consider it to be evildoing — not for a moment did he doubt that the inmates had every right to flee — they were being killed here after all — they're fleeing to try to live. Who dares forbid them?

But… Galia? What about Galia? She's probably done evil to plenty of people here — they'll certainly want to kill her. Those whom she forced to become snitches — they'll do it first. Those whom she gave over to her… what's his name? Tkachuk, who knocks out teeth. Can such a thing be possible? Or did she lie to Artiom about that?

What difference did it make? They'll still shoot her, knife her, stab her, trample her.

"What should I do?" thought Artiom in a fever. "To tell Galia that they're planning to flee? To arrest everyone and execute them? Horrible! That's just horrible! I can't even think about that."

To tell Galia that they need to quickly get back to Fox Island? And what? She'd listen to him?

To tell Afanasiev that they dare not kill Galia?

"Ha! Ha! Ha!" Artiom answered himself out loud, for some reason remembering Shlabukovskii.

To kill Burtsev? To call him into this room and choke him?

Madness, madness, madness, what madness.

Someone knocked on the door and it immediately opened. Troianskii's mother stood in the doorway.

"Forgive me, of course it's none of my business, but your mother has come to visit you," she said. "They won't let her into the monastery here, only Fiodor Ivanovich gave me a pass. You can get a pass in the IID to leave the monastery to see her. Everyone who comes for a visit is put in a barracks not far from the monastery. You can even get permission to spend the night with your family. They have special rooms for inmates."

Artiom nodded several times: yes, yes, yes. I understand, understand, understand. Good-good-good.

The door closed.

"And then there's mother, mother, mother," thought Artiom, clenching his head with all his strength.

* * *

When they announced the evening inspection, he wanted to hide and not go, but an unfamiliar duty officer appeared, swore at him horribly, even tried to hit him. Artiom looked at him with slight confusion: what? Have you gone insane?

"I'll break him into pieces right now and put him into the crate for dry rations," he imagined tiredly, lazily avoiding the swinging hand of the duty officer.

Artiom hadn't come up with anything concerning Galia — how would he talk to her anyway? Go to IID and order them: "Get me Galina!" They would definitely let him have it in the teeth.

He didn't go to his mother either; basically, he knew immediately that there would be no meeting.

The inspection was a general one for all brigades.

The inmates languished. It was a little warmer and yesterday's snow was forgotten, as though it was an inappropriate dream.

Over their head, young gulls flew. The rare older gulls who were supposed to take the young ones any day now to the south, far away from the nature on Solovki that had gone insane this year, walked around the yard and didn't waste their energy.

Artiom didn't know anyone in the brigade in which he stood, taking a place in the second row.

He saw many new faces even in the other brigades — they probably got sent here while he was on Fox Island.

He tried to find Vasilii Petrovich in the twelfth, but instead immediately saw Passport, who saw him too and bared his teeth…

Artiom turned away.

"Why did Galia bring me out here? What can I do here?" He asked himself again, but very weakly, as though his thoughts had gone hoarse. He knew in advance that there would be no answer.

Someone was trying to talk and immediately the guards and the brigade commanders descended on him with their bludgeons bared — they beat him with pleasure, angrily, taking pains.

"Things have gotten stricter," Artiom understood. He saw everything as though from the side and couldn't believe that he was the same as all the other inmates. No, he was here by accident and his place was on a small island, where Fura was on the roof, with Krapin and the fox-cook from the gambling den… "Well, I never…" Artiom remembered. "They incarcerated Krapin for shooting up an entire gambling den, and now look… he's living with the same sort of hustler side by side."

Artiom shivered, once again remembering where he was, and looked towards the St. Nicholas gates — they were so close! Just a minute's walk. And then he'd be off to his hut, if only he could find a boat.

One time, Burtsev walked along the line, full of himself and looking at no one.

Galina wasn't there.

They had been standing an hour already. Many tried to sleep on their feet, leaning with their shoulders against their neighbor. But those looking after general order didn't like that, and once again someone got it with the bludgeon, someone screamed from the unexpectedness, and the scream was so pitiful that people in the lineup laughed — it was funny, after all, when it was so unexpectedly painful for someone.

Another hour and a half later, Nogtev appeared. Artiom couldn't make him out at all — it was noticeably darker already.

The head of the camp loudly greeted the inmates of Solovki.

"Good!" they all yelled not together.

Artiom didn't yell.

Nogtev, evidently, remained unsatisfied with the greeting. He waved at some Chekist, who greeted the inmates one more time instead of him. "Good!" they all yelled again, a little better. Two, "Good!" Three, "Good!" all the gulls flew up as the guards ran along the lines searching for those who were not yelling with enough enthusiasm, and Artiom started to open his mouth and whisper out "Good…" just in case, or perhaps there was a snitch nearby…? Who cares, he still wouldn't stay here… but the tenth time, Artiom decided to scream and on the twentieth time, it all turned out really well, but to make it stick, they yelled another twelve times and thus the greeting was concluded.

They were so tired that they were ready to lie down and fall asleep in the courtyard.

The third hour of the inspection began.

Nogtev walked along the line in a sprawling gait, from time to time pointing at someone with his revolver; then that inmate would be pulled out by the scruff and immediately taken away. Evidently, some people got immediate solitary for infractions known only to the head of the camp.

"Put your beard higher, priest, you'll see your God soon," Nogtev bid Father Zinovii farewell on his way to the common labors.

Zinovii blinked often and kept whispering something.

It was the second brigade's turn.

Artiom decided not to look at Nogtev. He looked at the back of the neck of the inmate standing in front of him.

"Who here is going to the guard-less research trip?" Nogtev asked in a bass voice.

Troianskii was pushed out of line. Then they pushed him painfully in the back, and he, finally, said, "Me."

"Oh dear, Osip's here too," Artiom only then recognized him, but he didn't look at his former neighbor. He froze in place and didn't breathe, so no one would notice, distinguish, remember him.

"If you're not back by November 7, I'll shoot every tenth person in your brigade," Nogtev said to Troianskii directly into his face. "Got it?"

Troianskii was again poked in the back, but he couldn't for the life of him remember with what letter the proper answer began, and they all poured out of him mixed up, confused, and very fast, "You.. bz… Yes!"

Nogtev walked on, from brigade to brigade, with humorous catch-phrases and swear words coming out all the while, but at the same time boringly and drearily holding court — it all smelled of sorrow and emotional debauchery.

The submissive and oppressed look of the inmates loudly proclaimed that such inspections and personnel shake-ups had happened already more than once.

"… Such a person would easily shoot from his revolver at the newly-arrived work groups," Artiom suddenly remembered.

During the fourth hour, an uneasy pilot joined the rump of Nogtev's posse, and at the first available glance of the head of the camp, he shyly pointed at his watch.

He commanded them all to disperse.

For some time, everyone still stood: was it a joke? They're not going to push up back to our sleeping quarters with bludgeons?

Finally, not recognizing their own feet, the inmates, confused and bunching up, went each to his sleeping quarters.

Artiom also, trying to be inconspicuous and hurrying, moved in the direction of his room; to see both Passport and Shaferbekov, he had neither the strength nor the desire, but he didn't know how he would deal with Troianskii — would they come back for their last night or not?

As he was entering the abbot's wing, the duty officer caught him by the sleeve.

"Goriainov? You're ordered to go to IID," he called it "eye-eye-deez," tripping on the "z" with uneasiness, as though he guessed that letter wasn't necessary, but not knowing how to end on a vowel.

"What's going on now?" Artiom was slightly uneasy. "Not Burtsev, I hope…? I didn't do anything, did I…?"

"No, of course not," he answered himself habitually. "You've only deserved to sit the rest of your time on Sekirka…"

In IID, unexpectedly, several windows were illumined — either Burtsev's meticulousness had forced his new colleagues to work longer hours, or the new head of the camp required it of them; maybe it was both.

He announced himself to the duty officer; he felt a bit sick from worry.

A soldier came out to lead the inmate upstairs.

Second floor. Third. Galia's office.

He opened the door, asked, "Can we come in?" And pushed in Artiom.

Galia sat at her desk.

Looking at her now, he once again forgot to even think about the fact that this was the woman who…

In the room, it was dark. The white nights and white evenings had finished, and the single weak lamp didn't give the room enough illumination.

Artiom had never been here this late.

"Bastard, why won't you go visit your mother?" the question came immediately. Galia spoke through her teeth, as though she were letting out the words with difficulty. "Jackal! Do you have a conscience?"

"Why can't you open your mouth?" thought Artiom, making a face. "I know how it opens for you…"

He stood at the door still.

"Sit on the stool," said Galia and got up.

He walked to her desk and saw that under the glass there was now neither one nor the other portrait — only some papers with writing. Her hand was elegant and easy to read.

"Too bad I can't read upside down," Artiom was almost seriously upset. "What if this is written there: 'Assign a date for Goriainov's execution' with three question marks?"

Galia drank some water — she was trying to calm down.

"You're not at all ashamed, Tiom?" she asked in a completely different voice. "Before your own mother?"

He didn't want to talk about it so much that he actually felt sick from it. He didn't even want to remember it; he hadn't remembered it once during his entire time at Solovki.

And his mother's arrival was unnecessary also, because it was simultaneously a remembrance and an echo — and why? And why?

But he couldn't avoid answering Galia's question, especially in her office, where in one of the cabinets, his own file lay, and, probably, all the accusations from snitches. He had enough of those to cut off a single, huge life with a single, small death.

"No, I'm not ashamed," he said, feeling no saliva in his mouth, making his words dry and cracking.

"How? How did this happen?"

Artiom swallowed his saliva — oh, can't she understand the inappropriateness of such questions and all this emotional conversation in prison, in her office, where people sometimes break backbones and crush internal organs…

"My mother, my brother… and I… came home… from our dacha. My brother got sick, and we came back to the city in the middle of August, unexpectedly." He started talking as though it was a duty that needed to be done quickly. "I walked in first. My father was with a woman. He was naked… We started screaming at each other… screaming, helter-skelter… my father was drunk and he grabbed a knife, my brother was shrieking, my mother reached to choke the woman, the woman also attacked my mother, I attacked my father, my father attacked the women… and in that confusion…" Here Artiom grew silent, because he had said everything.

"You killed your father because of the insult to your mother?" Galia asked one more time, her brows knitted.

Artiom once again made a pained face, as though there wasn't too little light, but too much, more than the human eye could bear.

"That woman… It wasn't so much that I was upset that he was with her… It was horrible that he was naked… I killed my father for his nakedness."

Artiom suddenly spread his knees and let a long, sticky string of saliva fall on the floor. He didn't wipe it off.

Galia looked at all this, but said nothing.

She truly needed to understand Artiom.

"There is nothing in your file about any woman," she said quietly.

"I said nothing during my interrogation about the woman," said Artiom.

Galia yelped from her chair: "What do you mean? Why not?"

"My mother said nothing either — she was ashamed… before people. She's stupid."

"What about you? Do you have a brain?" Galia asked, her eyes wide. Artiom naturally understood what she was on about. If she and his mother had said that there was a woman involved that could have changed the verdict. The only thing was, he didn't want to tell Galia that not only was his mother ashamed. He was ashamed too, only not before other people. But before whom, Artiom didn't know. Maybe before the father he killed…?

There was no answer to her question, and who needed it anyway? Artiom definitely didn't.

"Yes," he said to Galia to conclude the conversation.

He kept thinking about whether or not it was a good time to talk about all the insane stories of Afanasiev.

During the evening inspection, seeing Nogtev, it suddenly seemed completely impossible to Artiom — everything that the red-head had been saying on Fox Island. What seizing of artillery? What flight? There were armed soldiers all around. What? Was Burtsev going to pull out his revolver and take them all prisoner? Insanity!

Tomorrow morning the ship would leave and, by the way, take Troianskii with it, and there would be nothing for the conspirators to seize and everything that so sickened and tortured Artiom would end up a fantasy of the red-headed fantasist, whose brain had been blown away by the winds of Solovki.

But at least he should say something about Burtsev — that he knows everything about them.

And also not to forget to speak about Avdei Sivtsev and Zahar, so that she would do something and let them both go.

What should he start with?

"Galia, you need to know," Artiom began and immediately, dumbfounded by the sound of firing somewhere either very close or on the next floor down, he jumped up, dropping his stool…

"Sit down!" yelled Galia, more in habit, as she screamed at many who ended up in her office.

"It's begun!" the thought rattled in Artiom's head. "They've decided to do it!"

"Galia, stop!" he called, running up to the doors. "It's a conspiracy! They're trying to escape!"

"Shut up!" looking back at him with a twisted face, she almost shrieked, like a peck across his forehead, and went into the corridor.

In the corridor, the Chekists were yelling in different voices, like they would in a fire.

"He's here! Here! Ready!"

"Dead?"

"Dead?"

"Is he dead?"

"Wounded! He almost got Tkachuk, the bastard!"

Artiom walked around the room several times — what should he do? Where should he go? Whose side was he on?"

In a minute, a pale, but calm Galia returned, with a darkened look. She put her revolver back in its drawer.

"They've arrested Burtsev in his office. He shot at them. Now they've gone to the sleeping quarters. They're going to arrest some more people. I know nothing about all this. Go back and spend the night in your room; tomorrow I'm sending you back to Fox Island. I'll get a soldier right now."

* * *

The soldier accompanied him only to the exit of the IID building.

It smelled of weapons, powder, nervousness, insanity, fear, whitewash pierced with bullets.

Every Chekist that ran past Artiom looked him in the face, as though they were suspecting him of being a detailed conspirator.

"We need to get all the files from his office," two of them were saying to each other as they rose up the stairs. Artiom guessed that they were speaking about Burtsev, about all the material he had gathered on them.

Afanasiev had been right, right, right.

There were unexpectedly many Chekists in the building, as though they had all come out of their cabinets, underneath tables, from behind couches, where they were all hiding.

"Who is that?" yet more devils in leather jackets asked the soldier.

Artiom started. The Chekists were looking for people to kill.

"He's coming from an interrogation, they told me to let him go," answered the soldier.

They kicked Artiom outside.

The Transfiguration church was filled with screams, as though monkeys had gotten in and were being beaten with whips all along the sleeping bunks and walls.

Black, leaning on his front paws, was fiercely barking in the direction of the church.

Sometimes soldiers ran along the courtyard.

Artiom hurried in the direction of the abbot's wing, but from there, walking towards him, they were pulling out a priest by his hair, while inside the building someone was screaming as though his most painful members were being crushed in a door… it's possible that's exactly what was happening.

The Chekist who was pulling the priest was drunk. Without releasing the hair from his fist, he vomited on the stones of the courtyard and then pulled his prisoner through that foul puddle. The long beard of the priest was unnaturally twisted and visibly heavy, as though it were made, not of hairs, but some boneless part of the body.

Artiom realized that the beard was soaked in blood like a soapy mop. Blood flowed from his mouth, his nose, his forehead, his ears.

Taking a step back, Artiom looked around in painful and sluggish indecision — where should he go? He couldn't go into the abbot's wing — they'd kill him there without asking who he was and whose neck he breathed on last night.

Why did he not go to his mother? He'd be on her knees right now.

"The wood stores!" someone suggested to him, and he trusted him.

Along the wall, avoiding the light of the lanterns, Artiom ran to the wood piles, his breathing ragged, breathing like he was crying.

It seemed to him that the earth careened and the Solovki Monastery, like a stone carriage on crooked wheels, was flying down a mountain and would crash into the horrifying earth, and everything would explode into small pieces, and that entire hash would be sucked into a black hole, leaving nothing behind.

He climbed between the logs, holding back a hoarse cry that tried to tear itself from his throat.

The logs were long — for the monastery heating. He scratched his cheek, got himself a palm full of splinters, but managed to get as far in as possible, where he sat quietly, seeing a single star over his head.

A few times, somewhere beyond the kremlin walls, they were firing. One volley. Another volley. Another volley. Then, many single retorts.

Somewhere a woman screamed, and the scream was cut off quickly.

Someone ran by, very close by, but they caught him and Artiom heard the sound of blows.

Artiom closed his eyes; what if they were shining in the darkness or reflecting the single star?

Around the nearest corner, someone was swearing in an amazing variety of words — the oaths poured from that person like scourings, cuttings and husks falling out of a bag of garbage.

The noise suddenly stopped.

It became so unnaturally quiet, as though all that had made a racket and screamed in the last hours had only been doing so in Artiom's head.

He opened his eyes: maybe he had dreamt it?

The star was still there.

Someone not far away started to talk, but the voice was completely calm, as though a person had woken up, come outside with a glass of milk in his hands, asked the passers-by what time it was, got surprised, stayed alone, sang an inaudible song, then drank a bit of milk.

Artiom listened carefully; that voice could calm him, let him know that there was nothing scary in the world, and if there was, it had passed.

First with his teeth, then with his nails, this action also brought order to his soul, because it relieved his pain immediately. Just before, it smarted in the most defenseless part between the thumb and index finger, but now it didn't smart any more. His own saliva in his own palm — that calmed him too. Artiom's entire face was dirty, because to get a splinter out of the very center of the palm with your teeth was hard, but very entertaining — it poured out of his mouth as though he had become a dog. But there was no one there to be ashamed of; in the wood pile, under a single star, there was a person with his own splinter. Everything was simple; nothing was strange.

He searched in his pants' pockets for something to wipe his hands and face on — he had never had a kerchief before, but maybe…? There was nothing in his jacket either.

"As for Krapin," Artiom said. "He cut his old shirts into accurate squares for kerchiefs… Here I'm always considering him to be beneath me — he's a policeman, after all, and I know by heart several long poems of Andrei Bely — but he's got kerchiefs, and I don't."

The thought of Krapin was a warm, familial one… Artiom for some reason was convinced that he would go back there tomorrow, and his bed would still be covered in Galia's sheets — the fox-chef hadn't taken them back — and all of it would happen, and no one, not a single person, would ever know how he, choking from fear, sat in a wood pile.

Artiom wiped his hands on his pant leg, listened one more time and only heard the sea — it was strange; he hadn't heard it during the day.

He got up and crawled back, sometimes stopping and looking around: everything was quiet now, or did he just imagine it?

No, it was quiet.

He got out and moved towards his room, careless as though he were walking along the Prechistenka.

"Hey, come here! Who are you, you bitch?"

They were calling him from the just-opened doors of the monastery's sauna.

Artiom came up and stood at the very edge of the square tongue of light that had fallen on the road.

Steam rose in the light.

Next to the doors lay either a drunk man or a dead body.

No, it was definitely a dead body.

Onto the threshold of the sauna walked out a man.

Black cuffs on his overcoat. A cap with a band… A familiar face. Gorshkov.

Gorshkov was in his uniform, but barefooted. He was nauseous, but he held onto the lintel.

He recognized Artiom too.

"Was it you who was looking for treasure with Eichmanis?" he asked with unkind mockery. "Did Eichmanis find his treasure...? We know many places to dig!" Gorshkov looked back, and there in answer, from several throats, laughed something many-headed and frightening.

"Let him come in here!" they commanded from behind Gorshkov's back.

Artiom took four steps along the square of light to the threshold.

In the anteroom of the sauna, at the very entrance, lay a pile of boots, all very dirty and shining with some unfamiliar, frightening light.

Raising his eyes, Artiom saw a few completely naked, wet and steamed-up men sitting on the ledges.

One of them had such a long scrotum, it was as though from childhood he had attached a weight to it and walked around like that, getting used to it. Another held his entire large endowment in his hand and was either clenching his fist or relaxing it. From the threshold, it seemed that he was holding a huge, boiled toad. A third was pouring vodka into glasses. He was also naked, but you couldn't see his nether regions behind the table and empty bottles. Someone was snarling and roaring in the steam room.

Another man, very strong, came out of the dressing room in his underwear. Having stopped in the middle of the anteroom, he attentively looked at Artiom.

"You found another one?" he asked. "Is he also for the firing squad?"

"Tkachuk," said Gorshkov, not having heard him, "let him wash the boots," and he waved with his free hand in Artiom's direction.

"Let him wash them for now," answered Tkachuk and went into the steam room.

"Wash the boots, jackal," Gorshkov said to Artiom.

All of the boots were covered in human blood, that's why they were sparkling so strangely.

Artiom, remembering nothing, thinking nothing and knowing nothing, took one boot, looked for its pair and even found it. With these boots, he moved towards the steam room, but one of those seated awkwardly pushed him, the one who hadn't yet released his hairy toad from his fist.

"Where you off to, fucker? You think you're just gonna walk back and forth with those boots? Pour water into a tub and wash them outside, brainless fucker."

In his other hand, the man held a glass with vodka and spilled it a bit while he swore.

Artiom saw clearly how the vodka poured down a red hand with thick hairs.

Artiom remembered him. It was he who walked into the iodine plant that time and took a rabbit.

Artiom walked into the steam room, took a tub, began to pour hot water into it. Then he changed his mind, and, raising the vat on one end, slowly poured it out, trying not to make a sound. He turned on the tap with the cold water. It poured and seethed in the tub.

On the threshold of the steam room lay a rag — to wipe your feet. Artiom went to get it, waited for the tub to fill, moved it, and not turning off the tap, rinsed and wrung out the rag several times under the water.

He pushed the door into the anteroom, and, trying not to hit anyone, walked with the tub and the rag back outside.

Having put the tub on the ground, he sat on the threshold in such a way that the light would fall over his shoulder. He looked askance at the body lying near the sauna. He finally realized that the body, when it was still a living person, had gotten a bullet in the head, and the former person, the current dead body's skull looked as though it had been moved to the side.

Or it all seemed like that to Artiom in the half darkness and in the night delirium that had begun.

The blood stank, and, combined with the dirt, was hard to wash out. The boots became slimy and smelled strongly of human internal organs — or at least Artiom would have thought that right now, if he could think, that human internal organs smelled exactly so.

He looked into the darkness and, as though thinking of himself from the side, not from within his own head, realized that he could easily get up and run away.

Those naked people would probably not run after him, washing as they were after the murder of other people.

"Grigorii," Gorshkov was trying to convince Tkachuk, who had come out of the sauna, "We have to kill him. If Nogtev begins interrogating him… anything could happen… Even though they seem to have burned all his papers already… Good thing that Nogtev flew to Kemi…"

Artiom got up and brought in the first pair of boots. He couldn't run anywhere. He could wash a few more pairs of bloody boots.

Tkachuk once again stood in the middle of the anteroom — healthy, with wet, bushy eyebrows, toothy — as though he had two of his own teeth in his strong, full-lipped mouth for every inmates' tooth he knocked out.

Someone, again from the side, whispered to Artiom — they're talking about Burtsev, whom they have to execute before Nogtev, who flew away to Kemi, can interrogate him.

The Chekists and the commandants had decided in advance to uncover and put down the conspiracy when Nogtev would be away. Then to set everything up in such a way for no one to know about the information that Burtsev had on the majority of the camp's administrative staff.

"We'll get our boots dirty again," said Tkachuk with the same tone, as though someone had offered him to go pick a head of cabbage.

"Come on, it's just one!" Gorshkov hissed his drunken, yet intelligible speech. "At least we'll get some clean girls from the women's barracks."

Artiom was sitting next to the tub with a new pair of boots, sometimes looking out into the darkness.

From the darkness came Black, smelled the air, and, growling, ran away.

Artiom, not getting up and even somehow getting used to the situation — what? I'm sitting here and washing boots, it's a normal enough activity — returned the clean pair to the anteroom and took two more, even three, no longer worrying about getting the pairs right — they'd manage on their own.

"They're going to shoot only Burtsev," someone whispered to Artiom. "They won't shoot you, because you've got nothing to do with anything. Gorshkov, though drunk, remembers how you dug for Eichmanis's treasure. So sit there and wash your boots."

Two men came out of the darkness, carrying a mat behind them.

Rubbing his slippery hands like fish, Artiom recognized Avdei Sivtsev and Zahar.

He expected that the guard would come get them, but there was no guard.

They had an unhealthy look about them that smelled of death. They looked like garbage-feeding dogs. Their eyes bulged and their faces were constricted from cold.

They stared at Artiom: why was he here, what was he doing next to a tub full of blood?

Their hands, their pants, their shirts, their lips, their foreheads, their cheeks — everything was covered in dirt.

"Did you dig them up?" Tkachuk's voice rose over Artiom's head.

"They took them out of the icebox to bury dead bodies," once again someone whispered to Artiom in his very ears. Artiom's cheek almost twitched.

Avdei and Zahar took turns nodding their contorted faces. Dried earth fell from their hair.

"Well, let's go then," Tkachuk said to his people, "They can bury this cigarette butt while they're at it." He nodded at the dead man who lay next to the sauna.

"Get to work, Jackal!" he hurled at Artiom.

Avdei and Zahar unrolled the mat and, getting mixed up, pulled the body on to it. Artiom stepped on the mat to keep it from hiking up.

"Pick it up?" asked Avdei quietly; his voice was shaking.

They looked at each other, took it, and carried it.

Artiom got the head, it was bouncing from side to side. His hands were slippery and soon he couldn't hold and dropped… what he was carrying.

He wiped his palms on himself, grabbed it more firmly and tried again.

Avdei and Zahar already knew the way — they walked as quickly as they could towards the holy gates.

Soon the Chekists and commandants gained on them. Three of them had gotten dressed — their overcoats slapped against the tops of the washed boots. The fourth had only found his pants and walked, naked to his waist, very fast.

Among them, wobbling, Burtsev shuffled with his hands tied behind his back. Where they had wounded him, you couldn't tell — his entire shirt was covered with blood in the front and the blood had poured lower, so his pants were distended and blackened all the way to his knees.

One after the other, several other people from the sauna joined them, hurriedly dressing as they walked, as well as some soldiers who came from nowhere, and one more, it looked like, from the camp's administrative staff. He was in a civilian coat and a dapper cap and walked next to Burtsev; looking at his face occasionally, as though he expected that he would look at him. In anticipation of that moment, the uncalled escort, apparently, had a speech prepared, or at least an insulting phrase.

One of the soldiers carried a smoking torch.

In the stone walkway towards the arched holy gates that were similar in shape to ancient princely helmets, the torch flared and spluttered.

Beyond the gates, they led Burtsev through a crowd, as though they were seeing off their dearest friend before his journey.

It became clear exactly how many people had come to hate him in a short time.

Burtsev himself didn't notice anything, he only sometimes tripped over his own feet and kept looking at the ground as before, as though under his feet some confused writing had spread out, and he was trying, without especial diligence, to read it.

The air began to get lighter.

Artiom, sensing the dawn, suddenly distinguished all objects clearly and sharply. All of his feelings returned to him, as well as his numbed consciousness.

They didn't have to wait till dawn, but the night was going to end soon anyway.

"They definitely won't kill me," Artiom realized for himself for the first time that night, without anyone suggesting it to him.

The dead head he carried no longer frightened him. Nothing frightened him. Everything had already happened. And what was about to happen — that was unavoidable.

"Hey, you!" the same civilian called to Burtsev.

Artiom was sure that Burtsev walked half-conscious, but no, he raised his head and spit powerfully in the direction of the man who mocked him.

"Who's that woman?" Tkachuk suddenly raised his voice.

On the road, facing the crowd, stood the mother of Artiom Goriainov.

She was immovable and straight; only the ends of her kerchief moved with the wind.

Artiom recognized her without any surprise, and, stopping, not blinking, he looked at his mother's wizened face.

She also recognized her son and stared at him, seeing how the eyes were in his face, is the burden in his hands pulling him down, was he planning on dying right now?

"No, I'm not," said Artiom in a whisper. "I'm sorry, mother. If we're found worthy of it, we'll see each other later."

She didn't hear him, but stared directly at his lips.

"Where are you from, old woman?"

"She's probably a hired worker," said Gorshkov, who liked to seem sober and all-remembering. "A laundress."

"Get out of here, idiot!" said Tkachuk and shot from his Mauser over her head.

At first, she crouched, then ran away in an ugly way.

Gorshkov, fingers lost in his holster, also got his pistol and shot upwards.

Artiom looked down, onto the hair made curly with blood, lest he see anything else.

Burtsev waited for all that happened to end, having lowered his chin and closed his eyes. From time to time, he wrinkled his forehead, as though he were trying to shake off the mosquitoes, though there weren't any mosquitoes.

They stopped him, not far from the female barracks, next to a badly dug trench, and they immediately began to shoot at him from three sides — they didn't line up and wait for a command. Everyone wanted to be the first to do it and to do it as painfully as possible. No one could find immediate satisfaction in his death; therefore, Burtsev was shot several times in the face, with some even running up to the body to do it. His face was falling apart.

In the female barracks, the women of Solovki once again woke up and started screaming. For the whole night, they had the honor of hearing executions.

The Chekists, immediately, barely having wiped off their foul-smelling sweat, remembered why they came here, in addition to the murder.

While Artiom, Zahar and Sivtsev covered Burtsev with earth — they put him face-down, so they wouldn't see anything, so that he wouldn't even look human, but like something else — several girls were pulled out from the women's barracks into the musty light.

The Chekists raised a lantern taken from the soldiers up to their faces, so they could see them better.

"Why did you bring that one?" Tkachuk complained cantankerously. "She's an old woman. Go to sleep, you damn poker."

Burtsev was already buried when Gorshkov returned, and having asked, "Here?" fired three more times into the ground, after which he ran after the women with burned-off eyebrows and fringe.

"Forgive us, Mstislav," said Artiom aloud, barely audibly.

Zahar even stopped moving his shovel, not to bother him and let him say his peace.

When the last soldier walked past them with a lantern, Artiom noticed a small, nickel-sized piece of skull on the ground. It still had hair attached. He turned away immediately. For some time, he stood still, not breathing.

The grave-diggers went back to the holy gates.

Black, smelling the ground, ran towards them unevenly, as though during the night he had become blind.

"The laundress is still there, looking," said Zahar, nodding over his shoulder. "She just walked away a little. She probably thinks that now they can't reach her."

Artiom knew that she was looking, but he didn't turn around.

His fingers were cramping, and he tried to clench and unclench them.

A crust of someone else's dried blood cracked on his fingers.

"We need to bring back the shovels and… you know… ask what's next," said Sivtsev in the monastery's courtyard.

Artiom didn't care — if they had to bring them back, then they had to bring them back — he remembered for sure that he would survive today.

"… A Russian *muzhik*," he thought only, "buried a body, asked, 'What next?' And if they told him, 'Dig him up again!' he would do it."

They returned to the sauna.

Inside was the sound of pained female moans, as though it wasn't a man who raped each of them, but a demon with charred black balls and a bull's member — thin, as long as one and a half bayonets, slimily crawling out from the depths of the stomach somewhere, full of worms and festering foulness.

* * *

Artiom remembered how one morning, instead of "God save the Tsar," the Spasskaia Tower suddenly rang with the "Internationale". He had sharply sat up on his bed and looked at his parents, who were already awake.

"Look out the window," his father had said jokingly to his mother, "maybe the sun's come up angular too."

Now, it wasn't so much a dream as reverie that the tower, continually transforming into the burned-out Transfiguration Cathedral, played some new, shrieking music, like a wainwright's wheel, and behind that music, barely keeping up, a drum hurried, pushing out its tight cheeks and slapping itself out of rhythm on its exposed Chekist stomach.

On the cart, lying in a heap, were a bunch of naked priestlings. Behind the cart ran a donkey tied to it. On its neck a bell tinkled occasionally.

Artiom slept little and came awake slowly, feeling a huge, boiling headache that was bigger than his own head.

It was a comical likeness to another awakening in the very first years of the twenties, when Artiom and his friends had gone to his dacha, had drunk far too much there and started a fire that they barely put out in their drunken stupor — the cover of the piano had a frightful hole burned into it which revealed the strings, his father's favorite rug on the wall, which he had brought from Kazan, was scorched. The ceiling was blackened, the china was shattered and crunched under their feet — his grandmother's inheritance, as well as a crystal vase, a milk jug and soup bowls from Muir and Merrilee's. To prevent them from choking, someone very decisively had broken the window with a chair and it was stuck with its legs outside, its back still in the room.

Artiom thought then, overcoming his alcoholic nausea and finding, with some surprise, that he was wearing a raccoon fur coat, that if he would hang himself in the midst of their small, pleasant sitting room in his fur coat, the spectacle would be complete.

Today, also, Artiom felt a natural kind of hangover, as though he had fallen into a nine-day drunken bender, and now, on the tenth day, he was crawling out from under ice, shaking, insane, trying to hold on to its hard, crusty edge.

His eyes ached. His hands woodenly shook. His mouth was dry. His clothing was incomparably dirty and foul-smelling.

When he appeared after the inspection, Troianskii's mother sat at her son's feet. Osip slept. She probably thought that Artiom had crawled out of a grave, because it was cold and uncomfortable there, while it was warm and clean in the room.

Artiom lay under the covers in his clothing and shoes and pulled up his knees, as he did in childhood, up to his stomach.

The Troianskiis probably left at dawn; he was insensate and heard nothing.

It's possible that they, having a pass in their hands, had decided to wait for the ship "Gleb Bokii's" departure in port, to avoid going to the morning inspection.

The hours that for years were passed under the ringing of the Spasskaia Tower lined up in Artiom's head, saying clearly that any minute now, less than a minute, the horrifying siren will scream the wakeup call.

It seemed now that they drove out everyone for the morning line-up — even those brigades who began work at eight, or even nine.

He had to somehow explain and justify the past night, so that he could find the strength to get up and the will to live and watch.

He found neither the strength nor the will, only a loud, insistent pain pressing against the inside of his skull. Artiom would have squeezed his ears with his fingers if he believed that his fingers were capable of unclenching.

Having overcome nothing inside himself, he still got up somehow and slowly sat up in his bed. In his head, yesterday's blood water in the vat was slowly pouring back and forth. His sheet, Artiom noticed, was almost black and wet as though a cow with a sick, bloody moth had been chewing it.

"Did they shoot Afanasiev too?" Artiom asked himself. It turned out he was capable of thinking in a whisper. "They were also supposed to shoot him. I was probably walking over an earth-covered grave, and he was lying underneath."

Artiom wasn't able to think about all this coherently for a long time, as though a hole formed in his soul, like in that piano, and if he were to go outside, snow would fall onto the exposed strings, his very soul. If you pressed a key, a sound would come out — short, strange, gravelly, immediately cut off.

The siren sounded, long and always unexpected — it bored into one of his temples and, with a bony drill bit on the sharp end, pushed its way through the other side of his skull, still spinning.

"Get up!" Someone yelled somewhere in the building, as though someone had unexpectedly poured a full bucket of leeches onto his exposed groin.

Artiom could only restore his understanding of the world with his own voice and through his own rational speech.

Several times, he breathed in and out. Having teased at the skin on his forehead and clenched his jaw muscles, he finally opened his eyes. He clenched his fists with force, then unclenched them, taming the shakes. He stomped his shoes on the floor. He licked his lips, as though he were getting ready to sing.

"Good morning, Artiom," he said to himself. "You're alive. And now you will continue to live."

His sleep-deprived eyes burned; in each of them, they had lit a candle, and the hot wax melted into his sockets. His head felt as though it were bandaged with coarse sand paper; a crazy janitor with bestial strength had wrapped it.

As much as he could, he also breathed in and slowly breathed out through his nose.

"If everything had worked out for Burtsev yesterday…" Artiom began with cutting hatred directed at himself.

He needed to overcome that hatred and take his medicine…

"If everything had worked out for him, then Galia would be lying in that hole in the ground. And if I was found in Galia's office, I'd be there too. They would have buried me next to Galia," said Artiom and got up.

The inspection passed as though quotidian, and the sleepy people all stood silently. Everyone, as much as possible, pretended that the empty spaces in the line-up were no reason to wonder or ask where this one or that one went.

Afanasiev wasn't there.

Artiom, over and over again, caught quick glances inside the lines. It seemed that the prisoners, today more than any other day, wanted to quickly get to work at the farthest possible work sites.

Tkachuk walked amongst the work group, looking for someone.

"Is he really looking for me?" Artiom thought, feeling as though his heart were falling down and turning into a piece of salted beef.

Tkachuk was springy, wide-faced and wide-hipped, quick in his movements, pink and fresh, as though, while Artiom lay in place for an hour and a half in a catatonic state, he had slept for three full nights without waking up, as in a bear lair under seven layers of snow.

"What a strong race they are," thought Artiom without any respect, only pain.

"I'll need you again today," Tkachuk pointed at Artiom with his large fingers. "I've told the work assignment clerk already. Wait in IID so I don't have to look for you."

Next to the building, Zahar and Avdei Sivtsev were waiting, for they knew not what. Both of them had a sickly color to their face, their lips caked up, their eyes shadowed in black.

They didn't say hello. Either they didn't feel like they had ever parted, or a greeting would have too obviously given meaning to their communal work of yesterday, and who needed to remember that?

Artiom sat on the ground.

Zahar and Avdei stood next to him, tortured by cold expectation and simultaneously not wanting anyone to remember their existence.

"I don't even know what's worse — solitary or here," said Sivtsev, chewing his lips.

Since the morning, Black seemed beside himself. He didn't come up to anyone and seemed to be looking for someone.

"They're pushing our brigade for the second day straight, so that no one else would see anything. Does that mean they're going to bury us at the end of it?" Sivtsev asked, looking at Artiom. He spoke strangely, making his words sound like jesters.

"Where's Galia?" thought Artiom, looking at Black. "Get me out of here immediately, Galia!"

Gorshkov appeared. He looked a little worse than Tkachuk, but also not bad — washed, shaved, well-fed. Not looking at those who stood in the department of grave-digging, he jumped into the doorway, but immediately, remembering something, returned.

He walked up to Artiom, who immediately got up.

"If you tell Eichmanis that we were laughing at him here, you'll end up in yesterday's hole in the ground," Gorshkov whispered in his ear.

"You weren't laughing at him," Artiom quietly answered, looking away.

Having blown his nose onto the stones of the yard, Gorshkov left.

On the back of his boot was a bloody blob — Artiom had washed that one badly.

Black, who had been planning something for a long time and was accordingly acting strangely, suddenly contrived to jump up and catch a gull. It screamed, calling its friends for help, but the maddened dog, helping himself with his paws, soon bit through its head and in a minute didn't so much eat the bird as tear it into pieces.

Everything around them was covered in feathers and small bird innards.

No one decided to shoo Black away; the rest of the gulls just screamed with their full bird voices and flew sharp zigzags in the air, made miserable by the treachery of the dog and yesterday's shooting and the sharp change in weather — three days ago it was still warm, and yesterday there was snow, and today was an indeterminate, windy haze — they needed to get out of here immediately — and here one of the oldest gull's was torn to shreds!

The soldiers hurriedly bustled back and forth, Tkachuk looked outside and again walked back into the building, someone uttered the last name of the new head of the camp, and Artiom realized that Nogtev had arrived from Kemi.

In his leather coat, the head of the camp walked out into the yard — Black seemed to be waiting for him — tearing from his place, he hurled himself at Nogtev.

The head of the camp was quicker than the soldier accompanying him, who only managed to get his rifle off his shoulder. With the first shot of the revolver he deftly grabbed from his holster, Nogtev lifted the dog off its feet, and with his second, he finished it off somewhere in the neck.

One of the gulls, incensed by yet another volley of shots, flew over Nogtev's head and left a white mark on his shoulder.

Nogtev shot at the gull, but this time he didn't get it.

"Kill all the gulls," Nogtev commanded, laughing. In spite of his miss, he was pleased with himself. "Let them forget the way back here."

A bunch of soldiers gathered, aroused like they were before the sauna. Unimaginable gunfire began.

The gulls, screaming bone-chillingly, couldn't believe that they were planning on exterminating them all. They flew up for some time, then again tried to fly towards the kitchen, especially since the forewarned cook kept carrying out, at first, all the leftovers, then in the heat of the moment seemed to have poured out the entire lunch of one of the brigades — probably the thirteenth.

One large gull, understanding what was going on, attacked a soldier in a terminal rage — scaring him in earnest — but they shot it down on the second loop of its switchback from three rifles.

The soldiers laughed, even the prisoners didn't feel bad for the gulls, not really.

"No one is going to fly away from here," thought Artiom, laughing through the pain in his entire face. He also couldn't care less.

He looked at Black for a long time, but then the duty officer of the IID showed up, pushed Zahar, pointed at the dog and swore. Zahar understood everything, got up, and, making sure that no one was pointing a rifle at him, ran to Black, took the dog by its legs and pulled it back.

The dead Black ended up being a small, not very pretty, and not very black dog.

Under this racket of gunfire, obstreperousness of the foremen and the shrieks of the gulls, Galia came out. She was without her jacket, in uniform, tired and also not very pretty.

In the yard, it was madness and confusion, people from the administration were running out, as well as the nurses, the cooks — it was almost like a holiday — the autumn culling of the birds.

Galia stood next to Artiom and asked, looking at the back of a soldier who was aiming at a gull, "Why do you look like this?"

Artiom was quiet, and after his second attempt — he had to wait for the nearest volley to end — he answered, "I was washing the Chekists' bloody boots. Then I buried the body of Burtsev."

"Did they beat you?" Galia quickly asked and just as quickly examined Artiom's face.

"No," he said.

Galia transferred her unseeing glance to a different soldier and announced, "Thirty-six people were shot overnight. There won't be any more. Nogtev forbade it."

"He… didn't know…" Artiom said.

"He knew everything," Galia answered immediately with anger. "He left on purpose."

A thought pierced Artiom: "Black ended up being the smartest of us all!"

He looked askance at Galia — should he share this revelation with her or not. He decided it wasn't worth it.

Artiom imagined that Galia didn't want to go back inside the building because she liked to stand next to him.

Except he didn't feel even a little bit better from her presence, he only wanted the gunfire to end.

"Did they shoot Afanasiev?" asked Artiom, noticing that it was very hard for him to say the last two words, as though they were magnets repelling each other.

"Why do you say that?" Galia looked at him again. "No. I didn't see him on the list. Why Afanasiev?"

"Idiot! What am I doing?" Artiom rebuked himself regretfully.

"No reason," he answered, as sincerely as he could manage. "He just missed the morning inspection, and I was afraid for him."

Galia didn't answer. She didn't care about Afanasiev.

"I'll try to send you back to Fox Island today," she said after a minute.

Artiom bit his lower lip; if only that were true, if only you could manage it, I'll put up your photograph, Galia, and I will pray to it. He thought that Krapin had managed to photograph her in the company of the foxes that were intended to warm her shoulder during the forthcoming winter of Solovki.

They stood another half minute in silence. Artiom sometimes jumped or at least made a face from the gunfire; Galia didn't even blink.

Sivtsev and Zahar returned. Probably judging by the bloody spots on their clothing and by the fact that Artiom moved a little bit, not completely surprised by their arrival, Galia figured out what they had been doing together.

"You haven't eaten yet?" she asked Sivtsev.

He looked at Artiom questioningly — what should I say? Should I tell the truth?

Artiom didn't turn his head.

"He was in the war," thought Artiom slowly, "but I wasn't. And he's waiting for me to tell him what to do?"

"Well, it's not clear where we belong now — neither solitary nor a brigade," Sivtsev answered distractedly, looking first at Galia, then at Artiom, then, finally, at Zahar too.

"Go into the infirmary," Galia commanded, for some reason putting up her collar as she walked into the building. "I'll make a call and they'll feed you and let you wash. Go wash your clothes."

"But citizen commandant Tkachuk commanded us to wait," Sivtsev called in her wake with a crying voice.

"I'll tell Tkachuk too," Galia answered, not turning around.

* * *

For lunch — or was it dinner already — they got pea gruel and millet cutlets with a sour berry sauce.

Artiom looked at the bowls for a long time, then dropped the cutlet into the sour soup and ate everything in a third of a minute.

Sometimes he raised his eyes either to Sivtsev — who ate moderately and turned inward — or at Zahar—who was trying to eat slowly but failing. Artiom felt a light itch from his desire to tell them that Galia had clapped them into solitary, though at least now she was feeding them — see how attentive she is? Not only that, but they were sitting in solitary because of his — the prisoner Goriainov, and one other — a reckless balalaika-player — sins.

In the infirmary's staff dining room, there was no one else. Doctor Ali himself had led them there, having pretended that he didn't remember Artiom — though perhaps he truly didn't — who knows how many lice-ridden inmate-brothers have lain here?

"Would you like another bowl?" Doctor Ali offered with his lovely accent, having once again looked in on them, caressing his beard.

All three of them looked at each other, Artiom, in a sign of approval, lightly tapped the edge of the spoon he held in his fist against the table.

Doctor Ali laughed as though he knew no greater joy than to feed three dirty grave-diggers — he had also figured out what these three unfortunates had been doing all night and why they had been recommended by the IID.

"What a nice man," thought Artiom with his previous, souring tiredness. "And here I was, I think, angry at him…"

Though it was possible that Doctor Ali just liked a certain Chekist lady named Galina and wanted to serve her; who knows? Maybe she'll suddenly remember this simple good deed and help him on a difficult day or, perhaps, will at least unbutton the top two buttons of her shirt one time, gifting him with white skin and light…

They brought them three more millet cutlets each and a mug of tea — real tea, not berry tea — but even that wasn't the most amazing thing. What shocked them was the ball of butter — gentle, sunny — heaped with a generous spoon onto the edge of every bowl.

Without agreeing in advance, all three of them attacked their cutlets and each one, leaning over the bowl, all stared at the butter as though it might disappear in a flash.

Artiom, once again dispensing with his food before everyone else, carefully picked up the magical ball and, putting it on the back of his hand, began to lick it off, squinting and trying to acknowledge every second of this blessed, head-spinning deliciousness.

He didn't notice how Zahar and Sivtsev ate their butter.

Ali didn't appear any more, but a worker that Artiom knew as well brought a pile of washed pants and shirts and jackets and an old padded vest and, though it was in holes, an overcoat.

"It's nobody's," said the worker. "You can give me yours — the women will wash yours and you can get them tomorrow."

Zahar seemed to have second thoughts — should he ask from whose back these were taken off — not from a dead man's?

"Who else, Zahar?" Artiom lightly slapped him on the shoulder. "Of course it's from dead men. This is an infirmary — here, they heal you if they can, but they bury you if they can't."

Artiom didn't care — from the earliest morning, he was cold, and all this was dry, soaped up with female hands, rinsed and wrung out.

He undressed to his undies and immediately chose those things that he thought would fit him — and he wasn't wrong once. Only on top of everything, he put on his own jacket.

Zahar followed his example.

Sivtsev parted with his rags unwillingly, he kept patting himself and looking for something in his pockets, where, except for lice, no one had resided in a long time.

"Don't be afraid," said the worker. "You can keep these, and you'll get yours back too. Its winter soon — everything is useful and will wear itself out.

The reminder of winter had an immediate effect on the *muzhik*.

They didn't go and wash; instead, they quickly returned to IID in their new clothes. What if they were looking for them, after all?

They had already taken away the dead gulls from the yard, and it was newly quiet, as though everything was ready for the coming of snow, because winter loves silence for its first appearance.

The Chekists, who were poking around all the brigades the entire day — they either lost someone or did it as a warning — brought an actor in this time. He was scared shitless and kept looking around to see if anyone from the recognizable authority figures might show up, who had applauded him the last time so loudly.

Zahar and Artiom stood next to each other, not looking at each other, but they had the same thought at the same moment — will we have to bury him too today?

Sivtsev looked to the side, as though he was tortured by guilt and couldn't find any accord with that shame.

"… I was mad at Burtsev and wished him ill," Artiom thought without any desire and even against his will, not so much in words, but with fragments or emotions that replaced words, "And now, he's a body underground. Who was I mad at? A dead body? And all my irritation — they've buried it together with Burtsev, or has my gall towards him, now orphaned, returned to me? And do I now have to carry all that rust with me now, because I can't put it anywhere, nor can I scrape it off?"

Bear the deer, having seen his fill during the day, tried to avoid all people and only run along the courtyard here, then there, smelling, listing his head towards the air, where it still smelled of power and the death of his canine comrade, and he flicked his ears — maybe the familiar bark of a gull-scream would sound again?

Even before, Bear didn't distinguish the inmates from the Chekists, though it would have been preferable if he would gently smell and lick the former, while kicking the latter with his hooves in their stomachs, but now it was even worse. He determined that the entire human species was evil. A few times, Bear came up to the gates, his sides quivering with worry, but the guards sent him away, waving ham-fisted at him. Those fists smelled of damp cloth, tobacco and gun oil.

Gorshkov, either cheerful or angry, but in any case extraordinarily agitated and talkative, was leading another inmate with two soldiers. Gorshkov walked first, and at first Artiom didn't see the inmate under guard.

"How many years have I been here, and I haven't even noticed you, you bastard," Gorshkov either laughed or was angry. He was drunk again, his tight cheeks quivering. "You put on a cap, you bastard. It was your good fortune, bastard, that you were sent out to a distant work group, or you would have long ago rotted in my swamp!" Gorshkov, looking around and tripping because of it, for the umpteenth time explained to the soldier what he had just told him a minute ago. "I'll remember this bastard for my whole life! Kolchak's counterintelligence. It was he who shredded chunks of flesh from my back! Not a bad place to meet again! Like sinking two billiard balls with a single blow! Your God hasn't forgotten you, you bastard! He rolled this bread roll exactly where he needed to go!"

Artiom at first remembered that yesterday Gorshkov hadn't undressed in the steam room. Then he saw that they were leading Vasilii Petrovich.

He was without his cap, which for some reason Gorshkov carried in his hands — evidently as vivid proof of his unexpected good luck.

"You've mixed everything up, citizen commandant Chekist," said Vasilii Petrovich, hurrying and strangely grimacing.

But even Artiom knew for some reason that the citizen commandant hadn't mixed anything up.

* * *

The knowledge that Vasilii Petrovich used to be engaged in the same — or almost the same — activities as Tkachuk or Gorshkov yesterday did not create a second black hole in Artiom's soul.

Into the one that now existed much could fall in and disappear without a trace.

"How did I not notice his paraffin eyes?" thought Artiom, without any sorrow, because there was nothing else to think.

It was better to remember the butter and to smell his hand from time to time — maybe that taste would come through once more?

Someone — Artiom didn't know who — had suggested to him that every person has at his core a bit of hell — if you stir with the poker, a foul-smelling smoke will rise.

He himself had waved the knife and cut open the throat of his father, as though he were a sheep. While Vasilii Petrovich shredded flesh from Gorshkov's back — so what? Everyone earns the Kingdom of Heaven in whatever way he can.

After the day's work, one after the other, the work groups of the twelfth brigade returned.

Artiom noticed Passport and Shaferbekov, and they, walking by, saw him as well.

Artiom sniffled, bit his cheek and stood on in an empty and wordless expectation of what life might offer him this time.

The gangsters came back very soon, walked past the IID in one direction, then another.

Zahar, recognizing the guests, kept glancing in their direction, though Artiom didn't.

The gangsters stood a distance off. Passport stared at Artiom; Artiom didn't turn around.

But dinner time came, and the gangsters left with nothing.

Over the courtyard, once again two or three still living young gulls flew by, seeking their parents or someone older. Their squeaking was heart-rending and pitiful.

The brave soldiers ran in to shoot some more.

Galia appeared again, when it was already late evening, in her leather jacket and gloves.

"Return to your sleeping quarters," she said to Sivtsev and Zahar, interlacing her fingers, so that her gloves would be more snug on her hands. "I've released you from solitary."

"We didn't even know about those sauna switches that..." began to mutter the unexpectedly happy and gently mocking Sivtsev. "And for what did we sit? Well, all's well that ends well! Sometimes you don't get punished for your own sins, so we can suffer for someone else's too. I guess it was our turn!"

"How agitated and jumpy he is, that *muzhik*," Artiom quietly wondered.

He remembered that Sivtsev wasn't like that in July when they were sent to break the cemetery. He had killed people in war, and he could have been killed — what was there here on Solovki that could put Sivtsev down?

"He came here with his truth, which hadn't abandoned him his whole life, but suddenly it did," Artiom found the answer, as though even this time the answer had been whispered to him in advance.

"I've started to think much too," he said to himself, immediately forgetting about Sivtsev — who cares about Sivtsev if he didn't even remember his own mother all day. "But I shouldn't think, because that's how you start to crack, and you'll break down quickly."

Artiom hadn't forgotten that not so long ago, even — it's funny to say — yesterday, when he was afraid for Galia, he had rebuked himself painfully for lacking the habit of thinking things through — but had he figured out much then? Did his overburdened reason save him?

Galia silently waited for Sivtsev to have his say.

"Go to your sleeping quarters," she said, not waiting for the end.

Sivtsev fell silent, but didn't stop smiling, and, looking back a few times, hurried after Zahar, who hadn't started to bother everyone.

For some reason, Sivtsev started to limp on one leg — maybe he had stood too long here during the day.

"Nogtev has forbidden the use of any boats," said Galia without any emotion, not looking at Artiom. "But the arrests have stopped, all the Chekists have gone home, only Gorshkov can't stop talking to your Vasilii Petrovich. You can calm down a bit..." She shook her head. "Wait till tomorrow," Galia added with the tiniest increase of the thermometer in her voice. Without saying goodbye, she left.

He should, if not feel sorry for him, then at least remember Vasilii Petrovich — are they torturing him right now? Are they burning him, cutting him into little pieces? But Artiom didn't want to, didn't want to, didn't want to.

"Tomorrow, tomorrow, tomorrow," he repeated either without meaning or in prayer, looking at this leaving woman who bore within her his salvation. And there, living as a near neighbor with his right to life, was preserved his delayed death.

Heartily believing in his own luck, Artiom slapped his own pockets and got caught, like on a hook, on his own sharp and painful thought — he had lost his pass that allowed him to work in the fox nursery.

"Tomorrow Galia will have to write me a new one," he thought frantically. Disappointed, he immediately tried to calm himself, but not without a pleased kind of malice: "Stop your hysterics! Burtsev doesn't need a pass any more. What, is it worse for you than for him?" But even this had a weak effect. "They put a stamp of approval on each pass — that's done by the head of IID. That means Galia will have to go to him, and does she need that?" Artiom asked himself. "And what if they ask Galia why she's suddenly so interested in Fox Island? And what if they don't issue such passes anymore? How stupid! How stupid it all turned out!"

His first guess was that he had forgotten the pass in the pants that he had left to be laundered in the infirmary, but no, he remembered clearly that he had turned out both his pockets, and only after that, very pleased with himself that he forgot nothing (because he had found his money): did he hand in his clothes? His sleepless head didn't remember the pass then; he had licked up his butter and lost his marbles.

Artiom pulled out the wad of money, folded it in half, from the pocket of his new pants, taken off an unknown dead man from the infirmary. Maybe the pass was stuck in the Solovetsian currency? Though he knew in advance that it wasn't there.

It wasn't there.

He stood, just like that piano with a burnt-through cover and twangy strings, and he twisted his face from self-loathing.

He had to go into his room and look there — maybe it had fallen out when he was asleep, but even here, Artiom knew that not once during that entire hour and a half, while he slept, did he even move. Nothing could have fallen out. There was no pass there.

"... And you laughed at Troianskii who carried a safety pin in his pocket for more than a month," Artiom rebuked himself with torturous sorrow.

"You should have pinned the pass to your own skin and carried it like that, you idiot."

"... And I couldn't have lost it in the sauna, nor next to the sauna," Artiom went through the previous day again, ready to walk behind his shadow along the entire courtyard, to the edge of the gravesite and back... then he suddenly remembered. He could have dropped the pass when he was hiding in the pile of logs and reaching into his pocket to find the handkerchief that he had never had.

Artiom walked to the wood pile, hurrying and afraid to scare off his luck and his clear premonition, so obvious that you could hide it in the palm of your hand like a coin.

Looking around, and seeing no one, Artiom crouched and crawled into the same place where he had hidden yesterday.

His fear was profound, sharp, but not prolonged. In the same place, another person sat in a student's cap, squinting his eyes.

Artiom was the first to take control of himself. He recognized Mitya Schelkachov.

"What are you doing here?" asked Artiom quietly, realizing with a start that he felt sorry for the young man, as though he hadn't been in the same place the previous day.

Mitya finally recognized Artiom, but he still hadn't calmed down.

"They executed four hundred people," said Schelkachov, his teeth chattering.

"Thirty-six," said Artiom.

"Eh?" Schelkachov didn't understand. "They're looking for me."

"Get out," said Artiom. "All the Chekists are sleeping. No one's looking for you. Who needs you anyway?"

"Eh?" Schelkachov didn't hear him again, even though they were talking face to face.

Mitya had the shakes.

"Move over," Artiom asked and pushed Schelkachov in his forehead — he still wasn't realizing anything.

Schelkachov moved over uncomfortably, evidently expecting Artiom to join him.

Artiom patted the place where Mitya had been sitting — well, there it was. The pass.

Just in case, Artiom raised his paper right up to his eyes.

He sighed so lightly, so calmly, so gratefully, as though it wasn't a ticket to Fox Island, but a full pardon.

Without saying goodbye to Schelkachov — let him sit there if he likes — Artiom climbed back out. It was tight and uncomfortable, but he still smiled while he crawled, and didn't stop smiling while he straightened out to his full height and saw Passport and Shaferbekov in his peripheral vision. They had noticed him, then probably had lost him, then found him again.

"They're going to write you another kind of pass," said Artiom aloud. Without looking at them, he grabbed the highest log, hugging its top end to his chest — like an overgrown child — and thus, not making it obvious, he walked back in the direction of the abbot's wing.

The bottom of the log covered his groin, the top one rubbed his temple.

It was dark outside, the light of the monastery's lanterns barely reached this place, and it was important to walk carefully, lest he fall over.

Artiom tried to walk fast, but not so fast that the noise of his steps and the beating of his booming heart would drown out the steps of the men running after him.

He had just enough self-restraint — or just tired stupidity from the last two days — not to rush. In the last possible moment, he loosened his hands, the log dropped and Artiom caught it by its very end and smacked it, swinging hard, right on the head of the one who was gaining on him.

It was Passport, who, having made two steps somewhere to the side, fell on his knee and got in Shaferbekov's way, who flipped over him, head over heels.

Shaferbekov had a knife in his hands — the knife fell and rolled along the cobblestones.

Artiom, immediately dropping the log and stepping back by inertia, saw everything — Shaferbekov, the knife — but he didn't have enough madness or courage in him to start knifing everyone here.

He kicked the knife so that it jumped somewhere far away, and, turning around, ran.

No one followed him.

"A beaten *friar*," whispered Artiom. "I'm a beaten *friar*! The beaten *friar* will beat up the unbeaten gangsters!"

Desperate anger was pulling him apart.

Not far from the abbot's wing, he slowed to a walking pace and once again checked for his pass. Is it here? It didn't fall out?

It's here, it's here, get out of the yard already!

* * *

In the morning, right after the siren, to which Artiom had almost become accustomed, a soldier came for him: back to IID.

"They're sending them out like postmen to get me," he laughed, thinking whether or not he should take anything to Fox Island or leave everything here. He hadn't managed to take the package from his mother. Well, Galia would bring it later.

"Hurry," said the soldier.

"I'll hurry you right now, blockhead," Artiom answered silently. He could have said it aloud, but what was the point?

He had slept well. His life, though twisted in the face and smelling shamefully, aggressively reasserted its rights. He didn't want to answer for anything. Those who flee the island and who prepare death for others know that they can be offered their own death in return. Those who cut others into pieces often remember that they themselves might be cut up and salted in Solovki's seas. Artiom, more than anything else in the world, wanted to clean up after the foxes.

The feed boxes on Fox Island had covers, and they absolutely had to be closed, because the foxes had the bad habit of shitting in the same place where they ate.

This knowledge about feeding boxes and fox characters was more than enough for Artiom to continue living. He did not require any other knowledge.

Several people walked into the room at once — the duty officer, the brigade commander, and two inmates with bags — they were probably moving in.

"What are you doing here, jackal?" the commander of the second brigade yelled at Artiom from the threshold.

"What? Have they all become animals from the morning?" Artiom thought, blinking slightly, as though flies were attacking his face.

"He's coming here the second day in a row, as though he lived here — I didn't know that he had been transferred," the duty officer said obsequiously, simultaneously looking askance with a frenzied dog-eye at Artiom. "I remember him, but he didn't say that he had been transferred; he keeps coming here as though it were his own apartment."

"Where's your place, jackal? In the zoo!" the brigade commander stepped towards Artiom to smack him with a fist between the eyes, but there stood the soldier, who for who knows what reason had come and was preventing quick justice from being accomplished. "You think this is an inn? Get out of here like a bullet."

Artiom got out like a bullet.

He noticed that judging by the distant look of the inmates eyes, his fellow prisoners felt no sympathy for him; on the contrary, he would have energetically supported the brigade commander if he had thrown Artiom to the floor and started stomping on him.

"Sleeping in a hole in the ground, you jackal mug!" the brigade commander growled in his wake. He pulled the sheet, covered in earth, from the bed and threw it at Artiom.

Artiom caught it, and not knowing what to do with it, twisted it onto his arm.

"No one dares hit me, the beaten *friar*," Artiom joked silently. "Look, they even gave me a sheet!"

Turning it around and slightly shaking it out, Artiom threw the sheet over his shoulder and wore it as though it were a white robe, even if it was dirty.

The soldier didn't care, and no one paid him any attention in the monastery's courtyard — on Solovki people walked around in all kinds of get-up… maybe the young man was carrying all his possessions on him.

"This is my handkerchief," Artiom mocked. "Let Krapin be jealous!"

The soldier, who walked into IID first, didn't go up the stairs, but in the opposite direction, downwards. Artiom even stopped to wait for him; maybe the soldier needed to get some tobacco from a buddy of his?

Though in his heart, he understood everything at once.

He even understood as he was fooling about with his sheet outside.

"Why are you standing there?" barked the soldier, who ran back towards Artiom, grabbed him by the neck and pushed him in front of him, adding a fist between his shoulder blades for good measure.

He walked down the ancient stone stairs, into the basement rooms. The soldier knocked on a metal door with his fist, and from there he heard a question, "Who is it?"

"I've brought Goriainov," answered the soldier, not mixing up a single letter of his last name.

They locked him in there, behind the metal doors, in a dark, musty room with no windows.

Artiom stood near the door, getting used to the darkness and listening in — is there anyone else here? Judging by the noise of the door as it slammed shut behind him, the room was not large.

And empty.

Well, settle in and live.

"He's already woken up, go ahead and bring him," someone said loudly in the corridor.

They opened the door again and commanded Artiom to come out.

"I was just getting used to it," said Artiom.

The soldier didn't answer, but only gathered his hatred for the next blow.

They went up the way they had come.

"They're going to put me back in my monastic cell and say, 'Go ahead and sleep some more, buddy, sorry for bothering you! They'll send a boat for you soon… right into the monastery's courtyard. Would you like a motor boat or a sailboat…?'" Artiom told himself, like a bedtime story.

In a second-story office, Gorshkov sat, looking horribly tired. His tight cheeks had wilted a bit, but he was in a good mood, with even a sparkle of mischief in his eyes.

"It's not the torture room at least," Artiom tried to buck himself up.

The whitewash was poked out in several places.

"Oh, it's Burtsev's office," Artiom guessed easily. "Look who's moved in now!"

The room was a badly cleaned mess — they had clearly pulled out the drawers from the cabinets, breaking some of them out in the process, then they had haphazardly put them back. Several papers, trampled, still lay on the floor; a pile of folders was dumped in the left corner behind Gorshkov's back.

"He's brought his sheet along with him!" said Gorshkov, but as though not to Goriainov, but to someone else, someone invisible. "He's going to gather his teeth in it!"

"What? Is he talking to Burtsev, the half-wit scum?" Artiom wondered.

The new inhabitant of the office nodded at the stool next to the desk.

Artiom sat, having folded the messy sheet onto his knees.

"Last name?"

He named himself and gave his conviction and time served.

"Vasilii Petrovich Vershilin — do you know him?" asked Gorshkov, sighing a bit wearily, but with the same kind of feeling that a person has when offered a second or even a third bowl of soup that he has to somehow plough through.

"Vasilii Petrovich?" asked Artiom. "Of course I do. We were in the same brigade. And bunked next to each other."

"What about Sergei Yurievich Mezernitskii?" Gorshkov occasionally noted something in his papers.

"Mezernitskii?" Artiom kept repeating the names, to have time to think, though there was hardly anything special he could come up with in the circumstances. "I've seen him."

"Did you ever meet with him before your incarceration here?"

"With Mezernitskii? Of course not. I've only seen him in the camp."

"How many times?"

"A few times."

"Under what circumstances?"

"Under what… at first living, then dead."

Gorshkov gathered his lips like the rump of a chicken, not so much thinking as resting. He had no time for Goriainov's jokes.

"Mstislav Arkadievich Burtsev," Gorshkov uttered a short while later, not without pleasure — it seemed that he, as he named each of them, built a wall from building blocks. "Did you know him?"

Artiom coughed, though he didn't want to cough.

"Burtsev was in our brigade too," he said. "The same as Vasilii Petrovich."

"I'm asking if you knew him personally," repeated Gorshkov, fixing Artiom with his small eyes.

"I knew him personally," said Artiom, "but we weren't close."

"Did you ever meet Burtsev in the cell of Mezernitskii at one of the evening parties that you called…" Gorshkov looked through his papers. "The Athenian nights?"

"Evenings," Artiom corrected him.

Gorshkov was looking at him with his small eyes, not blinking.

Artiom was quiet, then repeated.

"Athenian evenings. I saw him there once."

"Or twice?" asked Gorshkov.

Artiom coughed again.

"Interesting," thought Artiom. "Does Galia know where I am? Her office is exactly above this one. Maybe I should scream in an inhuman voice, and she would hear?"

"Did you and Burtsev discuss his work in the Information and Investigation Department?" Gorshkov kept on digging.

"The citizen commandant is looking for a new conspiracy, so that Nogtev would be impressed and would assign him his new best friend." Artiom guessed without any difficulty. The only thing that was still unclear was what he should do in this situation. The poor foxes were probably hungry. The covers of the food boxes aren't closed. Krapin is walking around, unhappy.

"On the other hand," he tried to think slowly, as though walking through a swamp, "I'm not involved in anything and am not guilty of anything. Other than seeing Burtsev at Mezernitskii's, they've got nothing on me."

It helped Artiom that he had watched Gorshkov that time on Lesser Muksol'ma and knew the pitiful agitation of this Chekist, remembering how Eichmanis had knocked the stool out from under him. Artiom wasn't afraid of Gorshkov, and he was, as much as possible, calm. Though, maybe that wasn't such a good idea.

"No, never," Artiom finally said. "We didn't get along. He beat me up once. It was because of him that I was in the infirmary. We didn't speak at all."

Gorshkov wiggled his burnt-off eyebrows and, it seemed, didn't believe a single word that Artiom had said.

"Then how did you know that Grakov was a secret collaborator with the Information and Investigation Department?" asked Gorshkov, and, extremely pleased with himself, leaned back in his chair.

His eyes had an affecting look, and, yes, they were cunning.

"Vasilii Petrovich gave me up," Artiom said to himself and even forget what he had to answer in the quiet, heart-felt surprise.

"How did you know about the informant?" Gorshkov suddenly yelled and jumped up from his seat.

"I didn't know anything about any informant!" answered Artiom loudly, as though that would be more convincing.

Gorshkov, clenching his fists, went around his desk and stood next to Artiom, bending down slightly.

"Maybe I should grab his leg too, like Galia," Artiom had enough strength to joke with himself. "Maybe I'll guess right again, like that time."

"Think one more time, jackal, and answer."

"... Then there's the stupid sheet..." the thought passed through Artiom's head.

Gorshkov was in his boots, and knocked the stool out from underneath him.

"... He didn't forget how Eichmanis did that to him."

Artiom fell on the ground and got a few kicks with the nose of the boot on his neck, though he was probably aiming for the teeth. The next blow landed on his ear — it hurt, for real! The third was on his hand, with which he tried to cover his head, though Gorshkov was aiming at the same ear.

"I'm going to go deaf, and then I won't be able to answer any question." Artiom was aware of everything to a sickening degree of accuracy, constantly asking himself with an angry scoff: "What do people do in these situations? What should I do? Grab the boot and kiss it? Say that Galia told me about the informant? Then they'll let me go immediately? I'll tell you, bitch, just you try…"

Gorshkov grabbed the stool from the floor and, in three generous swings, as though he were chipping wood on a gorgeous sunny morning, broke it over Artiom's back.

"They're so flimsy," he complained, throwing the stool, broken in half, on the floor. "The local woodworkers make them, the damn jackals…"

Straightening himself out, Gorshkov went to grab his own chair, and, returning, put it right in front of Artiom's face.

Artiom examined Gorshkov's boots. Then he noticed another broken stool lying in the far corner of the room.

"It seems… they're… redecorating," he thought, gasping.

It hurt in his ear, in the back of his head… his back felt like an accordion that a bear had played…

"The question was as follows," said Gorshkov, catching his breath. "How did you know that the citizen journalist of the Solovki newspaper, the inmate Grakov, was secretly cooperating with the Information and Investigation Department?"

Artiom pulled the long end of the sheet closer to his head — he wiped blood from his face… from where had it managed to flow already?

"I didn't know," he answered quietly, smelling the blood on the sheet. "I guessed."

He looked at Gorshkov from below — it was a strange thing. He was still not frightening… so why did his ear hurt so much…?

The door opened. The chair on which Gorshkov sat moved a bit. Artiom guessed that Gorshkov had turned to see who had walked in.

Artiom looked sideways and saw two more male boots, only about three sizes larger.

"He's got a sheet," said the new boots. "Why didn't he bring his pillow too?"

That was Tkachuk — it was hard not to recognize his voice, which had come out of his belly, where it lived among the huge tangle of intestines and a horse-sized spleen.

Tkachuk came to the prone Artiom. The heaviness of his step was such that the boards bent.

Artiom pulled his legs to his stomach, while his hands — with the ends of the sheet gathered into a knot — to his very face.

"He's moving like a caterpillar…" said Tkachuk. "Did he say anything?"

Gorshkov didn't answer. Evidently, he made some sort of gesture.

Artiom knew for a fact that it was time to screw up his eyes. And he did.

The blow was so powerful that he flew, like a bag of bones, to the opposite wall.

Artiom didn't think anything anymore, and only rolled into a knot, into a ball, into a wet, rancid, cockle-cockle-dough.

"Let's sit him up again," offered Gorshkov. "I can't see his eyes. You can always tell by the eyes if he's afraid or not."

"Why wouldn't he be scared?" said Tkachuk with the voice of a person who had never beaten anyone and wasn't even planning on it. "He's scared all right."

"… He's lying, so no," Gorshkov put himself straight.

"Why wouldn't he lie?" said Tkachuk. "He's lying all right… I saw another stool in the corridor."

He opened the door and immediately greeted someone, cracking a smile.

"What're you up to in there?" asked a woman's voice.

Artiom pulled away the sheet from his face and saw Galia. She stood at the threshold of the room and looked in from beyond Tkachuk, rising up a bit on her toes and still not even reaching his shoulder.

"Here," said Tkachuk indifferently, and, turning aside, indicated Artiom.

Artiom, moving his legs, rose up to his elbow, then sat with his back to the wall.

He looked Galia in the eyes, without any request, without any desperation, without anything.

"We're working, Galina," Gorshkov said in an unfriendly voice from his chair, not looking at her all the same, but at the conscious Artiom. "What business do you have with us?"

Galina hesitated for a moment and thought of something: "Nogtev was looking for you."

"He found me already," said Gorshkov. "The head of the camp knows that I'm working… What else?" And he turned to Galina.

"Nothing," she said.

Tkachuk led Galia away with his glance, looked in the other direction of the corridor, and announced, "There is no other stool. Let him talk standing… Get up, you branded bastard!"

* * *

The inmates talked quietly, like kidnapped children in someone else's house.

Artiom sat in his place in his underwear and listened to the never-ending wind.

In the space under the door, barely alive, a lamp smoked.

Along the walls of the cold church, in two levels, the bunks stood empty.

Artiom immediately, habitually, took a place on top.

He didn't even have time to think that if they had a stove in the church, it would be warmer on the top level. He just picked a place and, in contrast to the others who were driven together with him into the penal isolation ward, didn't just stand in place at the entrance, suffering from indecision. Instead, he immediately determined where he should live. Because he was planning on living.

Vasilii Petrovich was in the same column. The shirt on his chest and back was ripped to shreds. Even when he was undressing in the street, Artiom noticed many different-shaped bruises, as though they had sprinkled Vasilii Petrovich with many different kinds of berries and then crushed them. The spots then dried and now drily shone in different colors.

Without his usual cap, overgrown with a pathetic bristle, he looked like an old man. Looking around nearsightedly, Vasilii Petrovich saw Artiom climbing up and hurried to occupy the place underneath.

He wasn't acting normally.

"Maybe he's gone crazy and thinks that we're in the twelfth brigade still?" Artiom asked himself without any emotion, looking from above at the balding, and also somehow thinned-out, head of Vasilii Petrovich.

Sometimes, the head quivered slightly.

"And when it gets cold?" someone asked in a whisper not far away from them. "How do we survive here?"

"Survive until winter," hoarsely and quietly said someone, though everyone heard it. He had already been in the church when the new prisoners arrived in the church. Artiom could see his place from his bunk.

A few people came up to his bunk below, towards the voice. Someone asked, "How is it here? What?"

But the man who was dressed in two or three pairs of underwear, as well as some inconceivable rags several layers thick, said nothing more, as though he were preserving every word, knowing that he only had a few more left to say before his death.

"He has taken off the underwear from dead bodies," Artiom understood. Even before the cold came, it was already unpleasant here — a damp room, constantly moving air. It was no more than ten degrees outside.

Many people shivered, their jaws chattering, though it was unclear whether that was from cold or terror. Others, trying to warm themselves, walked back and forth along the church. Still, it wasn't clear if they were getting warmer.

Not far from Artiom, there was a window. He climbed up there, perhaps, without thinking about it, because there was at least a little bit of light, even through the shield that covered the window from the outside — everywhere else, there was a half-darkness.

One person in the lower levels lit a match — it was immediately snuffed out by the wind.

"Oh, dear," he said, as though getting angry at the match.

That was Khasaev the Chechen, the former duty officer of the twelfth brigade. Artiom recognized him. Khasaev was hairy, strong and, in contrast to most of the others, he didn't freeze, only slouched and looked around as though he knew for sure that there would be an exit from here as well, he just needed to figure out where it was.

After becoming a bit accustomed, Artiom understood that he would regret taking this spot in winter — there was no stove in the church; however, if there was a slanting, angry wind, the snowy powder from the window would fly right onto his bunk.

"... Later, everything later," thought Artiom, patting the walls.

It was as though he were in a half-drunk state that had not yet aired itself out and was still confusing his head; he hadn't yet come back to sufficient consciousness to remember what had happened yesterday.

The walls were covered in crude whitewash — the Bolsheviks, as the new masters, had probably covered the icons.

He had to understand how and with what he could get warm here — until the time it should all end — after all, it would end. Galia would come up with something, his mother would beg him free, or anything else might happen — the important thing was not to freeze right now. For now, nothing came into his mind.

They had forced everyone to take their shoes and clothes off to their undies at the entrance to the church. They piled it all together and promised to burn it. "You all won't need them anymore, and there's no point in freezing the lice!" the guards yelled, making each other laugh.

They only allowed them to bring spoons — whoever had them. Artiom had them. While he was still on Fox Island, Krapin had advised him to sew an extra spoon into the lining of his jacket. When he was undressing, he had pulled it out.

He also had, unlike many others, wool socks, also taken from Fox Island. And he still had the sheet. It was his good luck that as they dragged him from Gorshkov's office, he was still clutching the sheet in his clenched hands.

Later, as he lay in solitary, trying to overcome the pain in his entire body, Artiom had lowered his pants a bit, and, raising his undershirt, had wrapped the sheet around himself to keep warm.

"They beat, they kneaded the dough… the bride and the groom,"[45] Artiom said to himself, feeling that he was crying, and even the tears hurt his face.

He hadn't said anything to Gorshkov ultimately, only, as soon as they started to beat him, he yelled like someone in a fit, "I didn't know that Grakov was a snitch! Didn't know! I guessed! It's written on his forehead that he's a snitch! Who else can work at the newspaper on Solovki! I didn't know… I guessed!"

Gorshkov, you could see, had spent a sleepless night with Vasilii Petrovich, and he ended up not having enough meticulousness to break Artiom.

They only beat Artiom until lunch — only about six hours, no more, and even so without especial inspiration and with breaks — Tkachuk went to get some pies in the main kitchen, then he and Gorshkov ate them and discussed the counter-rev girls who had come into the women's barracks with the new work groups, not forgetting all the while to look sideways at Artiom to check that he was standing straight.

From his solitary confinement, Artiom was no longer called out to be interrogated. The next day, while it was still dark, even before the siren, they drove him here.

Along the way, Artiom didn't greet anyone or say anything; moreover, there was no opportunity — a downpour started, cruelly teasing, then stopped suddenly. Many thought that they were being taken out to be shot, until a wet, quavering whisper passed along the lines — they were going toward Sekirka.

Every prisoner knew that the hill of Sekirka was almost death. But it wasn't death yet.

Artiom believed that at least there it would be dry.

He wanted to get rid of that wetness and the endless dirt that crawled under his feet as soon as possible.

Artiom had time to notice the dome of the chapel on Sekirnaia Hill itself… the road went up from the chapel — there a red, broken cross extended its arms, meeting the new parishioners… the smoothly whittled white

45 A Russian nursery rhyme.

handrails, the stone rim along the road was painted with whitewash… on the seventy-meter height of Sekirnaia Hill stood a white church covered with red tin — the octagonal church of the Ascension… the windows of the church were also painted white. Red shields covering the windows… a drum-shaped bell tower with four openings for the ringing…

The onion dome crowning the church was covered in wooden scales, with a glass lighthouse lantern.

Like a madman in the bushes, not far from the church stuck out a yellow house, winking with the evil and frightful eye of its window. That, it seemed, was where the administration of the fourth division of the camp of Solovki was stationed.

The entrance to the church was on the western side. There was a wooden lean-to at the entrance.

In the narthex of the church were stairs leading through the bell tower to the lighthouse, but the entrance was boarded up completely. Someone had said that you could see that lighthouse fifty kilometers away…

A black dog on a chain barked at the prisoners.

The rain, which had come from Sekirka downward, ran its fingers and hurriedly pinched the trees, one after the other, like a blind man in search of his child.

Artiom's heart was dull.

He wrung out his socks and boxers, put them underneath himself, then rolled himself up in the sheet and lay on top to dry them out with his body.

He forgot himself in a difficult, frozen sleep for an hour, maybe two. A scream woke him up: "What is this? If they don't shoot us, they'll starve and freeze us!"

Everyone seemed to gather boldness from the voice and immediately started to yell — it wasn't frightening to scream in a crowd.

The boldest threw himself at the doors and began to beat it with his hands and feet.

Completely frozen through, Artiom sat on the bunk. His hands shook, either from yesterday's beatings or from digging the graves the day before, and they were covered in blisters, as though he had grabbed stinging nettles all day. His chest ached as though he had drunk water from the black depths of a well, his elbows were dislocating from their joints from his shakes, his feet danced…

At least his underwear had dried.

Artiom tore the sheet in two, took off his shirt, for a moment remaining completely naked, and he tensed all his muscles so that his hands would listen. Then he wrapped his pounded, but not quite fully pounded, body anew.

"Mommy, I've put on my diaper. Bring me your titty with the milk," asked Artiom, his teeth chattering.

Once again he put on his underwear and socks and together with the rest of the rampaging inmates yelled, "Stove! Stove! Food! Food! Stove! Stove! Food! Food!"

His blood warmed up a little from the screaming, many were screaming, dancing in place, or striking their bunks with their fists. Then someone said:

"Quiet! Quiet! What's that sound? Are they coming?"

Closer and closer sounded a gentle ringing.

The deadbolt rattled.

In the opening of the doors, a soldier and a Chekist in a leather jacket appeared. The Chekist smiled gently and hopefully, like a matchmaker. In his hands was a large bell, and he rang it. No one dared to interrupt this ringing with a scream or a word.

The soldier grabbed the first inmate near the doors by the scruff and pulled him out.

The door closed.

The bells rang in the opposite direction.

Everyone understood that while the bell rang, nothing would happen.

The bell fell silent, and immediately a shot rang out.

* * *

It got colder at night. Artiom, like almost everyone in the icebox, slept in several shifts. Over the course of an hour or two he froze so much that his mind grew turbid.

He was forced to get up, and, bumping into the other inmates, to walk in circles in complete darkness.

Then he lay down again, took off his socks and put them on his hands like mittens. He dreamed too that he had stretched them so much that he could climb inside with his whole body — that was the last good dream he had that night.

Soon he had to get up again — it got three times colder, though it had seemed that nothing worse was possible.

"What if it snows?" thought Artiom. "It's probably not even minus one yet…"

Once again he walked in a circle.

The lice returned. Artiom had had time to forget them after the twelfth. In the second, they had more or less exterminated them, while in the iodine plant and on Fox Island there were no lice at all.

Now the lice were bothering him, though they helped him battle his sleep.

Someone, managing to fall asleep on his feet, fell on Artiom. He caught the sleeping man, wanted immediately to get rid of this foreign creature, but instead of that, he held him in his arms a little longer he was warm, after all.

The person woke up and pushed Artiom in the chest.

"The important thing is to survive till the morning," Artiom begged himself, stomping. "The important thing — survive till morning."

After a third descent into dark dreams, which resulted in Artiom being covered in an icy crust that stuck to his body both inside and out, he didn't even try to sleep again. Neither walking in a circle, nor grimacing and jumping around could warm him enough to give him the will to lie down on the bunk. What would he do there? Freeze through?

The pain in his ribs was forgotten in the cold, as well as his deformed nose that had spread out over his entire face, and his hands, covered in blisters, and his dislocated jaw, because of which any loudly spoken word pained him sharply in the back of the head, as though a fishbone was stuck in his brains.

By morning, his state was such that if Artiom was offered another interrogation in Gorshkov's office, he would have run there.

It turned out that there is nothing worse than cold, even when Gorshkov beat him in the face. Artiom could, as if passed out, wait it out, then crawl into the corner and suddenly, through his half-wittedness and bestial sorrow, sniveling with a bloody nose, he remembered how upset he was at Krapin with his bludgeon — hilarious! Too funny.

Cold was more frightening than Tkachuk and Gorshkov put together — you couldn't make a joke about cold, because the mind refused to see anything funny in it, the world in general no longer waited for any answers or left any reason for hope.

The body froze and prayed for at least some warm thing, as for eternal life — Artiom couldn't even imagine how much he would have given for a hot mug of water… He would have even given up that same eternal life, not even so much for hot water, but even for a hot, empty mug.

But then the sun appeared and he climbed up to his bunk, and tried to lure it to himself, on himself, inside himself, at least a single ray.

By nine o'clock, they brought food — that same hot water and three quarters of a pound of unbaked bread.

Khasaev volunteered to take control, no one dissented.

He poured out the hot water into several clay cups; no one fought or got scared. There was enough for everyone.

Artiom drank, sifting each blessed swallow of the magical hot water, then he ate the bread without leaving any for later, holding in his mouth every bit of pulp, frugally and extremely carefully broken off, until it just melted in his mouth.

He had barely gotten warm at all, but his blood came back to life and was grateful to Artiom and to the sun, which finally became perceptible; the pain in his nose, back, lips, ribs, and back of head even returned. But that was OK. That he could endure. That would heal.

His vision, hearing, reasoning, ability to smile — they all returned. He decided to hold on to eternal life for the time being.

In the side altars, it turned out, there were even more solitary iceboxes.

"... What, do they put the completely naked ones there?" Artiom asked himself. "And don't feed them at all?"

The latrine stood in the place of the Holy Offering — a tub with a board.

Artiom visited this place as well. Coming back from there, rubbing his pained sides with his twisted finger, under-slept, he was still a bit more cheerful.

"What about the monk that lived in the hole — how was it for him?" thought Artiom. "They didn't bring him any hot water..."

The first thing that Artiom understood about Sekirka was that work, at least in autumn, was not the worst thing in the world. If they had driven them all outside, it would have been much simpler.

One of the long-time residents in Sekirka, dressed in several shirts and briefs, attracted attention to himself. He had firmly wrapped rags on his swollen feet, one layer on top of the other, like a cabbage.

From his behavior, Artiom understood another law of Sekirka — it was better to sleep during the day, since it was warmer then, while at night you had to move and survive.

In the morning, the old-timer of Sekirka, who hadn't lain down for a moment, walked past all the bunks, like a forest manager, touching the foreheads and cheeks of the prisoners who hadn't gotten up yet. Sometimes they yelled at him; he walked away silently, saying nothing.

He was watching for any night death — it had happened last night. One inmate died.

However, Vasilii Petrovich himself had figured out that any clothing, even taken off a dead man, is better than no clothing at all. So without any excessive conversation, he was the first to pull off the briefs from the dead man.

The spectacle was unpleasant, and Artiom turned around.

The old-timer, standing at the dead man's head, was planning on doing exactly the same. He inaudibly complained and tried to grab hold of the underwear.

Vasilii Petrovich straightened out, leaving the shorts on the dead man's knees, gathering the face of the old-timer in his iron fingers and sharply straightened his hand — the man, his legs buckling under him, fell on the stone floor, striking it with the back of his head hard. Having lived a week, or perhaps a month, on Sekirka, he ended up being much weaker than the merely two-day-beaten gatherer of berries with an unpleasant past.

Vasilii Petrovich's head especially shook now, but the movements were angry, jerky and confident. He pulled out his spoon from his pants, crouched down, pressing down on the chest of the fallen man, and, having pressed the edge of the spoon to his closed eye, promised, "If you come up one more time, I'll blind you." And he pressed.

This was a different Vasilii Petrovich, someone Artiom had never met, making himself seriously doubt that he had ever eaten berries from his hand.

Artiom quickly got up to his bunk to try to get at least a little bit warmer. Maybe the sun's generosity would extend to a single long ray reaching up to Sekirnaia Hill itself?

A little later, as in past times, the head of Vasilii Petrovich appeared next to his bunk.

"… To say hello would be stupid," he said quietly, as though continuing a conversation he had started in the twelfth brigade. "Good day — simply awful. I greet you — nonsense. Maybe the Bolsheviks will come up with a new word for decent people to use when greeting each other in such places… What do you think, Artiom? 'What, not dead yet?' — is that a possible option? Except it has to be pronounced in a single word. Whanodeayet? There's something Egyptian-sounding in that, from the age of Pharaohs… But I still want to tell you… hello."

Artiom was trying to catch a ray of sunlight in his palm, as though he were planning on storing up the warmth and washing with it.

"Hello," he said calmly. What? Should he be bothered about Gorshkov's back now?

"Did you know? My father finished his life as a 'wild landowner.'" Vasilii Petrovich put his hands on Artiom's bunk and petted the boards as though he were trying to warm himself on them. "You probably don't know what that is? That's a landowner who either sold or drank away his estate, but remained in those places where in past times he had the power to kill or pardon. At first, a merchant fed him by buying off our family estate for nothing, and garden, and stable, and… everything else. Later, the merchant got sick of him, and my father walked around the peasants' yards, and they would bring him out either an egg or some moonshine. And they called him, 'wild landowner'. And he thanked them in French, drank, then walked on… They say that he was accidentally shot by the merchant's guests when they were out hunting. I don't know. I despised him terribly… But if my own son would see me now!" And Vasilii Petrovich nodded at his new underwear, which Artiom couldn't see.

"You have a son?" asked Artiom.

"A son?" Vasilii Petrovich echoed. "Yes. Well, no. And I never did. At first I thought that you could become my son… And in some sense you have become him — you despise me as much as children despise their parents."

"I? Why? No," said Artiom, and, abandoning hope of the sun's ray, put his hands under his armpits — they were only getting cold.

"Then you're certainly not my son. You don't care," Vasilii Petrovich concluded.

It was strange, but his voice calmed Artiom, and he was already ready to remember the accursed life in the twelfth brigade as the good old days — right now, Vasilii Petrovich will call him to descend, then offer some berries and even a dried biscuit, and even some tea — how sad that it all had to end. Looking intently at the squinting eyes of Vasilii Petrovich, Artiom remained silent. Vasilii Petrovich was right. He really didn't care.

"Artiom, I would like to tell you, it's important to me, you see…" Vasilii Petrovich said and even looked around, as though his confessions could possibly be interesting to anyone here. "When you and I… socialized and were, I hope, friends… I didn't lie to you once. Do you understand? I just never spoke about certain things."

Artiom nodded. It would have made sense right now to tell Vasilii Petrovich that he could have not spoken about "certain things" during his interrogation — but what was the point? It was an excessive waste of warmth.

Clicking his tongue with suppressed and surprised pain, Artiom scratched his chest — a louse.

* * *

After the morning inspection, a soldier came and commanded Khasaev to choose orderlies.

As was his habit, Artiom hid, and they didn't choose him.

They told the orderlies to carry out the latrine.

According to the same habit, Artiom was happy that he didn't have to do that work, but then realized that he was being stupid. To carry out the latrine meant to be in the sun, to breathe the air, to look around, to stretch, to smell the light of the sun. If he were to do everything slowly, he could perhaps have a ten-minute walk — depending on where they emptied the latrine. Maybe even more!

Returning with the latrine, the orderlies immediately turned back — this time to carry out the body. Khasaev had told the soldiers about the body.

Turning around, Artiom fell asleep again, this time deeply. During the day, the air was a bit warmer. He had very many dreams; they constantly switched and got confused with each other. One pushed out another, and all he could remember was that somewhere nearby they had lit a stove, but, though the logs were already alight, the fire in the stove was still cold, as though it had to get warm first. Artiom waited patiently, sometimes touching the tongue of the flame with his hand — the sensation was similar to when someone sprays cologne or alcohol on his hand. Then he turned his back to the fire and began to wait for it to mature.

His entire dream was endurance incarnate.

By lunch, his body had forgotten about the hot water and the bread that had melted in his mouth.

The inmates who had started to talk to each other again fell silent, lying there soured and freezing. They kept their eyes half-open, as though even they were freezing.

For lunch, they fed them again: gruel.

In the gruel, there was neither fish, nor carrot, nor potato, nor cabbage — nothing. Only a few snotty conglomerations that stuck to the sides and the bottom — but at least it was extremely hot, and while Artiom held the cup in his hands, his palms managed to sweat and his blisters even sweetly ached.

After the gruel, they even offered some tea — that is, an entire bucket of hot water.

Khasaev had already come into his own. Someone tried to climb back into line a second time, and he hit him so hard in the chest that the stupid man kept sitting at the doors until the end of the hand-outs, yawning like a fish.

Artiom was frightened when the deadbolts crashed open after lunch — everyone froze in place, trying to determine if the bell would start ringing — but no, and another group of new prisoners were let in, about ten half-naked inmates. Among them was the immediately obvious *Vladychka* John in his cassock.

"They can't leave us without a priest!" someone laughed. "Why didn't they undress you, *Vladychka*?"

"Even Chekists are afraid of a naked priest," he answered, laughing, and many people thought it was funny, as though hope glimmered.

Vasilii Petrovich immediately got up from his bunk, overjoyed more than anyone else, as though his closest relatives had come to visit him. Artiom suddenly thought that his former friend probably had no one — no wife, no parents and no one to remember him.

"... Except perhaps some invalids wandering on the face of the earth, whom he didn't quite finish torturing, only tearing out a piece, like from Paschal bread," Artiom said to himself.

Vladychka took the place of the inmate who had died in the night.

A few people came up to him for a blessing; he had compassion for all of them and patted them on the head.

Artiom, his legs hanging from his bunk, nonchalantly watched all this and battled his silent desire to come down and also find warmth under the freckled hand of *Vladychka*.

He heard snatches of phrases: "... Let's not bemoan..." "Their feet run towards evil, and they hurry to spill innocent blood..." "They've grown up in evil, but are only children in good, but you must do the opposite..." "The Lord resurrected, and all evil and foulness of the world is doomed to die..." "... The almighty Hand..." "We are unworthy of Christ's sufferings, but..."

"Unworthy, but... unworthy, but..." Artiom repeated.

It was as though the entire place filled with *Vladychka*'s words. They rustled like falling leaves. With every burst of wind, the words, flew up to the vaulting and quietly circled up there. Every word could be caught on one's palm. If a word would have landed in a ray of light, you could have seen its thin, blue-veined body.

Vasilii Petrovich patiently waited for the visits to end. The priest remained alone, and Vasilii Petrovich quietly asked what had brought him to Sekirka.

"They informed me," *Vladychka* answered with the same cheerfulness and readiness to speak, "that I nudged Mezernitskii to kill Eichmanis. And they didn't listen to my protestations. Can I possibly nudge a person to place his soul into the fires of Gehenna?"

Artiom jumped down to take part in this curious conversation.

"You are here as well, my dear?" said Father John, looking up at Artiom quickly. "I had thought that your light heart — as your invisible rudder that knows that its ultimate care is in the hands of the Most High — would bear you past all sorrows. But it's too early to despair — I see that people live even here. How do you live here, God's people?"

"We drank two buckets full of hot water, *Vladychka*," said Artiom, waiting for the pain to recede in his leg, and his head, and his back — he needed to jump more carefully. He had even forgotten what it was he wanted to ask. "A bucket of gruel… Some bread to suck on."

"Oh, they feed you here?" *Vladychka* threw up his arms. "Here I was thinking that they were taking me here to starve, and they put me on the hill so that my exhausted spirit wouldn't have as far to fly!" *Vladychka* laughed. "That means that, trusting in our Lord, there is reason to hope that we may endure even the tribulation of Sekirka. Every time," he continued, enjoying to hear himself speak, "when you walk past a black cap-band or a leather jacket, when you bend your back next to a foreman or a brigade commander, you think — they're going to bludgeon me right now, and my spirit will fly up — catch it by the tail, like a dove. But they don't bludgeon you every time! And one time they don't, and two times, and then sometimes they even say a human word, not just barking or meowing! And you once again start thinking that people are good!"

Vladychka looked over Artiom and Vasilii Petrovich, as though expecting that they would share his strange revelation, but since they didn't hurry to do so, he agreed to contradict himself.

"… However, you only seem to get used to people being good, and then you remember that there was such a person as Putsha, and Talets and Elovets Lyashko, who killed St. Boris by the order of the accursed Sviatopolk. St. Gleb had a cook named Torchin, who cut his throat open. There were Muscovites, one of whom put St. Philip in irons — he who was the former abbot of Solovki, the metropolitan of Moscow and all Rus, another man put his foot in irons and a third put metal chains on the old man's neck. And when they led Philip into exile, the cruel Stepan Kobylin treated him inhumanly, torturing him with hunger and cold. And then there was Maliuta Skuratov, who smothered St. Philip with a pillow. And all these, who tortured and tormented our saints, all these executioners and torturers had children. While Boris didn't have time to give birth to children, nor did Gleb. And St. Philip lived in celibacy. And I look around sometime and think, maybe, that only the children of Putsha and Skuratov remain, the children of Elovets and

Kobylin? And they prowl all through Russia — these children of the murderers of holy martyrs, and even the new martyrs are children of murderers, because there are no other children left."

Vladychka suddenly broke into tears, quietly and helplessly, like an old man, ashamed of himself. No one dared to calm him. Only those who were walking around the church stood still and those who were talking at their bunks fell silent.

But even that lasted less than a third of a minute.

Vladychka sighed and wiped his eyes with his sleeve.

"But we have to love even them," he said and looked around at everyone. "If only I had the strength."

* * *

At nine o'clock, they had the evening inspection.

They didn't bring dinner.

Artiom sat on his bunk, hugging his knees, and firmly understood that to sleep tonight would be even more unbearable than yesterday; a freezing sleet gathered in the sky.

"What about the Indian Summer?" thought Artiom. "Did it happen already?"

In answer, a snowflake landed on his windowsill.

Artiom smashed it with his finger.

"It's winter; it's over," he said.

For some reason, with every hour he hoped less and less for Galia's help. For the last two days, he remembered neither her face nor, obviously, his encounters with her, even though the silent conviction in her quickly helped breathe life inside him.

But, having lived these days in a painful torpor of spirit — which didn't prevent him, for all that, from drinking hot water, speaking, examining the quivering head of Vasilii Petrovich, listening in on *Vladychka*'s speeches — he, without realizing it and without even trying, had lost that conviction.

… Only once, during the frozen-over leisure time of Sekirka, he looked into the corner of his heart, where his confidence in Galia was preserved. He found nothing there.

Immediately he convinced himself that in that place, from the very beginning, there was nothing at all. No Galia existed in nature; she could never have existed.

This seemed a much easier way for Artiom to survive.

Amusing himself, he, while it still wasn't dark, scraped off the whitewash from the walls. His hands were clumsy and crooked from cold, but at least it was some kind of activity.

Behind a layer of whitewash, he found an eye.

He scraped off some more and found an ear.

You could say something into that ear.

Artiom, unexpectedly inspired, continued his work, but the unhappy voice of Vasilii Petrovich sounded from below: "Artiom, why is it constantly flaking from up there? Are you cleaning out your wardrobe?"

Answering nothing, Artiom left his work until tomorrow.

Near midnight, feeling the constant cold and the sticky hoarfrost even in the roots of his hair, Artiom climbed down.

He tried to console himself with the fact that among the prisoners here there were many who were barefoot — how could they walk on the floor…? But others' suffering didn't strengthen his spirit.

Many coughed in the church, someone moaned from the cold, someone cried, someone prayed — there was an incessant noise, as though it were the waiting room to the sauna of hell.

Everyone tried to find at least some kind of source of heat — O, if only a hot knitting needle would appear in the middle of the church — what joy that would be!

Hugging himself with awkward hands, Artiom seriously wondered if a human being could curl up into a ball like a hedgehog. But then again, why was he wondering about human beings — he, the self-same Artiom — could he?

To curl up and roll away into a corner, to grow a bristle there, to fall silent, paws inside, the head breathing into one's own belly button, and nothing but the back exposed to the outside.

Eh? Why not? Why was Artiom torturing his mind with unnecessary knowledge, lines of poetry, why did he twist about on a pull up bar, work out his muscles, learn how to box, instead of learning the only necessary and important thing in life — to be able to curl up into a ball like a hedgehog?

The entrance door thundered open. Everyone stopped in frightened expectation, which could immediately become joy.

In the opening, a soldier appeared. A single one.

"Soldier, maybe you can bring a little stove?" someone asked so pitifully it was funny, as though he were a rejected man pining for his lover.

"A candle for the departed," answered the soldier in the same spirit and threw a pile of clothing on the floor.

It was immediately obvious that there weren't enough things for everyone, and even if they were to tear each thing in half, many would still get nothing.

No one had yet managed to grab a single shirt from the pile, but the crowd of inmates moved in a way that revealed a huge detachment from humanity — everyone only wanted something for himself.

"Hey!" yelled Khasaev. "I'm in charge here! I'll pass them out!"

But no one even turned his head towards him.

"There's going to be a fight right now..." Artiom understood. He had had darned good luck before — the only thing was that he didn't want to expose his bruised ribs again, but there was nothing else he could do.

"My children," said *Vladychka* quietly, but everyone heard him and stopped. "Lest we freeze, we'll have to not only live, but even sleep as true brothers in Christ. There are not enough things for all of us, anyone can see that."

"Tell us, *batushka*, tell us what to do," someone offered the opinion of the majority.

"We walk here and there, only making gusts of wind, while it would be wiser to conserve heat. And when the boldest, or the strongest, or the stupidest among us will put on these things, they will also not become much warmer, but will only incite the worst qualities of their neighbors — hatred, envy, or even, when the snows come (and my bones sense the coming of snow already), a desire to kill."

"*Vladychka,* quickly already!" asked someone, apparently even now barely holding off the desire to plunge into that pile, and also the hatred, envy, and all the rest he mentioned.

John offered to put down a few boards from the bunks on the ground and to lie down stacked up in rows — four people below, four across on top of them, and then another four, creating a kind of double lattice, then another four across again... On top, he offered to put the whole pile of clothing.

One such pile-up would be too large and heavy; therefore, it would be better to make two.

"Once in an hour, we have to get up and the top row must lie on the bottom, then the bottom goes one row higher. Otherwise, we'll crush each other," said *Vladychka*.

His voice sounded confident, as though this church of Sekirka had become a ship, and he, as it turned out, its captain.

He didn't have to try to convince anyone. The most frozen, in their lack of patience, lay down first.

Having lost all their shame and disgust and remembering only the warmth, these men lay on top of each other.

To one pile-up they added a second, next to it, side-to-side, ankle-to-ankle, head-to-head.

The last to lie down was Khasaev. Somehow, he managed to pile everyone with jackets and coats, and it seemed just enough.

"There's one cloak here," said Khasaev. "I'll take it and lie on my own, yes?" he asked with dignity.

No one was against it.

At first, everyone was surprised and even, as much as the circumstances allowed it, people were amused — the lowest patiently endured the heaviness in exchange for warmth, while the topmost laughed, trying not to move too much.

"*Vladychka*, tell us a story," someone asked. "We can't fall asleep without a story."

"I'll pray for you all, my children," said Father John. "Then you'll wake up, and the sun will come out, and the Lord will once again take you into His tender care."

Artiom fell asleep as in childhood, with hope for the morning and his mother's warm hands. As for his own actual mother, worrying near the monastery, he didn't remember her at all not once, and didn't start now. They wouldn't put her in prison, but they'll send her back home. It's her place there. The fact that her son is alive — she knows it. What else does she need to know?

In an hour, according to the word of the as-though-not-sleeping *Vladychka*, both pile-ups dissolved. But then, in the half-darkness the inmates took a very long time to lie down again; they pushed, were confused and argued. One pile-up got mixed up with another so much that in the first, there were twenty men, but only twelve in the second.

During the darkest hour of night, sleep became labor, no less difficult than carrying the logs. Bones ached, heads throbbed, tiredness threatened to overcome, someone was crushed so much that he couldn't get up and had to be helped. Then for a long time, stepping on some people's feet, some people's heads, he climbed up to the top level.

"You clumsy cow, what, are you calving over there?" They were yelling from below.

Vladychka sighed and, it seemed, was sad that he couldn't cross himself, all bundled up as he was. He only repeated, "Oh-oh-oh."

It seemed to Artiom that *Vladychka* listened to the heart of every person who was near him all night. As though he counted the people like a mother hen counts her chicks: there's one heartbeat, there's the fifth, there's the seventh, there's the tenth — everyone's hurrying, running, don't lag behind, my dears.

Further down, someone in the middle started to cough — again everyone was bothered — underneath they hissed for him to shut up, on top they tried to poke him in the side, but probably landed on someone completely different — how can you tell in such a pile-up?

By the morning, they all looked like they had walked around all night, attended three weddings, fought three fights, broke the bones of three grooms and suffered wounds themselves.

But no one froze to death.

* * *

"*Vladychka*, you figured out everyone's salvation," said Artiom, while drinking hot water. "Otherwise, we would have frozen to death one by one."

"I know it," answered Father John with his eternal smile, sarcastic only with reference to himself. For some reason, he smelled of dried apples. "I can't guarantee eternal salvation. Like all of you, I only hope in it. But at least I can provide the temporary option."

"Do you know it, really?" Artiom laughed.

And *Vladychka* too, as though flustered, chuckled very quaintly, looking at Artiom sideways.

"… I adore him!" Artiom suddenly thought with such an extraordinary feeling (for him). He had never before felt like this about another man, except his father.

He felt content and not very cold; in the morning, not thinking long about it, he took one of the jackets that the whole pile-up used at night.

Vladychka leaned towards Artiom's ear and told him with great, appealing secrecy, "In childhood, you play in the sandbox, and sit there thinking, there goes a lady, she's looking at me and thinking, 'What a good boy!'" *Vladychka* leaned back, and, still not laughing, but breathing more rapidly as though preparing to laugh, looked at Artiom. He had the same look that a boy has when telling his friend a dirty joke.

Artiom didn't admit that the same thing had happened to him. The conversation didn't require it. All the more so because *Vladychka* himself continued, "Every person, until his very death, thinks the same thing: 'I'm such a good boy!' Even I, one time during confession, thought about myself, 'What a good priest I am! Oh, how good!'"

Vladychka looked around to see if anyone was listening in on his admission. But he did this more for appearances or maybe even more for Artiom — Father John himself didn't care what people thought about him; he worried more that people might think badly of his friend.

No one, as it seemed to *batushka*, was eavesdropping. Though Artiom saw very well that one of the people in the next bunk constantly kept moving closer to them, lest he miss a single word. Of course, that was Vasilii Petrovich, who clearly was jealous of Artiom.

"Maybe I'm wrong, my dear," Father John said to Artiom in an audible whisper, "but you live in such a way that if you cut your hand, the wound immediately heals. I'm speaking of your spiritual wounds, though even physical wounds on your young skin cover up on the first day like a wave on sand. Some things I see myself, other things I'm told by others. Solovki is good in the sense that everyone here is exposed, like naked people and there's no need to undress anyone. Life is not commensurate with understanding. And you lived by life, not by understanding. Your soul led you lightly and without errors, in spite of much tribulation, slander and difficulty. It is said that with the righteous, you shall be righteous, and with a blameless man, you will be blameless, and with the chosen, you will be chosen, and with the devious you will become depraved. But you were with the depraved and with the guilty, as with the chosen and righteous. Not given to idle talk or laughter, not tending to self-justification, to foul and false language, cunning, hypocrisy, gossip, blasphemy, or despair — you were like a child among all. Like a stalk of wheat not yet full of grain, but filled with the milk of goodness. And if you had to act cruelly, then it was not because you were possessed by an unreasonable anger, but by virtue of the reasonable preservation of your body, which is a vessel into which the spirit of God is placed."

Artiom looked at the stone floor, not moving and clenching his fists tight.

He knew nothing of the sort about himself, nor did he wish to, but it still warmed his heart.

Vasilii Petrovich, it seemed, had completely stopped breathing.

"As for me," *Vladychka* admitted, "I accepted Solovki as a cruel school for the virtues — endurance, love of work, self-restraint. I thank God that I arrived here — here are the graves of righteous men. Before these icons, saints and ascetics crossed themselves, but I pray to them now."

"... Stepan Razin also prayed before these icons," Artiom suddenly remembered, knowing that the insane Cossack, beloved of the downtrodden, came to Solovki twice from the Don, across all of Rus, before the rebellion he had planned. That thought, in a strange way, did not argue with the words of *Vladychka*, but agreed with their truth.

"All who are fated to survive this," *Vladychka* said, as though he saw the future, "will live a long time. And they will no longer fear anything."

"And everyone who is fated to die will die quickly," Artiom laughed pleasantly, quietly and purely, like a good, though brazen, little boy.

"It is so, it is so," *Vladychka* caught up his laugh. "But no matter what your journey, remember that the Lord will watch every one and will give everyone what he deserves by his deeds and faith. It was said that whoever preserves his life will lose it, while whoever loses his life for the sake of our Lord will save it. When I look at you, I console myself with the hope that there are those who do not preserve their own life, and don't lose it. But if you strengthened yourself with the word of the Lord and with faith in Him, it would be a hundred times simpler for you and you would feel angelic wings behind your back. It's difficult, after all, without a guardian angel. If you're in mud to your knees, you won't be able to jump out. But if you prayed, look! He might even carry you over to the other side. You'd come back to your sleeping quarters and your pants are dry, and your shoes haven't fallen apart. If you froze in the snow, you'd look for that wing in the middle of the night, saying a prayer and you'd wrap yourself in it. Perhaps the feather is flimsy to the touch, but it warms by faith. You'll wake up in the morning, look around and there's snow all around you, the hoarfrost hangs heavy on the windows, and the air itself is drawing decorations with ice, but you're whole."

Artiom sighed.

Even looking down at the cold, trampled floors, he felt that Father John looked at him with hope and gentleness.

He raised his eyes at *Vladychka* and nodded: yes, my dear, my grandfather, yes.

Only now did Artiom notice that Father John held in his hands a Gospel that hadn't been confiscated. With his fingers, he patted the threadbare book, as though it were a living thing, and either he was caressing it, or being caressed by it.

"What, is it really that hard for you? Take the book, at least this one time," Artiom begged himself. "How many stupid little books have you taken from your friends without being embarrassed?"

But instead, he got up gently, like a self-styled animal, took the edge of his bunk and deftly threw his significantly-healed body up to his own blowing winds, the light fall of snow on the window sill, and to the ear and eye on the wall that he had yesterday uncovered in part.

Vasilii Petrovich, evidently gladdened by Artiom's departure, sat next to *Vladychka*, and they continued to whisper and laugh about something that they both understood. Or better yet, at first only Vasilii Petrovich laughed, even a little intrusively, while *Vladychka* was quiet, thoughtful about something, but then he also was carried away by the conversation and forgot about his sorrow.

"Well and good," thought Artiom.

He had no problem upsetting anyone — just not *Vladychka*.

Under his bunks, there was nobody, and Artiom continued his work.

The icon revealed itself more and more. Under the whitewash, a face opened up. The sunken cheeks of a person as though sick and suffering. Huge, strict eyes of a greenish-blue color. Black pupils, not quite exactly drawn in each eye, which often happens in icons. A straight nose, beautiful mouth, high forehead, eyebrows like a black bird had shared its wing. A beard — a full wedge, long hair…

Artiom leaned back and suddenly understood what was so attractive and strange about this face. If not for the long hair and beard, the person depicted in the icon would have looked very much like Artiom himself.

Hurriedly, sometimes leaving scratches on the brushwork, he continued to uncover the image, occasionally looking around to see if someone might stop him.

The doors opened loudly, Artiom turned around and covered the holy man who had revealed himself in the cold church.

They had just let in a new group: eight people.

The first was Afanasiev — alive and seemingly unharmed; he also noticed Artiom and waved his hand, simultaneously looking around: can we talk here or not?

"Can we talk in here?" he asked Artiom quietly, not understanding, as soon as the door opened.

"Yes, we can, we can," said Artiom. "Come up here. Here there are some free bunks."

Afanasiev didn't take long to convince, he looked around — should he say hello to anyone else? — and not having honored anyone with a greeting, not even Vasilii Petrovich, climbed up. Not as sprightly as Artiom, but also youthful.

"It's freezing out there," Afanasiev complained. "October, but some kind of awful grains are falling down and immediately melting. Not winter, not autumn. Devil knows what."

"Get undressed for now, let's dry your clothes," Artiom recommended. "I'll let you wear this jacket in the meantime, later you'll give it back."

"Ah, Tiomochka! How good it is to see you," Afanasiev admitted, doing everything as he was commanded. "No sooner do I see you than I… I know that everything has to get better. At one time, I thought that you wouldn't survive long. But now I understand that you have good luck, so I'm going to hold on to your leg when you fly away from this damn hill towards you… where did you live then? Zariadie? You can lower down over the Yaroslavl region a bit and I'll jump down. My village is right there."

Artiom couldn't for the life of him understand what had changed in Afanasiev.

It was immediately clear that he had developed a nervous tic. His right eye kept closing, and in a moment, Afanasiev started his convulsive efforts to open it — such things happened to people sometimes when they just wake up. He helped his eye by raising his eyebrow and opening his mouth, wrinkling his brow like an accordion — at first, nothing happened, but finally the eye opened. Moreover, all this didn't prevent Afanasiev from continuing to speak, which caused an almost frightening impression.

For some time, he spoke, then the eye, as though someone had put a nickel on it, closed again. Another moment, and the face began its work to open it again.

Artiom watched him again and again and realized that Afanasiev's face lived a separate life from Afanasiev himself — he didn't even notice that he had a nervous tic.

But the problem wasn't limited to the eye — there was something else, no less chilling… Artiom, suddenly understanding what it was, peremptorily took his friend by the chin and turned his head. Yes, it was as he thought — Afanasiev's forelock had been torn out — there was no more red bush, only some kind of wormwood shreds.

Squinting and examining him, Artiom noticed a grey tuft on the red head of Afanasiev. That tuft looked ugly, like a bit of molting fur on a sick, mangy dog.

"What did you find?" asked Afanasiev. "A louse?"

"No, everything's fine," answered Artiom.

People looked in the mirror rarely on Solovki. Afanasiev hadn't seen himself yet.

Sometimes he made the automatic gesture of reaching for his forelock, as though he were catching a fly near his face. But the invisible fly kept flying away, and he slowly lowered his hand, reaching with his finger in the air, as though adding flourishes to his never-ending speech.

At every new rise of intonation, the hand flew up, looking for the forelock… and again floated there, having forgotten, along the way, what it had been looking for.

* * *

"… as you know, they didn't take me that night… they missed me," Afanasiev said, wrapping himself in Artiom's jacket. "In the morning, I'm walking to the inspection, and the head of this new 'propaganda brigade' grabs me — they just created it. I know him from Petersburg — a total idiot, a real commie, but who messed up for something. I used to get easy work from him back in Petersburg, I wrote all kinds of slogans for him for the October celebrations. By the way, it was there that I met Grakov, in those distant days… 'I've gotta go to the inspection,' I said to this commie agitator, 'and then from there I've got a pass to go to Fox Island.' He said to me, 'Stand there! This is a new front for the work, I'll feed you seven rations, I won't let you go.' And I didn't… sleep all night from the nightmares… they shot them, you know…? I'm barely able to think and I've become submissive like a drunk coed. Basically, both of us went to Nogtev, but he, it turned out, persisted in his bad mood, unhappy with the absence of Bolshevik agitation in the camp and required immediately to have more signs everywhere. We come out, and the head of the new brigade says, 'Come on, Afanasiev, I need a new poster by evening. We'll have it on the Transfiguration Church, from window to window. What'll we write?' he asks. Without even thinking, on the fly, I answered, I didn't even want to joke: 'Solovki — for the workers and the peasants!' He said, 'Do what you need to, Afanasiev! Do it!' So I did."

Afanasiev's eyelid fluttered, then closed… this time he even shook his head, as though sticking his cervical vertebrae back in place, as though they were preventing his eyes from working.

"I grabbed an artist, and we d-d-drew it in three hours, and in another hour had it up. In time for the evening inspection," hurriedly and neurotically twitching, Afanasiev continued his story, intending it to be obviously comical.

Artiom didn't take his eyes off him, not really believing what he was hearing but at the same time understanding that everything he said was the complete truth. And Afanasiev's eyes, once again oppressed by an invisible force, were proof of that.

"The brigades lined up, those that were smart," Afanasiev continued, already chuckling. "And here Nogtev appeared, glanced around, nodded... then stopped and windup-punched the head of the propaganda brigade in the teeth. He happened to have been passing by."

Afanasiev wanted to laugh, but it wasn't coming, as though it had fallen into another throat along the way and was stuck there now, unable to climb out. What resulted was some kind of hawking sound.

"Are you really that stupid?" asked Artiom.

"I couldn't help myself," Afanasiev answered simply, raising his honest eyes.

"No, really, are you an idiot?" Artiom said.

"Well, I don't know," Afanasiev tried to think. "I thought I would force utter amazement onto my f-f-face, s-say that the commander of the brigade had commanded..."

"You didn't think at all," said Artiom, angry for some reason, as though Afanasiev had set him up, instead of himself.

Afanasiev, scratching first his chest, then his leg, became thoughtful, invisibly looking somewhere into the darkness.

"Tioma," he said. "They shot three of my comrades, with whom I was ready to escape from here all the way to Finland — I may have not known them that well, but still, they were living people... and what? I can't, at least once in my life, spit in the face of these dogs?"

Artiom sighed — a long sigh through clenched teeth — as though he blew on a candle standing nearby, not wanting to blow it out, just bend the flame a little.

"And what then?" asked Artiom.

"Later, Tiomka, came the f-f-unniest b-bit," answered Afanasiev, opening his eye and beginning to stutter even more. "They grabbed me and led me to the nearest old c-c-cemetery. I look, and there's already a coffin prepared for me. Its s-s-standing there, opening its maw: get in, Afanaska, I'll take you for a ride underground... And there was a hole too. The Chekists were laughing — the head, named T-tkachuk, I'll remember him now forever. 'What are you on about,' I said, 'comrades? I didn't do anything! I'm a poet, and I read you all p-poems right now!' M-myself, I'm still hoping that it'll all turn out OK, because the soldiers are smoking and it seemed n-not p-planning to shoot me. But Tkachuk took me by the scruff and threw me into the coffin — like, you know, a cat. Me, Tiomka, I tried to keep a leg outside, but the soldiers gathered, helped and put the lid and began to nail it shut. Have you ever h-heard how nails are driven into a coffin? It's… a horrible sound. But, Tiomochka, if only you knew how it sounds from inside the coffin! I keep thinking… right now they'll have their joke and let me go. I stop, I'm thinking, playing cards, I'll b-b-become a model laborer, I'll enter the Komsomol, anything they need. But instead of that, they raised the coffin and began to l-lower it."

Afanasiev fell silent and tried to breathe several times without success — it seemed that air had become uncomfortable for his lungs.

"I heard how the earth fell on top of it," he said without a voice. "I started screaming… I remember it badly." Here he made the usual gesture over his head, and Artiom understood when Afanasiev had pulled out his forelock — inside the coffin! He had tried to pull himself out by his forelock!

Not finding it now, Afanasiev, gathering his fingers into a bird's claw, began to scratch his temple, as though he were trying to hook one of the veins and pull it out onto the surface from inside his head, together with all the pain that was wrapped around it.

"I don't know how long I lay there, Tioma," he hurried, as though he wanted to quickly part with the remembrance, "but when they started to dig me out, I was already beside myself, understood nothing, started to choke. They opened it, and there was the sun. And here, Tiomka, I went insane."

Afanasiev looked at Artiom with a direct glance — probably the same kind of glance that people use when confessing to adultery, murder, the worst sins.

"Tkachuk," Afanasiev said, "crouched near the coffin… as though it were a boat that was about to disembark again into the depths, and he said, 'Tell me, jackal, who incited you to this counter-revolutionary action.' And I kn-know that no one did. And though I'm in a fog, I already understand that if I say that no one did, they won't believe me. I understand that I have to say something that will seem important to them. I breathed in and whispered, though I was trying to scream, "I know my oath and actions for the Tsar,[46] take me to the IID…' B-but they didn't take me there, forcing me to talk right there at the coffin, or rather… inside the c-coffin to admit everything. So I admitted that I wanted to flee with Burtsev and I named all the co-conspirators."

....

46 A reference to a law in Tsarist Russia maintaining that every civil servant was required to inform on any plot against the Tsar or his family.

"I hope you didn't add me to the list," it flashed, bone-chillingly, through Artiom's head.

"I c-c-couldn't name many of them," Afanasiev continued. "Burtsev had divided everyone into four groups, and no one really knew anyone properly. I think there were about one hundred people in the group, maybe even more… but they killed my fourth in the first night, and it was those that I snitched on… So Tkachuk took me by the ear into IID. There he asked me the s-s-same thing."

"Did they beat you?" Artiom asked.

"Me? No, they didn't," Afanasiev answered. "Oh!" he remembered. "I wanted to ask you personally about something else. When they were leading me down into solitary after the interrogation, a half hour later the keys clinked in the lock and… guess who came in. Galina! She brought me a pie and a bottle of vodka. She poured me a glass, I drank, then took a bite of pie. She poured another glass, and I drank it too. Then she turned around and walked out. Didn't s-s-say a word."

Afanasiev looked at Artiom significantly.

"Do you know this one?" Afanasiev poked Artiom in the side, laughing from who knows where. "Here on S-solovki, when five hundred years ago the monks Savvatii and Herman planned on living here, there was another couple — a young man and woman, like Adam and Eve… They floated here from the mainland and caught fish here, bothering nobody. But Eve, you understand, seemed a problem to the monks. And, lest she hinder the founding of the S-s-olovetsk monastery, two angels descended from the heavens and spanked that woman. Can you imagine, Tiom? The woman understood the hint and immediately left the island. And took her husband with her. And they spanked that woman exactly on the spot where you and I find ourselves now. That's why they call it Sekirnaia Hill.[47] Here it was that they… whipped the woman. Got the hint, Tiomka?"

"No, I don't get it," Artiom said quickly and angrily.

"Keep in mind," Afanasiev explained eagerly, "that joking around with women on Solovki ends badly."

"Judging by your example, it's better not to joke on Solovki at all," Artiom said without smiling.

"Ha!" said Afanasiev and waved his hand over his head, but the damn fly had disappeared again.

47 Sekirnaia comes from the word "sech", meaning "to beat or whip".

If Artiom could have seen them both from the side, it would have amused him to tears. They sat on the top level, their legs hanging down and sometimes even swinging them in harmony with the rhythm of their speech — like two boys on the beach. All that was left, looking carefully from side to side, was to take the cigarette stolen from their father and smoke it, dragging on it in turn, not swallowing the smoke because they didn't know how.

But if it was a beach, then this was some other kind of river.

Afanasiev, as though he had not just been talking about how they had buried him alive in a coffin, was in a good mood and talkative.

"You know, Tiomka, don't be angry about your Galia," he said placatingly. "I'm just jealous, you got it?"

Artiom didn't bother answering: he was probably lying, saying anything to prevent his tongue from stopping and he could say whatever popped into his head.

"I was never jealous of anyone, even Serioga, when after his trip to America so m-many people came to the concert that they had to be dispersed with horsed policemen… but you, I envied." He wouldn't back down; and something unexpected appeared in his voice, as though Afanasiev himself were speaking but there was a second voice that was also repeating the same melody. "That was supposed to be my story: on Solovki! And together with the girlfriend of the head of the camp! Tiomka…! She didn't even look at me once. Am I all that worse than you? I would have… taught her to play cards…"

"I think she knows how to," said Artiom, for some reason feeling more disposed towards Afanasiev. He even answered only to keep Afanasiev from falling silent.

"She does," Afanasiev nodded. "I think she knows how to do many things that I won't even mention here… But out in the free world, Artiom? Why do you need her out there? What, do you want to live with a tribunal?"

"Fuck," thought Artiom. "I shouldn't have kept him talking."

He even got a little upset, but it was clear that Afanasiev was fooling around and saying all this to forget about his coffin, and also because he truly, it seemed, was jealous and couldn't quite understand why he didn't have Artiom's luck.

"Every woman is a tribunal as it is," Afanasiev continued. "God," here the poet nodded at *Vladychka*, who had sat next to an inmate on the other side of the space to console him, "is One in Three Persons. And a woman also is a revolutionary troika. She interrogates, writes it all down, then brings her conviction into ac-c-tion. And that's every day, until she runs you ragged.

Or have you so gotten used to the idea of executions that now you won't be able to deal without a tribunal out there?"

"Enough, Afanas, stop talking about her, I'm sick of it," Artiom said.

"Sick of it! Fine. But why did she dump you here, my dear boy?" he said.

"... I called down the red-head on my own head," thought Artiom, mad for real this time and made a movement as though he would jump down from the bunk.

"I'm sorry, I'm sorry, I won't ask it," Afanasiev immediately recanted, holding Artiom by the hand. "Your business. I think that she'll get you out. Maybe you'll say a word for me there too, eh?"

There was nothing to do down there anyway, and they remained seated on their beach; maybe someone would sail by and take them along?

"Do they feed you here?" asked Afanasiev. "I can't w-warm up for the life of me."

"They'll bring some hot water tomorrow morning," answered Artiom, after a pause.

After another pause, he pulled off his wool socks.

"Here, warm up your feet," he gave them to Afanasiev, "take yours off. We'll dry them."

Afanasiev eagerly took them off and Artiom stuck them under his buttocks.

"I'll take them back for the night," Artiom warned.

"Sure thing," Afanasiev agreed, pulling on one sock; he looked as though he had just won the pair at cards. He even stood up on the bunk and stomped on the screeching boards — as though trying out something new.

Artiom sarcastically stared at his friend, thinking indistinctly again, "And that's him just out of the coffin... and he's already happy about the socks... what a devil!"

"O, the moon," Afanasiev pointed at the window into the crack between the boards. "L-listen, Tiomk. The moon's over there."

"Why, haven't I ever seen the moon before?"

Afanasiev sat down and began to massage his feet with his hands.

"Have you noticed, Tioma, that all of Dostoyevsky's suicides have names that start with 's'? Svidrigailov, Smerdiakov, Stavrogin. And I've lost the ability to say that letter clearly. 'S' is like the moon. It stuck out of the middle of the last name Dos-s-stoyevsky and hung on his neck. It whispered in his ear... satanic squabble... sensual she-devil... and salty sea-breezes... the sickle sliced the chest... and cessation... and S-sekirka. You got it?"

"Nope," said Artiom.

"But I can't figure out how you got here," said Afanasiev.

Artiom shook his head. Then he shrugged. It would be too long to tell. Unclear, where to begin.

"I want to eat," said Afanasiev, as though he hadn't asked anything.

They lay down to sleep in pile-ups again, and Afanasiev thought it was very funny.

He amused everyone, flapping his gums constantly from the middle of the cold human intertwining, "Listen, brothers, we'll get so used to this that when we get back to the camp, they'll announce the line-up, and — voila! — we'll lie down in a pile-up. The head commissar will come out, and he'll hear from this hut on chicken feet, 'The pile-up from the first brigade is assembled!' 'The pile-up from the second brigade is assembled!'"

They laughed so hard that the pile-up fell apart, and someone got kicked in the neck.

They had to pile up again.

They seriously promised Afanasiev that they would tear his head off if he didn't shut up. But he had no intention of shutting up.

* * *

The dreams were becoming more and more insistent, climbing into your head even when you weren't asleep. You're lying in the pile-up, feeling smashed, your rib cage compressed, someone's knee is sticking into your spine, you've lost your feet completely, and it's a strange feeling: with one frozen hand you touch another hand, but you can't tell for sure if both hands are yours, or only one, and if it's only one — which one? And on top of it all, the dreams come like a wave — a general dream that flows from one head to another, your dream gets mixed up with someone else's confused, unpleasant one, with a woman's back, it's naked, cold, like a toad's, then someone is harnessing a horse, someone is sharpening a scythe, cuts himself, then tries to put his hand under his armpit to stop the bleeding, but the hand won't come up, and it's a sinew that's been sliced in the arm, very scary — when your appendage suddenly becomes foreign and helpless, while in another dream, there's just a dark room, damp and a man is sad in this dampness, he's not a worm, after all, he's afraid of being dug in the earth and he doesn't believe in its warmth.

Artiom sat at the common table, where every dream looked like a plate with someone else's leavings, and the guests had left, and only a few had remained — faces, not faces — rocking in the air, moved their lips.

Artiom had his own plate, and he would have liked to embrace it with his arms to prevent them from taking it away. There was honey in that plate.

His mother stood behind his back, clearing up. Artiom wasn't supposed to see her, but he still did. When she walked past the table, the faces that remained after lunch floated away to the side quietly and hung in the air, as before, moving their lips without a sound.

She was piling up dishes to make the table look cleaner, but there were still many leftovers, and they looked vile.

"Have some honey, my son," she said. "Honey is healthy."

Artiom didn't like honey — everyone loved it, but not him. It was too sweet, pleasant to look at, but to eat — no, his jaw clenched shut at the thought of it.

But now he wanted the honey terribly — yet there was something missing, something necessary to be able to eat it — either a spoon, or the plate wasn't comfortable, with edges turned inward — and if you tried to overturn it into your mouth, it fell on your forehead, poured into your eyes, but you couldn't taste any of it.

His mother was about to take the plate: well, if you don't want it, you don't have to eat it, I'll give you some when you ask for it, and it was necessary to let her know that: yes, I'll have some honey, Mama!

"I'll have some honey, Mama!

"I'll have some honey, Mama!

"I'll have some honey, Mama!"

Artiom was about to either cry or scream, the faces at the table became worried, their lips moved faster, their cheeks were covered in turbid, hot, dirty sweat and mother's plates all fell…

That was somebody in the middle of the pile-up sneezing and the structure leaned, someone swore, and when the inmate Goriainov caught himself thinking that he was still repeating, "I'll have some honey, Mama!" loud, it was already loud enough for others to hear, but not too loud or pitiful.

"… I don't think anyone noticed," Artiom thought, half-mad, as he kept touching another hand with his own — was the other one his as well? — but no, it became clear that it was someone else's because it moved away. His own hand, when Artiom got up, hung at his side, completely numb, and you could have easily put it into a bonfire or cut it with a knife like cold cuts and even eat a piece probably (but only if someone had given it to him and not told him where the meat was from).

"When are we getting our hot water, Tioma?" asked Afanasiev with pain in his voice. It looked like he had slept under a pile of wood — his whole face was sideways, his eyes crossed, his head was dusty, his ears crumpled, one shoulder higher than the other, he was tripping over his feet, his fingers were crooked, each pointing in a different direction, as though someone had beaten his hand with a rolling pin, and he smelled of decay.

"Do I look like that too?" Artiom weakly tested himself, but in actual fact he didn't care — so what if he did, just give me some hot water, some hot water and gruel.

The body couldn't deal with the cold and the hunger; it was rebelling, tearing at him and knocking at his consciousness — find me food! Feed me! Don't think of anything else, think of me, I'm bigger than your woman, I'm bigger than your mother, I'm bigger than our child, I'm bigger than you!

"Get out of here, fool of a woman!" said Artiom. "You'll manage without your hot water."

He even repeated it aloud, quietly.

Afanasiev heard it, attached himself like a burr to Artiom's shoulder, walked after him, whispering, "You're not whis-spering poems there, are you, Tiomka? I'm creating new ones every day, but I haven't written down even one. Up to this point, I remembered them all, but tonight they all got mixed up in my head. Pull on one line, and it pulls another behind it, twice as long… It's as though I broke a pearl necklace, and now you can't put the different-sized beads back on the string… But at least a kind of music appeared — can't understand if it's mine or someone else's… I sing it… And sometimes I sing my poems, and they, Tioma, they seem to get somehow smarter than on paper. Music is magic, as though you looked over the edge, and there's a different life there, bigger than ours… I would like to c-c-compose music. My own songs. It's such a s-sweet sensation when you go after the song into the deepest unknown reaches of your own s-s-self. It's like the journey of a sea-vessel into India… like Afanasii Nikitin over the three seas… You understand, my dear? You can go and find nothing there — just dust and old cobwebs. But the boy from Yaroslavl went from the Varengians to the Greeks, from the Greeks to the Persians and from there returned to Rus and brought brocade, a concubine and a wild horse with the neck of a swan, all dappled and shaking — that's my song… You can only believe in music, Tiomka; there's nothing else. Heaven is music. I've finally figured it out… Can you hear the music?"

All the inmates in the church heard the music.

They stopped where they stood, except that no one stood at the doors.

Someone was walking towards the church, ringing a bell.

No one had time to tell Afanasiev about that bell, and he was just about the only person who was happy to hear it: "They're bringing the hot water and letting us know about it…" And he took three steps to the exit.

The door opened, and the bell stopped ringing in the middle of a peal — the same smiling, eyebrow-less, fish-like Chekist had stopped the tongue with his hand.

"Afanasiev?" he asked, looking at Afanasiev. "Come outside."

The Chekist rang again, very pleased that he had immediately found a person and didn't need to pull him outside by the leg.

"Oh, they're calling me to my lesson," Afanasiev said, turning to Artiom, not so much joking as trying to raise his own spirits. "I've learned my lesson… I'll go answer it right now."

Artiom unwittingly stepped back, pushing someone, and the one who stood behind him took a step to the side, and Artiom took another step back.

Afanasiev waved his hand over his head — if only he could grab his forelock and pull himself against the current…

One more time, at the doors, he looked back at Artiom — Afanasiev's eyes were completely different. He had understood everything in a single second and with a clanging voice, he said, "I did plant the cards on you, Tiomka. Forgive me."

The door slammed shut, the latch looked for its place and bit into its groove.

The bell continued to ring, but more quietly.

"Let Afanasiev go, you bitch's jaw, they'll curse you forever for my sake!" suddenly an insane cry rang out.

The bell fell silent, someone swore horribly and then, a quick shot, then another one, then another one. A man had run away from his death, but the bullet overtook him: here, did you forget this? Is this yours…?

A few minutes later, they brought hot water with some milk added and millet porridge — one spoonful for each person.

The red-head hadn't lived to see his hot water.

Everyone threw themselves at the food; no one refused to eat.

Artiom lay on the top bunk, face down, biting his hand.

But the smell of millet reached him, woke him up and pulled him out of his unconsciousness.

He jumped down, pushed aside the crowd and stood first in line.

Khasaev didn't say anything, then gave Artiom his spoonful, as well as a second one — he gave him a double ration.

Artiom immediately ate it, not even getting out of line. Without any emotion, he drank it down with hot water.

On the way back to his bunk, licking his lips, he noticed that only *Vladychka* didn't go into line; he stood in the corner on his knees, quietly praying.

They brought him some millet and hot water and put it on the floor not too far from him.

"*Vladychka* — here," someone said quietly, like you might say to a breastfeeding mother who had fallen asleep or a person you loved who was sick.

"He knew that they would bring it to him! He knew it!" the thought raged and seethed inside Artiom. "He knew it and decided to show off, the stupid old man."

* * *

"Maybe it's all a trick, buffoonery?" Artiom tried to convince himself, holding back tears. "They'll ring the bell, lead out the person, wink at him and shoot in the air. The person nods approvingly and runs into the forest, wherever his feet will take him… How else could it be? Who would dream of shooting Afanasiev? The red-head? Why? Because he planted the cards on me? I forgave him immediately… Why else, Lord? Lord, are you even there?"

Artiom wanted to lean back and look at the face that he had uncovered with his prisoner's spoon, into the very eyes — but he didn't have the strength, and his head was spinning.

Downstairs, Vasilii Petrovich pottered about, constantly mumbling something.

"Circus tent… this is our circus tent. I'm pouring cranberry juice. They've exiled the Silver Age to Sekirka… Here it lives out its days…! How many lice did the old man have, my God!" Awkwardly, not even like an old man, but somehow like an old woman, he took off the foreign underwear and started to shake it and pull out the lice.

"… I will never again shake his hand," Artiom promised himself in a fit of inexplicable disgust, looking at Vasilii Petrovich through the crack between the bed-boards. "He's truly gone insane, that wormy head of his…"

Vladychka returned to his place and quietly ate the porridge, taking such a long time that it seemed he had not one spoonful but thirty-three; he even smacked his lips a few times.

"I remember in childhood," Vasilii Petrovich shared, "I read the Lives for hours, couldn't calm myself down. At night, I'd throw off the blanket from my body — I'm lying there, freezing for the glory of God… until my father would come in. I was mad at him for covering me up with a blanket. And now, go ahead and lie here, freeze all you like, no one will cover you. But now I don't want to."

Vladychka's breathing quickened — not that he was laughing exactly, but rather supporting the story with his breathing.

"… In military school," Vasilii Petrovich continued, "after finishing our two-year course, we arranged a joke-funeral of a student. We put him on a door and carried him out. Before the coffin, dressed-up 'clergy' walked, behind, the wailing family… Oh, how we thought it was funny. The choir sang, the candles burned and went out… they put tobacco in the censer. We couldn't stop from joy, until the authorities suddenly showed up, and then, dropping the laughing dead man, we ran away… Like children, really… sometimes I close my eyes here and wait for the commanding officer from my school to walk in… and it'll all be funny again, and we'll all run away, bursting from laughter."

Vladychka ate his eternal porridge and grew silent.

"Free will, the gift of the All-good God, is the most important gift of all," Vasilii Petrovich whispered to him. "I always knew about this freedom. It lay in my inside pocket." He touched his chest with his hand, holding an invisible bundle — "it lay as an immutable proof of the right to my moving about freely during my whole life. With this document, I always remembered that I could always hide from death behind a bush, run back… surrender, finally, and it would have pity on me and let me go again. But here I feel that I'm caught, and my soul aches and trembles."

"… You wail, you executioner," thought Artiom. A feeling seized him inexorably, like nausea, that it was Vasilii Petrovich who killed Afanasiev, and now he was sitting there as though nothing had happened, rummaging about in other people's underwear. Maybe he had taken it off Afanasiev?

This feeling of hatred and disgust was a hundred times stronger because Vasilii Petrovich was saying aloud the same things that Artiom was afraid to tell himself.

That nausea was not only because of the underwear, because of the shaking head underneath him, but because of fear — a fear that had never yet grabbed Artiom so mercilessly.

Vladychka whispered words of consolation to Vasilii Petrovich, unheard by Artiom. He didn't even want to hear them, but only watched the quivering of Vasilii Petrovich's head, as he was listening, as though not believing anything. But at the same time, it was clear that Vasilii Petrovich agreed with *Vladychka* on all points, he just couldn't get enough of his words and wanted to hear more and more thoughts about mercy, goodness and inevitable salvation.

It's possible that Artiom also needed those thoughts, so that this horrible, sticky nausea would abandon him. But he didn't want these thoughts to be the same for him as for that head, quivering in constant tremors.

He would have cracked it like a raw egg, so that the birds could peck out that villainous brain.

Because... because... where was Afanasiev now? Who would console him?

Afanasiev was no longer creating poems, nor was he seeking the music within himself.

But how did he cease creating it, how did he stop listening to the music, what could have happened to him? Was it possible that a single, two, three bullets could pierce such a young body and it would break immediately? What was he? A phonograph? Was he worse than a phonograph? What, you couldn't just change the needle? To put on a new record, and then Afanasiev — fine, let him continue stuttering on his 's's' — would once again tell him about the cards, Sekirka, poems, and the salty sea-breezes of Solovki.

Because Afanasiev was somewhere — he couldn't just disappear, right? He's probably lying somewhere, exactly the same as an hour ago, only now he's quiet. How is he feeling? Did they already cover him with earth? And what? Is he lying there in the ground?

It was unbearable.

"... When I worked in counterintelligence, I used to hold sugar in my mouth. It calmed me down..." Vasilii Petrovich was saying below.

Artiom stuck his face into the chink between the rare boards so hard that it crushed against his temples.

"Shut up, you old devil!" Artiom screamed almost into Vasilii Petrovich's pate. "Shut up! Before I choke you!"

Vasilii Petrovich looked up in fear and locked gazes with Artiom. *Vladychka* couldn't understand where the noise was coming from, and in his confusion, he kept looking from one side to the other.

Artiom, getting up for a moment, moving the boards aside and once again leaning down into the open space, but now not just with his head but with his whole chest and one hand, as though he were planning on grabbing that foul head by its mangy, small ear.

"He held sugar in his mouth, the sweet tooth… while he choked and smothered other people!" He yelled, swinging his hand at the recoiling face of Vasilii Petrovich and almost clacking his teeth.

"I never… not one person…" he bared his teeth and hissed through them.

"Yes!" Artiom croaked. "Never killed anyone. Only cut out small pieces! And always left the biggest piece for others in his generosity! Viper! Die, you viper!"

Understanding that by stupidly swinging from above, he would never reach anyone, Artiom turned with a racket and jumped down.

Vasilii Petrovich was no longer in place, as though he had dissolved in the half-dark of the church, but *Vladychka* appeared in front of him, not even saying anything, only quietly blowing at Artiom, as though he were a lit firebrand.

Artiom himself had complicated emotions — he could have pushed *Vladychka* aside, but he didn't do that — not because he respected his status, he didn't have a shadow of respect inside him — but also in fear that if he touched this person, his beard and hair would catch fire, and he would have to do something then… maybe even put the fire out so that it wouldn't smell of burnt hair.

Making an angry gesture with his hand, meaning: piss off! Artiom turned back to the bunks and grabbed them as hard as if he were planning to tear them apart.

"I know that you, never pandering to anyone, seventy times seven forgave everyone," *Vladychka* said. "Afanasiev, because of whom you went to the infirmary that time… and the dissolute women, with whom you did not sin in the infirmary… and Vasilii Petrovich, because of whom you are here right now… and all those who wanted to destroy you, you forgave them every time… why now, Tiomon'ka, in your most difficult hour, are you angry? Maybe your goodness can save you and give strength to those who are weak of spirit?"

Artiom turned back at *Vladychka*, extremely surprised.

"How do you know?" he asked, dumbfounded, "About Afanasiev? About… all this?"

Vladychka himself was genuinely surprised — what do you mean how? His whole countenance said, how could I not know all that? Its written black and white, I just read it.

"Does he know about my father?" Artiom asked himself in fear. "Does he know that I adored my father? That I considered him the best person on this earth? Eh?"

"There is no goodness here," Artiom said, not waiting for an answer. "None! Got it, priest? I'm your failure."

And once again he turned around.

"My dear, do you know how I feel?" *Vladychka* continued whispering, not moving away. "Solovki is the Old Testament whale on which the Christians settled. And this whale is going underwater. The black water is closing in over our heads. But while at least one head remains above the black water, there's a chance for all the other perishable bodies to be saved, for all those gathered here not to be destroyed before their time. Don't go under the water, my dear, don't be covered in darkness. Everyone here is already there."

"Go away," said Artiom, feeling that he was about to throw up.

"He keeps talking to everyone about goodness," he wound himself up with fitful anger, clenching his teeth with all his strength. "To every inmate here. And every one of them is an evil creature that dreams of snuggling into his own rotted-through jacket and waiting until everyone else around them dies off."

Artiom stood there another minute, then looked around. Seeing no one there, he caught himself thinking that he had wanted to see *Vladychka* still standing there — why had he left? His mother wouldn't have left? No matter how much he would have yelled at her! His mother would have still been standing there in expectation, waiting for her stupid son to call to her. A mother is kinder than God — no matter who you killed, she would still wait there with her warm hands. But that one, with the beard, promises the world — but he might not even wait it out! He might forget!"

From his excessive anger, Artiom was suddenly seized by weakness.

At first, he sat down on Vasilii Petrovich's bunk and sat there in a half-daze.

Then he barely managed to gather his strength and climb back up to his bunk. Somehow he moved the boards back, curled up as much as he could, pulling his legs up to his stomach, hugging himself.

Exhausted by hunger, his whole body felt an eternal tickling.

His feet were completely frozen and his wool socks weren't helping.

As he fell asleep, Artiom felt as though his feet were no longer his own, but Afanasiev's — he had warmed his feet in these socks, after all… and even now, his dirty, twisted toes were still in there.

His smallest sepulchral toe, bluish and revolting, started to grow until it became a complete person, and now Artiom felt his whole self as though he were that little toe, and his face was as though a child's bloodless toenail.

Then he dreamed of a person who was shot through. The bullet was stuck in the bones of his ribcage.

The person was in a coffin.

It was impossible to understand whether that was Afanasiev or Artiom, because the person was rotting.

He was falling to pieces, then the pieces became dust, and one time inside the coffin for the first time — and for the last time for the eternal years — a meek sound was heard — from under the bones, freed by the rotted flesh, the bullet rolled out and fell to the bottom of the coffin — *plunk!*

That fallen bullet — that was the most frightening sound in the world! The thought boomed in Artiom's consciousness — the most frightening! The most frightening in the world from the very creation of mankind! It was impossible!

From the falling of the bullet, something moved — and a small cross worn on the chest, which had fallen through the ribcage, began to swing back and forth on its chain.

In the darkness of the tomb, the crucified Christ swung on the copper cross as on a swing set.

* * *

When Artiom woke up, he was unsurprised to see a few new inmates in the church — they had driven in another group of unfortunates.

Father Zinovii, with whom he had been in the infirmary that time. His eyes were inflamed, he took a place far away from *Vladychka*, and kept fingering his camlet cassock, which was shredded as though by wild beasts…

There was a homeless boy — also, through all his dirt, he seemed familiar…

Grakov, skinny and with a face as though bent. His mouth slipped somewhere down, losing its place.

Artiom had neither the strength nor the desire to speak with anyone. He sometimes caught himself in a faint spiritual rift — he wanted to sit up like a bird and watch the room with a single eye, his head cocked. Somewhere here Afanasiev was supposed to be. Why wouldn't he be? If he would correctly align his consciousness and his vision, he might see him. Or at least hear him.

Closing his eyes, Artiom listened in on the voices — very soon, he was sure to hear Afanasiev's laugh… or some kind of poetic joke, invented for audacity's sake, or even for bawdiness.

Once, Artiom remembered, they had left the twelfth brigade with Afanasiev. It was a July morning, very transparent — "Look at how the church is standing, all in morning dew, like a gentle girl who had just washed…" said that insane red-head. Artiom's shoulder twitched, and he had answered nothing. And now he suddenly thought — how much youth and purity were in that stupid phrase that in no way demeaned either the church or the girl.

But Afanasiev's voice didn't appear.

Everyone was oppressed and quiet.

Audibly, though quietly, only Vasilii Petrovich talked, again saying something pathetic and, judging by Artiom's heart's reaction, odious. Artiom recognized that he was speaking completely not out of any compassion for those killed and tortured here, but only to prove to himself that he was still alive — while he spoke, his life continued.

But, even while speaking, Vasilii Petrovich was listening, and nearly everyone was also listening, because any new sound could touch each of them with a hand of death.

Someone accidentally clanged his spoon and Artiom felt how everyone's hearts skipped a beat at the sound. Everyone thought the same thing — the bell was coming again.

The guilty party was revealed, and he found himself surrounded by a multitude of frenzied looks, and he quickly hid his spoon somewhere in his chest, where it could never clang against timid human flesh.

Father Zinovii wandered throughout the church, asking for a little sugar, a little salt, a little bread. They didn't even answer him.

Instead of sugar, there was only visible fear, which crunched like sand underfoot. Everyone chewed on his own fear, soundlessly breaking his own teeth.

Zinovii avoided the bunk of *Vladychka*, walking around him in an exaggerated angle.

From somewhere, the feeling emerged that all of this had already happened — Artiom had lived this life before at some point, with this chilling feeling of apathy, with these quiet and tedious voices of other people, with these ceilings, these bunks, sprinkled with whitewash — except he forget how the story ended.

If he had died, then how did he get here again? If he had survived, then why was he here for another round? He's not a gull — to spend one summer on the wild hill, overgrown with full bushes, then another among the monoliths of Solovki, and so for all eternity.

Grakov walked past Artiom several times — evidently, he wanted to talk. Artiom always managed to close his eyes and pretend he was asleep, absent, disappeared without a trace.

He didn't notice whether Grakov and Vasilii Petrovich had greeted each other. It's possible that they nodded at each other… but they didn't seem to be talking.

"The demons cover the earth with snares," Father Zinovii was telling someone without waiting for either the salt or the sweet. "When I was walking here, I saw a bird in the skies. Its name is harbinger of woe."

Artiom at first imagined a bird, then the sky, then the trees and the grass on the earth.

But you can eat grass, it seemed to Artiom. At first, it's probably not good, but if you chew it a long time, chew, chew, then it'll fill with human saliva, human warmth and it will become almost like soup. After all, they make nettle soup, they eat dill and onions — there's probably some grass left, even in October, why don't they let us out to eat it. Even dogs eat grass, after which they cough very curiously. Cows chew grass, then they give milk. That means grass is a healthy thing, since you get milk out of it.

Artiom went over and over these thoughts. They seemed very wise, and in his heart he wondered how he had never before thought to try eating grass, especially in the summer when there's a lot of it and it's green.

He even sat up and started to look through the chinks in the window-shield — was there any grass visible? He should tell Khasaev to make him an orderly, and when they'd be let out to carry the latrine outside, then he'd fill his pockets with grass. When all's said and done, if it's not as good as expected, you could always dress the gruel with it — the gruel is empty anyway.

His stomach contracted so powerfully that it was as though four hands were wringing out a shirt inside Artiom — the feeling of hunger began in the solar plexus and finished below the stomach, and from the constant wringing it became thicker, more painful, more insistent.

Sometimes, Artiom closed his eyes and began to pray to the plate of hot milk-soup. Then to a piece of bread with a piece of boiled meat. Then to a bowl with berries, and next to it stood a cup of cocoa. The prayers were debilitating.

No sooner had he seen that Artiom was sitting, Grakov, with a strange swiftness, ran up to him.

He couldn't get out of it. Artiom silently looked at Grakov who stood below, not finding it necessary to greet him — they had already spent several hours in the same closed space. What was the point of saying hello now?

Below, the homeless boy spoke with *Vladychka* with a whiny voice, complaining, "They beat me harder than firemen beat the alarm bell. It's not a childhood, but a funeral, uncle…"

"He's lying about everything, the little creature," thought Artiom dully, sensing all the while that the kid was uttering these words not for the first time by any stretch of the imagination.

Grakov took a step forward and put a hand on Artiom's bunk.

"Have you been here long?" he asked with his mouth, which had slid to the side.

"… Why did they drive you here, snitch?" Artiom asked silently, looking Grakov in the eye.

Grakov didn't hear the question and didn't answer it.

"I don't remember…" said Artiom unwillingly with a cracking voice. "A few days."

Grakov clearly wanted to ask, "How is it here?" or even "Do they kill people here?" but he was shy, couldn't, and only moved his face as though he wanted to return his mouth back to its rightful place.

"Come up here, tell me the news of the town," said Artiom, feeling sorry for him. He had nothing else to do, except to listen to the maddening itch inside him and dream at least about the green, meaty, fleshy grass.

In addition, the boy below had started to ramble — from hunger, his mind was getting confused, and he yelped and cried disgustingly, and it looked as though when *Vladychka* patted him, he looked for food in those hands.

Grakov got up with difficulty, awkwardly. It seemed that his legs had already stopped working, because, as he raised himself by his arms, he couldn't lift his knee and leaned forward with his body onto the bunk. Artiom pulled him up by his shorts, grimacing from irritation, already thinking about whether or not he should throw down that sickly body. Too bad it wasn't that high.

"Where did you get a jacket?" asked Grakov, having got up. "They took mine away… And it's cold. How do you sleep here?"

"We sleep well," said Artiom. "You'll see… they sometimes hand out a bit of clothing here.

"Really?" Grakov was immediately interested. "Maybe we can write some sort of petition here? About issuing clothing? Because it's completely unbearable. What a horrible autumn it is this year, it's not normal."

"Why not? Go ahead and write it," said Artiom, catching himself in genuine, sarcastic mockery. He wanted to see where Grakov would find a paper and pencil here, and how he would then knock on the door, awaiting his bell.

Grakov seemed to have figured that out; he moved his mouth back and forth and dropped the subject.

"It didn't use to be like this here," said Grakov, looking around the space where frozen people constantly moved about in frightening silence, in a half-dark reminiscent of mist.

"He probably visited here and then described Sekirka's daily life and miracles of correction in the newspaper," Artiom guessed, but he didn't say anything.

"As I can see, they've driven all the useless ones here," said Grakov quietly, turning to face Artiom. From the unexpectedness of it, Artiom even recoiled. Grakov's mouth was so frighteningly close that it seemed it might try, without recourse to its master's will, to bite Artiom. "… there, in the kremlin, Nogtev will have to answer for all these reprisals: there were many witnesses, no matter where you hide. And you could have total anarchy here."

"… So now you begin to speak…" Artiom thought caustically.

"… Or perhaps they sent him here with a secret assignment to learn the mood among the Sekirka inmates?" Artiom thought after a pause, but also without any fear. After the bell, it was hard to be afraid of Grakov.

"Why don't you write another article about it?" Artiom offered.

Grakov expressed neither surprise nor offence. He looked at the inmates, walking in a circle, blinking from time to time, as though invisible, painless tears were too heavy for his eyelids.

"Nogtev served on the '*Aurora*'. The revolution began with him," said Grakov a minute later.

Artiom rubbed his frozen toes through his wool socks, not even expecting to warm them.

"It began with him," Grakov added after another minute passed, "and here, it can also end with him."

In a different time, Artiom would never have dreamed of remaining silent when people were speaking to him, but now it was easy. He had absolutely no interest in what Grakov would think and how he would feel as a result of his reticence.

Now rubbing his knees, he slowly and icily thought, "Maybe I should tell Grakov that it was because of him that I ended up on Sekirka? Should I thank him somehow…? Or maybe warn him that if the Sekirka-bell begins ringing, he must immediately turn into smoke, into whitewash, into a dream, into the dirt under their feet, to lose his age, calling, name, face, to divide into pieces and not move, even if a strong wind blows… or maybe he should tell him that they killed Afanasiev — Grakov knew Afanasiev, let him be amazed that Afanasiev is no longer alive, but dead… after all, it's so pleasant to amaze people… or maybe he should ask Grakov why he's here? Did he commit an infraction, drop his work, get into hot water…?"

Artiom didn't say anything. He was just sorry to let out such warm and familiar words into the cold air. Just before, they had lain within him, but if he speaks, they'll dissipate.

It was a strange feeling, but not a heavy one — next to him was Grakov, below sat Vasilii Petrovich — people who were tied to Artiom by fate, completely unnecessary to his life and foreign to him, but it was exactly because of them that his existence on this earth could cease. Any minute now, the smiling Chekist would get bored in his room, would finish his tea in a big gulp, and, grunting, would get up, looking around as he did: where's my bell gone to, why is it so quiet? Ah, there it is, my little bell, still standing in its place, not moving, I can pick it up, ring it, go ahead and try grabbing it by the clapper — it's got such a tongue, that even if you bit it off, it'll still ring until it scratches its way out of your brains, and then — bang! — you fall on the table and you can catch a human soul with the body of the bell, like a fly — what, are you buzzing in there, you hairy-footed creature? Are you scared? You might be scared, but we're loving it. It's invigorating.

That evening, they brought some hot water and gruel, and the mists moved, the mouths opened, the noses began to tremble — everyone inhaled the new smells, trying to understand if there were carrots in the gruel, or if you couldn't find any in it, maybe it was boiled in the same water, or maybe if it wasn't boiled there, then, let's meekly suppose that it was at least washed in the same water. Or, let's say, our hope will come true about cabbage — white, crunchy, jovial — and maybe its boiled-over-boiled leaves would appear…

The kid forgot about *Vladychka*, yelled, "yummy-yummy! Potato soup! Yummy-yummy! Potato soup!"

Artiom noticed his hands — they were small and red like the feet of a pigeon. Each hand was missing its last finger.

The boy kept trying to get into the line and asked every passing bowl, "Where? What about me? Where? What about me?"

It seemed that he was talking to the bowls, not suspecting that people were carrying them — it looked to him that the gruel was flying hither-thither by itself.

"Where" he pronounced as "wheare," drawling out the vowels.

Artiom remembered, completely inappropriately, how Shaferbekov once teased a gull. He tied a string firmly to a piece of meat and tossed it in the air. A gull immediately swallowed the present, but as it flew up, Shaferbekov pulled it down, easily dislodging the piece of meat. The confused gull returned for its meat once, twice, three times, but finally realized the human's villainy and, having told of its wounded pride to its compatriots, it returned with twelve other gulls who almost pecked Shaferbekov's eyes out and poked his head enough to bleed.

The gangster thought the whole thing was funny; it was as though he had recognized a fellow thug, and, rubbing the blood off his head, he kept laughing. The meat that had been three times in the gull's stomach he ate himself, only untying the string, that's all.

The "wheare" kept falling out of the kid like that same piece of meat out of the gull. The word stank of insult, stupid surprise and sour stomach acid.

Today, Artiom decided to do everything backwards. At first, to drink the hot water, because it got cold quickly, and only then to suck down the gruel.

The hot water permeated, not his throat or his chest, but, for some reason, his head, his brain, all the way to the back of the skull, which for a short time, but almost to drunkenness, was enveloped in sauna-steam. To taste the gruel turned out to be impossible. It somehow disappeared immediately, and no matter how much he wiped the bowl with his finger afterward, he could find nothing on his finger — it was just a finger, might as well bite it.

Returning the bowl, Artiom saw that *Vladychka,* waiting for the kid to finish eating, then gave him his ration as well; that one, not saying thank you, as though the bowl had floated down from heaven, grabbed it with his pigeon feet.

All of it was unpleasant and foreign to Artiom. He didn't respect *Vladychka*; nor did he feel sorry for the boy.

Having climbed up to at least warm up a little from the gruel and hot water, Artiom clearly remembered where he had seen the homeless kid — in the attic of the Cathedral of the Transfiguration, where he was once with Galia…

Having eaten two bowls of gruel, the kid yelled again, "Yummy-yummy, potato soup! Yummy-yummy, potato soup!"

No one offered him any potato soup, and a minute later he fell asleep on *Vladychka*'s bunk.

"He didn't have a chance to grow up, and already he's climbed back to his childhood," Vasilii Petrovich's voice sounded from below.

Artiom, patting the uncovered saint on the cheek, lazily and coldly thought, "… He climbed back to childhood… but where do we go? In what direction? It's far away back to childhood… and forward to old age…"

"At least death is always close," the thought pecked him in the head, like a gull, and Artiom immediately forgot, either one second before the ringing of the bell started, or a second afterward, because there were more important things to think about.

His hunger disappeared, as did the dissipating warmth of the gruel, his memory of his mother's face, the sense of sticky coldness in his toes, the face of the saint on the wall became indistinct, the voices of the inmates disappeared, especially considering that they did actually disappear — only *Vladychka* prayed… no, Father Zinovii prayed too, and for the first time they were together, and it seemed that even their prayers were word for word, as though they were putting them up together cube by cube. But the bell ended up being stronger; it was like a grown idiot in a child's game who comes in and pushes aside all the cubes with his boot, and they all fly around and roll on the stone floor: red, orange, yellow, green, light blue, blue, purple. Every hunter wants to know, where sits… who? Who?

… Which pheasant was this hunter seeking?

"Ve…" began the Chekist.

Without even looking down, Artiom felt that the head of Vasilii Petrovich shook even more fiercely, as though he were holding a berry in his teeth, and someone else's icy, wildly strong hands were shaking him, trying to dislodge that berry to crush it under a boot.

"Ver… fuck, it can't read it…" the Chekist complained. "Is there someone here with a name beginning with Ver…" he looked down again. "Vershi… lin?"

"I believe!" Vasilii Petrovich suddenly exclaimed in a voice not his own.

The berry fell out.

"O Master Lord Almighty, accept my spirit in peace. Send down from Your all-holy glory a peaceful angel who will lead me to Your three-sunned Divinity, so that the lord of darkness and his powers will not stop me along the way," Vasilii Petrovich said, walking out.

His thin hair stuck out in all directions in a horrifying way; they stood on end.

The bell rang outside the door.

It rang for a long time, longer than usual and someone couldn't bear it and started to wail, at first quietly, then louder and louder and more horrifyingly.

Another inmate threw himself at the doors and, striking them with his forehead, knees, his arms, yelled, "Stop it! Stop! Stop!"

Grakov jumped from his spot and started to rush about the church, either trying to understand what was going on or in the hope of finding a crack that no one had noticed and hide his head there. His mouth had crawled almost to his neck.

The kid woke up and started to cry: "Potato soup! Yummy-yummy!"

Father Zinovii got up from his knees and waved his thin hand. "Herods! Anathema to you and your children for all time!"

The shot rang out — it was somehow very far, slight, even comical, compared to the whole man for whom it was intended.

Artiom turned to his side, rolled up into a ball and fell silent.

"They fed us and killed him off afterwards," he complained, whispering. "Better if they had given me his gruel first."

Below him, the bunks were empty, and that emptiness spread everywhere like fog or poisonous gas.

The smell of emptiness was palpable and caustic.

The inmates, it seemed to Artiom, tried not to breathe, lest they get poisoned.

Vasilii Petrovich didn't force Artiom to wait long. He returned quickly, no more than half an hour.

"I gave you berries, you know," he said to Artiom rather loudly.

He was sitting somewhere nearby.

Screwing up his eyes, Artiom tried not to move his hands or his feet, to avoid accidentally striking Vasilii Petrovich; more importantly, not to push over his basket.

The basket was already full.

The worms in the basket were of all colors — white, light blue, yellow, green, purple. A few were extremely small, nimble, quick, while others were larger, fat, viscous.

* * *

It turned out that you could sleep in a pile-up among many other bodies and feel completely alone.

There were ever more lice, and the cold made them angrier.

Where was that Galia, who wasn't there and had never been there? Where is she? That Galia, where?

"I can destroy her, after all!" Artiom told the saint on the scratched-off fresco. He called him "prince". "I can destroy her, prince! Now I'm, what am I now? Shall I knock on the door? Ha!"

He could have played a childhood game, when he and his brother knocked on the door, heard mother's steps and quickly hid under the bed or in an armoire. And mama pretended to be surprised, "Who was it that knocked?" And they would choke from laughter and hold it back, trying not to sneeze.

To knock, to hear the bell and then for everyone to hide. The smiling Chekist would come in and say, "Where is everyone? Who was knocking?" And then, perhaps, Grakov wouldn't be able to hold it in and would laugh under the bunks... Not a bad game, that!

In the morning, Artiom sat on his bunk, feeling like a bag of bones that had been mixed up with dough — and they kneaded, kneaded, kneaded those bones all night.

He took off his jacket to shake off the lice, but he quickly froze — it didn't seem to get warmer than five degrees outside, maybe seven — no one could tell anymore, while at night it dipped to around two or three, and they didn't bring any more clothing; the hot water today was only warm, and the gruel was no thicker than water and *Vladychka* once again gave his bowl to the kid with pigeon feet, who kept repeating his "Wheare? Wheare?" and sometimes added, "It's not a life, but a funeral, uncle."

Artiom tried to put his jacket on his legs, but his back immediately froze.

Through the crack in the window, he suddenly saw the distant lake and a fog over it.

Someone was walking outside — Artiom saw a shoulder, a cap and a leather jacket.

Recoiling, he listened intently — had he gone deaf? Had he missed the ringing?

No, it was quiet, and they opened the door quietly, and only one person came in — the same Chekist, drunk, with a wet, tired smile that seemed to have crawled down, like pants falling off a shameless rear end.

He stood in the entrance, holding the silent bell in one hand and the tongue in the other to prevent it from ringing.

The Chekist was looking for someone but couldn't find him in the half-dark among the humpbacked, crushed monkeys who had been beaten by their own fear.

"You tomb worm. Have you come to see whom you might eat?" Zinovii's quiet, insinuating voice resounded, lacking even the slightest quaver.

The Chekist smacked his lips, as though he were trying to hold up his drooping smile, and answered in the same smiling words, wet as his lips.

"The harvest is plentiful, but the workers are few... Have you thought to recant, Zinovii?"

It seemed that he was continuing a conversation that had been started earlier.

"I reject the Antichrist," Zinovii answered meekly.

At first, Artiom didn't even understand what he had said, but he quickly figured it out. Zinovii was saying that that demon was offering him a chance to reject Christ.

The Chekist rocked on the spot, and his smile rocked across his face, like a dead fish in a vat filled with foul water.

"What if I let go of the tongue?" asked the Chekist, raising the bell in his right hand and slowly moving away his left.

The metal string with its teardrop end shook, missing the inner wall of the bell by a distance of no more than an eyelash's width.

Every person shook on that string, as though they were on swings that launched you off, not into a patch of nettles, as in childhood, but into a worm-ridden deaf-dumb pit.

The Chekist looked around the entire church, sometimes licking his lips with a slow and disobedient tongue.

Nearly three dozen living souls attached their eyes to the bell, listening in and not breathing — what if the winds of Sekirka were missing only a single human breath to push the resonant tongue and receive in answer the quietest fatal ring.

Every single one of them wanted to stop his heart, lest its beating might rock the cosmos suddenly and make it tip over, covering someone, turning over, with wet earth.

Into the church, they brought in a vat with gruel and a few loaves of bread.

Something that promised life moved in the air.

The Chekist put the bell into his pocket and left, rocking.

Everyone breathed out, and the animation was so sincere, it was as if they all believed the Chekist couldn't come back immediately after they finished drinking the hot water, but instead walked far away, so far away that he might even forget the way back if he decided to come back.

"Father Zinovii, can it be that we are already in hell?" someone asked loudly.

"They're in hell," waved Father Zinovii in the direction of the doors; it was obvious who he had in mind. He stood first in line as he always did. "And it's us who are looking at them from the side."

Strangely, the behavior of both *Vladychka* John, who refused to eat every other time and never stood in line to receive it, and Father Zinovii, who had the habit of immediately downing his bowl and then walking around with it, empty, asking at least for another drop for the old man, seemed to everyone to be correct and appropriate to their priesthood.

Sometimes they did drop a few drops into Zinovii's bowl, some even gave him a full spoon, and if they complained, it was more for appearances — people treated him with a great deal more respect here than in the infirmary, and this respect only grew with time.

"… They… secretly hope… that he can save them," thought Artiom with tired mockery and an already constant tiredness.

Having eaten, Artiom quickly lay down in a fetal position, placed his hands between his legs in a vain hope to warm up at least his hands, since they hadn't been quite warmed up by the mug with hot water.

Zinovii, Artiom saw, ended up being not quite so pathetic as he had thought before, though his behavior smacked of purposefully imitating a fool for Christ. However, behind the foolishness, you could clearly see an extraordinary strength of spirit and angry human courage.

Artiom, for all that, didn't care — having lost his own strength, he was not in any state to value the willpower of someone else. He, on his bunk, was being carried down a dirty current full of snakes, and through a chilly fever he saw either a fanciful tree on the shore or a washed out blob of a star's reflection on the water, or long leeches that reached towards the underwater smell of flesh.

Here, Grakov passed by, driven by the wind, his crooked mouth looked for something to chew, and his eyes recognized nothing — it seemed that the event with the bell had driven him mad.

Having leaned over and looked down from his bunk, Artiom could see Vasilii Petrovich or Afanasiev lying below — both of them with their open eyes, the first was silent, while the second smiled; but it was better not to stare at them.

Artiom now neither slept nor was awake, but was constantly in an in-between state. Not only his skin, but his insides had frozen — he felt how cold and empty it was in his stomach, his groin, his chest and his brain looked like thawing meat, red and raw from one side and hard and white with ice on the other. Sometimes, a sober thought seemed to crawl into the icy area and get stuck there, becoming stupid, beginning to fall apart.

Unexpectedly, he saw before his eyes the text of a letter typed by Galina on a typewriter: "… I require… the transfer of Artiom Goriainov… into the brass orchestra…" the "b" key was stuck, and the letter came out indistinct, barely visible, while in the word "orchestra" all the consonants got confused, and it turned out to be a different word entirely, looking like cacophonous music, the woodwinds to the left, the violins to the right, the conductor in despair — "in place of… the inmate Afanasiev… in connection with his departure to… Fox Island…"

"He's not on Fox Island, Galia!" Artiom tried to yell at her. "I don't want to take his place!"

Galia didn't turn around and kept typing with firm and confident fingers, sometimes typing not with the soft pad of the finger but with her nail, and after, having clicked her tongue, quickly raised her fingers to her mouth, either warming the pained spot with her breath or straightening out the end of her nail with her teeth.

Artiom felt that this was not true — he could hardly expect to see from his bunk what it was that Galia typed, but he didn't hurry to leave her office, where Galia, for all that, was no longer found. Now he hurried down the stairs, trying not to be spotted by Gorshkov or Tkachuk; someone was carrying a coffin towards him, either empty or occupied by someone. Artiom moved to the side, sat, crawled between the bearers' legs, ended up outside, walked through the forest, past the iodine plant, crossed over to Fox Island, to which of course you had to go by boat and ended up on Sekirnaia Hill, on the top of which, the lighthouse blinked. He needed to get up the stairs to the church and, losing his breath one hundred times, he hurried, crawled, dragged himself up, and with every stop, if he turned around, the views became more and more incredible, but he didn't have time for them — on the top stood Galia, who talking calmly with the smiling Chekist who was sober, nodding often and trying, awkwardly maneuvering between her commandingly-intoned words, to stick in his equally commanding words, "… no, I understand everything… I also have my work… we have to take pains…"

"Turns out he's not such a bad guy," Artiom thought sincerely, wiping off his sweat. "You can understand him too."

"There he is, your Goriainov," nodded the Chekist. He stood face to face with the ascending Artiom. Galina looked around, and on her neck there was something like an abscess, not very pleasant to look at. Artiom tried not to look at her.

"Wait on your bunk for now…" said Galia, also not very pleased by the sudden appearance of Artiom. He hurried to accomplish her command, limping slightly from exhaustion, ran to the church and there, the smiling Chekist, as though in jest, pushed Galia, so that she would roll a bit down the ladder. The Chekist thought that she would roll down three or four steps and would then appreciate his friendly jest, but Galia awkwardly flipped head over heels and unexpectedly quickly fell into the depths of hades, her legs flailing uglily, all awkwardness, ugliness and foolishness, and during one of her many somersaults, Artiom suddenly saw that it wasn't Galia at all, but his mother — with her pies or something like them; there was jam on her face… the shame of it…

But he couldn't keep looking, he had to go back to his bunk, he returned, climbed up, opened his eyes and kept thinking worriedly for another minute, "Now she won't go back because she fell down the stairs… But really that was Galia, not my mother, I saw Galia for sure… as for the jam, that was just a mirage, there was no jam, I'm just seeing things…"

Artiom couldn't part with his vision for a long time afterwards, as though he were haggling with someone using such vivid and exact remembrances as payment for his rational mind. OK, so he didn't go back to the monastery, but he did read the text of Galia's letter… but then again, when did he read it, how…? He didn't get up any staircase, of course, but did he hear the conversation between the Chekist and Galia? The conversation had taken place of course! Eh? Artiom felt his tears very near the surface, and he bit himself on the hand, lest he start screaming: "Of course, you fucking bitch! It happened! They talked!"

"The demons are talkative; God is given to silence," Father Zinovii was teaching. "The demons scream in your ear; God shows you. The Bolshies are active, angry and incessant — have you noticed?"

Zinovii appeared first here, then there, and everyone went towards him, many stood on their knees, asking for a blessing. In the church, people started to cross themselves so often and so expansively that it was as though a cloud of flies had appeared, like in a cow bar and everyone was waving them off.

Artiom twisted his lips, seeing those stupid movements.

"Their speech is pernicious; to hear them is to dishonor your ears and befoul them! Flee from their words!" Father Zinovii said in another place, pronouncing many of the vowels twice as long: "Dishonor your ea-ears," "Flee-ee from their words!" This made what he said even more vivid and scorching.

"So what do we do, Father?" they asked him.

"The demons, even now, whisper in your ears that salvation is possible if you move the Chekist, if you make him like you, if you start singing and stand in a big Bolshie circle and dance around with him, around their chief foul-smelling dead man, even, if they allow it, to kiss that dead man on the lips as proof of your treachery. But don't you listen to the demons!" And Father Zinovii blessed the ears of the inmates, as Artiom saw from above, comically turning to him sideways, as though everyone were sitting on a chair at the barber's and had asked him to trim their sideburns. "Don't let him lead you into delusion; remember that only the Lord bears to us the word of salvation, and it is better to die merely one time and step into the Kingdom of Heaven, than be led by the demons into fiery Gehenna forever, to be destroyed eternally."

"How can we get into the Kingdom of Heaven when we are all sinful here?" They asked him again.

Grakov, completely mad, acknowledging neither himself nor what happened around him, walking around Father Zinovii and the inmates who stood with him constantly. He was only sure of one thing — if there were several people together in any one place, then it might be warm there, with some food.

"Christ came not to save the righteous, but sinners. The Church of Christ consists of sinners along," it was *Vladychka* John who continued. It turned out that they were standing together, back to back with Zinovii, and more and more unfortunates walked towards their warm hands and voices.

"We won't perish, fathers?" someone yelled over the heads of the crowd, addressing both fathers at the same time.

"You are the light of the world. A city that stands on a hill cannot be covered," answered Father Zinovii. "And, having lit the candle, no one puts it under a vessel, but on a candlestick and it gives light to everyone. We are all on the top of Sekirnaia Hill, and our light will be seen from the other side of the world."

"Please don't argue with each other, our fathers," the same voice begged. "No one can lead us, your children, outside into the light, except for you two…"

"And the apostle said that there would be dissensions among us," answered Zinovii strictly, but the answer itself was a sign that there was no more room for dissension between him and *Vladychka*, and there was no more time left to continue it.

The itch inside Artiom kept getting more frightening and insistent; his entire body laughed.

* * *

That itch was like a bunch of little bells under his skin, and the ringing didn't leave him anymore.

Artiom felt that he was full of dead, resonant, exposed fish who kept rolling back and forth, as they do on the bottom of a barge. Inside him, everything was horribly loud and noisy.

The ringing exploded out of him, and the entire room started to resonate with it.

The others also heard the ringing; it was hysterical, constant and now was found outside the church, reeling in a silver thread, like a cobweb.

"Lord, Lord, Lord!" cried one prisoner, then another.

An old man in a grey beard stood not far from Artiom's bunk, crossing himself without stopping and he began to do full prostrations in front of the saint that Artiom had uncovered and whom he called "prince".

Enveloped in the ringing, the church was becoming like a silver ball — someone pushed it and it rolled off the top of Sekirnaia Hill, filled with madness-inducing human screaming.

The Chekist had clearly gone bananas and was ringing from all sides at once, as though running from one place to another.

Grakov wept in between coughing fits, first grabbing his hair, then crumpling his cheeks and trying to stuff his never-silent mouth, full of saliva and fear.

"Confession and communion!" someone desperately begged first Father Zinovii, then *Vladychka*.

Artiom held on to his bunk, feeling a pitiless nausea.

But many other inmates, one after the other, came down from their rickety board, stood on their knees in the middle of the church in expectation of the promised confession and communion.

Zinovii had a cross on his chest that was carved out of wood — John had his own priestly cross of silver. They each had a Gospel book.

They came through the invisible Royal Doors to the place that had once been called the ambo, and, one after the other, switching with each other as soon as one began to gasp for air, began to preach.

"In the name of the Father, and of the Son, and of the Holy Spirit. Amen!" said *Vladychka* John; his voice was not loud, but firm.

"The king and psalmist David said: God looks down from heaven upon the children of men, to see if there are any who understand, who seek God. Every one of them has turned aside; they have together become corrupt; there is none who does good, no, not one," continued Father Zinovii in an exhilaratingly young and high-pitched voice.

"It is thus today," said *Vladychka*. "In corruption, everyone has forgotten about virtue, having applied their energy to save their own lives. But our attempts have proved vain and there is no oil in our oil lamp. Only the Lord alone can purify us of our impurity and give us communion with eternal joy."

The constant ringing beyond the walls didn't stop.

The church shook like a platter filled with fragile china that a drunk server carries while running along slippery stone floors, and on those floors lie puddles of someone's smelly blood.

Inside Artiom, the fish started to come alive, scratching with their sharp tails his weak intestines, liver, gallbladder — everything bled and smarted as though someone had poured out a pull dustbin of broken glass into his vivisected stomach.

"*Vladychka*! Father! Pray for us!" several people screamed, vying with one another.

Raising his head high like a bird and bulging out his red-rimmed eyes, Father Zinovii screamed out frantically, "The sins that you conceal at confession will remain unrepented and that means unforgiven, and they'll pull you down into hell! Repent!"

The inmates wailed. Nearly everyone cried and lamented loudly. But even above this wailing, you could still hear the bell which had caught everyone with an icy hook — some by the lip, some by the Adam's apple, some by the shoulder blade, some by the skin on their stomach.

"We will list all the human sins, and you repent and say, 'I am sinful,'" commanded *Vladychka* John, waving around his hand with the cross clasped in it.

"Repeat after me, "I, the greatly sinful one, confess to our Lord, God, and Savior Jesus Christ… all my sins… and all my evil deeds, which I have committed in all the days of my life in deed… or in thought, even until this day," Father Zinovii continued resonantly.

Pitiful voices, tripping over themselves in the confusion, rose up in the church.

"Forgive me, Father, I have sinned in lack of love for God and fear for God," *Vladychka* dictated.

"Sinful!" every single inmate uttered.

"And I," answered Artiom silently, and the fish swam even more furiously, trying to burst out of him into the outside.

"I have sinned by pride, including lack of humility in spirit, lack of a desire to live according to the will of God, self-will, willfulness, and self-importance," Father Zinovii yelled out.

"And I," once again Artiom nodded, baring his teeth.

"I have sinned by not fulfilling the commandments of God."

"I repent!" screamed the inmates, not seeing or recognizing each other, though they all heard the frantic ringing every second.

"I have sinned by idolatry!"

“And how,” agreed Artiom, twisting on his bunk, as though forty angry and wet hands were washing him with soap.

“I have sinned by excessive reliance on God’s long-suffering, including allowing myself to commit a multitude of sins!” the priests exclaimed, their voices no longer distinguishable.

“I am sinful!” the inmates yelled. “I repent!”

“I have sinned by vanity, excessive speaking and ambition!”

“Here I am! Here!” Artiom answered every sin, neither knowing it nor desiring to repent of it.

“I have sinned by weak faith, including the absence of Christ’s peace in the soul!”

“And that as well, yes!” Artiom laughed internally. “Including that!”

“I am sinful!” exclaimed the inmates with the same passion with which they had yelled “Good!” to the administration.

“… Ingratitude towards God!

“… Sinful sorrow and despair!”

“… I have sinned by a lack of patience during the tribulations sent by God, including a lack of patience during hunger, disease, cold!”

“I’m freezing!” Artiom agreed with demonic joy. “I want to eat and I’m freezing!”

“I have sinned by a lack of hope in salvation… by a lack of trust in God’s mercy…”

“I didn’t believe in it,” nodded Artiom with the same shameless face that a drunk man has when he’s expecting the barman to pour him another drink.

“… In thoughts and attempts at suicide…”

“Forgive me, Father!” someone cried. “I tried to hang myself! With a rope around the neck!”

“I have sinned by taking God’s name in vain… and with foul, dirty language…”

“I have sinned!” they answered here and there.

Every word sounded even louder, as though it were resonating even more against the echo that was trapped inside.

“… Not fulfilling my promises before God…”

“… Self-justification…”

“… Irreverent treatment of icons and holy objects…”

“… Not keeping the feasts of the church…”

“… Judgment of priests…”

“… Laziness in prayer…”

"I have been ashamed to admit to being a Christian, including being ashamed of crossing myself in public or wearing a cross on my chest!"

"That's me!" Artiom repeated without tiring. "I'm here! I! What riches I have! All covered, as in burrs, as in medals! Is there even any sin that I have not committed?"

The shouting was as loud as at a slaughter-house.

Even the kid joined the tail end of the crowd, and raising his fingerless hands, demanded potato soup — he probably thought that everyone else was asking for food.

Khasaev stood to the side with blackening eyes and didn't take part in anything, as though it were a bestial wedding, and he was the only one of a different species.

"I sinned by lack of love for my neighbor!" uttered *Vladychka*, his voice cracking.

"I sent my mother away!" exclaimed Artiom, holding down the mutinous fish in his chest and stomach.

"I didn't visit the sick, didn't help the poor, was miserly in my alms, condemned the poor!"

"Yes, yes, yes, and the leopards, and the weak, and the sick, and everyone — I despised them all!" Artiom remembered and poured it all, like coins onto the counter.

"I have sinned! I am guilty…! I repent!" the people coughed on their knees.

"I have sinned by not aiding the salvation of my neighbor!"

"Yes! Father, save us! Forgive us, Lord!" screamed the people, horrified by their sinfulness.

"… Lack of respect for the elderly."

Artiom was ready to turn onto his side, and, his head hanging down, to spit in Vasilii Petrovich's face, who lay there on the bottom, but he was afraid that the fish would tear him apart from within.

I have sinned by hatred and anger, by wishing evil on others, by malice. Yes. Wrath. Yes. I have cursed people near and far. Yes. I have sinned by gossiping. Yes. I have sinned by envy. Yes. Falsehood. Yes. Boasting. Yes. Condemnation. Yes. Flattery. Yes. Mockery and shamelessness. Yes. Eavesdropping and seeking out others' secrets. Yes, yes, yes.

"I have sinned by willful or unwilling murder!" Father Zinovii called.

"It's like an auction!" Artiom laughed aloud. "I'll take that one! And that one! Willful murder! Hey! That one's mine!"

"*Vladychka*!" someone wailed as though he were dropped in fire. "I killed my wife!"

Everyone grew silent, but only for a moment.

"I shot a Jew!" another one wheezed.

"My God! I robbed and killed an old woman!" admitted a third.

"I choked a child to death! Mercy! All-good One! I pray You!"

The shriek became so thick that a bird would not have been able to fly through it.

Vladychka and Father stood amongst the people as though they were in the midst of a conflagration — their feet burned and their eyes languished above the fiery pit.

"I sinned by being cruel to animals," called *Vladychka*, screwing up his eyes through the heat.

"Yes, Father!"

One admitted that he killed a puppy on Solovki to eat it. Another admitted that he had pulled out all the feathers off a living gull. A third confessed bestiality with a cat stuffed in a boot, its face shoved into the toe.

Father Zinovii's teeth shone in the fire.

"I committed fornication with a woman..."

"My entire life is fornication — I'm not married, father, forgive me!" yelled another in answer.

Artiom twisted on his bunk, as though the fish were sucking up his insides, pulling in all his organs — his tongue, his nipples, his eyes.

"I committed adultery!"

"It happened! I repent! *Vladychenka*!"

"Incest!"

"I am guilty! Don't destroy me!"

Vladychka wiped off the profuse sweat from his face.

"I sinned by unnatural union with another man!"

Many were no longer in a state to mouth "I repent", but just shrieked like birds, while others mooed, and others bleated.

Playing cards. Other forms of gambling. Immoderate laughter. Evil tears.

Every sin found its answer as the prisoners reached hysterical pitch, and still they were not capable of outshouting the ringing of the single bell, as they rubbed off their dirty tears on their dirty faces.

Masturbation. Impure thoughts. Remembrance of sins. Sensual viewing of debauched books and pictures.

"Oh, that's me again! Me again!" Artiom answered loudly, though his mouth was closed, as though he were lost in the woods, and now they found him by his many footprints, but he still didn't hurry to come out to answer the call, but only fooled around and confused his trail.

He started to hiccup, and was unable to stop it.

Excessive drunkenness. Here. Smoking. Here. Overeating. Here. Thievery and robbing. Here. Embezzlement and extortion. Here. Bribery and cheating. Here.

Everyone tried to be louder and more audible than his neighbor. Someone had even torn open his forehead and cheeks, someone was striking his head against the floor, as though knocking out his utter vileness and the unceasing, itching bell. Someone crawled on his stomach towards the priests, rubbing himself in dust and dirt.

Carelessness of God's gifts: life, flesh, mind, conscience. Yes, and again yes, and again yes, and one more time yes, Artiom hiccupped, holding back his laughter.

Out of nowhere, all kinds of vermin appeared — toads and slugs, scorpions and tapeworms, chameleons and lizards, spiders and centipedes… even the vermin were crooked and ugly. There were one-legged frogs that jumped sideways and landed on their stomachs, intestinal worms with an unblinking bird's eye on their tail, centipedes whose front half moved in one direction and bottom half moved in the opposite direction. Lizards with wet tinsel of eviscerated intestines, and on every intestine, holding on with all their might, were bloodsuckers and lice, spiders with the wet and meaty bodies of snails or flesh that looked like a human eye, rats turned inside out, with a stomach festooned with underdeveloped rat fetuses — blind, their insides exposed. Tarantulas on old women's fingers instead of legs… a hairy tail twisted about, having lost its animal rear… snakes lay around in foul coils, immediately giving birth to live-born young that twitched angrily as though they were being burned… the whole floor was covered with slime, human vomit and every possible foulness that the body could emit.

An unnaturally long, hairy, wooly caterpillar crawled out of someone's bellybutton; the person looked at it with pain in his eyes, expecting it to end, but it kept on coming out and coming out…

Another one had a worm on his finger that had sucked in the finger whole, and the inmate kept trying to pull it off, but it turned out that the worm had grown into the skin and was already digesting the finger, having broken it down with its stomach acid, almost to the bone.

One inmate, suffering and crying, jumped away, not for the first time, from a large, unnaturally fast crustacean; on the next, maggots crawled from his mouth, eyes and ears — and his entire bears seemed to be a badly chewed rise, might as well make soup out of it. A third was blowing some slimly, living, half-transparent, whiskered monstrosity out of its nose — but it, seeming to have come out almost entirely, kept jumping back into the nose with a sob, on the very last thread of snot, where it lived and fed.

From the continual hiccupping, Artiom's belly button got untied and from it slimy, half-rotted, large fish fell onto the bunks, and from them came out smaller fish that they had managed to eat, and from those came out even smaller ones, also half-eaten, then from the third, new tiny ones, and from those tiny ones came out a barely visible, disgusting, grainy detritus…

Artiom kept trying to put them all back — mine, mine, back into me, it's mine, where are you all planning on going…?

"Do you see how sinful we all are?" cried out Father Zinovii. "Do you see? Look inside yourselves and be horrified! Look around yourselves and cry from shame…! These are your traces, filled with slime and foulness! Every single one of you deserves utter punishment! But our Father in Heaven doesn't want the destruction of His children! And for the sake of our salvation, He did not spare His Only-begotten Son, He sent Him into the world to redeem us, so that He might forgive all our sins for His sake."

"And not only forgive us," *Vladychka* said, barely alive, but with consoling and pure eyes, "but even to call us to His divine feast! For this, He gave us a great miracle — the most-holy Body and Blood of His own Son, our Lord Jesus Christ. This miraculous feast is accomplished at every liturgy, according to the words of our Lord, 'Take, eat. This is My Body!' and 'Drink, this is My Blood!'"

"Go now with complete faith and hope in the mercy of the Father, because of the intercession of His Son! Come and approach the Holy Communion with fear and faith," Father Zinovii added.

"And now, my dears, bow your heads. And we, by the authority given to us by God, will read over you the prayer of absolution," said *Vladychka* John.

His neck became thin, and you could see three blue veins that were ready to burst.

It became quiet.

Everyone bowed his head.

Near every head, a bell rang, as though a butterfly, unafraid of the reptiles, vermin and insects, had flown in to drink nectar and was choosing the sweetest flower.

Father Zinovii read the prayer of absolution.

Together with *Vladychka* John, they made the sign of the cross over everyone.

"I forgive and absolve," said Father Zinovii.

"In the name of the Father and the Son and the Holy Spirit," said *Vladychka* John.

The communion began.

Everyone kissed the cross and the Gospel.

One of the priests dropped dried cranberries into plain water — was it prepared in a baggie in advance or did it roll in by itself? — but the berry juice became the Blood of Christ. The scanty, straw-like bread of Solovki became the body.

It was clean and resonant in the church, like a field covered in snow.

Only the ringing didn't stop — it came nearer, then farther; it got confused, then spluttered, then it was as though it had fallen down a hill.

Artiom, who had mastered his hiccup, sat at the window and laughed rollickingly, unable to stop. The Chekist had put the bell on the dog, untied it from its chain and it ran around the church, constantly jingling.

Artiom saw either its tail, its side, or its black head in the chink in the window.

If the dog stopped, the soldiers immediately made it run again, giggling at their ingenious joke.

No one in the church could guess what it was.

Grakov climbed onto the cold metal stove near the entrance and sat there, crouching, hugging the pipe. He had gone mad and had no more chances to come back into the world.

Artiom didn't take communion.

His hands were dry, powerful and angry; his heart was stubborn; his thoughts were empty.

* * *

In the darkest part of the night, a huge bell tolled over the sleepers — it was a single toll, a long one, ringing over many kilometers.

A heavy wind blew in almost equally-spaced gusts, as though someone was sweeping Solovki.

The human pile-up was so compressed that no one got up or could even cross himself, though everyone knew that the bell tower was empty, and there was neither ringer nor bell, nor could either have come from anywhere, because the staircase was filled in and boarded up.

In the morning, everyone woke up quiet, with sweaty and slightly crumpled faces, but their eyes were pure and filled with moisture — like they were just after a sauna.

No one hurried to their bunks, everyone kept standing in the middle of the church, looking up, as though the night's tolling still hadn't ended.

"Russia is the coming of Jesus," said Father Zinovii for everyone. Pointing up, he added, "There's the lighthouse. God lit a candle above our heads on purpose, so that we could see better. The one problem is that we're sleeping, while all we must do is keep vigil, for no one knows when the Son of Man will come! Do you hear, *Vladychka*?"

It was *Vladychka's* luck to be on the bottom row of the night's last turn.

There were still three layers above him — while they took off all the others' hands and legs, it became obvious that *Vladychka* was no longer alive — he had been crushed to death.

His body had become thin, broken, comical, as though he were a youth. The freckles on his hands had become greenish.

One eye was closed, and with the other he still seemed to look out, though his gaze was unconsoling and stingy.

Artiom sat down and caressed *Vladychka* on the head. The hairs ended up being coarse, dirty, and not living — as though he were caressing an old mitten.

He smelled his hand in hopes of smelling the familiar scent of dried apples, but instead he saw a louse crawling on his hand — it had hopped off the dead man.

He hurried back to his bunk, already knowing what he would do. In a single jump, he got up and took out his spoon. In several swings, he scratched up the face of his "prince", getting in the way of the prayers of several inmates who were praying to the holy man.

The eyes were the hardest to get at — Artiom gouged them out with the sharp end of the spoon.

He carved off the ears one by one. He rubbed off the lips. He pulled out the hair in bunches.

Above the prince's body, on his wide shoulders, there was no longer a head — you could easily put another head there like in the photograph on Miasnitskaia Road.

He worked quickly, full of wrath and baring his teeth.

"Oh my God…" someone breathed out below him. "He doesn't have a cross on."

Shrieking, Father Zinovii grabbed and pulled Artiom down by his shorts.

"They… they lie there under the whitewash like grass and berries under the snow… they're preserved there and wait… wait for their hour… how did it come into your head, you heathen, to first uncover it, then… to disfigure it? How?"

Without any effort, Artiom threw off the weak old man's arm, but several other arms came to help him, hurried and greedy. Artiom had nothing to grab on to; unexpectedly for himself, he fell backwards — it seemed almost funny to him — he feared no one among the prisoners and felt himself to be stronger than any one of them, what could they do to him?

... But to begin with, they just didn't try to catch Artiom. Having thrown him off the bunks, everyone together, without agreeing to it, stepped back and he fell onto his side, directly onto the stone floor with a crack in his ribs and with red sparks inside his skull. He hadn't had a chance to gather himself. At the same time, he felt a sharp burning sensation in his knee, which seemed to be connected with his brain by a good hundred fast telegraph lines that were beating a sharp message into his consciousness: horror, horror, horror, send a quick lighting, one hundred lightning's, there's pain here, pain, it hurts!

But they decided this wasn't enough. One hand grabbed Artiom by the ear, another hit his side, someone's bony fist jabbed him in the eyebrow... He tried to get up, but they pushed him back down, jabbed him in the chest, stepped on his stomach — only the multitude of weak and awkward, frozen and confused people prevented themselves from immediately tearing him into pieces.

The frightened Grakov once again sat on his stove, wailing from there, hiding his eyes in his hands.

"... Unrepentant one!" yelped Zinovii. "You're rotting alive... there's a foul stench inside you... your soul is rotting! O you of little faith, you're a thief, a rogue, an insolent man. I'll spew you out, you lukewarm neither-fish-nor-meat![48]... I'll spew you out!"

"Oh yeah, you'll spit me out..." Artiom had time to think, understanding for sure that they would kill him right now, though that didn't make it any less comical or hilarious. "But you wouldn't spew out the fish or the meat. You'd eat it..."

Cunningly, Artiom, turning around and lying face-down, tried to cover his head with his arms. They were pushing him, pecking at him, beating him, trampling him, kneading him, pinching him, rubbing him, rumpling him, mangling him, biting him, ripping at him, taking pieces off him...

"*Vladychka*!" he called with a plaintive but slightly mocking voice. He was ashamed to scream out in full seriousness. "They're killing me!"

Vladychka looked on with his eye and didn't move.

[48] The expression "neither fish nor meat" means "ambivalent" or "lukewarm" in Russian.

"Hey!" a confident voice rose up. "Enough! Hey! Russians! What are you doing?" That was Khasaev.

Artiom sensed that there were now fewer hands ripping at him, but Khasaev still wasn't managing — he yelled for the orderlies, but they, it seemed, didn't hurry to help.

However, the homeless kid ran into the crowd, and, not forgetting to yell either "Yummy-yummy, potato soup!" or "Wheare? What about me?" grabbed hold of Artiom's barely grown-out hair with four fingers — at least not five! — of his disfigured hand, ripping away the skin from Artiom's scalp with his dirty fingernail, as though Artiom were that potato soup that had finally been found and needed to be shared.

They screamed as though all the vile sins that had been crawling around yesterday had all crawled into Artiom and found their abode in him — that meant that they could return to any of their former domiciles — to that one's ear, that one's bellybutton, that one's nostril.

That cannot be allowed. You need to preserve and protect the purity of the soul…

"They're really going to kill me!" Artiom understood again, with that same almost comical feeling.

Only his heart jumped inside him like a foreign object, alive and disagreeing with him — OK, so they kill you, but what about me? Why me? Let them finish you off, but let me out…!

All that was left was a single fierce blow to the temple, so that his life would finally unchain itself and fly away — losing its last feathers along the way, with teary eyes, filled with new air.

Artiom's guardian angel sat on his bunk, pouring the scratched-off whitewash from palm to palm, like a child in a sandbox.

"Jackals! Get back in place!" the soldiers yelled. "Hurry the fuck up, jackals!"

Someone got it in the back with the butt end of a rifle, someone got a boot in the stomach.

They left Artiom in a flash — he lay there alone, still holding his hands on his head; they were stuck to his temples and the back of his neck, since everything was covered in blood.

"Where are we hurrying off to?" asked the Chekist in his leather jacket, still standing at the entrance with his bell — truly, he was afraid to drop it and break it in the fracas. "Are we not depriving you of life well enough already? You think we won't manage to get all of you, if you don't help us out, citizens…? Finally, isn't there any order, line? Why are you crowding?"

His voice once again gave away his drunken and crooked smile — white with puce — on his face.

"They were praying to God!" the fingerless kid suddenly complained loudly.

The Chekist looked at Zinovii.

"Zinovii, you hairy dog, have you considered recanting?"

"I reject Antichrist," the priest said, as though spitting.

"Well, keep waiting while we finish devouring your parishioners," said the Chekist.

"I will still have time to laugh at your destruction," Father Zinovii suddenly answered loudly and confidently.

However, the Chekist lost interest in continuing the conversation. Having taken out a paper from his pocket and unfolding it in the air, he read: "Goria…I! Nov…! Artiom…! Which one?"

* * *

Father Zinovii crawled after Artiom as they dragged him: "Forgive me, my son! Forgive me!"

Artiom looked around in confusion: what was he on about? What does he want?

Everything stopped being funny at once.

The world stopped, his consciousness turned into aspic, his heart pulsed blood with frenzied energy into his head and his fresh wounds bled even more hotly and abundantly. His back was covered in cold sweat. Sweat immediately formed even between his fingers and toes, under his chin, in his groin — it was as though they were carrying Artiom out of the frozen basement to have him for dinner.

"And if I forgive him?" Artiom looked around at Father Zinovii. "Is anything going to change…? They saved me from being trampled to death here… so that… what? They could shoot me over there?"

With a groan, the door closed behind his back, into his face blew fresh air from the sea, tinged with fir trees and dug-up earth, there was something missing in the world… but that absence didn't mean death… on the contrary, on the contrary, it hid inside itself an invisible, unexpected hope descended from above.

Artiom looked around — what had changed, what?

He needed to quickly — before it was too late — understand what had changed.

There was a great deal of light; he hadn't seen daylight for a while, but what did the light have to do with that?

Sekirnaia Hill stood in its place, the sky moved over the forests and seas, the black dog jumped back and forth near his doghouse, continually invigorating him with the jingling — … Artiom breathed out — … chain.

"What about the bell?" he quietly asked. "Where's my bell?"

The Chekist looked at him and nudged the soldier walking next to him, "What a peacock! He wants some exit music!"

They laughed cheerfully, like a pack of dogs. It stank unbearably of moonshine and tobacco.

They showed Artiom a cart and, indifferent to his subsequent fate, immediately gave him joy: "You're back to the monastery. Vacation's over. Sorry, we couldn't see you to the end. The documents are with your escorting guard."

Artiom didn't have strength to laugh — less than a minute ago he would have let them chop his arm off and would have agreed to eternal shameful slavery under any master, just for the right to live. But now, barely waiting for his smarty-pants blood — it had immediately understood everything before the man with all his idiotic reasoning capacity — to go back down from his head along his jugular veins and sleepy arteries, he already recognized nothing but the cold.

It was cold, cold, cold. His entire body shook with tremors, the wind blew from all sides, he was in his socks and underwear, the abundantly flowing sweat was getting cold and the already drying blood on his face didn't warm him.

With difficulty — his ribs creaked, his knee wouldn't bend — he sat down, gathered a handful of straw that had been strewn on the cart, and hugged it — maybe it could save him?

No.

"Hey!" he called at the soldier. His voice was not his own, his jaws were tight, barely moving. "Can I warm myself with something?"

"You can go back into the church, its warm there," said the soldier, baring crooked teeth and looking at Artiom for a long time, waiting for an answer with expectant pleasure. He had long convinced himself of his own power and right to consider all prisoners to be stupid cattle that would never be able to find a good answer.

In Artiom's case, that was true.

The guard came by — a thug with a bristle.

"Where are you sitting, jackal's muzzle?" he asked.

Artiom jumped off — the landing caused the back of his head to jolt with pain; it seemed that his kneecap had just about fallen to the ground.

"Giddy-up!" called the soldier. The cart started; the dog barked.

Artiom looked around and understood that he had to run after the cart; otherwise, they'd leave him here and, a little later, would bury him here too.

He hobbled off, tears gushed from his eyes, mixing with the blood and starting new trails in the dried-out crust. The dog barked even more viciously.

Understanding nothing, moaning and mumbling to himself, he hurried with all his strength and still couldn't catch up.

Luckily, there was a gate; while they opened it, Artiom reached the cart.

But then the same began again — another minute of such running and he would fall over without any strength and would only be able to move forward at a crawl.

Hot apples began to drop from out of the horse. Artiom immediately stepped in one, feeling the soft warmth.

"Whoa!" the guard pulled the reins.

He looked back at Artiom and wanted to swear again, but he was lazy, and instead advised him lazily: "Hold on to the cart, jackal."

Artiom fell onto the cart.

The soldier turned away, and Artiom immediately, as in childhood, leaned forward with his stomach onto the cart, letting his legs hang — it's not that he was riding, exactly, but neither was he running, though he could also hop off and pretend that he hadn't done anything really.

Now the soldier heard neither the pitter patter of prisoners' feet, nor his ragged and wheezing breath, but he pretended that he didn't notice.

And he didn't look around.

He was a kind man.

"How could I think that today I would be dead?" thought Artiom, looking at the ears and the back of the head of the soldier.

He had gotten a little warmer as he ran.

On his sole, the horse's manure was drying.

The bloody mush on his face dried up finally, helped along by the wind. If he smiled, an entire piece of red-black whitewash would fall off at once. He smiled.

"... If the saints... under their whitewash... knew how to smile," thought Artiom in the rolling quickness of the cart, "maybe... also... their faces... would be more easily seen..."

* * *

In the hazy heat of May or June, the monastery at Solovki, when you approached, could resemble a font for washing children. In October, under the steely, smoky sky, it now looked like a smoky kitchen range, covered in dirty, black pots and pans — what they're cooking there, who knows?

Maybe human flesh.

From the St Nicholas gates, Artiom continued on foot — in the paper, it was written that he was assigned to the brass orchestra.

Even by Solovetsian standards, he looked skinny — dirty, ragged underwear, socks in horse manure, jacket covered in blood and also ripped, a piece of black sheet sticking out from his chest, his chest, stomach and legs dusted with straw, his face bloody and wild, his nose swollen, one ear larger than the other — he couldn't even touch it…

"… I think," Artiom remembered, "that homeless scum had grabbed it with his disgusting pigeon claws: 'Wheare? What about me? Wheare? What about me?'"

Hobbled and beaten, he arrived at the designated place in the former cook's wing. Those walking past him were talking in full voice and laughing about trivialities.

Just a short while ago, he looked like these people.

Somewhere, a stove was alight. Just the knowledge of the existence of the stove was like a child's knowledge that he has a mother, that she will come for him some day, and that he will not remain without her love and care. With this knowledge, one could live.

… Finally, a fast-moving, tall person — he was concentrating on some thought, but two steps from Artiom he saw his guest, suddenly noticing him like a wall — stood and immediately put his hands behind his back.

"French horn?" he asked.

Artiom scratched his cheek, then looked over his monkey-like hand, with its crooked and hardened fingers, crowned with black fingernails, broken in places.

"I want to eat. And wash. Then — French horn."

"They're just mocking me," the tall man said, turning to the echoing and damp champers of the cook's wing. It appeared that he was about to leave.

"I'll pass it on," Artiom promised, looking at his fingers that he couldn't for the life of him straighten out.

The man stopped and patted his head with a careful gesture, as though calming himself down.

They brought Artiom to a faucet. The water was cold, but at least they had warmed up the washroom no more than a day ago. Artiom now could, like an insect, sense the smallest inkling of warmth.

He began to wash and scrape his head, but the water soon ran out. The surface of the sink was covered in a layer of dirt. You could see lice in that dirt who had survived the deluge.

Someone walked in without knocking and put soap on the edge of the sink.

"The water ran out," Artiom said, not looking around.

A short while later, they brought a bucket of water and put it down at the entrance.

Having taken off the cover from the sink, Artiom, swearing, poured half the bucket in there, feeling all the while that he had become weak and shaky.

Having sprinkled water on his hands, Artiom soaped up his face, head, and neck — and washed for a long, long time. The water was a little colder than the cold that he had brought inside him, while his face turned out to be very large, complex, and variegated — you could wash it all day.

Then he pulled out a piece of the sheet from under his jacket — it had stuck to his body; he had to, not without some pleasure, tear it off.

He wiped his eyes with the same sheet, though he was too grossed out to do it to the rest of his face. Though he had literally torn the sheet from his body, the smell of it was foul, not familiar.

He used the second sheet to wipe his hands, which he managed to wash off, by the fourth time, up to the elbows. He didn't have the strength left to wash any higher.

"Well now," said Artiom aloud, straightening out in front of the sink, "let's go and play some French horn. I'll play a Solovetsian waltz for you." For some reason he immediately thought of Afanasiev.

Two people — a man and a woman — hurriedly walked to the shack where he was splashing about. It's wasn't hard to recognize the sound of that heel. They clopped along quickly, while the boots, as though unwilling, followed behind.

"Where is he?" asked the woman agitatedly and indeterminately. "Here?"

"What a fool of a woman," thought Artiom. "She's lost all her fear…"

"Here, he's washing," answered the orderly. "But he… isn't in uniform… He's in his underthings…"

"I've brought him everything."

"Oh, the idiot," Artiom thought again.

The man in the boots remained silent; he, it seemed, was perplexed — why was this employee of the IID carrying pants to some over-ripe leopard?

Artiom quietly opened the door, looked out in the corridor, and said, "I'm here."

Galia looked at him point-blank and her eyes widened for a moment.

The question that arose inside her was directed not to Artiom: "You?" but to herself, "… Him?"

"… I hope Galia doesn't run off with my pants…" Artiom had time to think.

He put his hand out for the bundle.

She mastered herself. She nodded to Artiom meekly, gave him a soft package wrapped in newspaper — as only a woman can do.

"Get dressed," she said; she had to say something.

"One moment," said Artiom; he had to answer something.

In the package were a pair of pants, a shirt, and — how about that! — a woven sweater.

Artiom quickly, grabbing with his toes, got rid of his crusty and monstrous socks, leaving them for now to lie on the floor, then he pulled down his underpants, he wanted to throw them out into the waste basket, but, jerking his shoulders with disgust, remembered: "What if they send me back to Sekirka?" And, rolling up his disgusting underwear, threw it on the same newspaper, lying unrolled on the floor, with his niggling eye, he managed to catch a few iron headlines.

Having examined his black feet, he quickly put on his pants, right onto his naked body… then thought about it. And, standing next to the sink, washed his groin with soap — at least that.

Raising his socks with disgust, he shook them out, knocked them against the wall, turned them inside out and back again, and still ended up putting them on — the floor was stone cold.

The shirt and sweater were just his size. Clean clothing… there's something… humanizing in that.

He shook out his jacket and climbed into it with some difficulty, holding the sleeves of the sweater with his fingers so they wouldn't roll up.

He rolled up the newspaper with his things and looked out again.

Galia was alone now.

She weakly smiled at Artiom with a still incomprehensible hope, a little bit, as though she were nearsighted, as though she was afraid that if she were to stare at anything at all for too long, something difficult, unpleasant and painful would reveal itself.

"Let's go…" she called him with a whisper.

"I'm… you know… barefoot," he said, trying to smile.

She looked at his feet thoughtfully.

"We'll find something," she answered just as quietly.

Galia and Artiom — she walked first, he, limping, after her — walked into a green room — the same one where he had once been with Shlabukovskii and Eichmanis… At the entrance of this green room stood the orderly — evidently following Galina's order not to allow any actors or musicians inside.

"Thank you," Galina said dryly.

The orderly didn't answer, which seemed crazy to Artiom.

A bottle of milk and a while platter of hand pies stood on the table.

While Galia closed the door, he was already there, where it smelled of onion, eggs, cabbage…

He may have remembered something about the fact that it's better to eat slowly, but it turned out that he swallowed everything without chewing and he poured it all down with milk.

While he chewed one pie, a second was in his hand, and he was already eyeing the platter, or it might run away.

The milk was lukewarm.

When Galia came up, Artiom suddenly guessed why even dogs will growl at their masters when they're protecting their pile of meat — he found himself ready to growl at her, push her aside; there just wasn't any time.

Artiom didn't feel like he satisfied his hunger. He only saw that there were no more pies and the bottle was empty.

He once again tried to smile at Galia; once again, it didn't really work.

"You went wild in there," she said quietly and sadly looked at him a little longer.

Artiom licked his lips, may have shrugged his shoulders, and unerringly found the part of the wall that was especially warm — evidently there was a stove on the other side of the wall.

He sat right on the floor and leaned with his back against the almost hot surface of the wall.

"One more minute, and I'll come back to life," he promised, for some reason unable to raise his eyes at Galia, looking instead at her knees and stomach. Then he added a word that he really didn't like and never said, "I'm sorry."

Galia was in a short autumn coat and a long grey skirt with a few drops of dirt on the hem. She held her hands in her pockets.

"Did they beat you in there? What's wrong with you?" she asked quietly and crouched next to him. This movement of hers — careful and measured in a woman's way, very elegant, suddenly making her knees very obvious, though they were still under her skirt, her knees, the line of her hip — if it didn't quite return to Artiom the sensation of any possibility of there being another, peaceful life that lacked any physical pain, it at least reminded him that such a thing existed.

He raised his hands and fingers, disobedient and splayed like a rake, and touched her knee.

Galia quickly looked at the door: was it closed? Though she had carefully made sure of that less than a minute before.

Artiom took away his hand with the same slow movement; he carried his fingers through the warm air as though they were the paw of an animal.

"I can't have you in my office anymore," said Galia. "I don't even have an office anymore."

"How?" Artiom didn't understand.

She quickly bit her lower lip and finally allowed herself a very long look directly into Artiom's eyes.

"Do you love me?" she asked.

Artiom was in no state to wrap his mind around everything that stood behind that question, everything that preceded it, and everything that could follow it. To answer it after incessant, half-comatose coldness, after the bell and the groom's smile of the half-wit Chekist, after the potato soup and the pigeon feet of the kid, after Afanasiev's torn off forelock and Grakov wailing on the stove, after the morning's broken and crooked body of *Vladychka*, his unclosing eye, after dreaming itself — filled with men, their foulness, their ankles and their puny buttocks, their bony backs and sharp knees, after the sour gruel that was intended not to nourish but to kill all that was human in them, after the shrieks: "I ate human flesh!" and "I raped my sister!" after the holy man who was covered in dust from whitewash, after they tried to kill Artiom and accidentally didn't quite manage it only a few hours ago — how could he answer that question? He didn't have a word for it in his language.

Artiom wasn't even able to blink in answer.

"Did you come to Sekirka?" he asked.

"Yes," she answered hotly. "I was… At first I didn't even know where you were, and I had no way of finding out… then I came, and that obnoxious pig…"

"With the bell?"

"The what? Oh, yes, he did have a bell on the table. The deputy direction of the division, named Sannikov… I had to return here, and…"

"Oh, I knew that. That you came… and that they would put me in the brass orchestra."

"How? Did someone tell you?"

"No, no one... told me. Why don't you have your own office?"

"It's not important," she said. "Later. I have to leave here, understand?" She was quiet. "Fiodor called," she explained. "And he warned me that there will be an investigation... there's a report and some documents about me... I can't stay here. I know that myself. It can all end very badly. They might... I don't know... even transfer me to the female barracks. Damn."

Artiom, blessedly leaning with his back to the wall, asked, completely without being upset — why should he be upset when it was so warm and when he had drunk his fill of milk?

"Have you called me to say goodbye, Galia?"

"We can run away," she said firmly and with that thoughtless frenzy that replaces deliberateness in women. "But it has to be right now. In November, it will be too late — the cold will come. Are you... strong enough? Otherwise, they'll kill you here, Tioma."

"Yes," he said, meaning that they would kill him.

He didn't have any choice.

"What happened, did you have a bad tooth?" he asked, and if his hands weren't so disfigured, he would have caressed her on the cheek.

He followed the line of her cheekbone to her beautifully dimpled chin with two fingers.

"Is it obvious?" she asked.

She was upset that it was obvious.

"No," Artiom said honestly.

* * *

Galia commanded him to go into the infirmary so that Doctor Ali could examine him. She promised to talk to him in advance.

She left before him; Artiom sat another fifteen minutes at the wall in the green room. The actors and musicians appeared, walking back and forth, looking at the new person, but no one asked who he was.

He didn't care.

Artiom suddenly felt like a dog that was allowed to be in the presence of people — but no one knows what's on his mind. Here someone walked by in a skirt. There someone walked in wearing galoshes, наследил, his voice unpleasant. Maybe I should bite him?

It seemed that he feel asleep for a bit.

He woke up in time, got up with a groan, walked to the infirmary and once again noticed that there were much fewer people in the yard than previously — the new head of the camp was sweeping in and out again.

Galia wasn't there anymore, but he encountered Doctor Ali's beard at the entrance. That one immediately determined with his cherry eyes that this one was for him.

He examined Artiom quickly, touching him with very strong and very large fingers, and immediately concluded with his characteristic accent: "No breaks, can't let you in, otherwise I'll be punished. But I'll let you sleep here one night. And you can eat as much as you like."

He was kindly disposed, and, it seemed, he was telling the truth.

Artiom was given someone's old boots. They fed him in the infirmary's kitchen, alone. This time he slowly and stubbornly ate four portions of millet porridge, an entire mountain of moldy scraps of bread, rubbing off the mold with his sleeve, and he drank about twelve cups of hot water.

He finally got warm, but he couldn't trust that feeling at all. Even though he sat in the heated kitchen in a warm sweater and jacket, the chill occasionally climbed out from his waist to his neck, as though someone licked him with a cold tongue all along the spine. At other times the same tongue licked him from the bellybutton to the armpits, across the left breast, and also sometimes his feet froze unexpectedly and his groin iced over.

"There is no more millet porridge," said Doctor Ali, running into the kitchen. "Will you wash?"

Artiom looked into the dark, full-lipped face — big whites in the eyes, meaty ears — this person was very talented at being both unpleasant and good, and his beard was either frightening or kind.

Artiom got up and almost fell to the side.

"You should get some sleep," said Doctor Ali with somewhat forced assiduity. Artiom immediately remembered *Vladychka*'s "What a good priest I am!"

"I'll find you a place after your shower. Or will you eat a little first, then sleep? There's some fish left."

"I'll eat some more," said Artiom. After every word, his lips stuck together, and it took effort to unstick them.

He took off his clothes with a bit of regret and fear: well, I'll leave them here, but what if they take them away? It's a sweater, after all.

Holding on to the wet walls, he stood under the first showerhead, turned on the water, and almost boiling water poured on him. He, swearing, endured it and stayed in place, feeling how wonderful it was to be boiled, steamed, with his burned skin, his eyes popped from the heat… his bad knee ached — Artiom stuck it under the water on purpose… he slowly scraped himself off with his fingers, blew his nose, climbed into this ears — one hurt severely whenever he touched it, but he still climbed in — he nearly fell over without trying to help himself with his hand or move the foot onto which everything fell. He filled a full mouth of hot water, and, having no strength to spit it out, stood there with his jaw open, the water pouring out of it…

Tottering, he came out of the shower, somehow managed to dry himself with the sleeve of his shirt, since he had no towel. Once again, he came down to the kitchen and there was a bowl of fish already waiting for him. He ate the fish — it wasn't salted enough, not quite cooked, old and tasted bad. He poured a handful of salt from the bowl, gathering the broken-down pieces, joyful and smacking his lips — though his eyes were sticking together and he was falling asleep right on the bench.

The former monastic worker was there at the doors; Artiom remembered him; they had seen each other before here.

Guessing without words that the worker had come to show him his bed, Artiom got up and lumbered behind him. When he saw his bed, he immediately fell asleep, even though he was still a few steps away from it. Then, he even took his boots off and maybe did something else, but he could never, afterwards, remember it.

He slept until midnight; at midnight, or near it, he opened his eyes and immediately remembered what Galia had said to him yesterday, and he felt an onrush of fear — childish, huge, making his knees shake, but at the same time, he didn't forget to check if his boots were still there (they were), and the blessed joy of sleeping alone, under a blanket, in a warmed-up little room in the infirmary was far stronger than any looming death of tomorrow. Nearby, the sick were moaning, someone was calling for a nurse, but all this only made him calmer and sweeter; Artiom crawled with his head somewhere into the depths, into a hole, into his own warmth, into childhood, into his mother's womb, into his father's stomach, in a distant and trustworthy place, like the earth, beating of the heart and a badly distinguishable and half-bestial mumbling of his forefathers, who had preserved his insane, hilarious life from the primeval forests, between Estonia and Mordovia, from underneath the hoofs of the Pechenegs, from the cries of the Polovetsians, from the confused crossroads between Novgorod, Kiev, Suzdal, Riazan' and Tmutarakan, from under the sharp Mongol eye, through the times of trouble and the times of plague, through the fires of Sten'ka Razin's rebellion, through failed harvests once every three years, from under the hooves of the Oprichnina,

Peter's press-gangs, the Turkish wars, the German wars, stabbings in public houses, infertility, drought and flood, evil spirits of water, forest, horse, path, being whipped in the stables, hatred from the neighbors, all those in his family who died on the road, on their way out into God's light — and they had all led him here, to Solovki.

Artiom slept, screwing his eyes up with all his strength, and in his sleep, it was as though he floated on a narrow boat along a fast-moving and hot river of his own blood, and the current of that blood bore him further and further back to the times when just beyond the river bend, enemies were pulling back bowstrings, but only a hair too far, and the arrow fell behind the back of his forefather. On another bend, they were firing from cannons, but every single round met a headwind and few, no farther than a hand span, past the temple of his great-grandfather. On the third bend, his great-grandmother, still a maiden, or rather a girl, she wasn't even two yet — fell down the stairs while everyone was out harvesting and managed to crawl away just enough not to be immolated while the fire in the hut rose and rose. On the fourth bend, the great-grandmother of that great-grandmother didn't die after her first childbearing and she was fated to give birth to another seven, and the seventh was the direct ancestor of Artiom. On the fifth bend, his great-great-grandfather of his great-grandfather was scything grass on the shore, still a boy, got tired, fell asleep, got severe sunstroke in the back of his head, and could have never woken up; but an annoying angel pushed his dilatory neighbor under the arm, and that neighbor came to the same meadow, not even knowing why, and he found the great-grandfather of the great-grandfather, and he woke him up and held him under the chest while he vomited into the freshly-scythed grass. And on all the other bends of the river, all the rest of Artiom's many-faced and many-eyed family also fell into water, swelled up from hunger, burned, drank themselves into stupors, were beaten with whips, were wounded, fell from roofs and bell towers, got trampled by horses, got lost in blizzards and in forests, fell into bears' dens, encountered packs of wolves, tried to kill themselves, endured the instruments of torture, but every time just short of death — or at the very least they all didn't die just long enough for Artiom's boat to float past, and only after that were they allowed to descend into the earth and be dissolved in it.

His coming in the world was a direct consequence of a series of countless miracles.

Having made a full circle of his body, Artiom returned to the same place from where he disembarked, in the same day under the same sky to the same infirmary bed, and he opened his eyes.

Galia told him to stay out of the morning inspection and to come to the quay afterwards. She had given him a pass through the St. Nicholas gates.

Artiom, still lying under his blanket, found the document in his jacket and got it out — the document was supposed to prove that yesterday's hurried conversation was no delusion.

It seemed that he had once already lost such a paper and then found it in a pile of wood… but he couldn't remember whether that discovery had brought him happiness or not.

And he didn't want to remember.

At the quay, he and Galia were supposed to get on a motor boat and supposedly go to the islands of the archipelago — there was even a corresponding document attesting to that.

Artiom wasn't supposed to be in that motor boat at all, but they wouldn't be looking for him for a while, at least not immediately. Because, from the icebox on Sekirka, the inmate Goriainov returned to the camp with a transfer into the musicians' brigade and the commander of that brigade had received a phony health statement that proved that Artiom Goriainov wasn't physically able to join the musicians yet and was redirected temporarily to the infirmary. As for Doctor Ali, he was sure that the inmate who had slept for a day and a half on one of his couches knew where he had to go and he had no business whatsoever with him, because he never officially admitted him but only put him up for a night as a favor — or rather, because Galia asked him to — and now the only person responsible for this state of affairs was Galia herself.

The mechanic who was able to drive the motor boat was sent into the shop to rebuild an old motor. She knew how to drive it herself. Or at least that's what she said.

Where were they planning to go, Artiom forgot to ask; and he didn't really want to anyway, because no matter where they went, they would be chased and they would catch them for sure, because many people talked about flight from Solovki, but not a single person ever seemed to do it successfully. Everyone was returned and executed here, and they always announced it at the evening inspections, but more often than not they just killed them along the way.

Artiom came out into the white light of Solovki. His knee was as little better, his ear hurt a little less, his body breathed and asked to live some more, like a dog on a leash who begs to take a walk with its master, to bite some grass, to smell the air, to bark at a squirrel.

But he had little strength and his mind had been frozen on Sekirka — everything came to him slowly and more dully.

He looked like a typical inmate — his Muscovite bearing was gone, his eyes had dimmed, his hubris had run out, his gait had been rubbed out — Artiom seemed to switch his ace with a two of clubs. The winning card in his sleeve was no more than a beat-up penny.

As any Solovetsian frightened to his bones, Artiom walked with a clear sense of his own conspicuity.

It seemed that the Chekist walking towards him would stop him and ask, "Are you going to the quay, and then try to flee?" And he would have to answer, "Yes," how else could it be?

Two soldiers in the square laughed as they looked at Artiom, probably saying one to the other, "Look! It's a jackal in a woman's sweater — he's planning on fleeing!"

"Wait, is this really a woman's sweater?" Artiom thought indifferently.

The guard at the St. Nicholas gates let him through without obstruction, though Artiom still hadn't come up with anything to say if they were to ask him, "Where are you off to?"

Artiom walked to the quay and felt that two soldiers with rifles were already following him to finish him off somewhere near the female barracks, and now no mother would come to him — we've sent your mother away a long time ago, silly fool, she looked at you and that's enough, he's already a big boy, he's capable of getting into his own coffin and covering it with a lid.

He looked around: no one was there.

He remembered the Bay of Good Fortune well. He had worked here as a stevedore at the beginning of the summer.

To the right stood the female barracks, a wooden building with windows, which was recently painted with white paint and from there, you could hear the voices of former counter-rev girls and prostitutes. When he had worked here as a stevedore, these voices had seemed pleasant to him at first, then they weighed on him more and more.

The quay was empty, a brigade of several inmates sat not far away, awaiting their foreman.

Artiom saw Galia immediately; she sat in the boat, alone, very calm. On the pier stood a soldier, asking her something, she answered. The wind blew in the other direction, so Artiom didn't hear the conversation.

The soldier, feeling the movement of the pier-boards under his feet, looked at Artiom.

"What do you want here?" he asked rudely, though the smile from conversing with Galia still floated on his lips.

The soldier was good-looking, blue-eyed, straight-nosed, thin, with pink lips, dark skin and a cut on his cheek — he had just been shaving. Even the cut was handsome.

"He's with me," said Galia, holding on too firmly to the edge of the boat.

On the nose of the boat, there was a tarp that made a kind of hutch, which was filled with packed things.

The soldier looked at Galia, as though expecting to hear that it was a joke, and then one more time at Artiom with displeased interest.

"The new mechanic, is that it?" he asked, not looking away from Artiom with his disfigured face.

Galia didn't answer any more, but she did get up, at first fixing her belt, then touching her holster. The boat rocked. Galia had a long leather coat on — too long for her — in which she seemed to be fat and therefore unwieldy.

Artiom walked around the soldier, and with limp legs, with his breath gone, he awkwardly climbed aboard. His heart hammered as though it were falling down a mountain and would fall into the water any second now and quickly fall to the bottom.

"Wait," Galia told him, looking at him with angry eyes; only now did Artiom notice how pale she was. "The moorings..."

"Sit there, idiot," said the soldier mockingly, untying the rope and pushing the boat out.

Artiom stood up and waited.

The soldier threw the rope right in his face on purpose. The end of it thwacked him painfully in the ear and the pain jabbed in his eyes as well, as though it hung on a thread that reached back to the ear, and they had just sharply pulled on that thread.

Something burst inside Artiom at that moment.

"Protect the citizen commissar, jackal's muzzle!" said the soldier, baring his teeth.

"What an imbecile! Thug!" thought Artiom in a frenzy, screwing his face up from the pain. Having caught the rope and having pushed the boat from the shore, not even expecting it of himself, he growled through his teeth, "I'm going to suck your eyeballs out, you rotted whore! I'm going to pull out your guts through your mouth, you b-b-b-bitch!" He swung his rope that he still held in his hand at the smiling soldier; even though he understood that the rope couldn't reach him, he still jumped back, and from his own instantaneous and shameful fear, he turned white with fury.

"Stand there!" he screamed, beside himself, looking first at Artiom then at Galia and taking his rifle off his shoulder. "Give me that jackal!"

"Leave it!" Galia suddenly yelled even more resonantly and with greater authority. Artiom couldn't even imagine that such power and such hatred could hide in that already strong young woman. "Get back to you place, you filth! Get back to your guard duty!"

The soldier recoiled, but he kept holding his rifle at the ready, moving his twisted lips, as though they were sewn on from another body and hadn't quite adapted yet.

Galia pulled Artiom down sharply by the jacket: quickly down, you idiot.

She turned the motor on with her first attempt — her movements were all awkward because of her heavy clothing, but evidently her piercing anger helped.

"You're taking him for a ride too?" the soldier yelled over the rumble of the motor of the departing boat. "Maybe you'll suck him too, commissar? I'll inform on you! Rancid bitch…"

And he yelled something else, shaking his rifle, but you couldn't hear him anymore.

The inmates sitting on the shore were watching everything: some with a crooked smile, some with fear.

* * *

Not far from the boat, in its wake, a seal swam for a short time, appearing then diving down, as though he were teasing them and having fun.

Tears poured down Galia's face.

Artiom shook uncontrollably for one, two, three minutes.

Then his breathing returned and his disfigured heart returned to its place.

He looked back at the monastery — they should have already set off the rockets — flight! — but nothing like that was happening.

Even the people on the beach, while they were still visible, stayed seated.

From the sea, in the morning light, the monastery looked like a sugar cookie.

"Go ahead and chew it, you'll break all your teeth on it…" Artiom said, though he didn't feel any bravado at all, only a nauseous clump in his chest.

"I hate…" Galia quietly murmured. "I hate them all… I should have shot him. Why did I not… Idiot. I hate him."

Artiom looked first at Galia, then at the water. The water was cold, frightening.

Then once again at Galia. Jaw muscles rippled on her face, as starkly as on a man's.

She sped forward so fast that the boat shrieked and jumped, threatening to break apart. Her right hand, with her thin and not very long fingers, was white from holding and squeezing the control bar, which was a metal stick pointing at Artiom's chest.

"Who is that woman, Artiom? Do you know her?" he asked himself sincerely and simply.

Galia looked forward, driving the boat and not looking around.

She had beaver-fur gloves on, and her boots were beautifully tipped with the same animal's fur.

In a few minutes, Artiom firmly understood that they wouldn't catch them this very minute, and now he would have to somehow live in this boat, do something, play some game that they were floating away and no one would catch them… but that required him to find strength.

Soon the monastery's bulk lost its heft and grandeur, became smaller and lighter. The world around them ended up much larger. But before that, the opposite had seemed true — the world was small and the monastery was an overwhelming juggernaut.

Only a short time passed and already the monastery was nothing but a small dot on the shore. If you lifted your index finger, the monastery, like a louse, would fit under one fingernail.

But it didn't even occur to Artiom to think himself free. How could he be free with all this water around him, under this heavy sky that wasn't hurrying with them but immovably stuck over their heads.

"Maybe I should ask her to turn towards Fox Island?" he said to himself with unbearable self-pity and a foolish hope. "We'll stop over. Krapin's there; he'll be happy to see us. He'll warm up the sauna. The fox-chef will bake a pie… There'll be a feast… I'll let Krapin have Galia, let him use her. Just put me in a fox apartment; I can live there. I'll eat from a fox feeding trough and I'll open my mouth without complaining to receive my tablets against intestinal worms…"

Artiom looked at Galia again and barely stopped himself from uttering all that he had thought.

He understood that it was impossible.

Don't change anything, mommy. I'm going in the opposite direction.

The motor roared.

Artiom looked at the metal box with surprise — could you really trust two human souls to it? Could it carry them to another island, to the mainland, to foreign waters? Where are they planning on going? How can he hope in that? The motor would definitely break, any minute now.

Very soon, Artiom started to freeze and pointlessly raised the collar of his jacket.

"Here," Galia poked the package on the floor of the boat with her foot. "There's clothing. Get dressed quickly. There won't be any more chances to get warm."

Torturing himself for a few minutes, Artiom untied the heavy package.

There were many things inside.

A Chekist coat lined with seal fur — Artiom immediately climbed into it with an animal's care for his own hide. A Chekists leather hat with ear flaps also came in handy. Gloves! Winter gloves. Very appropriate.

Cotton-wool pants...Well, that's good too. Swearing, Artiom took off his boots and pulled the cotton-wool pants with difficulty on top of his own pants.

He became impressive and large; otherwise, compared with Galia, he had looked like a completely puny, louse-ridden kid.

Unexpectedly, he calmed down.

The headwind was airing out his head.

"Something's rattling up front," said Galia. "Go and check it out."

He crawled closer to the nose to see what was in the pile of things, all business.

Containers of gasoline. Oars and oarlocks. A hook. A lantern. An axe. A bucket. An anchor. Two short shovels. A knife. A machete. A kerosene stove. A pair of binoculars. A blanket. A tightly wrapped package with something heavy, like nails. Tow rope.

He rearranged some of the things.

A few loaves of bread. A package of tinned meat. A package of tinned fish. Two raincoats. Matting. A few flasks — Artiom shook them — maybe there was something inside?

He left some of the things lying about. There would still be time to look through them.

He looked at Galia with the maximum possible amazement and even respect that he was capable of: she prepared!

Galia didn't understand his expression and cried out, "It's vodka. Drink some if you like."

"You?" He asked, raising the flask.

She looked at Artiom and nodded.

She slowed the boat down slightly. The roaring became more uniform. Good thing too, because his head was getting foggy from all the noise.

Artiom opened the flask and drank a bit. In such a wind, he felt nothing at all. Everything that had burned and blown out inside him during the last few weeks, days, hours immediately dissolved with the vodka, or what was in there — moonshine? — without any leftovers. He drank a little, even held it in his mouth…

While the liquid was in his mouth — yes, it was definitely hard alcohol, yes — he could sense it. But no sooner had he swallowed it then it disappeared again. Only passing from one place to another. He gave the flask to Galia.

She took a quick and short sip and silently returned the flask to Artiom.

"Do you know where we're going?" he asked.

In the distance, he saw some islands. Wouldn't it be good to land on one of them and find a lasting vacation spot there?

Galia once again looked at Artiom. This was a new mannerism for her — to look him over before speaking, as though to check whether it was the same human being before her as before, and whether she could talk to him.

"We sailed here with Fiodor," she answered shortly and loudly, and added some speed to the motor.

Artiom nodded. They sailed and they sailed. Why, was he the only person here?

"Can I eat anything?" he asked. *They'll catch us right now, and again they won't let me eat anything,* he thought.

"Yes," answered Galia, looking not at Artiom but somewhere above him.

Knife, canned food. Quickly, he opened it. He got the fish out with his fingers and ate it. Broke off a piece of bread. The fish, the bread — it was good.

They opened the flask again, drank again.

Finally, he sensed something like a shot in the vein on his temple — the heat rose.

He didn't look at Galia — what if she didn't like what he was doing? Then he would have to feel awkward and would have to do something about overcoming that feeling.

In his dullness, with his covered-up ears, he almost felt good. The less he remembered who he was, how he was and where he was going, the better. It was twice as hard to remember when you didn't know in the first place.

The motor droned on a low tone, sometimes changing tone. Or, perhaps, Artiom had just moved the position of his head, so the wind began to blow on him differently, and then it seemed that the motor took it half a step lower.

If he squinted and tried to think and feel something with his own frontal bone, then the motor seemed like an insect that buzzed just overhead.

A huge insect, but not a dangerous one — more likely it was even protecting them from some even more terrible danger.

Sometimes, this insect seemed to wiggle back and forth. Sometimes it flew slightly ahead of them. But the further they went, the more confidently it flew just above the boat.

In the sea, there was a band of water of a different color — evidently that was a contrary and very fast current.

Belugas played in that band. Hearing the boat, they didn't float away, but stopped to look. One of the belugas flew water out of its air hole, like a whale.

"The coast-dwellers say that she carries her young on her back," Galia said unexpectedly, lowering the speed a bit. "If it shows you its back, you'll see them sitting there like kittens."

Artiom looked at Galia; she was completely calm and even beautiful, only the full spaces in the leather coat ruined the impression.

He suddenly smiled at Galia and she answered his smile.

He offered her fish; she, also silently, shook her head.

Artiom dipped bread into the thick porridge with fish oil that he had kneaded with his fingers in the can and wiped it back and forth. He repeated this four times, checked the can for the last time, then threw it out overboard. He put out his hands and caught the spray, from time to time rubbing his hands against each other, then against his coat, then against his pants.

He turned around, looked at the sky — it was tormented and dirty.

Ahead of them a dark, ragged blueness gathered to prevent them from going anywhere.

"Hug me," Galia said.

She had been waiting for that for a long time.

* * *

"I'm looking at you, and it's like I've stolen a child. You can't do anything," said Galia.

Artiom had no chance either to shrug or express something with his face; they sat next to each other.

"But at least you can do everything," thought Artiom; but it was true — she could manage. She drove the boat confidently and from time to time pulled out a compass and map to make sure she was on course.

He had never before seen a compass. This was only his third time in a boat, ever. He didn't understand maps.

"Where did you get the boat?" he asked, leaning back, looking at the beaver gloves.

Artiom had long sought a chance to move away; he felt awkward and sorrow had once again crept in. It was a strange feeling, experienced for the first time in his life — so much wind, so much open space, but his soul was still under a brick wall.

In his mouth too, inappropriately, he tasted brick. Brick and fish.

At the same time, he wanted to look around — was anyone gaining on them? From time to time he turned around and stared until his eyes burned.

But she didn't.

"It would be fine if..." Galia continued, and Artiom at first didn't understand what she was talking about. "You probably can't even shoot?" she asked. "Give me some more alcohol... I'm freezing... I thought you were so strong at first. But what can you do? Why are you just sitting there?"

"Maybe I can drown her?" thought Artiom slowly and painfully, feeling depressed from the very sound of her voice, the same way you felt from shooting pains in a stuffed-up ear. She tried to talk louder for him to distinguish her words, and in her efforts, there was something of the student, the school-girl about her.

They remained silent a long time.

"At first, I wanted to return you to Fox Island," she began after drinking from the flask. She had moved the flask to herself with her own foot, since Artiom hadn't got around to doing it himself. "But your Krapin's got a full house..." She drank some more, and, not breathing out, continued, turning away from the wind. "Then I thought I'd put you in the infirmary with Ali... but he wanted too much... There was one more distant assignment, but you could just as easily freeze to death there... In general, I found out that they were looking for musicians for the anniversary of the revolution and there aren't enough in the orchestra. I retyped your specifications and stuck it where it needed to go... Got it? Do you understand what that cost me?"

Artiom awkwardly sat on the bench in the middle of the boat, facing her.

"Three more would have fit in here," he thought, looking around. "We should have taken someone else with us... Burtsev, Afanasiev, Vasilii Petrovich. They would have made her laugh."

He raised his eyes, saw in the heavy twilit half-light that she was still looking at him and expecting an answer.

"What did it cost you?" asked Artiom silently, looking at her directly, but it seemed she didn't understand.

"I can clean your boots," he said, or maybe it was his demon.

Sometimes Artiom thought to himself that he didn't accidentally kill his father, but, quite the opposite, because he was accursed.

"Ba-a-astard," Galia drawled and slowly reached for her holster.

Artiom sat and watched her movements almost indifferently.

He guessed that she could shoot him and probably had already done it several times; or at least once.

"Shoot me, throw me overboard, and go home," he said. "You'll make it just in time for the play."

But he saw the axe under the seat and knew that if she reached for her pistol, then…

Galia was quiet, not looking away. The motor worked quietly, as though it were waiting.

"You've come to life finally," said Galia, as though with distaste, but there was something else in her voice. "… Too bad I can't see your mottled green eyes. Did you know that if you drown in the sea, then the water, when it gets into your eyes, turns from blue to green…? It was with those eyes that you looked at me when I walked into Gorshkov's office — no fear in them, nothing, you were just sitting and waiting. Some fearless dogs look like that while you're killing them. Except that you rarely find a dog with green eyes… I looked at you then and decided that I would save you. Maybe I would save myself too."

They seemed to have traveled a great distance — it was starting to get dark, but Sekirka's lighthouse continued to shine behind them, the foulness, it wouldn't come off them.

It seemed that while they could see it, they were still in bondage, as though on a long sea-line, and at any moment, they could pull it back, joyful in their catch.

If only he could tear it.

"I would pray for your salvation, if…" said Artiom without any bathos in his voice, not looking away from the lighthouse.

She nodded. She didn't believe in anything either.

"As for the boat," said Galia, answering a long-ago-asked question. "Some prisoners made it. Not mechanics, just… magicians. Fiodor wanted to start a factory making speed boats, but it would have been very expensive to set up — you know they give the camp very little money… Only four people have access to this boat. Fiodor added me to the list a long time ago… And those morons didn't notice. I didn't touch it on purpose, so that no one would pay any attention to the fact that I could take it out wherever I wanted to. Everyone is writing reports against each other here — they would have informed on me immediately."

"What about the one who was on the shore? Will he inform on you?" asked Artiom.

"Kolesnikov? The soldier? I don't even know… But no one's going to catch us anyway, Tiom."

"Really?" he didn't believe her. He still didn't believe in it.

"The other boat's broken. You can't catch us on a sailboat. 'Gleb Bokii' is in Kemi and will only arrive in three days. There is a plane, but I sent a fake order to the technician to rebuild the engine in time for the commission's arrival, and I went myself to check up on him. The entire motor is in pieces on the tarpaulin." Galia unexpected laughed, not very prettily, with one corner of her mouth. "I asked the technician how long it would take to put it back together and he got scared and said: two days if I start right now. I said, 'No hurry!'"

Artiom listened to all of this as though it were a fairy tale, afraid of breathing out or even blinking.

"Eichmanis is helping us…" Galia continued, and in her voice there was something vengeful, feminine. "There was a map on which the islands are all drawn. It was done by the monks — there are more than a hundred islands in the archipelago. Eichmanis organized a few expeditions, fixed the old maps and found a few new islands. No one has a map like this. I ordered Kabir-shah to redraw it."

"And what… what could happen?" asked Artiom, looking askance at the motor behind her back.

"It's already overheating," said Galia, not even touching the motor with her palm. "Those islands over there… We're going to land on one of them."

"Why?"

"We'll sleep for a bit. Don't be afraid. Today they definitely won't come for us… I'm already not comprehending anything…"

As they approached the island, both Galia and Artiom looked at each other in a way that made it clear they both had the same thought. What if the maps and compass both fooled them, and they were now approaching the farthest outpost of the camp?

“If this is part of the camp,” said Galia, “I’ll tell them we’re part of an inspection…”

“We’ll eat all their reserves and go on,” Artiom tried to joke, but he felt sick at heart. He didn’t want to see any more guards.

Galia thought for a moment, and, reaching for her pocket, extended something to Artiom.

“Take it,” she said, dropping speed.

It was a revolver.

“I have one. If there’s a group of soldiers… and they want to arrest us… we’ll have to kill them all. You hear me?” She clacked her teeth unpleasantly, as though her teeth were made of metal and they clanged against metal.

“Yes, Galia!” answered Artiom, and her name also seemed metal to him.

He was not afraid in the least.

* * *

They found a good landing spot on the slightly sloping shore.

Artiom jumped into the water three meters from the shore; he thought it would be shallower, but ended up in water almost to his wait, and the boots were slipping impossibly on the rocks — while he, swearing, walked those three meters then pulled the boat by the rope, he got as tired as though he had been carrying logs for six hours. He was shaking all over and felt nauseous.

Even so, he had more strength than what he had after Sekirka.

He could barely breathe and was completely worn out in a long string of saliva.

His feet were soaked through, everything squelched and slurped under his ankles.

When they turned off the motor, it became unfamiliarly quiet and uneasy. As though the droning motor had been driving away evil spirits, and now they could all descend on them.

It seemed there was no one on the island.

Artiom shook with the cold; he wanted to lie down as soon as possible and sleep for as long as possible.

But at first, to pull the boat onto shore, they had to unload it. He climbed here and there as though in a bad dream. He ripped off a nail. He held that finger in his mouth like a child. From under the nail, a salty liquid seeped.

Galia went somewhere on her own business. She returned when he had pulled the boat halfway up the bank.

"It's slipping back," said Galia strictly.

If Artiom had gone away for two minutes to heed nature's call — he had long been planning on it — the boat would have slipped back into the sea. They would have died on that island. Or waited for the Chekists like rabbits caught in a snare. They would have shrieked like them too from horror.

While Galia held the rope tight, not allowing the boat to slip back, Artiom, almost dead, turned over a boulder, wedging it under the keel.

"I'm going to die," he occasionally repeated. "I'm going to die…"

Galia picked a place to sleep.

The kerosene stove wouldn't light.

Artiom, still grimacing from the pain — the nail, the damn nail — cleaned the stove with horsehair and lit it.

Warth wafted from the stove, as well as the smell of kerosene — but it still wasn't very warm at all.

"A bonfire," said Galia. "We need a bonfire now."

Wet through, his eyelids drooping, in squelching boots, Artiom went to chop wood — he found two local birches. They leaned towards the ground but barely gave way to the axe…

Or his hands weren't listening any more.

When Artiom got back, the blanket was hung on the upwind side between two shovels, and a hole had been dug to more easily light the fire.

Artiom, managing more or less with the axe, chopped one of the logs into kindling.

The fire appeared — it was so joyful, as though salvation itself had lit up, and you could see it, touch it with a quick hand.

They sat at the fire, not warming themselves so much as protecting the fire from the wind.

Artiom took off his boots; one sock remained inside — he had to climb inside the boot to get it — he pulled out something that wasn't so much a sock as a porridge made of wool and manure. With such a porridge you could, for example, feed a small devil from a spoon. He clenched it in a fist shaking from exhaustion, and something thick and viscous poured down his fingers.

He dried it all for a long time, awkwardly, by the fire.

Galia watched all this with a sarcastic look — that ability, in short, was an ever-present aspect of the female mind. Artiom had learned that from somewhere before.

Half an hour later, Artiom found himself with a can of oil in one hand and a can of sugar in another.

He was handing them over to Galia, then she returned them. They ate everything with a spoon that became covered in sugar and oil. An incredible case of overeating — only the spoon ended up heavy like an iron ladle.

They drank it down with tea. Artiom, burning the entire inside of his mouth, had already drunk three mugs. In his mouth, scraps of burnt-off skin flapped about. Without any self-pity, he reached inside his mouth to tear them off.

His body was still cool and from time to time it became even colder, as though the tea only burned his throat and that place in the middle of the chest into which it flowed, while at the same time cooling the lower half of the ribcage.

Galia managed to somehow put down her half-drunk mug. Her eyes were closing on their own.

"I didn't sleep at all," she admitted. "I was nervous."

"Has anyone ever run away… from the camp?" asked Artiom, having chewed and wiped his lips with his sleeve.

"Seems like I'm not going to die yet…" he thought to himself.

"Just recently, in the summer… one…" said Galia. "He figured out the movements of the sea currents, tied himself to a log and departed. All the way to the mainland."

"And?"

"He got tossed out to shore," said Galia, not exactly empathetically, but with a measure of sympathy. "All his bones were broken, his skull was so crushed that it looked like he had been beaten with a sledgehammer. Probably against the cliffs… didn't have time to untie himself. Or he choked on the water before then… Don't know."

An autumn tree enchanted him.

Artiom wanted to be assured of their success and he once again started to ask Galia about what could possibly happen to them.

"The motor could break," said Galia. "But we do have a mast and sail, and we… can try to make it that way then. I know a bit about sailing, Fiodor showed me. His brother's a sailor… And the local monks taught me… the old man of the sea… he also showed me. There could also be a storm. If so, we'll drown and they won't find us then." She laughed as she could. "… Though in two or three days, probably, we'll go not far from the western shore, in case we need to land for whatever reason…"

Artiom had a sudden compulsion to kiss her on the lips and embrace her, like a sister.

She didn't see that so much as feel his childishly surprised and unexpectedly joyful state, and she was infected with it and laughed again at something.

In this inspired state, Artiom went to find something to add to the fire, wandering about in total darkness, falling several times.

"At least a single fir tree," thought Artiom, imagining how the branches would burn. But where would he find a fur on this little coin in the middle of the sea, what would it be doing here? What would it think about?

He bumbled into another scanty bush, broke it up, hacked it up, not even understanding in the darkness what it was.

Hurriedly, he returned to the barely alive, trembling fire, as though there he could find safety and a protective charm.

His legs didn't listen to him.

The waves rolled over the sandbank; the wind blew in his face and if he hid his face, it vengefully blew at the rest of his body.

Galia had laid out the tarpaulin on the shore, and a blanket on top, covering herself with a raincoat. She left Artiom the other one.

She lay with her head towards the fire. On her head she had put on a soldier's helmet, tying it under her chin — she looked very funny. She looked at him with a floating, sicky glance.

"In the blue, distance ocean… somewhere near the fiery land…" Galia sang. "Lie down quickly."

A bit of his stomach groaned, barely audibly.

"Maybe I truly love her?" he thought, very carefully weighing the question in his head, lest he scare it off with his sneering from a previous life. "Do I love her?" He repeated again, soundlessly uttering those words to feel them on his lips. "Or what do you call 'love' in my case?"

He added the last branch to the fire.

"Where are we going?" he asked, crawling under his raincoat and feeling that he was barely able to speak at all.

"I haven't decided yet," Galia said quietly, also barely reaching him through her half-sleep and exhaustion, but her tone was still the kind that you use when you're choosing between going to a movie theater or seeing a play tomorrow. "Everyone who flees tries to reach Kemi. And from there, to Finland. They'll look for us there too, probably… But we're going in a different direction. Maybe we'll reach Finland itself by sea… That's two hundred *versts*. Maybe we'll shift course and get out on the Russian shore near Arkhangelsk… or somewhere in those lands. Maybe we'll sail all the way to Norwegian waters… I don't know… I'm not sure how much our gasoline will give us. We still have three canisters full… I took them from the mechanic who… disassembled our airplane into one hundred pieces of metal… but maybe, as I was saying… we can finish it under a sail… let's sleep…"

With an uneven, but so familiar gesture, she raised her raincoat: come to me, Tiom.

With his last bit of strength, he laughed.

"What is it?" she asked, not opening her eyes and confusing the syllables.

"Your helmet… I just can't. It's like I'm lying down to sleep with a soldier from the guard brigade…"

Galia made a move as though to turn away from him, but more to keep up the appearance of her strictness.

Artiom hugged her and didn't let her go.

They fell asleep immediately.

* * *

Artiom slept with difficulty, as though sleep itself had become a kind of labor. Incessantly, like a bad tooth, some part of his consciousness ached: you have to get up, you have to sail further, you have to get up, they're already on your tail, they saw us from the lighthouse on Sekirka, they noticed us and…

In a frightening and confused vision, the soldiers were floating up to their little island on their horses — so that they couldn't hear them approach. The horses snorted and raised their heads with their red, insane eyes and the soldiers bared their teeth…

He needed to wake up Galia quickly, to roll away from her — they might still not notice them. But the boat! Where should they put the boat? They could sink it quickly… yes! He ran on long, tottering legs, as though he had drawn them as a small child, holding his pencil in his fist, towards the motor boat and began pushing it into the sea, and the boat immediately sank under the waves… "What are you doing?" screamed Galia beside herself with terror.

Artiom woke up with a splitting headache, as though between his eyebrows, onto his forehead, they had attached something foreign, sticky, dreary — and he wanted to tear it off.

In his head, the sound of the sea was incessant.

Galia was no longer asleep. She lay, it seemed, unable to get up from underneath the raincoat. Her face was sullen and no longer beautiful.

"What time do you think it is?" he asked. He had no saliva in his mouth.

"Four something," answered Galia quietly and unhappily.

She had a watch on her chest under the leather coat, Artiom saw how she took them out yesterday.

"Should we drink some vodka?" Artiom offered. "It'll be fun."

Galia looked at him and unexpectedly chuckled.

"Well, thank God for that," thought Artiom. "Otherwise, how could we have gone anywhere with that kind of a mood?"

He ended up saying exactly what he had thought aloud.

"Give some vodka, then," said Galia, pulling herself up, "to your mistress and lady..."

Yesterday's fire looked untidy, as though someone had eaten it, then vomited out something slimy in its place.

Artiom put on a cap. Galia drank some vodka and returned the flask. As he took it, he leaned over to her and kissed her on the cheek next to her lips. Her cheek was salty, her lips wet.

Galia made an annoyed grunt: I can't swallow it if you're bothering me! And immediately wiped her face with her hand — either to get rid of the kiss or the vodka on her lips.

Artiom wasn't insulted.

Each of them a little bit more cheerful, they gathered their things. They loaded the boat almost with zeal. They poured in the gasoline without rushing. Artiom moved the boulders with an intentional grunt.

They started the motor already in the water, after they had shoved off.

It caught on the third try — they didn't have a chance to get properly scared.

They looked at each other and, not saying a word, moved along the island and to the left — into the sea. Galia added speed, and the roaring of the motor woke them up fully.

They hadn't been caught. With every minute they were going ever further.

The sun rose triumphantly — it seemed that at any moment now, some kind of music would start.

But the further they went during that day, the more it seemed that the music would end up being ugly and evil.

The island disappeared.

They became lonely and cold.

Artiom drank a little more vodka.

This time, it didn't banish the haze in his brain, only adding to it.

If there had been land around them, he would have found the strength inside himself to get angry. That anger would have added to his life and faith. If there were people nearby, he could always get angry at them, but who could he get angry at here? And where would he go with that anger?

Yesterday, the weather scared them, but today it was something else — the sky. The sky and the emptiness around them. So much water — what was the point of it? Why did they pour so much of it here?

Artiom's heart never again found joy in water. He and Galia sat together on a single bench; they were silent. The waves were almost completely uniform. They moved like they did on a bad motorway, taut, jumping up and down. From time to time, Artiom unwillingly pulled his neck out, as though he were helping the boat overcome the waves.

He looked back almost every minute — it seemed to him that every cloud that appeared in the sky would find another, then the two of them with a third would join into a mass and begin to chase the motor boat.

The sun disappeared, and it was even hard to imagine where it had gone.

The further they went, the lower the sky became, as though the expanse were becoming narrower and they would finally be forced to turn into a narrow horizontal crevice that would crush the boat.

Beginning to believe in his own frightened fantasies, Artiom looked forward for a long time; what about that crevice? Had it moved closer?

Galia sometimes checked her compass.

She got the cart on the tablet. She looked at it, pressing down the tablet to her knees with one hand. She dropped the glove from that hand onto the bottom of the boat.

Not to get in her way, Artiom sat on a different bench. From here, he noticed for the first time how small Galia's hands were. If you gave her a large apple, she might have to pick it up with two hands.

While she was writing down his frightened responses, seated at her desk, he didn't notice it. While she caressed his back, his head and everywhere else with those hands — the same. But now, when all around her there were large, manly object — motor, mast, the anchor on the floor — it became obvious. Add to that her huge leather coat and her other warm clothing.

"Is it possible that such a hand could kill?" Artiom asked himself. He often asked himself questions that he never intended to find answers to.

From her hands, Artiom looked at the map and also looked at it for some time — upside down.

He destroyed the silence by saying, "Where are we?"

With a quick and uneven gesture — the wind made the map flap — she drew a cross on the map with her nail: here.

The monastery was still close, but Arkhangelsk and Finland were far, and Norway's waters were all the way beyond the edge of the sea.

"Really, this was a stupid idea. Soon the gas will run out; and does she really know how to sail? Women can't do that," he either doubted it seriously or was just angering himself on purpose.

He turned around on his bench — he didn't want to look at Galia and her strictness all the time.

He rubbed his eyes in the utterly foolish hope of seeing something beyond the horizon.

"If only I squint for a minute, then open my eyes, there… well, let's say, I'll see land. And above that land is a sign: 'Norway!' It need not even be in Russian… On the shore, there are people waiting with their Norwegian bread and salt… Boom! The cannon would fire. We've waited for you, Artiom and Galia, fellow travelers in woe, deserters, runaways! Let's go and find you some warm apartments with tubs filled with shampoo. They're already foaming, the hot water running with a hurried babble into the froth…"

He wanted to find the binoculars, but he was too lazy, or rather he had decided to deny himself that disappointment. The more emptiness you see, the better you understand what a dreary journey awaits you.

They had only traveled for two days, and he already felt that he breathed so much new air that had not been in his lungs for a whole year. The air constantly beat at his face, making his head spin, but not in an earthly way, as though they were on a different planet, with a different and wet intoxication.

Artiom took off his glove, touched his cheeks; the skin was so sincerely, joyfully surprised by the warmth — as though it was something foreign and completely unexpected.

He suddenly felt that Galia was no longer behind him but was gone. He turned around so suddenly that his neck cracked. Galia looked at him with repressed curiosity.

It seemed to Artiom that she had just been crying and he bustled over to her bench, still not knowing why — either to comfort her or to at least warm her cheeks with his hands, as he had just warmed his own cheeks.

He extended his hand to her face. Galia made a slow, but still a noticeable, movement to lean away: what are you doing? Why, Artiom?

"I wanted to warm you…" he said, smiling a bit crookedly. "You're not frozen?"

She didn't answer — just looked at him from top to bottom and said, "Sit down. You'll fall out."

He felt that Galia was unhappy with him. He even guessed why she was unhappy. He wasn't taking care of her, wasn't watching her, wasn't commiserating with her, wasn't trying to raise her spirits.

But how could he take care of her on a boat? You can only take care of a girl when it's dry all around and there's a place to stand, or better yet, lie down.

Artiom returned to his place, saying to himself, "He sat down, having eaten unsalted food…" and he chuckled immediately. That expression,[49] set against the endless sea around him, for the first time in his life sounded like a mockery — I don't want to eat your salted food.

Somewhere in the distance, behind Galia's back, lightning struck — it wasn't audible but clearly visible through the dark, unkempt, clumpy blueness.

Having had time to laugh at the fact that the weather matched Galina's mood, Artiom immediately realized that there was nothing funny about it: the storm would reach them anyway.

In some confusion, he looked back again — where do we hide, if…?

At least some kind of island, at least a hillock. It's easy for the fish — it's not afraid of rain. The thunder booms, and it goes down into the depths and stays there.

Why did they sail away from the island? They could have waited the rain out on land… But what if the downpour lasted a whole week? Two weeks?

At least some land, even the tiniest bit!

As though she felt Artiom's worry, Galia looked back.

"Is it a storm?" asked Artiom as calmly as he could — he was a man, after all. "Are there any islands on the way?"

The imminent terror, it seemed, made Galia more amenable and kinder.

"Yes…" she said. "There are islands. I accounted for them when planning. But if we don't make any mistakes along the way, we'll reach the island by evening. But that rain looks like it's going to start now."

Confirming her words, as though jumping from a hiding place, a driving wind rose up, and it immediately became harder for the boat to go forward. Artiom looked at the motor with sorrow and an inexpressible request: it had been dragging them for two days already without complaining or losing strength. But who knew what the motor was planning on doing under a downpour.

---

49 An expression meaning "with nothing".

Artiom's insides ached painfully, and he thought once again that it would have been much easier on land, even when they were planning on shooting you, you could always rip the rifle out of their hands, beg them, fall on your knees, beg for your life, run away into the forest, pull out the guard's Adam's apple… or even get shot, but not fatally, then crawl out of your grave. He had heard of such cases; or just pretend to be dead, though still alive, just bleeding through a hole in the chest… but here? In front of whom are you going to fall on your knees? Will you play dead in front of the sea? Will you show it the hole in your chest?

You'll never crawl out of this grave.

The sudden icy rain struck them backhandedly, from the right and from the left at the same time, smacking them on the back, so loud that it out-roared the motor.

The boat lurched sideways, the motor wheezed on a low note as though someone was pressing against its chest.

"Wake up! Wake up!" Artiom commanded himself loudly. "The motor — to hell with it! Galia said that there would be an island. That means that there will be an island! The motor will die, but we'll go on with the sail. We'll figure it out somehow. The monks sailed for almost half a thousand years, so what about you? What? Were you born without hands?"

The rain was so thick and dense that he had trouble even seeing Galia.

Her face seemed to be terrified and white.

"Galia!" he yelled, "My love! We'll get out of this!"

Artiom pulled sacking out of the hutch at the front of the boat and threw it to her: "Cover the motor! You have to cover the motor!"

He found a bucket and, helping with his feet, began to pour the quickly-gathering water out of the boat, so quickly that, even though he constantly rubbed his eyes, Artiom still managed to stare at the bottom of the boat to make sure there was no hole.

Over their head, with a metallic, horrifying boom, lightning struck. For a second, Artiom was blinded; his vision returned, and he immediately remembered that when the lightning struck, Galia shrieked like she was naked.

"Galia! My darling!" he yelled one more time.

"What if the motor…" she called out.

"There's a sail!" he answered. "The rain will finish and we'll put the sail up!"

The water boiled around them, not even so much from the wind and rain, but from some kind of madness hiding in its depths.

The wind beat them down. It seemed to Artiom that he could see it, this wind, as it was bearing down from the left, then from the right, completely off its head.

The waves were so huge that they seemed to be crashing over the top of the boat. Or was that only his fear and the watery confusion all around?

In a single instant, Artiom caught himself thinking that he had just tried to beat the water with the bucket, on its forehead, cheek, as though it were a living person.

These waves that were overcoming them were a total absurdity — in such a sea where they could grow to be two, three, eight times larger.

Artiom didn't remember how he had become soaked through — it poured down his chest, and his pants swelled outward.

He no longer noticed the lightning, nor did he hear the thunder.

He ladled out water like a man condemned to death. In this action, there was something mad: take the water, pour it into water, take the water, pour it into water...

He only woke up when Galia screamed, "The motor's out!"

He straightened out and through the downpour that made his face wooden and dull, he looked at her.

Galia, of course, wasn't crying, but her face was wet, twisted and her lips were a thin line.

"Damn it to hell, Galia!" he yelled. "It's OK!"

"Whoever hasn't been at sea has never learned to pray," he remembered a phrase he had heard somewhere, at some point in time.

It had absolutely nothing to do with him.

Artiom found another bucket, and now they ladled it out together, sometimes bumping into each other with their arms and not really looking to the sides. All around them was perdition, the same cold destruction.

The rain finished all at once, in a moment.

The storm moved on.

The wind came back for another round then left, cutting the wave with its sharp tail.

The relief was short-lived.

They only managed to smile at each other, barely alive, their faces beaten to a blue pulp. Her fringe hung low — wet, untidy, like a broken bird's wing. He didn't even know what he looked like, probably a tin-colored face with a diseased flush on the cheek, and a bucket in his hand.

The smiles remained on their faces, but it was already clear that the motor was silent and they were stuck in the open water.

Galia touched the motor, caressed it — in this gesture there was something telling and painful: why are you like that? How will we go on now?

"Maybe we can try turning it on?" Artiom offered, for some reason almost in a whisper.

The water sloshed against the boat.

"Eichmanis always said, before fixing a machine, make sure it has time to think," said Galia with difficulty, as though her chest were crushed.

The thunder boomed somewhere far away.

They both looked in that direction — forward. Maybe something would be visible there other than the storm? But ahead of them was a dark blue that was almost completely lacking in light.

Both Galia and Artiom knew that if they tried to turn the motor on now, and it wouldn't start, that would be the end, ruin.

They wanted to put that moment off.

They probably should have put up the mast in the morning, on land, and tied the sail to it, because they could have just raised it now. So that the people wouldn't have had to work in the middle of the sea, freezing in the wind, scared out of their wits.

* * *

They wrapped the motor up like a child.

They drank some vodka.

They finished pouring out the water.

They added some gasoline.

They sat and drank another sip.

Galia looked for a long time somewhere into the sky, then, as though not seriously, said, not looking at Artiom.

"Let's shoot ourselves."

"Uh-huh. So why did I survive for so long?" Artiom immediately answered.

He couldn't bear such conversations, and he answered in the kind of voice that allowed him to immediately close the topic.

They patiently waited almost half an hour.

They pulled the cord, and the motor started.

Artiom laughed. Galia smiled too. She put it on a loud setting, as though the louder the motor worked, the better it would be.

They took off across the sea.

For another half hour, they were quiet, looking in all the directions of the world.

Then Artiom looked at Galia.

A ray of the invisibly rising autumn sun on her face was the only ray in the entire world.

"Now really, Gal," Artiom said loudly, to out scream the motor, "where are we going?"

Galia moved her slow, squinting gaze away from the wind and on to Artiom.

"The Norwegians have sea-hunting concessions, and their ships go all the way from the shore near Murmansk to the neck of the White Sea and even enter it sometimes. I hope we'll meet one of them. Also, in Western Murman, there are some Norwegian colonists. No one has yet thought of escaping to them… In any case, it's too early to think about that… the important thing is not to miss the next islands…"

"Early, not early… what if I never come back to Russia?" Artiom thought in surprise. "What would I lose?"

He grimaced for a moment, saw a bumblebee on a wheat stalk, a horse, its sides quivering, a crow's nest, his younger brother, the photographer's studio on Miasnitskaia, a snowman at a house, lines of poetry…

He quickly waved it all away: it's all foam.

"No," he answered himself, but waved it off again.

"A woman has no fatherland. Her fatherland is her husband." Someone said that on Solovki. Was it Vasilii Petrovich… or Burtsev… or Mezernitskii? One of those former White Army officers and formerly living people. "A fatherland for a woman appears when her husband appears. The fatherland is there, where the heart of her child beats…"

Who had said that?

The light of heaven inclined him to at least some kind of thought, but the less light there was, the stupider and more ill-intentioned his abstract thought became. Their weight lessened with every second. What fatherland? What bumblebee on a stalk? What heart? There was only water and salt in the sea. Only water and salt.

"Do you know how to swim, Galia?" he asked, to avoid the silence.

"The monks didn't know how to swim, Tiom. The old man of the sea told me. Lest they have false hope in life… the monks didn't know how and we don't need to either. You won't swim away here. The water is ten degrees cold."

The darkness came so much more quickly than expected.

It was as though they poured it out of an inkwell. Turn to one side — the left becomes black. Turn the other direction, and the right turns completely dark.

While it still made sense, Artiom kept on staring — where was that damn island…

"Is it big, our island?" he asked several times.

"I don't know," she answered, without irritation, but also thoughtful and worried.

The time came when the darkness reached their very eyes. You could almost not see any stars, only one or two appeared sometimes and quickly disappeared. There was nothing but the noise of the motor, the wind and the splashing of water.

Artiom looked into the darkness and from time to time, he thought he saw a forest — tall and thick trees of incredible height.

He remembered how afraid he was of the night forest in childhood. How silly those childish fears now seemed: shadowy trees? That's calm, that's life.

The lighthouse over Sekirka disappeared. Who could have thought that its disappearance could be felt as a loss.

How small man is, how weak. And how huge the world, huge and black.

Could this pitch-black night even be compared with that one — when he had buried Burtsev, covered in someone else's blood?

So what if he was burying someone — at least it was into the earth, into firm earth on which you could stand. And all around there were people, even if they had wolves' eyes, at least they had minds, and their minds could inspire them to any decisions.

To pardon Artiom, for example.

You could at least talk to them. Have a conversation. Tell them about your life.

"I'm not afraid of people," Artiom thought. "I'm afraid of being without people."

The thought seemed to him incredibly profound, hiding ineffable meaning.

During the day, you could still seek the sun and hope to see it; but what is your hope when you're blind?

Galia looked at the compass, raising it to her palm and to her very face.

What if they suddenly sailed right into a huge open maw? They say that whales feed that way, by opening their huge mouth, and everything that falls in — that's whale-food.

The compass doesn't know that!

Artiom looked ahead so intently that he felt his forehead was cutting itself open.

"Find the lantern!" said Galia.

Artiom blinked, made an attempt to move and understood that during the last few hours he had gotten so cold that he couldn't even lift his arms.

No sooner had he fallen over to his side like a sack than he pointlessly began to fumble about on the floor in search of a lantern. He didn't find anything. Then Galia, forgetting that she had even asked, pushed the boat onward, and the motor was the only intelligent and calm being in this entire emptiness.

"I ended up here," Artiom was saying to someone silently, "in the midst of the cold sea, with a woman whom I barely know. It's possible that she has terrible sins on her soul, and it was fate that pulled her out to sea to drown her. I have nothing to do with that. I'm here by accident, on my own, without any guilt. I killed my father, but I was punished for that, I pulled logs, I was beaten, I was almost knifed. I saw death and I was condemned to die, I froze on Sekirka, slept under human bones, I heard the bell… Oh, if only someone would now ring that bell, somewhere in the darkness, and we would rush towards it so fast! Yes, Galia?"

He looked once again at his… who? His girlfriend? His wife? An unknown woman with a huge, boundless fate behind her?

What could possible save them now — him, them?

Maybe it was worth uttering his own name aloud — and then in the card catalogue of all human names, there would be an investigation and a revision — yes, there is such a thing, yes, behind this name a certain road winds its way, but for some reason we don't have the future of this name. Let's give this name, this blood flow, this apple of the eye the right for another day's life.

"Lord! I am Artiom Goriainov, look on me through this darkness. Next to me is my woman — look on her as well. You can't just take me in one hand, but leave the other empty, can you? Take her as well. She had my seed inside her — she is not a foreign person. I am not ready to speak for her past, but I'm ready to share her future."

Lord?

There's no one here, only two fates and two memories — hers and his. They trailed behind the boat, losing parts of themselves on the way — some words, some things, some voices.

* * *

Did we miss the island? Miss the island? Miss the island?

Of course, how could we not miss the island?

And now what?

Galia lowered their speed, the motor working at its lowest gears.

The air was becoming ever sharper, thorny, unbearable.

You could hear how Artiom's teeth were chattering.

"Artiom?" called Galia.

Evidently, she was dressed more warmly than he. Her voice still sounded.

"I'm dying," he barely got out, looking at her dully.

"Enough of that," she answered. "We haven't even started suffering yet."

"That's because I've had my fill of suffering!" Artiom suddenly exclaimed, holding his jaw in place for each word with difficulty.

He wanted to fall to the floor of the boat, to roll into a ball, to fall asleep without any dreams.

"Turn around, I have to… pee," Galia asked him loudly.

He, barely moving, threw his leg over the bench and sat with his back to her.

Galia let the rudder go and the motor fell silent.

She took a very long time to do it.

"Why are you so quiet?" asked Galia. "Say something. Sing. Don't be silent. Find some vodka. There's vodka there."

He understood by the sound — she was pissing into a ladle.

How strange — a woman, but a liquid poured out of her. Why? Who would have thought it? Up to this point, he never would have imagined it, looking at Galia.

She threw it overboard.

"Give me the ladle too," asked Artiom.

At least a bit of vodka first, Artiom thought confusedly and frozenly.

He suddenly remembered where he had put the flask, and he climbed to get it.

Barely raising his arm, he drank a great deal, then gave it to Galia. He found the lantern too, gave it to her. She switched it for the ladle.

He didn't need the ladle anyway — his hands weren't managing with anything, his penis had disappeared from the cold, and when it came out, it went everywhere except the ladle.

Did Galia figure that out? Doesn't matter. When he turned to her, she turned on the lantern. It was even a little funny — two blue faces in the dense, wet darkness.

If only his mother could have known into what latitude and longitude they had thrown the heart of her son.

Galia looked at the compass, at the map, at Artiom — their glances met as though they were complete strangers who had accidentally met here — right now, the light would go out and each of them would continue on his way.

In the light of the lantern, nothing was visible — only dark water.

She turned it off.

"Galia!" Artiom called her.

"Yes," she answered.

"Is it morning soon?"

The vodka had a slight effect — he definitely still couldn't feel his legs, but at least his tongue came alive.

Galia didn't answer. Artiom moved his tongue in isolation, examining his own mouth.

He tried to get up, to stomp his feet, to change position, but Galia told him not to rock the boat.

He closed his eyes.

The whale didn't swallow them after all.

Artiom fell asleep several times — his sleep was icy, dangerous and almost unyielding, but at the edge of his perception, the noise of the motor persisted. This noise mixed together with the roar of his blood. It didn't allow his blood to stop flowing.

When he opened his eyes one time, he was surprised that he was able to see more clearly and further.

Then he understood that morning was coming, morning was returning.

"Galia!" he called, though he had no voice. "Galia! Galia!" He tried, but only on his fifth attempt did something like a wheeze come out.

"What do you need?" she asked. Her voice was hard, sleepless — she truly was a strong woman, how about that? "You want a pacifier?"

To not answer, Artiom just kept his hand raised.

She put the flask into it, there was only a little left. He finished it off.

He believed that the morning would bring relief, but it was quite the opposite. The revelation of the wet, harbor-less spectacle confirmed everything that Artiom had experienced that night — they were nowhere, nothing to no one.

What is this? What? When would it finish? Maybe there is no more land on this earth?

* * *

Galia forced Artiom to take off his boots. She found some foot wraps among her reserves and a bit more vodka — "rub your feet!" she commanded. His feet felt like they were someone else's, like logs, completely white, might as well drive nails into them.

He rubbed them, drank a bit, rubbed them again.

"If I could walk a bit," he admitted to Galia.

This was a serious dream, unlike many others.

She nodded, finding strength to smile.

"I won't perish with her around," Artiom suddenly thought happily, gratefully and sincerely. "I will thank her properly for all this."

They ate some canned food.

Artiom even washed.

"… As for God, even if He exists, He's still bound to the land, right?" Artiom spoke aloud in the middle of his thought. "No, He walked on water — but where, and how far? The water, you said, is ten degrees, and He's barefoot. Why would He go out into the open sea, whom could He catch out here, other than two idiots? There are plenty of places in the world where the idiots live in larger groups. Yes?"

"Yes," answered Galia calmly.

No, but really, tinned food is a wonderful thing. Canned beef with vodka.

His legs still felt nothing, but inside, under his skin, in his veins, life still remained, Artiom knew that.

He was a witness to how a few people dear to him died or were killed — Afanasiev, *Vladychka* John… This did not poison his life. This did not make food any less delicious.

Artiom thought about that a little, but inside him the taste of canned meat interrupted all other thoughts.

"What if they had killed your mother?" he asked himself.

The question was unpleasant, insinuating, Artiom didn't want to answer it.

"Were you always like this or did you harden like this here?" He asked himself finally.

And again, he didn't answer himself.

The motor sputtered and died.

They were also both silent. Again it became horrifyingly quiet.

"It's out of gas," Galia said quickly, so quickly to prevent any other possibility from being spoken aloud first.

"Help me," she asked.

Artiom took a canister out of the hutch in the nose of the boat and pulled it with difficulty towards his bench.

At first, he picked up and carried the canister over, then dragged himself over. The lids from the two gasoline tanks were already lying on the bottom of the boat.

When he poured in the gasoline, holding the canister in his straining arms, Artiom saw how a snowflake fell onto his hand. It was sharp and it didn't melt for some time.

The wind blew and suddenly there were many snowflakes and even more wind, as though the wind and the snow depended on each other or were playing tag.

How frightening, fatal and icy can nature be! How little naked man has!

Raising and holding the canister balanced in midair, Artiom sensed his physiology, including the fact that yesterday he had eaten and there was a need to part with some of it. With doubt, he looked at Galia… How would they do that? The boat wasn't made for that sort of thing.

"It's better to think about the fact that the motor isn't starting," Artiom snarled at himself. But again, he guessed wrong — the motor, no sooner had they filled it than it once again gave its hoarse, blessed voice, and they moved on further… However, while he held the canister, Artiom did manage to freeze his hands. And the snow was gathering in greater and greater numbers, and visibility was about thirty meters, no more.

"Why does the snow fall onto the water?" Artiom wondered. "What's the point? When it falls on the ground, that's good, it's beautiful. But in the sea? It's stupid. For whom does it fall here?"

Galia held her left hand on the motor, calming the metal down.

Lest he freeze completely, he sorted through all the things, trying to move as much as possible, or he turned to Galia and they locked gazes and every time Galia wiped off the snow that was sticking to her face, and once again returned to their reserves, moving them here and there.

It got darker from the bright snow, or maybe the day was already close to sunset. Galia had the watch.

She gave him the binoculars.

"You're the lucky one," she said; by her voice it was clear that she was starting to freeze and was extremely, extremely tired. "Look."

From the binoculars and the rocking of the boat, Artiom's head started to spin, but he kept looking and looking. There, the unexpectedly close metallic water and the white, confused whirl of snow rocked with the boat.

There was a lot of sky. Much more than any person would ever need.

After some time had passed, Artiom got so seasick that he began to lose consciousness, then fell back into it, barely even noticing the change.

He felt like he was a motor that needed to have gasoline poured into it. Or he understood that his cheeks, neck and forehead were covered in seal fat that had gotten properly frozen, but if he were to poke it sharply with his finger — for example, into his forehead — then he would very easily poke a hole in it. Inside his head, there was also something cold, fatty and confused.

It was as though he had finally lost himself in the constant wind of the last two days — all that was left were some clumps, fragments, splinters, that no one would have recognized as the previous Artiom.

He raised his binoculars and felt that it was not he who was looking at the snow and grey sky, but it was the turbid, fitful, rocking world surrounding him on all sides that was looking at him.

Having thrown down the binoculars to his chest, Artiom tried to decide where it was colder — here or on Sekirka. But the cold didn't give him a chance to compare. His thoughts were also frozen and sharp-edged. They couldn't line up properly, like sheared-off and slippery blocks.

The boat turned sideways. Galia fell asleep.

He climbed over to her bench and took the rudder himself, not knowing where to go, aiming at the thorniest star he could see.

Galia wasn't waking up.

* * *

"Galia! Over there! Look! Can you see it? Over there…! Shit!" He looked in the binoculars, then started to take it off his neck, almost tearing his ears off with the strap in his hurry. "Look, there…"

The snow had long ago ended, but the sense of its presence remained in the air, as though the snow had only just been in every space that they now inhabited in their boat, and it had left a cold place behind it. They were forced to tear the air apart with their faces, like canvas. The air crackled in their ears.

The approaching darkness entitled them to make a mistake, but it wasn't just land over there, there was fire — a small, flickering flame.

Galia, now awake, saw it too.

Her face had frozen to such a degree that it was incapable of expressing any emotion at all.

"What is that?" she finally asked, barely managing to move her mouth.

"Whatever…!" began Artiom and cut off his own speech, because it was all dreadfully clear. All the more so because he felt himself, more and more sharply, as being not quite normal, close to going insane. In such a state, it's better to be quiet.

They both looked at that quivering bright pink spot.

No, no, no: how could the Chekists be here?

Or did they send the Chekists out to meet them, to catch them on the way?

Hardly. Impossible.

Galia grabbed the rudder and slowly moved it, directing their motor boat towards the light.

Artiom sat down in his place, as though it had become much more familiar to him, and constantly looked forward in expectation of coming to land.

Galia called him.

He didn't answer, only nodded.

"Shoot without thinking," she said.

"Yes," he answered.

He didn't want to jump into the water — that would be awful, who would warm him afterwards? But to shoot, why not? It might warm him.

"… I'll call the soldier to help me out…" he decided raggedly, as though drunk. "… And as soon as they drag the boat to shore… I'll shoot him in the back… in the back is best of all."

Only one figure met them on shore.

The person was quietly crying, barely gathering enough air to cry out even louder. It was exactly how abandoned, frightened, or hungry children cry.

He waved his arms and didn't stop crying out, even when it was obvious that they had seen him and were coming towards him.

About twenty meters away, it became clear that it was a woman. Her movements and her cries were simply too stupid to be male.

When the boat came up very close, Artiom awkwardly threw the rope to her to moor the boat.

The rope didn't reach her, falling into the water.

And another time. And another.

Every time, the woman waved her arms stupidly, as though she were scaring off birds. Then she just raised her hands and stood there on the shore, as though frightening those who approached, or surrendering to them.

Artiom felt that Galia, who sat behind him, already wanted to shoot her.

Finally, the rope reached land. Naturally, the woman didn't catch it. Having awkwardly crouched down — it looked like she had about seven layers of clothes on — she raised the rope and pulled.

They landed.

Behind him, a light turned on. Galia had lit the lantern.

Artiom got up with difficulty and somehow, almost falling, jumped off, not feeling his feet, hands, body, or life at all.

Together with the woman, they, slipping and leaning forward, managed to pull the boat to shore.

It seemed to him that the woman was laughing with some kind of completely inappropriate laughter.

Then he understood that she was crying without stopping, tears of joy that were freezing on her cheeks.

They could see no one else around — only the bonfire and various rags and garbage thrown about next to the fire. It's possible that one other person was lying there. But no more than one.

"Give me your hand," said Galia, either with an angry or a dead voice.

He helped her get onto land.

"Who are you?" she asked the woman, barely lifting the lantern.

Not able to stand in the wind, the woman took a step back, but it seemed that it happened because of Galia's voice and the lantern-light.

"We… are going…" answered the woman with a thick accent, trying to smile. "From…" she continued in English.

No sooner had she opened her mouth than Artiom guessed that before him stood someone who wasn't Russian.

The woman looked first at Galia, then at Artiom, expecting that they would help her answer.

Galia, it seemed, couldn't understand why she wasn't explaining what was going on.

Artiom climbed back into the boat to pull out the heavier things, so that they could pull the boat further ashore.

"Do you speak English?" asked the woman in English, smiling with such a pleading look that it seemed she was asking for bread or money. She rubbed the tears off her face and sniffled from time to time.

"Who else is on the island?" asked Galia firmly and loudly, as though she hadn't just heard the previous phrase.

"There…" the woman waved, speaking broken Russian. "Friend… Husband!" And something long and confused in her own language.

Galia looked in the direction she indicated for some time.

"French? Deutsch?" the woman asked.

By her voice, it was obvious that she was truly happy and really wanted to be pleasant, lest her good fortune disappear, because she had evidently already lost hope in it.

Galia didn't answer.

No sooner had they pulled the boat a little further than Artiom went to the fire, as though to find the friend and husband, but in actual fact, just to be near warmth. He stuck his hands in his pocket; in the pocket lay the revolver, though he now guessed that he wouldn't have to kill anyone here. Those rags were a perfect hiding place for twenty soldiers.

At the bonfire, Artiom crouched with difficulty and stuck his hands right into the hottest part. For a moment, his palms seemed golden in the flame.

Having looked closer, he understood that there were boards feeding the fire. There was no way for any boards to end up on an island. That meant that these people were burning their boat.

Artiom slowly, as though they were animal meat, pulled out his hands from the fire. They were smoking. Now he inclined his face to the heat and screwed up his eyes. With a crackle, his eyelashes burned off — he didn't care.

The women approached.

"Bring some food, Artiom," asked Galia.

Artiom nodded, but he didn't move, he only removed his face from the fire. His bristle had also burned off. His lips were sweetly tingling. The saliva in his mouth had gotten warm — that was strange.

Galia crouched next to him. Now she extended her hand to the fire.

"She's not Russian," Galia informed him.

Artiom nodded.

"… My lips have split now," he thought, touching the edge of his mouth with his lips.

"What's there?" asked Galia, nodding at the rubbish. "Did you look?"

"I'll look now," answered Artiom and finally got up.

"I," the woman pointed at herself with her thumb — her hands were in heavy black mittens, "… Marie."

"I'm Artiom," he answered and asked, stopping after each word, "Where. Is. Your. Friend?"

"Yes!" Marie answered readily and even triumphantly, nodding and stepped towards the hill of blankets, tarpaulin and pieces of sailcloth. Artiom walked behind her.

The hair of the friend stuck out in all directions, either sticky because of dirt and blood, or frozen stiff… lips covered in sores, an open mouth, breathing… you could see his tongue, his nose was filled with black… Artiom recoiled a little.

The man lay next to the bonfire, he was easily visible in the light of the fire. Galia took off her gloves, moved a bit, extended her hand and touched the forehead of the man lying there.

After a minute of silence, she said, "You can warm yourself against him… He's going to die soon."

The man tried to open his eyes and his face, as though surprised, twisted.

He couldn't manage with the eyes, but he unstuck his mouth.

"Ma…" he called.

"Water?" Marie asked Artiom. "Water…? And… hot! Friend… hot! Medicine?"

"No medicine," said Galia. "Artiom, bring some water. And something to eat. And some vodka to rub the sick man down. Please."

* * *

Ultimately, they didn't understand from where, or why, these people came here.

Marie started crying a few more times, still smiling all the while, often asking for help, for salvation, adding something hurriedly in one tinny language or in several at once.

Artiom tried to remember his Latin from his school days, but immediately gave up.

The man was insensate. Marie tried to give him water, then tea, but he only coughed, got in the way and everything poured to the back of his head.

They fed Marie — she ate greedily, but constantly raised her grateful and pleading eyes, and even when she chewed, she still smiled.

Galia, using the light from her lantern, rummaged through their things without asking, looking at their maps and some kind of notebooks.

"She thinks they're spies," Artiom decided, having at first eaten a tall tin of canned food, then heating it over the fire and using it to warm his hands.

Having eaten, Marie once again bustled around her friend or husband, rubbed his chest with vodka, but he only moaned.

She wanted to feed him — no point…

She kept looking at Galia.

Having wiped his face, Marie confidently walked up to her and began to explain something important.

Galia, sitting down and putting the lantern nearby, wasn't even listening, only nodding sometimes, not so much to Marie as to herself.

Leafing through the notebooks in gloves was uncomfortable, so she took one off and stuck it under her armpit. Her clothing was large, and so her glove soon fell. Marie immediately picked it up and gave it to Galia, continuing to talk.

Galia didn't return the notebook to its place, but put it under her coat. She took the glove back but didn't put it on. Her naked hand was red, taut, almost like a man's. She extinguished the lantern. Sat nearer to Artiom. He passed his hot can to her. Galia, not understanding, looked inside.

"Warm yourself up," he explained.

Artiom, even now, didn't think about anything, sure that Galia had to make the decision: who was he anyway? He was nobody.

"As far as I can understand, their boat broke when they came ashore," said Galia quietly. "They've been here a week, and they burned their boat so they wouldn't freeze. Because there was nothing else to burn."

Marie sat across from them and nodded at every word Galia said, as though she understood what they were talking about.

Artiom didn't answer.

"She said that they were at sea for a week. Seven days."

That news didn't make him feel more energetic.

Artiom looked around — it was completely dark, and the invisible sea was loud.

Or maybe that wasn't the sea, but the wind? And the sea, for example, had frozen over? And they could keep going on foot? On foot would be longer and more difficult. But at least you couldn't drown. Only freeze. And that would happen very quickly…

Better say that it's the sea making that noise.

"If we leave them here, they'll both die. If we take them with us, the man will die on the way. He won't survive a week."

"Save!" begged Marie, nodding, and once again began to uncover her beloved under the rags, so that everyone would understand what she meant.

The man was truly unwell, Artiom noticed again.

But he felt absolutely no pity.

"… And our gasoline will run out more quickly, because the boat will be heavier," Galia finished.

"Where did they come from?" asked Artiom.

"I couldn't understand," said Galia. "But reaching Norwegian waters is still further than going back. And the weather's getting worse."

"Interesting," thought Artiom. "Are there any other such crazy people anywhere else in the world who are sitting in the middle of the sea and thinking how best to die — at sea or by going home?"

"There is hope that we'll get there, where we're planning to go, alone. But we'd have to leave these people here. Even though the motor doesn't start in cold weather, and if it hits below freezing, it'll stop working… But if we go back… If we go back, I don't know what will happen. More than likely everything will be very bad," Galia threw the empty can into the fire and looked at Marie. She also looked at Galia.

Galia could have said, "Well, at least we'll save these people," but Artiom understood that it wasn't necessary to say it. Galia understood it well enough. Two hours ago she was planning on shooting any soldier, down to the last one, whom they might encounter on this island. So to now start talking about saving some unknown foreigners — was madness, utter madness.

"We need to go there," said Galia to Marie. She waved towards the darkness of foreign lands.

"No, no!" answered Marie in English, crossing her hands over her face; but to show where they should actually go, she had to uncross her hands.

She pointed at Solovki, directly towards the invisible hill of Sekirka.

* * *

In the morning, Artiom, though it was impossible to consider, woke up in a good mood. Several times during the night, Marie got up to her husband, kept the fire alive, throwing the last kindling in there, then the oars as well — for some reason she had kept an oar for last.

Really, she was warming her husband, but Artiom liked to think that all this care was taken for his sake, so he slept even better.

In essence, Artiom was right.

Yesterday, Marie had found dry fur-lined boots and wool socks for him, and he changed his footwear.

No sooner had it gotten light than Marie began to prepare some kind of porridge — she had some unknown spices and unfamiliar grains left over.

The porridge quickly came to a boil, and even though the aroma was soon taken away by the wind, Artiom had a chance to smell it.

In expectation of breakfast, he, still in a morning haze, imagined himself an explorer discovering knew islands.

"... I'll name them myself," thought Artiom in a half-daze. "Afanasiev Isle is where we are now... The first one is *Vladychka* Isle... Burtsev should get his own island too."

Artiom didn't doubt that they would go back to Solovki.

For some reason it seemed that the road ahead was the road home.

It's possible that's exactly what it was.

The man, husband, friend moaned.

His moan proved that they had to return.

It also proved that Artiom was healthy, young and his lips were not covered with sores. He even felt the lightest, barely jolting sexual desire, which almost made him feel light-headed — what an idiot he was, stuck in the middle of a frozen sea, and still he was planning on continuing his useless race.

It smelled slightly of rot, either from the ground or from the sick man, but that didn't affect or turn off the desire to eat.

"Flesh from flesh, flesh into flesh, flesh against flesh, flesh for flesh, flesh, flesh, flesh," Artiom repeated in a whisper.

Somewhere nearby Galia began to move. Judging by her movements, she wasn't asleep and she had slept badly the past night. Artiom also guessed that she was mad at him — not bad, they hadn't even started their life together, and already he knew everything about Galia.

She was mad because she had to make the decision.

Though, in actual fact, there were no other possible decisions left in reserve.

"... They'll bring me back to Sekirka," Artiom thought calmly, because Sekirka still seemed far away. "I'll tell them, 'Greeting, brothers!' Where's my spot in the pile-up, the third from the bottom?'"

While they were eating, Artiom tried to smile at Galia a few times, but she didn't answer and looked away with cold eyes. By a barely noticeable movement of her strict jaws, Artiom realized that she was sometimes biting her cheek. Her soup was getting cold, sitting at her feet.

The pots of the foreigners were sparkling and clean.

Marie kept looking at Artiom and Galia either with hope or with horror and was afraid of speaking today, as though yesterday she was drunk and now she was shy.

In the morning light, Marie was revealed to be ugly and with a large nose. But she did have kind eyes.

The soup was delicious. Possibly the most delicious soup in Artiom's life... Except for the one when Troianskii's mother came to visit him... But there he knew what he was eating, here, he had no idea.

A slippery drizzle fell on them and got into the soup, but Artiom wasn't upset by that.

The island, in the light, was dirty, no good. He didn't want to live here.

Marie uncovered her husband — he hadn't died yet. Not only that but the necessity of changing his underthings had arisen, which is exactly what Marie began to do.

"In a similar situation, Galia would have just shot me," Artiom decided darkly as he got up. He thought for a bit more and concluded the thought, "And she would have done rightly."

Wet snow lay on the bottom of the boat. The boat was strange, cold, slippery — only yesterday it had seemed almost like home.

Seeing the snow falling into the water, it all became much viler and a shudder ran over his body, just like when he had a cold or right before throwing up.

He got warm by putting all the things back. Galia helped him. During the entire morning, they had not said a word to each other.

"They must have some kind of weapon," Galia said when they had finished loading. "Find it; we have to confiscate it. And all the other notebooks with the maps. Do it all yourself, OK? Here she comes."

Marie ran to them in fear and confusion, ready to fall on her knees, cry, wail, kill them, break the motor of the others' boat…

But when she came up very close, she couldn't speak. She only sobbed and shook.

"We're going together," Galia told her firmly. "Life for you, execution for us. But for now, together. Take your… whoever he is to you…"

With every one of Galia's words, Marie, in contrast to the horrible weather, lit up more and more like a spark and her face became warmer and more grateful with every moment.

"If only my fate looked at me as Marie looks at you," he said to Galia on the way back to the dying fire and the bed of the sick man.

He unexpectedly started and looked at the foreigners with terror, as though they weren't people at all, but, for example, recently arrived angels, salted by the local winds.

"Maybe he was pretending?" Artiom asked Galia cheerfully.

She smiled unexpectedly.

"Look out, pirates!" said Artiom. "You've found a good time to sleep!"

Galia laughed.

Marie fretted around them, not knowing what to do.

You don't need to do anything, just take your beloved by the legs and let's carry him.

They sailed home on a light wind. The way back to the monastery seemed short. All that was left was to see the lighthouse.

* * *

On the second day, they had a fight.

The boat barely moved forward, as though a current was meeting them headlong.

The motor was angry.

The waves gathered and grew.

There was constant water on the bottom of the boat.

At first, they threw away all the things that they had considered necessary to take from the island — the others' pots, blankets, crowbar, shovels — why was there so much stuff? You can't take it all…

Marie sighed, started and accompanied every thrown-out thing with a sad, thin, barely audible shriek.

Those shrieks drove Galia mad, but silently.

Artiom threw away the things with pleasure, as though they wouldn't have accepted him back at home with these things.

"Why did you throw out the axe?" Galia suddenly barked.

"You told me to," answered Artiom.

"I did not," she yelled.

"Should I dive for it?" asked Artiom.

Galia was greenish in color, very tired, and she was starting to get seasick. The foreigner — Marie called him Tom, so Tom, he was just as bad as before. Artiom watched life leaving him with a certain amount of interest. It was like sand flowing down an hourglass.

A few times, Tom came out of his comatose state and began to tell Marie something important, but she couldn't make it out and put her fingers on his lips. Her fingers were long and pretty. Galia's hands were smaller, more weathered, stronger.

Tom lay in the middle of the boat on a mound of blankets. With his feet, he pushed against Galia's knees. His feet shook in the rocking, as though they were separate things, not alive.

Galia was nauseous from the salty air, from Artiom, from the rocking, from the foreigners in the boat and she couldn't hold it in any more — she vomited.

"That's for the axe," thought Artiom, sloshing the water on the base of the boat. He felt sick too. He looked for something else to throw out.

"Soon Tom will depart and we'll throw him out," Artiom calmed himself, looking askance at Marie.

He felt sorry for her — it seemed she couldn't even admit that her husband was dying.

The more Artiom looked at them, the better he understood that these were just two weirdos who had arranged some utter foolishness for themselves, something like a honeymoon. Neither Tom nor Marie were older than thirty, probably, though she looked older by about fifteen years, and he — twice as old as himself.

As he went through the things, Artiom once again bumped into the firmly tied, heavy brick that lay there — he kept on planning to ask Galia what that was, but kept forgetting.

He tried to untie it.

"Leave it!" yelled Galia, and added fierce speed to the motor.

Marie, from time to time helping to ladle out water, shook from the unexpectedness and almost fell over.

Artiom looked at Galia with a smile and began to rip the knot with his teeth.

Galia dropped the rudder and got up.

The boat went sideways, around, threatening to flip over. Galia sat, or she would have been the first to go overboard.

The motor died.

"Give it back, bastard!" Galia yelled.

Marie shrieked thinly.

"Where do they teach them to yelp like that…? It's pretty…" thought Artiom in passing.

"You're the bastard!" he exclaimed and threw the brick at Galia, between the half-dead Tom's legs.

Everyone's nerves exploded.

Galia was crying.

The motor was silent.

The snow fell again. The tips of Tom's pretty winter shoes were in snow, whitened.

Twenty meters from the boat was a ragged darkness. In the interstices, you could see that beyond was the same darkness.

"You're nobody!" sobbed Galia. "You could have been whomever you wanted. I chose you. But you're an empty space. I've lost everything. How dare you!"

She had a knife, she cut open the knot on the brick, opened the packing. Gold coins fell onto the floor of the boat. Galia caught a few as they were falling, threw them into the water.

"So Eichmanis did find his buried treasure…" thought Artiom distantly.

He didn't care about the gold.

Marie looked at Galia.

She couldn't stop herself and kept getting up, extending her hands to the gold, shrieking something bird like.

"Sit!" Artiom grabbed and pushed her down by the bottom of her coat. "Sit, don't bother us! We're sowing gold. We have the right."

The fact that he didn't care made Galia cry even more.

"I stole it!" she said, almost growling. "I stole it from Eichmanis because of you! You! Oh, you!"

"So it was for me…" thought Artiom, looking at Galia.

"You were the most insignificant!" she yelled, having taken a breath and once again beginning to throw the gold into the water. The coins sank quickly, as though they were created for that purpose. "The most! Of all of them! Only Passport is worse than you! I could have done it with Burtsev… He crawled to me, the filth. Or better yet, it should have been Vasilii Petrovich, that God-fearing torturer… I would have pulled out my tit at any moment and said, "Suck!" And all of them would have gotten in line…"

Artiom continued to slosh the water with his feet, sometimes looking up to see Galia picking up a coin then throwing it with an awkward, feminine gesture.

Marie looked to the side, disconsolate, but with every one of Galia's gestures, she slightly started and winced.

"There was no pretense about you — you were the only worthy one," Galia was explaining to someone. "But now I see that you have nothing to pretend with."

Galia grabbed a handful from under the bench, between Tom's legs and threw them across Artiom, through Marie, beyond their backs.

Artiom deftly caught one and threw it back to Galia's feet with a gentle motion: a second attempt was necessary.

"Bastard, you bastard!" Galia swore at him, looking around as though blind. "He knew that I would be with you. He pulled you out on purpose to distract me. So that I wouldn't bother him. Leaving him with his whores…"

Artiom, at first thinking these words referred only to him, then understood that she wasn't only talking about him.

"Do you know why he didn't kill any gulls?" asked Galia, though not talking to Artiom at all. "Because he himself looks like a gull. Have you seen his profile? I put Trotsky's portrait on the wall on purpose; he was sure that I slept with him. But I was just making him mad!"

"And what? You didn't sleep with him?" Artiom wanted to ask, but didn't.

He had no love for this stupid woman.

Nor did she have any for him.

* * *

They reached some little island only on the next evening.

It was impossible to understand whether this land was the same that they had encountered before or a different one.

Along the way, their fresh water ran out.

There should have been another flask, but it was unclear where it had gotten to. Maybe they had forgotten it on the island where they had met the foreigners.

They started a fire and hung their things up to dry — they were dripping wet. They put pots under them.

They waited, quietly, until at least half a bowl of water dripped out.

It ended up being salty. In the sea, salty snow fell and salty rain dropped.

Galia threw the metal bowl down in anger. It fell on stones, then jumped back up with a bang.

Artiom walked over the island looking for wood. Everything near the water was bare and rocky — the waves and undertow had washed away all living things. A pitiful grass could still be seen on the hills. In the troughs, he found a few unknown shrubs and small trees.

On the way back, he met Galia. It seemed she had been looking for him and found him by the sound of the axe.

She acted as though nothing had happened.

"We have to go on immediately," said Galia. "Or he'll die. How he hasn't died yet…"

Artiom shrugged — he didn't care. They could go on or not.

"To look at you, you'd think freedom and prison, water and land — it's all the same," she said, with only gentle mockery.

"I like land and freedom better," Artiom answered simply.

"There's this word: freedom-loving," said Galia, and added after a pause, "It doesn't describe you."

Artiom silently carried the crooked branches, hugging them against his chest. They kept getting into his face.

"We're not going to Solovki, but to Kemi," Galia continued with no break. "We'll let them out there; they'll figure out their way on the mainland themselves. But we'll try to find a train and go in any direction. How are you?" She stopped.

Artiom stopped too. For half a minute, they stared at each other.

"And I kissed that face..." thought Artiom. The feeling was as though it had all happened two lifetimes ago. But it wasn't a bad life. Or not the worst.

"Of course, Galia," said Artiom. "We'll be together."

They went the rest of the way arm in arm, though they didn't touch each other.

"Artiom, I'm sorry," Galia said quickly.

"No need. I understand."

Tom was still lying in the boat. Marie was waiting for them to carry him off together.

"Rub him down with vodka and we'll leave immediately." Galia waved in the direction of Solovki.

Marie understood everything. She had started understanding everything from the first attempt.

"I'm not walking on plush... not on velvet..." Artiom sang, pushing the boat into the water.

Marie, sitting in the boat, looked at him with a frightened expression, as though Artiom might not have time to jump in and would stay on the island.

Artiom sang the second phrase already in the boat and hugged her rakishly. She didn't complain.

Galia looked at them and chuckled. He thought it was without any rancor.

The wind was fair.

In an hour, it started to get darker and the light of the lighthouse became clear.

Galia was the first to see the light and called Artiom, who sat facing her: look.

The lighthouse looked as though someone was holding a burning branch right in front of their faces.

Artiom stared at it for some time, then turned around — his eyes started to hurt.

No, they couldn't go back to prison. They had to go to Kemi. They had to run away.

It was frightening to go on in the darkness, so Galia lit the lantern again.

Artiom put it on the nose of the boat. The black water seemed very deep in the light of the lantern.

"All the time you forget that death is all around," Artiom thought coldly. "Without the light it's awful, and with it, it's terrifying."

The lantern blinked. The lighthouse blinked.

Marie often touched her husband's head — that was irritating too.

It seemed that Artiom fell asleep a few times. He acknowledged that he dropped into sleep only because of the shards of icy nonsense that was going on inside his head.

… They met the barge with Red Army soldiers unexpectedly; evidently, they had noticed the light of the lantern and were waiting to find out what sort of travelers these were.

… The travelers noticed the barge when they were about thirty meters from it.

"Turn the motor off," they both yelled in several voices.

Galia listened and turned off the roar of the motor.

By inertia, their boat flew right up to the barge. The soldiers caught the boat with a boat-hook. Galia struck it with her fist, but didn't try to throw it off.

"Should we shoot them all?" thought Artiom feverishly, looking first at Galia, then the barge; the revolver was still in his pocket, while a rifle with extra rounds lay on the bottom of the boat. Artiom, as Galia had told him, had taken it away from the foreigners. If only he had time to get it…

Galia, it seems, was thinking about the same thing, holding her hand over her holster.

But three soldiers at once aimed their rifles at them from the barge.

They lit a lantern as well.

"Well, who's this then?" asked the Chekist with the lantern, looking at Artiom. "Take your hand out of your pocket."

Marie at first was happy to see the barge, but now, seeing people with guns, she was scared. Artiom felt that she was shaking. Though it's possible she had been shaking for a few hours. You could hear her teeth chattering.

"What's the matter? Have you gone completely blind?" Galia barked, getting up, either making her voice rougher on purpose or having truly gone hoarse because of the wind.

"Oh, it's the commissar from IID," someone said.

The Chekist raised the lantern higher.

"Commander! Report on the reason for this night raid!" Galia growled.

For some time, there was silence. Only the creaking of the barge and the night wind.

"You're not my commanding officer," said the Chekist with the lantern. "I don't report to you. Who are you looking for out here in your own boat?"

"Special order of the head of the camp!" Galia continued barking like a hoarse bird. "We've detained and are bringing into the camp two spies. Move the barge immediately! And put down the rifles finally!"

"Show me the special order!" said the Chekist.

Artiom finally recognized him: Gorshkov. Only fear had prevented him from recognizing that awful voice sooner.

"Put down the rifles, I said!" Galia exclaimed.

… These insane screams, like in an extended dream, in the light of two lanterns, the metallic water all around…

Artiom shook.

… There was still much noise, they forced them to open up the rags and see Tom — what if they had a machine gun hidden there…? They decided that the barge would pull the motor boat to shore.

They floated in a torpor.

Marie stared at the barge, simultaneously holding her hand on her husband's head, as though telling him — wait, wait a little longer.

Galia sat, her chapped lips pursed.

"That's it," said Artiom to himself. "They shoot you for trying to escape…"

"… Except, why don't the soldiers know that we tried to flee?"

Not for the first time, he wasn't surprised that though he wasn't able to think much during normal days, he was capable of thinking through everything that happened during the moments when, other than terror, there was nothing else to experience.

"Galia," Artiom decided. "Let Galia get us out of this. It's easier for her… I'll say that I was following her orders."

It's as though she heard his thoughts and firmly said, "Act as though nothing's wrong. As soon as we get there, go to your sleeping quarters. Don't speak to anyone about anything. I think they don't know anything. They didn't even take away our weapons." She suddenly raised her voice, "Hey! You on the barge! You're barely moving! Let us go, we'll go the rest of the way on the motor!

In answer, they were quiet for a long time.

"We'll get you there," said Gorshkov finally.

It seemed he was suspicious about something.

Galia pulled on the motor's cord in frustration. It still didn't start.

That was probably supposed to calm them down — the motor died when they were already on their way to land, not in the middle of the sea.

But it didn't calm him down in the least.

* * *

It was already morning, and Artiom alone, without a guard, walking with difficulty on his numb legs, descended to the land of the monastery, following Galia. He had given her the revolver while he was still in the boat.

"In three hours, I'll expect you in the IID," said Galia to Gorshkov, who had quickly jumped off the barge. "Let's sort this out."

The rest of the soldiers and a few Chekist coats with seal fur for some reason weren't in any hurry to come down to shore.

The guards at the shore also didn't really understand what was going on.

"... How's that for nerves," thought Artiom, looking at Galia. "Maybe we'll really get out of it?"

Gorshkov, during that time, was looking at Artiom. He couldn't recognize him in his new clothes.

"Why is this jackal with you?" he remembered finally. "And who gave him that coat? Or did you raise him to the level of Chekist?"

"I'm expecting you at ten," Galia interrupted him. "We'll see who's going to be reporting to whom. Get ready to explain your business. We'll find out exactly what you were looking for fifteen *versts* from here."

"We'll see who's going to do the explaining," Gorshkov hissed.

Galia presented herself to the commander, by uniform, of the shore guard.

"Here are my commanding papers. Here's my document authorizing a special mission. During our mission, we detained two spies," she said distinctly, pointing at Marie, who was still sitting in the boat. "We must immediately get them to IID for interrogation. The second is sick, unconscious — he must first go into the infirmary. Quickly."

Artiom stomped in place.

"Why are you standing there?" Galia turned to him. "Immediately report back to your brigade."

"They won't let me in," Artiom wanted to say, but Galina had already walked forward, her hand waving as she stepped.

The walls of Solovki stood like black bread in dirty, sweet pollen.

At the gates Galia, handing in her documents, nodded at Artiom: "He's with me."

In the yard, she turned towards the IID at once, without saying goodbye. Artiom made his way towards the twelfth working brigade of the camp of Solovki.

Evidently, the work assignments were just finishing, and the first groups were moving towards their jobs through the autumn drizzle.

A brigade of ten people walked towards him. Two of the workers at the back were in heavy overcoats on top of underpants, another was in felt boots without galoshes, a third in shoes — he raised his feet high to avoid all the puddles. All were wearing caps.

In general, there were not many people in the yard, as had now become usual. Those who appeared looked nervous.

Along the courtyard, a few infirmary attendants carried the sick, but for some reason not into the infirmary, but from it.

"Those are bodies," Artiom explained to himself.

The attendants were in masks. They had never before worn masks like that.

It was unclear why Artiom thought that they would just let him in to sleep. He was simply dead, and it seemed enough of a reason. It also seemed like everything that was going on had already happened, and in the sleeping quarters he would find Vasilii Petrovich or Afanasiev, or maybe even Krapin. That meant that everything was in its proper place and would take care of itself, as it did more than once.

In the wooden lean-to, he did indeed see two Chechen orderlies sitting at their post.

"Ai," one of them recognized Artiom. "You were out to sea? You haven't been around in a while. Did you kill a whale?"

Artiom wanted to smile, but couldn't, so he just nodded and tried to pass.

"Hey," said the Chechen without any nastiness, but firmly. "Wait. You're in our brigade?"

Artiom nodded and looked at the clock, as though it would confirm the truth of his words.

He suddenly remembered that this was the younger Khasaev — the brother of the one who was in Sekirka with him. The brothers had always had a touching relationship — the elder took care of the younger, as though he were a child.

"No, I have to call the commander," said the younger Khasaev, a little sadly. "Listen, I don't care, but I haven't seen you… in a very long time. Do you have a transfer back to this brigade? They told me that now you're only working with the commanders, why do you want to come here? You're not drunk? Are you frozen? Here, warm up at the stove."

Khasaev left, Artiom quickly drank three mugs of water from the vat and, getting immediately drunk, he sat on the floor, leaning, with his back against the stove.

He closed his eyes and fell asleep.

The Chechen returned with some commander.

They kicked Artiom, not very hard, like a yard dog that was in the way.

He got up — he felt that his back had stuck to his shirt, his shirt to his Chekist's coat, and the coat itself was as hot as an iron.

Through his sticky dream-state, he looked into the commander's face… no, he didn't remember that face.

"Where's Curly?" asked Artiom.

The younger Khasaev barely noticeably chuckled.

"Re-PORT!" the commander ordered with rising fury.

"Artiom Goriainov." For the first time in his life, he got confused with his own last name, as though he were naming a foreign country. "I was on a special mission, now returned to my brigade by order of the IID."

"Where are your papers?"

"They are in IID."

For some reason, Artiom felt that he was riding a sled down a hill; he really wanted to close his eyes and fall asleep again.

"How am I supposed to know who you are?" The commander yelled in Artiom's face. "Take him to IID for the papers," he commanded the orderlies.

Khasaev grabbed Artiom rather rudely — but as soon as the screaming commander left, he loosened his hold.

"What? You don't know what's going on?" he asked on the road, leaning towards Artiom's ear. "You left a long time ago, probably? For three days now there's been an inspection. They've arrested them all — Curly, Chekists from the IID, commanders of the distant stations. Serious business… You should be less conspicuous. But you stick out like a sore thumb. In that coat especially."

The Chechen smelled strongly of onion and agitation. It was a good smell.

"Go, figure it all out, then come back to the brigade. I'll wait for you, brother," he said, very sincerely. "They said that you worked with Eichmanis, yes? Then they said you hit a Chekist in the yard, yeah? Then you beat up the gangsters? You're a strong lad; come back for sure to the brigade. What sort of mission was it, tell me in short?"

Various inmates walked around the yard, going to their work. Almost everyone's footwear was useless, only the orderly Khasaev, who walked next to him wore excellent boots. They looked Cossack. Artiom couldn't lift his head any higher.

They walked into IID, the duty officer showed up in a minute, also upset about something, but Artiom managed to sleep for a full minute while standing.

He felt that he was standing in the middle of the ocean, underwater, but dry.

The duty officer floated to him like a fish with an elongated face — he was all flattened, that duty officer, as though he grew not downward, as was proper, but kept on growing in the region of the back of his head, and kept getting longer and longer. If you looked the duty officer in the mouth — you'd find a tunnel there. In this mouth, you could fit your entire arm up to your elbow and find the swallowed bait.

Artiom was starting to get feverish.

He kept repeating to himself several times, "It's just lack of sleep," to explain his state to himself. But it was impossible to delve into the meaning of that word — in a frightening way, it was connected with a mug of tea into which they had poured some lumps of sugar, and the sugar was connected with snow, which fell, not with an icy dust, but in heavy pieces, as though they had dragged it to the very edge of the sky, like the edge of an ice floe, then threw it down into the water, which as before wasn't sweet at all.

Artiom didn't remember the beginning of the conversation with the duty officer, though he did take part in that conversation.

Even though he came back to himself long enough to finish the conversation — it was already late and the Chechen had gone without saying goodbye, but at least there were two soldiers leading Artiom through the yard. The word "solitary" was attached to his leg and struck the pavestones of the yard with each step.

"Why don't you give me your coat; they're going to execute you anyway," said the soldier while walking along. "I'll give you some tobacco. Look, you've already burned it in the back. They'll add some holes to it as well. Is that a good idea?"

Artiom moaned his disagreement.

The soldier grabbed him by the neck and pushed him against the wall. Artiom managed to spit at him; the saliva remained on his lip, but it did scare the soldier. Somehow, he then turned around and pushed the momentarily confused soldier in the chest.

The second one cooled down his buddy: enough, leave him alone, do you even know who he is? Maybe it's not worth undressing him.

"They're still going to put him under the store, don't you see?" The soldier snarled, but stepped back.

But as a parting shot, he said to Artiom, "I'll be the one to shoot you. It's too bad you didn't give me the coat. It would have been the nice thing to do. But you wanted it yourself. I'll shoot you just to make a point."

Artiom wiped the spit off his face.

While he was walking, he momentarily forgot where they were taking him.

There was a metal clanging — the lock opened.

Screech — the door opened.

Bang — the door closed behind his back.

Another clanging — once again the lock.

The entire bunch of keys, as they locked the door, rang in Artiom's brain.

A room and another room. In the room there were several people. Their faces were familiar.

He didn't remember a single name, but he knew them, and he knew them well.

There were three levels of bunks.

One bunk on the lowest level was empty, Artiom hurried there.

They called to him: stop, not yours! But he didn't listen.

* * *

He couldn't have figured anything better himself — he slept.

He slept in a place where no water would get him.

He was barely asleep when they, swearing, pulled him by his feet, but he kicked them off, got up on one elbow, forgot all words and growled — and for some reason this didn't surprise anyone. If they had thrown him to the ground, he wouldn't have woken up. They didn't.

He didn't know how long he slept, and no one ever told him.

When Artiom woke up, they had just brought in a bucket of hot water.

He didn't have a mug, and he was the last to drink what was left, picking up the whole bucket.

He drank it all and suddenly realized that his fever was gone.

Soon they took the empty bucket, though they did push in a confused, red-faced — his buttons all the way to the stomach were either unbuttoned or torn off — Gorshkov.

Artiom rubbed his eyes for a long time, not understanding anything.

Gorshkov sat on a bench exactly opposite Artiom, at first not recognizing him in the half-dark.

"Did you receive your report?" Artiom asked.

He had slept so well that a good mood descended on him.

Or maybe he just finally went mad.

"What?" said Gorshkov, peering ahead.

One more inmate looked intently at Artiom — that was Tkachuk, which was also unexpected.

"Shut your mouth, jackal," Gorshkov said.

"Woof, woof," Artiom answered, smiling and walked to the latrine.

Though he didn't understand anything yet, he had many guessses.

The prison guard stood at the entrance, confused by their papers and not understanding who they were supposed to take out of there.

"Oh, there it is… what the hell is that last name? Goria… Goria?"

"Goriainov!" Artiom suggested, doing his gurgling business.

"Look, he's already pissed himself," said the prison warden, impatiently rustling his keychain.

Sideways across the floor, fearing no one, a rat ran by and climbed into a crack in the wall, not very effectively — her tail stuck out so long that it seemed she was teasing someone.

Artiom was already coming out, and with difficult he was tucking his shirt in his cotton-wool pants. But the tail still hadn't disappeared.

It was daytime outside. Only it wasn't clear whether it was the same day or the next one.

The inmates vigorously swept the yard. No one smoked or yelled in the yard.

Marie walked out of the IID, saw Artiom and was inexpressibly happy, then finally realized he was under guard and was just as inexpressibly surprised.

"Where does he go?" asked the duty officer.

"How should I know?" said the guard. "To look at him, you'd think he was planning on running away at the first opportunity."

"Take him to the secretariat, they'll tell you," said the duty officer to his assistant.

In the IID it was just as unusually quiet and empty — either there was no one left in the offices or everyone had stamped their mouths shut and closed the doors.

"Does Goriainov go here?" the duty officer's assistant asked the secretary — a nervous fellow, slightly slanting and prematurely bald. He had absolutely no hair exactly up to the middle of his head, then it grew very thickly. This gave the secretary a simultaneously intelligent and idiotic look.

Artiom didn't know him. Something in his face suggested he had arrived in Solovki not long ago. Here everyone was more weather-beaten, older. In everyone's eyes something special glimmered, something of Solovki.

"In the corridor…" said the secretary; evidently, it wasn't part of his job description to utter complete phrases.

They put Artiom on a bench in the corridor, then the assistant to the duty officer left. They left the door into the secretariat open, so Artiom could see the secretary and the secretary could see Artiom.

Someone a floor above them ran by. On the floor below, the telephone rang, but the voice of the person who had picked up the receiver wasn't audible.

No one guarded Artiom — he could, for example, walk here and there. Or so it seemed to him. But he sat.

The secretary was called into the next room, and he left. A cup of tea was left on his table. It steamed.

Ten minutes later he heard steps — it was a woman, and Artiom knew that woman.

It was Galia. She was alone.

Artiom got up and looked in her direction. The expression of her eyes could have explained much. He looked, but didn't understand anything until she came close.

Stopping next to Artiom, barely audibly, almost with her lips alone, she said very quickly, "They've concealed our flight completely. The very same day when we left, an inspection arrived from Moscow. There have been many arrests among the Chekists in Solovki. Devil only knows what's going on." Galia looked forward, past Artiom, and only from time to time did she look at him, and then only for a moment. "Don't admit to anything. Nod at me when you don't know what to say. Tell them that you were working for Eichmanis and by his command you went to work for me. Tell them that we were studying geography and the local fauna. I was writing things down and you weren't involved in the process at all. Tell them that we went no further than fifteen *versts* out. Then the motor broke and we lost time. Then we found the spies and brought them here."

In the depth of the secretariat, the door opened and a powerful male voice sounded.

Galia calmly walked on.

Artiom watched her pass. She felt it and twice, without looking around, clenched and unclenched her hand fiercely.

That could have meant many things. Artiom interpreted it thus: be strong.

The secretary returned and took his tea. He had probably not prepared it for himself.

Artiom felt his heart beating. Like in school before an exam.

"It's strange," he thought. "Evidently, fear can't overcome a person completely, even if a test is a little scarier than possible execution. The same thoughts, the same gestures, the same dullness in the whole body..."

In the far office, the owner of the powerful voice began to dictate. A typewriter clacked.

For some time, Artiom listened in. Then he stood up and came to the doors; well, yes, the secretary's door led into a different office, without a name tag, and what was happening there was quite audible.

"The commission had expected to find in the regimen of Solovki, the first camp of the USSR, a more or less established order," the voice dictated. "The seeming order of the factories, the time-consuming labors, the extensive living space, the presence of comparatively decent Chekist cadres — all of this should have allowed for a firm, regular regimen of work... It's quite different in reality. Based only recently acquired information, the commission has come to the conclusion that mockery, beating and torture of the inmates has quantitatively passed into quality, that is, into the very system of the regimen..." The man coughed vigorously and the typewriter carefully waited until the coughing finished. "The method used by the commission to investigate the camp includes personal interviews of all those arrested during investigative and disciplinary procedures and those incarcerated in the common barracks," the voice continued. "As a firmly established fact, it is necessary to constitute that general fear exists amongst the prisoners: all complaints regarding the cruelty of the regime were only aired in the absence of any members of the administration, and only when we guaranteed that there would be no more beatings."

For some time, there was silence and it seemed to Artiom that he heard the rustling of papers.

"An objective assessment of the regimen at the lumber mill is as follows," continued the voice. "First of all, the commission investigated solitary confinement. This was a wooden shed, two square meters in size, without a heater, with huge holes in the roof, through which water flows copiously, with a single row of bunks. In this space, literally on top of each other, at the moment of the Commission's arrival, sixteen half-dressed people lived, the majority of whom had been there from seven to ten days. Only on the eve of the commission's arrival did the arrested receive hot water. Before then, it was considered an excessive luxury. Eight people were investigated as a result of complaints. Their bodies and arms were covered in what was obviously, even to the naked eye, contusions and abrasions from beatings. It is characteristic that the medical attendant, who was called to examine the beaten and who authoritatively applied his ear to various parts of the inmates' bodies, was actually a priest, convicted under article 58/10 of the criminal code. He was immediately moved to the common labors. The reasons for the beatings — slight disciplinary infractions, sometimes flight or attempted flight. The ones performing the beatings were guards, escorts, sharpshooters, foremen, military commanding personnel — and the vast majority of them were themselves inmates."

Artiom listened and dimly recognized that almost nothing of what he heard surprised him. That they didn't shoot people immediately for attempted flight, but merely put them in solitary — that even calmed him down.

Someone hurriedly came down from the top floor, Artiom heard it in time. He turned around and stood at the wall near the doors to the secretariat — just a humble prisoner awaiting his call.

Two Chekists walked by, who immediately fell silent when they saw Artiom. They were clearly not locals. One, a curly, big-nosed, big-eyed fellow, looked at Artiom in such a way that he stopped breathing just in case.

The Chekists left — Artiom went back to his place.

"Especially bestial were the punishments on the island of the Revolution at the hands of the commander of the fifth quarantine brigade, the inmate Kurilko," Artiom heard. "His most elaborate artwork: he forced inmates to commit the act of urination in each other's mouths, built a special room for beatings, left people outside naked in the snow, forced them to jump into the bay in winter, etc. Only in a slightly more moderate form did the other administrators show themselves. The worst spectacle appeared before the members of the commission at Raznovoloki station. In spite of the intense preparation for the coming of the commission — extra dressing of the undressed at night, taking inmates out of solitary, destruction of lice with help of the fire brigade, etc., the commission still managed to bring to light such a heavy spectacle of the general regimen that I remembered the favorite expression of the afore-mentioned Kurilko: 'Here, it's not the Soviet government, but the government of Solovki.'"

Artiom chuckled. He had heard the like many times.

"When investigating the beaten men, we found not only abrasions, wheals, contusions, but also considerable inflammation, and one with a broken pelvis… There are no bunks in solitary, and the snow falls into the large gaps in the walls. The incarcerated are held there regardless of the weather from two to five hours in nothing but underwear. They only let them out when the freezing victims begin to scream deliriously. One of the inmates in this 'covered wagon', a few days before the investigation, sliced up his stomach with a piece of glass. The inmates in the general barracks also complain of occasional beatings. This system of torture is cultivated by the commander of the isolation barracks, is acted upon by the guards and is approved by the commander of the military detachment, a member of the Communist Party."

For some reason, Artiom thought that at any moment now the man would start speaking about something that had to do with him personally, and he almost guessed right, but not quite.

"The employee of IID named Burtsev systematically beat not only other inmates, but also members of the guard of the camp. Not once did he ride around the camp on horseback, he arranged races with obstacles, he rode into the barracks and into the kitchen, arranged debauches everywhere and required that he and his horse have first dibs on meals. Seated on his horse, Burtsev drilled the inmates, beating them with his revolver, forcing them to run. A few times, he arranged stagings of executions, including a situation when he lined up, apparently for execution, former members of the Cheka from the third brigade. Subsequently, he was himself shot without tribunal by a few members of the administration of the camp, including Gorshkov and Tkachuk."

"Atta boy Burtsev…" Artiom thought with respect.

"The member of the IID, Gorshkov, forced women to cohabit with him, embezzled money and stole the inmates' property. Every one of the women he forced to live with him were issued a number; by number, these women were summoned to orgies in which another member of the IID, Tkachuk, took part, as well as a series of other members. Three more people have been arrested for similar reasons."

"Oh, my dears, they're going to fry you all soon," Artiom said aloud.

"The commander of the twelfth workers' brigade, Curly, beat inmates many times. Eight of them have been sent to the infirmary, two died from their wounds. In a drunken state, he confiscated the property of inmates…"

"Did they count me or not?" thought Artiom in agitation. Something completely extraordinary was going on.

"In the fourth division of the camp, inmates were systematically beaten, held outside for hours at a time and tied to posts. Not one of the accused had been arrested before the coming of the commission. I recommend that this issue be transferred to the OGPU," the voice announced and drank some tea. "Reports on the guard contingent of the Engozero work station, Zolotarev and his helpers, who systematically tortured the inmates, as a result of which three deaths were officially registered. All the accused have been arrested. I recommend the issue be transferred to the OGPU." Another sip of tea and it seemed that he lit a cigarette. "Report on the commander of the work station at Parandovskii's Road, 63rd kilometer, Gashidze and eighteen sniper guards, orderlies and foremen, all of whom were inmates. The accused beat, to the music of accordions, other inmates with felt boots filled with metal barbells. They drove undressed inmates under the bridge into the water, where they would force them to stay for several hours. They tied their feet with ropes and forced them to march to work in this way. A special form of punishment was standing in the latrine. One inmate was beaten to unconsciousness and laid down next to a bonfire, which resulted in his death. Gashidze himself built a solitary cell no higher than one meter, the ceiling and floor of which was covered in sharp thorns. Those who were put into this solitary cell, in the best cases, were laid up in the infirmary for a very long time. Several cases noted of open murder of the inmates in the forest. A few people died in solitary. Many, driven to madness, committed suicide or ran away in sight of the guard detail screaming, 'shoot!' and were indeed shot by the guards. The official report on these infractions was repeatedly delayed, lying for months without any movement and it was also concealed from the commission. When the members of the commission found out about its existence, it was first declared to them that the report had been sent to Moscow, but then it was in the procurator's office, and only now has the report with the accusatory conclusions reached the commission. Many episodes of this report are clearly redacted and some of the accused, led by Gashidze himself, remained free. Appended to this report is a detailed investigation for the colleagues of the OGPU."

"That I hadn't heard," Artiom admitted. "Even if someone told me, I wouldn't have believed them probably… I'll tell Galia later. Let her have the joy of hearing this news."

"Report on the assistant commander of the solitary confinement found on Sekirnaia Hill, Sannikov. He became the initiator of a series of lawless and ill-intentioned executions of inmates. To this moment, we have established thirteen such cases. Appended to this report is a detailed investigation for the colleagues of the OGPU."

"Isn't that our… with the bell…? I think Galia had named him…" Artiom thought in passing; his heart was beating even more furiously, he was suddenly hot and he unbuttoned his coat.

"… Eight cases of clearly unlawful closures of disciplinary investigations with clearly justifiable proof of the torture of inmates. Moreover, eight closed cases or analogous cases that were sent to the administration of the camp were not found in the archives… June 15 of this year, comrade Eichmanis gave an order concerning an official investigation of inmates' complaints concerning beatings and arrests in cases where these complaints were found to have occurred. Despite the fact that the fault of several guards was clearly established, they were not arrested before the arrival of the commission. Taking into account existing reports of the IID, the commission has called in seventy-four people, forty-seven of whom have been arrested, decisions concerning arrests of the remaining twenty-seven are pending."

"That's why there's no one in IID," Artiom chuckled. "They've all been arrested! Who's going to guard us now?

"… Our attention," the voice hammered irreproachably, like a mint, "is fixed for the most part on the main defects in serving the inhabitants of the camps and the main questions and needs of the prisoners. Complaints from the inmates concerning the absence of regularity in working days and days of rest are universal. The majority of the camp's work is seasonal in character — lumber preparation, fishing, road building, agriculture, etc. Arranging normal conditions in such a situation, especially with respect to the specific atmospheric conditions of this area, is impossible. The work is arranged by time periods and the impossibly difficult nature of the latter appears in a mass of complaints. Days of rest are only observed in the small shrub gardens." The voice grew quiet and in a single loud gulp, as though his throat were a puddle, the man dictating finished his tea. "… The officially assigned normative ration can be considered in essence adequate, but thanks to infractions or pilfering by the staff, it is a matter of routine to have limited rations as well as the preparation of excessively repetitive food. The cultural and educational needs of the inmates are met with adequate regularity. Almost everywhere, there are recreation rooms, very presentable newspaper printing and lectures on a variety of topics are offered. However, the objects of our service, because of the extreme difficulty of the assigned work, are not in any state to spend time becoming enriched with culture. Moreover, the work of cultural illumination in most of the distant work stations clearly does not correspond with the difficulty of the schedule. The living conditions of the inmates are excessively difficult and we cannot speak of any regularity here, since the inhabitants, as a result of overpopulation of living quarters, sleep in close proximity to each other. There is not even a hint of bedsheets or blankets. The newly built barracks leave a slightly better impression, but that only makes the contrast between them and the old living spaces all the more stark. For the entire population of the camp, there are only twenty-eight doctors, the vast majority of which are found in the administrative section of the camp. The qualifications of medical attendants, which work independently of the doctors in nearly all cases, are not adequately checked. During the last two quarters of this year, 24.6% of the population of the camp was sick at one time or another. During this same half year, 6.8% of the population died."

"Exactly right, exactly right," whispered Artiom. "Let's dissolve this camp, comrades!"

"In the interest of cutting off additional growth of this cruel regimen and to improve the daily life of the inmates, the commission is undertaking the following measures." The inclination of the voice suggested he was coming to the end. "First. We recommend immediate cessation of the system of incarceration as inappropriate, including in unheated buildings. Second. We recommend that all dormitories be fitted with bed bunks, etc. Third. We have included in our cost sheets an allowance for the physical needs of the inmates: we mean sheets, blankets and the like. Fourth. Twenty-four members of the administrative and military staff, as mentioned before, have been arrested. Fifth. The commander of the division of Labor and Accounting, the administrator of the retail division and the commander of the road-building division of the camp have been arrested. A proposal has been made to remove the assistant to the head of the camp. Sixth. We are deepening and further developing the investigation into existing cases and beginning new ones. Seventh. We have begun an outreach campaign for the workers of the camp who are members of the Party. As a result of the energetic actions taken by the commission, the systematic beating of inmates has been limited."

"What are you doing there?"

Artiom jumped, but why did he need to jump? Everything was obvious already.

Before him stood another Chekist from the capital, smoothly shaved, good-looking, with white teeth — any moment now, he would bite through one of Artiom's important veins.

"They told me to stand here and wait to be called," Artiom boldly lied.

The secretary, hearing the voices, looked out.

"Who's this?" asked the Chekist, nodding at Artiom.

"A detainee, we're just going to start his interrogation," reported the secretary.

"What detainee? I came here myself," snarled Artiom. All that he had just heard inspired him to speak in a certain way.

"Is he one of Gorshkov's bunch?" the white-toothed Chekist, staring point-blankly at Artiom, loudly asked either the secretary or the owner of the powerful voice and puddly throat from the neighboring office. "The one who took a trip out to sea as soon as our commission appeared?"

"We'll take care of this now," the voice resounded, and even the glass in the windows resonated from it. "Bring him here."

As he entered the office, Artiom began to seek the owner of the indomitable bass with some confusion, but all he found was a puny man no more than a meter and a half in height, with long hair, glasses and bushy eyebrows to boot.

"Where are your documents?" he asked. The voice belonged to him. He stole that voice or caught it in a snare, then tamed it, like a predator. Now the voice served him.

"What documents?" asked Artiom.

"Your commanding documents." With such a voice, you could crack nuts.

"Ask Galina. She had everything," Artiom quickly answered, trying to convince himself not to hurry.

The white-toothed one asked something of the secretary and soon walked in after Artiom.

The secretary closed the door quietly, but firmly.

"Where did you get that coat?" asked the white-toothed one. "IID?"

"I am an inmate of the twelfth workers' brigade," reported Artiom, then immediately redirected their attention, not even knowing why, by saying, "and was temporarily transferred into the second brigade."

"I haven't seen any such coats in the workers' brigade. You're not mixing anything up, sonny?" The white-toothed one was possibly mocking him.

"How am I your 'sonny'?" Artiom quickly thought. "I'm not sure that you're even old enough to be my older brother."

"I was rewarded by comrade Eichmanis for exemplary work," Artiom lied, not even expecting it of himself. Something suggested to him that this would be best. What else would he have said? That Galina had issued him the coat on the day of their intended flight?

"And what exemplary work was that?"

"We worked alongside comrade Eichmanis in studying the local geography, flora, fauna," Artiom reported as though he were laying out cards.

His life depended on the outcome of the gamble.

"And where did you sail with the member of the IID… what's her name…" The half-metered man with bushy eyebrows asked, moving to his table. Artiom slowly looked at him and didn't understand if he was sitting down at his table or was standing behind it. It was characteristic that the bearer of the puddly throat wasn't bothered by his own shortness. Having such a voice and a Mauser on his side was more than enough for him to feel manly.

"An island fifteen *versts* from the camp," answered Artiom.

"The purpose of the journey?" Now only the big-voiced one talked.

"As much as I understood, the creation and improvement of maps of the Archipelago of Solovki." Artiom firmly answered.

"How did you find the foreign nationals?" the short man smoked a cigar that looked huge next to his small head.

"They lit a fire on the island, and we saw them."

"Did they try to resist you?"

"No, one of them, the man, was unconscious. He was feverish, lay in a comatose state. But they did have weapons. We confiscated them."

"Did you speak with them?" the small man knocked the ash right onto some papers on the table.

"No, they don't speak Russian, nor do we speak foreign languages."

The white-toothed one also came up to the table, stood behind the back of his short comrade, looked at the paper — evidently, he was allowed to do this. The owner of the voice looked back. The white-toothed man nodded questioningly: well, what do you think?

"According to the papers, everything you say is correct," said the short man, turning back to the table. When he lowered his eyes, his eyebrows hung over them so thickly that it looked like a few furry, slow bumblebees sat in the region of his supraciliary arch.

* * *

They sent Artiom back into the prison cell: "Let him sit there for a bit," commanded the big-voiced man, getting up from his table in search of his ash tray, which he himself had left on the small monastery windowsill. "Or he'll float away again… Find me his file!" he commanded the secretary. "All orders concerning internal transfers. I need to understand what it was he was doing with Eichmanis… or else, flora…" And he laughed so hard that the spoon in his cup of tea rattled.

The prison cell smelled acrid and full of human sweat.

Gorshkov and Tkachuk frequently walked into a corner and either mumbled something there or stood silently.

Tkachuk slouched and scratched himself often.

Here, together with Artiom, sat ten people, but there were only eight beds, and so people took turns on two of the spaces.

Artiom, though he did occupy someone else's bed, didn't take part in any turns, but just lay in the place where he fell when he had come in. He didn't bother finding out who slept there before him.

Probably such an opening chord immediately gave him a sense of brazenness and made him want to start a fight. What he had heard in the secretary's office only deepened that mood.

Curly — he was here too — almost didn't get up and looked as though he was in a heavy hung-over state for the last few days. His face was puffy, his ears hung, his cheeks hung, his nose hung. He drank ten mugs of water at a time, until they chased him away from the bucket.

Here no one respected anyone.

The ringer of Sekirka ended up being the most restless; as opposed to the rest, he was always hot, he walked in a floral shirt alone, as if he had been taken during a wedding, and he made such movements with his face as though a caterpillar had crawled on the back of his neck, but it was impossible to get it off.

He looked everyone in the eye, sometimes stopping next to Gorshkov and Tkachuk, but he didn't speak to them.

He came up to Artiom, who asked him loudly, "Sannikov?"

The ringer started, "Yes, that's right. And you are, please?"

"Where's the bell?" asked Artiom, not answering the question. He firmly felt that it would cost him nothing to kill this person right now, preferably by choking him.

Sannikov started doing something with his cheeks as though he had no control over them.

Artiom turned away.

"Don't you dare!" said Sannikov to his back.

Sannikov couldn't calm down for another hour; he kept walking back and forth, looking sideways at Artiom until they called him out for an interrogation.

"Ding-ding!" said Artiom as he left.

"I'll come back for you," he promised furiously.

Artiom winked at him with unusual frivolity: sure thing, I'll be waiting.

Everyone wanted to believe that they would soon be let out: they'll figure it out and be done with it.

No one showed any solidarity with anyone else, even Tkachuk and Gorshkov's conversations were becoming more and more nervous, as though each of them suspected that he had been informed on by the other.

Finally, Tkachuk said something rude to Gorshkov, reminding him about the barge: Artiom heard.

"You should have surrendered to the Norwegians," Tkachuk said, showing an unusual amount of humor. "You should have told them that you were a victim of the Bolshevik regime. You could have also written a book with revelations… 'The Red Exile', Fuck!"

Artiom didn't understand one thing yet — did Gorshkov go out on the barge because he was looking for something, did he decide to fish in October, or did he leave without thinking of a proper reason for his search? In any case, he hadn't called Tkachuk to go with him, preferring to save himself alone.

"… Did they put me here because of my coat?" Artiom thought. After what he heard in the secretary's room, the price of his wet excursion no longer seemed so high.

Hardly any time had passed at all, and he had already convinced himself that he and Galia had never planned on going anywhere, only that they were preparing maps and were riding around the islands not far from the camp. This faith had a tinge of emotional madness, but it really helped him calm down; it made him feel as though he was on firmer ground.

After all, not everything here was Sekirka, not everything was Sekirka.

Artiom was also warmed by the feeling of an unexpectedly-realized power that he had in the midst of all this vile rabble.

The formerly huge Curly was nothing more than an elderly and sick man who was always whispering something to himself. Artiom caught himself thinking that up to this point, he had only seen the former commander of the brigade in two states — drunk and hung over. But this was a completely different creature — sober and without cigars. Curly begged a smoke from the guards; one time they did give him a cigarillo, then they stopped reacting to his pleas.

The guards showed no sympathy to the incarcerated — they tried to avoid any interaction, as though they were lepers.

It turned out that everyone here was squeamish about what they could eat. Whatever Artiom ate, even with pleasure, they looked at as something exotic. They smelled it, examined it, pushed the snotty grains here and there with their spoons, Curly spoke with the food assigned to him, Gorshkov swallowed it, grimacing. Tkachuk threw his portion out into the latrine and threw the plate at the doors.

In the evening, they returned Sannikov. He looked at no one, especially not at Artiom. He sniffled and frequently blinked.

Three times in the space of half an hour, he went to the latrine and kept moaning about his bad luck.

One time, he was pulling his pants up as he walked and he started speaking to the first person he encountered, "I think they've forgotten that there's such a thing as revolutionary expediency. We'll have to remind them."

But he didn't have enough of a voice for it, and the first phrase, which began confidently and boldly, by the end was barely crawling forward, in an almost falsetto voice. To save face, Sannikov decided to start coughing and quickly climbed into his bunk.

Artiom couldn't stop himself, and, getting up, stood next to Sannikov's bunk, saying nothing and almost whistling. The ringer turned to face the wall.

Something was egging him on to be impertinent to someone here. Artiom's self-confidence had no rational explanation. Nevertheless, no one wanted to have anything to do with the stray wanderer.

Only Tkachuk presented any kind of danger, at least because of his size, but by the evening, he slept most of the time, or tried to fall asleep.

The room was full of rats — even the kitchens didn't have so many — evidently, it smelt especially rank of garbage, rotting meat, cowardice and filth.

At night, Sannikov howled — a rat had begun to gnaw at his ear.

He jumped down, holding his ear in his fist — it was bleeding.

Artiom woke up in the morning also not alone, but with a neighbor — it sat calmly next to him, right on the bunk, looking at him with an eye, while the scabrous tail lay unmoving.

He wasn't in the least bit afraid.

Because of old habits, Artiom hid his bread from lunch and decided to be generous. Quietly, not to scare the rat, he got the bread out from his pants and rolled two bread-balls.

"Here you go. Just don't bite me on the ear, please."

It slowly approached its feast — like a peasant it didn't hurry, doing everything short of crossing itself. In every movement, it revealed dignity and exactness. It hurried nowhere and feared nothing.

"Teach me to live, rat!" Artiom asked with a quiet smile.

It seemed that the rat was pregnant — its huge ratty belly was bulging.

* * *

After lunch, they called out Curly.

He stood in the middle of the room, as if he had immediately forgotten whether he had to leave or whether he had just come back.

The soldiers pulled him outside. Curly walked, leaning his head back far. In the room, a sickly smell was left after his exit.

But at least they brought in Artiom's old friend, Moisei Solomonovich.

He wasn't inclined to sing, as in former times and was in a certain state of mental distress.

They asked him about news from the camp, but he had nothing to say, either that, or Moisei Solomonovich for some reason didn't want to share his knowledge.

Somehow he had hardly changed; he had the same long face, the same large tongue, almost cow-like, the same bulging eyes — only now he wore glasses, his eyebrows had become bushier and his ears were also covered with many hairs. He sometimes touched and picked at these hairs.

Artiom felt no need to converse with him, but Moisei Solomonovich himself sought an opportunity to talk.

"Artiom," he said, sitting down on the edge of the bed. "Hello."

"Fancy meeting you here, Moisei Solomonovich," said Artiom, rubbing his face with his hands.

"You've still preserved the ability to smile," said Moisei Solomonovich poignantly, though, here, no one seemed to be smiling.

In a few minutes, Artiom already knew that Moisei Solomonovich was now a manager in the economic division, or at least had been that morning and was sitting in the administrative building in his own office: "Well, not really an office, a small room, it was muggy…"

"Muggy — that meant they heated it," Artiom decided, but said nothing. Moisei Solomonovich had landed here due to his extremely diligent accounting work.

The point of his conversation became obvious to Artiom from the first word — the frightened man was running through his own truth in his head, getting ready to offer it during his imminent — immediately following Curly's — interrogation. And he wanted to check how convincing this truth was, or was it a story, a substitute for the truth?

"You act completely freely and don't look like any of them," quickly whispered Moisei Solomonovich, indicating the others with his eyes. Then he took off his glasses and began to rub them with the end of his jacket, as though he were trying to hide the fact that he had indicated the other prisoners.

"I still don't understand, did you work in the administrative division or not?" Moisei Solomonovich suddenly asked. "I saw very little of you."

Artiom sat up on his bunk — after all, talking while lying down wasn't proper — and now he looked either at the glasses of his friend — one of the lenses was tied in place with a piece of string — or at his jacket, which had also seen better days, and had seen so much in fact that by wearing it he was showing a certain degree of deliberateness. Not answering, Artiom shook his head in a significant way: Yes, I was in the administrative division or, maybe, no I wasn't, but I did see many things and go many places.

"Do you know that they're going to blame everything, everything on the Jews again?" whispered Moisei Solomonovich, not waiting for an answer and not upset at not receiving one. "But comrade Gleb Bokii, who runs everything here," and Moisei Solomonovich, having quickly put on his glasses, made a narrow gesture with his hands, as though Bokii had direct control of their life in this very room, "I have it on very good authority that he's a Russian nobleman. Comrade Eichmanis is half-Latvian, half-Russian and everyone knows that. And they're both baptized Christians. Comrade Nogtev — that's obvious — he's fully Russian, it's written all over his face. Yes, there is a comrade Frenkel here — a Jew, and a noted Jew, a protégé of comrade Eichmanis, the head of the production and maintenance division — but he's one of the inmates. And what do we see? No sooner do they start detaining people — and for good reason, we understand — then, immediately, 'Do come behind these bars please, Moisei Solomonovich!' Twice they put me in prison, Artiom! Or maybe even three times! At first, we get stuck in the Soviet Republic. That wasn't enough, so they hid us in Solovki. But Solovki wasn't enough for Moisei Solomonovich, and they found an even more trustworthy prison, this room! And all I did was try to balance the books of their idiotic management!"

Artiom shrugged. It was also strange that this person spoke of himself as though he were the only person on Solovki and all the others here weren't really imprisoned. It was also strange how much he had changed in the past few months. Artiom remembered him constantly singing, the gangsters had even nicknamed him "operetta". Who could have thought that "operetta" could be capable of such sweeping generalizations?

Artiom had some bread left over from feeding the rat and rolled five balls for himself. He put them in his mouth one by one.

"And what sort of management they have here — you yourself can imagine well enough," his conversant looked at Artiom over his glasses, and Artiom thought that Moisei Solomonovich couldn't care less what Artiom understood or not, but just needed to correctly line up the words in his speech. "It could not have happened in any other way on Solovko. Former White Army officers ran all of the industries here, counter-revs everywhere, priests, as though they had set it all up on purpose, to give the management roles to the least trustworthy people. I told Comrade Eichmanis about this, I even wrote it in a report. I asked them at the interrogation to find that report and append it to my file, but… they have enough to do without me."

Moisei Solomonovich described the circumlocution of Solovki's production plants for a long time, though somewhat confusedly. He explained in detail how the brickmaking enterprise had been ruined. The mainland had returned a ton of bricks from Solovki because they had ended up being useless for building and they tried to save the failed brickmaking production plant at the expense of unwise timber exploitation, the excess profit of which went to the various nurseries to which Comrade Eichmanis brought rare animals. Basically, as a rule, they didn't breed in captivity… The shoe factory produced crap, the journal of Solovki, though it had subscribers all over the country, ended up in the red, even the numbers of fish caught were insignificant…

"It's not management, but a series of failures!" insisted Moisei Solomonovich, getting more and more angry, as he somehow roundly accented the letter "f".

"You're lying! You're lying! A lot was done, you counter-rev. You should be the first to be smashed!" Gorshkov dully barked from above, eavesdropping on the conversation.

Moisei Solomonovich took off his glasses with a frenzied movement. It was as though he believed that if he could not see without his glasses, then no one else would see him either.

Gorshkov hurriedly got down from the upper bunk, wanting to shake Moisei Solomonovich by the chest, but he saw Artiom, who was only waiting for someone like him, so he just laid out his reserves of bad language, swearing foully, abundantly, strenuously.

Artiom listened, his mouth agape and then started to grimace, teasing Gorshkov, pretending to conduct his speech with his grimaces, tongue and nose.

Gorshkov, turning red, rushed to the doors, as if he planned on leaving. He thundered with his bones there for a while against the metal, and, squinting with one twitching eye, returned to the small barred window that he couldn't reach — he tried to get his breath of air.

For a few minutes more, the heat rose from Gorshkov in all directions, as though he were a pot with boiling, but already soured, borsch.

Moisei Solomonovich moved to the place of the absent Curly and was silent.

Until dinner, Artiom dozed. He kept dreaming about cold, salty water and he felt a uniform and warm pleasure from the fact that he was no longer sailing anywhere.

"What about Curly?" Tkachuk asked the prison guard, who had brought in a vat with gruel. "Did they let him go?"

"They've already buried Curly," he answered.

Everyone fell silent.

In a single minute, the temperature in the room fell.

They ate slowly, trying not to utter any noises.

All conversations ended and everyone was left to his own oppressive loneliness.

Sannikov's intestines sang loudly.

Artiom suddenly understood that his strength for being joyful at their misfortune was running out. He was suddenly overcome by a thick nausea.

At first, he had waited for his turn on Sekirka — but there, everything was clear. It was a distant isolation prison and who needed the inmates? You chop down half, new ones will grow. But now he ended up here, and it was all repeating itself.

Who could have guessed that they would also pick off the administration?

Artiom lay still, his body pined. His bones felt brittle and weak — you couldn't pick anything up with such hands, you wouldn't go far on these legs, this neck wouldn't hold the head up.

He lay on his side, facing the wall — with the intention of falling asleep, but he lay sleepless, dully convincingly himself — maybe you'll still get up? Manage to live a little longer? Get some final pleasure from life?

It was all stupid — pleasure? From what? From walking in a room among badly smelling filth?

"Will they really bury you together with them, Artiom? In a single grave? Will we really have common worms?" He asked himself constantly.

He thought that at least here, among the black hat-bands, everything would be pretend, but it turned out that for them everything was very real.

"How many times have they tried to kill me already?" Artiom complained with tears. "I can't count anymore! The gangsters cut me. They let me rot on the logs. They beat me to death for someone else's cards. They buried me together with the conspirators. They shot me on Sekirka. The inmates trampled me, unable to forgive the defaced icon on the wall. They shot me another time in Galina's boat. The sea drowned me and that which my mother petted on the head was eaten by fish. I slowly died from cold and hunger. Why should I die again? It's not my turn anymore! I've had my turn ten times over! Lord!"

He didn't see, didn't hear, but with some bestial sixth sense he felt that the rat had returned. Yes, it was there.

He had some bread from dinner with him — Artiom hadn't really wanted to eat much the last few days. He ate by habit, for the future, not thinking whether or not he wanted to.

He threw the rat the entire piece: eat, no one is going to shoot you.

He closed his eyes. The rat wisely managed the gift — it ate a bit, then took the rest away with her.

Artiom heard its rustling, but he didn't open his eyes.

His thoughts had begun to grow confused. He slept for a minute, two minutes, three minutes, then jumped, woke up, opened his eyes and tried to remember what he was just thinking about, nothing, nothing, he remembered nothing.

During yet another momentary dream, he suddenly saw himself from above — he was naked, though he was also asleep in the seal-fur coat and in wool-cotton pants, not getting sick of the warmth.

"I have to return, my body's about to wake up," Artiom asked himself and tried to fall back into his body, into his skeleton, awkwardly falling back-first, risking the possibility of missing the body completely. At the same time, another dark sense tortured him — he couldn't talk about it out loud, as though these words made him grow numb.

Finally, with incredible effort, he said, pushing the words out of himself as out of a rock, "God is naked here. I don't want to look at a naked God. God is naked on Solovki. I don't want Him anymore. I'm ashamed."

He fell into his own body, woke up, caught himself realizing that he saw, not God, but his own father — naked — and he was speaking about him.

He squinted, buried his chin into his coat and once again fell into a half-daze.

It was unsettling; it was maddening.

God is my father. And I killed my father. Now I have no God. Only I, the son. I'm my own Holy Spirit.

"…While my father was alive, I hid from death behind his back. Father died, and you walk out on your own… where? To God? Somewhere… And I myself, I pushed my own father from my road and ended up here — where is he who will meet me? Hey? Who's here? Is there anyone here…?"

He listened to the dense dream of the night — no one.

"God doesn't torture. God abandons forever. Come back, Lord. Kill me, but come back."

Open unto me the doors of repentance, O Giver of life.

Silently, not so much a huge hand as a huge finger appeared… and squished a louse.

* * *

Right before morning, an angel appeared to Artiom. He put his hand on Artiom's chest and promised that everything would be well — nothing is going to happen to you.

Or rather, he didn't promise anything and Artiom didn't actually see his face, but he knew for sure that it was a messenger who had come to tell him that your fate was still warm, my dear.

Artiom woke up, felt a hot trace on his chest, exactly in the middle of it and fell asleep incredibly deeply and calmly. Not even on Fox Island did he sleep so well.

He opened his eyes and the room appeared large, sunny and expansive. Inside his heart, there was unheard-of freedom.

Not thinking of anything on purpose, but moved along by an elemental feeling of defiance, Artiom jerked up from his bed — it was probably around six in the morning — and in two steps he was next to Sannikov's bed.

Pursing his lips in a ribbon, Artiom portrayed the wailing ring right into the ear of the sleeping man: "Bbrrrrrrrrrring!!!! Ding-ding-ding! Sannikov! Time for your lesson! To the exit with your things!"

Sannikov jumped up like he was doused with hot water.

"No!" he shrieked frantically.

"Get your things!" commanded Artiom joyfully and impudently. "The worms are waiting for you; they're ravenous! Into your forehead — bang!"

and Artiom pushed Sannikov firmly with his finger in his forehead. "Your head cracks in half, come on flies, they've opened up a Chekist head for you, like a can of beans!"

Sannikov, his eyes bulging, looked at Artiom, unable to understand what was going on.

The rest of the rumpled prisoners woke up on the other beds. But no one wanted to raise his voice, to say a single word to Artiom: the frenzied smile on his face, the mad passion and the free-for-all — it was better not to get involved with any of it. Every one of them had been beaten up by his own irrepressible fever.

Artiom circled the room like a bumblebee, nagging and annoying everyone.

At six, they announced wake-up time, then they brought some steaming hot water. Artiom grabbed a mug from one of the Chekists — he thought that was the same Gashidze mentioned by the big-voiced Chekist in his report. Then he stood first, began to drink without rushing, not walking away from the bucket, preventing everyone else on purpose. Gashidze, baring his teeth, was quiet, looking at the bucket from time to time.

Sannikov didn't get up at all, but, twitching in his bed, waited for Artiom to finish.

But since Artiom wasn't planning on going anywhere, even after he gave the others room to get their hot water, Sannikov decided to get up and, hiding behind the others' backs, passed someone else his mug saying, "Please pour me some, would you?"

Artiom grabbed the mug, "Let me!" And, taking three steps, threw it in the latrine.

"Hell!" yelled Sannikov. "Why? That's my mug! What are you doing?"

"Would you like to drink?" asked Artiom. With a quick gesture, he grabbed Gashidze's unfinished mug and with sincere pleasure threw the hot water in Sannikov's vile face.

That's how the day began.

The keys rang, the door opened to take out the bucket; by the way, they also took out another Chekist. He hurriedly grabbed his things and didn't walk, but almost ran out. No one watched him leave.

Lying down on his bunk, Artiom happily squished the lice on the nearest wall — they were all engorged, and each left a bloody stain.

"Sannikov!" Artiom quietly named each of the lice. "Where are you going, my dear? Ding-dong! Hear it? The bell is calling you under its arch! Dilly-dilly-dong! An act of revolutionary justice transpires! Bang! Yuck, how disgusting… Next! Gorshkov? Stay there! Chin up! Where's your swagger, Cheka? There it is! Would you like it in the head or in the stomach? As you wish! From a rifle or a revolver? Bang! Bang! Oops. One minute, we didn't quite get you that time. Encore! Bang!"

"Stop it, reptile!" someone shrieked from above.

Artiom kicked the bunk above him as hard as he could.

Closer to lunch, when Artiom had his fill of fun and fell silent, half-sleeping, Moisei Solomonovich sat near him and quickly whispered, "They're planning on choking you to death. All together."

Artiom, instead of answering, laughed.

Tkachuk approached their bunk, looking at Moisei Solomonovich darkly.

"… and it wasn't only economic management," he continued, as though continuing a conversation, "I have to take part in the educational division. Not many people know that there were eight schools here, twenty-two campaigns against illiteracy, twelve professional courses, eighteen libraries, including moveable ones! Who had to make sure that all this received the necessary love and care? Moisei Solomonovich!"

"What are you doing there, horse-belly?" Artiom asked Tkachuk.

Tkachuk was thinner than before, but was still twice as muscular as Artiom and everyone else in the room.

"I'm going to…" said Tkachuk, though he didn't move from his place.

Moisei Solomonovich once again took off his glasses quickly.

Artiom didn't get up on purpose — otherwise, it would have been too obvious how he was shorter than this castrated horse by a head and a half.

Except Tkachuk was rocking in place and his hands shook — this gave Artiom a certain advantage.

In the room, there was one stool and one table, but both were bolted to the ground.

Listening to himself, Artiom realized that he wasn't afraid at all.

Nothing happened. Tkachuk gnashed his teeth, spat on the floor, and walked away.

"Might as well have pissed yourself here, you castrated horse," said Artiom. Moisei Solomonovich looked at him with pleading eyes.

Lunch was buckwheat, and they added the same Chekist whom they had taken out in the morning.

The mood in the room changed immediately — they didn't kill him. They let him return, though he was completely rumpled, beaten, scared and wet for some reason — were they pouring water on him?

The returned Chekist hid in a corner. He was shaking.

When he asked for something to drink in half an hour, someone immediately brought him a half-drunk mug of water.

He tried to explain what had happened — everyone waited for at least some news — but it didn't work out. He tripped on the first memory of the interrogation: "… they were screaming, 'Shoot him in the forehead, shoot him in the forehead!' They got the revolver — poked me in the forehead and yelled…"

He did have a bloody abrasion on his forehead.

"I told them everything, and so?" the returned man admitted. "Everything. But I was following orders, only orders. Question: who could have given them — them! — such orders against us?"

All this still gave hope to the locals. To yell, "Shoot him in the forehead" and to actually shoot someone in the forehead — those were two different things.

From boredom, and to make the human cattle angry, Artiom measured the room diagonally by walking back and forth. It was ten steps. During one of his turns, he noticed that the way along which he walked was a different color than the rest of the room — an irrepressible prisoner like him had walked this path before.

He remembered mixed-up poems and prayers that he was supposed to know, but — what a pity! — he didn't know them completely.

"That's one of the things I repented of, on that day! It was like purgatory working inside me… With inexpressible speed… I confessed my sins… before myself…"

He made about a dozen circuits, unnoticeably switching to new paths. All the more so since it wasn't in Artiom's nature to repent anything, he had no knowledge of how to do it, and the words that he had somehow managed to learn by heart meant nothing to him at all.

"… It seems to me that in the magic circle… the demons of past centuries appear…"[50] Artiom turned around on his heels, whispering, "The wounds of Godunov are seeping slowly… the captured have their spines snapped into two…"

For some time he walked with the demons on his lips, crunching on the word "spines" like it was sugar. He kept staring at Gorshkov, but he was lying down with closed eyes. Suddenly, he switched his poems to the ragged bits of what he had heard during boring church services or from his long-ago-dead grandmothers.

---

50 Citation from a poem by Konstatin Balmont.

"… You live on high, O Christ the King… fighting fiercely against the passions… save us by your prayers, O Seraphim… all of creation serves You… For you are the Savior…"

And another turn.

And again about creation and salvation.

Moisei Solomonovich listened in to his mumbling, his head cocked and sometimes began to move his lips as well, as though he were preparing to help him out, to sing with him, but these words he didn't know.

The prisoners at first glared at Artiom, expecting a new outburst of his nasty game, but then they got used to it.

Someone even said aloud, hoping for the others' understanding.

"I'd love some boiled potatoes with onion."

To calm down at least somewhat, the human cattle began to reminisce, little by little, naturally about the grub that they used to swallow in days past.

Open pies, steaks, Kiev borsch, cutlets, smoked fish, aspic, sweetbreads, ribs and cartilage began to float into the room.

Gashidze got down from his bunk as if he had just come down from a mountain, bringing with him a just butchered young lamb.

"I once fried a grouse in a fruit candy box," said the one who had a gun aimed at his head two hours ago. He kept soaking his bloody abrasion with a horribly dirty handkerchief.

Moisei Solomonovich didn't quite start singing, but, not able to contain himself, he did begin to utter some sort of melody in his nose, through a single nostril.

"I remember that during the imperialistic war, I was surrounded," Tkachuk interrupted him. "My horse was wounded, and it was winter. We killed it right then and there. Kept our hands warm in the stomach, dressed it, and divided it… but how to prepare it? We went into a hut where we were spending the night. You stick the horsemeat into a little pot, put it into a warmed-up stove — by morning, the meat is ready. It's sinewy and it smells, but if you sprinkle a lot of salt, then…"

Artiom kept moving for some time, but he forgot about his poems mixed together with prayer, and even started to listen, not really remembering that the storytellers, during their not very long lives, had already digested human flesh in as much volume as horsemeat, beef and lamb.

But either from these conversations or from his long and monotonous walking, his head started to spin, so Artiom lay down on his bunk.

As though interested in the conversation, Artiom's rat appeared — he was already used to it and was prepared for its coming. He had poured aside a bit of lunch's buckwheat and without any disgust hid it in his jacket pocket. Now he started to dig there, grabbed it in his finger, brought one pinch, and then brought another: here, have your fill.

He looked around: Tkachuk was looking at Artiom directly with a strange expression, but definitely without hatred.

As Artiom examined the rat, its movements, its black, intelligent eyes, he remembered Galia for some reason — where was she? What if they had arrested her as well? What if they're beating her?"

"No," he answered himself. "No. Everything's fine with her. Otherwise, I would have known."

It's not that she was important to him — Artiom didn't want any memories of her, and all his feelings for Galia had blown away on the sea-winds.

No one expected it, but that same evening, they took Tkachuk, Gashidze and the one who fried a grouse.

"But they've already interrogated me today!" he yelped. "How much more of this?"

"Tkachuk!" Artiom called him, having come back to life and smiling in his new way.

He walked last, slowly. It seemed he didn't want to look around, but against his will, he turned. His eyes were almost completely empty, but they still sought any possible hope.

"May the earth sit lightly on you!" Artiom said without any pity or shame.

Some kind of final vein popped inside Tkachuk, and he only blinked.

It became expansive, pleasant in the room.

None of them came back.

* * *

On this new night, he slept well and had no fear that they would choke him in his sleep. With Tkachuk, they might have managed it, but without him… who here would do it?

"… There was something important but also shameful in those words that Tkachuk said last, about the horsemeat cooked in a pot…" thought Artiom, slightly more awake. This was his first morning thought.

He felt that there were about seven minutes left before the wake-up call and the hot water — in the corridor, he heard the voices of the guards and the banging of a full bucket against the wall.

It was quiet in the room. No one even snored.

"Sannikov!" Artiom barked from his place. "Confession time! Communion! Unction! Rrrrrring! Sannikov, who am I talking to? Enough sleeping, they've already sewn the burial shroud! They've fried the grouse, they've butchered the lamb, they've cooked the horsemeat — now they're going to eat you, you tow-headed roach."

Artiom's aggressive voice woke up everyone at once — someone jumped up, someone started swearing frantically, but not at anyone in particular this time, someone moaned from a horrible headache... Sannikov wept. He wept and ripped at his face with his long nails. He didn't have enough hair, and so he ripped his shirt into pieces — rip! — colored tatters hung down.

Artiom watched this from below with interest.

"Well then, you've got your fairness now," he said. "Up to now you've been treating yourself like a schoolboy. Now rip your pants."

Sannikov's eyes were huge, slightly insane, his neck was veiny, his Adam's apple was unnaturally large, his cheeks were sunken, like a Jesuit's, his lips were wet and always slightly open, his ears were large, his thin eyebrows almost didn't grow, his forehead was dirty, uneven — it seemed that sand or dust had stuck to him.

"At the same time, in childhood he was probably the nicest boy — a mischievous, big-eyed lad," thought Artiom distantly.

"Still, it sounds a bit clumsy," he goodheartedly shared his thoughts with the rest of the room. "Listen: the sentence is brought to accomplishment. Let's look, for example, at Sannikov — let's try to apply that phrase to him. Well, it's literally like a tie on his neck: 'seeeentence... is brought... to... accc... o... mplish... ment!' Or... are you listening, Sannikov? It feels like a worm is crawling along the stomach, extending its annular body: the sentence is brought to accomplishment... Can you feel it, yes?"

The room listened to Artiom as though he were unconquerable evil, something like a radio stuck inside a wall.

"Though it still sounds stupid and pompous as I don't even know what..." Artiom sneered slowly, once again sweetly stretching and massaging his temples with his strong hands. "First of all, 'the sentence is brought'. What sentence, where? What does it mean? Where in these words, for example, can we fit comrade Gorshkov? Then even more stupid: 'brought to accomplishment...' accomplishment? What has been accomplished? What is this? A school? A museum? A theater? Why should we bring the sentence there? Will they feed it there? After which ring will they let it into the hall? After the third or immediately after the first? What sort of accomplishment can you expect there? Will this be Gorshkov's favorite accomplishment? Will he be appreciated for it? Maybe he has no talent and there will be no accomplishment? He'll leave… unaccomplished? Maybe he'll write a complaint!"

"Gangrene, they're going to shoot you too," Gorshkov promised in a suppressed voice from above.

Artiom grabbed himself by the earlobe with two finger and held it. For some reason, his head worked better that way and his anger didn't recede.

"I'll let Sannikov's mommy know that he died properly," Artiom continued matter-of-factly. "Sannikov! You hear? I'll say: you sang the International before being shot. Then a few more songs… The execution was long, unhurried, triumphant. They gave speeches, honored him properly, poured out hot water for everyone. 'Sannikov sang about the monotonous bell too, Mommy, about the bell — that one was his favorite…' With the song on his lips, in short, he met his bullet… They didn't kill him with the first try. They had to, you know, finish him off… Then they added a bayonet in the stomach — Stab! That's just to make sure. He died beautifully."

Sannikov held his jaw in his hands, as though he were afraid that something vitally important would be vomited out.

"Why are you doing this?" even Moisei Solomonovich couldn't contain himself, and, getting up, stood in the middle of the room to cover Sannikov with his body. "What are you doing, Artiom? Where's your heart?"

He was truly bewildered and upset.

"Hey! Get out of there!" Artiom commanded, seriously angry and made a gesture as though he were planning on kicking Moisei Solomonovich. He ran away.

When they opened the door, everyone fell silent, even Artiom. Sannikov stopped weeping, only his lips quivered.

Everyone had memorized the order of noises — key, two turns, screech and the door opens.

If they're carrying hot water or gruel, there's two guards. If they're taking someone away, then there are three — the commander and two soldiers. If they were bringing out several, you could hear by the voices that there was a whole division of soldiers greeting you.

This time, two appeared in the doorway with the bucket. Everyone breathed out, but then everyone's restarted heart stopped again — after them appeared three more, and the senior of them held a paper in his hands.

"Attention! Up on your feet. Who's Gorshkov?"

Gorshkov stood closest of all to the exit, holding a mug.

"Who, I'm asking?" repeated the senior officer, looking past Gorshkov, who had frozen on the spot before him.

"What about the hot water?" asked Gorshkov quietly.

"You?" asked the senior officer. "Come out. You don't need hot water."

Gorshkov returned to the bolted-down table and with a too-fluid motion put down the empty mug. The weak clank of metal on wood sounded.

Turning around, Gorshkov loudly proclaimed, "Yes, we know about all of them. Kurilko, Gashidze, Curly — they're villains and con men. Tkachuk is a screwed-up Chekist who stayed longer than his term as a hired worker, a sadist and a lowlife. But me? I'm a Bolshevik, a communist, a member of the party since 1918, I fought in the war — how dare you take me! Take me to Nogtev, I order you! Immediately!"

He probably needed witnesses for this speech: he had decided that it would sound more convincing in front of witnesses.

"Yes, sir," said the senior officer with a sneer and waved his tobacco-stained fingers in a parody of a salute.

Gorshkov, not understanding, nodded and walked out.

For a minute, everyone stood without moving — what if they came back for someone?

Artiom's insides rejoiced and raged in equal measure.

He didn't really feel anything heavy or vengeful at that moment; on the contrary, he was filled with lightness and joy.

He took a mug left over from one of yesterday's doomed men, went to get some hot water, and they immediately made way for him.

Having drunk a little bit and not looking around, Artiom asked with fake solicitude, "Sannikov! Can you see how quickly they've started working? They're already cleaning the revolver for you. Let me wash you properly beforehand. Or else, who will think to wash you there? They'll just shove you in the earth as you are — dirty and snotty. Is that fair, I ask you?"

Dunking the mug right into the bucket, Artiom walked to Sannikov's bunk.

Sannikov pressed himself against the wall. Finding no words to answer, he bared his teeth and looked like an animal.

"Oh," said Artiom, looking the ringer in the mouth, "what excellent teeth! But tomorrow, it'll be a mouth full of earth."

Even though Sannikov only slept in a shirt, he smelled acrid and foul, as though he were hiding a rotten egg in his pants or in his cheek.

Suddenly he jumped up — Artiom didn't even understand the point of the gesture; turns out, that's how wretchedness gets up.

Jumping down from the bunks, Sannikov threw himself at the door, screaming and begging for help.

Artiom, despite the fact that everything was happening wildly and in a frenzy, managed to think with pleased malice, "… Oh, they'll help you, all right!"

Along the way, Sannikov overturned the bucket and all the rest of the hot water poured on the floor.

A rat ran across the puddle. It left a wet trace behind it.

No one appeared to answer the noise.

Sannikov wailed at the door like a homeless and abandoned child. His back shook.

* * *

Artiom now called his Chekist neighbors "corpses". Good morning, corpses. Corpse, move over. Corpse, get off the latrine, how long can it take? Corpse, don't stand at the window, you won't get enough air before you die. And you're blocking my sun.

All the next morning, Artiom walked the room and either evenly, or in a rattling ill-temper, beat one plate against another — all the ones who had been sent "under the store" had left plates — and at the same time he moaned something unpleasant, as though he were accompanying Sannikov on his final journey.

Once again, it was Moisei Solomonovich who complained first, pleading: "Artiom, please stop, I beg you."

"Shut up," answered Artiom shortly.

Having thought about it, he explicated, "The lads asked me to serve a humane memorial service."

For some time, Moisei Solomonovich was quiet, which made his eyebrows even bushier and his glasses slipped all the way to the edge of his porous, seemingly eternally oily nose.

Then he asked, "What lads?"

"Afanas, for example, asked me," answered Artiom, stopping the resonant "dong-dong" of the plates for a second.

Moisei Solomonovich, it seemed, didn't understand and only looked at Artiom a few times — at first over his glasses, then without his glasses, then in his glasses.

Sannikov lay with his face towards the wall, his legs pulled up, hugging his head with his arms, as though he were dead already.

At noon, those whom Artiom had taken to calling the "funeral company" appeared.

The unpleasant thing was that the senior officer was the soldier to whom Artiom didn't give his coat — for which he had promised to kill him not nicely, but unpleasantly.

Artiom swallowed his suddenly-disappearing saliva and begged, "No. Please, no." He stood there with the plates still in his hands.

"Get up! Sannikov!" barked the one who entered, paying no attention to Artiom or the plates.

"Him!" Sannikov, who was standing leaning against his bunks as though he were broken, unexpectedly pointed at Artiom. "He's Sannikov!"

Artiom, at first understanding nothing, looked around, then laughed and banged the plates, as though getting ready for a dance. It's a devil's comedy, when it's your time to die.

"Name?" the soldier asked Artiom.

"Ivan," Artiom answered readily, fooling around and enjoying himself immensely.

"What Ivan, moron?" said the soldier.

"Mitya."

"Which, damn you, Mitya?"

"Aliosha."

"Jackal! I'll kill you!" the soldier walked to Artiom. "What's your name? Last name!"

"I'm a Russian man. Goriainov Artiom."

"I'm just going to kill you all right now," yelled the soldier. "Where's Sannikov?" and he pulled the rifle from his shoulder — by the way, it had a bayonet affixed.

Sannikov was pushed out by his own fellow messed-up Chekists with black faces and eyes burned-out like alcohol.

Taking an unhappy step towards the doors, Sannikov sat down for no discernible reason. The soldier grabbed him by the hair and threw him out. Sannikov screamed.

Artiom waited half a minute, then jumped on the table, kicking off Gorshkov's mug, which was still standing there a day later. He looked through the window. He wanted to see it one more time — how they led him.

"A guard with a bayonet," said Artiom, as though mad. "Moisei Solomonovich, did you know that they call bayonets 'candles' here? They 'put up candles', get it? Afanasiev would have liked it. Enjoy it, Afanas. There is truth in the world. There is righteousness."

Before lunch, they took the last of the Chekists. Artiom didn't enjoy their exit — he was bored with it all. To accompany every single one of them was to give them too much honor.

Only when they closed the door did he sit down on his bunk, slowly stomping his feet.

He and Moisei Solomonovich were left alone.

For a moment, they sat opposite each other, silently looking each other in the eyes. But neither said anything.

During lunch, Moisei Solomonovich asked something of the guard in a whisper, and he unexpectedly answered, even pleasantly, and the answer wasn't short, but with certain details.

They brought enough gruel, if not for ten people, then for six at least. Moreover, Artiom had lost his appetite during the first days of his incarceration here and he wasn't planning on eating now. He was nourished by something else.

He poured a full bowl of gruel, then poured some directly into his mug — it's like fish soup, almost. He chewed half a piece of bread and sat down, awaiting the rat.

Other rats ran across the floor from time to time, but his bulging buddy was nowhere to be seen.

Moisei Solomonovich, as it turned out, was extremely scared of rats and as soon as he saw them, he hopped away to the other side of the room.

Not able to bear the utter silence of the room, he announced, "Your behavior, generally speaking, is loathsome and revolting. But I can respect your self-control. It sometimes seemed to me, Artiom, that you had gone mad, but now I understand that that's not the case. But I wanted to tell you something else. You and I have known each other for a while, and I couldn't keep this from you… the commission is leaving today… they've already gathered their things. Today or tomorrow morning. But more likely today. They've already executed all our neighbors. The neighboring room is also empty; they shot them all too. It's just you and I left. If we survive the coming hours, at most another night, we have… hope. Do you see how it all is?"

"Of course we'll survive," said Artiom and winked at Moisei Solomonovich: he was, after all, a fine chap. And he sang well.

Moisei Solomonovich smiled. His half-blind eyes expressed, in some way, exhilaration with this inappropriately strong young man.

"Perhaps then, at least, you won't play the plates anymore?" asked Moisei Solomonovich.

* * *

Artiom woke up very early in the morning, without even realizing that — he survived, he endured, it'll be all right! — he was quite sure of that anyway. It was dark outside, over the door was a vile lamp, someone was squeaking and moving under his bunk. He looked underneath and immediately recoiled in fear: there was an entire brood of rats tossing and turning there.

"What sort of an idiot are you?" Artiom swore furiously at his friend. "You gave birth to them and now you've brought them here for me to be impressed? You long-tailed creature!"

Moisei Solomonovich turned over and weakly called out, "What is it? What's the matter?"

"Sleep, I'm not talking to you," said Artiom. "The commission's left; now you'll live forever."

Overcoming his disgust, he once again looked under the bunk — yes, that's his rat, all right. She — much thinner than before — and her — one, two, three, four — ratlings.

The rat, seeing Artiom, stood on her hind legs.

"I got it, I got it," said Artiom. "You see me as your bridegroom. Well, I prepared yesterday."

On the top empty bunk stood a full plate of gruel, with thickly sprinkled bread in it. It was already covered with another plate. Artiom carefully lowered the feast down and put it at some distance from the rat.

Waiting until the rat started to eat — the plate started to rustle across the floor, and the sound was unpleasant, though for some reason it calmed him — Artiom began to fall back asleep.

Judging by the rustling, he guessed that Moisei Solomonovich had put on his glasses and was looking at the rat, experiencing an exceptional bout of disgust.

"Yesterday or the day before, Gorshkov ate from that place, stuffing his taut cheeks that only turned white for the first time when they were taking him away, and now, a rat is eating from there; there's some fairness in that. Maybe God is taking part in that," thought Artiom.

The dream that descended on Artiom was the sweetest.

That morning, another wonderful thing happened. No one woke them up at six.

As he was getting ready to wake up, untangling himself from his dream as from hot, sunny snares, Artiom explained to himself — the man is coming back inside me — I haven't quite become a beast. That's probably because we saved those foreigners, didn't let them die. A good deed preserved my soul and now my soul is in flower, and grasshoppers are tickling it.

The rat with her ratlings also took part, in some way, in his dream — it turned out that Artiom and Galia had also saved the rat and brought it back in their boat. That, naturally meant that Tom and Marie in that moment were under his bunk eating gruel — which wasn't quite true; though that would be their business, their business… The important thing was that everyone was warm — Artiom, the rat, Tom and his wife, or girlfriend, or bride…

He barely woke up right before lunch, having become even younger, as though there had never been any camp behind him, as though almost everyone that he knew hadn't died here.

They brought an amazing lunch — milled porridge with butter. The porridge smelled insistently of something meaty.

Artiom finally felt how hungry he had gotten during these past days. It's not even worth mentioning Moisei Solomonovich — he was almost dancing. The smell of the porridge inspired him extraordinarily.

He put himself two heaping plates — the guards had no problem with that. He and Moisei Solomonovich winked at each other, and no sooner had the door closed than he, holding those two plates in his hand, exclaimed, opening his already bulging eyes, "Artiom! Artiom! The commission's left! They've established order and left! Comrade Nogtev will once again take his place as head of the camp! Let's hope that they'll send us back to work soon! Do you have any technical or economical talents? I would take you in? What do you think?"

There was no point in hiding it — Artiom was also overjoyed. Premonitions are one thing, but news from the guard is something else. A guard is far more trustworthy than any angel.

"God exists, and we'll eat; God exists, and we'll eat," Artiom repeated quickly, mixing his porridge.

Suddenly he saw meat on the bottom of his plate — a huge, thick piece, not some tinned beef here, but — devil take it! — veal, probably! Or maybe even pork!

What a day!

Artiom slung the meat into his spoon and wanted to boast about it to Moisei Solomonovich: look here, have your fill! There is a God, there is! What do you think of His gift for long-suffering and torture?

Not able to wait for it, he attacked the piece of meat with his teeth. He immediately realized that it was a piece of rat dropping that had fallen from above.

He opened his mouth — everything fell out of there in a wet mess.

He licked his own hand for a long time after that.

He said nothing to Moisei Solomonovich — why ruin his lunch?

By that time, something indescribable flowered in his chest — as if he was about to throw up any moment. His chest seized as though in a fit — Artiom opened his mouth — damn it, let it be on the floor, I won't make it to the latrine in time, who cares… then he realized that he was weeping.

He wept and wept, and his head spun and shook, and his temples were breaking apart from the inside.

Moisei Solomonovich jumped up at first, then somehow realized that it would be better not to approach, so he sat down.

Artiom was woozy and felt vertigo. With all his strength, he grabbed the bunks. His chest was ripping apart and aching, his heart was pumping painful blood.

The fit ended in five or seven minutes.

Artiom, still shaking from the intensity of it, caressed himself on the face — calm down, calm down, calm down.

When he dropped his weak hands onto his knees, he immediately realized, by looking at his own palms, that there was not a single tear on them.

Ten minutes later, as he spit lightly on the floor, he whispered, "Well, that's OK, Lord. That's OK. I'm not mad at you. And don't be mad at me. I appreciated your joke. I hope you appreciate mine."

Artiom no longer paid attention to the rumbling of the locks — the fright had passed, and the rest would come, leaving only shit on his teeth.

They took Moisei Solomonovich along with his things, letting him know at once that he was to be returned to his work group.

They embraced in parting.

"Think of it, think of it!" Moisei Solomonovich kept repeating. "I'll find you some work when you come up with something you're good at."

The room was completely empty.

"Am I supposed to think about something important, my last thought?" Artiom asked himself.

Only now, in loneliness, did he realize how horrible it smelled here. They hadn't taken out the latrine today — from yesterday — it stank. They had finished shooting all the people and burying them in the icy ground; let their shit rot here, so to speak, in the warmth.

"Maybe that was the most important thought?" Artiom reflected.

Total exhaustion was just around the corner, for all his strength.

* * *

They finished interrogating Artiom and Galia together.

None of their story was being seriously accepted as possible.

The interrogation continued for more than an hour, and it turned out that the two Chekists — more than likely Galia knew them pretty well — didn't know what to do with them. On the one hand, it was some kind of idiotic, confused story, but on the other hand, she was the former girlfriend of Eichmanis himself — everyone knew about that.

It's possible that in their own time, these Chekists had watched Galia's walk with pleasure, and now look how it all turned out!

They asked Artiom little — what were you incarcerated for, how did you end up in Sekirka, what do you remember from your schoolboy days about geography and the natural sciences, do you have any technical know-how? But in general he had the feeling that in their understanding Galia had taken him with her like you might take a dog — and what can you ask a dog?

Everything happened in the same office of the IID where Artiom had been interrogated the last time. On the windowsill, the full ashtray still stood. It's doubtful that it had been standing there from the time the commission left, but Artiom liked to think, for some reason, that no one here dared throw out the ashes left over from the Muscovite guests — what if they came back?

Galia looked irritated, old, flabby — a dilapidated, middle-aged woman. But she acted with some dignity. The commission had left, so who would kill her now? Who would touch her? Nothing would happen to her — that's how she acted.

Artiom looked at her rarely and thought that it was impossible that he could ever have been with her — that was some kind of dream, some kind of delusion… and even if he had been mad, then even so, she was no wife or sister to him, but… a passer-by.

Galia didn't look at Artiom at all. And she was right — why should she look at him?

"… Yes, I heard you, I get it," the young Chekist grimaced, looking first at Galia, then at his fellow interrogator, but never at Artiom. "Just explain one thing to me. Why did you go with an inmate who really doesn't know much, as far as we can tell, about flora or fauna…?"

"He worked on Fox Island. He worked with Eichmanis. I have reasons to trust him. I couldn't just take anyone," Galia repeated, looking into the small window where it uncomfortably snowed in the dim pre-winter sun.

It seemed that what most irritated her was that they spoke to her using the informal "you".

On the table of the one asking the questions, Galia's papers were laid out — a map that she had used, with notes that she had made in her own hand and the notebooks taken from the foreigners.

"It's hard to avoid the suspicion that you wanted to flee…" said the Chekist after a pause, raising his eyes from the map.

He wanted more than anything for Galia to resolve these doubts for him.

"You're all so useless," said Galia quietly. "We found spies for you. We detained them, brought them into the camp. If we were fleeing, why would we bring them here? We would have continued on our merry way! Call Eichmanis already, will you? He'll tell you all about me."

Ignoring the proposition to call Eichmanis, the Chekist rocked on his chair and said, "We still need to determine whether they're even spies."

"So go and determine," answered Galina, grimacing as though she had a headache. "And stop wasting my time on these… conversations. The commission already interrogated me. Do you have any reason to think their work was unsatisfactory? Or perhaps that they were too humane?"

The Chekists looked at each other. One of them sneered. The other grimaced.

In the next room, a noise erupted — someone, probably the secretary, got up from his place, the chair rumbled, and the objects on his table sang in concert.

The head of the camp, Nogtev, walked in. His glance was heavy, and it looked like someone had poured sand into his eyes — they were dull and vague.

He didn't even see Artiom.

"What is this creature going on about?" asked Nogtev, not speaking to anyone in particular. He came up to the table, picked up some paper, and threw it back down again.

Two people answered at the same time — Galia herself and one of the Chekists.

"She's sticking to her story — they were making maps, she's still referring to Eichmanis," the Chekist said quickly, getting up from his place.

"I'm a fighter in the Red Army," Galia said slowly.

Nogtev's jaw twitched.

"Three years for the bitch," he said, not looking at Galia and already on the way out; then he remembered something, and, stopping in the doorway, even a little more cheerful, added, "Burtsev's papers include a report from one of the leopards that she was messing about with an inmate… right on the roof! Maybe it was with you?" and he moved his eyes, full of dull sand, at Artiom.

Turned out he had seen him after all.

"No," said Artiom, feeling that a huge monastic wall was falling on him, and there was no way out. He had never heard himself utter anything with such a voice — it was the voice of a man who had the right only to speak one word, but that word wouldn't change anything.

"Like anyone here cares," laughed Nogtev, showing unexpectedly white and very strong teeth. "You're still going to die, jackal."

"What sort of nightmare is going on here? I'm going to write to Fiodor. What's going on?" said Galia, getting up.

Every phrase uttered by her was strained and fell flat.

"She's only talking about herself…" Artiom understood. No one was talking about him anymore.

Though they still hadn't condemned him to death. They had said nothing about him yet.

"Three years for 'willful AWOL.'" Repeated Nogtev, not looking at Galia. "Let her be glad that we aren't finding out about her prostitutes, or we might find something and…" He left.

The door slammed against its frame and squeaked, staying half open.

The secretary slowly went — for some reason everyone listened to those steps — and firmly shut the door. Probably that was his constant work responsibility.

Galia, without strength, lowered herself onto the chair and sat, biting her lip. She couldn't believe it.

The young Chekists looked at each other again. What their glance meant, Artiom couldn't guess.

"You'll all be punished for this, you understand?" Galia said, barely audibly, as though in that moment, her voice had disappeared.

"The administrative board of the camp has the legal right to convict, Galina. You know that," said the Chekist, not looking her in the eye. While she was almost an equal, he used the informal "you", now he switched to the formal address. The quick transfer of the former employee of the camp into the number of prisoners seemingly had raised her in his estimation… or rather, it made her more distant.

"Nogtev gave an illegal order. The commission will return and he will have nothing again, and they'll bury you on Sekirka," said Galia, drawing in air. By the time she said "Sekirka", her voice returned and almost rang out.

The Chekist who was standing and who hadn't spoken yet, looked at Galina with a long look and answered impartially and heavily: "No need to scare anyone here. Or you'll be the first to get to Sekirka."

Galia suddenly looked at Artiom: helpless, like a woman, open. It was so unexpected. "Can it be true?" that's what her glance said.

"What about him?" asked the seated Chekist, nodding at Artiom.

Artiom felt his blood rush to his head — just as stupidly and furiously as the snow in the window, only it was hot, hot.

The second Chekist, waiting very briefly, decided: "He said three years for her. So we'll add three years for him too."

He pulled on his cigar contentedly. Their ashes were on the windowsill.

* * *

Everything in Artiom's face became small — small eyes that never looked straight, thin lips that never hurried to smile. His gestures became impersonal, erased. A not very sick, not very well person.

He adopted the strange habit of never showing his naked body — neck, chest, hands — his hands were always in his pocket, but if he was working, they were in old mittens.

He also never showed his teeth.

The words he uttered were rare, ragged, as though they were merely the wrappers of his words — weighing nothing, impossible to grasp. If the wind blew, the words would disappear.

It was better without words, completely.

His every movement was quick, but invisible, having no direct reference to any object or action. He looked like he was eating, but then he wasn't really, and he never really sat where he was sitting either. He looked like he was darning something, but then there wasn't a needle and thread in his hands, and he himself disappeared as though someone had pulled him by a string and then loosened them.

No gesticulations.

Always a little unshaven, but not enough to call it a beard. Always a little unwashed, but not enough to attract attention with his smell — no smell at all.

He was always ready to steal, and would sometimes even give some food to others. But when he saw food, he showed it absolutely no preference.

If a prostitute offered him to join her line, he might agree, but in any other moment, he felt nothing about women and didn't even watch the women's brigade walk by.

He no longer divided people into good and bad. People were divided into "dangerous" and "the rest". Towards both he felt no emotions. People are people — he had no more questions to ask them.

He could smile at the commanders, but he could also push any one of them into a hole in the ice and wait until he drowned.

He never counted the remaining days of his incarceration; he was filled with the days of his previous life. But he couldn't remember that life any more.

Memory is like a cold. Your head hurts from it and your eyes tear up.

His life was chopped in half by a shovel, like a worm — what he left behind lives on its own. His childhood doesn't ask to be returned.

He knew nothing about the world beyond the boulders of Solovki, and if he dreamed of freedom, it was like the autumn, icy sea — that freedom had no boundaries and no pity. It was naked and empty.

"Both in prison and in freedom the skies are the same," said *Vladychka* John, but Artiom, if he even thought about it, would have found his words unnecessary and pointless.

Vladychka John wasn't around anymore either, because nothing exists unless it's in front of your eyes.

Father Zinovii had been there a short while back.

Artiom had seen in passing how he had said to Nogtev, "It wasn't enough for you to betray him; you wanted to kill Christ a second time. After all, the soldier who pierced His side is a saint! And the Red Army, if you look closely, also wants to be holy."

Nogtev answered, "You don't say!"

Zinovii was mocking; Nogtev was mocking.

Only Nogtev's mocking was more dependable, because they soon sent Zinovii back to Sekirka.

There were always many people who wanted something — they're all attracted by something, like children.

The inmates drew on themselves — crosses, skulls, cupolas, nasty notes about the Chekists. What can be stupider than that useless activity — to draw on oneself? You can sew a metal can to your leg, and walk like that — why not if you can draw on your own back?

The inmates sought protection, entertainment, friendship, conversation, amusement, warmth. From this entire list, all they really needed was warmth. You have to answer, even for favors.

His brigade, for now, was the fourteenth — the untouchables. Here they put all the people who were inclined to run. They couldn't leave the monastery walls.

Everything in its own time.

The best place was in the shade; the best work was at night. At night, the dangerous people were tired, the guards were stupider and saw less. At night, it was easy to get mixed up with other people, to not even distinguish yourself from other people.

It was also easier to not think or remember at night.

Krapin sent his things from Fox Island, including his mother's pillow. He felt something human towards that pillow that poked his heart, so he soon traded it for something else.

Those who just arrived in the camp read the newspapers as though it was news from the other world, not this physical world, but news still came from there.

In his brigade, nearly no one knew him by name. They heard his last name during the inspections; that was enough.

Artiom acted as though he had no name. He was a citizen of Solovki.

On the last boat of autumn, the last group of inmates arrived.

There were many green, young, toothy, stupidly smiling, stupidly scared people. They were afraid, and, overcoming their fear, they asked those who they thought might answer them.

One of them came up to Artiom in the yard, at the shop, for some reason distinguished him among the rest, or maybe he asked everyone he met and hoarded the answers.

He asked: how is it?

Artiom looked to the side. He breathed in and breathed out. Nodded: go be.

He could have answered: like this.

If in more detail, then here you go: God exists, but He doesn't need our faith. He's like air. Does the air need us to believe in it?

What do *we* need, though? That's a different question.

Later on, they'll say that here was hell. But here was life.

Death is also a kind of life. You have to grow into that thought, you won't just understand it if you think superficially.

As for hell? It's just one form of life, nothing too scary.

But he said nothing, shrugged, nodded at Schelkachov — Schelkachov had come to the shop to buy paper and a pencil; he loved to explain everything.

Artiom bought himself a cup of milk and drank it slowly, standing, not facing the people, or they might see his face, but not with his back to them either — they might push him in the back. He stood sideways.

Rare snowflakes fell into the milk.

He returned into his sleeping quarters, lay down on his bunk. It was neither on the top nor on the bottom. It was in the middle.

He had pulled his seal coat inside out and had sewn some kind of rags on top — what turned out was exactly the kind of ugliness that was necessary. At the very least, no soldier would ask for it. He never took it off, not even in his sleeping quarters. He even slept in it.

* * *

The same boat, named "Gleb Bokii", returned Osip Troianskii into the camp.

He had disappeared. They had to look for him on the mainland and take him under guard.

In honor of catching Troianskii, they lined up the fourteenth brigade, including the female contingent of untouchables — it turned out there was a decent number of them too.

November was waning.

The inmates stood facing each other.

The male brigade was lined up in two rows, but only one for the women — both the first and the second were lined up by height.

On the wall of the Transfiguration Church, only recently, they had drawn factory chimneys, an airplane and a red star. Over all this was emblazoned the slogan: "Long live free and joyful labor!"

Artiom at first looked at the airplane.

He thought: airplane.

Then he saw Galia.

Galia had cut her hair. She stood without a hat.

"In three years, that hair will grow out and be like it was. As if nothing had happened," someone whispered to Artiom.

She nodded at him.

He didn't answer. What was the point? He just blinked. She would still not understand from that side of the square whether he answered her or not.

They stood for a long time — Galia now had a head covering of snow on her head. She didn't notice.

The untouchable women were talking to each other and joking, but no one turned to Galia. It seemed that they treated her as a pariah.

She had rubber boots on, awkward and dirty. Artiom had never seen her in such boots. Moreover, some of the untouchables were dressed well, even in modish boots with a heel — but that was easy to explain. Many of them worked in the stables, taking care of the Chekists horses, and… well, the Chekists too.

Troianskii stood four people to the right of Artiom. Only Artiom was in the second row, Troianskii was in the first. There were several bruises on his face — they probably beat him upon arrival, to congratulate him on his return.

Troianskii slouched and held his arms strangely, bent at the elbow — as though they wouldn't extend properly. With such arms, he looked like a bird. All the birds had flown away, but this one had just flown in.

By the second hour, Nogtev finally arrived. He looked drunk, he walked heavily, as though filled with wet sand, but firmly.

The inmates loudly exclaimed, "Good!" Here, for the most part, were experienced inmates. They didn't want to stand outside any longer than necessary.

The inspection began unexpectedly. They read the inmates a short report concerning the work of the commission on the liquidation of all infractions committed by the administration of the camp.

This number of people were found guilty and disciplined. Those that were taken off their posts and moved into the ranks of the prisoners were this many. That many were convicted and shot.

The untouchable brigade drew themselves together and frowned. The numbers sounded cruel and sharp, as though they were metal.

"If only there were such inspections every day," said someone in front of Artiom.

Artiom didn't like the fact that such words were spoken right next to him — they might think it was him.

Then they announced an order that all personal clothing was to be confiscated — all inmates would now wear the same uniform.

Nogtev, listening how they were reading his command out loud, slowly turned his head, watching the inmates. He was in a cap, raincoat and boots. It all looked good on him.

The third order had to do with the complete exit of all former inhabitants of the monastery — the monks and monastic workers. They were going straight back to the mainland to take full part in the life and construction of the Soviet Republic.

The fourth order informed them that due to the many infractions of order and insufficient work standards, there would be no early pardons this year. By the beginning of the spring seagoing weather, the inmates of the camp of Solovki had to show worthy results. All those who deserved an approval, including pardons, would then be approved and pardoned.

At these words, Nogtev slightly rocked in place, and this movement seemed to wake him up. He moved his jawed and unexpectedly walked along the first row.

The Chekist who had been reading the orders immediately fell silent.

"Discipline!" said Nogtev; his voice was full and powerful, as though it was made of meat. With such a voice, it didn't matter what he was saying, any word had immediate weight. "We require discipline!"

The head of the camp walked to the place where Troianskii stood and stopped.

He had sought and now found the one he needed.

"Inmate Osip Troianskii," announced Nogtev, "was sent on a free, unguarded research journey as a specialist-scientist. He needed to do some necessary research, but he had to return in time for the holiday of November 7. The day of the revolution. Osip Troianskii attempted to flee. A special division was sent to find him. Osip Troianskii was detained."

Nogtev beat Troianskii with every word, as you beat a nail into a cobblestone. The nail was bending.

Artiom felt his front teeth ache, as though he was holding something hard in them.

"When inmate Osip Troianskii left, it was announced to him that if he failed to return within the allotted time, every tenth person in his brigade would be shot," Nogtev uttered his heavy words in a quotidian manner. "The administration of the camp is required to keep to its word."

Nogtev waved his powerful arm in the air — let it be so! The hand was gloved.

Two Chekists ran out — one in fidgety indecision stood next to the women's division, as though they had offered him to pick a wife, while the other, counting off the frozen people, walked along the male rows.

The first Chekist, after a few seconds, poked the tenth woman and immediately turned away from her and went further. She screamed as though they had torn her skirt to pieces, and under the skirt her hidden child hung by the umbilical cord.

The Chekist who was walking along the men's row got confused and started counting again.

Artiom saw how those who were counted from seven to nine melted and the one who realized he was "ten" became so white that you couldn't distinguish it from the snow on her cheek.

The first Chekist came to the end of the female line and pointed at Galia who stood second to last.

"How small she is," thought Artiom distantly.

"All because she's without heels," he understood.

"If she was in heels now, they'd have counted differently," Artiom kept thinking faster and faster.

His heart pumped cooled-off blood.

Everyone who stood next to him was trying to count those to his right — that wasn't hard, but everyone was getting confused and starting over, their eyes running back and forth. Their pupils jumped from place to place.

Galia stood before her row, bewildered like a child. The second doomed woman quietly wailed.

They pulled one out of the male row — like a tooth.

Those who stood not far away from him seemed to feel better; their soul became light as silk or down.

But around Artiom, everyone was oppressed as though their spirit had swollen up in advance, engorging with blood, hanging like a sack filled with stones.

The Chekist miscounted again. He couldn't figure out whether he needed to count Troianskii or not. What about the foremen? The commanders of divisions? He looked at Nogtev, but didn't dare ask — the head of the camp was looking down somewhere, at the cobblestone under his foot, barely rocking his massive body. His boots frowned in the places where they bent as though they were predatory, alive.

The Chekist started counting everyone.

Artiom measured out his fate with his eyes one more time. He was number eighteen. Number twenty, his old acquaintance Zahar, stood near to him and understood everything already.

"It's me," he breathed out with his second to last hot breath into the snow at his face. "It's me, my God. What on earth? It's me."

Artiom raised his eyes and looked at Galia.

Galia looked around herself as though she saw nothing, moving her fingers as though wanting to touch the air around her and afraid to do it. She was completely alone, as though on an ice floe. She looked like her hair had turned white.

"Switch places with me. You hear? You'll stay alive," Artiom suddenly commanded Zahar.

He, understanding nothing, uncomplainingly switched places with him, interlaced his fingers into a lock and stared with mad eyes at the counter, to read the salvific "eighteen" on his lips. Or "eight", depending on how the Chekist started his new ten.

"You!" commanded the soldier, poking Artiom with a finger.

They parted before Artiom so respectfully as never before in his life.

He walked forward.

Galia jerked and came to herself — she saw him.

"… What sort of vigilante justice is this?" yelled Troianskii, as though they had just pulled out the gag from his mouth. "What sort of vigilante justice is this!" he repeated, shrieking. After all, two such phrases should cost more than just one.

"Guards, line up!" commanded Nogtev, lightly out screaming Troianskii.

They had never before shot people in the square, but after the way the commission did its work, nothing would surprise them.

The soldiers, hurrying and stomping their boots, lined up.

From the male group, they quickly — they were themselves disgusted by what they were doing — pulled out another twelve people.

Troianskii kept shrieking until the one who had long ago finished counting the women and who now stood without anything to do came up to him and swung his revolver right at Troianskii's teeth.

Holding his mouth, Troianskii fell on his knees.

On the faces of the soldiers appeared a slow, glassy, almost drunk expression, typical of people who were about to kill their own kind. A few held their rifles more firmly. Their knotty fingers were wet from melting snow.

Artiom smiled at Galia.

Galia looked him in the eyes and breathed with an open mouth.

Artiom remembered that mouth, its warm, feminine, impossible breathing.

Nogtev, it seemed, had grown tired of the show and suddenly laughed.

Having had his fill, he walked away from the square in the direction of the gates.

"Get to work, jackals!" he commanded, raising his head somewhere to the sky, as though he were speaking to angels.

The Chekists looked at Nogtev's back in indecision.

But it was all obvious already.

They dismissed them all.

AFTERWORD

The phone number of the daughter of Fiodor Ivanovich Eichmanis was given to me by a retired colonel of state security, a reader of patriotic newspapers, a demagogue filled a sense of his own dignity and false significance. However, he wasn't all unpleasant, a good host, not bad to have a drink with. At a certain moment in life, former soldier and old comics become similar; there's something to that, isn't there?

The colonel was showing me the photographs of his children. He offered to play chess. I watched as he placed the pieces — the last time he played was twenty years before, and I was worried I'd embarrass myself. But in vain…

I lost terribly, bringing him great joy.

"Another cognac?"

I hope you're not also an amateur fencer, comrade colonel.

He cited this and that acquaintance, pointing either up or down or sideways with his eyes, as though he used to work as an air traffic controller in his former job. He had nothing good to say about his highly placed colleagues, who had remained in power one way or another, though he did it generally, not concretely. He didn't like the opposition — it seemed that he knew something only known to the elect about every single one of them. However, he clearly understood nothing about the subject that he himself started. Behind every word, you could hear: now if only he had been the one in charge, not all of these jokesters and troublemakers, then…

He could never have been able to take care of any of it, as though they had a long time ago cut out the organ that was in charge of making his own contrary or defiant decisions.

A clean cut, six stitches, the scar disappeared a long time ago, you can't find it with any magnifying glass, where that organ used to be. You can hit it with a little hammer to listen how his strong body (his garden helps him keep his physique) is completely empty inside. But that requires a different legend, and it's not my job. I pretended to be a journalist, not a masseur.

The colonel, in general, lived not very richly. Looking past the children (the children were typical, well fed since childhood) on the photographs, I approximately understood what his country house constituted — well, it was funny, but in such houses, only one floor higher and one floor deeper, the drivers of these same officers, for whom the rank of major was the absolute ceiling, now live.

I tried to guess how many such colonels and generals, not to put too fine a point on it, or even marshals, sit and burn with the fire of their words a shot glass of cognac, a flowery tablecloth on the table, a clock over the fireplace, their own portrait with medals from governments of half the known world (part of the aforementioned countries have already run off the map, while the medals — there they all are, longer-lived than any empire), a portrait of the commander-in-chief — "Who else? We are servants of the government" — an icon with a namesake saint of the colonel, only with a beard, but an excellent intercessor, as God sees — he had saved him many times while under fire, "... I remember, in Afghanistan, our forces were already retreating..." a German shepherd on a leash in the yard (it barks like a moron, the doghouse hopping from its anger)... I imagined, basically, a whole number of these humiliated and insulted, angered and uncooperative soldiers, and I understood that you could fill any Winter Palace with the bodies of such men. Put them all up in a single phalanx, and it would be a stronghold that even the Americans don't show in their movies, you can fall over from terror!

... He helped me out with the phone number, and I no longer saw him; not even to thank him. He had the idea to write the thing together — his idea, our collaborative effort, so I immediately decided that the acquired number (in essence, it's just a bunch of numbers, I know them all, it's just a matter of putting them together properly) didn't require any gratitude from me.

Interestingly, the colonel didn't know the last name "Eichmanis" — though he had a stout bookcase filled with books on the subject in his office: why people were incarcerated, who destroyed it, the breakdown of the underground resistance, the death of the empire, the demons of the revolution, destruction, then renaissance, then destruction again.

I told him who he was — Eichmanis. The colonel only offered the possible nationality of my hero. He guessed, but I didn't press him on it.

The daughter immediately picked up the phone.

She had never heard of me and saw no reason for meeting me. Naturally, her last name was different. Her voice wasn't so much young as energetic, its sound was like — you know when dry twigs burn and loudly crack — it was like that.

"But he's your father?" I pressed her, already understanding that nothing would work out.

"What do you need?" she asked.

She waited while I searched for the answer, which had got lost in my throat, and, not appreciating my throat-singing, hung up the phone.

The next day, she called me back herself: come by, I'll help however I can, though I doubt I'll be useful.

I would never have guessed her age based on her appearance.

That is, by most tragic calculation (she was born a few months after Eichmanis was buried on the Butovo polygon), she was born in 1939.

But she didn't look at all seventy-five! No. She was a calm, middle-aged woman given to smiling. She wore a conservative suit without any jewelry on her fingers.

Elvira Fiodorovna.

Her apartment was clean, there was a lot of wood, good rugs on the floor, a chandelier with kerosene lamps — everything was precisely planned, though there was no sense that a man lived or even visited there regularly. It seemed she lived alone. It was even unclear whether or not any guests visited — the air was that empty.

I sincerely shared my pursuits with her and gave her a few chapters. She put them on the table, petting them reflexively. Her hand was thin and strong. Her nails were feminine, looked-after, unpainted or covered in colorless polish, I can't tell the difference.

"Do you have any photographs of him?" I asked and looked at the walls.

For some reason, as I walked up the staircase, it seemed that there should be some likeness of the father on the walls — here he's overseeing inspections in Solovki, there he's walking in the Red Square, there he's with his wife and they're laughing.

There were no photographs on the walls. None at all. In the bookcase, there was nothing but the classics — the latest of them was Chekhov. Not even any Gorky. Well, yes, there was Nabokov, but only the Russian Nabokov. There was probably Bunin as well, but I didn't see.

She got up, opened a panel, and got out an album — it lay on top, seemingly prepared for my visit.

"Here, a few."

Eichmanis hunting, that was a photograph from Solovki. He was smiling, with a mustache for some reason, very good-looking, in a sweater, without a hat, tall boots, a rifle…

And that one's on Vaigach: the impressing architecture of his powerful face — half in shadow, half in light — a powdered eyebrow, the nostril of a predator, a proud lower lip, eyes with a large, egg-like white — all of this fate molded carefully in the icy winds; fate put in the effort, and it worked. Eichmanis looked like an inquisitor, but not in a black cap, but in a white fur coat.

Eichmanis in uniform, a late photograph, looking older than his years, a straight glance, straight lips, straight line of the forehead.

Eichmanis in a group of soldiers; moreover, it even looked like those in civilian clothing were also soldiers. That's probably Gleb Bokii. Strange, but in other Soviet photographs similar to this one, it was always clear who was higher in status, even without epaulets and with indistinct diamonds on the shoulder. The pose, the expression of the eyes, the place in the center or on the edge — these signs are always telling.

"Here he's with mother." The "he" sounded detached.

What can I say? In this sense, his taste was ideal. Perfect eyes, eyelashes, breasts. Such women look wonderful next to military men and at parties.

Even on the photograph, it seemed that her cheek was cold, almost icy, while if he were to come very close, he could see the tiniest, almost invisible hair on the cheekbones. If you were to grab her neck with your hand, a bit rougher than was necessary (with the thumb and index finger resting on the base of the skull), and not let go.

For some reason, I searched with my eyes to see if any gramophone was still in the house.

"They lived here?" I asked.

"Mama lived here," answered Elvira Fiodorovna.

"Is it true that she was the daughter of an inmate and Fiodor Ivanovich promised an immediate pardon to her father if she would agree to marry him?"

"I think that's an apocryphal story."

"But she was the daughter of an inmate?"

Elvira Fiodorovna gave me the album, which up to this point she had held on her knees, and calmly answered, "Yes, my grandfather was incarcerated on Solovki. He lived to be ninety-six years old and never spoke about that time. He recently died…" And Elvira Fiodorovna looked somewhere to the side of the kitchen, as though I came about forty minutes late to the conversation about Solovki, which had been drinking tea, and then a white-winged team came for it and took it away.

A teapot whistled in the kitchen.

Elvira Fiodorovna — I quickly leafed through the album while she was gone — used to be good-looking in youth.

A few minutes later, she returned with a platter — two cups, a silver sugar basin and chocolate.

"Will you write about Mama as well?" Elvira Fiodorovna asked, putting the platter on a low table next to the couch.

"Your mother? No."

"Good," it seemed that she was sincerely happy to hear about that.

I had many questions about Fiodor Eichmanis, and I, trying out the hot water with my lips (she made strong black tea without asking for my preference), asked a few of them. Did she know…? Did she remember…? Did she ever meet…?

Seven times Elvira Fiodorovna answered "No." She didn't want to upset me: just—no.

"I have a few archival videos. A few years ago, my friends made me this complication; they thought I might find it interesting."

"But you're not interested?" I was surprised.

"I watched it," she answered after a pause. "I'm not sure what sort of feelings I'm supposed to experience when I watch it."

Two crossed white lines on the black screen, and immediately, a line of energetic inmates walked somewhere, moving forward, almost at a trot.

The stone interiors of the monastery of Solovki, the quickly etched-out faces of the Red Army soldier — all of them, as though chosen in advance, had insane eyes. They all stared at the camera.

Nogtev — strong jawed, speaks as though he chews old, sinewy meat. A few times, he tried to smile, but he's not capable of it.

Oh, there's Fiodor Eichmanis. The deportment, the thinness. Very calm; he doesn't see the camera, though there's probably such a racket around it.

"I think that's… that's Galia," I said aloud. "Galia, there you are. I've recognized you!"

I was a little disillusioned. She was angular, a bit fat, not as pretty as I thought.

Though that was just the camera, the camera. In life, everything was different.

Elvira Fiodorovna quickly looked at me.

"You know who that is? Galina Kucherenko? You know?" I hurried to ask her, even nudging the platter with my knee, making my tea spill over. She drank two thirds of her cup.

Without answering, Elvira Fiodorovna looked at the screen, and I looked back again — there was Nogtev again, Eichmanis again… then it was only railroad tracks and "Gleb Bokii", the ship.

"You would like to kill my father one more time?" my hostess asked me. "That's a pointless task; he's not going to come back to life."

"No, not to kill him," I said, not looking away from the screen. Maybe Artiom Goriainov might run by, maybe Burtsev might ride by on his horse, demanding to taste the lunch in advance, Shlabukovskii might walk by, swinging his cane.

"Not to justify him? Do you even have… the words… for that?" Elvira Fiodorovna looked at me, and, naturally, I turned back to her. My God, she was ready to laugh! If she didn't do that, it was only because of her excellent taste — women of her age don't look good when laughing, especially in the presence of a young man.

"I have very little love for the Soviet government," I answered, slowly choosing the words. "But those who especially hate it are the kind of people whom I abhor, as a rule, even more."

She nodded: I understand.

"And that helps me make my peace with it," I added.

This time, she didn't react at all, as though she suddenly understood everything about me.

It was time to leave.

"One last question, with your permission. Maybe your mother told you? Did he speak French?"

"He spoke German."

"But not French?"

"No. I think not."

We parted rather formally. I went outside and walked to the closest café. There was a free spot in the corner, with its back to the entrance, as I prefer.

"Hello," said the waitress.

I nodded amicably.

"Do you know why no one ever greets the waitresses?" she asked.

It was an unexpected, but in my case an appropriate statement.

"I apologize," I answered. "Hello."

I ordered some tea and a little bit of vodka. To drink vodka and finish it off with tea — that's not bad at all. You can do it with sweet tea or without sugar — tastes differ.

The waitress went to wait at other tables, but I kept an eye on her — she deserved to do more than work in a café. But I thought about something else.

Russian history gives examples of extraordinary degrees of vileness and infamy. Still, we're not an anomaly among all nations, though we do have the habit of trying to convince all other nations that we are an anomaly, and they believe us. Maybe that's the only thing that they do believe about us.

However, our distinction from them lies in the fact that we punish ourselves very quickly and with our own hands — we don't require other nations to do it for us; though, sometimes, they still try, and always at the moment when we, let's say, have already broken our own legs, have pulled out a veiny eye, and, bleeding and gurgling, we lie, gently caressing the earth with our hands.

The Russian man doesn't feel sorry for himself; that's his most unique characteristic.

In Russia, everything happens by God's permission. He has nothing to do here.

No sooner has He, tired and wrathful, raised His punishing hand and turned at us, He suddenly sees — we've done it to ourselves already. Our ribs are exposed, our intestines have been pulled out, there's a compound fracture of the spine, the head had been crushed. Countless insects are crawling over what's left of the face.

"At least don't play the fool for Christ, you, Russian man."

No, you hear me, I'm not playing the fool for Christ, no! I'm singing.

... It's exactly in a café that you should think about such things, slightly the worse for wear, because if anything like this comes to you when you're sober, standing in the autumn field or next to a ruin of ancient walls or on the shore of a sea that is white from cold, then there's something wrong with you.

Elvira Fiodorovna called me a week later and offered that I come back for a short visit.

I took my things and drove; why should I tell her that I don't live close enough just to drop by?

I thought that she would have some comments on my manuscript, but that wasn't it. She just announced laconically, "I read it." Then she calmly added, "It's your business."

On the table where the telephone stood, there lay a rather heavy folder of papers.

"This is for you…" said Elvira Fiodorovna. "These are the diaries of that woman whom you recognized on the photograph during your last visit… They were in my mother's archives. Evidently, my father somehow confiscated them and took them off Solovki when they transferred him to Moscow. It's strange that he never destroyed them. It's possible he was sentimental — such people are often sentimental. I don't know. I read them a few times in my youth; it affected me deeply. A quarter of a century ago, I read it again, with much less enthusiasm and even thought about publishing them. But I decided that hardly anyone needed it, and basically considered it lacking in usefulness. Though, as I now understand, you think otherwise. So take it: in any case, it might help with your work."

When I opened it, already in the entryway, my head spun. This was impossible; this doesn't happen and just couldn't be. In my joy, I dropped all the pages. I gathered them from the staircase as I descended, laughing.

APPENDIX: THE DIARY OF GALINA KUCHERENKO

December 17:

I wanted to fool myself, to start my diary with what should worry me. About what I imagined the path of my life would resemble, or the way of our revolution. And yes, that does worry me.

But I still want to write about something else.

I remember him constantly. From the morning, even before I get up. I imagine what he's doing there, in his huge house. He always wakes up cheerful, a face as though he just ate snow — his teeth shining, his lips red, his eyes exhilarated.

He's so cheerful that he just doesn't care about anything. He's going to hunt today.

December 20:

Yesterday, we sledded down the hill on icons that we had covered in water, then frozen. He came and started to yell at us, even picking up a few icons. D. (he had just been writing) immediately ran to pick them all up and carry them away.

F. handed them over, cursing crudely all the while, and I saw those white spots on his as-though-frozen skin that I love so much.

All this because he has some kind of new passion — a museum. He was probably talking with one of the inmates, who had explained how much an old icon could cost. Or something else about culture. F. didn't have enough culture in childhood, and he wants there to be culture. It's funny sometimes. Or I'm just mad at him.

For his eyes, they sometimes call him "Engels". Fiodor Engels, or even "Engelis". In front of me, they try not to call him that. Everyone knows about everything.

(Evening of the same day, I remembered.)

It was in September.

F. didn't go, but I did. It was in the church of the Transfiguration. They found two cases walled in a niche in the southern wall. On one was written "Zosima", on the other — "Savvatii". It was funny — like a cookie or furniture. So they wouldn't get mixed up.

They brought in the bishop of Tula, the bishop of Gdov and *Vladychka* John was there too — that's how they call him here, "*Vladychka*". Kogan was head of the commission. They opened the relics of St. Zosima. They put them next to the coffin. There was nothing but bones and debris. Just as I thought. Even as they opened it, I didn't have a moment's doubt.

Kogan asked, "That's the patron saint?" He kicked the skull against the wall with the nose of his boot.

At that point, F. didn't care about it at all.

(Even later.)

Women always like to read others' letters more than men do. I take notes from the inmates, I read them and it arouses me. I want to be able to write like that to someone.

"Come to the woodshed, my beauty. Your famous lover."

I want to come to the woodshed. What stupidity, my beauty. I have to take myself in hand, finally.

(Even later.)

F. allowed the inmates the following — if a person bought two tickets to the movie theater, he could give the second one to a woman in the female barracks. He could even sit next to his friend during the showing.

They sit in their heavy overcoats (its cold) and fondle each other under the coat flaps.

No one will send me a ticket. I'm free.

December 22:

Summer passed so quickly.

I remember spring — the snow lies thick, but the butterflies are already flying about — nature hurries to do everything it must, summer is so short here. My summer is just as short. I have to do everything in time.

I still remember how I walked in the forest in summer and saw a huge caterpillar. I think it was almost a meter long. I was covered in sweat from horror. I still see it in my dreams. What sort of a caterpillar was that? Where was it crawling? What, did it forget to become a butterfly?

Today I called in Ivan Mikhailovich Zaitsev for an interrogation. He's the former chief of staff of Dutov's army. A general of both the Tsar's and the White Armies.

F. once said, "Do you know who killed Dutov? I killed Dutov."

He was drunk and happy. He allowed me to caress his face (usually, he doesn't allow that).

They killed General Dutov in China, where he had fled. That's all I know.

Today I asked Zaitsev a few questions about that, but he answered very measuredly and slowly, as though afraid to slip up. He doesn't know anything specific about Dutov's murder. Only that Dutov was very well guarded, and that someone who had earned his trust had shot him.

Zaitsev probably thinks that I'm gathering new information about him, and he's afraid. Very many who come to me into my office consider everything that happens to have special significance. But often, there's nothing meaningful at all. Often, I'm feeling bad or again thinking about F.

All the time, I had this stupid and girlish desire to say to Zaitsev, "Do you know who arranged the assassination of your general?" And to tell him the name.

Now I ask myself: why did I want to do that? Probably the answer is something like this: I want for someone else to feel the same intensity of feeling towards him that I have. It doesn't have to be love (do I only feel love for him?), let it be whatever, even hatred. But at least I wouldn't feel alone.

December 23:

At night, we were drinking again, and again I heard my name from the corridor. They don't knock on my door, because they know about F. But we've not been with each other for a month already. I've begun to count the days. I never thought it was important, but I still have to start my count from that. Especially since everyone does.

How quickly the former soldiers and heroes of the Red Army turn into wanton pigs in this place. The Chekists and Red Army soldiers have to live near death all the time, sidling up to it. Only then do their faces begin to reflect a feeble light and a pride for the great work. Here, they've fallen into filthiness from their shamelessness and impunity.

December 24:

The flowers on Solovki don't smell in the summer.

The snow doesn't smell in the winter.

I'm frozen. I want to fall in love. To stick it to him.

But he'd only be happy, ha ha.

How stupid that "ha ha" looks on paper. Ha. Ha. It looks like a soldier leading a child. The soldier is girded with a belt. The child is small, in a coat too big for him, only his feet stick out, and he's in a fur hat with ear-flaps.

I want a fur coat, to run along the Red Square at night, for him to run after me and beg me: "Stop, already!" He grabs my sleeve. I hide my face so that I don't see his eyes and start laughing. A very steady snow falls and immediately melts.

Where did I get all this? From the fact that it will never be? Then why did I think of it?

December 25:

A month ago, I gave him a bunch of documents concerning infractions amongst the supervisory staff and administration.

There was no answer.

Today, I saw him in the administration building. The documents were just a reason to see him, of course. I stopped him in mid-run (he's always walking fast, and everyone hurries after him).

He says, "If everything is to be properly in order, we'd have to shoot all the Chekists. Because all the ones they send here are penalized soldier, sadists and villains. There's no point in trying to reeducate them. But if I shoot them all, they won't give me any more. So, I let everything continue as it is."

January 3:

Sometimes I try to calm myself. So much has happened in my short life, it wouldn't have fit in most long lives.

At night, I had a dream. We were again in Trotskii's train, and once again we accidentally met in the secretariat.

F. was trying to convince Rudolf Peterson, the director of the train, of something. He was thin, but the leather jacket made him look larger in the shoulders. It sat very well on him. That jacket looks good on everyone. When they — the guards in leather jackets — accompanied Lev Davidovich and everyone left the train, it was pleasant and yet horrifying to look at. They walked like black demons. All the Red Army soldiers from all the fronts — apathetic, hungry, and eaten alive by lice — were gathered together and were all shot down. But the demons were always forgiven, because they always brought victory.

We came to Peterson with Ustinov the journalist, whom I was helping. Ustinov needed clarification on some questions. They discussed something for a short time, then Rudolf Avgustovich said, "Eichmanis will accompany you."

We went into the second car, F. showed us everything. Ustinov left to meet someone else, and F. and I talked for the first time.

I immediately felt that I could fall in love with this one. I wanted to fall in love with him.

His eyes. It was as if there was moisture within that would never come out. The line of his cheekbones was indistinct, though I still called them "slanting cheekbones", as Mayakovskii wrote in his poetry. Slanted in the sense that they were scythed down, mowed down.

But then he laughed once, and triumphant flames danced in his eyes, as though somewhere beyond the river, the grass or a hay bale caught fire. The wind blew, and the sparks flew. I looked at those eyes for so long that he understood everything immediately. He invited me to see him again. His jacket creaked. He tried to stand without moving — maybe the creak would have distracted me?

I rejected him. He nodded, as though I had rejected him for a perfectly good reason that he respected.

Then Ustinov walked in.

It did happen a month later, and it was short and the memory of it is murky. I held on to his leather sleeve, and all the while, my hand was sliding off. I was falling the whole time, falling, and I wanted to land.

Anyway, I had been writing about the dream. I dreamed everything exactly how it was, except with some new, confused, completely unnecessary details. This time, Peterson talked more, Ustinov talked more, everyone kept talking, and I wanted them to get on with it.

I so wanted to experience it all anew. What happiness would that be — to relive it all anew.

January 17:

In the summer, he had had his fill of parades and inspections; in the autumn it was the museum; and now, he can only think of the hunt.

I'm angry, but every time, I unwillingly get inspired by everything that he does. In the summer, I thought it was all so terribly important — all the inspections, the marching step, the calls: "Good! Good! Good!" Then I was ready to work in the museum myself. I constantly called either the artist Braz in to interrogate him (I almost gave him a heart attack — he didn't understand what I wanted from him), or anyone else who appeared in the know, intelligent. Finally, I called in the priests. They also didn't understand why I kept asking them about the value of the icons and the ecclesiastical accoutrements. I so wanted to be useful to F.! I just caught myself thinking that I want to go hunting, after all, the hunt is glorious — the sun, the freezing cold, we killed an animal, it's lying in the snow…

I went to the library, looking for something about the hunt, but I could only think of the scene with the wolf in *War and Peace*. I reread it and became sad.

Who's he sleeping with, I wonder?

I would have forgiven him. Just curious.

I'm lying, lying, lying. I'm shamelessly lying to myself.

F. grew out a mustache. Maybe she asked him to?

January 19:

In the morning, I read my own file and caught myself thinking that, on the one hand, everything is so clear, but on the other, I don't recognize myself in a single line. Where I am in these descriptions?

My father was a student. He divorced my mother when I was six. I only remember his bad teeth, bristle, his shabby jacket. I was ready to adore my father. Where is he? Probably killed somewhere.

I lived a year and a half at my aunt's in Odessa. I was fourteen years old. My neighbor in the house across the street sold cakes, grapes, wine, homemade ice-cream from her window. I used to go to the sea with my uncle. He taught me how to hoist sails. I understand the sea and charts a little bit. My uncle was always breathing on me. I was very skinny; he was probably afraid of breaking me, he had very big hands. He stank of fish.

But the sea — the sea was like happiness. Only a single summer, but it was enough for a whole lifetime. I used to buy ice-cream from my neighbor for a penny, but my hands also stank of fish. That's my Odessa.

Then Petersburg. Mom finally got married, but I didn't get along with my stepfather. He was a vulgar man, a failed factory owner. I finished the Transfiguration Gymnasium in '17. Tried to enter university to study natural sciences, was hungry, fell in love for the first time, though now I hardly remember it. It just occurred to me that I hadn't remembered for a whole year, goodness. And it was such a love!

I became "red" immediately. At least, that's how I think of myself now. At lot of it was youth, irritation and resentment at being without a father. Because of my stepfather. But much of it was sincere.

Yana, a friend from the gymnasium, was the first of all my acquaintances to get an abortion. She arrived in March of 1919 because of her ill health.

She said that she worked as a stenographer in Trotskii's train and said the salary there was huge. She also talked about men, of course. Everything she said was unpleasant, but (I didn't want to admit it to myself) it attracted me.

But I still wanted to go to the front. Plus, the famine.

The final scene with my mother — we already hated each other.

The salary was almost two thousand rubles; Yana hadn't lied. I never sent a penny of it home. I justified it by saying that it would never get there. Mama got sick and died. My stepfather disappeared, and I didn't look for him.

When I read all this, it seems that it was sad and difficult. But at the same time, we were young, there was hope and poetry all the time.

F. knew some poems by heart. I was so surprised. Something horrible, maybe Severianin. He has terrible taste, it seems to me sometimes. But because he's a man, he can carry off his terrible taste as though it were the best taste.

I'm getting angry again. He's brilliant. I can't bear it.

March 14:

I felt it for the first time, intensely, today: spring. How much I want to survive this spring in full strength. I've begun to feel my youth, it's still there, but it's like gasoline that's running out. I could still run on this gasoline quite a distance, but I'm standing still.

I have nothing: no love, no child, no parents. Only people on whom I inflict pain.

But they deserve it. Everyone lies like a child and they think I can't see it. Everyone's innocent. Everyone hates the Soviet government. Everyone is ready to lick my boots. When I see them, I begin to love our revolution more. It stands behind me like a wall.

March 15:

It's disgusting that it happened. Disgusting that it happened with D. He's an idiot; he has neither a mind nor thoughts. Only brazenness and self-opinion. And he caught me with it.

Today he came, and I told him firmly: "Forget it. If there's even a rumor that you told someone about this, it'll come back to me, and you know what I'm capable of. You know what F. is capable of. You have to think of your safety."

He was surprised and left quietly. His face was red, even his ears blushed from surprise. His eyes hate me.

April 29:

At night, I couldn't stop myself and rode to his house. Suddenly I realized that the horse knows the way.

I stood there, looking at the window. One window was illumined.

I imagined that he would see me, come out and embrace me.

"Stupid girl," he would say. "I've been waiting so long for you."

Delusion. What foul delusion.

I rode back in tears.

The red army soldiers at the gate look at me crudely, as though they understand everything. How good it would be to shoot them all.

May 3:

Z. told me how F. canceled the May 1 celebration. The beast. I had already guessed. I even overheard a conversation about it once, but I convinced myself that I had imagined it.

May 17:

F. used to read avidly, then he stopped completely. He said that he loves to read orders and decrees most of all. He's being coy, because he's on vacation here, he could even get fat, but his inner fire burns away the consequences of his eternal parties.

And, of course, his masculine flame and the orgies with his favorite counter-revolutionary girls. Foul wanker. Oh, how I want to kill him. How I want to stare in his eyes when he hears me say the words: "Enforce the sentence."

(Evening of the same day; I've calmed down.)

Then F. said that with time they'll read only newspapers or, in the worst-case scenario, diaries and memoirs. I swear, that's exactly what he said. What nonsense! All diaries and memories are filled with more lies than any novel. In a novel, the writer thinks that he's hidden himself, revealing himself fully in one of his heroes or in two or three of them, in all his vulgarity. But in a diary that is always written with the expectation that it will be read, the writer (anyone, me, for example) fools around, puts on a show of himself. To judge by diaries is stupid.

If I were writing a novel about F., I would have… Everything would be quite different than in here. I only write the truth here, the truth as I see it. But to describe life, truth is not enough! The truth of events, writing them down or even reflecting on them only captures a small, external, laughable part of life.

You write the truth, but it turns out to be lies.

(I remembered, how curious!)

I summoned Shlabukovskii, whose file was labeled "order of Russian fascists".

Shlabukovskii knew Yesenin well, he knows that milieu very well. I interrogated him for a whole hour about Yesenin and Marienhof. He couldn't figure out why I was interested, but he carefully talked, then later even got inspired and softened up.

I suddenly thought: what a strange fortune that I ended up on Trotskii's train, then here, while I could have stayed in Moscow, I could have befriended the poets, started living with one of them. Would I have lost or gained more?

I would not have known much. I would not have understood the cost of the revolution. I would have been younger and stupider.

In conclusion? I don't regret a thing.

Shlabukovskii is a cocaine addict. There is some opportunity to get cocaine, even here. F. is a lover of the theater; he wants to let him leave the camp early, pardon him. But he should add five years to his time.

May 19:

Yesterday they brought me perfume and mascara from Finland.

F. came into my office. Funny: it's as though he smelled it. He's a hunter, after all. Like a hunting dog. Smelled the scent and lost his head.

Everything happened again. It's funny, but my laughter is happy.

Sometimes the painful thought about his women bothers me, his beastliness, the fact that he can infect me. I've seen what goes on around here. But I quickly, quickly, quickly banish those thoughts.

What joy. What bourgeois pettiness — I dreadfully want to put on makeup.

I sing loudly:

I will sew a modern bustle.
Whatever I can't hide, I'll stick in a chest.

He said that he expected me tonight, that I should come. He didn't make excuses, and I even liked that — it would have been too painful and repulsive if he had made excuses. (But inside, the thought still flared up: he's just shameless, he's long crossed the line).

All day I couldn't do anything. Before leaving the office, I am trying with all my might to stop smiling.

F. also said, "Get rid of Lev Davidovich's portrait if at all possible." But he said it nicely. So I put it away. Into my writing desk.

Trotskii's personal chef is an inmate in the camp. I, and probably F., often met him in the train. He only cooked for Trotskii — we cooked for ourselves — but I remember that he once treated me to a cooked apple with sweet filling. This was about one hundred years ago. I was just a girl. But I still want that apple.

F. doesn't speak to him; he sent him to work in the infirmary, where he never goes himself.

If it wasn't for Trotskii, the revolution would have failed. I know this; F. knows this too. We saw it with our own eyes. The revolution doesn't feel gratitude. That's probably correct. The future tramples the unnecessary. That's how it should be.

I should order some more perfume. I don't give a damn about anything. I went to the warehouse, picked some boots taken away from the counter-revolutionary dames. I don't want to think about that. I just took them, and that's that.

May 23:

F: "Here everyone has an invisible ring in his lip. If I have to, I grab that ring and pull him to the abyss."

I've noticed also that the inmates are incompetent in their attempts to hide. They look like radishes — every one of them has a tail sticking out of the ground. At any moment, anyone walking by the garden could grab that tail and pull it out.

I could do that with any one of them here.

(Later.)

I think I know why he took me back. He wants to speak to a woman. He has no one to talk to here. He could have talked to the counter-revolutionary girls, but he's not in a position to allow himself to do that. Or so it seems to me. He needs to be listened to, and that silence of listening has to have a feminine intonation. I've mastered that intonation.

As for the rest, he doesn't love me. I can tell myself that.

Sometimes we don't do anything and only talk. Then, I look at his face as I would look at a lamp. I feel the warmth, but I can't touch it.

The boots are tight.

May 24:

I took another pair of boots. To hell with it.

But these boots need a different skirt, but I don't have that skirt yet. Its OK, I'll get it later.

In general, I need to go shopping in Kemi. I really want him to notice me.

And here I realized something funny. No sooner do our relations start again (in all seriousness, this is already the fifth time, not counting petty arguments and those first arguments were all my fault, now I think — what a moron I was) — anyway, whenever we're together again, I begin to believe with some kind of new power and passion in all that we're doing here, and the revolution in general, which, of course, didn't bring all that we had expected, or at least not quickly enough.

Everyone understands this, even F., who never speaks about it.

He only talks about what's happening here and now. Sometimes I memorize his words, and when the "political types" try to argue with me during an interrogation, I answer them with F.'s best conclusions.

He (and the rest of the Soviet government) is blamed for the severity of the regime, but he said to me, laughing, not long ago, "You know how it was in 1917. It's true, the Bolsheviks didn't close the prisons, though some wanted to. But there were no iceboxes, no taking advantage of the prisoners, no single file strolls — what am I talking about! The rooms were open! If you want, go ahead and talk to each other! Then in 1918, we even abolished the death penalty. So why did we bring it back, do they ask? To kill more people? We brought it back because no one wanted peace except us. Now it turns out that we're the only ones who murder people. What, they didn't murder us?"

(But he probably heard that from someone else, probably from Bokii. F. was in the hospital all of 1917).

A little more about why, sometimes, innocents end up here (yes, it does happen, I knew about several cases).

F. says (I'm paraphrasing) that the Bolsheviks don't have the luxury of waiting for a crime to be committed, so there is a whole group of those inclined to anti-Soviet activity or those observed engaging in it that are imprisoned and isolated for the safety of the Soviet government.

Are they his own thoughts or not? It doesn't matter.

Everyone here insists that he's innocent, everyone! Sometimes I want to punish them for that. I know their files and some of them are so filthy that I wouldn't mind burying them alive, but they look at themselves with completely honorable eyes. Man is such a horrible creature.

Burtsev, the White Army officer, wasn't imprisoned for being part of the White Army, but for a series of robberies with a band of thieves that he himself ran (but what an aristocrat, what tone!). That priest John, though a Renovationist, is sitting because he gathered a group of parishioners, then transformed then into a secret anti-Soviet political organization. The poet

Afanasiev (I just called him in) wasn't imprisoned for his poems (though they're terrible), but for taking part in opening a gambling den and for trading in moonshine and prostitution.

And a little more about our so-called bestial discipline (in actual fact it's all a lot more complicated. Sometimes it's beastly, but other times the reins are completely slack).

F. says that discipline is inescapable, otherwise everything would fall apart. The political prisoners in Savvatievo showed that perfectly. If they gave everyone free rein like they did with the politicals, everyone would walk by the watchtowers screaming "idiots!" at the Reds and would get scurvy from boredom.

I think he's right, and when I say as much to the politicals, or to any of the intelligent inmates (the minority), or to the snitches, I always see that they don't want to understand it. They have, as it were, their "own truth".

May 26:

Today I told him about what Grakov had heard *Vladychka* John say at the camp get-together: "I was ready to believe in the Soviet government and to help its work in whatever way I could, if only not for the bestiality going on here."

F. waved it off. Quickly and almost indifferently, he said that no one knows how to run the camps; they don't teach it anywhere. But those who blame us for our cruelty didn't spend a single day on the front. He talked about Trotskii and the shootings in those years. I didn't see it, but I heard a great deal. Yes, it happened, and it worked. Horrifying, but often only horror works.

"Seven thousand people, and each one has an immortal soul, but I imprisoned it," said F. "The soul is oppressed and strives upwards, and in all four directions. But if I loosened my grip for only a minute, the leopards would devour the priests, the punished Chekists would kill the leopards and then all of them would be eaten by the counter-revs, while those would be choked by the socialists."

And he showed me with his hand, how he would loosen his grip.

His fingers are thin, white, but very strong. Sometimes he hurts me with them. Now I miss them, I want it to hurt at least one more time.

June 1:

F. examined the church near the cemetery where he allowed services to resume. I was with him. It's always such a joy to be with him, even if he's paying me no attention. I've become so much more accommodating, it's funny.

While he talked with the priests, who always have a whole scroll of desires and petitions, I walked in the cemetery. I love to do that.

I looked at one of the memorials — a very heavy headstone. I thought, how did they bring it here? Or did they bring the dead man to the stone and bury him under it?

Vladychka John quietly came up, greeted me companionably, and I answered.

He looked at the stone with me for a moment, then suddenly said, "Love is inside the parentheses, while death is outside the parentheses."

At first, I had no idea what he was talking about, but then I thought about it for the rest of the day. It's all priestly nonsense, of course… but for some reason I kept thinking about it.

(Later.)

Once, I interrogated John about his arguments with the Polish Catholic priests.

John said, "They're sure that we Orthodox have no grace, but we don't deny that even they might have some of it."

"What about us?" I asked.

He didn't answer as I would have liked.

During that same interrogation, he said, and I memorized it: "There are no un-crucified people in heaven" and "In Russia, there's open space everywhere." Both of those comments were about our camp.

(Even later.)

I remembered how F. laughed: "The emigres write that on Solovki we're killing Russian clergy, but all the while we only have 119 clergymen inmates, while 485 of our inmates are Chekists, and 591 are former Bolsheviks. Why don't they write that we've decided to kill off all the Cheka and the communists?"

June 2:

What do I really know about him anyway?

I know his silence. Silence has its own intonations. And I can distinguish them.

Of course, I know his voice. They say that the eyes have no expression, that people's eyes don't differ, but only the expressions of the laugh lines change, the mimicry. Whatever emotions a person feels most often — that determines the web of laugh lines developing on the face.

Laugh lines indicate character and fate. He has a young, white face, younger than his years, as though he never fought and never saw all that we saw. But when he smiles, he smiles genuinely. His laugh lines arrange themselves in such a way as though he had much good in him, though less than his self-will and his fury. When he smiles, I can forgive him much.

He has a very full voice. The voice, like laugh lines, has its tell-tale signs. Most often, he talks like a wind-up doll, but sometimes (when he drinks wine; when he's hunting; at night when no one else can hear him; when he's managed to succeed as something he wanted; after a good play; when Bokii comes) his voice is full of laughter, power, will and all of it intermingled. It's strange, but his voice gives him away as a man who's had a hard life, much more than his face does. If I stood at the doors and listened to F., but never saw his face, I would have thought that he was a middle-aged man over forty, a heavy man, even an overweight one.

I know that he's a choleric. He could become a Napoleon, but he's always on the lookout for that putrescence in himself.

But, even though he's a choleric, he's modest. For example, he was always sure that not only Trotskii was greater than he, but even Bokii was greater, stronger, smarter. He trusts Gleb and puts his confidence in him implicitly.

I remembered that Troitskii always had a photographer and a film camera operator near him. F. would never have allowed anything like that for himself. It wouldn't have even occurred to him. He considered himself to be a soldier.

But at the same time, he can speak duplicitously and sometimes starts talking in religious references I don't always recognize, as though he's sermonizing. Not like a barefoot preacher, but as though sitting on horseback. I once heard how he, clearly mocking us and very drunk, said, "You've all left the path and are, to a man, unfit. You don't listen to me, but if any of you do surpass each other, it's only in lechery and unfairness. It's easier to talk to the Lord than to you, unfaithful ones."

The people present were *Vladychka* John, a bunch of actors and former Chekists from the third brigade.

One of the actors guessed that F. was quoting Sacred Scripture.

Vladychka John said, as though to the air, not to F. in particular, "If anyone takes away from the words of the book of this prophecy, God shall take away his part from the Book of Life."[51]

F. pretended not to hear. Or he truly didn't hear.

Later, F. said, "We've made a deal with death, and death is working for us."

Everyone knew where he got that from. Lev Davidovich used to say that.

---

51 Although Eichmanis's scriptural reference is unclear, John is quoting Revelation 22:19.

Before, when F. began talking about how he established a dictatorship here, I used to think: he's trying to justify himself (after all, the war's over). But now I understand: no! He's satisfied with himself. I'm the one looking for justifications. But he, from time to time, assures himself of his eternal rightness.

(At night.)

His father is a Latvian, his mother's a Russian.

He said once, "Latvians don't have their own character. Instead of a character, they have diligence and accuracy. They thought that all of Russia would become their country — they didn't have their own country, only German overlords. But Russia turned about and became itself again. It's like one of the boulders on Solovki — you can't get inside it. The Latvians were left with nothing, but they figured it out too late."

(When I saw that stone in the cemetery, I remembered the boulder that he was talking about it, and so in my mind they became one and the same).

F. finished thus: "The work of the Bolsheviks is not to allow Russia to become itself again. We have to eviscerate it with a cleaver and fill it with new internal organs."

Of course, F. has no nationality.

June 3:

I came to Moscow in the autumn of 1921, when F. was serving somewhere in Central Asia. I worked in the Cheka and lived together (unhappily) with a certain failure of a man. Now, I can no longer have children.

F. returned in June 1922, and everything began again.

I want to say that we lived together, but we didn't live together. We were together sometimes.

I only really got to know him here. At first, he left, disappeared. Later, he wrote a letter, and I answered. I rewrote the answer many times.

Then he called me to Solovki. He said that there was a place for me here.

But now there is no place for me here.

June 5:

The amnesty committee arrived. F. included three of his orgy whores on the list for early release. I couldn't contain myself and demanded that he take them off the list, since some of them were open counter-revolutionaries.

Here was the conversation:

"Fiodor, why are you releasing them? You have to give a lawful explanation."

He thought about it and wrote a resolution: "For exemplary care of the bulls."

And he laughed in his vile manner.

(A few days ago, I wrote about how I love his laugh. I'm an idiot. It's the most revolting laugh in the world. His vulgar, vile smile.)

Shlabukovskii wasn't released. He wants to see a few more plays with him. "If I wish, I will execute; if I wish, I will pardon."

I didn't come to him. I went to sleep in my own place. Until night, I thought he'd call me. But that was complete madness. He has never been in my place and never called me from here.

It seems to me that everyone notices each of our quarrels and begins to whisper about it: look, she's sleeping here tonight. Or she's not sleeping here tonight. What filth.

Even Doctor Ali feels it, though what would he know about it, anyway? He still hopes, brushes his beard. He understands that I'm not F.'s wife, and that he can still hope.

It also seems that it would be very important for Doctor Ali that he had the same woman that F. had. That would, as it were, allow him to commune with authority, with power. How do I know that? I don't even know where this horrible knowledge comes from or what to do with it.

June 8:

The amnesty committee left.

They freed 450 people, sixteen of them were sailors who had taken part in the Kronstadt riots. And not three, but seven counter-revolutionary whores.

F. was half-drunk, and I already knew that I would have to appear before him that day. He's been active these days, and he's had an influx of energy, including masculine energy.

He immediately noticed me and told me to come to him, to "the villa".

He himself came after me very soon, half an hour later.

He smelled of smoke, but I didn't care. The heat rose from him; he was insane. It all came together — the smell of wine, his self-willed hands. I felt like an apple tree full of fruits, and they're falling off me, and it felt so good, I felt so light, as though the apple tree could fly up.

Later, he said, "Galia (he called me by name, though he tries to do that more rarely, I've long noticed it — he doesn't call me by name so that he doesn't have to tie himself to me), I hate all those whores, the sauna orgies. Every time, something dies inside. I'm starting to hate myself. But I've become accustomed to respecting myself."

"You're lying, you scum!" I said silently. I didn't say anything aloud. If only it was even a little bit true! But maybe the fact that he said it meant something?

He had never been so open with me before.

I think I knew what else he wanted to say.

He wanted to say, "I could live with you, Galia. But, Galia, I don't love you."

How can I live with this sense that I understand everything? Why do I have this knowledge?

I want to scream.

June 9:

F. is bored. He's constantly conversing with one of the inmates. I looked over his file. Masonic lodge. A mason. Speaks German. They meet every day.

June 13:

A new passion. Hidden treasure. F. is once again searching for buried treasure. He's sure that it exists. Last summer, he found a few things. They dug in the autumn, found nothing, then it snowed and I forgot about it.

With spring, it seems, he started again. They brought papers from the monastery archive into his office. He's reading, then sneezing. Sometimes it seems that he's fourteen years old.

At the same time, the parades, the hunts, the treasure, the saunas, the drunkenness (not very frequent for all that) — none of it prevents him from working on all the projects he started — the manufacturing, the nurseries, the zoos, the workshops, the factories, he even decided to do a Spartakiade. Every day, fifteen, twenty, thirty people visit him, and he speaks to all of them about their questions — with the inmates, the actors, the priests. Sometimes he gets inspired, but more often he speaks like that wind-up doll. He remembers several hundred names, some completely unnecessary personal details about each one. He truly thinks that you can re-forge people here, and it works for him. If it doesn't work, then he breaks that person or several people at once, like a child breaking a toy. Only F. does this, not in hysterical fits, but he just breaks them and doesn't give that action any significance. In other words, he doesn't care that he ordered someone's death or allowed that death to happen.

For him, the war didn't end. Or even better: his world is no different than war.

June 15:

Vladychka John: "Russia needs ascesis, not debauchery, and you are giving us that. May God grant that you yourself do not fall to debauchery, and the fact that your fellow brothers in atheism kill you is also good. The monastery saved all who wanted to be saved. You put all Russian people into your monastery behind the barbed wire, having given ascesis to everyone, the possibility to become monks equal to Peresvet and Osliaba."

You're lying, priest, and you're rude to boot. We want to feed everyone; we're just hiding the socially dangerous.

July 1:

F. to *Vladychka* John (verbatim): "I know what you're getting at! You think that everything will come back to us. It already has! The peasant Semen Shubin spent sixty-three years on Solovki — only for uttering blasphemy against the holy gifts and the holy church! Sixty-three! And half of them in solitary! This is your all-merciful and all-good Rus! These are her gifts... The last nomadic Cossack ataman of the Zaporozhian Sech', Petr Kal'nyshevskii, was imprisoned for twenty-five years here, sixteen of them in an oubliette. He was taken out for a walk three times a year — on Easter, Transfiguration and Christmas. That's very Orthodox, oh yes! The monks betrayed Metropolitan Philip, the former abbot of Solovki, to Ivan the Terrible. It would have been better if they were silent! And Philip had visions of Christ, in the Phillipov Hermitage! But still, his own monks gave him away, and he was smothered to death. What do you want there to be on Solovki now? Palm trees?"

(He was drunk and agitated; it was all uttered with bitterness.)

(*Vladychka* John listened, smiled, quietly nodded his head, as though he was listening to a beloved child who was reciting the Creed.)

July 2:

I remember that in Trotskii's train, we had a secretariat, a publishing house, a newspaper editing office, a telegraph station, a moving infirmary, a radio, an electrical power generator, a library, a garage and a steam room. F.'s own task force. A guard made up of Latvian sharpshooters. A group of political propagandists. A brigade of railroad maintenance technicians. A machine gun squadron. Then they added two planes, a few cars, and even an orchestra.

What does it remind you of? That's right. The camp at Solovki. He's building a new Trotskii train here. That which he saw in his youth, he's building that now. That's why he brought me here; I'm from there.

July 6:

The medical commission arrived. They checked the administrative staff and guards, including me.

Then I accompanied them everywhere, as F. ordered. There was a lot of work and a lot of stress.

The results were horrifying.

(Later, trying to calm down.)

Here are my notes from the conclusion of the medical commission:

"Among the 600 people checked amongst the hired workers and incarcerated Chekists, we have found 40% with psychopathic and epileptic tendencies. Nearly 30% exhibit psychopathic hysteria, and nearly 20% show other psychopathic tendencies and severe psychoneurotics."

Where I am living? Where am I? Where?

What if it's infectious?

We could have thought whatever we wanted, but it turned out that a band of cretins, sadists and psychopaths had dressed up in the uniform of the Cheka, the Red Army, and they received administrative positions. So, they torture people, they devour them whole and their teeth grow in such a way that their roots grow into their skills. If you pull off their lower jaw, a bloody mash of brains will fall out too. Yuck! It's all a nightmare. A nightmare!

(At night.)

I knew it all, there's no point in lying. What, you needed to see the paper to believe it? I knew it all, all of it.

The last time I was with him, I saw that his hands were covered in ink. He writes rarely — usually, he dictates. This means he was signing something. I remembered. There was a firing squad. He signed the death warrants and now he's caressing me with those inky hands.

July 8:

I had a hysterical fit at F.'s house.

For the first time, he hit me and threw me out.

I only remember one thing he said in the beginning of our conversation:

"The Solovetsians are here, but the reason for their coming here are on the mainland. We see the consequences. But their backstory isn't clear."

I just can't listen to it anymore.

July 11:

I got drunk. Pretended to be sick. Drank some more. Was "sick" all week. Maybe I'm an actress. It's just chaos all around.

July 12:

F. knows that that scum was bothering me. He didn't do anything. On purpose. It's strange that I expect something.

I don't expect anything.

July 26:

The aide of the citizen comrade. That's how it is.

(A few notes without dates.)

...

Yes, I'm taking my revenge. I wanted to. Not with a Chekist, not with a foreman, but with someone like that. Someone who is always in front of his face.

Probably, I shouldn't write about that.

...

I caught myself thinking that I'd like to write someone a long, huge, forty-page long letter about everything. And immediately I thought: I can't do it to anyone but F. I even laughed.

Yana is married now. Maybe to Yana. I need to find her.

...

He made Violar the head of the biological garden. (Before yesterday, he sold milk in the camp store. He put him, together with his wife, the Georgian princess, in the neighboring estate, not far from his villa. Violar is thrilled, and he almost kisses F.'s hand when he sees him.)

F. is learning English again with him. Still, it's not about the English. I know why he put them nearby. Because of the princess. What a scoundrel!

That's none of my business.

...

They caught a monk-hermit near the biological garden. The camp has been here seven years already, and he's been living there all this time. They interrogated him for a long time, but it was all obvious. He wasn't lying. One of the former monks had been bringing him food.

I went to see it — it was a hole. He lived there like a mole.

It's time to get out of the hole.

...

Turns out, he's planning to go to Moscow! Turns out he's getting married! To a maiden whom he saw a week ago for the first time. So much new news all of a sudden.

Its winter soon, and I'm going to ride down the hill. I'll prepare myself a frozen icon and I'll ride it. I'm sick of your boulders.

...

You're somehow not sugar-coated.

(An hour later, I can't remember why I wrote the last phrase.)

SOME NOTES

Galina Andreevna Kucherenko was pardoned a year after she was convicted — most likely thanks to Eichmanis.

She returned to the mainland to Kemi on one of the earliest spring crossings. She disappeared after that.

A bit more about Eichmanis: from these building blocks you can build a tall, shaky tower. The important thing is to walk away when it falls over, otherwise you might get crushed.

So, Fiodor Ivanovich Eichmanis was born on April 25, 1897 in a peasant family of the village Vec-Judup of the Gros-Ezersnkaia *volost'* of the Gol'dingensk *uezd* of the Courland *gubernia* (if you read all that geography out loud, it's like one of those Russian pre-tales).

His family (father, mother, three children — Teodor, as he was called at first, had a brother and a sister) lost everything in 1904.

He finished the two-class village school and the gymnasium by correspondence.

From 1909, he worked in a publishing house as a messenger boy (in Vindava). Then, he was a storekeeper, then a proofreader, then the accountant of that same publishing house. He rose quickly in the ranks from the age of fourteen to seventeen. He was a smart kid.

At the same time, he finished Riga Technical University and the military school in Riga.

Where next, Teodor? To Moscow! Eichmanis became a worker for "Muir and Merilees" in the capital. Here's a photo — high forehead, attentive eyes, thin lips — he was a thoroughbred, though from a peasant family, standing under the advertising garlands of the department store; it looked good. Another photo, according to the rules of the genre, is tragic. Above his head, like childish scribbles, is a cloud. The storm's coming.

In 1916, Fiodor Eichmanis was drafted as a solider of the Ahaltsisk infantry regiment.

He made a quick transition to commander of the scouts of the staff of the 41st division. The reason: frequent acts of bravery, two degrees (some documents suggest that he finished the technical university by correspondence as well), excellent proficiency in German.

For nearly a year, he was in battle constantly. That is, he periodically kills people, commands a series of war operations, is always working. No time to take photographs with his commendations.

In spring of 1917, he's gravely wounded. For several months, he lies in the hospitals of Petersburg.

In November of 1917 (some sources say it was half a year later), he joined the Russian Social Democratic Labor Party. In spring of 1918, he was discharged. For some time, he worked as a metalworker at one of Petersburg's factories (he does everything well — if you want, he can be an accountant, if you want, a proofreader, if you want, a metalworker). From there — pay attention — he transferred to the war control department of the Revolutionary Military Council of the Republic.

By the summer of 1918, according to the recommendation of the vice-director of the Cheka Yakov Peters, he was assigned as a secretary for the All-Russian Extraordinary Commission for Combatting Counter-revolution, then the supervisor of his department.

In June 1919, he jumped up yet again. The twenty-two-year-old young man became the commandant of the task force of the train of the Chairman of the Revolutionary War Council, the leader of the Red Army, the second man in the country after Lenin — Lev Trotskii.

Trotskii's train rides throughout the republic with unique, feverish speed. It unexpectedly appeared first on the Eastern, then the Southern, then the Western fronts, sending out lightning-fast orders, concluding arrest, enacting immediate judgment, shooting down deserters and plunderers, agitating, mobilizing the peasants into the Red Army, setting up anti-retreat forces, attacking, throwing off groups of parachuters, interrogating, taking military specialists as hostages and forcing them to work for the Bolsheviks, being shot at, even crashing. Trotskii called his train "the flying apparatus of the government".

Eichmanis was at the epicenter of it all, and he was constantly in Trotskii's full view.

In September 1920, along with the transfer of the front to Central Asia, Eichmanis was assigned to a special division of the Turkmenistan front as commandant of the Kalanisk division of the Cheka.

In November 1920, he become the chairman of the Cheka in the Semirechensk region. He developed a successful plan to destroy a Cossack division led by Colonel Boiko.

In the beginning of 1921, we see the twenty-four-year-old Eichmanis as the chairman of the Cheka of the entire Turkemnistan Republic (a geographical area equal to any large European country).

He organized the assassination of one of the most dangerous enemies of the Soviet government — Ataman Alexander Dutov. During the night of February 6, 1921, in China, in a place called Suidun, in his own personal quarters, Dutov was just short of point blank range. His large and well-trained guard was unable to save him.

In that same year, during the night of July 8, during the catastrophic mudslide in Alma-Ata, the first wife of Fiodor Eichmanis perished.

He led the crushing of a local uprising of peasants and soldiers of the third border brigade in Naryn.

He led the obliteration of the guerilla divisions of Israel-Bek and organized his subsequent assassination in his own quarters.

(Here in the record you begin to notice the very particular hand of Eichmanis. He could hardly imagine — this organizer of the first political assassinations in his country as well as abroad — that one day in the near future they would use his handwriting to sign the death warrant of Trotskii, his former boss, who was also killed in his own home.)

The next assassinations that were either ordered by Eichmanis or involved him tangentially: the head of the Basmachi revolt, Dzhanuzakov and one of the leader Basmachi commanders Enver-Pashi.

(It was wartime — he would have been killed too, and some tried. All Basmachi, Bai or Babai hated him, ascribing to this inventive demon even the deaths that he had no hand in.)

Later Eichmanis, bringing into action the special order of the Central Committee of the Communist Party, moved to Bukhara, where he successfully removed the last Bukhar emir beyond Pyanj.

On June 2, 1922, Eichmanis was transferred to Moscow. He was assigned as the commandant of the second division (the Middle East and Central Asia) of the secret operation of the GPU at the NKVD. One more time, let us stop for a moment and calmly note that a twenty-five year old man received the operation control of the entire Middle East and Central Asia — these are Macedonian proportions.

In the beginning of 1923, Eichmanis is offered work in the office of the director of Solovki — the first concentration camp created by the Soviet Republic on the territory of the former monastery.

(His simultaneously horrifying and yet staggering biography will continue to develop along these unexpected zigzags.)

The purpose of his new assignment was formulated gradually — to work out a mechanism to effectively and completely utilize the work capabilities of inmates.

Here was an important moment — the work of Solovki was not subject to the laws of the Soviet government. That is, do what you consider necessary, comrades. You have a great deal of experience of independent work, for example, in Soviet Asia.

This new transfer wasn't exile for Eichmanis (the south, Moscow, the north). On the contrary, he was entrusted in the organization of yet another extremely important government experiment.

In addition, it was in Solovki that all the worst enemies of the Soviet state were now sent. To whom if not to Eichmanis's personal care could the Bolsheviks entrust these people?

On the ship "Gleb Bokii" (who was Eichmanis's oldest friend from Turkmenistan and his new benefactor, after Yakov Peters — not only the ship, but the man himself, a member of the Cheka and a curator of Solovki) he arrived at his new post.

Now some curious details.

On March 13, 1925, the Solovetsk division of the Archangelsk Society for Regional Studies was organized by order of the administration of the Solovki Camp of Special Operations. The chairman of the organization, as strange as it may seem, was Fiodor Eichmanis.

On May 12, 1925, the same administration ordered that the north-eastern side of the great island of Solovki be declared a natural reserve. On the territory of this reserve, all timber felling, hunting, egg and feather gathering were prohibited. Later, thanks to Eichmanis's initiative, a nursery of deciduous and evergreen trees was established, which then provided small trees to be planted throughout the island.

(My obedient imagination draws a young man. He has a seedling in his hands. Now he's holding the softest lemon-colored chick in the palm of his hand.)

The regional experts on Solovki (who were also inmates), headed by the former organizer of political assassinations, successfully managed to incorporate musk beaver into the local nature and continued to study questions of the proper use of forests.

Eichmanis and his specialists studied the islands of the archipelago, the sketes on Anzer, the Neolithic labyrinths on the Great Zaiatsk Island, the Tabor chapel on Great Muksalma Island. They found and examined the dugout holes of the hermits.

An interesting number: 138 scientific organizations of the USSR regularly correspond with Eichmanis's regional experts.

In the summer of 1926, Eichmanis was visited by guests from the capital — Professor Schmidt of the Academy of Sciences of the USSR, Professor Rudnev of the Central Bureau of Regional Studies, Professor Benken of Leningrad University. To put it lightly, the professors were amazed by the results of his work and they insisted on making the local Solovki division of the Archangelsk Society for Regional Studies into an independent Solovetsk Society for Regional Studies.

It was officially organized in November 1926.

In December, the society published its first collection of scientific papers. In subsequent years, twenty-five more collections would be published. The value of some of these monographs is still indubitable.

Later — and this is another curio of the Latvian sharpshooter — a museum was organized, which included the Church of the Annunciation and an insulated curtain wall of the old Kremlin near the White Tower.

After the fire in the monastery (contrary to the legend, the Bolsheviks had nothing to do with it — why would they burn their own camp?), 1500 papers from the monastery archives went into the museum, 1126 old books and manuscripts, 2500 icons, wooden and tin crockery belonging to the monastery's founders, a white stone cell cross belonging to St. Savvatii, the miracle-working Sosnovsk version of the Chersonesse Icon Mother of God in a handmade silver-gilded cover, an icon of Christ Not Made with Hands painted by St. Eliazar of Anzer, parchments, a collection of restored old poleaxes, axes, arrows, cannons and arquebuses. Over 12,000 items.

Add to that programs of the camp theater, the camp journal and newspaper, photographs of the vigorous life of the camp inmates, their own literary work and other handmade objects. Well, that's history too.

At the same time, Eichmanis ordered that another museum be opened in part of the Transfiguration Cathedral. In the altar was an exhibit about iconography, in the Archangels' side-altar was a collection of original metal engravings of the eighteenth and nineteenth centuries along with their prints, a painted canopy for the altar dating to 1676, a collection of oil lamps and candle stands of the seventeenth century.

The remains of Zosima, Savvatii and Herman, earlier exhumed by the curious Cheka, once again ended up in their silver reliquaries.

(Maybe Eichmanis thought they would save him for this honor? They didn't.)

It's worth remembering that in May 1926, thanks to Eichmanis, Naftaly Frenkel's sentence was twice reduced. Later, Frenkel became a lieutenant general of the NKVD and to this day bears the glory of being an unsurpassed rationalizer of inmate labor.

In August 1929, Eichmanis returned to Moscow and became the head of the third division of the Special Department of the GPU — foreign counter-intelligence. The work suited him. He had long been working in that direction.

The next year: a new assignment, higher and more horrifying still — on April 25, Eichmanis was given authority over all the concentration camps of that time — Solovki, Vishera, Northern, Kazakhstan, the Far Eastern, the Siberian and the Central Asian.

He was the first commandant of the administration of all the camps of the GPU, the emperor of what later would be called the GULAG archipelago. (The formerly thin-legged, cute messenger boy kept running and running, and finally he arrived. He stands on the zenith and looks around. This is where he was going all along, no?)

Still, there's no point in overkill. He remained in this post for a little longer than a month, accepted the documents, then handed them in (Lazar Kogan replaced him).

(To be perfectly honest, Eichmanis never ruled over the GULAG exactly, because the abbreviation GULAG — with such a rusty, clanking sound, the axe should fall on the neck — only appeared in November of that year.)

On June 16, 1930, the party moved its Latvian sharpshooter even further.

Eichmanis became the organizer and leader of the legendary Vaygach expedition.

(Here we list the table of the contents of the previous chronicles and sagas: 1. Scout during the First World War; 2. The Petrograd Cheka; 3. Trotskii's train; 4. In the heat of the fire in Asia, Turkmenistan, Bukhara; 5. Solovki and surroundings; 6. Moscow, foreign counter-intelligence, four diamonds in his collar, and personal reports to the Kremlin; 7. The camps of all Rus, the greatest slave-owning empire of the world, under his personal control; 8. And now, the Vaygach, the Arctic, eternal freeze, minus fifty…)

Eichmanis arrived on Vaygach Island, as was typical, on the already familiar ship named "Gleb Bokii". This time, the ship, it's true, sailed in the wake of two ice-breakers through the plains of ice and aggregation of ice flows.

The word "expedition" sounds romantic, so let's blow it to pieces. It was actually called the Special Site for a Camp at Vaygach. The administration of this site was in the bay of Varnek on the island of Vaygach and was itself subject to the Administration of Northern Camps of the GPU.

On the surface, it might seem that Eichmanis had been seriously demoted, but that's all nonsense. The Vaygach expedition had a tremendous significance for the Soviet government and Eichmanis answered to no one on the frozen island. Everyone listened to him.

(There was a single Nenets there named Vylka with his family — only they didn't listen to Eichmanis.)

One hundred and thirty-two people wintered in the bay of Varnek with Eichmanis the first year. One hundred of them were inmates, both political and convicted criminals. Twenty-five were hired workers.

That is, only six members of the Cheka came with Eichmanis.

Columbus had a lot more decent people on his crew. They weren't sailing into the Arctic.

As for why the expedition had come to that island, the six members of the Cheka were not informed.

The people Eichmanis trusted the most were the geologists, miners, engineers and surveyors — real scientists, but all, unfortunately, were convinced under article 58. From the time of Solovki this particular kind of inmate was basically his favorite.

Wasting no time, from the summer they built warm barracks in this new place from timber Eichmanis had prepared back in Arkhangelsk. They assembled a diesel station, a radio broadcasting station, an infirmary, a refectory, correct foodstuffs (potatoes, onions, carrots and even a bilberry extract to combat scurvy). And then, work, work, work!

(A little later, they built an airstrip, a steam room and a post office.)

Metal ore from frozen Vaygach were sent to Arkhangelsk, then by airplane to Moscow, where they were analyzed and the results quickly shared with the Kremlin.

A quick word from a former inmate of the Vaygach concentration camp: "Eichmanis was a rather energetic administrator. He organized the building of the village effectively, as well as the establishment of daily routine and order. In the village, there was no difference between inmates and hired workers. Everyone lived together, worked together and associated with each other freely. There were no zones, no prohibitions. The inmates could walk around the environs at any time, as they wished, together with the freemen, without any special permission or pass. People even organized races on skis."

Here, so that everything doesn't look quite so positive, it would have been appropriate to mention the tragic tale of how Eichmanis put down a potential mutiny of inmates, but that would be all from the evil one. The truth is that no one even had the idea of rebelling, even if they could have smothered all the Cheka in the area in the space of ten minutes.

Interestingly, Eichmanis took advantage of several practices perfected in Solovki. Every inmate who did his work well could count every year of work as two years off his sentence. Specialist inmates had the right to have their wives and children join them on Vaygach Island, and this actually happened (the geologist Klykov, the geologist Flerov, a former brigadier of the Red Army of Archangelsk, the surveyor Perepletchikov, the cartographer Bukh all had their families join them, and Professor Wittenburg had his wife and eleven year old daughter join him from Leningrad: basically, it was all a fairy tale). The hired workers and the specialists lived in the same conditions. There was a single kiosk for purchases opened for all people, including the Cheka. It is true that the inmates were not allowed to buy alcohol (but in Solovki, oh yes, they were allowed).

In the subsequent years, fifty-eight lodes of lead-zinc and copper ore were found.

They even hoped to find gold, silver and platinum, but even this fairy tale had its limits.

The government's mission was accomplished, and in 1932 Eichmanis returned to the mainland on the "Gleb Bokii".

He was once again intent on Moscow.

Now he became the deputy commander of the ninth division (his boss was the very same Gleb Bokii) and at the same time the commander of the third sub-division of the ninth division of the Main Directorate for State Security of the NKVD of the USSR.

What was his job? His sub-division oversaw the cyphers of Soviet intelligence, developing them and applying them, and maintaining a crypto-correspondence with foreign representatives of the USSR.

Basically he (and Gleb Bokii) ran the entire apparatus of Soviet counter-intelligence.

He traveled on several business trips abroad to Europe and Japan. He had learned all there was to know about Russia. It was time to feast his eyes on the wider world. The world is huge, dangerous, so he zealously prepared himself for more massive villainy.

His entire fate was dedicated to armored train cars, counter-attacks, camps, interrogations, politicals, criminals, leopards, sweaty Baschmaches, the frozen Arctic. But suddenly, hell! A fine umbrella in hand, a doorman at the entrance, “Please, let me help you…” sidewalks, bridges, café's, *coffee, please.*

… The Soviet scout lies in a hotel room. He hasn’t taken off his beautiful shoes; he stares at the white ceiling. There's a chandelier hanging from the ceiling. Soon it’s time to go home.

In 1937, the last name of Fiodor Eichmanis appears in a list personally assembled by comrade Stalin. It’s not a list of those up for advancement; on the contrary, it contains 134 names of members of the NKVD facing trial before military tribunals of the Supreme Court of the USSR. Stalin and Molotov sanctioned the list, then the 134 people were slowly directed towards the scaffold.

At first, Eichmanis was fired from the NKVD.

(Do you remember, you Latvian sharpshooter, how you left those kids “to the mosquitoes” in Solovki? Now a huge ice mosquito has come for you, sat on the back of your head, and plunged his proboscis into your skull.)

For a short period of time, he regretted losing his apartment on the Petrovka and kept waiting for it all “to resolve itself”. His pregnant wife looks at him with pleading eyes.

Why didn’t he dig a hole and hide there?

On July 22, 1937, Eichmanis was arrested and accused of “participating in a conspiracy in the NKVD”.

He was under investigation for more than a year. That is a long time. Did they beat the evidence out of him for that long? More likely, there was a lot of talking, in all seriousness.

Let’s assume that at first, after a few “events”, that he told them all how it was in actual fact. Or at least part of the truth. They considered the facts and made their conclusions. Then, together they made up a good-sounding, impressive charge, something for the front page.

In Eichmanis’s case file, the following accusations are noted:

1. Recruited by Yakov Peterson to work in English counter-intelligence in 1921, when he was actually head of the Cheka in Turkmenistan (which is a pile of nonsense).

2. Failure to eliminate all Basmachi bands (which is black Bolshevik ingratitude).

3. Membership in the commando-terrorist organization "The One Brotherhood of Labor" (a typical Masonic name), led by Gleb Bokii (Eichmanis was, of course, both a commando and a terrorist in some sense, but still not in the one that was offered to the court; even though the Masonic connection… maybe that one is worth noting).

4. Member of a Spiritism circle organized by the same Bokii (this could be true, because Bokii was famous for his Spiritism tendencies and everyone knew about this strangeness of his. The devils tried to summon their own kind to themselves). The circle, among other things, liked to predict the future (judging by the results, very ineffectively).

5. He was the intermediary between Bokii and Trotskii (this could very well be, in one way or another; in that case, we can add another monogram to his biography by which they then hooked him by the ribs and pulled him to the slaughterhouse).

Some details from his case file follow:

1. In 1935 (the thirty-eight-year-old Eichmanis, by the way, had been promoted to major of the NKVD) traveled to Copenhagen. He found the Trotskyite Jorgenson and with his help soon met with Trotkii himself. "Ah, Lev Davidovich! How many years has it been? How are you here?" Trotskii gave Eichmanis a letter for Bokii. (In actual fact, there was no such meeting. Though Jorgenson was. Maybe the letter was real too?)

2. In 1936, during a trip to London, he gave Trotskii secret materials concerning the defense forces of the USSR, details of the NKVD's work abroad and cryptography codes. (Its absolute nonsense, but the readers of the front page are supposed to experience trembling and fury.)

3. In the same year of 1936, he took part in the preparation of an act of terrorism that would eliminate the chairman of the Committee of National Commissars, Molotov (if he had been involved, he would have definitely killed Molotov).

Having appeared before the military tribunal of the Supreme Court of the USSR, Fiodor Ivanovich Eichmanis confirmed all accusations, was sentenced to death and that same day, on September 3, 1938, was shot on the Butovo Polygon.

He was forty-one years old.

Later, his sister was informed that he died of heart failure on February 13, 1943. At the same time, they wrote to his daughter in 1955 that he was shot on October 15, 1939. These are the particularities of the Soviet mail. Somewhere in a cavern, an insane secretary sits and constantly sends letters to relatives and friends of the convicted. He guesses the dates and rejoices.

Don't ask for whom the post office doorbell tolls.

… We still have a few characters left.

Alexander Petrovich Nogtev, sailor of the Baltic Fleet, participant in the storming of the Winter Palace, head of Solovki in 1923-1924, later worked in other camps and returned to Solovki in 1929. In 1930, he retired (evidently for reasons of health, because he was only thirty-eight years old), and this saved him from being shot. He lived in Moscow from 1932-1938, he worked as the manager of the trust company "Mosgortop". He was arrested in 1938 (Eichmanis was just shot and then they suddenly remembered, what about Nogtev? How's he doing? Is everything OK with him?), sentenced to fifteen years of hard labor, sent to the Norylsk Concentration Camp. There he was recognized by Osip Troianskii, who was serving another term. Troianskii slapped Nogtev on the face. In 1944, he was transferred to live in the Krasnoiarsk region. He was granted amnesty in December 1945, but he never made it back to Moscow, didn't have a chance to find a place of residence there before he died in 1947 because of his ruined health.

Troianskii finished his term on Solovki and received another fifteen years in 1935. He was released early. He was a candidate to receive the Stalin prize in biology in 1949. He lived to be very old.

Gleb Ivanovich Bokii, a Russian nobleman with the face of a kind village teacher who sometimes falls to the ground, then turns out to be a shapeshifter… He had the idea to build a concentration camp in the North only for the intelligentsia and for the White Army without any hard labor, but it turned out differently. In August 1918, he became the commandant of the Petrograd Cheka, then he ran Solovki, ran the cryptography division of the NKVD for fifteen years, had a series of other important positions, and for that, on November 15, 1937, he was shot.

Naftali Aaronovich Frenkel, in his youth a financial risk taker and bootlegger, then inmate of Solovki (arrested in 1924, given ten years), then, suddenly, head of the financial department of the Solovki Camp. In 1931, he was already the assistant to the head of Belomorstroi and administrator of all projects. In 1933, he became head of Bamlag, and so on, and so forth, up and up along the skulls…

In 1947, he retired. He was one of several organizers of the GULAG that remained alive and wasn't repressed himself. He lived alone in his final years, not approaching the telephone at all. People called him, worried about him, maybe something happened? Maybe I can bring you a packet of Belomorkanal cigarettes? After all, it's hard for him to go to the store by himself; or, maybe Frenkel just died and is keeping quiet. But he kept on living and living… He died in 1960, at the age of eighty-three. All that time he could have written his memoirs.

Shlabukovskii tried to write his memoirs but changed his mind just in time. He died three years after Solovki from a morphine overdose.

Passport finished his days on Solovki during an epidemic of typhus. Boris Lukianovich escaped to Finland in the early years of the thirties. Moisei Solomonovich was released early, then again arrested, and he died in 1937. Krapin was well decorated during World War II.

As for the others, nothing is known, and all this isn't important anyway.

As for Artiom Goriainov, as my grandfather told me, retold from great-grandfather's account, he was finally murdered by the gangsters in the forest in 1930. He was walking past a forest lake and decided to bathe. There he was on the shore, naked and they stabbed him to death.

Now I think — what if I had looked at all that had happened from another point of view, with the eyes of Eichmanis? Galina? Burtsev? Mezernitskii? Afanasiev? Would it have been a different story? A different life?

Or would it all have been the same?

EPILOGUE

February came in like a lion, but March cried like a lamb. The cold was dry, but the puddles were salty.

In March, the gulls came back, but a lot fewer of them, and the crows left.

In April, it was still windy, difficult, but in May, it was fine, quiet. They killed off the rest of the gulls, so they wouldn't scream any more.

In June, Artiom tried to live again. He gave a ruble, he gave ten, then left the untouchable brigade and once again landed in the berry brigade.

In July, Fr. Zinovii unexpectedly joined them. Sekirka didn't kill him, after all.

Today they saw a snake in the forest. No one was afraid.

"July 7 is not an accidental day," whispered the priest, who had lost all of his teeth, "On this day, a frightening event occurred in the history of Solovki." He rustled on, amiably squinting his small eyes. "A huge English fleet approached the monastery and bombed it for many hours, demanding that it open its gates and surrender. Tons and tons of bombs then fell. The whole time, the monks prayed without ceasing. When the fleet departed, it became clear that the walls were pierced through in a hundred places, but not a single monk died, or even got hurt. It was a miracle of the Lord on this day." Fr. Zinovii brought his wrinkled face close and for some reason spoke, not in Artiom's ear, but into his mouth, "Every July 7, I pray for the Bolsheviks to depart."

"Better pray for me," Artiom wanted to say, but he was too lazy, plus Fr. Zinovii never let anyone get a word in edgewise.

"So the seventh day of July has come, and I pray, and I pray. Then I pray on all the other days as well. What's that you got there?"

"Bilberries," Artiom answered, "the grapes of Solovki."

"Berries, my soul," Fr. Zinovii was visibly moved. "But I can't find any," he added, chewing with his toothless lips, as though all the berries were in his mouth and he would find them growing there.

"Look for them where it's drier, father," Artiom recommended. "In the grass. You keep walking in the swamp."

"But the moss is soft for my feet." Fr. Zinovii laughed. "The bunks have sharpened all my bones; I've become frail, dried up. If you stick me in the ground, I'll show you all where the wind blows."

To help gather the berries, Artiom had inventively adapted a comb with thick teeth, which he then attached to the bucket.

He brushed the grass, and the comb gathered the berries.

Later, he would pour all of his spoils onto a wide board covered by a rough bag. All of the weeds stayed on the board, while the berries rolled off as needed — everything was as humane as you like.

He did all of that after he finished his work, on the straight path towards the monastery. In the brigade itself, he wouldn't have been able to manage it.

From a distance, the monastery looked like a basket. From that basket stuck out several big-headed mushrooms, being eaten up in some places by worms.

Nogtev was walking, probably from the Phillipov Hermitage, together with his posse of Chekists and guests. Among the adults there was a single boy, one of the homeless kids. He was pink, well-washed, scented. All he lacked was a sailor's cap.

Everyone was happy and, laughing a little, watched the berry pickers as though they were forest animals who had approached a human settlement.

"Have a berry, comrade commandant!" said Artiom gently, in the tone of a grumpy old man who had unwillingly succumbed to the general hilarity.

The head of the camp mechanically took a berry, rolled it in his palm and smashed it with his fingers.

An invisible bird rocked a prickly branch.

After these forest ambles, every time, there was so much sky that the expanse seemed to make people lose their hearing.

Soon the bells of the monastery would ring and all the living would hurry to the evening refectory, while the dead would watch them from above.

Man is dark and terrifying, but the world is gentle and warm.

ABSOLUTE ZERO

by Artem Chekh

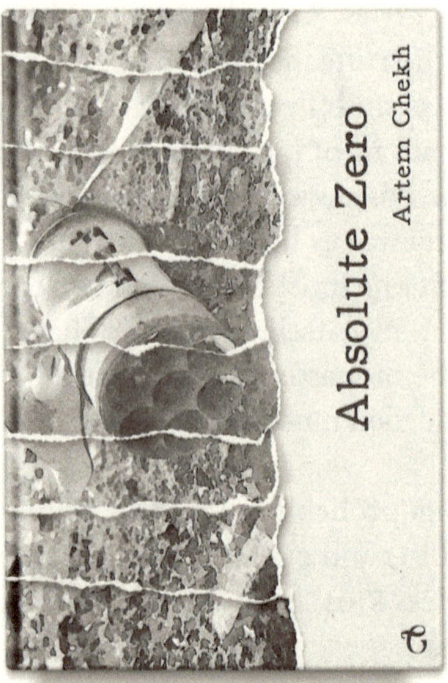

The book is a first person account of a soldier's journey, and is based on Artem Chekh's diary that he wrote while and after his service in the war in Donbas. One of the most important messages the book conveys is that war means pain. Chekh is not showing the reader any heroic combat, focusing instead on the quiet, mundane, and harsh soldier's life. Chekh masterfully selects the most poignant details of this kind of life.

Artem Chekh (1985) is a contemporary Ukrainian writer, author of more than ten books of fiction and essays. *Absolute Zero* (2017), an account of Chekh's service in the army in the war in Donbas, is one of his latest books, for which he became a recipient of several prestigious awards in Ukraine, such as the Joseph Conrad Prize (2019), the Gogol Prize (2018), the Voyin Svitla (2018), and the Litaktsent Prize (2017). This is his first book-length translation into English.

Buy it > www.glagoslav.com

WAR POEMS

by Alexander Korotko

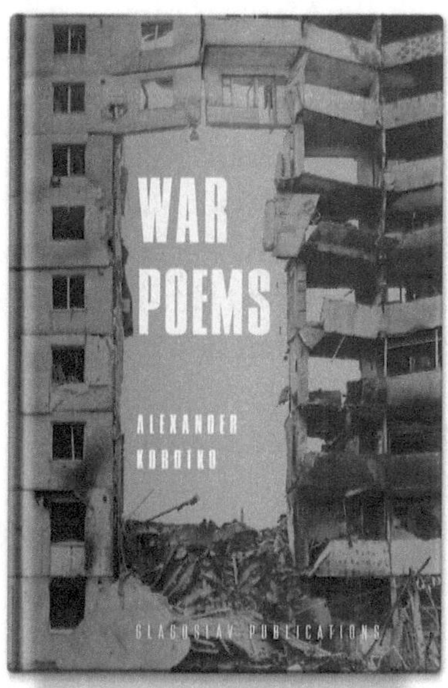

Soon after Russia invaded Ukraine on 24th February 2022, author and poet Alexander Korotko began to set down as poetry the turbulent responses at the emotional, philosophical and simply human levels evoked by the resulting war. Thus, we read in the 88 poems in this volume – completed in just less than 100 days – of the seemingly endless wail of sirens; of sheltering in cellars and tunnels; of the celebrated Ukrainian steppe, churned by tanks; the dead – "our killed, have become our Saviour Angels"; and whole poems devoted to Irpin and Mariupol as the atrocities there and elsewhere became known. Korotko is not without compassion for the Russian soldier – "Russian soldier, what did you forget in my land? We had grief enough without you." – and the soldier's mother when she receives his dead body as "cargo 200". Neither does he conceal his frustration with Ukraine's allies – "we pay the West for help with blood, but the West makes no haste to deliver."

Glagoslav Publications Catalogue

- *The Time of Women* by Elena Chizhova
- *Andrei Tarkovsky: A Life on the Cross* by Lyudmila Boyadzhieva
- *Sin* by Zakhar Prilepin
- *Hardly Ever Otherwise* by Maria Matios
- *Khatyn* by Ales Adamovich
- *The Lost Button* by Irene Rozdobudko
- *Christened with Crosses* by Eduard Kochergin
- *The Vital Needs of the Dead* by Igor Sakhnovsky
- *The Sarabande of Sara's Band* by Larysa Denysenko
- *A Poet and Bin Laden* by Hamid Ismailov
- *Zo Gaat Dat in Rusland* (Dutch Edition) by Maria Konjoekova
- *Kobzar* by Taras Shevchenko
- *The Stone Bridge* by Alexander Terekhov
- *Moryak* by Lee Mandel
- *King Stakh's Wild Hunt* by Uladzimir Karatkevich
- *The Hawks of Peace* by Dmitry Rogozin
- *Harlequin's Costume* by Leonid Yuzefovich
- *Depeche Mode* by Serhii Zhadan
- *Groot Slem en Andere Verhalen* (Dutch Edition) by Leonid Andrejev
- *METRO 2033* (Dutch Edition) by Dmitry Glukhovsky
- *METRO 2034* (Dutch Edition) by Dmitry Glukhovsky
- *A Russian Story* by Eugenia Kononenko
- *Herstories, An Anthology of New Ukrainian Women Prose Writers*
- *The Battle of the Sexes Russian Style* by Nadezhda Ptushkina
- *A Book Without Photographs* by Sergey Shargunov
- *Down Among The Fishes* by Natalka Babina
- *disUNITY* by Anatoly Kudryavitsky
- *Sankya* by Zakhar Prilepin
- *Wolf Messing* by Tatiana Lungin
- *Good Stalin* by Victor Erofeyev
- *Solar Plexus* by Rustam Ibragimbekov
- *Don't Call me a Victim!* by Dina Yafasova
- *Poetin* (Dutch Edition) by Chris Hutchins and Alexander Korobko

- *A History of Belarus* by Lubov Bazan
- *Children's Fashion of the Russian Empire* by Alexander Vasiliev
- *Empire of Corruption: The Russian National Pastime* by Vladimir Soloviev
- *Heroes of the 90s: People and Money. The Modern History of Russian Capitalism* by Alexander Solovev, Vladislav Dorofeev and Valeria Bashkirova
- *Fifty Highlights from the Russian Literature* (Dutch Edition) by Maarten Tengbergen
- *Bajesvolk* (Dutch Edition) by Michail Chodorkovsky
- *Dagboek van Keizerin Alexandra* (Dutch Edition)
- *Myths about Russia* by Vladimir Medinskiy
- *Boris Yeltsin: The Decade that Shook the World* by Boris Minaev
- *A Man Of Change: A study of the political life of Boris Yeltsin*
- *Sberbank: The Rebirth of Russia's Financial Giant* by Evgeny Karasyuk
- *To Get Ukraine* by Oleksandr Shyshko
- *Asystole* by Oleg Pavlov
- *Gnedich* by Maria Rybakova
- *Marina Tsvetaeva: The Essential Poetry*
- *Multiple Personalities* by Tatyana Shcherbina
- *The Investigator* by Margarita Khemlin
- *The Exile* by Zinaida Tulub
- *Leo Tolstoy: Flight from Paradise* by Pavel Basinsky
- *Moscow in the 1930* by Natalia Gromova
- *Laurus* (Dutch edition) by Evgenij Vodolazkin
- *Prisoner* by Anna Nemzer
- *The Crime of Chernobyl: The Nuclear Goulag* by Wladimir Tchertkoff
- *Alpine Ballad* by Vasil Bykau
- *The Complete Correspondence of Hryhory Skovoroda*
- *The Tale of Aypi* by Ak Welsapar
- *Selected Poems* by Lydia Grigorieva
- *The Fantastic Worlds of Yuri Vynnychuk*
- *The Garden of Divine Songs and Collected Poetry of Hryhory Skovoroda*
- *Adventures in the Slavic Kitchen: A Book of Essays with Recipes* by Igor Klekh
- *Seven Signs of the Lion* by Michael M. Naydan

- *Forefathers' Eve* by Adam Mickiewicz
- *One-Two* by Igor Eliseev
- *Girls, be Good* by Bojan Babić
- *Time of the Octopus* by Anatoly Kucherena
- *The Grand Harmony* by Bohdan Ihor Antonych
- *The Selected Lyric Poetry Of Maksym Rylsky*
- *The Shining Light* by Galymkair Mutanov
- *The Frontier: 28 Contemporary Ukrainian Poets - An Anthology*
- *Acropolis: The Wawel Plays* by Stanisław Wyspiański
- *Contours of the City* by Attyla Mohylny
- *Conversations Before Silence: The Selected Poetry of Oles Ilchenko*
- *The Secret History of my Sojourn in Russia* by Jaroslav Hašek
- *Mirror Sand: An Anthology of Russian Short Poems*
- *Maybe We're Leaving* by Jan Balaban
- *Death of the Snake Catcher* by Ak Welsapar
- *A Brown Man in Russia* by Vijay Menon
- *Hard Times* by Ostap Vyshnia
- *The Flying Dutchman* by Anatoly Kudryavitsky
- *Nikolai Gumilev's Africa* by Nikolai Gumilev
- *Combustions* by Srđan Srdić
- *The Sonnets* by Adam Mickiewicz
- *Dramatic Works* by Zygmunt Krasiński
- *Four Plays* by Juliusz Słowacki
- *Little Zinnobers* by Elena Chizhova
- *We Are Building Capitalism! Moscow in Transition 1992-1997* by Robert Stephenson
- *The Nuremberg Trials* by Alexander Zvyagintsev
- *The Hemingway Game* by Evgeni Grishkovets
- *A Flame Out at Sea* by Dmitry Novikov
- *Jesus' Cat* by Grig
- *Want a Baby and Other Plays* by Sergei Tretyakov
- *Mikhail Bulgakov: The Life and Times* by Marietta Chudakova
- *Leonardo's Handwriting* by Dina Rubina
- *A Burglar of the Better Sort* by Tytus Czyżewski
- *The Mouseiad and other Mock Epics* by Ignacy Krasicki
- *Ravens before Noah* by Susanna Harutyunyan

- *An English Queen and Stalingrad* by Natalia Kulishenko
- *Point Zero* by Narek Malian
- *Absolute Zero* by Artem Chekh
- *Olanda* by Rafał Wojasiński
- *Robinsons* by Aram Pachyan
- *The Monastery* by Zakhar Prilepin
- *The Selected Poetry of Bohdan Rubchak: Songs of Love, Songs of Death, Songs of the Moon*
- *Mebet* by Alexander Grigorenko
- *The Orchestra* by Vladimir Gonik
- *Everyday Stories* by Mima Mihajlović
- *Slavdom* by Ľudovít Štúr
- *The Code of Civilization* by Vyacheslav Nikonov
- *Where Was the Angel Going?* by Jan Balaban
- *De Zwarte Kip* (Dutch Edition) by Antoni Pogorelski
- *Głosy / Voices* by Jan Polkowski
- *Sergei Tretyakov: A Revolutionary Writer in Stalin's Russia* by Robert Leach
- *Opstand* (Dutch Edition) by Władysław Reymont
- *Dramatic Works* by Cyprian Kamil Norwid
- *Children's First Book of Chess* by Natalie Shevando and Matthew McMillion
- *Precursor* by Vasyl Shevchuk
- *The Vow: A Requiem for the Fifties* by Jiří Kratochvil
- *De Bibliothecaris* (Dutch edition) by Mikhail Jelizarov
- *Subterranean Fire* by Natalka Bilotserkivets
- *Vladimir Vysotsky: Selected Works*
- *Behind the Silk Curtain* by Gulistan Khamzayeva
- The *Village Teacher and Other Stories* by Theodore Odrach
- *Duel* by Borys Antonenko-Davydovych
- *War Poems* by Alexander Korotko
- *Ballads and Romances* by Adam Mickiewicz
- *The Revolt of the Animals* by Wladyslaw Reymont
- *Liza's Waterfall: The hidden story of a Russian feminist* by Pavel Basinsky
- *Biography of Sergei Prokofiev* by Igor Vishnevetsky

More coming . . .

GLAGOSLAV PUBLICATIONS
www.glagoslav.com

www.ingramcontent.com/pod-product-compliance
Lightning Source LLC
Chambersburg PA
CBHW020719310726
48979CB00004B/980
9781912894796